THE EMPIRE'S LION

THE IMPERIAL ADEPT BOOK ONE

NATHAN TUDOR

Edited by Celestian Rince

Cover designed by MiblArt

ISBN: 978-1-957611-00-6

nathantudor.com

For my dad, who has waited the longest.

CONTENTS

PART III

FIRE AND DEATH

PART IV
THE LION AND THE WOLF

THE SIBYL

Now I will tell of a thing yet to come, a marvel:
   A Lion and Wolf, born from the same womb, nursed at the same breasts,
   Born under a far-off sky where Four Gods hold sway.
   Both behold Death and know him as a counselor.
   Their teeth grow long and blood-washed; one takes hold of the other's throat
As the Many-eyed Eagle watches, slavering.
   This I see, and nothing more.
   —Collected Oracles of the Avernan Sibyl

PART I

BLOOD AND ICE

1

PAGAN HANDS WITH PAGAN MAGIC

IT WAS her first campaign as a fully commissioned Adept. A girl from the deserts of Talynis sent to a land of snow. Who could have guessed at the way fate would twist—or perhaps, the way she twisted fate?
—*The Memoirs of Flavia Iscator*

~

ELEVEN BODIES LAY amidst a frosted splotch of crimson.

Frozen blood never looked right. Ice—that was something Reiva could get her head around. It was even beautiful to look at sometimes. But ice made of blood? There was something wrong about that.

"Adept?" Captain Scanlon grumbled from atop his horse. He'd been in a bad mood since they set out this morning. All of them had.

Reiva stood, dusting snow from her woolen leggings. She kept her eyes on the corpses. "Middle of the night, based on how stiff they've gone. Done with axes and saw knives."

Scanlon grunted. "Brutal way of fighting if they managed *that* with just some axes and knives. How many enemies do you reckon, besides that bastard over there?"

Reiva spared a glance for the dead Hyrgallian. Eleven bodies—and only one of them belonged to an enemy. He had been killed with a spear through the mouth and out the back of the skull.

Disturbingly, that was the only wound he'd taken. Did that mean a legionnaire had gotten him with an expert strike right away, or did that mean he had evaded injury throughout the melee until a lucky thrust did him in?

"Based on the tracks," she said, "it's hard to say. They left in a line to hide numbers, and the prints around the battle are too hectic to read."

Scanlon grimaced. "Could've been quite a few then."

She looked again at the ten mutilated legionnaires lying in the red-stained snow. A full squadron on patrol. "Could've been," she echoed.

Reiva took a moment to regard the captain, who was scratching at his beard. Facial hair wasn't regulation, but in a land as cold as Hyrgallia, that sort of thing wasn't enforced as strictly. Not in the Fourth Legion, at least.

"The tracks head west. Nearest village is Hamstadt," she offered. "Could be worth asking around."

"Could be," echoed the captain. "Farreban, see to it that these men get full rites."

"Of course, sir," said Sergeant Farreban. He would ensure they were cremated properly, their belongings (those that had not been robbed) returned to families in Lazarra.

For a moment, Reiva remembered what it was like to have death visit the household, sent there from a distant battle line.

These legionnaires, though, they had not died in a line. They had been ambushed in the dark by Hyrgallian insurrectionists. Their greatest strength —the shield wall, the unity of heavy infantry in lockstep—lost to them in the gloom of a pitch-black winter night.

Reiva turned away from the corpses—from the gaping wounds in their skulls and chests, from the vicious hacks in arms and legs—and trudged back to her horse. He was a dull mount, not much bothered by the biting wind.

Not that Reiva was particularly affected by the cold either, but it would have been an annoyance if her horse was always shivering beneath her.

Once she was in the saddle, Scanlon told the company they would head to the village of Hamstadt. Reiva was glad for it, and not just because it vindicated her suggestion. The Hyrgallian countryside was a brutal place. The chance that the killers were in Hamstadt was non-trivial, especially since the village was known to harbor sympathies for Duke Faydn's insurrection.

Hamstadt was about two miles away—a trifle for Reiva and Scanlon, and the soldiers on foot were no worse for the wear. A legionnaire was no good if he couldn't march twenty miles in full kit—making the way to Hamstadt was practically a stroll, even through the snow.

The killers' tracks vanished as they came to the main road. She couldn't help but wonder why the murdered patrol had gone so far from the road in the first place, but there were plenty of possible reasons. Perhaps they had been lured, or maybe they were following the Hyrgallians when things turned violent.

Hopefully she would find those responsible today, and find some answers.

Hamstadt lay in a valley that supposedly filled with wildflowers in the spring. If all went according to plan, though, they would be back home long before they had the chance to see that. Tendrils of smoke wisping into the sky gave the first indication they were drawing near. Some clouds were on the approach, which put a knot of unease in Reiva's gut. If it began to snow, that would obscure any other trails left behind.

As far as villages went, Hamstadt wasn't too bad. Based on the size, Reiva estimated a population of four hundred or so. Enough for someone to disappear into, but not impossible to flush out a group of killers.

It was close to midday by the time they descended into the valley and reached the village wall. The sun set the frosted landscape all aglitter as they approached.

A burly, bearded man with a heavy staff stood at the gate—though gate was a generous word for it. Like many Hyrgallians, the guard was blond of hair and blue of eye—something that always struck Reiva as exotic.

"Legionnaires," said the man, not bothering to hide his distaste. "What brings you to Hamstadt?"

He spoke the thick, flowing tongue of Hyrgallia, so Private Hansan had to translate.

Scanlon looked down from atop his mount, but the man did not seem cowed. "This morning, we found several men from our company murdered. The killers' tracks brought us to your village."

As Hansan translated, the man's expression grew darker.

"There are no murderers in my village, Imperial."

"Then," Reiva said, "you will have no problem with us coming within the walls to look around."

The man did not hide his interest—and wariness—for the red mantle around her shoulders. The Adept's mark of office.

She felt Scanlon's eyes on her as well, but she held the Hyrgallian's gaze while Hansan translated.

Eventually, he shook his head. "No problem," he said. "Cause no trouble."

After a sharp rap on the gate with his staff, the man stepped aside to observe the company. The gate swung open, manned by a young lad on the inside who kept his eyes down.

Scanlon nudged his horse into motion, and Reiva kept pace.

"Just because we are of equal rank, Adept, does not mean you should speak out of turn."

Reiva fought a frown. "I don't—"

"If he was a more skittish sort of man, he might have felt cornered being addressed by an Adept. The situation could have escalated."

The captain gave her a significant look. "I know this is your first campaign on your own. I understand what that means. But don't rock the boat too much. We're far from help out here, and I'd rather avoid a fight."

Reiva dipped her chin. Her cheeks burned. "Yes, sir."

Scanlon smirked. "Don't get all formal on me now. Come on, ease up. They need to see you looking intimidating."

"The villagers or our men?"

A snort. "Both."

She made herself sit straighter in the saddle, but still felt abashed by the reproof. The Flame in her soul was unsettled, flickering with an admixture of anger and embarrassment. It thrashed inside her like a caged bull, desperate to be free.

Her horse huffed, trembling beneath her. Animals tended to have a sharp sense for emotional disturbances, but when that emotional disturbance came from an Adept, it created a subtle shift in the unseen energies that powered their magic, a shift in the aether.

Reiva stroked the horse's neck. She went back to the foundations of her training, stilling herself by shifting her awareness to the flow of her breath and the state of the world around her. She focused on the texture of the horse's coat, the warmth of his flesh.

The Flame quelled.

All Adepts had a heightened awareness of their internal state—it was the nature of their magic to affect and be affected by their emotions. Reiva's Art of Fire reacted most strongly to passions such as rage, thrill, and shame.

As they approached the center of the village, she held onto that state of self-awareness. At the drop of a hat, she could rouse the Flame to a blistering storm if needed. Hopefully that wouldn't be necessary, but things rarely went as well as one would hope.

Somewhere in this town were the men who had killed those soldiers. She knew it in her gut. Or if they weren't here now, then they had been.

As Reiva and the legionnaires made their way, folks peered out from windows and stopped along the side of the road. Some bore fear in their eyes, others hostility.

Hyrgallia was part of the Lazarran Empire—these people were subjects of Emperor Dioclete, and they were obliged by law to comply with all legion needs and affairs.

That did not mean they would do so happily—if they were even loyal. Many villages and towns in this region had cast their lot for Duke Faydn's rebellion.

In the town square was a well, a shrine of some sort, and a wooden effigy carved into what Reiva guessed was a folk hero or local god. The town's magistrate was waiting for them in the effigy's shadow. A balding man with a thick mustache and a larger gut than most could afford, he was wringing his hands—and Reiva guessed it was not just from the cold, for his voice trembled when he addressed Scanlon.

"*Ave Imperator*," he said.

"*Ave Imperator*," answered Scanlon. "Do you speak Lazarran? Karellan?"

Understanding lit the man's eyes. "Karellan, I know Karellan."

Scanlon seemed glad to not have to go through a translator. "I am Captain Scanlon of Ironback Company, Fourth Imperial Legion. Some of our men were murdered in the night, and we tracked the killers here."

The magistrate wiped his brow. "I assure you, Captain, Hamstadt has no part in the rebellion. We are happy with our king, and with our Emperor."

"I never said otherwise, but I'm glad to hear it. So I'll thank you in advance for your cooperation in our search of the town."

The man seemed to wilt. "Captain, it has been a difficult winter. Many of us have known the pangs of hunger. If—"

Scanlon waved his hand. "My soldiers won't take anything of yours—is that what you're worried about?"

"My lord! I would never accuse you or your men of—"

Scanlon snapped, "That's exactly what you were doing." He turned to Reiva. "You take the east side of town with Tharrick and Meridi's squads."

Reiva nodded, slipping out of the saddle. The snow crunched under her boots as she led the horse by the reins to the magistrate. "See to him, will you?"

For a moment, she thought he might pass out or piss himself, but he managed to take hold of the reins. When Scanlon tried to pass his own mount to the man, he almost seemed to forget he had a second hand for a moment.

"Your hospitality is appreciated," she called after him as he scampered off. Then, in the Lazarran tongue, muttered, "They don't build people right out here. He's what passes for a leader?"

Scanlon shrugged. "This far north, might be he's never seen a legionnaire in person. Certainly never an Adept."

Reiva frowned. "Still, these people are under the Imperial dominion. They should know what constitutes a well-formed person."

The captain snorted. "You expect a lot from barbarians."

She bit her tongue.

Scanlon winced. "Ah, I didn't mean—"

"It's all right, Captain. Let's just clear the town and be on our way." She was too busy wresting control of the Flame to respond further. She motioned to Sergeants Tharrick and Meridi, who stepped forward from the ranks. "We've got the east side of the village. No looting."

Tharrick frowned. "After these last few days, the troops will be looking for some release, Adept."

Meridi nodded, casting a wary glance toward the buildings around them as she said, "Besides, something's not right about this place. You saw how people were looking at us? I'd wager half my pay these people are with Faydn."

"I feel the same way," said Reiva, "but Scanlon wants to avoid any more friction than necessary. The magistrate claims they've had a hard winter."

Tharrick scoffed. "Is the captain going soft for savages?"

The Flame roiled again. Reiva did her best to keep a neutral expression as she shrugged. "Just make sure your people don't start anything they could avoid. Any signs a household supports the rebellion, lock it down and call for backup."

The sergeants saluted and went to spread the word to their subordinates. Reiva watched them, keeping her breathing measured.

'Barbarians.'

'Savages.'

Nearly a decade in Lazarra and she still felt a twinge of anger. Still felt like she had something to prove. She folded those emotions into her Flame, let them dissolve. All that mattered was the mission—the task in front of her. The Emperor's will.

She oversaw the proceedings, walking along the pathways as legionnaires under her command knocked on doors, sometimes shouldering aside the inhabitants when the language barrier was insurmountable.

Now and then, a crash echoed through the crisp air, and she was glad they were not followed by any further sounds of conflict. She had no doubt the order to take it easy had been disseminated properly, but there was only so much you could do to restrain soldiers at war. Discipline was the way of the warrior—but discipline was not domestication. That was the ugly truth of the matter, the necessity of it.

Again and again, legionnaires took their leave of a home, then moved on to another. Oftentimes they were followed by baleful glances, muttered words, the evil eye.

Reiva picked out Private Hansan from the soldiers under her command and called him to her. He hustled over and snapped off a crisp salute—fist to heart.

"*Ave Imperator*, Adept!" he said with the appropriate vigor and eagerness of a legionnaire as green as he was.

"At ease, Private. Tell me what the people are saying."

A flicker of confusion crossed his face, then understanding. "Curses, Adept. Some of them are invoking their gods."

Reiva hummed. "And how do you feel about this?"

"Excuse me?"

"You're Hyrgallian by blood, aren't you? Does any of this"—she waved a hand toward the ongoing search—"disturb you?"

Hansan nearly snapped to attention again. "No, Adept! My mother has always been loyal to Imperial rule, and my father raised me as a proper Lazarran. As the Emperor wills, so it shall be."

That was a good answer; the correct one. One that had been drilled into Reiva's own mind every day for over seven years. She believed it, too. She had to believe it.

"Come with me, Private. I'd like to speak with some of the locals."

"At your service," he said, falling in behind her as she set off for a home that had not yet been searched.

The denizens were already standing outside their door, faces marred by worry. When they caught sight of her approaching, Reiva thought she could see the life drain out of them even more.

It was a powerful feeling...also a wearying one.

A couple and their little girl, all blond. The girl did not seem as anxious as her parents, though she was obviously affected by their fear.

"Greetings," Reiva said, and Hansan relayed it in Hyrgallian.

The man hoarsely responded in kind, his wife nudging their girl behind her skirts. The child peered at Reiva with bright eyes, curious and wary in equal measure.

"What do you think of Duke Faydn?"

The man and woman looked stricken. "We do not care for the rebellion," he said.

The woman added, "It's only brought us trouble. The harvest in autumn was frail. The gods are displeased with it, we are sure."

"So why," Reiva said, "do you think so many of your countrymen follow him? Speak truthfully. The more I understand, the sooner this whole thing can be finished."

To Reiva's surprise, it was the girl who talked. "The duke is a hero."

Her mother blanched, but Reiva put up a hand as Hansan translated.

"Why do you say he's a hero?"

"He fought bad men who wanted to hurt us. Everyone knows."

Reiva looked at her parents. "The Northland invaders last year?"

The man nodded, a haggard look on his face. "It was bad. Many villages were overrun. Men killed, women and children taken away. And..."

"And the legions were far away," Reiva supplied.

"Yes," he whispered.

"Well, tell me honestly, would Hyrgallians be grateful if the Empire were to maintain a stronger military presence?"

"No, ma'am."

"I see. You want more men like Faydn."

"That is not what I—"

She waved off his fright. "Thank you for speaking to me. I am grateful for it." Out of the corner of her eye, she saw a pair of legionnaires approaching. "If you will allow these two to search your home, we will trouble you no further."

They said nothing to this, only stepped aside and watched.

Reiva motioned for the others to go inside and sweep the place, telling them to be gentle in particular with this home. They looked a bit dismayed, but Reiva knew it was important, when possible, to leave an impression of mercy upon people. She could understand people not wanting a strong legion presence in their land, but perhaps that could change with the next generation.

The girl, she noticed, was waving at Hansan. Reiva watched in amusement as the private kneeled down so she could whisper something in his ear. She glanced at Reiva as she did, and Hansan laughed.

"*Da hexen*," he said.

The girl gaped at Reiva, eyes round as Karellan shields, before retreating back behind her mother's skirts.

Reiva arched an eyebrow at the private, who returned a sheepish grin. "She asked why only you are wearing the red mantle."

"And you told her?"

He scratched the back of his head. "That you are a witch. There's not much of a better word for it," he hastily added.

Reiva snorted. "Fair enough. Come on, I want to—"

She stopped in her tracks. Goosebumps rippled up her arms.

"Adept?" Hansan sounded far away.

Reiva held up a hand, shushing him. She turned, eyes narrowed.

From the early days of their training, Adepts trained to sense the flow of aether—both passive and active.

But what Reiva sensed right now was a sort of blend between the two— like a runner's footprint left behind on a damp forest floor.

She might have missed it, if not for some random shifting of the currents, much as a shifting of the winds might carry a new scent to a tracker.

Her feet were already carrying her back to the home. The legionnaires were stepping out, and one of them was already telling her they had found nothing. She swept past them. Hansan was at her back as she stepped inside.

Now that she knew what to seek out, its signature in the environment was unmistakable.

She heard a dispute behind her. She didn't hear metal clearing a sheath yet, but she moved quickly, just in case.

The home was sparsely furnished. She ignored most of it, having eyes only for the hearth at the center. Like many Lazarran homes, there were objects of devotion near the hearth—carved idols, trinkets, charms.

Reiva picked out what looked like a belt buckle. It seemed old—no doubt her legionnaires had thought it was merely an heirloom of some sort.

Reiva channeled aether, fortifying herself against any potential power that might lash out as she touched it.

Nothing—just cold bronze.

And then she felt it stir. Beneath her fingertips, deep within the metal— something only a person attuned to the invisible flow of aether could recognize.

It was, in the Adept Corps' terminology, a relic. An item imbued with magical power. It was almost impossible to create them, but now and then you heard of findings such as this one—a relic made by pagan hands, with pagan magic.

Reiva turned, relic in hand. The man and woman were at the threshold, blocked from entering by the legionnaires. "Arrest them," she said, and in moments, her soldiers had them restrained. Their daughter began to shriek and batter at a legionnaire's calf—he shook her off without a second look.

Hansan stared at the bronze buckle, mystified. "What is it, Adept?"

"Something beyond your rank, Private." Which was true—but also, she herself did not understand what type of relic this was. This sort of thing fell outside her own expertise. It could have been a crude imitation of one of the arcane Arts known to the Adept Corps, or it could have been something more savage.

Reiva approached the man and woman, who looked pale as death now. Drawn by the commotion, more legionnaires were coming, forming a cordon around the area.

"Where did you get this?" she asked.

The man swallowed. "It is an heirloom."

"Lie to me again, and there will be consequences. Where did you get this?"

Hansan's voice seemed to quiver as he relayed her words. Perhaps he worried for the little girl. Perhaps it was harder for him to see these people —distant kinsmen of his, for all they knew—suffer retaliation for acts against the Empire.

The man shook his head, casting his eyes down. "You have no right to be here."

"I have every right, given by your king, who is loyal to my Emperor."

A dark shadow crossed the man's face, but he said no more.

"What is your name?"

Silence, and then, "Lars."

"People make mistakes, Lars. I understand that. I think you made a mistake, and you don't understand what's happening. Maybe you don't even understand what this is I'm holding. Is that right?"

A flicker of emotion crossed his face, but he kept his eyes down.

Reiva's Flame tinged with frustration. She turned to the woman. "And you, what is your name?"

"Hilda," she said. "Our daughter's name is Astrid."

"She's a lovely girl. You should be here to raise her up into a fine woman."

Hilda was nodding, tension in every muscle.

"Your husband is not speaking to me. He is loyal to his master, which is something I respect, but a mother ought to be loyal to her family first, shouldn't she? You should think of Astrid first. No child should see her parents dragged off in chains. Or worse."

Lars made a strangled sound. "You are cruel, Imperial."

Reiva swallowed.

Remember what the Empire gave you.

"I am only a woman charged with her duty, and I have lost brothers-in-arms on this day. I would not see further bloodshed if it could be avoided. Tell me who gave this to you, and where I can find them."

Hilda licked her lips. Astrid was crying, held away from her parents now by a legionnaire, clutching her like one might hold a rambunctious dog.

Reiva counted off ten seconds in her mind.

"Corporal Maurgis, take these two and—"

"I don't know his name!" shrieked Hilda.

Reiva let her order die, turning her attention back to the woman. "I don't need a name. Tell me whatever you know."

A shuddering sob racked her frame as her husband cast a distraught look at her. But she spoke.

"They came through the village this morning. It was early, most people were still asleep. I went outside to draw water, and they came while I was cracking the ice in the well."

"They came from east of here?"

A nod. "They were covered in blood. They moved very fast, even in the cold and dark. I thought they were going to hurt me, but the first man in their group pressed that buckle into my hands. He said that a week from now, a man in service to Duke Faydn would come here to collect it. It was covered in blood. The next thing I knew, they were gone, going north. He said...he said that if we did not keep it, he would kill us."

As Hansan related all this in Lazarran, Reiva ran her thumb along the engraved bronze. She still felt the rushing energy within, the wild potential eager to be unleashed.

"You're lying again," she said.

Hilda stammered, but Reiva pressed on.

"Something this valuable—whoever they are, they would not have handed this over to a stranger without confirming you are loyal to Duke Faydn's cause. No, I think they already knew you—or at least knew of you. Are you a supporter of the revolt? Be honest with me."

Before Hilda could answer, Lars snapped, "My wife and child have nothing to do with this!"

"So *you* received this artifact from the men who murdered a squadron of legionnaires?"

Lars' eyes were pained. Hilda shook her head. "Please, Imperial, we didn't have a choice. Times are hard. The duke will help us."

"Well, let me help you now. Swear your loyalty to the Lazarran Emperor, renounce your loyalty to Duke Faydn, and cooperate with me. Recognize that this was all just a mistake on your part. Be wise, for your daughter."

"You mean be cowards," muttered Lars.

"If you would rather die on my sword, I can oblige you. But I would rather there be no more bloodshed today than what my company has already suffered."

Hansan relayed the words. Hilda's lip curled. "We will swear. We will, Lars. *Lars*, my love. We will!"

For what seemed an eternity, he hung his head. Then, with eyes still low, he nodded. "We will swear."

"Good. Now tell me the whole story—including who else in this village is loyal to Faydn."

And so Hilda did—the list of names was long, and it included the magistrate. But what worried Reiva more was her account of the men who killed the legionnaires.

There were six of them, all of them burly and taller than average, and they reeked of a stench Hilda could not describe. Reiva suspected it was the strange odor that sometimes emerged when great quantities of magic were channeled.

The men had come to Hilda because Lars' cousin was an active member of the rebellion. The buckle had been left behind by accident, Hilda vowed, so they had cleaned it and decided to hide it in plain sight until they devised a plan by which to get it back to Faydn's men. Of course, now they never would.

"Do you fear retaliation?" asked Reiva.

"From the duke, or from the gods?" moaned Lars.

"Hyrgallia's gods serve Lazarra's," answered Reiva, "and your duke will be dead or in chains by winter's end. Now tell me where they were headed."

Hilda tilted her head. "Northeast. There is...there is a fortress in the mountain pass. An old castle, long abandoned. They might be going there."

At last, Reiva felt a surge of satisfaction in her heart. Not only was this a clue toward bringing down the murderers, this very well might be a step toward crippling the rebellion.

Who knew...perhaps the duke himself was in residence at this castle.

Reiva motioned for the legionnaires to release the family. They did so with some hesitance, but they did not dare defy an Adept's order.

"Your service to the Empire is noted and appreciated. Another will come to you before long to take down the names of those allied to the duke's cause. You made the right choice. Your daughter will grow up safe under the auspice of Imperial rule." She put a hand on each of their shoulders. "You did what is best for Hyrgallia today. Be proud of that. This violence will end sooner, now."

Lars regarded her from under a furrowed brow. She could tell he didn't believe a word of it, could tell he hated himself for this. "Do you truly think so, Imperial?"

Something flickered in Reiva's memory—a cold washcloth in her hands, her father's forehead burning with fever, the distant clink of chains...

She shoved the thoughts down, let the Flame burn them away, like deadwood into ash.

"I do," she said, and then took her leave.

As she passed little Astrid, the girl looked up at her, tears spilling down her cheeks. It put a knot in Reiva's gut. She ruffled the girl's hair. "Easy now, it's all going to be okay."

As they left, Private Hansan said, "Permission to speak freely, Adept?"

After a moment, she granted it.

"We are going to send Legion Intelligence to them. They will have to inform on their neighbors. They named even the magistrate as a supporter of Faydn's rebellion."

"They did."

"And if the village does not agree to take the same oaths of loyalty as they did?"

Reiva kept her eyes forward. "Do not let it trouble you, Private. After all, they're barbarians."

She ground her teeth.

Just like me.

2

A DEVIL OF ICE

MUCH IS MADE of Lazarran virtue. But there is no greater Lazarran vice than pride—and it was our wounded pride that drove us to resort to such underhanded treachery as happened in the siege of Dav-maiir.

I commanded that assault, and I can say now, without reservation, that we would have spent half our legion's blood taking that city, were it not for Tamiq, the traitor.

What an ugly truth.

—*The Memoirs of Flavia Iscator*

～

THE SUN BLAZED hot over a city at war. Smoke billowed from the western gate—Avi guessed the Lazarrans were already inside the walls.

It wasn't the first time the Empire had tried to conquer Talynis. Avi had been but a child, then. His father had joined the defense. Had given his life for the defense.

Avi had never dreamed he would have the chance to spill Lazarran blood in return.

He was not dressed like a soldier—indeed, if he had not been carrying the sword, he might have seemed like any other man about his business, caught by ill fortune on the day war came to the city of Dav-maiir.

But Avi had his weapon, and unlike everyone else in civilian clothes, he was running *toward* the fighting.

Four Gods, preserve King Malik, he prayed. *Make brave the defense, and send protection to the helpless.*

And when he caught sight of Lazarran legionnaires, he sent up one more prayer—this time to one of the Four in particular: *Warrior God, forge my arm into iron, work my bones into granite.*

But he did not jump into the fray—instead, he scaled a wall, expertly springing from hold to hold. He had grown up on the streets, and to survive, he'd learned to leave them for the rooftops.

Leaping from building to building, he scanned the carnage. The Empire's legionnaires were pushing their way through the principal thoroughfare—that was where King Malik's fighting men were offering the most resistance.

Avi longed to join them, but he had another role to play today. A very particular role.

Where are you...

On a hunch, he turned toward the south. That district was mostly merchants and shops. Avi could see from here the tall facade of the Grand Bazaar where bright textiles waved in the air. By day's end, it would almost certainly be looted. From the din of clashing metal and wailing men, there was a fight there too—maybe some desperate merchants trying to defend their wares.

But then, amidst the ringing iron and the screams, Avi heard something else. A strange crackling, the *whoosh* of wind.

The temperature, Avi realized, was dropping.

He had found his target.

The Lazarrans' greatest asset was their Adept Corps. Oh, they had engineers, they had great ranks of men (and women, Four Gods only knew why) —but any army could replicate that.

The great secret of Lazarran conquest was the means by which they made those walking horrors. They looked like humans, but they fought like monsters bred for nothing but the kill.

Today, they had sent a devil of ice to the field.

And today, Avi would kill him.

It was easy to follow the unusual sounds and the rapidly cooling temperatures. Within seconds, Avi had sight of the man. Adepts wore short red cloaks around their shoulders, supposedly as a way to intimidate their opponents—to send a warning.

Avi did not see the point in it; the sight of a man hurling great spears of ice did more to jar the nerves than a scrap of fabric.

The Adept was blond and pale—two things rarely seen in this part of the world. As he pushed forward, he swung frost-dusted arms in sharp gestures, conjuring from thin air blades of crisp blue, steaming under the desert sun.

Avi watched as one crackled into being, then soared forth, whistling an eerie tune, to skewer a man through the chest and erupt from his back in a spray of blood.

Avi's legs pumped under him.

More spears of ice. More valiant Talynisti men slain.

He dropped to the streets, rolled, and popped up into a fighting stance.

The Adept honed in on him, a cold and cruel grin on his face.

Avi's fingers closed around his weapon's grip.

Wait. Wait for the last moment.

The Adept raised a hand. The temperature plunged. Glittering air congealed into a foreboding weapon forged by foul sorcery.

With a flick of his fingers, the Adept sent the frozen weapon flying straight for Avi's heart.

Now!

From the sheath on his hip, he drew the blade—blacker than night, singing a strange song as it sliced the air.

And when Avi thrust it forth into the ice—*CRACK!*

In a puff, the conjuration vanished.

"Blessed are the Four," breathed Avi. The thing had actually *worked*.

The Adept looked gobsmacked, his pale blue eyes ratcheted to the black blade. A savage smile split Avi's face.

The Adept babbled something in the ridiculous Lazarran language. Though he did not know the meaning, Avi sensed the fear like a predator scented blood.

And from behind him, among the fighting men who still stood against the foe, he heard the call taken up: "A King's Viper! He's sent one of the Vipers!"

Avi charged, and the roar from behind told him he was not alone.

More spears of ice hurtled toward him, and every last one shattered at the touch of the blade.

He saw the horror on the Adept's face. The bastard knew what he was facing, then. Good—let him cower and die wondering how a man of Talynis got hold of such a weapon as this, the *Nihilo* Blade, the relic that destroyed all magic save its own.

Legionnaires pressed forward, finally seeming to realize the danger Avi posed to their witch. The Adept drew his sword, and Avi laughed. The men of Talynis crashed into the legionnaires, leaving Avi and the Adept in a pocket.

The Adept stabbed forward—he had more reach, both of arm and blade —but Avi had the relic. He deflected the thrust, and with a single, deft flick, scored a shallow cut against the Adept's arm.

The scream that erupted from the man—it was inhuman in its agony.

The *Nihilo* Blade's eerie hum became a *roar* as it drank of the Adept's power. The frost clinging to the Adept dissipated. The desert sun's warmth cut through the chill.

Fearful eyes fixed on Avi for just a moment. The sod was too horrified even to lift his sword in defense. Avi skewered him through the neck.

"The devil of ice is dead!" he shouted. "Push them back to the gate!"

The fighters roared in exultation. The legionnaires began to give ground, inch by inch, then yard by yard. One slipped in the blood and gore perished beneath a rain of blades.

Yes! Yes!

Talynis would win the day. Without their witch, the legion was nothing more than any other enemy. Let them learn this day the fury of Talynis, favored nation of the Four.

Avi let the men carry forward, slipping out from the press. This part of the defense would succeed. So he would return to the rooftops and seek out any other pockets of conflict where—

The tramp of feet pounding the earth, the rattle of armor.

Avi spun, looking down the road. He gave a sigh of relief.

Prince Tamiq's elite guard rounded the corner. Now there was no doubt—

It was instinct that saved him, screaming a warning before his conscious mind could recognize the danger.

He dropped to the ground as a spear whistled overhead.

Tamiq's men barreled down on him, murder in their eyes.

Treachery.

"Betrayal!" he yelled, scrambling to his feet.

He danced back, ducking a thrust spear, then turning tail and sprinting for all he could manage. By blind luck or divine favor, no other missile struck him.

"Traitors! Behind!"

But the fighting men at the fore were locked against the legionnaires— legionnaires who recovered their vigor now.

Caught in a crab's pincer.

A javelin sprouted from the back of a man ahead of Avi. He went down with bewilderment in his eyes. The men at his sides realized the danger, took up the warning cry.

Avi grabbed men by their shoulders to turn them around, shouting all the while, "Behind! Traitors from behind!"

Prince Tamiq's guard crashed into them like a battering ram. A dozen loyal men died in seconds. Avi was knocked to the ground, his shoulder screaming in pain, hot blood pumping across his skin.

Get up.

Against all the pain and fear, his higher mind gave the order—the only way he could hope to survive. The first threat was getting trampled. He scrambled to his feet, only to be knocked down again, kicked in the chest. All the while, he clutched the precious relic in a white-knuckled grasp. He would not lose it—not before death took him and the Wandering God snatched his soul away.

An iron grip clamped on his collar, hauled him to his feet. A man whose name he did not know had rescued him—and heartbeats later, the man fell to a vicious blow from one of the traitors. Avi screamed and returned a strike, driving the black point into the traitor's eye.

At Avi's back, just a few men away, were the legionnaires. He was caught between two walls of death. Spears leapt forward, swords milled down and out, shields clashed and clanged.

But Avi knew a lost cause when he saw it. He knew they had no chance.

And he knew what he had to do.

'A *glorious death,'* Crow had told him, '*is a blessing for warriors. We of the shadows have no such luxury.'*

Avi slashed open another traitor's throat. The man at his left fell, clutching his gut, wailing for his mother and his gods.

'*We are cowards, so others may be bold.'*

The man at his right made a mad push forward, cutting down a single member of Tamiq's guard and wounding a second before he was made into a crimson fountain.

'*We die in wretched silence, so others may die to the tune of a war choir.'*

Tears burned Avi's eyes.

He stepped back, slipping into the narrow space between the two killing fronts, and he shoved his way through. "King's Viper!" he yelled, hating the sound of his voice. "Make a path!"

And somehow, even amidst the crush of bodies and chaos of battle, they made way for him, opening a channel barely wide enough to admit him passage.

If any of them begrudged him for fleeing, they did not show it. Avi ran between them, making for the wall of some ransacked shop.

He vaulted to catch the lip of a window and heaved himself up to grab the edge of the roof. A javelin clattered against the stone. His wounded shoulder screamed as he levered himself up.

"For King Malik!" he roared over the clash.

"Malik!" answered a few men who still had the breath and presence of mind.

Avi saluted them with raised blade as he turned and fled.

They would be dead in minutes, if not seconds, their souls taken by the Wandering God to the place of rest prepared for the righteous.

May the Warrior give strength to their arms and hearts—may they slay a dozen foes for every righteous man that falls!

Such prayers echoed in an endless litany as he scrammed across the rooftops. He had killed an Adept—an impossible feat. An achievement worthy of song. And it meant nothing to him.

Because in his heart, he feared the city was lost.

The palace was far—too far. Prince Tamiq, Tamiq the traitor. The king's own brother working with the Lazarran Empire! Was Tamiq's betrayal already within the palace walls? Did it start there?

A terrible fear seized Avi's heart and guts as he ran.

What if Malik is dead? What of his sons?

What if Tamiq is king by right?

Such fears dogged his heels as he scrambled across the city, paying no heed to pain or risk as he vaulted across the city. On the streets below, bloodshed and burning buildings marked the incessant advance of the Lazarran legion.

And by now, Tamiq's guard was out in full force, aiding in the conquest of Avi's city.

Too many...when did Tamiq amass such a force?

That was a failure of his own office—it was the task of the Vipers to keep watch for all subtle machinations and unseen threats to the throne. Right under their noses, the king's brother had been working against them, and they had been blind to it.

Avi leaped across the thoroughfare, catching the opposite roof with his fingertips. Someone below shouted after him, but he was already gone by the time javelins whistled through the empty space where he had been.

How could we have missed this?

And as if in answer, another horrifying possibility raised its head.

What if we *are corrupted?*

He didn't even have the time to consider the ramifications of that before he caught sight of the Temple.

It flew Tamiq's banner. The priesthood had thrown their support behind Tamiq's claim to the throne.

That meant the gods were against Malik. The gods were against Avi.

For a tremulous moment, all the world seemed to hang in stillness.

"No," Avi hissed, breaking forward, carried on by rage and fear and blind determination.

Wrong—they're all wrong! Malik is king, so long as he lives! This is the law of Talynis.

So long as he lives. So long as he lives.

The Temple lay at the center of the city, and the palace was not so far from it, nestled in the northeast quarter. The legionnaire assault had not yet reached it.

But they had not needed to, for Tamiq's men were all over the place. They had done no damage to the palace itself, but strewn all across the roads, atop the wall parapets, along the lawn and throughout the gardens—bodies hewn and hacked unto gory demise.

Avi saw it all in his mind's eye. He knew already how Malik's loyal men had been surprised, overwhelmed. In the traitors' hands were Lazarran steel swords and steel-headed spears. They strutted about in breastplates that shone brightly under the noon sun.

The palace had fallen. The only hope, then, was that Malik had escaped. Tamiq would have known the plans for such a retreat, though. It was the duty of the king's brother to oversee such things, to ensure that the king was secure.

There could be no greater treachery—handed over unto death, or worse, by one's own sibling.

Could the gods abide such a thing? Never—not in the slightest.

The poison had infected Four-only-knew how many Talynisti warriors. It had even infected the priests—but Avi knew it could not have reached everywhere.

His training asserted itself. First, go to ground.

In any other situation, that would mean headquarters—but he had no reason to believe it was secure. If he were Prince Tamiq, then he would have either destroyed or taken hold of the Vipers' base by now. It was not far from the palace, and though disguised, known to Tamiq and his advisors.

That path was closed to Avi then, though he would scope it out at a later date. Now came survival, living long enough to retaliate another day.

Avi turned his back on the palace and ran south, seeking the one place he could trust for certain. It would be a narrow thing, but he thought he could make it there before the legion's advance reached him.

Already, he heard cries of surrender going up, the rattle of weapons thrown down. A part of him resented that, wanted to scream out, *'Stand and fight till death!'* But he too was setting aside the blade—for today. Lose the battle, prolong the war.

His shoulder wound was not severe, but blood loss was taking its toll. The blessed, vigorous shock of adrenaline was fading, and his head spun.

Four streets. I can make that.

The first one, he jumped. The second, he barely cleared, tumbling into a roll and earning bruises all along his good shoulder and back.

At the third, he had to clamber down—only to be surprised partway down by a gaggle of three legionnaires ahead of the main force.

On instinct, he jumped from the wall, crashing atop one of them and gashing open the man's throat. Then, a roll to the side, slipping under the attacks of the dying man's comrades.

As he popped to his feet, Avi batted away a messy spear thrust, grabbing the shaft and pulling the legionnaire off her feet. Taking her spear, he jammed the butt into the throat of the last standing soldier before hastily planting its head into the base of the tripped soldier's skull, right beneath her helmet.

Avi pounced forward, deflecting a clumsy slash from the choking man's sword, and ramming the *Nihilo* Blade below the armpit, into the heart.

He sighed once, then took off again at a run—before wincing and dropping to one knee.

He'd rolled an ankle in the melee.

Always one thing after another.

Picking himself up, he limped along, huffing and grimacing against the pain. Thank the Four, the last street was nearly empty—only the distant backs of still-retreating Talynisti were visible to him.

But he could hear the legionnaires' march, the shouted orders he could not understand but could guess well enough at the meaning.

'Find anyone who hasn't surrendered. Kill them.'

"Good luck with that," he snarled, tucking his still-bloodied blade through his belt.

Avi slipped into an alleyway, passing one door ajar, another shut tight—and then the third.

He rapped quickly against the wood, ignoring the faded lettering. "Madam Sahir," he hissed. "It's me."

Silence.

The approach of the legionnaires grew louder. Avi's neck prickled.

"Sahir?"

She couldn't have fled, could she?

"*Sahir!*"

He was half-turning tail to seek out some other desperate possibility, when the door opened and revealed a wizened old face peering out at him with two glimmering eyes.

"I don't care if the stars themselves are warring in the heavens—you call me *Madam*, boy."

A firm grip clamped down on his shoulder and pulled him in from the street.

Madam Sahir shut the door and slammed home the bar, plunging the home into darkness.

Avi scanned the room. "Children in the basement?"

"Aye, and I won't have you near them. Get down the ladder—Samara! Clean this blood."

A pretty young woman swept into the room, fear written in her eyes, determination set in her jaw. When she saw him, the fear morphed into shock. "Avi?" she whispered.

He grunted in acknowledgment as he pulled aside the carpet and opened the revealed trapdoor. "Samara." He set his foot on the first rung of the ladder, then groaned and nearly fell as he tried to place the other.

"Four Gods, boy," snapped Madam Sahir, "have you got any legs under you?"

From outside, the raucous thunder of doors pounded on, then kicked in. "Help him down! I'll take care of the blood." And with all the speed of a desert falcon, the Madam set upon wiping away the blood with her skirts.

Avi grunted, bracing with his one good arm, leaning on his one good leg. Next thing he knew, Samara slipped around him and dropped into the cellar with a muted thud.

The pounding was at the neighbor's door. The shouting was barely muffled.

As Avi descended, Samara took his weight and helped him down, step by shaky step. At the final three rungs, his arm seized up, and he collapsed onto her. She muttered some words the Madam would not have been pleased to hear, but helped him to rest against the wall.

"Hells but you're heavy," she sighed, then swore again. "And now *I've* got blood on me. You remember where the bandages are?"

He winced, but nodded.

"We'll check on you later."

Samara scrambled up the ladder and shut the trapdoor, plunging the cellar into darkness. No sooner had the heavy carpet been dragged back into place did Avi hear banging at the door.

In a moment, the door opened. Soldiers' thunderous footsteps stormed in.

Avi lay still as he could manage, one hand clamped over his wound, the other over his mouth as he breathed as shallowly as he could.

"What's all this!" squawked Madam Sahir. She was speaking Karellan, the trade language.

A gruff voice answered in the same tongue, a heavy Lazarran accent on his words. "Any soldiers? Young men? Hand them over—the fighting is done."

"If it was over, you wouldn't be waving that spear in my face. Look at this, you're tracking blood in here. This is an *orphanage*, if you can't read the sign."

"Orphanage," drawled the legionnaire. "Where are the orphans?"

"In the basement, with my granddaughter. Not a boy down there over the age of ten, mind you! None strong enough to hold a sword. Go look for yourself and bleed me if I lie."

The heavy tread rumbled through the house, marked by the faint jingle of armor.

Down the stairs, they went.

Avi held his breath.

The muffled sound of another exchange reached Avi. The basement was adjacent to this cellar, but he couldn't make out words through the thick stone.

And then the footsteps went back up.

"King Tamiq rules this city, with the power of the Ninth Imperial Legion under command of Legate Flavia Iscator. Anyone who harbors enemies to that reign and alliance will be punished."

"I'm sure," snapped the Madam. "Now if you're done traumatizing my children, please be along."

"*Ave Imperator*," said the Lazarran. "Means 'Hail the Emperor.' Get used to saying it, crone."

The door slammed shut.

Avi waited a breath, then two.

He finally allowed himself to relax.

Now, where were those bandages?

3

CLICK-CLACK-CLATTER

THE MASSACRE IN HYRGALLIA...HOW strange now to think of all the ways it foreshadowed what was to come.
—*The Memoirs of Flavia Iscator*

∽

IT DID NOT TAKE LONG to track down Scanlon and apprise him of the situation. She showed him the engraved buckle, though he was hesitant to look at it. Soldiers were a superstitious sort—which often made them wary around Adepts even in the best of times. Actually being brought face to face with an arcane relic—no wonder the captain looked uneasy.

When he had heard all Reiva had to say, he scratched his chin. "We need to go back to the camp then. We'll muster what forces we can, perhaps send for reinforcements from the main body. A Scout team can be sent to seek out this castle they mentioned."

Reiva shook her head. "That will take too long—based on what the couple hiding this relic said, the ones we're after passed through just this morning."

"There's no way we could catch them—it's going to snow soon and cover their tracks. Besides, the men won't be happy if they have to spend a night at forced march through the cold."

"Captain, ordinarily I would defer to you, but this is a matter of the arcane. Under normal circumstances, tracking them from this point would be a fool's errand, but now that I have this relic in hand, I can seek others like it. Lars and Hilda said that all the men had one just like it. I've already stretched out my perception, and I can sense a trail of similar power to what is held inside this one."

Scanlon looked skeptical, but also curious. "So you could sniff them out like a bloodhound."

"More or less, but the trace fades with time. If we're going to do this, we need to go now. I can take a small detachment—two squadrons—and we give chase while you and the others return to camp and bring reinforcements. But we'll have to leave now. Hilda said the castle they are going to is about three days' walk. With a small force and my abilities, we can overtake them before they escape our reach."

He was wavering. She needed to hit home one last time.

"Scanlon, whatever these things are, they're powerful. I don't know what they do exactly, but we both saw how those men brutalized those legionnaires. There's something wild about the power contained within this relic. Perhaps it's a corruption of the *Ars Theron*." Then, seeing his perplexed expression, quickly added, "The Art of Beasts. Maybe it lets them call wild animals to aid them—it would explain the wounds."

Scanlon sighed. "I understand the value of putting a stop to these enemies before they do more harm, but if they're as dangerous as you say, then you very well could be walking into a death trap. If I lose an Adept in the field, my career's deader than you'll be."

Reiva didn't have a response to that. Truth be told, she had been thinking of her own career—how great the renown would be when she reported to the Sanctum that she recovered a half-dozen pagan relics on her first campaign as a fully commissioned Adept.

"Give me a third squadron then," she said, hoping she didn't sound too pleading.

The captain frowned. She was asking for nearly three-fourths their current number.

"This will all be on my head, Scanlon. But I can't let this chance slip away. Give me these legionnaires, or I go after them myself."

The captain rubbed his nose. "Hells, Adept, you're giving me no choice here."

She felt a twinge of guilt, but she did not relent.

When he let out a sigh, she knew she'd prevailed.

"Take Gascal's squadron with you, then. You'll need to be on foot to hold pace with them and replenish their stamina, so I'll take your horse and send a rider ahead of us back to the camp. Tomorrow morning we'll follow with a full cohort, hopefully with more from the main force on the way, if the winds let me send a messenger hawk."

Reiva nodded, exultance filling her to the brim. The Flame was roaring in response to her anticipation. "Sacrifice an extra sheep for us, would you?"

Scanlon scoffed. "I'll sacrifice two if we can spare them. Gods be with you, Adept. For Emperor and Eagle."

"For Emperor and Eagle," she echoed.

QUICK AS THEY COULD MUSTER, Reiva and the three squadrons set out from Hamstadt at forced march pace. Reiva was at the fore, clutching the strange artifact in her hand, eyes scanning ahead feverishly.

The trail was hours old, so it was faint. She could name some senior Adepts who no doubt could have followed it as easily as a ship follows a blazing beacon in a clear night, but she did not have as many years under her belt. It took nearly all her concentration to pick out the residue of the artifacts. It was a good thing, too, that the group they were tracking had several in hand—only one or two and the trail almost certainly would have been invisible to her by now.

Then again, the more artifacts there were, the greater the risk to her and her soldiers.

Don't worry about that, she told herself. *Scanlon doesn't know how strong an Adept truly is.*

That set her at ease a bit. Though the Adept Corps was regarded by many of the Empire's best military minds (and nonmilitary minds who felt the need to comment) as the key engine of the Empire's unstoppable conquest, most legionnaires had not actually served in close proximity to an Adept. They heard stories, of course, but there simply weren't enough Adepts for every cohort to have one. At any time, a given *legion* might receive an attaché of two, maybe three Adepts given the need, and given how plentiful the numbers of the Corps were at the time. The Sanctum's ranks were thin at the moment though, so Adepts were a precious resource, and Scanlon had never served beside one.

Let alone one who bore the coveted *Ars Vulcana*, the Art of Fire.

The men they were after may have been able to slay a few legionnaires caught off-guard, but they were in for a very rude surprise once Reiva found them.

After an hour of marching, Reiva called a brief rest for the troops. During the rest, she moved among them, laying her hand on each. To all she bestowed a channeling of aether—just a drop, so as not to overwhelm them —but the effect was instant and marked. As soon as the infusion hit, soldiers stood up straighter, their breathing evened.

When Reiva had first done this for the soldiers during her early days with Ironback Company, people had been nervous—now they were eager for it.

Reiva had to be cautious not to overextend herself, but no symptoms of aether sickness had manifested yet, so she felt no qualms about re-infusing the troops once an hour. With regular refreshment, they were able to keep a hard pace, covering far more ground than they might during a normal march, even given the rough terrain.

Still, Reiva felt a growing uneasiness. When she led them at the front, she always kept her aether sense attuned to the energy of the artifact and the trail their quarry left behind.

The trail's signature had grown in strength a bit—unless that was just her own wishful thinking playing tricks on her—but not as much as she would have hoped.

That confirmed, then, that these men were likely able to fortify their own bodies using the artifacts. That was disconcerting for two reasons: one, it meant they were also gaining ground faster than the ordinary human might, so the chase was going to be harder than expected.

Two, it meant that Reiva possibly needed to revise her assumptions about what sort of relics they were using. She wasn't ready to abandon her theory that this power was some sort of lesser form of the Art of Beasts, but perhaps she had to assume that it was a more sophisticated craftsmanship than she had been willing to grant.

Subconsciously, she touched at the arcane focus around her neck. Its cool touch grounded her perceptions, and she sensed it resonating to the frequency of her own soul, like two singers harmonizing.

It was an Adept's focus that enabled her to interact with aether and shape magic. Without a focus, an Adept was almost powerless, since channeling aether without the controlled gateway of a focus was a sure road to rapid onset aether sickness—and usually death.

It was why being stripped of one's focus was considered the most severe sort of punishment for an Adept, worse than even execution. She had never even tried explaining it to someone outside the Adept Corps, because it was impossible to understand how precious an Adept's focus was. It was, in some ways, the linchpin of their entire existence after being inducted into the Corps. It was at the touch of an arcane focus that a child was identified as possessing the capacity to shape aether—that had happened to Reiva when she was about twelve—and soon after, the focus became a constant companion. To lack it was worse than to lack armor, sword, or shield—it was to miss a part of oneself.

The arcane focus was the miracle of Imperial engineering—the secret of their construction supposedly handed down by the High God Arkhon himself to the First Emperor.

But if these Hyrgallians could channel aether to reinforce their own bodies...could that mean that others were beginning to scratch the surface of crafting focuses of their own?

Reiva's head swam with these possibilities as the snowy ground rolled underfoot, pine forests passing by.

Again, her mind turned to how significant it would be for her when she brought these relics back to the Sanctum, with a report of how they had been used by the enemy.

She thought of the golden laurel crown worn by the Empire's champions when they marched through the capital in triumphal parades.

"Rest!" she called. "After this, we move double time. The bastards aren't getting away from us."

If anyone had doubts, they did not dare voice them to the Adept as she set about infusing them with aether.

And though a headache began to throb behind Reiva's eyes, she paid it no heed.

She was an Adept, fully initiated and brilliantly forged by the Sanctum; she could bear a minor case of aether sickness. She'd sleep it off tonight.

∿

THEY PUSHED on for an hour after sunset until they found a suitable place to make camp for the night. They chose a cave in the nearby forest, where the snow had not penetrated far inside. Legionnaires carried what they needed to survive on their backs, so they quickly set bedrolls out and devised a watch. Reiva allowed herself the luxury of a full night of sleep, knowing she needed to rest off as much wear on her soul as she could. Aether sickness was a dangerous condition, and one liable to advance more and more rapidly as an Adept pushed herself.

The last act of magic she did before bedding down was to light the fire. Of course, the legionnaires could spark it themselves with flint, but Reiva saw no need to refrain from more plainly practical uses of magic. Some Adepts spurned that sort of thing, she knew. They thought it better to reserve magic for grand acts of war, not something so pedestrian as lighting a fire.

Reiva's mentor, Alyat, had very simple words when it came to Adepts who held onto such notions—"However much honor or power you give someone, that's how far they're able to shove their head up their own ass."

Laying her head on her arm, she smiled at the memory. Sleep had her in moments.

Her dreams were not as pleasant as her final waking thoughts.

She was in a dark place—perhaps the cave, though she could see no walls. She tried to take a step, but her foot struck bones. In a heartbeat, she kindled fire in her hands, bright as she could.

For as far as the light reached, all the earth was bones, picked clean entirely of flesh. Skulls, scapulas, ribs—the thought of how many people were represented before her was staggering. Entire legions would have to die to leave a spectacle such as this.

And then she heard them rattle.

She spun to the sound, but all she saw was a far-reaching expanse of bleached white.

Someone was moving amongst them, just beyond the reach of her light. The *click-clack-clatter* sounded in the void like some macabre instrument beating an unnerving tune.

She threw a jet of fire—*there!*

A dark form leaped into the shadows. She caught just a flicker of it, but she thought it looked furry and rugged. A bear?

And then she heard the howling.

Reiva snapped awake, a cry of alarm in her throat.

The legionnaires nearest her roused immediately, scrambling for their weapons. Reiva had her own sword in hand before she realized the howls were gone—they had only been in her dreams.

"At ease, at ease."

It took a moment for the command to get through to the adrenaline-soaked legionnaires, but she managed to get them to stand down.

She also knew, though, that dreams were one of the ways the mind responded to the flow of aether. She checked to make sure the relic was still in her hip pouch, then told the legionnaires to begin rousing the others to prepare for the day's march. A quick glance at the cave's mouth told her dawn was approaching. There was no sense in waiting any longer; not while there was still a chance they might catch their quarry.

Still, Reiva made sure to walk about the outside of their campsite on her own as the troops woke up. She stretched out her aetheric sense, probing for any indication of danger. Nothing. The trail from the previous day was nearly gone, though. They would have to push themselves.

Hilda and Lars had said the castle was about four days' travel, but at the pace these rebels were moving, that could easily be cut down to two. Already, the mountain range was well within sight. They would probably hit the feet of the jagged formations while the sun was still up.

Reiva sighed, confronting the reality of the situation.

If they didn't catch up by tonight, she might have to call for them to turn around and head back. That would mean admitting defeat.

She needed a new plan.

And by the time she returned to the camp, she had one. She addressed the troops as a whole, not bothering to speak with the sergeants first. She was going to be taking volunteers for this, and she didn't want to spend any more time than absolutely necessary.

"If we're going to succeed in catching the men we're after—the men who killed our comrades—then we need to go faster. But I can't keep a force of thirty people replenished and be fresh enough to fight. So I need one squadron to go ahead with me, as fast as we can, with minimal gear. You'll run like you've never run before, but I'll keep you strong enough for it. The other squadrons will follow as close as they can, so they can reinforce us, but odds are we will be facing these opponents with diminished numbers."

She took a moment to look them all over once more. "Scanlon gave me all of you because of how dangerous these foes are. Many of you saw what they did to the patrol they fell upon. But those brave legionnaires killed one of them, and I'll be with you. We can kill them—I wouldn't propose this if I didn't think that—but it will be dangerous as marching on the hells themselves. So anyone who comes with me: double pay and honors for the month."

That got them thinking. That could mean early promotion, and besides, hardly any legionnaire was satisfied with how much pay he got for the sweat and blood he gave. It was Sergeant Tharrick, though, who spoke first.

"Adept, be honest with us. If we decide to go back, will you continue pursuing them on your own?"

Reiva had considered that, but the answer was painfully obvious. "No, I cannot do this on my own—not given the enemy numbers. With a squadron though, it's possible."

Tharrick sucked at his teeth. "Right then. I'm with you." Turning to his squadron, he said, "Rest of you don't need to come with me, but I'm telling your wives and husbands you thought the wind was too chilly to bring home some extra denarii."

Instantly, the mood among Tharrick's squadron changed, hesitation and curiosity bursting into uproarious protest. Every single one of his legionnaires volunteered. Reiva had to fight to keep a relieved sigh from bursting forth.

And then, Sergeant Meridi shouted over the clamor. "Are you sure you can only take one squadron with you, Adept? I'd hate for you to end up dead in the snow because Tharrick and his half-wits forgot which end of a sword was sharp."

Now Reiva couldn't help laugh. She did some estimation in her mind. "I can bring a second, but I won't be able to keep you all fresh. It will be hard going for all of us. We'll be fighting tired."

"As if we're not used to it—you think Scanlon ever cared? Bastard once made us fight while half of us had the flu."

There were ample laughs as people confirmed their presence at the infamous event, some readily calling out other instances where bodily miseries hadn't been enough to keep them from battle.

The Empire's greatest military minds said the Adepts were key to Lazarra's conquest—but those who had served on the ground, among the rank and file, knew that equally important was the veteran legionnaire's unflinching ability to be miserable, and enjoy it.

"Tharrick and Meridi will come with me then. Gascal, can you bring up the rear with our excess equipment?"

The sergeant gave a lopsided grin. "Aye, we can be pack mules while the rest of you get all the fun."

Reiva thanked him for stooping so low, and Tharrick chirped up, "Always thought you had a face like an ass—now you get to work like one!"

The joking and ribbing came to a hasty end though, as Reiva mustered the two squadrons—having shed everything save a day and a half's rations, their armor, sword, shield, and a heavy cloak. They'd be counting on Gascal to follow them, and everyone knew that without the Adept's reinforcing magic, the third squadron would suffer a heavy march.

So, as Reiva led the two squadrons out, she felt the Flame burning strong again—burning with expectation for the fight, certainly, but also burning with pride. Pride in herself, and pride that she was part of that brilliant and unbreakable force known as the Lazarran Legions.

As she honed in on the trail, she almost felt sorry for their quarry.

4

THE CHASE

Duke Faydn's rebellion seemed a minor nuisance when it first began—an ideal theater for a young Adept to prove her quality. Well, what happened to Reiva is well known. But the duke remained a thorn in the Emperor's side for quite some time, even after Reiva left.

Who could have imagined, though, the way the world would change by the time Reiva and Faydn at long last met so many months later?

—*The Memoirs of Flavia Iscator*

～

The chase was indeed a brutal one. Reiva had to ration herself when it came to channeling—her poor sleep meant she could still feel some of the previous day's wear on her soul. The pace would have been grueling even on a nice day, but of course, today the weather took a turn for the worse.

The winds whipped at Reiva's face like a thousand knives raked across the skin—she could only imagine how bad it was for those not blessed with the *Ars Vulcana*. She longed to summon her magic to further ward off the cold, but she forced herself to persevere through the frigid lashings. She couldn't spare herself such luxuries, not when there was a chance she'd be in battle soon.

At midday, they took a slightly longer rest. Legionnaires huddled together, backs to the wind, as they chewed on salted jerky. It was tough as shoe leather, but it revived them enough to keep going. Magical refreshment was potent, but the body still needed sustenance.

Reiva was more experienced in subsisting off aether, so she ate a smaller portion than most, taking the time to go on further ahead.

The trail was getting stronger—she was certain of it. That meant they were catching up. The harder pace was paying off. When they set out at dawn, it had been faint as a distant candle—now it was more like a bonfire.

They were also getting closer and closer to the mountains, though, and Reiva doubted they would be able to give effective chase at that point. They needed to catch up before then, ideally while the sun was still up. Given the short winter days, that did not afford them much wiggle room.

She called an early end to the rest. There were no complaints, only grim determination. They could tell this would be the hard push at the end. Reiva had specifically taken veteran soldiers for this reason.

This sort of test separated the consummate warriors from the failures. It was a test of will and discipline. After one final rejuvenation from Reiva, they broke out into pursuit.

Reiva kept her attention honed to the trail. It became stronger in her perception. She thought for a moment she could even smell that strange odor Hilda had reported. Whether it was just in her head or whether they were really that close, she didn't care—she just let it drive her harder.

Her legs had been burning for some time, but she didn't call a stop. The sun was drooping. They had perhaps two hours before it set.

The legionnaires kept pace with her, the sergeants calling out the rhythm with unfaltering strength.

On they went, always dogged by the fear their quarry would slip their grasp after they had come so close. That meant failure. That meant their chance to avenge the deaths of their comrades was foiled, and their enemies lived to kill another day.

Sunset painted the sky with brilliant colors—angry orange streaks, pink hues. The clouds turned red like blood in a frothing river.

On they went. On they went, and with every step, Reiva's heart pounded with terror at the thought of failing after having come so far.

The sun slipped behind the knife-edge peaks of the mountains.

The sky was dimming.

The trail was brightening. But it was not bright enough.

Reiva felt herself falter—then shoved that thought away. That was weakness talking. She was forged of steel, wasn't she? A perfect weapon crafted for the Emperor's own hand. That was the essence of an Adept.

So she did not stop, and neither did her compatriots. Though they were huffing, too spent of breath and energy even to curse their situation, they kept pace with her. They pressed on, on into the dark, on into the cold.

"*Enough.*"

Reiva hardly even realized she had said it. She marveled that her own feet had halted beneath her. She was surprised to hear the clatter of almost two dozen legionnaires arresting their motion.

But she had given the order. She had brought them to a stop.

She stood there, the only sounds the ragged breathing and eerie wind.

It's over.

She knew they were too late. She knew she was doing them no good, running them hard in the dark of winter like this. She knew she was only deluding herself.

When she turned to the legionnaires, she saw her own bitterness reflected back at her. They knew. Perhaps they had known longer than her, but pressed on out of duty and obligation. Out of hope, even.

"They're in the mountains by now. They're too far ahead of us. We're not charging up a snow-laden peak in the dark of night." She shook her head. Were these words even coming out of her own mouth?

"We're done. We make camp for the night, then tomorrow morning turn back to meet with Gascal."

She saw them deflating, weighed down by failure and dejection.

"We'll return," she said, putting as much strength into her voice as she could. "With a stronger force—Scanlon is going to marshal troops from the main body, and then we'll be at the tip of the spear when the time comes to take the castle."

It was meager consolation. There was precisely zero chance of a siege beginning in the winter—it would be suicidal. At *most* they would scout the area. They would need to wait months, during which they could be transferred to another part of the campaign, and some other hands would complete the work they had set up here.

Meridi's voice cut through the fog of disappointment. "We passed some sort of rock structure, about a half hour back. An old temple, maybe. We can spend the night there."

Reiva affirmed the suggestion, and they began the grueling walk back—harder than the run had been.

The troops did an about face, so Reiva brought up the rear now, with the sergeants at the front. She let herself drop back a bit. Following the shuffling footsteps of the legionnaires, she hung her head.

I was sure I could do it.

Well, you were wrong. It happens. Who were you, to think that you could pull off something so grandiose on your first campaign? Now you'll write a report about the relics, and some senior Adept will be dispatched here to handle this.

And that was the heart of it. Beyond any ordinary dejection she would feel from a failure like this was the knowledge that she would almost certainly be relegated to a supporting role. The Sanctum would likely leave her here to support whichever senior Adept was sent out, but then she would only receive the glory of an assistant. This was beyond someone such as her.

She held out the bronze buckle engraved with those strange runes. Under the bright light of the full moon, she could just barely see her face reflected in it.

She looked pathetic. A spurned child. Petulant.

An Adept, a flawless weapon in the hands of the Emperor?

Get over yourself.

Her fingers traced along the engravings in the bronze. Thin lines, expertly marked. And still, within the metal, the arcane power straining to be free.

Straining to be...to be...

She stopped. Something had changed.

She hadn't noticed it—she had been so focused on the trail. So focused she hadn't noticed the change in the relic she carried on her very person.

She had recognized its bestial aura early on, but she had only felt that insofar as the power longed to be free. Now though...

Her heart was hammering.

Now it was longing to be together—together with its kin.

How could seven men get ahold of relics like this?

If they were made as a set—if their power came from their unity.

The howl from her dream echoed down through her consciousness, sending goosebumps rippling down her arms.

If they were a pack.

"Company halt!" she bellowed, cursing how frantic her own voice sounded.

There was confusion up ahead as the legionnaires realized she had fallen behind. The sergeants were giving orders to turn about, but Reiva was already running to them.

"This isn't over!"

Tharrick muscled his way through the ranks to her. "What do you mean? I thought they were too far. And now we've spent time walking away."

Reiva shook her head. "They're not too far, not anymore."

Damnation, how to explain?

She barely understood it herself beyond raw intuition.

"This relic, it's connected to the other ones, and now I can feel that it's responding to their presence. Like a bell, ringing louder and louder with every strike."

Meridi frowned at the object. "Well, we got pretty damn close, I'm sure, but now won't it start quieting again?"

"That's just it—*it's getting louder.*"

It only took a moment for the significance of that to strike the company.

"They're coming back for it," muttered a legionnaire.

"How close?" Tharrick was nearly frantic as he asked. The thrill of impending battle was creeping into his eyes. Others looked the same as expectation jumped from person to person like a wildfire through trees.

"I don't know," she admitted, "so we act as fast as we can. Meridi, how defensible did that temple look?"

The sergeant twisted her lips. "From the glimpse I got, it's not ideal, but better than open ground.

"I'll take it. Double time, and we dig in. When they get to us, we'll be ready to fight like hell. For Emperor and Eagle!"

"Emperor and Eagle!" roared the company.

All fatigue evaporated from them as adrenaline surged.

Reiva was glad the darkness hid her smile, because she must have looked mad.

This wasn't over—but it was about to be.

5

DREAMS

THE WOLF CAST a ghoulish shadow over the Ninth Legion during our time in Dav-maiir. Many times I woke in the middle of the night, clutching at a dagger secreted under my pillow, certain he had come for me.

Well, I live, but many of my best officers from those days do not. Even now, knowing what I do about him, it seems impossible to see him as a mere human. I think, like the Lion, he was possessed by a need to survive though all the world conspired against him.

It is a bit of divine humor that the two of them bore such eponyms.

—*The Memoirs of Flavia Iscator*

∿

IT WASN'T long before there came a soft tap at the trapdoor. Avi came to attention from his near-stupor. For a moment, his heart jolted, but then he remembered where he was.

Madam Sahir came down the ladder, huffing with every step, an oil lamp in one hand. "Soldiers. Always the same. I've seen a thousand like them and I'll see a thousand more before my death. Mm? Boy, don't tell me you've gone and bled out."

"You know my name," he murmured. "And I'm all right. I'm just feeling the wine."

"That stuff's light as water."

"Well, I did lose a lot of blood before I got these bandages on."

Madam Sahir grumbled, holding the light over Avi. "Stitches?"

Avi thought for a moment. "Think so, yeah."

"Should've left a needle and gut down here. Well, I'll bring my kit. Try not to burn from the heat of this lamp."

He would have snorted, but all he could do was lean his head back against the wall.

Now that he'd come back to awareness, the guilt began to creep into his gut. The shame. Far worse than the pain pulsing in his wounds.

The city is lost.

That brief moment of glory he'd experienced when he killed the Adept —it seemed so childish now. The blade lying in the dust beside him was one of the rarest, most fabled weapons in all the world—a relic that could strip Adepts of their magic, turning them into humans as frail as any other. So pointless. The Lazarrans had taken the capital of Talynis, and it had only cost them one Adept, thanks to Prince Tamiq.

King Tamiq, now.

When the Madam returned, Malik's health was the first thing on Avi's lips.

She shook her head. "No one knows anything yet. If I hear anything, so will you."

Avi nodded, appreciative that, at least on this subject, she was not so rough. Madam Sahir was a hard woman who gave no undue respect to anyone who did not deserve it—but she had always spoken of the importance of a good king in Talynis. Evil kings brought evil times.

With a small knife, she sliced away the bandages Avi had tied over his shoulder. With a sniff, she shook her head and got to work. "It'll need a poultice first to keep the rot away. Some hot water. Samara!"

The younger woman's head appeared at the trapdoor. She spared a glance for Avi as she listened, then disappeared to carry out the Madam's directions.

Madam Sahir fixed Avi with a glance.

"What?"

"I see that look in your eyes, boy. You're wishing she was down here instead."

Avi frowned. "She said she would check on me."

"Not under my roof. I was young once too, you know."

Avi sighed, wincing as she rubbed a cloth against the dried blood clotted around the wound. "So are she and Bareli still...?"

The Madam nodded. "And I won't have you ruining her prospects."

"I wouldn't."

"You say that now, but I remember what you two were like." She hushed him when Samara returned with the kettle of water and the poultice. Avi kept his eyes low so he didn't have to see her face. He felt heat on his cheeks.

She washed out the wound twice, scrubbing it out with another clean cloth, before stitching it closed with the needle and gut. Then she fastened the poultice against the sutures and packed it all beneath expertly wound bandages.

"I'm sorry to bring trouble to your door, Madam."

"Hm? Oh, this is calming for me. Reminds me of simpler times."

Now it was Avi's turn to scoff. "Simpler times like the Raider Tribes?"

"Bandits are always simple—there were just a few more of them in those days. Learned plenty about medicine I did, tending to my Olaub and his brothers. Four Gods bless their rest."

"Four bless," Avi murmured.

The Madam sat back on her haunches, as if inspecting Avi. "You were always so like him. I should've known you would grow up to hold a sword."

"My father did," he said, hollow.

"Aye, and where did that leave him? Same place as my Olaub. Least we never had children before then."

He snorted. "And what did you do? Get a half-dozen."

"Closer to a whole dozen now. Some of the old ones have done well for themselves, though. They support the house."

Avi's half-grin faded, his chin dipped down.

"Oh don't mope like that. You sent when you could."

"Not always."

"Well, you should've been saving up for a wedding gift. Course, wouldn't have had to worry about *that* if you and Samara—"

"It wouldn't have worked."

"I know. I told her as much, and when you proved me right, I held her when she cried over it." She *tsked*, gathering up her medicinal trappings. "Little Avi. King's Viper. What do they call you again? Dog?"

"Wolf," he muttered.

A snort. "Wolf, right. That ankle looks all right—just keep weight off it. You can stay here until you're well enough to be on, but I won't have any risk to the children. And—look at me, boy—that means any risk that would happen from you putting thoughts in their heads about going to war. This country has lost too many fathers and sons already—that's why most of them are here in the first place. I won't have you becoming some sort of role model to them, or gods forbid, a hero."

"Don't worry, Madam. I'm no hero. Just a King's Viper."

She sniffed. "Aye. Just that. I'll see that you get some food when dinner's made."

"Thank you, Madam."

She left him with the lamp flickering in the cramped room and shut the trapdoor behind her. In the gloom and silence, guilt returned, throbbing in his chest as blood throbbed in his limbs.

He lowered himself into the place of pure awareness, that chamber of the mind where thought became a running river. He allowed the thoughts to slip by, observed but untouched. Sensation also he regarded as though his body were not his own. In that place, time became nothing to him.

At least, so it was for a moment. The flow of his consciousness shuddered; the river of thought frothed like the cataract waterfalls of Mizkhar, always bearing the same message—reminders of death, of failure, of defeat. And those last two were worse than the first.

His muscles tightened, his breathing went shallow, and it took some time to restore the blank flow of his inner being. He shifted like that, back and forth between the purity of impassiveness and the discord of thought.

A sound pulled him back to his surroundings—the creak of the trapdoor. The lamp still burned, though weakly.

Samara stepped off the ladder, bringing in one hand a small wooden bowl. The scent of roasted vegetables and barley reached him, and his stomach made him acutely aware of how he had not eaten since before dawn.

"The Madam," he said, "told me she didn't want you down here."

Samara shrugged. "She wants the children down here less. Besides, she's gone to bed."

Avi nodded, accepting the dish. With his good arm, he fed himself, keeping his eyes low. "Thank you," he muttered around the barley loaf. "I'm sorry to bring you trouble."

"It's all right. No one can avoid trouble today."

He shrugged. "There's trouble and then there's harboring a King's Viper."

"Well, someone has to."

He grew more and more aware of the fact she had not left. "What time is it?" he asked eventually.

"The moon is up. There's a curfew now, from sunset onward. That was about two hours ago."

A curfew? That would make his plans more difficult. Gods willing, it would be lifted by the time he was well enough to take to the rooftops again.

"These roots are good. You cook this?"

She shook her head. "One of the girls. She has a good head for the kitchen."

"Mm. Hopefully that will help her find a place."

"Hopefully."

Avi tried his best to sound casual as he asked his next question.

"Madam told me you and Bareli are still betrothed."

There was the slightest pause. "We are. He's in Shugrith now."

That shouldn't have stung, but it did. "My city," he murmured.

"Right, you were born there. I'm glad he wasn't here."

"Would've been killed."

She just nodded, making a small sound.

"Or surrendered like a coward."

"*Avi.*"

"There's no judgment in that—look at me. I ran. I'm hiding under an old woman's floor. Cowards live to fight another day."

Tension hung between them.

Then she got down and sat against the wall, almost close enough to touch shoulders. Unlike the basement, this cellar was designed to hide a few select goods—or select people, depending on the need—and so it wasn't particularly spacious. Avi went rigid, then kept eating.

You were supposed to leave then.

"You're not a coward," she murmured.

He stopped mid-bite, eyeing her sidelong.

"You're stupid and headstrong and you have a heart of stone sometimes. But I know you wouldn't have come here if you didn't think it was the right thing to do. You probably hate that. You probably wish you could have justified dying out there, like who knows how many others did today. That's not cowardice."

"Shut up," he muttered. "I left here years ago—you don't get to read me like that anymore."

"Well you haven't changed since then, so why shouldn't I be able to?"

"Hm."

When the dish was empty, he leaned his head back against the wall.

The lamp still flickered, though the oil must have been low by now.

"Thirsty?" he asked, eventually.

"Sure."

He reached for the jug of wine he'd opened earlier, handing it to her. She drank from it, then handed it back to him.

She smiled wanly. "Remember how we used to sneak down here? With Uri and Danae?"

"And get sick afterwards," he snorted. "Stuff's thin as water."

"Well, we were kids."

"We were." He realized he was smiling too, and then his smile faded. "What ever happened to the two of them?"

Her smile dropped away too. "I think Uri joined up with some merchants. He always wanted to see the world, remember? Danae...I heard rumors, but I don't know for sure."

"Maybe she found a good husband."

"Maybe. Maybe."

Another silence settled on them. At some point, the lamp went out, plunging them into darkness. It seemed to him that the ghosts of all the childhood friends (and not-friends) who had grown up in this house swirled around them. If he listened closely, he could almost hear their voices—and his own voice was among them. Younger, lighter. Memories of games played, of little adventures. Bold dreams of what they would do when they grew up and left. Bold promises—promises he made and broke.

"You should go to sleep," he said, a part of himself kicking him for it.

"Yeah," she sighed. "I should." As she stood up, she took the wooden bowl from him.

She stopped with one foot on the ladder. "Avi?"

"Hm?"

"Don't...don't die. Even if you think you need to."

He sat in the darkness, but she didn't move.

"I'll try."

"Good." And then she left.

Another promise I might break.

He shuffled around to lie on the ground, spreading a blanket over himself. Sleep evaded him, then came all at once, bringing dreams of death.

6

SHIELDS READY, SWORD ARMS STRONG

WE KNEW the history books and the arcane texts had been doctored or destroyed, but even we did not realize the extent of lost knowledge. The massacre in Hyrgallia impressed that upon us.
—*The Memoirs of Flavia Iscator*

THE PLACE they chose to make their stand was, as Meridi had guessed, some sort of ancient holy site. At the center was a proud menhir, carved with scenes of gods and spirits—probably the local deities. There was no roof, and four wide openings at the cardinal directions gave ample opportunity for the attackers to approach.

If anyone had worshiped at this place recently, there was no trace of it. No ashes from old offerings, no wilted floral decorations or proffered portions of the harvest.

The ground was covered in snow, which the legionnaires quickly took to clearing and packing into low barriers at the entrances. Their enemies would be approaching from the north, so Reiva directed a third of the force to stack up along that entrance, with the remaining two-thirds split to cover the remaining ones.

All the while, she held the relic in hand, attuned to its resonance. Every passing minute, it seemed to sing louder in her mind, and she kept casting glances toward the tree line.

She built and lit two fires on either side of the menhir, using iron braziers that had rusted from the elements. The light from the fire would spoil the attackers' night vision as they approached, leaving the legionnaires as little more than fearsome shadows, backlit by the flame. At the same time, it gave Reiva and her soldiers an ample field of vision.

Tharrick approached and asked how long she guessed until their enemies appeared. Reiva couldn't say—the relic had been steady for the past few minutes.

Tharrick grimaced. "So they're preparing."

Reiva concurred. The tension frayed her nerves, but every extra minute was more time for the legionnaires to build up their snow barricades. If the attack didn't come soon, then—

A long howl pierced the air.

Then, more joined in, until it seemed a veritable chorus was sounding in the darkness. The sound echoed from every which way.

They were surrounded.

All movement stopped as the company froze to listen. There was something primal deep in the human mind, some old memory of what it was like to be prey in the wilderness, that set the body on edge at such a sound.

The howls died away.

Reiva had already briefed them on what to expect, but she shouted, "Expect them to send the wolves first. Keep your shields ready, sword arms strong!"

The call bolstered the legionnaires, and they set their feet, ready for the enemy charge.

Reiva checked her helmet strap and made sure her focus was tucked securely beneath her breastplate. Lastly, she took one last look at the Beast Relic. It almost seemed to glow in her perception.

And right as she moved to tuck it into her hip pouch, a ragged voice came from the shadows.

"You have something of ours."

Reiva put up her hand, ready to kindle fire as she spun northward.

The man was out of sight, but his voice carried as well as the howls had.

"Who are you?" she said. "You are speaking to Adept Reiva."

A sharp chuckle. "What an honor! So kind of you to bring us a dead friend's treasure. Hand it over, and we'll leave you."

"You murdered our own. You'll die for that."

That same chuckle. "I was hoping you'd be difficult."

Reiva waited, eyes flitting side to side. They had every approach covered, they had the defensive advantage. She was sure of—

Tharrick bellowed, "Ready!"

He was at the western entrance—two dark, massive shapes had broken from the night, dashing into the light on all fours at inhuman speed.

Wolves. Despite the surging adrenaline, she felt elation—she'd guessed right at their magic. She had given the right orders to prepare. They were ready for this.

A heartbeat later, another three wolves attacked from the east.

Reiva's mind raced. A true Adept of the Art of Beasts could control a great many animals at a time, but this was a cheap imitation. Perhaps they could each only control one wolf—which meant there was only one more.

She couldn't help smirking. This was going to be—

The western attackers reached the shield line—and *leaped over them*.

The second line of legionnaires yelled, scrambling for their shields, desperately trying to pivot to face the threat, but the bloodshed had already begun.

And Reiva couldn't throw fire without endangering her allies.

She drew her sword, yelling a warning to the other lines. Her instincts told her to reinforce the western lines, but they had Sergeant Tharrick. The north had Meridi.

The eastern lines were about to be hit by three—and the wolves jumped them right as she arrived.

And one was coming right for her.

Reiva threw her shield up right before the beast struck. It was like getting hit with a boulder—even with aether reinforcing her legs, she was nearly knocked off her feet.

She heaved her shield left, chucking off the wolf.

All around her was disarray. The tight lines had been ruined by the enemy's surprise gambit, and there was chaos as legionnaires tripped and struggled to face their foe. Every heartbeat of confusion was capitalized on by the enemies, who tore out throats and ripped apart calves, killing and maiming legionnaires with abandon, spraying blood like rain.

All this, Reiva saw from the corner of her eye, because her attention was fixed on the monstrosity in front of her—as it *stood*.

She had been wrong. They weren't controlling wolves with magic.

The thing before her snarled, jumping forward with gleaming fangs that flashed beneath all-too-human eyes.

They were becoming wolves.

Reiva took the charge on her shield, stabbing around the side with her sword. The steel struck flesh—then turned away.

Her heart caught in her throat, instinct driving her back a half step as knifelike claws swept under her shield. Too slow—she felt the sting of parted flesh, warm blood seeping into her leggings.

She shunted a wave of aether to her thigh to heal the wound—at least enough to stop the bleeding—and then she braced again.

But the wolf-man had turned away, seeing another opportunity. She couldn't do anything but watch as he batted away a legionnaire's sword like it was straw and flayed open the man's throat.

She roared and lunged to skewer the wolf-man through the skull, but without even looking he ducked the strike and returned a body slam.

The blow threw Reiva off her feet, and she slammed into the cold standing stone, helmet *clanging* against the unyielding rock.

Their flesh could turn a blade, their reflexes were inhuman...

In the back of her mind, a panicked thought told her it was not a marvel that so few attackers had killed ten legionnaires—it was a marvel that the legionnaires had managed to bring down *one* of them.

She scrambled to her feet, head ringing, vision swimming.

The vague shape of Sergeant Tharrick interposed itself between her and the wolf-man, weapons thrown aside as he *grappled* the monster, struggling to hold the claws at bay. Reiva flooded her system with aether, feeling a rush like jumping into a glacial river.

Her sight realigned just in time for her to see the wolf-man close his jaws around Tharrick's head.

It was like seeing a child rip apart a straw doll.

Gore splashed over her. Reiva's gut turned.

The Flame roiled with raw rage and fear—and it would not be contained.

She screamed and dropped her sword, thrusting forth her hand.

A jet of red flame burst from her palm, frothing with steam in the cold night air.

It engulfed the wolf-man's head and chest, and for a moment he howled in fury, the aether of his magic resisting hers.

But a pagan relic, no matter how strong, was no match for an Adept.

She poured more power in, feeling her soul strain under the weight of so much channeled energy.

The monster's howling turned to agony, then—silence amid the clamor and din of war.

She cut off the fire, gritting her teeth against the headache already pounding behind her eyes.

The thing's corpse was a half-charred wreck, twitching and ruined beside Tharrick's headless body. Already, the fur and warped musculature was beginning to recede as magic faded along with life.

At the sight of it dead, all Reiva's fear transformed to wrath, and her Flame burned ferociously.

She didn't pick up her sword—she almost threw aside her shield, held back only by years of discipline.

The western legionnaires were fighting with all the courage and vigor they could muster, and she watched a swarm of them bring down another monster, raining down blades upon it, stuffing its maw full of steel.

She recalled the image of the single dead attacker found alongside the murdered legionnaires in the snow—a spear still impaled through his gaping mouth.

"Eyes and mouth!" she yelled. "They're weak at the eyes and mouth."

She hoped someone heard her as she charged into the fray at the eastern lines. They were still beset by two of the wolf-men, and at a glance, almost half her soldiers were either dead or incapacitated.

Reiva locked her eyes on one foe and charged straight for him. Right before her shield struck, his wild eyes swiveled to meet hers. Infusing her legs with as much aether as she dared, she launched him through the air, sending him soaring into the snow with a yelp.

Now, he was clear of the legionnaires.

She bathed him in fire, this time pouring on as much as she could from the start, blasting through his resistance and torching him in seconds.

A knife hammered through her temple. For a blink, she thought it was over. But her helmet was still in place. There was no knife—only blinding pain.

Aether sickness.

She grit her teeth, not even bothering to stifle the primal groan building in her throat.

Numbers. Think numbers.

Three dogs dead, three to go.

An abysmal trade—half the enemy for half her forces.

Today was a loss. The only question was how complete it would be.

"So kill three more," she hissed to herself. "Easy."

Her feet trudged through snow, the battle an eerie interplay of shadows backlit by the watch fires. She had thought that would work against their enemies—now, it just made everything more horrific.

By the time she made it back to the fighting, the legionnaires' shouts had turned from war cries to terror.

The lines were dissolved, any semblance of order lost to a frantic melee of limbs and swords and claws and fur. Some broke and fled, slipping in blood and tripping over maimed bodies and they dashed into the black night. Others stood over the bleeding and broken forms of their brothers and sisters, in a last, desperate show of valor.

Sergeant Meridi got in a lucky stab, impaling a wolf-man through his blood-soaked muzzle, right through the top of his skull. Claw marks scored half her face, and she looked up at the monster with one eye as it shuddered from the deathblow.

Then in one final, spiteful act of wrath, the wolf-man grabbed hold of her shield arm and ripped it clear from the socket.

The scream shook Reiva to her bones. She ran to the sergeant's side, clamping her hand over the spouting, ragged wound.

With something this serious, there was no time to channel aether to try to heal it. Reiva lit her hand aflame to cauterize. Amid the acrid stench of burning flesh, the sergeant passed out—or maybe she was already out from the shock of losing the arm. It was all a blur now.

Two left. That was all she had to ground her. *Two left.*

Stumbling to her feet, she whirled about. The last wolf-man in sight slashed open a legionnaire's throat, then picked her up and threw her into another, who went down in a mess of viscera. He pounced onto the pile, his jaw snapping bones and ripping flesh.

Were there two left, really? Maybe only five had come back from the original six—maybe this one was the last.

One. She could kill one. She had to.

With a roar, she stoked the Flame as strong as she dared, putting all her being into that singular core of rage and fury. Her skull was a churning mess —spikes of pain, incoherent recollections swam and stitched together like a patchwork of decade-old songs and yesterday's weather. She heard whispers behind her, her vision flickered with black splotches.

She had never pushed her soul so far before—not even when she had feared death.

But she could only see the wolf-man, standing from a mound of corpses, and not a single legionnaire still standing. He turned, and the bastard *grinned* at her.

She threw her shield aside and set her hands out, thumbs touching, fingers splayed, and drew an ocean of power through her.

He leaped, howling in violent ecstasy, tongue slick with her brethren's lifeblood.

The inferno blazed, and she felt the wolf-man's aether resistance *shred* like parchment.

She blinked, and she was on her hands and knees, panting. Her helmet weighed a ton. With fumbling fingers, she unfastened it and tossed it aside.

The wolf-man was a heap of charcoal, bits already dusting off in the harsh winds. Only his relic remained intact, unbroken despite the pressure Reiva had subjected it to.

Her arms were shaking. She needed to lie down, she needed to...

Everything was going dark.

A hand struck her across the face.

She gasped, fumbling to get her hand up for another volley, knowing it might well kill her.

"Adept!"

Reiva blinked. That face, she knew that face.

Sergeant Meridi.

"Adept!" she hoarsely yelled again.

"Your arm," Reiva mumbled.

"I'll manage," she hissed. "I need a bandage over this eye."

Reiva nodded, looking at the messy right side of the woman's face. "I can do—I can—I ca..."

She was tipping.

With a visceral grunt, Meridi caught her. "Come on, Adept, on your feet. You can't die on us now."

"Us?"

Meridi spat a glob of bloody saliva. "You really think we'd all go down as easy as that? Come on, *work with me*. One arm isn't enough to heft your ass."

She was right—Reiva needed to act. The fight was over, but the night was sure to be long yet.

Bracing an arm against the stone wall, Reiva took a deep breath and righted herself.

Then she took a long look around.

She was no stranger to the aftermath of a battlefield. The red and black gore. The stench of death. The heavy, haunted silence, so terrible it made you wish for the screams and ringing steel that had shattered your ears just minutes before.

And it was the silence that was worst, because it was nigh unbroken.

Then, a groan—wordless, incoherent, agonized.

A life that had not yet been snuffed out. A candle still flickering after the storm, against all odds.

The sergeant had said people needed help. There were survivors.

Alyat had taught her that so long as there were souls depending on her, her life was not her own. The trust one warrior placed in another—the faith that the shields at your left and right would hold—that was the one thing that held the legions, and so with them, the Lazarran Empire, together through strife and toil.

She let a trickle of aether in. Her head was still spinning, shadowy tingles creeping up and down her skin, but she needed that balm. The battle was over; she could afford to inch her condition forward a smidge if it helped her function now.

"How many are still alive?" she asked. "Have any of those who run come back?"

Meridi sighed in relief now that Reiva was finally speaking. "I've counted seven still alive. At least three have a good chance. No one has come back, but gods willing they do and we'll have some more hands here."

Reiva opened her mouth to speak—but the words died as another voice rolled through the air.

"The gods can do nothing for them."

A low voice, masculine and gruff. Sadistic, almost.

It was the same one who had spoken to Reiva before the attack.

Six after all, she thought, feeling her stomach drop to her boots.

Meridi scrambled along the ground, picking up a fallen legionnaire's discarded gladius. Reiva clenched her free hand, letting the rough grit of stone beneath her other ground her in this moment.

The fight was not over.

7

VALOR UNTO DEATH

WHETHER BY RAW WILL, divine intervention, or blind, bloody chance, the Lion survived. She refused death, and even when she longed for death, someone else refused it for her.

She survived, but always did the shadow of death lurk behind her eyes.

—*The Memoirs of Flavia Iscator*

ONE MORE—REIVA could kill one more.

Out of the shadows stepped a hulking form seven feet in stature, both taller and broader than any of the others had been. Unlike the others, his eyes had lost their human quality, instead glinting yellow like a true wolf's. The chains and relic about his waist gleamed in the brazier fire.

He carried a legion shield scored by claw marks and badly dented. His other hand dripped a constant patter of blood, and when he grinned with that horrible lupine maw, red oozed between his teeth.

"I spent a long time rearing those whelps," he growled. "If I had thought you were so dangerous, I might not have savored my hunt of the cowards for so long. You've cost me much tonight, *Adept*."

He said it like it was an insult. Reiva sighed, fingernails cutting into her palm. "Don't speak to me of cost."

The wolf-man looked about as though just noticing the carnage. "Impressive. I will mount your skull in my den so I never forget this night."

"You won't live to see the morning."

His grin widened, and then he moved.

It was immediately clear that this one's command of his transformation was far more deadly than the others they had faced tonight. All had been fast. He moved like the wind, bursting forward in an explosive blur.

Reiva shoved the sergeant aside, bracing her legs and locking her arms in an X, reinforcing her limbs with as much aether as she could stomach.

The impact threw her clean off her feet. The next thing she knew, she was rolling through the snow—and even once she stopped, the world kept spinning.

Get up.

The command to herself was easier issued than obeyed, but it wasn't just her own life she was fighting for. Sergeant Meridi. Those few legionnaires clinging still to life. She had to get up for them.

And so, more by will than strength, she forced herself to her knees, then her hands—

And then fell again, a lance of agony erupting in her right forearm.

She stared dumbfounded at the bone jutting from the skin.

In spite of her aether reinforcement, the bastard had broken her arm.

Adrenaline and shock were coursing through her, so she had felt no pain until she tried to lean on it.

Well, she didn't need to hold a sword to kill.

She scrambled to her feet, stumbling forward.

Sergeant Meridi had her gladius held out, her left arm unsteady as she went through a sequence of flourishes. It might have warded off a less confident foe, but the wolf-man saw through it. Instead of attacking the sergeant, he walked over to a pale, supine legionnaire, and stomped on his skull.

Meridi roared, jumped forward. The wolf-man let the blow spark off the pilfered shield and slammed it forward. Such a casual gesture, but it knocked the sergeant ten feet into the standing stone.

Reiva leaped the snow barrier, now more red than white, and shouted to get the wolf-man's attention.

He turned. Then scoffed. "Come here—I've done enough chasing for the night." And he moved to another legionnaire clinging to life.

Reiva grit her teeth, held out her good arm, and desperately hoped she could stay conscious through this.

Fire burst forward, steaming in the chill air.

The wolf-man hefted the legion shield, and the jet broke against it like a river against a rock, spraying to the sides in twin tails.

Every drop of aether shunted through her was like a shard of broken glass dragged through her veins. Blackness creeped at the edges of her vision.

She had to stop, swaying and barely catching herself against the wall. *Deep breaths. One to kill. Five dead, one to kill.*

Her enemy snorted, glowering over the rim of the shield. A choked sound burst from Reiva's lips as he slashed the legionnaire's throat. His long tongue flicked over bloody claws.

Reiva's exercises fled her. Her head was spinning, her breath turning more shallow by the second.

The wolf-man sneered. "Tired? Would you like a mug of ale? A warm bed?"

She rocked onto the balls of her feet, steeling herself against the tilting world. Blessedly, she did not collapse. "You talk too much for a dog."

A half-laugh, half-howl. "Then no more talking."

He exploded forward in a blur, leading with the shield. Reiva braced for another impact like before, but instead of striking with the shield, the wolf-man raked his claws in a whistling arc.

Reiva half-ducked, half-tumbled under the strike, drawing her side knife and lunging for his face. She needed to get at his weak points. She needed to—

He caught her wrist. For a moment, their eyes locked. And then he wrenched with preternatural strength, and something inside her arm *snapped.*

A wail tore itself from her lungs. The knife clattered to the floor.

She couldn't enforce her body against this anymore. Any more magic would just kill her before her enemy could finish the job.

That was not how a legionnaire died. Certainly not an Adept.

She jumped and smashed her forehead into his muzzle. At least, she tried. With reflexes too sharp to account for, he dropped his head so their foreheads crashed together.

Everything went black for a second. Reiva crumpled, her legs giving out completely. No orders she gave her body were obeyed.

And the wolf-man's feet were before her eyes, impossibly large and clawed, a thing from myth and stories told to frighten children.

He nudged his foot beneath her shoulder and kicked, flipping her onto her back. He moved to stand over her.

Reiva lashed out with a kick to the groin—but he caught it. And after he threw down her leg, he stomped straight on her knee.

The sound she made was more animal than human.

Now he was looming over her. And he lifted the legion shield high above her.

She knew it was coming, knew nothing could stop it—but she shut her eyes as though it might spare her somehow.

When he brought the shield down on her chest, all the air *rushed* out of her, and she could not get it back. Like a gaping fish, her mouth hung open, her insides spasming in some desperate bid to breathe life in again.

She tasted blood.

Like an observer of her own doom, she analyzed the wounds. *Snapped wrist. Broken arm. Shattered kneecap. Crushed ribs. Lungs likely punctured. Extreme magical intervention necessary.*

Magical intervention—she was the only person here who could do that for her. She couldn't save herself.

She was going to die in a land of snow and ice, far from anywhere she had ever called a home. That was a warrior's fate. But she had to die well— even if no one lived to see it.

At last, she sucked down a breath, and it was molten iron in her chest. Her breastplate had actually caved inward from the blow, crushing her already-broken insides.

A shadow lurched into her field of view. The wolf-man turned from Reiva, looking almost amused.

Meridi.

Tharrick had died like this, trying to protect her.

Get out of here, Meridi! Get away! I'll hold him here.

She wanted to say that, but she could not. She could not. She knew she could not. But she could not let another comrade die.

"*Run*," she hissed, coughing another trickle of blood.

"Like hell I will." Meridi's voice was strained, like a lyre tuned too far. But she was standing there. One-armed, one-eyed.

The wolf-man actually offered the sergeant a small nod. "You do not cower, though the stench of fear lies heavy upon you."

"It's just been a while since my last bath."

He swung out with the shield, then followed with a vicious sequence of slashes. The shield she evaded, the claws she warded off—managing to execute a textbook parry even using her off-hand.

Get up.

Reiva couldn't count how many times she had said it to herself tonight— but one more wasn't much worse. You could always get up one more time, so long as you could narrow your focus to that single action. One movement was always possible, then came the next—and you never dared think further, not when things were this bad.

Get up.

She rocked onto her side, groaning as bones shifting inside her chest. Every breath was a wisp of air and a mountain of pain thanks to the warped breastplate.

The wolf-man snapped a kick to Meridi's gut. She took it with a grunt, but stayed standing and returned a stab to the face.

One more dose of aether.

Reiva screwed her eyes shut and grit her teeth. The aether hit her like a storm wave washing over a rowboat. Torn flesh knit together, bones fused—not as they ought to. She would pay for this in the future, but now she needed it.

Putting as much weight on her good leg as she could, she teetered upward, clawing at the wall. Her bad leg was crooked, and bones were grinding together in ways they shouldn't have, but she could use it as a prop. All the while, she heard Meridi fighting for her life—maimed and alone.

Valor unto Death. The Fourth Legion's motto—the legion she was sworn to on this campaign.

She did not have the right to stand back.

She focused on them—on the wolf-man and her sergeant.

She didn't have a clear shot. She didn't have the luxury to wait. Precision —she could do precision. She had trained for this.

With trembling fingers, she raised her arm. One breath in, one breath out. She prepared to let the aether flow through her and become fire.

And, perhaps because he was attuned to that unseen energy, the wolf-man's ears pricked up.

He glanced at her, and he must have thought she looked pathetic, because he sneered, steam puffing from his nostrils.

Just as Meridi struck out at him, he deflected the blow off his shield and stepped inside her reach. His claws shred her arm to ribbons, and her grip failed, the sword clattering to the stones.

Reiva unleashed a wave of fire, her skull seeming to split under the pressure.

It happened in slow motion. The wolf-man pulled Meridi between them. Fear and pain flickered in her lone eye, and so did lashing tongues of fire.

Someone was screaming. At first Reiva thought it was Meridi—but no, Meridi was silent. It was her throat, her voice.

She banished the flames, and the world returned to gloom under the moon's light.

Laughter. He was laughing. "Quick reflexes," he snarled, clutching Sergeant Meridi in his sharp grasp.

Then he hoisted her above his head and threw her straight for Reiva.

She didn't have the stamina to dodge—she could only take the impact as it came, her head snapping against the wall.

The two of them groaned. Reiva opened her eyes, but everything was dark and blurred. Her face was wet. She wiped the moisture away—blood glistened in the light of the braziers. And not just her eyes. Her nose, her ears too—blood vessels had burst all over her head. She had pushed herself too far, and her body could no longer bear the strain.

Meridi grunted, fumbling for something. "Knife," she hissed. "Give me my knife. Sword's too heavy."

Reiva swallowed. "It's okay. You can stop, Meridi. It's over."

The sergeant fixed her with a horrified look. It gutted Reiva to see. At least that was better than a look of shame.

"Valor unto death, Adept."

Reiva couldn't hold her eyes any more. She had failed the company. She had failed Meridi, and Tharrick, and every other legionnaire who died tonight. She had failed her Empire and her mentor.

Meridi groaned as she shifted, and the glint of metal in the night caught Reiva's eye. It was a small knife—more suited for paring fingernails than warfare.

"Too small," Reiva muttered.

"It'll have to do."

The wolf-man came back into view. Reiva had hardly even realized he had walked away for a time. Her head was packed with cotton and jagged rocks all at once. "Still alive?" He chuckled, as though that were the punch-line to a joke only he knew. "I admire your spirit. Did you hear that last one crying?"

Reiva's stomach twisted. So he had finished off the wounded.

She couldn't tell if she was crying, since her eyes were already running with blood.

He approached. The shield was gone. Maybe he had broken it on one of her comrades. Her chest flared again with pain, and she hoped it had been enough to bring a quick end to a normal human.

But then she felt Meridi shift atop her, felt the tensing of muscle, and she thought no, there are no normal humans—not among the legion's finest.

Maybe there was one more thing Reiva could do. Limply, she raised her hand, and touched the flow of aether. The wolf-man snapped his attention to her trembling fist, tensing as if to roll away.

It was enough. By gods or devils, it was enough.

Meridi sprang to her feet, whirling with her knife clutched in an icepick grip.

The wolf-man's face ratcheted to the sergeant, right in time for her to bury her little knife deep into his left eye.

His terrible howl scraped Reiva's ears like a ragged blade.

Good.

The wolf-man scampered back, one hand over his eye, the other blazing with hatred.

"Shit," huffed Meridi. "Too small after all."

It was the last thing she said before he grabbed her head and smashed it into the stones.

A strangled sound burst from Reiva's throat.

That will be you.

The wolf-man's breathing was ragged, agonized.

And as he fixed her with that one burning yellow eye, she knew he wasn't going to die from this. With a wretched snarl, he pulled the blade out, the wound weeping dark crimson blood that steamed in the winter cold.

Contempt in every fiber of his being, he flung the knife aside like he might have shooed away a bee.

Reiva watched, pain scraping every nerve from crown to toe, as he got down on all fours. Step by shaking step, he approached, pinkish drool slavering from fearsome fangs.

So the last thing she saw in this world would be a hideous half-man, half-beast.

To the hells with that.

Her sight drifted off. She saw the bodies. Some she could recognize, others were too ruined by violence. She saw blood. She saw swords and rent shields.

She saw the coals of one brazier that had been knocked over. There was still a glimmer of heat left in them, though. One last wisp of flame, defiant against the cold.

Now, she was certain there were tears in her eyes, mingling with the blood.

She turned back to the hunching form of the wolf-man. He had stopped to regard her—his final prey of the night.

For a moment, it was just them and the wind.

Then a growl built deep in his chest.

The fingers on her arm—the arm with the less severe break—twitched.

He pounced, maw wide and dark and washed with the blood of her brothers and sisters.

She stretched out her hand, straight ahead, straight between his razor teeth, as they sliced a dozen trails through her flesh and clamped down with crushing fury.

And she screamed, not from the pain of the bite, but from the unyielding pain of one final burst of fire, coursing through her soul, her skin, her fingers.

From the inside, she burned his life away. He howled and scrambled back, tearing more gashes in her arm. He beat at his chest, his stomach. The wolf-man writhed in agony.

And then, he stilled, and his form shrank, and his fur faded to reveal splotchy, bright-red skin.

Six enemies.

Twenty-two legionnaires.

All dead.

Reiva's gaze drifted to Meridi's body. Her head rested in a pool of crimson, with little rivulets seeping into the cracked stone.

It was all too quiet.

Reiva tried to close her eyes, but even that was too much. So she stared at the massacre, wind stinging her eyes. Then she looked down at her arm. Broken even worse now, worse so than the other, and with heavy lacerations. Blood. She was losing blood. She needed to treat that.

But her head was so light now. She could hardly breathe. She was suffering blood loss. She was deep into aether sickness. She could just drift off. That would be easiest, wouldn't it? Earned, even. She had done her job. She had killed the enemy.

It all worked out, then. She could let go.

"Six dogs? That's all it took to bring you down?"

Her head lolled to the side.

Alyat was sitting at his desk, staring at her with his signature gruff demeanor.

"I'm delirious," she muttered.

"Damn right you're delirious if you're going to waste years of my time, going off and dying on your first campaign. How much is an Adept worth?"

She heard coins clinking. Or it might have been chains. "Thirty silver."

Her brow furrowed. That was wrong. Where had that come from?

"Priceless," she amended.

"Priceless. Exactly. I didn't make you what you are so you could quit in some gods-forsaken snow bank. So make yourself useful and staunch that wound, Adept."

"Aether sickness," she drawled, but she had blinked and Alyat was gone. She stared at the spot he and his desk had been.

Hundreds of leagues away and he won't let me die.

She sucked in a breath. The pain blossomed anew, but she let it focus her, drag her back to awareness of her surroundings.

Meridi's knife lay a few feet away.

She swallowed. She could do a few feet.

But the seconds rolled past, and she just lay there, staring at the knife.

Her Flame was weak, barely pulsing.

Then she looked again at the corpse of the enemy leader. A faint trail of steam curled from his mouth—so much smaller now that his magic had abandoned him.

She hated him.

The Flame burgeoned.

A rasped sigh escaped her lips.

Hatred. She still had hatred. She could live with hatred.

She hated him for how he had hunted down the stragglers. She hated him for how he had killed the wounded. She hated him for how he had not died when Sergeant Meridi stuck him in the eye.

The Flame built within her, and she felt its power thrumming. She dared not call upon it, not yet, but she let her every thought burn with the Flame.

Groaning and cursing, she lurched forward, practically dropping onto her stomach. Then she crawled, both arms screaming in pain, her insides ragged and raw.

Hatred. She had hatred.

She hated the darkness of the night. She hated the magic of the relics.

Her fingers closed around the little knife. First, she cut the straps on her breastplate and shrugged it off, letting it clang unceremoniously against the stone. She could breathe a little easier now. Next, she cut a strip of crimson cloth from her Adept's mantle, then wound it around her shredded forearm. Not as good as proper bandages, but it would do. It would hold the blood.

"Hold on," she breathed. "Hold on, just a little longer..."

She swallowed. Blood. She had been losing blood. She needed to bind her arm.

No, she had just done that. She needed to...needed to...

She pitched, nearly striking her head.

Too much blood loss. She would lose consciousness.

She needed to heal again.

Her Flame was burning strong. She could tap into her magic.

She took a shaky breath. Fifty-fifty odds this knocked her out anyway—but at least it would be something she could wake up from.

Hopefully.

She closed her eyes. She'd need everything she had for this. She needed to stoke the Flame one more time.

Hatred. She hated this snow. She hated these rocks. She hated...she hated herself for calling this mission. Hated that she had pressed for it, and now she alone still drew breath.

The Flame roared.

Reiva channeled aether—and the world went black.

8

MANGLED AND MALICED

SUFFERING IS THE GREAT PUZZLE. No sage I ever met has solved it.

But I met a beggar who did. He told me he stopped trying to find an answer and started trying to make one instead. He was happier than kings. He was wiser than philosophers.

He died in great agony at the age of thirty.

—*The Life and Wisdom of Simeon Binkhok As Told by Himself*

～

PAIN.

Pain was all Reiva knew.

She tried moving—pain.

She tried breathing—pain.

Her ribs—broken or only bruised? Could she stand up? Crawl even?

The world was a shifting spectrum of black, white, and red.

The black. Night? Unconsciousness?

The white. Snow? Yes, snow—she had been in Hyrgallia. She remembered the crunch of snow beneath her boots.

Red. Blood. It could only be blood. Blood flowing like a river, collecting tribute from shattered skulls and oozing bodies. Already, some of it was freezing into dark crimson ice.

Death. Death all around her.

She was not about to die.

With a bestial groan, she pushed herself up. The right arm screamed in agony—the bones grinding against one another in a horrific manner. She could only use her left, and gingerly at that, desperately trying to get purchase with her feet to stand.

Her legs gave out. Her face struck the snow. She hardly even felt it—a pinprick added to a thousand gashes and fractures.

The desire to just lie there, to let herself slip away, like the rivulets of red slipping across a frozen patch of earth and ice. She wanted it more than anything else.

But she was not about to die. Not now. Not here.

So, with another wrenching groan, practically a scream, she heaved herself up.

Everything spun. Her vision swam with black spots, then black curtains, closing on a world of red and white. The final act in a short life.

Head-to-toe, it all hurt. Her body felt *wrong* somehow. It had ever since she'd come to. Internal damage? Blood loss?

She still couldn't stand. But her arms were strong enough to crawl, if she mastered the pain.

Inch by inch, yard by yard, she hauled herself across the frozen earth.

A face on her right, disfigured and mangled, but still decipherable in identity and agony.

Tharrick. How had his head gotten this far?

She turned aside and vomited a foul admixture of bile and blood. Then, she kept crawling. The world became a series of landmarks. A hand here. A dropped sword there. A helmet further along. She couldn't look any farther than what lay right before her. An inch, a yard. She could manage that. Anything farther, and she would lose her drive. Her will.

Anger was all she had at this point.

Anger at the monsters who wreaked this havoc.

Anger at herself for bringing these men and women to chase it down.

Another inch, another yard.

Snow was falling. Little puffs of diamond dust, drifting down and resting on her skin. How could snow fall when the sky was clear? Was this too a delusion? Yet where they touched, she felt cool kisses so soft they tickled.

And then Reiva realized why everything felt so wrong.

She was *cold*.

And she was terrified, because she had not been cold in years. She *could not* be cold.

She was an Adept of Flame. A disciple of the *Ars Vulcana*.

And she was freezing.

Clear of the worst of the carnage, she counted her progress by dead branches peeking out from the wintry powder. Spring, she missed spring. She missed grass. A heated bath in the capital, spiced wine in a bronze bowl. Such things seemed lifetimes away.

Her fingers were numb. One of them was wrenched the wrong way, and she could not put it back.

Her vision was swimming again. Black dots, black curtains. She had closed up her wounds, but the wooziness from the blood loss was coming back with a vengeance. Adrenaline could only take her so far.

A tree. An evergreen pine, lonesome and proud against a star-strewn sky. She could go that far.

She could die under that tree, if it came to that. Her father used to tell her trees were sacred.

She hoped the gods—whichever gods regarded her, be they Lazarran or Talynisti—overlooked years of paying them no mind. Was a last-minute sacrifice to Marbellus before setting off on campaigns enough to pay her way to the heavens?

The boughs of the evergreen stretched out over her like a tent, like a funeral shroud. With one last heaving effort, she brought herself to rest against the rough-barked trunk.

She stared at the macabre display of blood and guts. It seemed so far away now. Had she really crawled from all the way over there?

Shivering, teeth chattering. With awkward movements, she rubbed her arms, curled in on herself as best she could.

She cupped her hands, that one finger sticking out awkwardly, and huffed a shallow breath. She barely felt it.

She took a shuddering gasp, cast her awareness to the unseen power hanging around her. Another breath—this time, she blew a puff of fire and nearly blacked out again.

No good.

Reiva clasped her arms as tight around herself as she could manage.

She wasn't shivering anymore. That was a bad sign.

The mangled and maliced bodies of her compatriots still lay there in the snow. She hoped it had been quick for most of them. She hoped they had not had the chance to blame her, to curse her name. She would not have spited them for it, though. She deserved it.

But she could not look at them any longer. She rested her head against the tree, looked up at the boughs.

A thought popped into her mind—the possibility of setting this lonesome arbor ablaze, a beacon so their bodies could be found before the Hyrgallian winter hid them beneath a snowy blanket. They could be burned then, their ashes scattered. The officers would be returned to Lazarra. They could receive the proper rites, they could escape a long, murky existence haunting this cursed patch of earth. Sergeant Gascal and his men could bring the relics back to the Sanctum.

But this tree was vibrantly alive, defiantly green. The night was cold; the snow was falling faster. It would not burn. At least, not given her current frailty. Her soul would dissolve, shatter under the effort.

It would be for naught.

She had been beaten. She had killed her enemies, though. She remembered that now. With blood spouting from every limb and eye and ear, she had turned her foe into a living torch.

That gave her some solace. She had not failed entirely then. She had done one last thing for the Empire.

But now she had been beaten by a tree. She could not help but laugh, then wince.

Fine—let the tree stand proud, immortal with its ever-verdant boughs and branches. It was not so bad a place to die.

She let her eyes close on the starry sky hanging over a foreign land—candles in the night, blown out into total darkness.

～

ROUGH FINGERS ON HER SHOULDER. The echo of a distant, but familiar voice. "—alive! Get a litter!"

Pain. Waking meant pain.

But pain meant life.

She opened her eyes.

Sergeant Gascal. His expression was nearly manic. There were tears on his cheeks.

So he had seen the massacre.

"My fault," she murmured.

Gascal bellowed again for a litter.

Her gaze drifted over his shoulder. His squadron was moving among the dead, desperately shaking friends they had known, spitting upon the corpses of their enemies.

They held torches.

It was still dark.

How had they found her so quickly?

And then she realized Gascal didn't have a torch, though his face was lit by the familiar textured light of flame. From where?

Fire—she needed fire. She was cold. Too cold. Cold as someone like her should never have been.

Gascal looked around, cursed. "Worthless sods." Though she knew he didn't mean it. He was almost certainly as torn up as his charges were. More so, perhaps. Leaders had a strange way of carrying the pain of a dead comrade—they felt the pain more acutely at the same time they needed to bury it the deepest.

His thickly corded arms scooped her up. With the slightest motion, her knee and chest screamed in sharp agony, like a thousand thorns of glass were raking her insides.

She stifled the cry of pain as best she could, but she doubted it was convincing.

"Hang in there, Adept. You're not dying while I have a say in this."

Reiva had thought much the same, just hours ago.

She almost said as much. Almost told the sergeant to let her die here with everyone she had failed.

But her head lolled to the side, and all words fled from her.

The tree. The tree was engulfed in flame.

"Impossible," she murmured.

Eventually, Gascal got two legionnaires to make the litter. They moved her beside a rekindled brazier and covered her with cloaks.

As the legionnaires moved to and fro, gathering the relics, closing their fellows' eyes, Reiva floated in and out of awareness. Every time she drifted nearer to lucidity, the realization of where she was and what had happened struck her anew. Again and again, she awoke to the nightmare.

Scanlon. She would have to face Scanlon.

The thought, as she watched the landscape go by, was yet another arrow of grief to her heart.

I should have died.

She lost track of how many times the thought bubbled up. It became a constant refrain echoing inside her skull. Whispers, whispers everywhere. Everywhere she looked, blood and broken bones.

She closed her eyes, and when she opened them, day had come. The crackle of a campfire. Stars overhead. A morsel of dried rations slipped into her mouth. Screams on the winter winds. The musk of wet fur.

Distant shouting.

Hoofbeats, muffled by snow, thudding closer.

Captain Scanlon's face appeared above her. Shock and worry and fear.

"Reiva! What happened?"

She tried to swallow, but couldn't. She couldn't speak.

She just shook her head.

She had failed.

9

TO KILL A KING

The Vipers trace their history to long before the monarchy. According to legend, the first of their fraternity was an old, blind man.

The *roshbet* of another clan wanted to marry the blind man's granddaughter, but the family refused the offer, knowing him to be a man of great violence and rage.

And indeed he was. In the night, the *roshbet* and his men slaughtered the whole family, even the woman he had longed to marry. Only the blind man was left alive, and this was done out of cruelty.

Months later, when the moon was new and the night dark, the *roshbet* awoke to dead silence. Unsure what had disturbed his rest, he called out to his wives, then his sons, then his fighting men.

When he finally left the tent, he found the old, blind man waiting for him, a gore-spattered club in one hand, a blood-washed blade in the other. Every last soul in the camp lay dead, slaughtered with hardly a murmur.

He left the *roshbet* alive.

—*A Chronicle of Talynisti Reign, Vol. I: Temple and Throne*

∾

To finally return to the rooftops, Avi imagined this was how a bird felt when it left the nest and took to the skies.

With stars above and cool winds around him, he clambered up the side of a building, finding footholds deftly. At first, he was careful not to set too much weight on his ankle, or to pull too much with his stitched shoulder, but as he began to warm up, his body tingled with excitement.

Soon enough, he was running the rooftops like he'd never left.

In the weeks since the occupation began, the curfew had not been lifted. The typical symphony of a Dav-maiir night was hauntingly absent, replaced by the rattle of occasional patrols or sounds drifting up from windows.

It was an eerie sensation, one that kept Avi checking over his shoulder.

Thankfully, there were very few rooftop guards. They would certainly be placed near the Temple and the royal palace, but Avi knew how to keep out of sight, and he wound a wide arc to avoid any hotbeds of activity.

Now and then, he would stop to observe a contingent of Tamiq's so-called Revolutionary Guard. They were Talynisti to a man, but Avi would not have called a single one his brother. More than once, he had to turn aside and quell the angry drive to descend upon them in a violent storm.

Sure, go ahead and die in a street fight—kill maybe three traitors. That will serve Malik.

Though it took him longer than under ideal conditions, he eventually caught sight of the palace. Sure enough, Tamiq's banner was flying...and beside it flew the Lazarran standard.

He had not seen many legionnaires tonight—most of them were concentrated in the western half of the city, near the garrison they had constructed beside the gate they crashed through.

Moving slower, more discreetly, he stalked nearer the palace, eyes and ears hyper-alert for any guards. Once he found a suitable nook in which to conceal himself, he hunkered down.

And then he waited and watched.

He counted patrols around the area, marking numbers of guards, numbers of squadrons, and how long they took to make their rounds. He noted too when shifts changed and how much of an opening they left.

In that spot, he waited some two or three hours, and then he slipped out, seeking another vantage point on the opposite side of the palace.

There was something profoundly strange about applying his infiltration training to a building he already knew so intimately—but he had to treat the place like he had never set eyes on it before. It was tempting to assume that, since he already knew the internal layout, he was well-prepared to sneak inside. That was a quick road to death. Almost certainly, the interior patrols would have changed—maybe there had even been some interior renovations done to alter pathways. He certainly couldn't rely on any of the old secret passages.

After another couple of hours, he vanished into the night, making his way back to Madam Sahir's before dawn.

Every night, he repeated this. As the days ticked past, he ventured out during the day, always being careful that none of the Madam's neighbors noticed him as he came and went. The basement of Madam Sahir's home had a false wall that led to an old, disused tunnel system, and sometimes he would leave or return that way, depending on where he was headed.

It took every ounce of his will not to bolt when the gaze of a Revolutionary Guard or a Lazarran legionnaire fell upon him, but he managed it just fine. If anyone stopped him, he would say he was running errands for his grandmother (which was almost true—the Madam never accepted him back inside unless he brought something from the Grand Bazaar, which was up and running again).

What he didn't have with him on those daytime excursions was the *Nihilo* Blade, which he left secreted in the room under the floor. Without a weapon, he felt naked—but it was the law now that no man could go about with a blade.

Inconveniences and obstacles abounded, but he went about his work all the same.

At dinner, he spoke with the Madam and Samara about any new information they had gleaned from neighbors or friends. By now, it was well-established that King Malik was alive—safe in the city of Shugrith, where he had established his court anew, partially of those who had fled Dav-maiir and partially of new men harvested from Shugrith.

It was a weak court, Avi knew. A new court always was, especially when so many of the old had been lost to violence. A mixture of old hands and new might have been even worse though. He imagined there would be disputes about how to proceed—some would call for an assault on Dav-maiir (almost impossible, given the Lazarrans' legendary capacity for siege warfare as both aggressors and defenders). Others would push for Malik to establish Shugrith as the new capital, which would never do—Dav-maiir was the holy city, its site chosen by the Four Gods from time immemorial.

All that amounted to Avi having little hope for aid from beyond the walls.

That was fine—he was used to being on his own. He was used to forming his own plans.

And one night, he was ready to put one into action.

He fastened the *Nihilo* Blade beneath his outer cloak, finding comfort in its presence. The night seemed charged with energy, with possibility. The moon was weak—a narrow crescent like a bull's horns in the sky, glimmering faint light upon the city.

Darkness was good—darkness was his ally tonight.

He picked his way along the rooftops, using a route he appreciated for its blend of speed and relative security. He wanted to avoid risk tonight—at least, for as long as he could.

The patrols walked about with extra torches tonight, given the gloom. That would spoil their night vision, making it nigh impossible to spot Avi as he swooped from building to building.

Soon, the palace stood resplendent before him.

Avi settled into one of his little hiding nooks—this one was atop a moneychanger's office—and he waited. He watched the guards.

Then came the shift change.

His heart picked up its pace. Now was the moment.

He left his alcove.

He would drop to the streets, dash to the wall, then scale it and be over. It would only take seconds, but he would be on the grounds long before—

"Off to kill a king, lad?"

Avi exploded into motion, hand closing around the *Nihilo* Blade's hilt as he dove into a sidelong roll.

When he popped up into a fighting stance, he found himself staring into a plainly amused face.

A familiar face, one marked by little scars with a half-gray beard and a head of hair to match.

"What," scoffed Crow, "forget my voice after a few weeks?"

Tension bled out from Avi. His heart was still pounding, but with elation. "Four Gods, Crow. I thought you were dead."

"Could've said the same to you," he mused, turning to examine the palace. "Caught you snooping around here a few nights ago, though."

Embarrassment and anger flooded through him. "You saw me? And you didn't *speak to me*?"

Crow gave him a dry look. "I was doing reconnaissance of my own, lad."

Avi scoffed, shooting a glance down at the streets. If he went now, he still had time...

"You'll die if you try it."

"I can get to him first."

"And then what? The legion installs a puppet ruler—maybe a cousin, maybe a priest, whoever—and then all you've done is make our rightful king look like a coward who strikes from the shadows."

"That's what we *do*, Crow."

"And don't forget who trained you *how* to do that, lad."

Enough of this—Avi was going to go. He was going to make Tamiq pay for his treachery, and that would be sufficient revenge to justify his own doom.

"One more step and I drop you."

"You're too old for that."

He sprang into motion, only for Crow to swoop in and get him into a hold, dropping them both to the tiles.

Avi hissed, struggling against the hold. "You want the guards to hear us?"

"I warned you, and you moved."

Avi glared as another detachment of the Revolutionary Guard came to patrol around the palace. Torches were moving along the nearest section of the enclosure wall again.

His window had passed.

"So," Avi sighed. "You have a plan of your own, I'm guessing?"

Crow loosened his hold, letting Avi slip out. "Aye. We run this like we're in an enemy city—which we are. Disinformation. Sabotage. We target the legion primarily. The people are unsure of Tamiq—you know how they always loved him, but ousting his brother has raised questions."

Avi nodded. "If we cripple the legion, though, there goes Tamiq's power."

"And opens the door for Malik to take back his throne."

Some gentle light kindled within Avi. Hopefulness.

"That...would do a lot more than just killing Tamiq," he admitted. "How many hands do we have?"

A grim solemnity ridged itself into Crow's face. "We lost almost everyone. They raided the old headquarters and performed executions without trials. I brought Malik to Shugrith with two men, and I left both with him."

"Insurance against any strikes from the shadows," Avi drawled. "So we're doing this on our own? Might as well go back to my plan—it's more feasible."

"I didn't say *that*. You remember the operation we pulled across the southern border two years ago? In New Mizkhar? I got one of the contractors we used."

Avi searched his memory. There was a Karellan man, more of a face than an actual operator. What had his name been... "Theimos?"

Crow nodded. "And I tracked down Jackal. Remember her?"

Avi's eyebrows went up. "I do. She'll be useful. Doubles our numbers. But tell me you've got more than just two."

"One more—a new acquaintance I made in Shugrith after I got Malik situated. Endric fellow."

"I don't want new people in on this."

"Wait till you meet him—absolute monster of a fighter. I'm calling him Mouse."

"Glad to see your sense of humor hasn't changed."

"Change is for young people. I'm too old for that."

Avi snorted. "Right. Headquarters?"

"There's an old safe house I kept off the books. Silk District, across the street from that old warehouse."

Avi whistled. "And here I thought you'd want a low profile."

"It'll do the job. Oh, and when you come, bring an intelligence drop. We've got a contact inside the palace. Get the drop from her around midnight tomorrow."

Avi perked up. *That* was good. "Meeting place?"

"Third level, eastern face. Balcony."

Avi went cold as he recalled who had taken up residence in that apartment. "*What?*"

Crow sighed. "Be a professional, lad. And do you really mean to tell me you haven't gone to see her yet? You're good with a blade, but sometimes I wonder if you've got anything going on inside your skull."

"Why would I talk to her—we haven't spoken in at least a year."

Crow raised an eyebrow.

"At least six months. We aren't anything."

"Wrong—you're colleagues now. And don't overcomplicate that, or I'll make Jackal her contact."

First Samara, now her?

Avi shook his head. "Fine, I'll get the drop."

Crow nodded, setting a hand on his shoulder. "Listen. We're in a bad spot now, but our enemies have no idea how many we are, or how strong. We're going to manage this. Gods willing."

Avi sighed, taking one more look at the palace. "Gods willing. I'll see you in two days, Crow. Stay alive."

"Same to you."

10

STRENGTH AND HONOR

I FEAR a reader of some other culture—be it removed from us in time or space—may not understand the force of the Lazarran virtues. The virtues that guided us. The virtues that taught what it means to be human.

To die for one's fathers, to die for one's state, to die for one's gods, to die for one's brothers and sisters. What could be a greater glory than these?

It is not that there was shame in survival—for to survive is to live and serve another day. The shame lay in surviving when all who had followed you to battle lay on the pyre.

—*The Memoirs of Flavia Iscator*

~

REIVA WAS IN A WAGON, of that she felt sure, drifting endlessly through fragile layers of consciousness, up and down like a rowboat tossed on storm-whipped waves.

Everything else? Everything else was a rolling tapestry. Snow, trees, ice, rivers, grass, skies dark and light alike. Reiva would turn her head, and a town would become a valley would become a dock. All the while, figures loomed—and upon every waking, her heart would seize with fear before she recognized the familiar silhouette of a legionnaire's helmet.

Sometimes after she closed her eyes, she'd open them and find hours had passed without recollection. Other times, her dreams seemed to stretch for years. She saw the wolf-men at a banquet table, feasting on the bones of her comrades. She heard the voices of Tharrick, Meridi, and twenty others crying out to her, crying out *against* her.

"You killed us, Adept," said Tharrick's severed head.

"I was counting on you," hissed Meridi.

"How can you call yourself an Adept?"

"Emperor's finest? Don't make me laugh."

"Go back to the sandpit you were born in."

"You are no Lazarran."

And through the endless challenges, her lips faltered. She could say nothing to them, because their words were her own, bubbled up from deep within herself.

One day she closed her eyes, and next she knew—hard, cold stone was at her back. A pillow had been tucked under her head.

No longer in the wagon, then.

She cracked open her eyes. There were windows overlain with thin, waxed paper, so as to let light in without leaving the room exposed to the open air.

She was naked, a sheet draped over her. Gingerly, she lifted the sheet, wincing as the motion brought new flares of pain.

For a moment, she thought it was another dream. The sight before her—that couldn't be *her*?

Purple-black bruises painted her body. Skin stretched where bone had fused improperly after a break. Scars ran in senseless tracks, some still bearing their stitches.

Surgery room.

She swallowed. But that would mean she was in Lazarra—a journey of hundreds of miles.

Her head fell back to the pillow. "Weeks?" she whispered to no one. "Months?"

The world seemed abuzz, as though she could feel every thread of the sheet, every ridge of the stone slab. Compared to the drifting state of consciousness she had endured for the last...who even knew how long, this was like the noon sun appearing at midnight.

Stimulants. They need me awake.

Just then, the door opened. In stepped a man with dark, curly hair and deep-set eyes. Reiva was not surprised to see him.

"Gylos," she muttered, her voice rugged from disuse.

He nodded. "Adept Reiva. Glad to see you're awake—the drug is working then. I must say, it is...my displeasure to see you." He added a half-smile.

Reiva swallowed. "Likewise."

She had only spoken with him once before—when Mylla, a friend in training, had come down with aether sickness and, full recovery eluding her, washed out from the Corps. Now that Reiva was the one lying down with Gylos looming over her, she found herself dreading a similar outcome.

"You have never undergone major *Viva* surgery, correct?"

She shook her head. "But I've heard."

Gylos nodded somberly. "It is an intense process. Your injuries are severe: numerous broken ribs, others cracked. A collapsed lung. Broken kneecap, torn ligament. Several breaks in your arms. There are others, but those are the most pressing. And all of that lashed together by haphazard aether channeling. Your self-healing in the field saved your life, but it's wreaked havoc on your internals."

He paused for a moment. "If you want a full recovery, I will need to re-break several bones so they may be properly set and healed. And because I need to be in full control, you cannot channel aether—otherwise we'll be back to square one."

There was the reason for the stimulant. An Adept's body, when wounded and unconscious, would automatically begin channeling aether. She needed to be fully aware.

Gylos took a deep breath. "Is this what you want? Adepts have declined full surgery before—I can focus on just the critical problems and repair you well enough so that you may live a normal life. But you would never be able to enter combat again, and your leg in particular may have a permanent limp."

Reiva closed her eyes. A life as a cripple. A life outside the legions.

'Emperor's finest? Don't make me laugh.'

"Do it," she whispered. Then again, stronger: "Do it."

Gylos hummed. "I will alert my assistants and we will prepare for surgery. May I take your focus for the duration of the procedure? Some Adepts find it helpful in reducing the urge to channel."

Her arcane focus, a treasure earned by years of blood, sweat, and tears. She shook her head. "I'll keep it on."

Gylos seemed to approve of this, which gave Reiva heart. He left, then returned soon after with two Initiates, a girl looking about thirteen or fourteen, a boy a few years older. They would be training in the *Ars Viva* under Gylos' tutelage. The Art of Life.

They brought with them a tray of fearsome-looking instruments. Reiva steadied her breathing. *No worse than a weapon on the battlefield*, she told herself.

The Initiates set to work applying restraints—chains with padding.

Reiva didn't bother protesting—she had her pride, but she also had years of combat training and the raw, fundamental human instinct to escape pain.

As if he knew her thoughts, Gylos said, "Do your best not to thrash, but I've seen some of the hardest warriors you've ever seen fight like hell on this table. Scream and groan however much you need, we're used to it. If you lose consciousness, we'll use smelling salts to revive you—worst-case scenario, we'll need to give you more stimulants. Do your best to hang on, remember your mental exercises. Oh, and bite down on this." He proffered a wad of cloth, which she clamped between her teeth.

There was a moment of tense stillness.

"Are you ready, Adept Reiva?"

Slowly, she nodded.

"Good. Strength and honor, Adept. And I am sorry."

She screwed her eyes shut.

For Emperor and Eagle.

11

A COLLEAGUE

It is the young who fight our wars. We need them for their strength, their brashness, their vainglory and foolhardiness. I also know firsthand, as does anyone who served in their more vigorous years, that no amount of military bylaws or regulations will rein in youthful passion.
—*The Memoirs of Flavia Iscator*

When Avi left the Madam's house for the last time, he left a small note with what little coinage he still had. Part of him wanted to say goodbye in person, but he didn't want emotion stewing inside him when he invaded the palace grounds.

The night was calm; the rooftops presented no surprises. Avi's familiarity with the guard patrols came in handy again, even though he wasn't going after Tamiq this time. Some part of him thought that would be easier than what he had lying ahead of him now, though.

When the gap in the patrols opened up, Avi scampered across the street, then climbed the enclosure wall—not too difficult, given all the ornamentation and symbolic carvings.

Then he was within the grounds, striding across a lawn. Trusting the guards' night vision would be spoiled by their torches, he stuck to the darkest patches as he slipped by.

The eastern face of the palace didn't have many handholds, but there were enough. Bit by bit, he scaled the structure, pausing now and then to check the guards' movement.

Once he was halfway along the second story, he relaxed a bit. Once you got to a certain height, people just didn't look up anymore.

He had worked up a sweat by the time he reached the balcony. That was somewhat undesirable.

Just a colleague, he reminded himself. *Just a colleague.*

Keeping low, he tapped rhythmically at the small door.

There was a pause. The wind rustled along.

And then the door creaked open just an inch, revealing two gleaming eyes in the dark.

Avi swallowed.

For a moment, they held one another's gaze.

"You were supposed to knock back, by the way," he whispered. "Well, are you going to invite me in, or shall we do this out here?"

She blinked. Then, an almost imperceptible nod.

He slipped into the palatial apartment, easing the door closed behind him.

"Can't have a princess talking to a strange man on the balcony in the middle of the night, hm?"

"Must you say it like that?" said Asrah, her voice soft as a moth's wings.

"Say what?"

"*Princess.*"

"Congratulations, by the way."

She scowled, shaking her head as she crossed to a small desk. She picked up a small set of folded papers, then stuck them out at him. "If that's how you want to be, then that's fine. Just take this and go."

Avi suppressed a sigh. "No," he breathed. "I'm sorry. I know you didn't ask for this."

"I didn't. And I'm risking a lot by doing this, and I will not stand for your *remarks* as if that doesn't matter."

"It does," he said. "And I'm sorry to be like this when we haven't seen each other in so long. I've just...it's been a lot."

Something softened behind her eyes. "For all of us, it has been. I'm...glad you're alive."

"Yeah, well, it happens. Most Vipers are dead now, but here I am."

"Don't feel guilty for it."

He gave her a look.

"I say that because I know you would."

Avi suppressed a sigh, weighing the fact that it really wouldn't pay to tell her he'd already heard this all from another woman not even one month ago. "It would be wrong not to feel guilt."

Her shoulders drooped. "You don't do yourself any favors thinking like that."

He looked away. Six months without a word, and so quickly they had returned to their old patterns. What had Crow said? Keep it professional?

Yeah, right.

In some other part of his mind, Madam Sahir was telling him she remembered what it was like to be young.

"Why work against your father?" he asked.

She stiffened at the change in topic, but didn't flinch from it. "What he did to my uncle isn't right. He might be my father, but he isn't my king. And the gods judge us for the opportunities we are given. I couldn't live with myself as a princess if it meant living with what was done to hand that to me."

Asrah held out the documents again, and Avi accepted them—using just the tips of his fingers, no contact between them. He tucked them away in a pocket inside his cloak. "What's in here?"

"My father's court and his military leaders, as far as I've been able to ascertain. It also contains...his schedule."

Avi's eyebrows went up at that. A schedule provided ample opportunities.

And he could see the weight on her for that. "We're not planning on assassinating Tamiq," he offered. "That doesn't mean we never will consider it, but it's not on the table for now."

Still, he could see the words had set her at ease, if only a little.

"Before you go," she whispered. "Tell me, was it you who killed that Adept?"

Avi nodded. "Small good it did."

"No, it did more than that. All across the city, my handmaids tell me, people whisper that the Wolf of Talynis killed an Imperial Adept. They say you cut his throat with a blade forged from night itself." Her voice ticked up in a half-scoff, almost like she was sharing a joke with him. But when she saw his face, the humor faded.

"It's an Imperial relic," he whispered, not sure why he was telling her, but also realizing if he didn't talk about this, he might talk about other things—things that would certainly jeopardize this *just colleagues* business. He also wondered how word about 'the Wolf of Talynis' as the culprit could have spread. Crow must have already gotten to work on the information campaign. What else was he putting out there?

Slowly, so as not to make a hiss when he pulled it from the sheath, he drew the *Nihilo* Blade.

"How did you get something like that?" she breathed, staring at the cold gleam of the iron.

"Better you don't ask. Some secrets are best left to the Vipers, Asrah."

She swallowed. He could see she was dissatisfied. It wasn't the first time the necessities of his vocation had put a gap between them.

The gap had widened, though. Not only was he a Viper—she was a princess now. The daughter of the man Avi wanted to kill more than anyone else.

"So many things you'll never tell me," mused Asrah. "What if I were to order you as your princess? Would you tell me then?"

"You're not my princess." He regretted how coldly he said it, but she didn't seem bothered.

"You're right. I'm not my own princess either."

"Colleagues," Avi muttered.

"Yes, colleagues." A strange light glimmered in her eyes. "And shouldn't colleagues know each other's names?"

Avi's throat closed up. "Sorry. For what it's worth, not even other Vipers know. We leave our names—"

"For the honor of your fathers," she sighed. "I remember. Still Wolf."

"Still Wolf."

"Well...I'm glad you killed that Adept. I'm glad it's you who wields that sword. If you'd prefer, I could leave future drops on the balcony, but..."

"I'll knock," he muttered quickly, turning his face away. "Better to speak when possible—some things don't come through as well in writing."

"Yes, good point."

He nodded a few times, then turned to the balcony door.

"Good night, Asrah. Stay safe."

"Four keep you."

He slipped out, the cool night air brushing his warm face.

Colleagues. Allies. Nothing more.

'I'm glad it's you...'

A ball of fire burned in his chest.

"Right, sure, Crow. Just colleagues."

12

THE JAWS OF DEATH

PRIDE CANNOT EXIST WITHOUT SHAME, and for as proud as we Lazarrans were of our Adept Corps, there was always a secret shame that went along with that. We wondered why our bloodlines could not produce those superb specimens who seized power divine. We wondered why the greatest civilization the world would ever know had need of foreign stock. We wondered why we needed barbarians.

—*The Memoirs of Flavia Iscator*

∼

REIVA EASED HERSELF INTO A CHAIR, letting out a long sigh. The night air breezing through the window was a godsend as she wiped away the sweat beading on her brow.

Adept Gylos had told her the surgery lasted nearly six hours. She took him at his word—time had ceased existing for her. When you went through hell, every moment was eternal.

She was past the worst of it, thankfully. Already, she had full range of motion. Theoretically, at least. Her mind had not yet acclimated to her body's recovery, and so she often had to concentrate and exert her will to do something as simple as bend her arm.

All that added up to deep-set fatigue. After Gylos' work was done, the exceptional healing and rejuvenation factors from his *Ars Viva* had seeped away. Her wounds were gone, but her body was wrung out in a way she had scarcely felt before—maybe her first week of training as an Initiate came close.

It would have been easier if she had clearance to channel aether, but Gylos had made clear that was forbidden to her until she was examined by another Adept who specialized in aether sickness. That put a knot of worry in her stomach—how badly had she suffered that Gylos needed to defer to another Adept on her recovery? She was wondering who that other person might be when a knock sounded at the door.

"Yes?" she called, startled by how tired her own voice sounded.

"Are you decent, kid?" came the gruff reply.

Despite her body's protests, Reiva sprang to her feet and rushed to the door.

She swung it open, her heart lifting at the sight of the perpetually scowling, bearded face that met her.

She caught him in an embrace, which Alyat somewhat stiffly, then more warmly returned. "Glad you're not dead."

Reiva nodded into his shoulder. For a moment, she felt small—not in a demeaned way, but in the same way she'd felt small when her father picked her up and put her on his shoulders.

Her mentor pushed her off, gently, keeping his hands on her shoulders as he looked her over head-to-toe. She was wearing a loose tunic that fell to the knees, but even that left ample scars visible. "Everything in working order?" he ventured.

"Yeah. Gylos did good work. Painful work," she added, wincing.

Alyat nudged her back to the chair, and she didn't object.

As she lowered herself, he inspected her room. "Didn't have such nice recovery rooms back in the day," he snorted. "We're going soft."

Reiva rolled her eyes, smirking. "One day it's ridiculous how hard you had it, the next day it's ridiculous that things are easier."

Alyat cast one of his famed side-eyes at her. "And? Paradox is the path to wisdom."

"Uh-huh." She winced as another lance of pain went through her arm.

Alyat's brow furrowed. "Sure Gylos fixed you up right? He's young."

"Younger than you is not young."

"He's thirty—that's young. Hard as that seems to be for you to get your head around, since you think barreling headlong into the jaws of death before you're twenty is a good move."

Her grin faded. Something in her chest knotted. "I'm sorry."

Alyat sighed, leaning against the wall to gaze out the window. He stayed quiet for a while, and the nightly sounds of Lazarra echoed around them—mules braying, drunkards reveling, birds keening.

"You don't need to apologize to me, kid. Was it a stupid move? Yeah. Excuse me, it was a *gods-damned stupid* move. Six relic-bearers. Only three squads with you way outside controlled territory. Six!"

He shook his head. "You should be dead ten times over."

Her eyes dropped to the floor. "I know."

Another heavy sigh. "I know you know, kid. Sergeant Gascal's write-up mentioned how bad a state you were in—not just your injuries, but your mind. You kept murmuring about how it was all your fault, how you should've died with them. I know you know. Maybe I shouldn't be kicking you over this, but I don't want you to forget. You won't always have reinforcements coming to carry you back to camp. You won't always survive the journey back. And major *Viva* surgery is a heavy thing—most people can't go through that more than two or three times before they quit, or just up and die on the table. Not out of any physical deficiency, either. Their minds just can't handle the pain, so they lose consciousness and never wake up again. Hey, look at me."

When she raised her eyes, he fixed her with a piercing gaze—and she realized his eyes were shining with held-back tears. "Most Adepts don't get another chance like this. Don't waste it."

Her throat constricted. She gave a small nod. "I won't," she croaked.

"Good."

They lapsed into silence again for a time. But eventually, the need to know something urged her to speak again. The need to know something she had feared for some time now.

"Am I being censured?"

He snorted. "What do you think? You pushed for that mission against the express wishes of the company captain. And on your first campaign as a commissioned Adept. It's not like these were auxiliary troops, either. *Twenty-two legionnaires,* Reiva. More than a *third* of the company, which had already lost a patrol of ten! Lazarran citizens, some of them with important relatives in the legions—or worse, the government. If it was an ambush, that was one thing—but you *pushed* for that mission." He pinched the bridge of his nose. "I know. I'm doing it again. But old gods burn me if I didn't fail you somehow for you to not only make that call, but persist in carrying that out despite repeated opportunities and reasons to pull back."

"You didn't," snapped Reiva. "Alyat, you didn't fail me. This was all my fault. If anyone tries to blame you for how I acted, then—"

He put up a hand. "I've been playing this game longer than you've been alive, kid. But thank you. To get back to your first question, yes, you're being censured. Nothing extreme," he added quickly.

Reiva let out a breath she didn't realize she'd been holding.

The punishments for an Adept, at the harshest end of the scale, were stripping of the regalia, exile, and even execution. And it wasn't necessarily true that execution was the worst of those. There were plenty of horror stories about what happened to Adepts stripped of their mantle and focus. Most ended up committing suicide—intentionally or not—by attempting to use their Art. Without a focus to regulate the flow of aether through the body...it was a gruesome way to die. Seizures, hemorrhaging of the brain.

"Your one saving grace," said Alyat, "is the recovery of those relics. Plenty of folks in the Sanctum are desperate to do research on those, not to mention how badly you must have crippled the Hyrgallian insurrectionists by taking them out of play. So, extreme failure, but also extreme success. You remember what I told you when you earned your mantle?"

She nodded solemnly. "People would be watching me."

"Aye. Graduating heads-and-shoulders above the rest of your cohort. Carrying the *Ars Vulcana*. Well, as always, I was right." He crossed his arms. "You've caught a praetor's eye."

Reiva swallowed. "What? Who?"

He grimaced. "Cassia Vantelle. Ninth and Tenth Legions."

Reiva's stomach dropped into the underworld. "*The* Vantelle? The Genius of the Aspagnian Counter-offensive?"

"And the Southlands Colonial Recapture. And the Myrmidon Resurgence." He rubbed his eyes.

"Is it...true she was a legate by the age of thirty?"

"Twenty-seven," drawled Alyat. "A woman of iron, a flawless blade in the hand of the Emperor. And I'd bet my focus Dioclete plans to name her as the Imperial Heir before long. Soon as his son proves he's too incompetent for the job—meaning less competent than Vantelle."

"What does she want with *me*?"

"Can't say—she'll only talk to you." He seemed to deliberate, then went on in a lower voice. "Whatever it is, kid, be careful. Vantelle's as sharp as they say—probably sharper—but she's also tough as steel. More than one of her subordinates cracked under the pressure. Remember, as an Adept, your ultimate loyalty is to the Emperor and the Corps. If she tries to recruit you into something, we have enough pull to deny her. She's not Empress yet."

"Yeah," murmured Reiva. "So you think it's a campaign she wants me for?"

"Probably—the Tenth has been mustering for mobilization. But even if she wants you for that, you still need to be cleared by Sharasthi for aether use."

A strangled sound emerged from Reiva's throat. "Sharasthi?!"

Alyat made a strange face. "Yeah. She's the other eye you've caught."

Reiva looked down at her feet. Part of her was excited that Adept Sharasthi would speak to her, but...if Sharasthi was involved, how badly did the Corps think she had damaged herself?

Alyat put a hand on her shoulder. "Easy, kid. I know it's a lot, but right now, you just need to recover. Take it easy. In a few days, this will all blow over, and you can focus on some rehabilitation, maybe spend a year training the new Initiates before heading back out for campaign."

His lips twisted into an even deeper scowl than usual. "Assuming we can even find enough recruits for a full cohort this year."

"Numbers still going down?"

"Yeah—and for some reason the Circle decided to put me on the task of investigating how to bolster them."

The Circle of Peers consisted of the most distinguished and senior Adepts in the Corps. If they wanted Alyat on the job, he couldn't refuse, but...

"Any breakthrough with the foundationals?"

Alyat shook his head. "Nothing, and there never will be. Gods only know why so few people manifest magical potential, and why none of them are of Lazarran bloodlines. The Empire will be chasing the answer to those questions long after you and me are dead."

Reiva nodded absently. Initiates had been taught about the foundational mysteries of the Adept Corps early on in their training—mysteries that had persisted ever since the end of the Dark Days, when the First Emperor rose to power with the might of the First Adepts at his back.

Alyat tapped his knuckles against the windowsill. "Well, those are *my* problems. You just worry about yourself, kid. Talk to me after this business with Vantelle and your examination with Sharasthi—we'll figure out what to do with you. Get some rest."

Reiva nodded, forcing a smile. "Thanks for coming, Alyat."

He grunted, slipping out the door.

Alone again. She slumped in her chair, looking out over the city. The capital of the greatest empire the world had known.

She blew out the candle, plunging the room into darkness, and watched the stars roll through the heavens, and she felt painfully heavy, chained to the earth and weighted by failures of the past and fears of the future.

13

FOR THE SAKE OF THE EMPIRE

IT IS a strange twist of fate, and a testimony to the havoc of the times we lived in, that history shall best remember Cassia Vantelle for her connection to the young Imperial Adept. It is not surprising the Lion was so enthralled by Cassia. A little girl without a mother—it is no wonder Reiva latched on so strongly. I know that impulse, for I too adored her.
—*The Memoirs of Flavia Iscator*

～

REIVA'S HEART was in her throat, her feet scarcely seeming to touch the stones as she walked.

In the hierarchy of the Lazarran Empire, a praetor was second only to the Emperor himself. And though Adepts were remarkable figures, it was rare even for a member of the Sanctum to be summoned personally by one of the seven praetors.

For someone as young as Reiva, that was only more unusual.

Her anxiety was little helped by Cassia Vantelle's foreboding reputation. Though the seven praetors were, in authority and autonomy, technically equal, Vantelle commanded a unique respect. She was about to meet the woman who might one day be Empress of Lazarra, ruler of the world.

She did her best to keep her breathing even, to not look rushed. She was to meet the praetor at noon, precisely. She certainly did not want to meet the praetor in a sweat, but she also did not want to be too long in reaching her.

Legion headquarters were located near their respective gates. Lazarra was a city of seven gates—and had been planned as such by the Founders, long before the walls were raised.

Seven gates, seven praetors. Vantelle was the fifth praetor, and so her legions were headquartered near the Fifth Gate. It was also called the Gate of Courage, and legend held that of all the city's gates, only the Fifth had never fallen in a siege.

Of course, it had been many decades since Lazarra was ever under siege, and Reiva doubted she would ever see one in her lifetime. She had no doubt she would take part in many—but those would all be against the enemies of the Empire. It was almost impossible to imagine a day when the fires of war would burn the gates of Lazarra once again.

The Fifth Gate, like all others, was manned by the Second Legion—the Orphans, so-called because they had lost their praetor, their Eagle, and their sister legion in the Dark Days.

The office of the first praetor still existed, of course, but it was technically absent. The legate of the Second Legion served as a sort of 'acting praetor,' until such a day that the First's *Aquila* standard might be recovered and a proper praetor installed again over both legions.

Reiva asked one of the Orphans stationed at the gate where to find Vantelle, and she told her the praetor was inspecting the Tenth from the parapet.

Reiva wished she could pull aether to steady her nerves, but Gylos had her under orders to refrain from any magic for a few weeks. The Flame flickered as it might before a battle, and she had to exert her will to quell its desire to lash out.

It was not difficult to pick out Vantelle—Reiva had seen her from a distance before, but even if she had not, it would have been impossible to mistake her: straight-backed, with close-cropped blonde hair beginning to silver from a life of hard campaigns. She had a gladius strapped to her side, and her uniform was impeccable. Her toga was fringed with Imperial Purple—one of the rarest honors in all the Empire, reserved only for those who had the Emperor's greatest favor. Steely gray eyes swept across the green, where the ranks of the Tenth were arrayed.

Something hitched inside her. From where she was standing, Vantelle was in profile, like the face of an Empress stamped on a coin. And if the rumors were true, her face very well might grace Imperial coinage someday. Would they keep the scar etched from beneath her eye down across her jawline, or would that be elided?

Everything about the woman spoke of control—control of herself and control of the men and women in ranks below.

Attending Vantelle were several senior officers, all having the insignias of prefects, save one—the legate. These were the highest-ranking leaders of the Tenth, and Reiva noticed more than a few carrying tension in their jaws and shoulders.

When Vantelle spoke, her voice was calm and firm, and it carried easily. The voice of someone well-accustomed to being heard over the din of war.

"A good display, Livus. I want five companies on the way as soon as possible. Heavy infantry primarily."

The legate stood a little straighter, and several of the prefects seemed to ease. "Thank you, my praetor," said the legate. "It will be done." Just then, his eyes drifted to the side, and he noticed Reiva. His eyebrows twitched for a moment, but aside from that, his face was a mask.

Reiva felt her stomach knot as he leaned closer to Vantelle and whispered.

The praetor's gaze swung to Reiva. She did not look surprised or much affected by her presence, which was hopefully a good sign.

"I think I will retire to my office, Livus. No need to attend me."

The legate saluted. "I will see that all necessary arrangements for transit are made straight away, praetor."

As the legate and his prefects dispersed, Vantelle gestured that Reiva approach. She did so, snapping off a salute. "*Ave Imperator*, my praetor. Adept Reiva, reporting."

"*Ave Imperator*. At ease, Adept. Will you walk with me?"

The question was rhetorical, of course, and Reiva fell in behind the praetor. Her heart pounded so hard she feared Vantelle might hear, and she hoped to the heavens that she would not miss a step on the way down the steps, or otherwise humiliate herself.

Before Vantelle went to the legion headquarters, though, she turned aside to inspect the forward ranks. Many of these men were rookies. Veteran soldiers stood further back—in battle, they would swoop in when the forward ranks (both theirs and those of the enemy) had begun to tire. The major exception to this—for the sake of inspection—was the aquilifer, the man who held the Legion's Eagle in battle. He stood at the fore, tall and proud. Legionnaires would readily die to protect him, for there was no greater shame than to lose the *Aquila*.

Vantelle addressed him, "How many campaigns does this make, Batro? Fourteen?"

The man nodded gravely. "Aye, my praetor. My third since I received the honor of bearing the Eagle. "

Vantelle clapped a hand on his shoulder. "I hope you will forgive me for sending you to the Ninth with a flag."

"To bear any standard is a glory, my praetor. I have already recommended to the legate a suitable man to carry the Eagle in my stead."

"I am glad to hear it. Strength and honor, Batro."

The aquilifer saluted as Vantelle moved on, Reiva trailing behind.

Reiva had to admire the man. When cohorts from one legion were detached to reinforce another, they carried a standard of their parent legion instead of the Eagle. He could have easily seen it as a slight to be downgraded to a vexillarius—a flag-bearer—but instead he had turned it into an opportunity to elevate another man, likely someone who had served as part of his guard while carrying the Eagle.

It was those sorts of things that Reiva loved about the men and women of the legions. Not all were like that, to be sure, but for those who were...

A pang of grief struck her as memories of Scanlon and Ironback Company bubbled up.

Everywhere Vantelle went, legionnaires saluted. Not a small number took notice of Reiva as well. She couldn't help but wonder if any of them had heard of what happened in Hyrgallia.

As it turned out, Hyrgallia was the first thing Vantelle spoke of. "How are your wounds healing, Adept? And do walk at my side, I would rather not talk over my shoulder."

Reiva hoped she managed to stay dignified as she scampered forward to come abreast with the praetor. "I am well, my praetor. Adept Gylos' skill is exceptional."

"So you have been cleared for service."

A lump formed in her throat. "Not yet, I regret to say."

Vantelle shot her an inquisitive look. "For what purpose?"

Reiva's face grew hot. "I have not yet been deemed psychologically fit." The words tumbled out, and for a moment Reiva worried she had dropped her voice in shame.

If she had, Vantelle did not comment on it. "And do you think that is a fair assessment?"

"Pardon me, Praetor?"

Vantelle stopped to examine a line of Legion Scouts. Reiva felt a stab of sympathy as she noticed a bead of sweat on one's temple. Vantelle nodded, then moved on without comment.

Reiva found herself wishing she could stay behind with this line—but her examination had only just begun.

"I was asking if *you* think that you are unfit to serve, Reiva."

It was surreal to hear her name on a praetor's lips. "It is not my place to question the judgment of—"

"I would not repeat myself." She said it coolly, but it may as well have been a slap to the face.

Reiva swallowed. What did she believe—truly? She had failed. Not a moment went by that the weight of the massacre did not crush her shoulders. Many nights she lay awake, thinking how those men and women might have been better served by another.

Maybe if she had paid more attention during logistics classes instead of throwing all her effort into combat training. Maybe if Tolm had been around after that last field mission...maybe if he had graduated first in their cohort instead of her, then those legionnaires would have had a more competent Adept with them—someone who would not have made such a daring gambit.

Maybe—so many maybes.

But there was one thing she knew for certain: that she had fought long and hard to get to where she was. That not a soul in the Sanctum had labored like she did to earn her mantle—and she had earned it with highest honors. Of all those who had stood before the Emperor and received their mantles on that fateful day months ago, she had been the best.

Reiva lifted her chin, speaking more from faith than confidence. "I am capable. I long to serve so I might redeem myself from the shame I bear."

"Good." The praetor stopped for a moment, looking Reiva in the eye. "Consider yourself cleared for service. I will have the paperwork handled by evening."

Reiva's heart skipped a beat, and then she realized Vantelle had already moved on, trudging up a grassy hill. "Thank you!" she blurted out.

"Do not thank me just yet. I have a condition."

A condition?

"I live to execute your will, my praetor."

"I am glad to hear it, but you do have a choice in the matter. This is not an order, so much as a request. You can reject it, and then you will return to the regular process of receiving clearance from the Sanctum."

Reiva's stomach was tying itself up again. Whatever it was, she would say yes—she *had* to. She would sooner go to the hells than spend a season convalescing.

"Were you acquainted with Adept Havan?"

Reiva racked her mind. The name was familiar. An image resolved: blond, solidly built. A Hyrgallian, she thought. "He holds the Art of Frost, if I am not mistaken."

Vantelle nodded. "He was attached to the Ninth."

"Was? He has been recalled from the field, then?"

"He was killed in action. Around the same time you suffered your injuries in Hyrgallia."

The world seemed to spin. Adepts died in battle, of course. That was something you were prepared for from the beginning. But to hear it so soon after nearly meeting her own end...

"Do you know why I inspected the Tenth today?"

Based on what she had heard so far, she could take a guess. "They will be reinforcing the Ninth."

"Correct—just a few companies, as the majority is needed elsewhere."

"And," Reiva said, "you will send me with them? As a replacement for Adept Havan?"

"If you accept."

"Of course! It would be—"

"I appreciate your enthusiasm, Reiva, but not so fast."

They had reached the top of the hill, and Praetor Vantelle stood atop it with one foot planted on a stone. It looked like a scene out of a victory monument.

Reiva stood slightly below and behind her, hands folded behind her back, sweat trickling down her neck—though not from exertion. The praetor's eyes were on the legion, yet she got the sense Vantelle was inspecting her far more closely than the ranks.

"The Ninth Legion," she said at last, "is currently stationed in Talynis. I would have you serve there under Legate Flavia Iscator."

Reiva blinked. She must have misheard, she must have—

She must have been seeing things, because Vantelle was looking at her with a small smile. "Pardon me, it is a rare privilege to see an Adept look startled. Normally you are iron-faced engines of power."

Was...was that a joke?

Reiva floundered for something to say. "That is impossible."

"No. That an Adept may not serve in the land of their birth is merely military law, which I am at liberty to dispense with for the sake of the Empire."

She said it simply, but she might as well have talked about changing the weather with a wave of the hand.

"I...pardon me, Praetor, but the Adept Corps—"

"I will handle the Corps. Of course, there will need to be some compromise—you will probably need to serve *qua paenitentia* for the campaign. All I need, Reiva, is to know whether you will serve me in this matter."

"Then pardon me again, but there are far better suited Adepts—not only Adepts born elsewhere, but Adepts with more experience."

Vantelle nodded along as she said these things, but put up her hand. "I want to send you *because* you are from Talynis, Reiva."

She was starting to wonder whether this was all a dream, and she was still recovering from her wounds. Maybe she was still lying in the snow in Hyrgallia and everything that had happened since was just some strange, final vision filling her last moments.

"Come, stand beside me. Look—is there anything more glorious than an Imperial legion kitted for war? The Eagle gleams with the sun's reflected glory. Hundreds, thousands of shields at the ready. There is no greater engine of war than the Lazarran Legions...but Talynis, as I am sure you know, presents a unique challenge for the Empire."

Lazarra had tried to conquer the country ten years ago before being repelled. The legions were ill-suited to desert warfare, and they had barely been able to establish a foothold. The Talynis campaign was one of the great shames of the Imperial military, famed and feared for their legendary ability to adapt to any necessities of war.

It had also left great scars upon the land of her birth. Reiva knew *that* firsthand.

"It has long been thought prudent," Vantelle continued, "to keep Adepts from serving in the lands of their birth, and the reasons are obvious. I think it may be worthwhile to try a new approach. Talynis is at war with herself. The Empire is backing Tamiq's bid to take the throne from his older brother Malik."

Reiva frowned, scouring her mind. Malik had been king when she left Talynis. Tamiq was always very popular, though. He had been more of a warrior than his older brother. He had probably led the defense efforts against the Empire.

Maybe he had even led her father.

"If I may ask, what purpose could sending *me* serve?"

"Tamiq has agreed to bring the country into the fold as an Imperial province if we can help him consolidate his rule. Tell me, Adept, as best you can recall, what was the attitude toward the Empire when you were a child?"

Reiva felt that lump rising up in her throat again. "Hateful, my praetor. Many people suffered greatly from the war."

"And you?"

Reiva clenched her jaw. "I am grateful to the Empire for welcoming me. The Emperor is a father to me, Lazarra my home."

Thankfully, Vantelle did not press her further on that. It was the truth— she *was* grateful—but as a child...well, it had taken some years for her heart to come to where she was now.

"I want to send you, Reiva, because I want you to spread that sentiment among the people. Tamiq has already begun that work, of course, but Talynis is a proud nation. If you were there, as a symbol of Lazarran and Talynisti unity, it may be a boon to our efforts. I do not intend to let this campaign fail, and I will use every option at my disposal to that end."

Reiva could see the logic behind what the praetor was saying, but... "I'll need to talk to Adept Alyat. I'll need approval. I do not have the privilege to—"

"I am giving you the privilege, and I am requiring of you an answer." Vantelle's eyes glinted as she surveyed the troops. "You will be on your way within a few days. I do not intend to let my war effort get tied up in bureaucratic back-and-forth. Either accept this charge, or be on your way, Adept."

Reiva's hands clenched at her side.

She should have said no. She *needed* to say no. The word of a praetor was great—second only to the Emperor himself—but this was against the codes and laws of the Corps. She did not have the right to do this.

Vantelle turned to her again. "I will tell you one more thing, Reiva, and then I will send you on your way. It's true that I want you in Talynis because I think you could serve the war effort there in a unique way—but I also want you there because I read the reports of what happened in Hyrgallia."

An ache flared in Reiva's arm, the one shredded in the wolf-man's maw. "Praetor?"

"The enemy relic-bearers eviscerated three squadrons to the last soul, two of them on the night you faced them. More than one legionnaire who rescued you grew ill at the sight. Is that accurate?"

The smell of burning flesh in the air, the sound of blood-squelched snow underfoot. The frantic certainty of death.

"Yes," she said quietly.

"And you survived that. You survived that, and then you endured a trip back here with badly fused bones and twisted-up insides. Hundreds of miles. You are responsible for the recovery of seven arcane relics—a formidable achievement for any Adept, more so one so young as you."

"I failed my company, Praetor."

Vantelle's hand came down on Reiva's shoulder. She nearly flinched away, but Vantelle's eyes held her like a lodestone holds iron. "Listen to me,

Reiva. I have lost count of how many legionnaires have died under my command. They were counting on me, and now they are gone. As a leader, that is the responsibility you bear. And I see the potential for you to be a great leader someday. But for that to come to fruition, you have to decide today whether you will carry that weight. It was ill fortune that put you and your company where you were, and a risky judgment on your part to pursue those Hyrgallian relic-bearers. But now you have the chance to turn yourself into something greater. I need an Adept in Talynis—will you serve me in this way, or shall I seek another?"

Reiva's heart was pounding. Her head was light and feathery. The grip of the praetor's hand on her shoulder was like iron, and yet it was also comforting. Anchoring.

But then, an old memory broke through. A cold, wet rag in her fingers. She dabbed it against the feverish forehead of a supine man. His face—she couldn't bring herself to recall his face.

'Take care of him.'

And she saw herself as they would see her in Talynis—clad in legion armor, her Adept's mantle red as fresh blood, her hands blazing with arcane fire. Over her head glittered the golden *Aquila* of the Imperial armies.

Staring down at the grass, lump in her throat, she said, "I am sorry, my praetor. But I cannot."

Vantelle hummed, turned back toward the arrayed army. The silence seemed to stretch. "I see. As I said, it is your choice. I will not order you to do this. You are dismissed."

Reiva saluted, not trusting herself to speak another word. She turned, descending from the height the praetor had brought her to. Level ground was the place for her.

But before she could get away, the praetor called to her, arresting her retreat. "Adept Reiva. Three days from now, at noon, I will select another."

Reiva bowed her head. "I am sure you will choose well, Praetor."

Some strange, proud light kindled behind Vantelle's eyes. "I always do, Adept."

14

VIPERS

A Wolf, a Jackal, a Crow—and Vipers all. I have never found an answer as to why the secret warriors of the Talynisti throne (throneless though their monarch was) took the identities of beasts upon themselves. It is particularly strange, given the ancestral terror their people bear toward serpents. Perhaps they adopted that mantle because they understood that only one who knows the spirit of the beast—who knows the inner monster—can ever hope to do what is required of a true human.

—*The Memoirs of Flavia Iscator*

Beneath a thin moon, Avi stalked across the rooftops of the Silk District. This area of the city was close—uncomfortably close, even—to the palace, so he took care to avoid any patrols by the Revolutionary Guard, or private guards positioned to protect the estates of the wealthy.

On the other hand, basing their operations so close to Tamiq's stronghold provided an unusual form of security. So long as they kept their heads low enough, their enemies would likely be so focused on threats from beyond, they would never suspect what lay right beneath their noses.

Following Crow's directions, he hopped to another roof, and there it was, stretched out before him. He couldn't help raising an eyebrow. By the standards of the Silk District, it certainly wasn't the most opulent estate around, but it also wasn't exactly low profile.

The exterior of the house was detailed with mosaics of fountains and rich flora. Two stories high, with a terraced roof ideal for entertaining guests in the evening cool—Avi found himself wondering how on earth Crow had gotten hold of something this grand.

It was also well-designed to protect against assaults. There was an enclosing wall around the property, too high to simply hop over. Avi guessed the tiling atop the wall was loose enough to slide off and shatter if a human put weight on it.

The house was set far enough back from the wall that anyone who got inside would have to approach without cover, since the grounds were barren of trees or ornamentation—just paved tiles. That would have been expensive, and he guessed they fit together in such a way as to create noise if any stepped on them. Also, some of those tiles probably hid tunnels. In the event hostiles breached the house, the inhabitants could escape to the yard and scamper over the wall.

Then again, this was Crow. There may have even been a tunnel stretching out beyond the reach of the property itself. Avi wouldn't have been surprised. He looked forward to hearing all about the place's surprises.

First though, he had to get inside.

He couldn't vault inside from this distance, so he checked the streets were clear before descending. Then he scampered up to the perimeter wall. The gate was locked and likely barred from inside. Though built of bricks, the wall was fairly smooth. He was skilled enough to scale it, but those tiles still made him uneasy. Maybe if he—

The rattling of wood jolted Avi into motion. His fingers were closing around his weapon when a door set into the gate opened.

"Oh do hurry up," sighed a vaguely familiar voice. A head poked out through the door, and a wry smile twisted handsome features. "What— scared a legionnaire was letting you in?"

Avi relaxed. "Nice to see you too, Theimos."

He snorted, stepping aside so Avi could enter. He was dressed in fine clothing, and rings glimmered faintly on his fingers in the dim night. "It's 'Stag' now, by the way. Crow insisted I join the costume party."

"Fine. How did you know I was here?"

Theimos—Stag—locked the door with a large key on a ring. "Mouse was on lookout when he saw you approaching. Don't look insulted—nothing gets by that man. I don't know how Crow found him, but whatever he's getting paid, he's worth it."

Avi grunted. "High praise from you."

He shrugged, unsettling ringlets of dark hair draped over his shoulders. "Come along, it's late and we've all stayed up in eager anticipation of your joining us."

Avi fell in behind Stag, carefully placing his steps just as the other man did. Though he didn't look back, the Karellan made a sound of appreciation when they were halfway to the house. "Observant as ever."

So I was right about the tiles.

The front doors were unlocked and gliding smoothly on their hinges. After they stepped inside, Stag locked them and set the key ring on a hook. "The old man is tight about these—there's no other set. When you enter in the future, use the servant's entrance at the back."

"Trick lock?"

Stag nodded. "Same method as the house in New Mizkhar."

"Makes sense. What have you been up to since then?"

A shrug. "Little things here and there. Yourself?"

"The same."

"Killing an Adept is hardly a little thing."

Now it was Avi's turn to shrug. Stag didn't press him on it, and he didn't press Stag.

Sometimes, Vipers had to work with contractors, but that didn't mean there was absolute trust. Betrayals happened both ways in their line of work. Stag wasn't here out of any sort of loyalty to Malik or Talynis; he was here because it benefited him somehow. Whatever Crow was paying him, plus— Avi guessed—there was some other way Stag would profit off all this. The man had connections to the Karellan underworld. There were plenty of ways to come out ahead when a civil war was raging, if you placed your bets wisely.

Stag led him into a great room, lit by oil lamps placed haphazardly around the place. In an ordinary manor, this space might have been for dining, but instead of plates and utensils, the large table in the center was strewn with maps of the city, architectural plans for key structures (Avi recognized the palace and Temple), and letters written in various ciphers, some of which he recognized, others he did not.

Crow was seated at the head of the table, poring over one such letter. Avi made his way over, retrieving the documents he'd received from Asrah and setting them in front of the commander. Crow thanked him, then stood up and stretched. "Welcome home. Gather the others, Stag."

"We're here." From the other side of the room, a woman dressed in dark trousers with a matching tunic and vest entered, her hair tied back in a braid. Loose around her neck was a mask that could be pulled up over the mouth and nose.

He had not seen Jackal since the early days of his recruitment to the Vipers. She hadn't stayed—despite Crow's best efforts, the brotherhood was insistent it remain, well, a brotherhood. And a Talynisti brotherhood, even more crucially. A Zarushan woman was out of the question—though that hadn't stopped Crow from training her on the side before she went off on her own.

She'd gained a bit of height and filled out with muscle tone—a far cry from the malnourished orphan she'd been back then. Avi wondered if she was thinking the same about him. She had the look of a typical Talynisti woman—dark eyes, tan skin, strong nose. It was the slight accent that gave her away as coming from their northern neighbor of Zarush. Other than that, she could blend in perfectly—which would come in handy, no doubt. She gave a slight nod to Avi before taking a seat at the table.

Following her was a startlingly tall, broad-shouldered man. His attire was Endric—loose linen trousers with a vest that left much of his well-muscled torso bare, along with arms as thick around the biceps as a normal man's thighs. With skin like bronze and a great beard that looked like black fire, he would have made for a fearsome sight on the battlefield.

"Good to see you, Jackal. And you must be Mouse," said Avi, suddenly conscious of how small he must have looked in comparison.

"And you are the Wolf," he answered. The accent was Endric, but his command of Talynisti was impressively smooth. The man's eyes went straight to Avi's weapon. "Is that the blade that killed a Lazarran Adept?"

For a moment, Avi thought he had a strange look in his eyes, but the moment passed. "It is, and it will kill more."

Mouse grunted. "Good hunting to you, then."

Stag had taken a seat as well, so Avi and Mouse followed suit. Avi was in the seat closest to Crow—not as much by choice as because the others left it open for him.

Crow took his seat last, bridging his fingers as he looked at each one of them in turn. "Now that we're all here, I might as well lay out exactly what we are going to be doing. You've all heard some of this in bits and pieces. Most of the King's Vipers are dead. There are only four that I know of. The two of us in this room, and the two guarding King Malik in Shugrith. We've lost access to almost all our resources, save a precious few loyal contacts I still have in the city. The three of you"—he looked at Jackal, Stag, and Mouse in turn—"are going to receive a dubious honor. Under my authority, you may consider yourselves honorary Vipers for the duration of our operations."

Jackal perked up. Stag's expression was studiously blank, as was Mouse's.

Avi had started at the announcement. He saw Crow note his reaction, but his commander went on.

"What that means is, when we get the throne back to Malik, you'll enjoy his favor and rewards beyond what a contractor would receive. I know I'm asking a lot of you all for relatively little in terms of compensation, but when this is all over, you'll get more than fair recompense...and perhaps the opportunity to stay on as full members."

Avi curled his fingers into a fist beneath the table. "Hang on, Crow. If you're giving outsiders that much, then I want to hear what they're in this for." He glanced at Jackal. "I know you owe the old man a favor, so I'm not surprised to see you here."

She smirked. "Can't I be here because I believe in the cause?"

Avi snorted. "Right. And Stag, I never did find out exactly who you are, but I'm sure you could be turning a fine profit somewhere you don't need to risk life and limb. I don't think you care all that much about who rules Talynis."

The Karellan examined his fingernails. "If you must know, I have a long-standing interest in Talynisti imports and exports—enough that I was already in the city when all this happened. You're right. I don't care whether Malik or his darling little brother is on the throne. But if the Lazarrans bring Talynis into the Imperial fold, that would make it more accessible to the western nations, which would increase my competition and spoil my profit margins." He turned his eyes toward Crow. "So, while I'm honored by the offer, I would never accept it. I have other loyalties."

Avi nodded. He and Stag had never gotten along particularly well, but the man was forthright. And he felt eased to hear that Stag had no interest in joining the ranks of the Vipers.

Mouse didn't wait for Avi to address him. "I am the stranger here, so I am sure you want to know why I have involved myself. Crow has heard this already. I came through the mountain pass for religious reasons. In Endra, I have...you would call him a priest. He sent me here for purposes of, of *pilgrimage*, you might say."

Crow nodded along and chimed in, saying, "And he's a devil with his swords."

Avi felt a knot forming in his gut, though. He had never cared much that Jackal and Stag were foreigners—as far as he knew, Stag didn't even observe his gods' rites. But *this* man was devout.

As if Mouse had read the source of Avi's unease, he spread his hands. "I serve my gods. But my purpose here is aligned with yours. I want to see Malik restored to the throne—we have felt in Endra the ripples of what is beginning in Talynis. The Lazarran Empire must not capture the Endric Pass."

Stag scoffed. "In other words, you just want to maintain the buffer between your nation and the Imperials. No paying taxes to Lazarra, no erecting altars to the Emperor and Arkhon."

Mouse shrugged his massive shoulders. "I do not deny that these things matter to us, but rest assured, Lazarra could not conquer Endra, even if she took the pass through the mountains. I am here to prevent that war from beginning at all."

Stag crossed his arms. "Yes, well, everyone thought they could handle Lazarra, up until they invented those damned Adepts. Don't forget, Karella had an empire once too. So did the Zarushans. But now my islands are patrolled by Imperial marines, and the Immortal Empire of Zarush is quite notably dead."

Jackal leaned back in her chair. "If going up against the Imperials is so hopeless, then why are you even here?"

Stag sniffed. "Admittedly, Talynis is the one nation that has successfully repelled the Empire in our lifetimes. They managed it a decade ago; they might do it again. But the legions learn quickly, and they'll no doubt be better prepared to brave the deserts. According to some of my sources, they've bought out entire Wanderer tribes."

Crow cut in. "The Mithallkiym would never ally themselves to the Empire. If they are working together, it is only as guides. For now, the desert is our ally—but as time passes, yes, the Lazarrans will become a more formidable presence, taking more cities. For now, they only have Dav-maiir, so if we take it back, we put an end to this. Time is of the essence. The Tenth Legion is sending reinforcements to bolster the occupying force in the city."

Stag raised an eyebrow. "The Tenth? That makes sense—the Ninth's sister legion. But how do you know they're on the way?"

Crow bridged his fingers again. "Show them your sword, Wolf."

Avi hesitated, feeling the weight of four gazes settle upon him, but he followed the order. Carefully, he drew the stark black blade and laid it on the table.

Jackal's eyes glittered. Stag whistled. Mouse leaned back.

"So it is real," breathed the Karellan.

"How the hell," muttered Jackal, "did you get hold of something like that?"

"I said I have precious few contacts left in the city," said Crow. "Well, I have some outside as well. A figure from the Lazarran underworld who goes by Ego."

Stag's head snapped up. *"What?* He's a phantom—no one has ever so much as caught sight of the man's shadow."

Crow nodded severely. "And I still haven't. We've only ever communicated through intermediaries. But Ego, like you, has a vested interest in keeping Talynis out of Imperial hands for business purposes. And that blade was placed in our hands by Ego."

Stag leaned back in his chair. "Damnation," he whispered. "Relics are almost impossible to get ahold of—*this* kind of relic, I wasn't even sure it existed until you drew it. An anti-magic weapon." He swore again, louder. *"When* did you get it?"

Avi felt a tingle on his neck. "A few weeks before the Imperial army was at the gates."

Mouse crossed his arms. "As a gift?"

Crow nodded. "A gift with the expectation of creating a relationship. It was with the *Nihilo* Blade that we first received word the legion was marching on us."

"Who delivered it?" asked Stag.

"An intermediary named Zageth—a man who is returning to Dav-maiir sometime in the coming days. He is a close servant of Ego's." Crow straightened. "We have no real reason to trust someone as infamous as Ego, of course. He would hang us out to dry in a moment if that benefited his own purposes. But to send something as rare as a *Nihilo* Blade—maybe the only *Nihilo* Blade—shows that he's invested in our cause. We don't have many options."

Everyone sat with that for a moment.

"If any of you want to leave after learning what you have, I don't begrudge you for it. But after tonight, I have no interest in working with someone who might quit on me. If you stay, you're committing to the end."

Stag brushed a ringlet of hair from his face. "So dramatic. I already gave you my word, didn't I? I don't renege on business deals."

Jackal rapped her fist on the table. "I'm here."

Mouse nodded solemnly. "I am with you."

Crow clapped his hands. "It's settled then. Tomorrow, we begin preparations to strike back. Rest well."

The group dispersed with little more said. Crow indicated Avi's room to him—a small space with a bed and a trunk containing everything he might need for operations. Rope, light armor, civilian clothes, throwing knives, weapon oil. The door had a lock, and it seemed sturdy enough to take a strong kick.

He lay awake for some time, struck by the surreal experience of not sleeping in a cellar anymore. Still, even in a secure place like this, he kept the *Nihilo* Blade in easy reach and slipped a knife under his pillow. His mind spun with thoughts of violence until he drifted off.

15

THE LAZARRAN HEART

IF THE RUMORS ARE TRUE, she was sold for a price that would have been paltry for any slave girl—let alone one strong, young, virginal. A mere thirty pieces of silver? It boggles the mind to think how such a precious thing could be sold for so little.

—*The Memoirs of Flavia Iscator*

THE WATER MIGHT HAVE SCALDED someone else, but Reiva's constitution had been too changed by years of fire magic. Still, a part of her wished she could feel the bath as a normal human might have. There was something pleasurable about letting yourself soak right at the edge of pain, breathing the steam.

"Esca," she called.

Almost immediately, the attendant poked her head around the corner. "My Lady Adept?"

"Can you heat the water more? I would, but I'm meant to be resting right now."

Esca blinked. Reiva had already asked the bath be brought to the highest temperature. "I will...see what we can do, Lady Adept. And the *frigidarium*?"

"It's fine." Reiva nodded her thanks, and Esca zipped off.

Esca was a kind young woman, but Reiva wished Marali had been here —the woman who had first shown her these baths long ago. She was not well, apparently, feeling less and less capable of doing her work in the muggy air of the bathhouse. That put another knot in Reiva's stomach.

Seeking distraction, she took a moment to look around, inspecting anew this room she had spent a fair deal of her time in during her training. Yes, Lazarra had its pleasures.

Most baths were public—something that had startled Reiva when she first arrived—but aristocrats often maintained a private bath at their estate. The Sanctum did as well—it had several, in fact—and Gylos had ordered Reiva to spend at least an hour a day here during her recovery.

That should have been a lovely thing. Instead, she felt guilt.

How often had she dreamed of returning to laze in a Lazarran bathhouse while braving the Hyrgallian snows? How many soldiers in Ironback Company had held that same fantasy?

Her fingernails were biting into her palms, she realized.

Slowly, she took a breath, let it out. Barely warm, despite the thickness of the steam.

She eased her hands open, massaging at where her nails had dug in. Her eyes drifted down her arms, taking in the host of fresh scars. Worse marks scored her torso, and one knee would likely be discolored for the rest of her life. Gylos had removed all the internal scar tissue, so she wouldn't suffer any lack of motion. He had said she could return to have the surface-level damage healed another time—he had been at risk of aether sickness himself after how long the operation had stretched on.

She'd thanked him for the offer, but she had no intention of availing herself of it. She would keep these scars.

"Lady Adept!"

That was fast.

Reiva glanced up as Esca breezed in, followed by a pair of sweating, well-muscled men carrying a bronze cauldron between them, its bottom blazing red.

One of them, Reiva noted, had a slave mark on his forehead. They were all slaves—Esca as well—but if he had a mark, then he had tried to run at some point.

An old hollowness opened in the pit of her stomach.

The men (though by Lazarran standards, they were not men) set the cauldron at the edge of the pool, then tipped it over, pouring a mass of red-hot stones into the water, each hissing and popping as they *plopped* in.

Reiva nodded to Esca. "That helps, thank you."

Esca nodded, looking relieved. She started to hustle the men away when Reiva raised her hand. "Actually...could you just set the cauldron in here?"

The attendant blinked, but quickly directed the men to acquiesce. It was awkward, but they managed to get enough water into the cauldron that it came to rest at the base of the pool.

"*Ah,*" Reiva sighed. "Thank you."

Esca smiled easily before flitting away with the men in tow.

Once they were gone, Reiva slumped forward, wrapping her arms around her knees. She took a long breath.

"Just think about the water," she muttered to herself. "Just water."

The water *was* hotter now. Not as hot as she'd have liked, but it was better.

"Just water."

Instead, she thought of the clinking of chains. The grit of sand between her teeth, caking her hair. Harsh laughter. A baking sun.

Why couldn't the water be hot like the sun had been?

She screwed her eyes shut. "Why couldn't I have died under that sun?"

She was starting to feel light-headed. Not because of the heat, but that didn't matter. She got up, padding from the scalding waters of this pool to the bracing waters of the *frigidarium.*

It hurt. It reminded her of Hyrgallia. The falling snow. The ice-encrusted hills. The frozen lakes.

She sunk down to her chin, then to her nose, every breath disturbing the surface.

Tharrick's head lying in a red circle of snow.

She plunged under, opened her eyes.

Painted tiles. Stones. Ceramic decorations. I'm in a bath in Lazarra.

She stayed down there until her lungs threatened to burst. When she gasped her first breath at the surface, she winced. Gylos would have chided her for straining her lungs so soon after the surgery.

"Why would it matter?" she hissed, setting her head against the stone edge of the pool. "I'll be a minor Adept my whole life. Maybe ten years from now they'll toss me a promotion, if I haven't died under some distant sky."

Esca's voice sounded from across the thick steam over the heated pool. "Did you call, Lady Adept?"

"No," she snapped, then sighed. "No," she said again, softer. "Sorry, Esca."

Esca murmured something apologetic, and Reiva sensed she was alone again. She was glad to be alone, and she hated that she was alone. If only Domi had been in the city—they could have come together—but no, she was still on assignment using her Art of Sea to chase down pirate ships. Had she been here, Domi would have chattered away, telling her all sorts of stories from her service with the marine legionnaires, telling her about the places she'd visited, the people she'd met...

Reiva closed her eyes again, feeling her forehead furrow. Hiding behind fantasy was a childish thing. She was alone with her failures, and no one could save her from that.

"Can't keep my men alive. Can't heat my own bath. Can't keep a bleeding promise, even to myself."

She almost called Esca back to make sure the woman knew she had done nothing wrong. It would do no good. To Esca, she was a Lazarran, and she had the Lazarran heart.

And didn't she? Hadn't she adopted their virtues? Their laws and culture?

She hadn't even blinked twice when those men had stepped in.

What would she have done seven years ago? Screamed? Curled up in a ball, turned her back?

She thought of the chains again. A high scaffold in a city square—she passed through that square, now and then, though she did her best to avoid it—and a man standing atop it with a booming voice. There were other people on that scaffolding. All naked, all in shackles. Heads bowed. The man with the great voice would prod at muscled arms, pert breasts, thick legs, chattering on in a language she didn't know as people in a crowd called things out. Now and then, one of the people on display would be taken down and handed over to someone in the crowd—money was exchanged at that point.

She was going to get up on that block. They were going to strip away her worn and ragged dress, put her up there for everyone to see, and then they'd—

And then someone touched cold metal to her forehead. A man with a severe face and a red garment around his shoulders.

Unconsciously, Reiva closed her hand around her focus. When had she started shivering?

Her Flame stirred at the touch and the memory.

"I can't do anything," she murmured. "I said I'd be better. But I can't..."

She swallowed, feeling a sudden tightness in her throat.

She had said no to Vantelle. Today was the last day the praetor had given her to change her mind. By noon, she had said. It was almost time—maybe it had passed already. It was hard to keep track of things in here.

She had chosen this for herself. This was her penance. Didn't she deserve this? Everything she had—it was a mistake, it was luck. And the facade had come crashing down in Hyrgallia.

She was the Adept who couldn't keep two damn squadrons alive, and she was supposed to go to *Talynis*? Fight and kill Talynisti?

"So what?" she hissed. "I was thrown away." She opened her eyes, looked around again. The elegant mosaics on the wall. The surface of the water, rippling with her shivers.

Cold—she still wasn't used to being cold.

She pulled herself from the water, then stopped, standing between the two pools. A breath, in and out.

Why couldn't she move?

She stood like that, and then she realized she was waiting.

Waiting for what? No one was coming for her. If she needed someone, she could call.

But she would not call. She needed no more help.

Someone had already thrown her a rope. She just had to take hold of it.

She was still shivering, standing there, dripping frigid water into a spreading puddle at her feet.

"I said no," she whispered, her voice lost in the shroud of steam.

Just get in the water. Just wait. Let it pass.

She stared at the pool. She could hide in there, underneath the roiling steam and simmering water.

But there was no one to hide from. There was only her.

Everything in her said to just get in, enjoy the heat.

And everything in her said, *No.*

She walked around it, straightening her shoulders. "Esca," she called, "is it midday yet?"

Esca looked startled to see Reiva stepping into the antechamber. "Not yet, Lady Adept. The sun is perhaps ten minutes from crossing the Pillar of Triumph. Do you need—"

Ten minutes...I can do that.

"A towel, my clothes. Quickly!" She swallowed. "I have a praetor waiting."

16

LIKE PHANTOMS

THE LEGIONS WERE and are the greatest fighting force the world has ever known—and I will not be convinced otherwise until all Lazarra is conquered (though I doubt such a thing could happen so long as we adhere to our traditions).

But time and again, Talynis frustrated our best efforts in a way no other foe managed. We knew urban warfare, we knew guerrilla warfare, but we had never known such fighting spirit as theirs.

And, foolishly, we underestimated what a handful of Vipers cut off from the king's treasury could manage.

—*The Memoirs of Flavia Iscator*

~

TWO NIGHTS HAD PASSED since Avi met the crew—and they were all itching to act. Not only was Avi eager to move against their foes, he was also curious to see Mouse in combat.

Now the time had come.

The Ninth Legion had just established a supply depot along the southern wall of the city, near the Market District. However, the depot was lightly stocked—the plan, so far as Stag had surmised from his merchant contacts—was to fill it with goods and equipment shipped in from New Mizkhar. Since it wasn't fully kitted out yet, the legion kept a light guard.

A perfect opportunity.

Avi, Jackal, and Mouse composed the strike team. Crow, as usual, had sketched the plan out and would wait at headquarters. Avi knew little about his commander's life before he had come to Talynis, aside from that he had lived all over the place—Karella (where Avi guessed he had been born), Lazarra, Mizkhar. And he had acquired a diverse skill set, including medical expertise. If anyone came back in a bad spot, he would patch them up.

Stag would act as set-up and support. Avi knew he worked in the arms trade, and apparently he had set up in Dav-maiir in the guise of a textiles merchant. During the day, under the cover of moving his merchandise, he had gotten the strike team's weaponry into place near the depot.

Avi left the headquarters with Jackal and Mouse two hours after dark. They slipped out the back, padding through the alleys of the Silk District. Compared to the rest of the city, the Silk District's alleys were basically just slightly narrower streets—not as fraught as the Northwest Quarter—but they kept out of sight. They took a circuitous route along the eastern wall, which had the weakest legion presence relative to the rest of the city. Tamiq's Revolutionary Guard was on patrol, but they were easily skirted.

Once they were within a quarter-mile of the depot, they moved to the rooftops. Despite his bulk, Mouse proved an agile climber, moving far more deftly than Avi would have guessed him capable.

Buildings in the Market District were densely packed, perfect for roof travel. As they alighted from building to building, Avi and Jackal pulled up their hoods and kerchiefs. Mouse did not bother with such things—he would be identifiable by size alone. That would make moving him around the city difficult during the day, but if Crow's testimony was right, the extra trouble would be worth it.

Avi's *Nihilo* Blade was small enough that he could keep it strapped to his person, but the others only had daggers. After they jumped another roof, Jackal pointed out the warehouse where Stag had stashed their gear. Gliding like phantoms, they moved toward it.

The building was supposed to be locked, both at street level and at the roof, but Stag had pilfered a key for them. It turned smoothly in the lock, and they were in. One by one, they dropped inside.

Inside was nearly pitch black. Avi's neck tingled—this would be the perfect setup for an ambush. He read tension in Jackal's posture as well. Mouse seemed at ease as he scanned the looming stacks all around them.

"Here it is," rumbled the tall man, brushing his fingers against a large wooden crate that looked like any other. Avi crept closer, and sure enough, there was the subtly carved mark Stag had drawn for them earlier.

He and Mouse used daggers to lever out the nails, the gentle creak of metal against wood painfully loud in the gloom. Then they slid away the top. Plain-looking rugs packed the interior of the crate. These they pulled out and unfurled. Avi retrieved his belt of throwing knives, which he shrugged over his head and fastened cross-body. He also delicately retrieved a small pouch with rattling contents. This he carefully strapped to his thigh.

Jackal eased visibly when she got hold of her shamshir—an elegantly carved saber with a thin cross-guard. She cradled it almost reverently in her arms before slipping the baldric over her head and buckling it at her waist, the hilt sitting high at her hip. She also slipped a small, oblong shield of boiled leather over her left arm.

He didn't know precisely why the sword meant so much to her. Maybe because the shamshir was a sword of Zarushan make, a memento of the once-great land that lay in ruins to the north of Talynis.

Such things were left in the dark. They were comrades; they got their jobs done and then parted ways. Any personal information was irrelevant, even dangerous. That was the cause for the cognomens used by the Vipers and imposed upon their contractors.

Mouse hefted his twin swords out from the base of the crate, where they had lain beneath a thick fold of canvas. The blades were broad and square, with intricate cross-guards. Strangely, they did not rest in scabbards, but sat in a leather harness that left most of the blades bare. Mouse strapped the harness to his back, where the swords sat in a foreboding X.

"You hold one of those in each hand?" Avi whispered, incredulous. He had seen men wield smaller swords double-handed.

Mouse flashed a toothy grin, but said nothing.

After they had repacked the crate and slipped the nails back into their holes, they exited via the roof, locking it behind them.

By now, night lay heavy upon the city. Not far from here, they could see the torches of the guards. The flickering fire reflected off their distinctive helmets and segmented armor.

Avi ran through the plan in his mind. According to their intelligence, there should be at least ten legionnaires, though they lacked an exact count.

They would strike just before the on-duty guards roused their compatriots to change shifts.

The depot was a sizable building, rectangular and squat. It stuck out like a sore thumb compared to the Talynisti architecture all around, clearly showing that Lazarran hands had built it. It butted up against the city wall, not far from the Southern Gate.

In this section of the city, the Revolutionary Guard patrolled the wall.

When the fighting started, they would only have so much time before Tamiq's goons arrived to aid the Imperials.

That was fine—Vipers struck fast and slipped away.

Avi flashed a hand signal. *Ready?*

Jackal and Mouse returned the affirmative.

Then it was time. He held up the signal for *Go*.

The raid was on.

Jackal moved first. She dropped to the street, coming at the guards on a diagonal. Two legionnaires were posted at the door. She dragged her left leg behind her, presenting her right shoulder—deftly obscuring her shamshir and shield. She slipped down her hood and mask.

"Ah! Help!" she sobbed. "Help!"

The guards, their eyes heavy with fatigue, suddenly snapped to awareness, their armor rattling as they honed in on Jackal's cries.

"Hey!" barked the one on the left. "Show yourself!"

She crept into the ring of illumination. "Help! That brute!"

Under the cover of Jackal's cries and the legionnaires' clanking, Avi and Mouse dropped to the streets. Avi palmed two throwing knives. Mouse pulled his blades free of the harness.

"Get the medic," said Left to Right. He was already stepping forward, spear in hand—but not held across his body as it should have been. Instead, he had it to the side.

It was a small mistake. The instinctive gesture of a man trying not to look hostile to a woman crying for help in the night.

"Are you okay?" asked the legionnaire.

Really, Avi had expected better of 'the finest army in the world.'

Jackal answered him with a draw-cut. The saber flashed in the night.

He didn't even have time to cry out before his head went rolling.

Avi and Mouse burst forward. The legionnaire on the right must have had more of his wits about him, because he hadn't immediately gone for the medic as his now-dead ally had instructed him.

The cry of alarm croaked in his throat as Avi's throwing knives buried into the soft flesh beneath his chin.

A third legionnaire was stepping out from inside. "Oy, what's all the—!"

Mouse strode forward with the speed and strength of a raging storm, slashing with his gargantuan blades. One took off the man's arm, the other flayed open his throat.

Three dead—a quarter of the enemy detachment, according to their intelligence. From the time Jackal had cried out to the moment Mouse dropped the third, it had been about twelve seconds.

Avi smiled beneath his mask.

It was good to be back in the game.

The rattling of weapons and armor from around the building reached Avi's ears. That would have been the guards on the opposite side.

"Hey!" called a gruff voice. "Private, report!"

Mouse was already moving to intercept them.

Avi kicked in the door, trusting Jackal to be at his back. He drew the *Nihilo* Blade in his right hand, palmed another throwing knife with his left.

One of the Lazarran legion's great strengths was its regularity. They constructed every camp, every outpost, *everything* according to the same basic plans. Wherever a legionnaire went in the world, he could quickly settle in.

This also meant, of course, that Crow had been able to draw a precise floor plan for the strike team.

As soon as Avi got inside, he encountered a legionnaire with bleary eyes, his breastplate half-buckled, a gladius sword clutched in his hand. Avi stabbed for the thigh, but the legionnaire deflected it with a wild parry.

"Duck!" yelled Jackal.

Without a moment's hesitation, Avi folded at the knees, feeling the whistling passage of her blade right over his head.

His senses were honed by years of combat training and adrenaline rushing through his system—everything seemed to happen in slow motion.

The legionnaire's eyes bulged, his mouth opened in a half-gasp, half-scream. The saber slipped right between his gawping jaws, shearing his head in two.

Avi kicked the mostly headless corpse aside, grimacing as hot blood spattered him and painted the walls in messy spurts of red.

He could clean himself up later. Another pair of legionnaires appeared around the corner. Like the fellow Jackal had just killed, these two looked exhausted and frantic all at once. The one on the left had an iron manica fastened to his sword-arm—a segmented piece of armor covering the wielder from shoulder to wrist—with a shield in his off hand. The one on the right had a gladius in one hand and a dagger in the other, with a breast-plate and helmet strapped on.

Avi named them Shell and Blades.

Here, the building opened up enough for two people to stand abreast, so Avi and Jackal came even, facing the two legionnaires. Avi threw his knife diagonally at Blades, but Shell blocked for his compatriot with his broad shield.

Jackal went for an overhead chop, which Blades stopped with a cross-block. She kicked out, striking at a knee, but he danced backward.

Avi feinted left, as if going for Blades, then quickly struck forward with a sequence of stabs and slashes once Shell moved to cover his ally.

Shell parried two of Avi's strikes, taking the rest on the manica before bringing his shield in and bashing it forward.

Avi jumped back. His heart pounding, he barely had time to parry Shell's darting blade as it came around the shield.

Jackal stepped backward, deflecting and dodging a vicious sequence of attacks from Blades.

Man-to-man combat rarely stretched into lengthy and elaborate dances of whirling metal, as happened in legends or stories told around the fire. Duels to the death lasted seconds. Every passing moment presented a dozen opportunities for one's life to end.

Time to change things up, thought Avi.

He stuck his hand into the rattling pouch at his thigh, grabbing hold of two little spheres. He took a big step backward and yelled, "Sparks!"

As Jackal stepped back, he threw them against the ground.

Two puffs of fire burst alight.

The legionnaires cried out in shock. Avi looked to see them stumbling away, Shell holding his shield high.

His night vision had been spoiled, but he could still see well enough to whip a throwing knife into Blades' throat. Jackal followed up with a horizontal slash, then shifted into a low cut across Shell's shins.

He bellowed in rage, but Avi quickly brought his relic forward in a determined thrust. It took Shell square in the nose, piercing through to the brain.

Jackal huffed. "That's five."

"And Mouse has at least two more outside. More than halfway."

They moved further in, stepping into the central, expansive room. A few crates were piled against one wall, some of them open. Cots lay spread out on the floor, with pieces of armor strewn about helter-skelter.

The door on the opposite side of the storage room burst open, two legionnaires soaked in blood stumbling in, tripping over their own feet.

Avi's stomach lurched—before he realized their blood was their own. One was missing an arm, the other leaning seriously on him and dragging a limp leg.

Avi moved to hurl another throwing knife. Jackal strode forward, already raising her shamshir for a deadly blow.

Neither of them got the chance, as Mouse appeared through the doorway, looming a full two heads taller than the legionnaires. His broad twin swords came around from either side, cutting like whirling iron fans.

Both legionnaires crumpled, their heads hitting the ground before their bodies.

Mouse bellowed, "Four and five."

Avi's eyebrows shot up. He glanced at one of the heads, shivering at the look of horror carved in the face.

If anything, he wondered if Crow had *undersold* this man.

Mouse stiffened. "Behind you!"

Avi threw himself into a sidelong roll. A blade tore into his side, and he sucked in a breath as he tumbled along the ground.

He popped to his feet, clamping one hand over the wound, ready to counterattack—but he was already out of range.

The bastard must have been hiding among the crates. He was fully armored, too, but with boiled leather that hadn't clanked as he moved. He had a shield in one hand and a sword in the other.

Mouse brought his swords down in a thunderous double-chop, battering against the man's shield. Jackal stepped around, cutting at his legs.

The legionnaire stumbled under the rain of blows—then turned tail and ran.

Jackal moved to chase, but Avi called for her to stop.

"We've been here too long," he grunted through gritted teeth. "If he didn't go, someone would've come for the sounds anyway."

Avi sheathed his blade, then grabbed a handful of the spark bombs and tossed them to Jackal, who caught them deftly.

Mouse was breaking open crates. "Here!" he proclaimed. The last crate he'd cracked was full of tunics.

Perfect.

There was oil for lamps in another crate—this they poured over the tunics, draping them over the various supplies, hanging them from the wooden rafters. While they worked, Avi cut a strip of cloth from one tunic and tied it around his midsection, stuffing the rest of the tunic against the wound. When that was done, he shut the door he and Jackal had come through.

Then, through the walls, he heard a muffled commotion, like a distant stampede. "There's Tamiq's goons," he huffed.

"Then let's ditch," snapped Jackal.

Avi and Mouse went through the door Mouse had entered by, Jackal going last. One by one, she chucked the spark bombs into the room. In an instant, the rushing, crackling roar of a devouring fire sprang to life.

She slammed the door shut behind her, and the three of them burst into the open air.

Avi threw the quickest of glances over his shoulders. Sure enough, the Revolutionary Guard was bearing down on them—but then they saw the smoke billowing from the supply depot. The supply depot that was supposed to jointly provide for the Lazarran and Talynisti forces.

Avi knew he should have turned to run full out, but he couldn't help peeking over his shoulder, just so he could see the—

FWOOM!

They had closed the doors leading to the storage room, which meant the fire had been contained and relatively stifled. As soon as the first guardsmen had opened the door, fresh air rushed in and gave the fire explosive new life.

Not for the first time that night, and in spite of the pain and blood at his side, Avi grinned.

Sure enough, the guards gave up the chase, desperately working to put out the billowing fire. The supply depot had been set apart from any other buildings for security purposes, and the city wall was stone, of course. Odds were, there would be no severe damage to anything—anything besides their enemies' cause, that was.

The team was a bit reckless in getting back to headquarters, though they could afford it. Word of the fire spread quickly, sending much of the city into a panic and pulling night patrols from everywhere. With all eyes on the alert for smoke and fire, nobody took note of three shadows scampering along the rooftops and through the alleyways.

Avi's wound, thankfully, turned out to be rather shallow. Once they were back at the headquarters, Crow stitched it up in moments, applying a cleansing salve to ward off infection.

After weapons had been cared for and bloody clothes shucked off for clean ones, the Vipers raised a toast to their first successful mission. As the warmth of the wine curled through Avi's limbs, he felt hope kindling within. Hope that they really could win this.

No matter who Tamiq or the Empire sent after them, they would match and surpass them.

He was glad, actually, that the one legionnaire had survived. Let him tell the story of how three warriors had undone three times their number.

Once again, he slept with the *Nihilo* Blade in reach, and he silently dared the Empire to send another Adept for the Wolf of Talynis. He would be ready.

17

THE BLADE THAT DOES NOT BREAK

THE LION HAD many mentors during her rise. If I can count myself among them, even in some small capacity, it is a disproportionate and unusual honor. But if she were asked herself, I suspect she would name Adept Sharasthi as the greatest among them after Alyat. Sharasthi was one of those rare and precious heroes who does not disappoint. The world is poorer for her absence.

—*The Memoirs of Flavia Iscator*

~

WHEN REIVA WAS new to Lazarra, new to the Adept Corps, she and all the other children in her cohort were given a day off. There was to be a triumphal parade, they were told—a celebration of Imperial glory, glory won with blood and steel by the Seventh Imperial Legion.

The Seventh Imperial Legion, and an Adept.

Dressed in a simple uniform—much like those worn by full Adepts, except the mantle lacked a gold fringe—Reiva stood alongside the central promenade. The widest road in Lazarra, it wound from the First Gate, past the major temples, and directly to the Palatine Hill, where the Emperor himself would await the procession.

It had been impressed upon Reiva that it was essential she act with decorum, as she would be standing among senators, aristocrats, military veterans —she was to be a shining example of the Adept Corps' future.

It didn't seem to matter much, though, since every eye was fixed upon the procession.

At the head of the march, a legionnaire carried the Seventh's Eagle. Their standard bore the motto *By Vigilance and Preparation*. The crowd roared as the sun glinted off the golden *Aquila*, as though the gods above shone forth their acclaim upon the legion.

Even louder, though, were the cheers for the captured standards of the enemies. Reflexively, Reiva clapped her hands over her ears, only for Alyat—standing behind her—to flick her fingers.

The captured flags and banners were many. Many bore horses, so Reiva guessed the Parthavans fought with a lot of cavalry, markedly different from the infantry-driven Lazarran army.

Carts laden with plunder trundled through the streets. Gilt belts and fur tunics, beautiful works of pottery, countless religious fetishes and idols—all these, taken from the enemy. An enemy that was now subject to Lazarra, surrendered to the will of the Emperor and the High God Arkhon.

As the rank and file of the Seventh entered the city, laurel wreaths rained down from the rooftops, strewn across the street. Legionnaires plucked them from the air and set them atop their heads with broad smiles and gleeful laughter. They had not only survived war—they had won it.

If Alyat had not flicked her fingers before, then Reiva certainly would have covered her ears at *this* scream.

Atop a magnificent horse—more beautiful than any Reiva had seen in Lazarra—rode a man dressed in spotless formal kit, every bit of metal polished to a gleam.

Even if she had not memorized legionnaire insignias already, she could have guessed this was the legate, the commander of the entire legion. But her eyes only flickered over him, because another glint of gold caught her eye.

She had been told how, in a triumphal parade, the legion selected one person to wear the golden laurel—the second-greatest honor to be bestowed in the entire Empire. Only a dispensation from the Emperor to wear Imperial Purple was more cherished.

Generally, it was the legate whom the army furnished with the golden laurel. Sometimes, it was a lesser officer who had led some daring, suicidal charge that turned the tide of battle—that was the sort of honor that could change a legionnaire's life and career forever.

But on that day, the laurel crown sat atop a head of dark hair, coiffed in curls that flowed starkly over the crimson red of an Adept's mantle.

Reiva's heart pounded in her chest. Alyat had said she would see an

Adept today...but she had not thought the Adept would wear the gold. From the gasps and murmurs spreading amongst her fellow Initiates, they were just as awed.

She almost turned around to ask Alyat about this, but her gaze stayed riveted on the woman. Adept Sharasthi, that was her name—Reiva remembered being struck by how Talynisti it sounded. Now that she saw the reddish-brown complexion, the strong nose, thick hair, she was almost certain this woman was from the eastern reaches of the realm. Mizkhari? Zarushan?

Wherever she was from, when her eyes (so self-assured, so impassive) flitted over Reiva, the girl almost thought she'd fall to her knees.

That memory—the image of Adept Sharasthi riding through the gates with a crown on her head—had been a source of drive for Reiva, in the grueling years to come. She had only interacted with Sharasthi on a scant few occasions—including a rather grueling interrogation regarding the fate of Tolm, an Initiate who had gone missing during a mission—but countless times she heard and told others the incredible story of her valor on the Parthavan campaign.

And now, years later, Reiva found herself seated in a garden cultivated behind the temple of Somnus, god of sleep. The sun was shining through the olive trees' boughs. The hint of burning incense from within the temple tinged the air. It was...nice. Lovely, even. A day to be enjoyed.

"Adept Reiva."

But Reiva could not enjoy any of it, not today.

She snapped to her feet, fist to heart as she turned toward the temple.

Adept Sharasthi had looked imposing, seven years ago. Now, Reiva still sensed the self-assured weight of a career warrior from her, but...well, she did not seem much of a conquering hero. Her hair was streaked with gray, even though she must have been barely past thirty-five. The crimson of the Adept's mantle also did not suit her—it seemed too bright for one of the greatest covert operatives in the Empire's service.

This was the Adept who had spent two weeks trapped behind the Parthavan enemy lines, surviving by raw skill, divine favor, and unrestrained application of her arcane discipline that Alyat had once described as '*insane in the extreme.*' The *Ars Tenebrae*, Art of Shadows. Her unit cut off from the legion by an ally-turned-traitor, only she made it back alive—and having killed no fewer than three key Parthavan commanders on her way. Legend had it, they still told ghost stories about 'the Night-cloaked Witch' in that part of the world.

"*Ave Imperator*, Adept Sharasthi." Reiva's mouth was dry.

Sharasthi nodded imperceptibly and returned the greeting. "Thank you for agreeing to meet me here. Somnus' temple is not often visited, but I've found it to have a soothing effect on the soul. Sit."

Reiva did so, and Sharasthi took the other chair. Both had been there already when Reiva arrived, and she wondered whether the priests had set them up at Sharasthi's request, or whether they were always here.

"It is my honor to speak with you. I...was inspired by your triumphal parade after the Parthavan campaign seven years ago."

Sharasthi's voice was even, almost flat. Not harsh, but not warm either. "Is that so?" She tilted her head, gray eyes scanning Reiva head-to-toe. "Did you desire the same glory I received?"

Reiva found it difficult to swallow. "I did."

"Hm. Perhaps you should not have. One of the greatest cruelties the gods send is the granting of wishes."

Her hands tightened in her lap. "Perhaps."

"There is no *perhaps* about that. What is still in question, though, is whether what you suffered will have a long-term effect on your career within the Corps. The praetor is quite insistent you be cleared, but I would be remiss in my duties if I were simply to roll over—even for one so illustrious as Cassia Vantelle."

This woman held the power to clear Reiva for service. She guarded the final gate separating her from going to Talynis.

"I've recovered almost completely from my physical injuries, and I haven't suffered any symptoms of aether sickness since Adept Gylos operated on me."

"Good signs, but that sort of thing passes quickly by the time one is a fully commissioned Adept. Tell me, have you suffered nightmares?"

Reiva swallowed. "Some. Recollections of the battle. I see the faces of my allies and enemies. I see death."

"Death as in people dying, or *Death* as in..." She waved toward the temple. "The brother of Somnus."

"Dying. I do not dream of gods."

"Never?"

Something went taut in Reiva's gut. A memory of burning sand under a bright sky. A face that did not look quite right. *'Rebbaelah, you are not to die today.'*

She smothered the thought.

"Not for a very long time. Before I was brought to Lazarra."

Sharasthi hummed, and Reiva was not sure what to make of that.

"Your nightmares, then, are likely from shock. That can be a deadly

thing in its own right, but you've trained in how to manage that. Hallucinations—major or minor?"

"None since the battle. I experienced minor auditory hallucinations, and
while suffering blood loss, I thought I saw my mentor."

The senior Adept nodded, but seemed far off.

Reiva fought a frown. "Excuse me, but this was all in my report, and I'm
certain you've read it."

An arched eyebrow—that was all it took to send a wave of hot shame
across Reiva's face. But before she could backtrack, Sharasthi waved her
hand. "Yes, I read it all, but sometimes you get a different sense when you
speak to a person than when you read carefully thought-out writings. Particularly important when dealing with something that can affect the mind as
starkly as extreme aether sickness."

The burning in her cheeks abated, but now she couldn't hide her frown.
"I don't think I suffered *extreme* aether sickness. Nausea certainly, and minor
hallucinations. When I thought I saw Alyat, I was suffering blood loss and
felt certain of imminent death. Even normal soldiers have those sorts of
experiences."

For a moment, Reiva almost ducked her head, but no, she would hold
her chin high. She had the will of a praetor behind her. She was not about to
let herself be written off. "I could not perform magic without blacking out.
That suggests my soul was fatigued—sensible, given the rate and intensity
with which I called fire to destroy those wolf-men, not to mention chan-
nelling to heal."

The ghost of a smile flickered on Sharasthi's lips. "Passionate—Art of
Fire indeed. Good. And fair points."

Warmth kindled in Reiva's chest. For a moment, she was that little girl
watching a triumphal parade march through the city, beholding an Adept
crowned with glory.

"However," she continued, "I have testimony from the legionnaires who
transported you from Hyrgallia to Lazarra that you often muttered in your
sleep—and some say while you were awake—in nonsensical babbling.
Other times, you frantically whispered to yourself about fire. Not to mention
your eyes wheeled about as though you saw things that were not there."

Reiva's hands closed into fists. "I...I don't remember any of that." A lead
weight settled in her stomach.

Sharasthi stabbed a finger into the air. "Exactly. Memory loss, delusions
—maybe even a psychotic episode. I know it's uncomfortable to consider,
Reiva, but you were almost certainly suffering the third stage of aether sickness. It's a miracle you even survived the transit."

She cast her eyes down again, fighting the prickling threat of tears. "Fire —but it makes sense I would talk about fire. Gods' sakes, it's my Art!"

Sharasthi seemed to be waiting. Observing her, most likely.

Focus—you can't look broken. Not now. You need to prove you're strong enough to go back to the field. Otherwise it's all over.

She took a slow breath. When she looked up, Sharasthi's expression was impassive.

No, not impassive. With a shock, Reiva realized...there was pain in her eyes.

Two weeks alone in the wilderness. How far did she have to push her magic to survive?

"It's a hard thing," breathed Sharasthi. "Coming back when you've been so far gone. It's an experience that changes you forever. Never try to hide that truth from yourself, Reiva. It will only harm you worse when you can't run from it anymore."

Before she knew it, Reiva was saying, "But I can't show weakness. An Adept is the blade that does not break."

"Forged for the Emperor's hand, yes, so we are told. A flaw in the indoctrination procedures, if I am to be honest. Blades shatter, but you can reforge them, and then they are blades again. But if the blade was convinced it would never shatter in the first place, it might start to question whether it was ever *really* a blade. It might start to think things are better as a pile of steel splinters—for it and for the world."

Sharasthi frowned. "You are not to repeat that bit about the flaw in the Corps' indoctrination curriculum. That's a project of mine and I'd rather not preemptively spoil the attitudes of my Peers by rumors fluttering through the Sanctum."

As a member of the Circle of Peers, Sharasthi held one of the most honored positions in the Adept Corps. She partook in the leadership and shaping of the whole organization. And she had just let Reiva in on something even some on the Circle did not yet know.

"I understand," said Reiva. "And thank you, Adept Sharasthi."

She nodded slightly. "Now, you mentioned fire. Tell me about the burning tree. Based on your report, you were unconscious when the blaze started. You have no memory of how it may have been set aflame."

"My will was shattered; the slightest draw of aether threatened to drive me into darkness. I passed out expecting to die in the cold."

Sharasthi pursed her lips. "You were the only surviving human there, so far as we know. So the possibilities are scant. Either the gods intervened for your sake, or you did it yourself in a fugue state. What you thought was loss of consciousness may have been an *alteration* of consciousness."

Reiva scowled. "Impossible if I could not draw aether, though. This was an evergreen in Hyrgallian winter—the amount of power needed to turn that thing into a torch would have undone me."

Sharasthi looked askance, as though inspecting the temple's masonry. "I admit, it is a difficult theory to swallow, but not without precedent. Even allowing for the inflation of rumors and the way soldiers tell their tales, the reports of what I accomplished in Parthava seven years ago... I would have called it impossible as well, and yet if there's even some accuracy to the stories, I must assume that it is possible for an Adept to draw upon a greater well of power under certain conditions related to the lowest hells of aether sickness."

Strange as that was to hear, it struck a chord with Reiva. A warm glimmer of hope. She felt *understood*.

Sharasthi turned back to Reiva. "I've decided."

Reiva snapped to awareness like a thunderclap had split the sky.

"I will clear you for active duty on two conditions. One, you must refrain from using your Art for another two weeks, so your soul may rest and cleanse itself."

"Done," she blurted out. The world seemed brighter. Her Flame burgeoned within, and her shoulders bore less weight.

"Temper yourself—the second condition is harder, since it is out of your control. After your rest is complete, you will be in one of three states. You can guess two of them."

Reiva nodded. "Either a full recovery, or...or I'm a cripple, effectively."

"A dreadful fate for one who has tasted the arcane Arts. Possibly the end of your career with the Adept Corps, unless you could finagle some other way to be useful. It goes without saying that if magic deserts you, you will not be cleared to serve as an Adept.

"But there is a third possibility—one I do not inform many Adepts of for fear of...hazardous behavior. This third possibility is what I experienced in the wake of my time in Parthava."

Reiva leaned forward, all the world condensing to the person before her. Sharasthi was a living legend in the Corps and even in the wider culture. Could this have been part of the key to that? Could she follow in that path?

"You may develop a new awareness of your powers. If that happens, write to me immediately. I will see that one of my personal ciphers is delivered to your quarters—use it for any letters you send me."

"I'm honored," she said, and she meant it, "but also confused. What do you mean by new awareness? Expanded aetheric sense?"

The senior Adept tilted her head. "That might be part of it. I cannot say for certain. You would be able to manipulate aether in ways that previously seemed impossible. Imagine waking up one day with a third arm—all of a sudden, all the limits of your reality have shifted. I have no records of a Fire Adept experiencing this before, so I cannot predict anything specific—*if* this happens, mind you."

She rolled her jaw from side to side. "One more thing, Adept Reiva. The reason you need to use the cipher. This is one of the deeper mysteries of the Adept Corps. You are not at liberty to tell *anyone* about this—not even Alyat. Even some of my colleagues in the Circle are ignorant of this."

That shocked Reiva. "But why?"

A haunted look eclipsed Sharasthi's features. "Think back to how it felt, Reiva. The dread, the certainty of doom. The pain, like rusted nails pushed through your veins. Your nerves scoured by a brush of shark's teeth. Now imagine what would happen to the Adept Corps if it were known that surviving extreme aether sickness could awaken deeper powers in an Adept."

Reiva swallowed, sweat trickling down the back of her neck. "I understand."

"Good. I will see that the cipher is delivered by tomorrow—well before you are due to leave." She rose, and Reiva mirrored her.

Before Reiva could salute, Sharasthi stuck out her hand. "Good luck, Adept. May you find strength and wisdom on your way."

It sounded like it could have been a desert blessing. Perhaps it was.

Stunned, Reiva took her hand. "Thank you. Thank you, I...I hope I do. But what if I fail again? What if this is just a painful extension of something that should have ended in the north?"

Sharasthi looked off to the side, toward the violet flowers just beginning to gain strength with the coming spring. "I have an intuition for these things, Reiva. I do not expect failure from you. You may think I'm wrong—you may even have evidence in the coming months to show me I *am* wrong—but life winds and weaves in strange ways. Today's failure is tomorrow's door to opportunity. Never forget that. And don't die, would you? I did enjoy this meeting."

Reiva's heart seemed about to burst. "Thank you for this honor, Adept Sharasthi. I will give Praetor Vantelle the good news."

Something flickered behind Sharasthi's features. Amusement? Sardonicism? "See to it that you do."

18

THE MAN IN THE RING

HE CALLED HIMSELF 'YAROS' in those days. A thin disguise for one so renowned as him, but he wanted to be found. Some part of him wanted to die. But instead of death, the Lion found him.
—*The Memoirs of Flavia Iscator*

~

THE ROAR of the crowd was like getting boxed in the ears. And the stink, the mingled odor of alcohol and sweaty bodies—patrons of the Nine-knuckle House called it 'our perfume.' No one liked it, but no one tried much to freshen the place up.

After all, if you weren't tough enough to brave the smell, you sure as hell weren't tough enough to get in the ring.

Reiva slipped through the crowd with ease. She hadn't been here in a while, but the Nine-knuckle House never changed. There was the old dogs' table, where the grayhairs moaned on about how no one *really* knew how to fight anymore, always eager to give a mountain of advice in exchange for a round of ale—or two.

She was glad to see that she recognized the man currently working the bar. He did a double take as she walked up.

"Gods save me. What sin have I committed to bring Red Reiva back down here?"

She smiled easily. "Good to see you too, Jalis."

Reiva had left her Adept's mantle at the Sanctum, opting to dress like most other folk here. Roughspun tunic, well-worn shoes. It's not that Adepts weren't welcome—it's that the only status allowed in the House was what you earned with your hands. Here alone in Lazarra did senators and sailors mingle in common dress and speak frankly with one another, no pretenses.

If anyone brought their pretenses in, a round of drinks or a round in the ring squared them away.

Jalis poured a mug of ale, sliding it across the bar.

Reiva took a sip out of politeness. Alyat had sent her here for a reason, and she didn't want to get comfortable.

But Jalis gave her a flat look.

She knocked back half the mug.

"Atta girl!" The rough-faced bartender went back to polishing his countertop. "So, come here to watch or come here to make me rich? I'm down in the betting against Polnoff."

Reiva smirked. "I thought 'no one sees talent like Jalis'?"

"Aye, well, I'm old and my eyes are going bad. Picked you out, though, didn't I? Gave you your name too."

"You're acting like I should be grateful for that."

Jalis cackled. "Blushing like a boy on his first visit to the Belletranes."

Reiva scoffed, shaking her head as she went for another pull. "Like I said, things are different where I'm from."

"Probably stone *me* on sight ever I set foot in there."

"Now that's something I'd put money on."

Jalis groaned, bowing his head. "I'll beat Polnoff yet. Any day now luck will turn my way."

Reiva glanced toward the ring. From where the bar was situated, she could only see about a quarter of the sand pit, illuminated by the ring of torches. Now and then, the contestants would yell—either a war cry or an insult foul enough to crack the ears off a statue of Vestali—and then the blows would commence. The smack of flesh on flesh, the crunch of bone, the roar of a crowd drunk on blood.

She was tempted to go watch a few bouts, but first, she needed to ask Jalis a question. After she had told Vantelle of her intent to join the campaign, the praetor had given her more details—and one in particular haunted her dreams.

Adept Havan had been killed with a *Nihilo* Blade, a type of relic so rare and mythic that many within the Adept Corps doubted it even existed. If her enemy truly possessed such a terrifying weapon, then she was walking into almost certain doom.

She needed insurance.

"I hear," she said casually, "there's a new fighter in town."

Jalis cocked an eyebrow. "Ice tell you?"

She nodded. Alyat was upset by her decision to go to Talynis—quite vocally upset, in fact. But he also knew she was not about to be dissuaded, especially now that she had Adept Sharasthi's clearance. So when she had broached the topic of hiring some extra protection, he had pointed her toward the Nine-knuckle House. He always kept on top of such things—the result of years of service with Legion Intelligence, no doubt.

Jalis puckered his lips. "Lots of new folks been trying the ring lately. Most aren't worth spitting on."

"Said he fought drunk."

"Really narrows it down, that does—but I know who you're looking for. Hasn't got a proper name yet. Just calls hisself Yaros."

"Sounds Karellan."

"That it does, and that's all I can suss out about him. Figures Ice would notice him, though. Right bastard in the ring, this one is."

Reiva leaned forward on her elbows, eyes intent.

Jalis took the opportunity to steal a swig of her ale. "Fights too good, he does. He's not amateur, that's for sure. But he's not legion either, not a chance."

"Mercenary?"

"I'd guess, but no clue who he'd be with. No tattoos, no friends—he just walks in here drunk off his tits, thrashes a half-dozen sods, then wanders out. Bets on himself too, but just spends it here."

"Drink of choice?"

Jalis snorted. "Karellan wine at first, then rotgut once he's been going for a bit."

"What, does he wear silk robes with sackcloth underwear too?"

"Like I said, odd fellow."

"And you actually stock Karellan wine?"

Jalis looked offended. "You'd ask the best damn barkeep in the city that question?"

"I just would never think to order it."

"Well, unlike that mug of ale, it wouldn't be on the House. But if memory serves, the man you're after is due to be in the ring soon. Pour you another to pass the time?"

"Just *posca*. Half-cut."

Jalis produced a bottle of the sour-smelling drink, pouring it into a wooden cup and mixing in as much water. It was closer to vinegar than wine, but it also reminded her of being on campaign.

And she would need to see this like she saw a campaign. This was a mission, and one she intended to see turn a victory for her.

First, though, she needed to see the man in the ring.

∿

KNUCKLES SMASHED INTO CHEEK, and teeth went flying. The force of the blow carried its victim off his feet, and he crashed into the sand, going limp.

The man who'd knocked him out didn't even wait for the referee to call it; he just strolled on over, hauled the man to his feet, and hefted him up to the waiting arms of his friends, who pulled him back into the stands.

The crowd's roar was deafening. Reiva took another sip of her drink, never letting her eyes leave the fighter.

Jalis was right. He was too good.

He was also too drunk to be fighting as well as he was. His face was flushed, his gaze lazy—but gods, he moved like lightning and hit as hard.

He was also courteous to everyone he beat up, taking the time to hand them up to their friends, not to mention popping into his opponent's cell to retrieve their clothing and hand that up as well.

Like Jalis had said, the man didn't have any tattoos to identify him as part of a mercenary band or legion. No slave brands either.

Unless he was hiding something under his loincloth, but you'd have to be a special sort of cracked to get marked up down there.

His close-cropped beard and his hairstyle—long and dressed in a warrior's braid no Lazarran man would ever dare attempt—confirmed him as a Karellan, or at least an adherent of Karellan fashion, but that wasn't much to go on.

Reiva slipped back through the crowds, making her way to the bar. She declined Jalis' offer for a refill, sinking into thought.

"Tell me when he comes by," she muttered.

Polishing another cup, the barkeep nodded.

How to start the conversation?

"He's coming."

Reiva shut her eyes. Could the gods not give her one shred of spare time nowadays?

"More of the stiff stuff, Jalis." Yaros knocked on the bar with bruised knuckles. He hadn't been wearing fist wraps—which was about the only stitch of fabric men were allowed in the ring besides a loincloth.

He'd pulled on some trousers, which was odd, since hardly anyone wore such clothing in Lazarra. They were considered barbaric attire—only cavalry or northerly-stationed legionnaires wore them out of necessity.

The barkeep slid the requested drink across the polished wood. "Good fight?"

A shrug. "Same as before. When can I do a real one?"

"Gotta find a full member willing to stand toe-to-toe with you."

"And how do I do that?"

"Insult their mothers."

"Seems rude."

Jalis snorted. "One of my drink runners said you've broken two jaws and eight fingers so far tonight. Maybe you're too scary."

"I'm gentle as a dove."

"And I'm a virgin consecrated to Vestali."

Reiva watched the back and forth with interest. His speech was slurred a bit, but still mostly coherent.

A huddle of folks were hovering around. Probably either looking to speak with this Yaros, or to challenge him to a fight themselves. But they respected the sanctity of a fighter enjoying a post-match drink.

Just as she was working out the best way to approach without getting shooed off, Jalis cracked a devious smile.

"By the way, Yaros, you're sitting not three feet from a longstanding member of this establishment."

The man's gaze swooped over to her, somehow dazed but intensely focused all at once. "This one?"

Reiva arched an eyebrow. "*This one* earned her place when she was fifteen."

"Fight me," he said immediately.

And there was her opening.

"Before I agree to that, you have to agree to something."

"You're not my type."

"And you're not mine. I'm talking business."

Jalis frowned. "Red, you know the rules—"

She shot him a withering glance. But he was right, of course. No external affairs were to be discussed on House grounds.

Still, Yaros downed the rest of his drink, slammed his cup on the bar, and said, "You want me to kill someone, I have a fee. I don't do merchant escorts. I don't get involved in romantic disputes."

"I need a bodyguard on retainer, indefinite contract."

He made a face like he'd bit into a lemon. "Make it definite."

"Talynis. I have no idea for how long, but we can negotiate payment in cycles."

He perked up at the mention of Talynis. "Are you legion?"

"In a sense."

"You've got the look."

"Aggressive?"

"Like you've got a stick up your ass." He downed his drink, turned, and meandered down toward the ring. "Fight me and we'll talk."

Reiva shared a look with Jalis. "Went well, all things considered."

The barkeep nodded. "Question is, who do I bet on?"

Reiva did her best to look insulted.

THERE WERE two cells branching off from the pit where fighters could prepare for their bout. As Reiva wound strips of cloth around her fists, she could already hear the crowd's anticipatory rumbling.

It wasn't often that a newcomer to the House managed to fight a full member so soon. What's more, Reiva hadn't stepped into the ring in years. People would be wondering whether Red still had it.

If Yaros beat her, he'd earn status as a member of the Nine-knuckle House. Reiva considered whether it was in her best interest to throw the match, but quickly dismissed the notion. For one, she had her pride. Two, if Alyat found out, he'd be ashamed. And three, if she wanted this man working for her, then she needed his respect. Losing on purpose wasn't the way to get it.

As she tied up her hair, she wove her focus in. She wasn't going to cheat and use aether, but she also wasn't about to just leave her focus behind before going into combat.

No one knew exactly how the focus functioned, insofar as it came to what constituted 'wearing' one. Most Adepts wore them as necklaces, but some tucked them into pouches sewn inside their clothes, others did what Reiva was doing now and hid them in their hair. Even if it wasn't touching skin, the focus worked so long as it was on the Adept's person. Various experiments throughout the Corps' history had shed no light on the limits of that though—supposedly someone had once given up after putting five layers of clothing between him and his focus with no loss of effect.

The drawback of going into the ring with her focus was that she'd need to dedicate conscious thought to stop herself from reflexively drawing on aether. That could leave her slightly vulnerable, but she'd take that over just leaving it behind. The psychological vulnerability that came from not having her focus on would have been far worse.

By the time she was satisfied that her hair was securely in place, she heard the crowd getting uppity again. Yaros had probably gone out, then.

Hope this makes you money, Jalis.

She turned and walked out of the cell, into the sand pit and the wild acclaim of the House.

Sure enough, Yaros was already there, as was Polnoff—Jalis' betting rival, business partner and referee (if he could really be called that). The House didn't interfere much, so long as no one was dying—his real job was to stoke the energy.

Polnoff was a wiry man, so the depth and projection of his voice was always a bit of a surprise. "Friends of the Nine-knuckle House, we have a special treat tonight!" His voice carried well over the cheering and stomping, but he also had the dramatic flair to wait until just when the crowd's enthusiasm was quieting, always keeping them at the peak of excitement.

"For the first time in ages, a man so new to the House he doesn't even have a name yet will be trying for his stripes. This man, Yaros, seeks your approval!"

The crowd was deafening, stomping their feet and screaming themselves hoarse. But if Yaros really was interested in the crowd's approval, he didn't show it much. He looked focused—more focused than she'd expected a man who'd just drunken so much to be.

"And his opponent," boomed Polnoff, "a woman we haven't seen here in quite some time, but we are *oh so happy* to have her back, a fighter who was cracking bones while her voice was cracking—you know her, you love her —Red!"

Reiva let the thunder wash over her—she'd never been one for showmanship. Alyat had drilled into her from day one that all that counted was a clean, fast win.

But she did take a *bit* of satisfaction in just how uproarious the people were at her introduction.

Polnoff waved the two of them in closer. "Same rules as always. Stop at a knockout or submission. No lethal hits or holds. No touching anything you'd pay for in a brothel. Easy on the head and neck. And give 'em a good show, eh?"

He shot a glance at Reiva. "And, not that I don't trust you, Red, but in case any sore losers come by the betting table later—"

"You've got my word it's fair."

Polnoff nodded, then stepped back. "At the bell, contestants."

Yaros had observed that last exchange with narrowed eyes. He cocked his head at Reiva, who just shrugged her shoulders. "Talk to me after and you'll find out."

"I'll try to leave your teeth in then."

Reiva cracked a half-smile. "Likewise."

For a moment, they were both standing there, totally relaxed.

Then Polnoff struck the bell.

Yaros exploded forward with a haymaker. Reiva ducked under and stepped right, locked his arm in hers, and retaliated with a jab to the face.

Instead of ducking it, he took the hit straight-on and pulled her in, throwing up his knee.

Reiva flexed her abdominals and took the hit, pain blossoming in both her fist and stomach. She untangled from the lock, dancing backward across the sand.

They circled one another, breathing slowly, hands up to block. A part of her brain knew the crowd was roaring, but it faded to the back of her mind like waves on a distant shore.

She could see the thoughts spinning in Yaros' head as he looked her up and down. With her stance, her tattooed shoulder was presented toward him, and he spared it a glance.

Reiva seized upon the split-second distraction, lashing out with a lightning-fast sequence of jabs. Hands high, Yaros blocked nearly every strike, then swept out with one of his long legs.

Reiva hopped it, but then she took the follow-up hook right on the jaw. Stinging pain exploded across her face. She rolled with the hit, then came back with an uppercut.

A flash of surprise crossed Yaros' face just before the impact. A breath of air puffed out from his lungs, and Reiva pressed her momentum, moving into a volley of rapid strikes, always bobbing out of the way just as he made his counter.

Yaros had the advantage of reach and raw strength, but Reiva had speed. So long as she could maintain control of the engagement, she'd—

Just as she snapped out a kick to the side, he locked it down, then *hurled* her across the ring.

She hit the sand on her back, coming to a quick, and painful, stop. The skin all over her back was screaming like she'd been burned—the first time in years she'd felt that sensation. Wincing, she wanted to just lie there for a moment.

But Yaros was barreling down on her.

Get up.

She scrambled to her feet just in time to duck a wild swing, answering with a strike to the ribs that earned her a satisfying *crack*. He hardly even flinched as he took the blow—in fact, he stepped *into* it, then grabbed her around the shoulders and yanked her in.

His chest slammed into her face like a galley at ramming speed. Everything flashed black, and on instinct she launched another two punches at his wounded side.

Finally, he groaned and shoved her off. She stumbled back, barely holding her balance.

The deep, even breathing was gone. Yaros was lightly sucking in air, favoring his rapidly purpling side. Reiva blinked away tears, wondering if her nose was broken.

Years of training had drilled into her the instinct to channel aether right now and mend all her wounds. But not only had she said she'd play fair—now that things were really going, she *enjoyed* it. The pain fueled a rush all along her nervous system.

More than feeling hurt, she felt alive.

And she was going to win.

Yaros came in with a feint to the left, then a vicious cross. She blocked it, the impact jarring every bone up to her shoulder, and threw a gut punch.

He *caught* her at the wrist, twisted her arm to the side, and hit her elbow. A shock went up her arm, leaving the whole thing numb and limp.

She barely ducked his next punch, took the one after square in the mouth. The copper tang of blood was on her tongue.

She spit a red glob of saliva to the side, then charged back in.

Whatever he'd been expecting, it hadn't been a full-body tackle. Reiva hooked her leg around his, tripping him and taking him down to earth.

She threw her weight on him, pinning him as best she could and raining down blows.

She had him. Any second he'd submit and—

He bucked and rolled, throwing her off balance enough to free an arm and shove her off.

Yaros rolled in the sand, popped up to his feet, and burst forward.

Reiva barely had time to put up her arms before his kick lashed out, slamming into her like an iron rod and breaking her guard.

Before she could recover, he had her in a lock. Then a chokehold.

She struggled against the hold, but he leveraged his size and weight against her. In seconds, blackness was washing in at the edges of her vision. She felt her muscles begin to slacken. The crowd was a distant whisper.

"Yield," he hissed.

Fat chance.

With her last ounce of strength, she jabbed her elbow into his wounded side. As he flinched against the pain, his grip loosened just enough for her to gasp in a breath. Her sight and strength returned.

She got her arms up and broke the lock, rolling away and springing to her feet. She dashed for him, seeing him wobble.

Just as she punched, he kicked. Right before her fist made contact, his shin collided with her temple.

She felt a flash of pain, and next thing she knew, she was lying in the sand.

Yaros was looking down, surprise writ plainly on his face.

Realizing what had happened, Reiva quickly put up a hand. "I yield."

Yaros eased off slightly as Polnoff announced the result to thunderous acclaim, though he continued to stare at her with confusion. Hesitantly, he stuck out a hand. Reiva accepted it.

"Congratulations," she said between breaths.

He accepted the praise with a slight nod. "Could've sworn that kick put your lights out."

She nodded, reading the skepticism in his voice. "Come talk at the bar."

"Suppose I'll have to."

Back in her cell as she washed off the smears of blood—mostly her own, from her nose—she began channeling aether. A *little* bit of healing probably wouldn't harm her soul. By the time she had gotten dressed, every bruise and scrape was gone. She made her way back to Jalis' bar feeling even better than she had before the fight.

Jalis slid her a cup—he always gave fighters a free drink, whether or not they won.

"Sorry if I lost you more money," she said sheepishly.

The man shrugged, half-smirking. "I put it on him after all."

"I would be offended if you hadn't turned out to be right."

"Well, you've been out of the ring for a while, and he was, well, him. Don't let it bother you too much, Red."

Reiva tried to accept that, but deep down she was smothering frustration with herself. First she failed in the field, now she failed here. If she couldn't get back on her game soon...well, she knew what was at stake.

The upside was, her best chance at finding success in the near future was walking toward the bar.

As Yaros walked, he got a great deal of backslaps and drunken compliments. He did a remarkable job of interacting with people as he glided past them, refusing to get tied down.

Once he took up residence at the bar, accepting the free drink from Jalis, people pulled back a bit, though they continued to orbit around. The bar was sacred territory, far as the House was concerned—you didn't bother a fighter when they had a drink in their hand.

"I hear they're calling you 'Purple' now," said Jalis.

Yaros nodded absently. "The teeth, I think, from your excellent wine stores."

"Perfect—you're a pair of colors."

Yaros sipped his drink, nodding to Reiva. "Why 'Red' anyway? Blood?"

Jalis snorted. "Turned bright as a tomato first time she got in the ring."

Yaros looked to Reiva for confirmation. She shrugged. "I was born in Talynis, came here at twelve. Took some getting used to the attire choices people in this part of the world make for athletics."

"You would have hated Karella then." Yaros' eyes narrowed. "You're an Adept, aren't you? Talynis, military tattoo on your shoulder, you said you're 'sort of' legion. You're also much stronger than any woman your size has a right to be."

Reiva nodded. "I yielded," she explained, "because you *did* knock me out with that kick. My body started healing itself on instinct, so I woke up right away—wouldn't have been fair to keep on going."

Yaros stuck out his hand. "Show me."

She decided now was not the time to explain that she should've been on rest from aether use—especially since she had clearly healed herself from the fight. She took his hand, channeling aether through her body and into his. In seconds, the purple bruise over one of his eyes cleared away, and his breathing evened out.

He shook his head, eyes wide like he'd just gotten dunked with cold water. "Did that...burn off my wine?"

"The effects of alcohol are treated by the body like a minor poison, and aether accelerates the body's natural healing processes."

"Fascinating. Jalis—two more cups."

The bartender was happy to oblige.

"So," Yaros continued, nursing his next drink, "you wanted to contract for Talynis. My memory must be failing me somewhere. If you're an Adept, you can't go back to Talynis."

"Under ordinary circumstances, that would be true, but there are exceptions."

"What sorts of exceptions?"

"Nothing you need to be aware of if you're not in my employ."

"Well that sort of information is deeply relevant to whether or not I decide to contract with you, considering how foundational that requirement is to Lazarran military law."

"And why would a mercenary be so well informed? I assume you're a mercenary."

Something flickered behind his eyes. "I am. And it's professional curiosity."

"And in your profession, what sort of work have you done before?"

He shrugged, taking another drink. "Odds and ends, mostly. Used to do more high-end contracts but it becomes a pain dealing with the sort of people who can afford that. Now I just kick around, taking whatever interests me."

"And does working for an Adept interest you?"

"It does," he said without hesitation, "but everything about this just gives me reason to suspect that if I go with you, I'll be at significant risk of an early grave."

"That's true of all soldiers."

"Right, but let's add to that. You're an Adept looking for a bodyguard—tells me you can't rely on legion protection for some reason or other. That means you're serving penance as a shieldless, and that means you're being punished for something. You're going to your birth nation, which suggests highly irregular circumstances. And right now the Empire is currently fielding its...*Ninth* Legion to Talynis, if I'm not mistaken. All this conspires to tell me that, if I take this job, I should command a high fee from you."

Reiva listened to all of this with a neutral face. "If you're serious, then let's talk figures."

Jalis, who had moved off to tend to some other customers, shot her a withering look—which she ignored.

"Four hundred denarii."

She scoffed, rolling her eyes. "You're mad."

"In hard silver."

"You're a good fighter, but I'm not about to drain the Empire's coffers for you."

He waved it off. "Drain your own then. Adepts receive a handsome stipend, I'm told."

"Not as handsome as you seem to think. I don't have room for you in my budget."

"Why?" He smirked. "Spend it all on whores?"

She raised an eyebrow. "This is how you endear prospective employers? Exorbitant rates and speculations about their sex lives?"

"I assure you, my rate is perfectly in keeping with what I can offer you."

"You're competent, but there are other competent mercenaries. Three hundred."

"Three seventy-five. I speak Talynisti better than nine out of ten foreigners, I've been to the land, and I'll even taste your wine for poisons."

"I can't be poisoned...usually."

"Then I'll taste your wine for quality assurance purposes."

"And I'd prefer you stay sober if you're going to be guarding my life."

"Mm, I'll go down to three-fifty if you waive that requirement when I'm off duty."

Reiva considered the man again. Alyat had seen him and encouraged her to go after him. Alyat's insight was never a trivial thing.

She had also gone toe-to-toe with him, and she knew firsthand that his skill was indeed exceptional. Anyone could throw a few punches and kicks, but he fought with a precision of form that betrayed extensive training. He probably had some sort of background with an elite mercenary company—maybe left or got kicked out before he could take the oath and get inked.

And, most critically, she felt how the Flame had reacted to their combat. With excitement, tension, fury—whatever he was, her spirit was moved by it in a way that reminded her of the best parts of war. The vying for excellence, the exercise of talent and attainment of glory.

"Three-fifty." She stuck out her hand. "If you can be ready to leave the city within two days."

He took it, smiling easily. "We should probably seal the actual contract somewhere else. Jalis looks about ready to throw a pot at us."

Reiva agreed. "Tomorrow at noon, come to the temple of Orcaes and we'll have the contract witnessed."

Yaros made a face. "That won't do. I have some acquaintances there I'd rather not run into."

Reiva frowned.

"I'll swear to any god you want," Yaros added, "but I won't go to the temple."

Reiva considered that for a moment. Truth be told, for her it didn't matter so much whether a god witnessed the contract or not—like many Adepts, her view of religion was tendentious at best. Her real curiosity—and concern—was with precisely who Yaros would want to avoid.

Orcaes was a god of death, but he also had the divine function of upholding oaths. Contracts were often made with him as witness. So either he didn't want to be around the priests who certified their witness...or he didn't want to be around the death clerics.

"We can meet elsewhere," Reiva said eventually, "but first tell me—does this have anything to do with your mercenary work?"

He nodded.

Reiva leaned in, lowering her voice. "Off the record, no consequences, just tell me now whether you've ever killed anyone of import in the legions or government."

"It would be best," he murmured, "that we leave anything like that in the dark. I'm willing to forge the contract with you, so long as we both respect one another's privacy. I don't need to know all the details of what *you'll* be up to, and you don't need to know about what I've been up to in the past. Client privilege and such."

Well, any answers besides 'No' told her enough—but now she was at an impasse. She was already in dire straits. Was now really the time to attach herself to someone like this? A cold hand touched her heart as she considered whether this man just inches away—this man she had fought moments before—might have killed legion officers, Imperial governors, even senators...

On the other hand, she was shieldless. And much as she hated to contemplate it, Alyat was right. She needed someone outside the legion to be her guard—someone who would be loyal first and foremost to her.

"One last question then. Have you ever tried to kill the Emperor?"

Yaros actually cracked a smile at that. "I haven't, swear on all hell's rivers."

"Good enough."

19

THE OLD FISSURE

THE ADEPTS HAD their own culture, in many ways. Rare was the one who wore the red mantle, yet could still mingle amongst the rank and file of the legions as an ordinary soldier might. And the greater the reputation one enjoyed, the more difficult that task was. Had I not served so closely to so many, I might have forgotten that they too are merely human.

—*The Memoirs of Flavia Iscator*

∾

ALYAT KNOCKED ON THE DOOR.

"Enter."

He stepped in, memory stirring as he caught sight of the familiar office, memories of a time he would not have been so formal in entering.

Adept Sharasthi raised an eyebrow, glancing up from some paperwork on her desk. "Alyat. This is about your protégé?"

"It is."

Sharasthi leaned back, scanning him. Alyat knew she was using her aetheric sense to feel out the flow of power around him. A particularly practiced Adept could intuit faint cues about a person's emotional state from how their soul interacted with the ambient aether.

But even a man half-blind could have read the anger in Alyat's manner as he stepped up to her desk and leaned on his knuckles.

"Reiva nearly died a half-dozen different ways in the past month. She's under a mountain of pressure—from herself and from the Corps. And you think it's a good idea to send her to *Talynis*."

She kept observing him with that damned impassive expression of hers —the one she always used when she was playing a game with someone. And Sharasthi saw everything as a game. That was part of what had made working with her such a pain over the years.

"I respect you, Sharasthi," he said, truthfully. "You're clever and strong. But this is my apprentice we're talking about, and I'm not about to roll over and accept your usual brand of secrecy and half-answers."

A faint smile quirked across her lips. "*Lumens contra Tenebrae.*"

"Don't reduce this to our Arts."

"I'm not reducing anything. The longer a person practices their Art, the more they align to its essence—whether it be virtue or vice. You need to shed light on things; I need to keep things close to the chest. We couldn't live any other way, and neither could the Empire. If it were otherwise, there would be no need for the two of us to exist."

Alyat pinched the bridge of his nose. "You're evading."

"Such is my way," she said with a shrug. "But no, I'm trying to get you to think about Reiva. *Ars Vulcana*, Alyat. Fire. She needs to burn bright—if she does not live up to the ideal that her Art creates within her, then she will fizzle into smoke. Or worse, she'll descend into the vices of her Art. Unbridled hatred and resentment. She would want to burn the world into which she could not fit."

He sighed. "I never said, nor would I ever say, that she should be caged in Lazarra. But Sharasthi—*Talynis!*" He slammed a fist down on the wood.

Sharasthi didn't blink. "Alyat."

He knew that tone. He hated that tone. That was how she talked when she was about to pull back the curtains and expose something. Something he knew deep down, but wasn't willing to look at.

"You're worried about her."

"Plainly," he snapped.

"And you are letting that worry overcome your better judgment. You come from the Northlands."

He sighed, already seeing where she was going.

"Isn't it true that they send boys out into the woods in the dead of winter with nothing but a hatchet and the clothes on their back and tell them, 'Come back a man, or not at all'?"

"*I* told you about all that."

"And yet you've forgotten it."

His hands clenched, fingernails digging into his palms. All throughout their time working together in Legion Intelligence, this had been the thing that flustered him most. He was the one who dragged things into the open. She was the one who shrouded what needed to be concealed. They had grated on each other for it, but had always known the value of one another to the Empire.

But the damned thing was that no one was able to drag *his* secrets into the light like the woman who breathed shadows.

Her hand slid across the desk, her fingers folding over his.

A lump appeared in his throat.

All right, espying his secrets was *part* of how she used to fluster him.

"*Our* mentors took a chance on us, Alyat. They took the chance we would die, or come back maimed for life, or shattered in body and soul. Your protégé went out into the world, and it nearly killed her. And now she needs to go back, because if she does not, then she will never truly live again. You know this."

He looked at her hand over his. Her touch had always been warmer than he'd expected. He had assumed, when they first met, that she would be cold, but he'd come to know her warmth well.

"Shara, she left as a slave. Now she's going to go back there, and she's going to have to kill people who speak the language put in her mouth at birth, people whose veins flow with the same blood that flows in hers, people who worship gods she was made to turn away from. There is a *reason* for our codes. And if someone is to overstep one of our most fundamental, then it cannot be Reiva. Not now, not so soon after what happened in Hyrgallia."

Her thumb brushed across his knuckles, sending a shiver up his arm. He should have pulled back by now.

"Or maybe facing the demons in her native land is exactly what she needs to do, in order to heal from every wound she has carried since she left."

"That's a monumental *maybe*."

She pulled her hand back. Something in his chest twinged.

Her face was still impassive as ever, and he knew his was too. He also knew that neither of them believed one another's masks, but they were not about to take them off.

"I wouldn't have cleared her if I hadn't thought she has the potential to become one of the greatest Adepts of our time. If I hadn't thought she could do what will be required of her."

He scoffed. "Because it is always best that we do what is required of us."

It was almost imperceptible, but something flickered behind her features. She did not answer him, but instead held his eyes for what seemed like minutes. He wanted to take her hand again. Wanted to erase the fissure of time and distance they had dug between them.

Instead, he said, "I also came here because I need to consult you on a matter of intelligence. I've caught wind of some sort of organization—criminal perhaps, though I haven't heard anything specific about them. The Order of the Sleeping Dragon, they call themselves. Do you know them?"

He was watching her eyes, and she was watching his. And he knew her well enough to see that she was lying when she said, "No."

Of course, she also knew him well. Well enough that she had almost certainly discerned he was hiding things from her too.

"You will tell me if you recall anything, or come across anything new?"

"Of course."

He straightened, stiff in his motions. "Thank you, Adept Sharasthi."

She nodded, turning back to the papers strewn across her desk. "You are welcome, Adept Alyat."

He left, feeling the old fissure widen again.

20

MARBELLUS AND BELLETRA

RELIGION WAS ALWAYS a strange thing for Adepts. Perhaps because they came from foreign lands, with foreign gods. But even after integrating into Lazarran culture in every other way, that aversion to our pantheon persisted.

Perhaps because, even then, they had some inkling of the truth deep in their souls.

—*The Memoirs of Flavia Iscator*

～

THE MORNING WAS cold and crisp when Reiva made her final preparations for departure. The sun had not yet risen, and the city was slow in waking. What few people she encountered parted and made way, some of them muttering obeisances. The exception was the drunks, a few of whom called out to her asking for magic tricks.

She ignored them—even if she could have obliged, she would have ignored them.

Since she was not to use her magic yet, she drew her mantle up over her mouth and nose, puffing breath to warm her chilled face. She would meet Alyat and Yaros at the easternmost gate, the First Gate, around sunrise. But first, she needed to make the sacrifice. The temple she sought was on the way—it was one of the most important in the city, so it enjoyed a prominent place along the central promenade.

Religion in Lazarra was a strange thing—an important thing, but a strange one. Strange ever since it had been explained to her when she first came to the city.

There were the gods—many of them, too many to remember—and then there was *the* god. The High God. The one called Arkhon, whose name was literally 'Ruler' in the Karellan tongue. Why he had a Karellan name, Reiva had no idea. There was probably some sort of historical reason for it—but what mattered was what Arkhon had done for Lazarran history.

In the depths of the Dark Days, when all faith in the gods had collapsed, when the world was in chaos, one man had united the disparate factions and families of the broken Lazarran Republic. The First Emperor. Bearing word of divine inspiration from Arkhon, a then-unknown deity, he forged the Lazarran Empire.

It had been a great step forward for Lazarra. Religion mirrored the Imperial project quite well—one god over all the others, one city over all the others. Arkhon and Lazarra—the heights of power in this world and the one above.

But the cults of the old gods had not gone away. They had simply been subsumed into the overarching cult of Arkhon. All the old temples still stood, just as all the nations Lazarra conquered still stood. Arkhon gave the gods a unifying rule—a divine Empire that inscribed the earthly.

And it was customary that all warriors, before going on campaign, visit the old temple of Marbellus, god of war. Lazarra had multiple war gods, of course, but Marbellus' favor was sought before an offensive. The goddess Menrv, on the other hand, would be beseeched before a defensive war. Reiva had never needed to visit Menrv, but tacticians and artisans often implored her, so Reiva assumed she didn't go hungry up there in the heavens.

Reiva stepped through a crossway, almost to her destination. She could see it now, in fact. It was just across the way, and—

"My, is that an Adept?" crooned a smooth voice.

Reiva stopped in her tracks.

The speaker smiled when Reiva looked up at him. "Up so late, warrior? Whatever could you be searching for?"

He was lounging on the portico of the temple directly opposite Marbellus'. His eyes seemed to glitter as she surveyed him and his surroundings. His attire was elegant, woven of fine silks, and it was sparse. Quite sparse.

"It's early," drawled Reiva. "I have duties to attend to, none concerning the temple of Belletra."

He pouted with full lips, glancing toward the sky. "Is it early? I could have sworn it's late in the night. Ah, let the philosophers muddle that out— why not come in for a drink, hero? Salisa!"

Before Reiva could reply, out from the temple stumbled a lovely woman, her hair mussed but interwoven with finely cut gemstones. She was swathed in a gossamer-sheer shift, and if she hadn't been standing on temple grounds, she'd likely have been fined for it. Even at this distance, Reiva caught a wisp of her perfume as she found her footing, leaning against a pillar carved with acanthus leaves. It must have been an expensive perfume to have lasted all night, and its aroma mingled with the heady smell of wine.

"Hmm? What is it, Lastro? Oh! An Adept." She smiled easily, teeth wine-stained and her eyelids heavy. "Come to pay reverence, my lovely? How pious. Oh, but you're a pretty face. I've never known you to come here. You will come in, won't you?" She clapped her hands, giggling. "No charge for a noble hero of the Empire."

Reiva felt heat creeping into her cheeks. "As I told your fellow...priest, I am not here for the services of the Belletranes. And don't disrupt the peace."

The two deflated. "You'll visit us another time, though, won't you?" beseeched Lastro.

"Please?" added Salisa. "Adepts are always such fun. Such gifted lovers. They're *so*—mm, how would you put it, Lastro?"

"Vigorous?"

"Yes! That's it. Positively magical constitutions, they have."

The pair lapsed into another round of giggling, during which Reiva turned her back and started walking. As she went, the Belletranes went on in their ramblings, calling out now and then to passersby, some of whom eagerly climbed the steps and vanished into the aromatic recesses of the temple.

Marbellus and Belletra were consorts, supposedly. War and Love. Whether or not that was true, thought Reiva, it was certainly convenient for the soldiers.

Stepping quickly, Reiva made her way up the steps of the temple. A priest of Marbellus was immediately at her disposal, and she pressed a handful of coins into his hands before he could even get two words out. "A bull. For strength and honor in war."

He was speedy, thankfully, and he assured her that her donation would fund a fine sacrifice before midday, as well as the ongoing support of the temple. He bowed deeply to her. "Blessings upon you, Adept. May your arm never falter and your sword never shatter in the vocation of war."

She dipped her head in acknowledgment, and with that she was off.

By the time she reached the gate, the sun was peeking over the horizon. She had arranged for the horses to be ready at the nearest stable—typically used by Second Legion cavalry patrols—and it was there that she found

Alyat. They embraced briefly, then folded their arms and waited beneath the eaves of the stable. They typically had little to say on occasions such as this.

This time was different though, because as they waited, Alyat muttered something. "Looks like I have even more on my plate than I thought. New outfit's come out of the woodwork—call themselves the Order of the Sleeping Dragon."

Reiva knit her brows and began to speak, but he made the signs for *quiet, danger.*

Frowning against the chill morning air, she knew she'd hear nothing more of that—just another thing to stow in her mind. Another thing to be wary of.

That was like Alyat though—just drop something like that and then move on. Well, fine. It wasn't as if she'd have to worry about this Order anytime soon—she'd be hundreds of miles away.

Her horse was laden with supplies for the journey, though there would be ample availability along the way—at least, until they left the borders of Lazarra. Demman, the quartermaster of the Adept Corps, had personally repaired her armor. He was a reliable and strong-hearted man, long retired from the battlefield but always devoted to keeping others safe on it. He had fixed up her shield too, even though she was serving penance.

Despite the requirement to forego a shield, however, she still had the right to wear the red of an Adept, and she also had rights to make use of the Sanctum's coffers when it came to purchasing supplies. Even the horse she had selected was requisitioned from the stables of a Scout regiment—a hardy mare, bred for endurance of distance and the elements.

She had similarly gotten hold of a mount for Yaros, who arrived looking sober and professional, and relatively on time. He kept the hood of his cloak up, and Reiva wondered if that was merely for cold, or whether he was intending to keep his face hidden. Eventually she would need to get a better handle on exactly who he was—why he would make such a ruckus in the Nine-knuckle House while also wanting to keep a low profile.

Well, there would be plenty of time for that in the days to come. And if he decided to stonewall her, that was fine too. She needed him as a guard, and if he preferred to keep personal details to himself, that was not a problem, so long as it didn't somehow place her or the Empire at risk of harm.

She and Alyat exchanged a few more brief words—nothing too sensitive, given Yaros' proximity and the fact that he had not yet shown himself trustworthy as anything more than hired muscle. As they spoke, though, Reiva couldn't help thinking back to a morning not so different from this, when she had set out from Lazarra early in the day. Going to Hyrgallia had seemed exciting, then. Now, she wished that, at the very least, the weather could have been different. Even though spring was drawing near, the cool gloom matched her last departure from this place so uncannily that she couldn't help but wonder if it was an omen of some sort.

Maybe I should have paid for an extra bull, she mused.

Again, Reiva marveled that she was preparing to attack the nation of her birth. She was about to cross the world to do so. The capital of Talynis had fallen under Imperial control, but doubtless there would have to be further struggle until all subsided.

She tried to think of the gods of Talynis. There were only four. The Four on High, they were called.

The Worldfather. The Windmother. The Warrior. The Wanderer.

If she had never been brought here, what would she be doing right now? Would she be praying to the Warrior that he grant victory against Lazarra? She would probably have been married by now—maybe to a man about to fight and die to expel the Empire from Talynis.

There were women like that in Talynis right now. Women who had been made widows.

Women she was about to make into widows.

Alyat put a hand on her shoulder, snapping her out of her ruminations. For a moment, they held one another's eyes.

Then she nodded, and he returned the gesture.

"See you in some months, kid."

"See you then. Gods willing."

Alyat grunted. "Try to avoid any situations where the gods' favor has anything to do with whether you come out alive."

"Well, I'd hardly be a good Adept if I lived like that, could I?"

"At least avoid repeats of last time. I'd rather not have my pupil be known for getting shipped back to Lazarra in an oxcart twice in one year."

"I'll keep your reputation at the forefront of my mind."

"Good. And you, mercenary, you be sure to earn your keep."

Yaros offered a lazy salute. "And how, sir. At the rate she's paying me, I'll be sure she lives a long and healthy life."

Alyat seemed satisfied with that—Reiva had never known him to have prejudice toward mercenaries, unlike many in the legions and Sanctum. She was glad for it; had she learned under another master, perhaps she would have been averse to hiring someone like Yaros. The common logic went that anyone whose loyalty you could buy was not someone you could count on. And certainly, mercenaries had been bought off mid-war and changed sides, but that happened less often these days. Mercenary companies nowadays worked hard to cultivate their reputations, and it was a bad business decision to draw the ire of the Lazarran Empire.

Besides, Reiva thought to herself, *maybe we can't even trust people inside the legions anymore.*

She bit her tongue, wanting to banish the thought. She had faith in the legion. She owed her life to it.

But she also had not been able to shake off what Praetor Vantelle had told her when she had accepted the commission:

'When you are in Talynis, do not only keep your eyes on the enemy. Be watchful of the Ninth itself—in particular, be wary of Legate Iscator. She was once an officer without peer. I shepherded her rise myself. But now I fear the legate has begun to harbor anti-Imperial sympathies. Or perhaps she has simply begun to go soft. I pray it is nothing, but I will rely on you, Reiva.

'I will arrive in Talynis not long after you. I want to know how Iscator comports herself when I am not present. I want to know whether she is worthy of the position I have handed to her.'

Reiva swung up into the saddle. *Well, I'll have plenty of time to puzzle that out as we ride. It's a long way to Talynis.*

After a final check on their provisions, Reiva touched the reins. The mare was surefooted and confident, and Reiva hardly had to pay much mind to navigating. She focused on the passing scenery—the dewy grass on the rolling hillsides, the fog evaporating as the sun crept into the sky.

The only time she called a stop during their first few hours was right as they crested a high hill to the east of the city. She turned in her saddle, taking a long look at Lazarra, at the glimmering surface of the Mother River slicing the land.

Then, she turned back to the road, and the city was lost to her.

All that existed was the way ahead, and the land that existed at the end —a land she had left, never believing she would return. A land she was going to as a conqueror.

21

REMEMBER THE DARK DAYS

MANY HAVE WRITTEN that it was the vanities and delusions of the Republic that brought about the Dark Days. It was the belief of the Order that whatever vanities and delusions those were, the rise of Empire was no soothing balm, no fit replacement.

—*The Memoirs of Flavia Iscator*

ALYAT LEANED back in his chair, heaved a great sigh. A pleasant nighttime breeze drifted in through his window, carrying with it the muted racket of a city trying to sleep, but never quite succeeding.

Reiva had left this morning. He did not believe Vantelle's logic. Praetors were not infallible, of course (much as they would have enjoyed such a reputation), but a woman like Vantelle was too competent to not grasp that her blatant disregard for the codes of the Adept Corps would draw attention, even ire, though it would be spoken of in hushed tones and with furtive glances.

The praetor had some greater designs. Of that he was sure.

But what could have drawn her eye toward Reiva? The girl had always been a prodigy, which tended to turn someone into a target in the military, for good and ill alike. She had borne that scrutiny well, ever since she was young. But she also did not fully appreciate the danger that came with such attention from so high an office.

Reiva was desperate, Alyat knew. He would be lying to himself to deny that he did not also worry for her sake after the incident in Hyrgallia.

But he also would be lying if he did not admit that he feared she was walking into an even worse set of trials.

It was a strange time—and it had been made only stranger by the letter sitting on his desk. A letter he had read dozens of times since it arrived without a name or point of origin recorded.

To learn the truth, come to the old temple beneath the lone umbrella pine atop a sloping hill in the Old City. One hour past midnight, alone.

Ordo Draconis Laevisomnis.

Every one of the arcane arts practiced by Adepts brought with it certain emotional and spiritual effects. Classic texts on the matter written by the founders of the Corps referred to them as the attendant virtues and vices of the arts—something Alyat found rather pretentious, but the effects were true either way. What was more, as an Adept honed his skill and leaned further into the nature of his Art, the more his personality molded to suit its contours.

His *Ars Lumens* brought with it the virtues of curiosity and insight. It was why he had excelled in political and diplomatic matters—he was quick to seek out and comprehend the complexities of a situation.

It could also be a curse, however, because he could not for the life of him bring himself to just burn the letter and be done with it.

With a grimace, he glanced out his window. The moon was setting. The night would grow darker soon.

"To hells with it," he growled under his breath, shoving back his chair.

He threw a heavy cloak on over his clothing, checking to make sure that his Adept's mantle was covered before setting out into the night.

The streets were mostly empty now, save the occasional cart of goods being shuttled somewhere, or the beggars snoring, shouting, mumbling.

A man dressed in tatters struck his head against a wall. A bandage was wrapped around his eyes. "The foretold comes into being! Their teeth grow long and blood-washed!" he wailed. "With endless vision, the *kakodaimon* watches!"

Another man, oddly dressed, stood beside the first and pulled him away from the wall, eased him down to sit. He glanced up at Alyat as he passed.

Alyat kept walking. But as he went, he slowed, frowning. There had been something odd about that second man. Something about his eyes...

He looked back, but only the blind beggar was there, sleeping peacefully with a clean tunic folded under his head.

Alyat's frown deepened, but he went onward.

The Old City was not far from the Gilt District. The new seat of rule had been constructed so close by to draw some measure of heritage and authority from the ruins of ancient Lazarra.

Sometimes you heard of young people sneaking off to the ruins, then getting robbed in the middle of their tryst. Robbed or killed—there had been murders, but the culprits were always found. As a rule, they never strayed far from the Old City. That was why, although it was open to the public without restriction, hardly anyone went there. The area had a strange atmosphere about it. Stories abounded of ghosts drifting without aim, weeping, raging—the casualties of the Dark Days, never properly remembered in rites of veneration, their names lost to time.

The boundary was marked by an archway—a more modern construction of smooth marble and neat engraving.

Remember the Dark Days. Honor the Emperor.

The First Emperor had rescued Lazarra from those times of ruin and murder. As Alyat passed through the arch, he hoped he was not about to run headlong into another manifestation of that past.

As he walked amid the torn-up streets and burned-down wreckage, he drew upon the *Ars Lumens*. He pulled ambient light toward his eyes, enhancing his night vision. It slightly fuzzed things, but with decades of practice he had learned to overcome that.

Perched in the boughs of an olive tree, a golden-eyed owl spun its head to him.

"*Hoo.*"

Alyat passed under its branch. He didn't look back, but couldn't shake the feeling that the owl was still watching him.

By now, the ground beneath his feet had turned to grass. Toppled columns lay strewn about, many of them carved with graffiti—names, lewd jokes, cartoonish drawings. Alyat picked his way through them, sparing an extra glance for those gloomy patches where some unknown danger might lurk. If anything, at least it would take a rather bold person to try to kill an Adept in the heart of the Empire.

The temple the letter referred to was half-collapsed, its open side facing the distant horizon. Alyat crept to the front, casting his vision about. He took the added precaution of bending light around himself, obscuring him almost perfectly in the dim lighting.

Over the gaping doorway was a cracked and ruined sculpture of a woman's head. Blank-eyed and mouthless, she stared out across the ruins of the Old City. Alyat imagined she was looking directly toward the Imperial Palace.

She would have been an oracle in the old days. They still had women like that in Karella—illegal, heretical under the cult of Arkhon, which forbade any attempts at divination. The future was a mystery to mortal minds, a fog-laden valley. It was not the place of humans to steal from the gods secrets of what was yet to come.

As Alyat passed beneath the oracle's eyes, he wondered at why the meeting had been called here. None of the possibilities seemed favorable.

Raising a hand, he cast a soft glow of light into the ruins. Sure enough, someone was standing there, dead center of the room, not even trying to hide. He wore a mask, like the sort actors wore in stage performances. An exaggerated frown, a tear hanging from the corner of the eye.

"Adept Alyat," he murmured, his voice soft.

"I would know your name, since you already know mine."

"My name is insignificant." He stood up straighter, as though he were proud to say it.

"Tell me or I leave," he snapped, letting a bit of Northlander burr creep back into his voice.

He spread his arms, as though wanting to envelop Alyat in an embrace. "Then call me Nuntius. What matters, though, is for whom I speak. The Order of the Sleeping Dragon."

"Yes, your letter said as much."

During his time with Legion Intelligence, he'd kept tabs on every secret society in the Ixian Reach—and there were many. Most were harmless, even pious and loyal to the cause of the Emperor, but once in a while you found the madmen. The prophets. The revolutionaries.

But of the Order of the Sleeping Dragon, he knew nothing.

"Since I must admit," he began, "that I know nothing of your Order, maybe you can explain why you're so interested in me. Enough to invite me out to a clandestine meeting in these damned ruins."

The masked man waved his hand expansively. "Do you know what they called this place once?"

"An oracle's dwelling. Fortune telling. Heathenry. The sort of abominations that brought the Dark Days."

The man's laugh was silken, haughty. "Yes, we all are told as much. This was not the greatest oracle's dwelling—that would be the Sibylline House up in the mountains. But what if I told you there was someone even now, within the walls of this very city, who still peered into the future?"

Alyat snorted. "I'd ask you to hand them over for interrogation."

"Execution, you mean."

Alyat shrugged. "The law is the law. All must obey, from the lowest slave to the Emperor himself."

"Ah, there it is. *The law.*"

"If you have called me here because you thought I would be charmed by the promise of glimpsing the future, I'm telling you I'm not. Aches and pains, a gray head, weak eyes—I already know my future."

"You misunderstand me, Adept. It is not my Order which practices the forbidden sight." He paused, gauging Alyat's reaction. "I speak of none other than our illustrious Emperor."

Alyat scoffed. "Ah, so you're insane." He turned to leave.

"The Emperor is an Adept."

Alyat stopped mid-stride. Slowly, he looked back.

"He is the sole practitioner of the *Ars Prognoscens.*"

"There is no such Art."

"Many things 'stopped existing' after the Dark Days."

Alyat came back, slowly. He examined Nuntius with a new interest. None of what he was saying made sense...but he could not deny his hunger for knowledge. He had to know for himself.

"Where's your proof? And I won't accept some 'my-teacher-learned-it-from-his-teacher' bullshit."

The man seemed pleased, and Alyat got the sense he was smiling. "Come here."

"I may be interested, but I'm not stupid enough to get within knife range of you."

The man nodded. "A fair point—I suppose there are many dangers in being an Adept. You must be worried for your young apprentice."

A cold hand gripped Alyat's heart. "What did you say?"

"The Order has many eyes, Adept. In many places." He produced a scroll from inside his cloak. "Do be careful with this."

"You should make copies of things before you go handing them out. I would think that's essential secret order protocol."

"I meant be careful for *your* sake. This is a highly proscribed text. You would not want anyone to know that you were indulging in such indecent material."

"You're telling me that the Empire erased the memory of an entire arcane Art—one capable of revealing the future—and that Emperor Dioclete, a man of *Lazarran* blood, is a wielder of it. It's unthinkable. If your book is empty wind, I'll know."

"Many things are possible with the power of the so-called 'High God,' Adept."

Alyat fought the urge to roll his eyes. "Now you cast doubt upon Arkh—"

"*Shh!*" The man nearly leaped for Alyat, finger pressed to his mask's exaggerated lips. Alyat marveled as he swept his gaze around them, as if he expected the Palatine Guard themselves to spring out from behind the crumbling masonry.

"He hears his name, Adept. Do not speak it if you are not prepared to bear his scrutiny."

At this point, Alyat was nearly certain the man was crazy...but he had in his hands a scroll that supposedly no one in the Empire had read for centuries, save this Order, and he could not deny that something strange was happening with regard to Reiva's commission to Talynis.

"I'll investigate. Discreetly. But in all things, I serve the Emperor. Don't forget that."

The man gave a perfunctory bow. "Adept Alyat, it is for your hunger for the truth that we approached you. I have faith you will understand. The Order watches. The Order waits."

More than a little perturbed, Alyat made his way home, leaving the masked man in the shadow-swarmed ruins of the temple. Now and then, he checked over his shoulders, thinking he heard the patter of footsteps, glimpsed fleeting movement in the corner of his eye.

'The Order watches. The Order waits.'

If someone were particularly motivated and sufficiently well-positioned in the government or the military, they could have made a case that by even accepting the scroll—by leaving Nuntius free and alive after hearing him speak—Alyat had committed treason, or at the very least acted as an accessory to conspiracy.

Well, it wouldn't be the first time he'd run afoul of protocol. He knew Legion Intelligence well enough to stay a step ahead if they came knocking.

Then again, he was certain Sharasthi lied to him when he'd asked whether she knew of the Order of the Sleeping Dragon. His gut instinct said she was involved in this somehow.

But logically, that didn't make sense. Over the years, he'd heard her say plenty of things that would have gotten her in hot water. Even today, some of the ways she used her authority in the Circle raised eyebrows. She would know he'd hear her out—what Nuntius had said was outlandish, but barely worse than some of the stuff she'd said in their younger days.

There was another possibility—she did know about the Order, but she had lied because she was afraid of getting anywhere near them.

He wasn't sure which possibility unnerved him more.

22

THE UNCONSCIOUS MIND

IN ALL THE lands my father showed me and all the lands I traveled after his death, I did find practitioners of the arcane arts. Magicians, sorcerers, druids —they call themselves by many names, but always they can be found. Some have been hostile, others hospitable, but always we have recognized one another by the way the old teachings mark the soul.

And though all vary in certain traditions or trappings, we are united in the central mystery of the arts: the Binding.

—*The Life and Wisdom of Simeon Binkhok As Told by Himself*

~

"COME ON, *NEVER*?"

Reiva snorted. "For the tenth time, yes. Swear on my sword, my armor, and my mantle."

Yaros shook his head. "You've got to be joking."

"What part of swearing an oath do you not understand? I'll even swear on my focus if it makes you happy."

"Still wouldn't believe you." He leaned forward to look her horse in the eye. "What about you, eh? You believe this?"

"What would a horse know about lying?"

"Come now, everyone knows horses are experts when it comes to sex."

"Is that so?" she drawled.

"Almost as expert as we Karellans."

"That I believe. But in Talynis, your expertise would not be so well-regarded."

"Ah, so that's it. Desert prudery. Well, if I burst into a ball of flames when I set foot in the holy city, promise me you'll do something about it."

"I can only create fire, not suffocate it. So how about I just burn you faster—put you out of your misery?"

Yaros smirked. "Should've inked that into the contract before we left."

Reiva cast an exaggerated glance over her shoulder, squinting against the nighttime gloom as she surveyed the sparse landscape. "Lazarra is only, what, a few hundred miles back? We can turn around."

"I'm not going through that one village between the rivers again."

"They probably wouldn't want you to go through again either."

Yaros muttered something under his breath.

Reiva shrugged.

Hard to believe we've already come so far.

Traveling in a pair had cut the travel time remarkably compared to moving across the land as part of a full legion. The reinforcements from the Tenth would beat them there, since they were going much of the way by ship, but Reiva had never been one for sea travel. Besides, after the first two weeks, Reiva had been clear to channel aether to rejuvenate their horses, further expanding the amount of ground they could cover in a day. And once they left the well-patrolled roads of the Ixian Reach, the lands at the heart of the Lazarran Empire, Reiva's mantle had served well to ward off any would-be bandits.

Now and then, though, she had considered stowing the mantle, just to break up the monotony. She had not had much opportunity to use her magic beyond lighting the evening campfire.

She glanced at the sky, noting the moon already on the rise. Her throat was dry from a full day of riding (and far more talking than she'd have had to endure were she traveling with Alyat or a legion detachment), so she took a drink from her waterskin.

"Tell you what, boss," chirped Yaros. "Henceforth, consider it part of my contract to get you laid."

Reiva choked, spitting a mouthful of water into the dust.

She cast a baleful look at him. "You did that on purpose."

He beamed shamelessly. "But I wasn't joking. I'm quite the romantic accomplice—I'll have paramours lining up at your doorstep before you can say 'snuff the candles.'"

"Did it perhaps occur to you that I was just never interested?"

"Come on, you grew up in a military enclosure training with some of the best young warriors in the world. There must have been some strapping young lad who caught your eye."

She shrugged. "Never like *that*."

"A pretty girl, then."

"Also no." Domi and Phetan were both rather attractive—even Tolm, she had to admit—but she'd never seen anything romantic in any of them.

Yaros arched an eyebrow. "I'm going to need you to swear on that focus of yours after all."

"I know I asked when we first met, but did it ever occur to you that interrogating your employer's sex life is not a wise decision for future career prospects?"

"You also said I'm not your type, which implies you have one."

"If I do, I haven't found anyone who fits it. Now, am I going to have to invoke the 'shut up' clause of our contract?"

"I realize I have been little service to you aside from my entertainment value and culinary skill, but soon as we come to violence, you'll see I am more than worth my fee."

She hoped so—in fact, most of the reason she had hired him in the first place had been so someone could watch her back against the Wolf and his *Nihilo* Blade. But she wasn't about to let him get overconfident in the security of his position. "At three hundred and fifty denarii, you had better be. Otherwise I might haul you before a court for fraud."

The mercenary snorted. "You may be a Talynisti prude, but you've got the Lazarran bureaucracy deep in your bones."

Reiva's smile strained a bit. If Yaros noticed, though, he didn't remark on it. Maybe this was another way of probing her, trying to get a sense of just who she was. That was fine—it was only natural he would want to know what sort of person he was working for, and he was often irritatingly curious. But for how much he asked, he was also remarkably obscure about his own past.

"From now on," she said, "any time you want to learn something about me, you have to reciprocate."

"Now who's asking who about their sex life?"

She gave him a flat look. "I meant, I would like to know more about why you're worth so much as a warrior. No identifying tattoos, no heraldry on your weapons. You must have worked with some sort of mercenary outfit in the past."

He shrugged, and Reiva noted his expression had gone impassive, like he'd slipped on a mask. "I've worked with plenty of mercenary bands. Never swore on to any of them though."

"But one of them must have given you the bulk of your training. What style were you using in the ring? It felt like *pankration* but I didn't recognize some of those holds."

"And you're not going to answer any more of my prying questions unless I give something back?"

"Not a one."

"All right. Well, you're correct, it's an offshoot of Karellan *pankration*."

"What sort of derivation? Who developed it?"

"If you want to ask more questions, first you'll have to give me something more."

"Hang on—I've already given you information about the *Nihilo* Blade, which is privileged beyond belief."

"Yes but one, that is directly relevant to your hiring me so I can keep you safe, so it's impersonal, and two, you told me weeks ago and we are all past any valid period for redeeming that."

Reiva frowned. "On second thought, let's stop for the night. I can only take so many deep revelations about my traveling companion."

While Yaros set out to gather firewood—a task becoming increasingly difficult as they drew closer to the eastern realms—Reiva rubbed down the horses and rejuvenated them with a measure of aether. The horses' coats carried more dust than they had just a few days ago.

She sighed, thinking of the shifting sands she had crossed years ago. Years that seemed a lifetime.

Her hand drifted toward her saddlebag, where she'd stowed two copies of the Talynisti scriptures—a Karellan translation and one in the original tongue. Every day she'd been working through a bit, trying to refresh what she had lost of the language over the years.

'I do not dream of gods.'

'Never?'

'Not for a very long time.'

In truth, there had only been one dream. One dream, and one god, encountered among the desert sands, beside a muddy river as a dying man wailed.

At least, she told herself it had been a dream—a viciously real nightmare brought on by desert heat, dehydration, and despair. The alternative...

She shook her head, shoving away the memory and muttering to herself. The horses pricked up their ears, turning big, curious eyes toward her. Reiva smiled faintly. "At least you never bother me with questions."

"Talking to the horses—finally cracked?" called Yaros.

"If I am, you drove me to it." She ignored the twisting uncertainty in her gut, ignored how Sharasthi had said the legionnaires reported her mumbling in her sleep, speaking to things that were not there.

Yaros set to work building the fire. "If I really do drive you insane, I'll reduce my fee."

"Astute business practice," she observed.

"I try. Now get over here and light this."

She turned from the horses and took a step forward, then stopped, staring at the wood and kindling.

Yaros arched an eyebrow. "Not up to your standards?"

She waved him off, frowning. It seemed...off.

It's just a pile of wood and dried twigs. I've done this thousands of times.

So why did something seem different?

And then it clicked.

It wasn't that the wood *looked* different; it was that she was *perceiving* it differently.

Reiva's heart pounded. What had Adept Sharasthi said?

'Imagine waking up one day with a third arm—all of a sudden, all the limits of your reality have shifted.'

"Stand back."

Now he looked curious, but he took a few steps away.

Seeing his excitement, she suddenly felt self-conscious. *I don't even know what I'm doing.*

But no, she did. She just didn't know what she knew.

When she had begun her training as an Adept Initiate, Alyat had taught her that she already knew how to use her magic—that it was ingrained into her. All she had to do was reach out and bring it to bear, bringing what the unconscious mind knew into the provenance of the conscious mind.

Why did the wood seem different to me once I took a step toward it?

Experimentally, she took a step back.

There!

Another step back. Then two steps forward.

She spun around, casting her gaze.

She focused on a tree—yes, she could see it there. Then a scraggly shrub. Even Yaros and the horses.

Something was different about everything in her environment, and it shifted depending on her distance from it. It was also easier to recognize that difference the more flammable the object was.

She turned back to the wood and kindling in the center of their campsite.

Distance...it couldn't be, could it?

Her Flame burgeoned, as if eager to be used. It almost felt like it was speaking to her, shouting 'Yes!'

She raised her hand, as she would any other time she'd conjure fire. But instead of sending out aether through her fingertips, she focused on the little twigs and dried leaves, the kindling. She attended to the subtle difference in the way it appeared.

'You would be able to manipulate aether in ways that previously seemed impossible.'

Burn, she thought.

And the kindling *burst* aflame.

Reiva gasped, stumbling backward.

The little flame grew, consuming the kindling, spreading to the logs.

Yaros swore, crossing his arms. He turned a bewildered expression toward her. "New trick?"

Reiva stared at the fire, the fire she had lit without *throwing* anything at it. "Guess so."

She also felt a deep fatigue in her soul, as she might have felt after a great deal of working her Art. Like exercising a muscle unaccustomed to heavy labor.

And then, elation. She laughed, slapping her forehead.

She needed to write a letter to Adept Sharasthi. As soon as she reached Dav-maiir, she'd send it.

She turned her eyes heavenward, picking a point in space ten feet above her head, and concentrated, *strained*—and sure enough, a ball of fire flickered there, just for a moment, before she lost her grasp on it.

The ball fizzled out as soon as her hold lapsed, but she had sensed something there. Like a potential well of power straining to be let free, an ocean held back by a dam. A tremendous, explosive power.

Reiva let out a slow breath. If she could harness that potential, if she could master it...

Yes, she needed to send a letter to Sharasthi.

And she needed to start training like it was day one in the Sanctum.

Let the Corps see what I am capable of.

23

PRIMITIVE DESERT DRIVEL

HIGH PRIEST BARMOSHE ZADIQ SAID, 'The Mithallkiym cling to an old way of life—perhaps the oldest in Talynis since the withdrawal of the waters. What earns the suspicion and ire of the Talynisti people is the undue reverence they give to the Wandering God, as though he were distinct among the Four.

'But I must wonder, if our people gave ha'Mithalleik the reverence that was his rightful due, perhaps there would be no need for the Mithallkiym to follow his ways so extravagantly. Perhaps they are a living indictment of our sin.'
—*A Chronicle of Talynisti Reign, Vol. I: Temple and Throne*

∾

ADEPT REIVA ARRIVED at the border of Talynis on a scorching day, much the same as the day she left seven years ago.

It was a sand-swept land, a scrap of desert ignored by most other nations.

It was the land of her birth, the land of her blood—it was the land she would conquer in the Emperor's name.

She tugged her red mantle up over her mouth and nose, trying to ward against the dust and sand kicked up by the hot winds.

The border town of Amrun was a bustle of activity. Many legionnaires were already here, easily identified by their plated armor, their gladius swords, their massive shields. They seemed irritated. Antsy. Exactly the sort of soldiers you would not want in your town for long. These were the men and women of the Tenth Imperial Legion, sent here to reinforce the Ninth Legion, currently spread thin across the nation.

"I'll figure out what's going on," said Yaros. He nudged his horse into a trot, seeking out whatever local officials he could find. He would try to avoid the legionnaires if he could, Reiva knew, but if he couldn't help it, her name would get him out of any binds. A foreign mercenary like Yaros would draw a great deal of suspicion trying to enter the country.

Still, simple though his command of the language was, he spoke Talynisti better than Reiva did. One of the many complexities of being an Adept. She should never have set foot in Talynis again, so she had never bothered to keep up with the language—well, besides that brief, blessed period of life she had known Levin and Artha. Her being here was, by every written law and code she was sworn to, illegal.

And yet, here she was.

Tugging down her mantle, she spit in the sand. She could already feel the grit in her teeth. It had been a daily reality growing up. Even within the more temperate oasis-cities of Talynis, sand always found its way in. She had never thought she would feel that sensation again, once she reached the coastal lands of Lazarra. The weather there was balmy, the air pregnant with moisture and life.

People here hid their faces from the sun. Truth be told, it amazed Reiva that the Empire was even trying to take Talynis, given how spectacularly it had failed on its last attempt. That infamous campaign had wounded the Empire's pride.

It had also destroyed many families in Talynis. Reiva knew that well enough.

Another reason she should not have been here.

Another shadow of the past she would have to keep buried.

She was here to serve the Emperor. To earn back something lost. She would have to cut down people in this land where she had been born. She might have to burn cities. And she would serve her new home—the home that had welcomed her and raised her up to a position of power—in doing these things.

At least, she told herself that.

Some legionnaires had taken notice of her. They cast wary glances when they thought she wasn't looking.

They were on the same side, of course, but it was not uncommon for the rank-and-file of the legions to feel uncomfortable with the Adepts. Particularly if any of them had heard of what happened in Hyrgallia.

Reiva had stopped taking it personally a long time ago. You had to, to survive in this career. *'Either get thick skin, or go cut some off someone else so you can wear it,'* Alyat used to say to her. She'd been a little girl then, teary-eyed, hating that she had been born with this thing called magic in her soul.

Now, that magic was the one thing keeping her from squalor. Her performance in Talynis was her last chance to prove to the Empire that it still needed her.

She scowled, nudged her horse into a trot. What was taking Yaros so long?

The locals of the border town were small in number—this place was neither close enough to the fertile regions of Parthava to the west, nor was it built around one of the famed oases of Talynis further into the desert. It existed in an uneasy limbo between those two realities.

She watched women with headdresses draw water from a well. One of them, the younger one, stared at Reiva as she passed, taking in her braided hair, her uncovered legs. The older one smacked the younger's elbow and tugged her away, whispering.

Her mother had worn a headdress like that. She had always expected to wear one when she grew up. Instead, the only way she covered her head was with a helmet.

Reiva felt an odd stab of embarrassment. After her initial shock years ago, she had acclimated to Lazarran customs of dress. She hadn't even considered that coming back to Talynis might evoke this inner tension.

She wondered what her father would have thought about this return. She avoided thinking about her mother.

As she drew closer to the edge of the desert proper, she caught sight of several legion officials—captains and a prefect by their insignias. There was also a deeply tanned man with a thick beard and loose robes, talking animatedly with his hands. She caught the flowing, clipped sounds of Lazarran, the gutturals and sibilants of Talynisti.

And between them all, Yaros was there, arguing with everyone at once from the look of it, switching between languages as deftly as he switched between weaponry.

It was irritating, of course, but she couldn't help but crack a smile. Yaros prided himself on getting along with everyone. "People trust my face," he always said, then added, deadly serious, "unlike yours, which looks like you are contemplating whether you'll roast them alive."

She would shrug then. "It's a good guess, usually."

Reiva did not begrudge legionnaires who trod warily around Adepts. Even if you were on the same side, it was a bit like having a raging bull in your ranks. You just hoped it kept its horns pointed toward the enemy lines.

As Reiva approached, Yaros' expression flickered with a meld of relief and *don't-mess-this-up-even-more.*

"*Ave Imperator,*" she called to the legionnaires, sliding off her horse.

The prefect blinked, then his eyes fastened on the red-and-gold mantle. He snapped off the legion salute. "*Ave Imperator,* Adept."

The captains looked uneasily between their prefect and Reiva.

The Talynisti man—village elder, she guessed—looked at her with not a little fear, but also firm determination. Even in the face of someone who could end his life with a wave of her hand, he refused to be cowed.

It reminded her of her father.

Yaros slid over to stand beside Reiva, his movements smooth and cat-like. "As I said, I travel with an Imperial Adept on a mission of great importance. Whatever your guides charge, we will pay." He spoke in Karellan now, not the more elaborate form of his birth tongue but the dialect of trade.

The Talynisti man began spouting off in rough, but comprehensible, Karellan. Even though Karella no longer dominated the world as it once had, its tongue was still the most widespread.

"Again, coin is not the issue! There have been ill omens." He spat over his shoulder. "We are not sending any guides out—not until the full moon when the proper rituals can set things right."

The prefect crossed his arms. "I place no stock in barbaric superstition. You are obstructing the will of the Emperor of Lazarra. When your civil war is over, the Empire will remember who aided her."

The Talynisti threw up his arms. "Civil war, no civil war—we don't care who is king. All that matters is the safety of our people."

"What sorts of omens?" asked Reiva.

The prefect shot her a baffled look. "Adept, surely you do not imply that you believe this primitive desert drivel."

For a moment, she was sitting around the hearth with her brother, listening to her mother tell them about the poet-king who charmed a wicked spirit with nothing but the sweet sounds of his lyre and faithful prayers from his heart.

Primitive desert drivel.

"Anything keeping me from fulfilling my orders is of concern, prefect. I would not have this campaign fail because the Empire was not prepared." She nodded toward the Talynisti man.

The prefect's nostrils flared, fists clenched. The implication of her words had been clear. The last Imperial campaign in Talynis had failed because the legions were unsuited for desert warfare, too slow to adapt.

The village elder clearly looked uncomfortable speaking of these things, but he answered. "The camels hide from the wind. My own brother heard a she-demon's song not three nights ago."

Yaros scratched at his beard—shorter than the Talynisti style, but it made him fit in far better than the legionnaires with their smooth cheeks and close-cropped hair. "We all have a common interest here. We need passage, and you"—he gestured to the town elders—"want our coin, as well as the goodwill of the Empire. I'd say the compromise is simple."

One of the legionnaire captains snorted. "Trust a mercenary to think he can do a better job. What are you going to do—bribe a ghost? Hopefully they're as greedy as your sort."

Yaros took it in stride, flashing startlingly white teeth. "I guarantee they are not, and besides, everyone knows you can't bribe ghosts with money—you need a virgin's blood."

The legionnaires were bewildered; the Talynisti seemed frightened.

"Either way," Yaros said, "that was not what I hoped to do—unless any of you are willing to admit to never knowing a woman."

Reiva rolled her eyes. However great a warrior Yaros was, he did little to dispel the stereotype of Karellan libertinism.

"My thought was that the Adept and I shall go out and put an end to whatever nefarious forces are at work."

The elder blanched. "You are strangers to this land. Any man who steps into the wilderness courts death."

"Reiva's not a man, so the plan holds water." He clapped, as though congratulating himself for solving that particularly wrinkle. "Which way shall we go? I can follow the stars here as well as anywhere else, I'm sure."

The prefect threw up his hands. "I'm not wasting my time with this. If no one here is ready to take my men into the desert by tomorrow, then we are striking out on our own."

Reiva watched the man stride away, stepping like he had a spear up his backside.

"My apologies, honored *av*," she said, bowing slightly. *Av*—father—a term of respect. She hadn't called anyone that in a long time.

The man's eyebrows shot up. *"Talnishte debar?"*

She made a *so-so* gesture. "I was born in Shugrith, but left very young."

Something changed in the elder's posture. She could read the uncertainty written in his face—he could process her as an Imperial...but a woman from Talynis? Dressed in legionnaire's armor?

Yaros clapped a hand on her shoulder, then chattered in Talynisti for a bit, too fast for Reiva to follow every word, but she caught his meaning. He wanted the elder to know that she would do great things on behalf of the Talynisti people.

And she knew as she listened that she could not have said it so confidently as Yaros—not in any language in the world.

But some of the tension bled out from the old man. He chuckled, then spoke in Karellan. "Well, if there is a Talynisti with the Lazarrans, then maybe this civil war won't turn out so bad, eh? My name is Kalum."

"Yaros." The mercenary crossed his arms. "You're not a supporter of Malik then?"

He shrugged. "Out here, it does not matter so much. Further south lies New Mizkhar, I'm sure you know. More trade goes through the port there. That is where most of the Imperials are; these ones got fed up with waiting for their turn to cross and came up hoping to find someone else willing to take them."

"Fewer hauntings down there, I'd imagine," said Reiva.

The man rubbed his eyes. "May the Four on High spare us. From the desert *and* your lot! You truly mean to go out there tonight? You cannot fight the desert with swords."

Yaros stuck his thumbs through his belt, which bore no fewer than one Karellan xiphos sword and two long knives. "Now that the prefect is gone, I'll admit that I'm nervous about the wayfinding issue."

Reiva snorted. "What happened to following the stars?"

Yaros' genial expression muted slightly. "Strange things happen in the desert."

The Talynisti nodded sagely. "You have crossed the sands before."

"Twice, and I spent about a year in Dav-maiir between."

That had been a large factor in Reiva's decision to hire him. She had never seen the capital of Talynis, even as a child.

Well, she'd caught a glimpse of it on the horizon once—but she had been in chains at the time.

Kalum seemed appreciative of Yaros' time in the country, but he did not waver. "If you go out alone, you will die. None of us will risk the passage—not while something so disruptive as a civil war is going on. Like ripples in a pond, such things affect the world in strange ways."

Yaros took a breath, but Reiva held up a hand to forestall him. There were times you could bargain—this was not one of those.

She had another idea, though.

"What about the Wanderers? Would they be willing to take us?"

A spark lit Yaros' eyes. From their conversations on the way, she had garnered he hadn't interacted much with the nomad tribes of Talynis.

Kalum nodded slowly, though he looked wary. "The Mithallkiym. They would. There is a small tribe of them near here. They got out of sight as soon as word came that the Imperials were coming, but they have not left yet."

Yaros raised an eyebrow. "And they would take us? I heard nothing good of the tribes."

Kalum shrugged. "They are heretics, many would say. But coin means much to them. They go by different routes—older routes And they do not fear wicked spirits."

"They don't believe in them?"

"They believe in too many of them," Kalum scoffed. "But they also believe ha'Mithalleik protects them—the god from whom they take their name."

"Where are they exactly?" asked Reiva.

"Cross that dune," he said, pointing, "and go east until you hear their music. The *roshbet* is a man named Jaibul. Honest, but a hard negotiator. Tell him I sent you, and perhaps he will hear you out.

"Thank you, Kalum." Reiva extended her hand.

The man looked at it uncomfortably.

Right.

She let it drop, settling for a brief bow, which he returned more readily before shuffling away, back slightly bent with age.

She imagined him going home to his family. There would be at least three generations in the home—grandparents, parents, children. Four was considered a blessing; one generation for every god on high. They would eat bread cooked in the public ovens. Barley, most likely. There would be wine —thinner than the stuff they made in Lazarra, and slightly sour. At night, they would perform their prayers, sing their songs.

Yaros snapped his fingers, pulling her out of her reverie. He looked uncharacteristically concerned.

"Not that it's my place to pry, boss, but when we get to Dav-maiir..."

Reiva set her jaw. "I will do what I must. For Emperor and Eagle, Yaros."

"*Imperator et Aquila*, yes, yes, I've heard it all before." He didn't look ready to let the matter drop, but he did.

"Come on," said Reiva. "Let's cut a deal with the Mithallkiym. I'd rather not fight any ghosts if I can avoid it."

Yaros waved her on. They mounted up on their horses and struck out according to Kalum's directions.

24

OF DEATH AND THE UNKNOWN

WE STRUGGLED to build alliances with the nomads of the Talynisti wilderness, who seemed almost a nation unto themselves. A strong-blooded people, hard in body and spirit. Perhaps the harshness of their environment bred all weakness out of them. Or perhaps they possessed such qualities intrinsically, and so they had sought the rigors of the desert out of necessity. The fervent worship and imitation of the liminal deity called ha'Mithalleik, the Wanderer—this too lies at the core of their strength.

—*The Memoirs of Flavia Iscator*

❧

SURE ENOUGH, Kalum's directions brought them to a tribe of Mithallkiym. They were set up in tents decorated with furs, fabrics dyed in all manner of colors and cut in all manner of shapes.

As Reiva and Yaros approached, the Wanderers did not seem to pay them mind. They went on preparing meals, singing songs, pounding drums, plucking harps, playing flutes.

Yaros glanced over at Reiva. "Did you ever know these sorts?"

"I met a few, but never knew them well. Plenty of Talynisti don't trust them."

Yet watching the children playing, going about their chores, tending to camels and horses, even the occasional falcon—you would never have thought most of the nation looked down on these people.

Though 'looked down on,' Reiva thought, was not quite right. Feared—
that was more appropriate. No one quite knew what to make of the nomad
tribes with their strange fixation on the Wandering God—the god of death
and the unknown.

"I take the lead?" Yaros asked out of the corner of his mouth. They were
nearly upon the camp.

Reiva shook her head. "They'll see it as dishonest."

He raised an eyebrow at that, but said nothing.

They dismounted, and at last, one tribesman came over to them. He was
a young man, with sharp eyes and an easygoing grin. From one ear dangled
a talisman carved with Talynisti letters: *MTHLK*. Wanderer.

"Peace, friends," he said. "I am Faizal beyt'Jaibul." So he was the son of
the man they were seeking—maybe next in line for leadership after Jaibul's
passing. He spoke Karellan well; she wondered if that was common in this
tribe.

"I am Reiva, and this is my guard, Yaros."

She had been expected a look of shock—but to his credit, Faizal didn't
seem fazed by the news that Reiva was in charge. He simply said, "You are
warriors," and looked openly at their weapons, taking an extra moment to
appreciate the javelins on Yaros' back. "Do you hunt men or beasts with
those?"

Yaros' smile easily matched Faizal's. "Depends on whether I'm hungry or
getting paid."

Faizal laughed, and it seemed genuine enough. That did not tell you
much in this part of the world, though. Negotiating was as much a part of
life as breathing. Reiva was sure he could become belligerent and stone-
faced at a moment's notice if he thought it would better serve his interests.

"We are seeking your father," she said. "A man named Kalum sent us to
you."

Faizal rubbed his beard, pensive. "Kalum, sure. A friend to our family. He
is not as...hostile as others."

"Interesting you say that," Yaros said. "We hear there is some desert curse
causing trouble out here at night."

"Of course, of course. I am sure your Empire would love it if the towns-
people were not so concerned, eh?" He smirked at Reiva.

A prickle of irritation ran up her back, but she let her own smile appear.
A test, all part of the dance. *'Can you deal with us, outsider?'*

Reiva spread her hands. "I'm sure the prefect would also love if he could
lounge in a heated bath while women feed him dates and hold a cup of wine
to his lips—but we cannot all have such things."

Faizal laughed again, and a satisfied glimmer shone in his eyes. "An interesting way to speak of your ally—unless your armor is stolen, in which case I am in for a great reward."

"I am an Adept of the Lazarran Empire. I am also Talynisti by blood, born in Shugrith."

This piqued Faizal's interest. He peered more closely at Reiva's features. That sort of thing would have been rude in the Empire. In the oasis-cities of Talynis, it could have cost him an eye depending on who Reiva's father was. The Wanderers lived differently.

"I have been to Shugrith many times. Would I know your family?"

"No," she said, then cursed herself for how quickly she'd spoken.

Faizal seemed further intrigued, but covered it with another easygoing mask. "Well, then ha'Mithalleik has brought our blood together for the first time on this most blessed of days. *Hakham ha'Mithalleik.*" *Wise is the Wanderer.*

"Wise indeed," Reiva replied out of politeness. As she said it, old memories rose like bile.

Wise enough to let good men die, she thought to herself.

"So, you come here to speak to my father, and you serve the Empire—but you do not travel with those scaled soldiers back in town." He shrugged. "I have heard of stranger things across the sands. But my father is a busy man, friends, and at his age he cannot give so much time to hearing the requests of strangers. And this business of the curse—he is not so interested in that. The people of the cities have never respected our ways, except when it stands to benefit them. We are not some tool to be used when you brush up against something you do not understand."

As he spoke, his tone shifted just slightly, his shoulders squared a bit. He crossed his arms, cocked his head. He was waiting for a counter; he would have been disappointed, insulted even, if they did not offer one.

Reiva obliged. "We have coin—Lazarran and otherwise—and we can extend to you the favor of the Emperor. I am sure a people as well-versed in the value of trust as yours would appreciate the significance of that."

Faizal shrugged. "Coin I can get from anyone. The Wanderer has been kind to us; we must say no to more business than we say yes to these days."

"A great blessing," said Reiva.

"Indeed." He looked off toward the horizon, shielding his eyes, pursing his lips.

"An Emperor's trust," he continued, "is no small thing. But why should it mean so much to the Wanderers? For thousands of years we have lived among the sands, following the thousand paths of our god. Kings live and die; nations rise and fall. The desert is always here, and so are our people. We do not play politics, Imperial."

Imperial. Maybe he did not believe her when she said she was born in Shugrith. Maybe he did, but just did not care now that she wore legion gear and had donned the red mantle.

Yaros stepped forward—just one step, but the gesture was not lost on Faizal, who looked the mercenary up and down.

"Just take us across, Faizal. Take our coin, and be done with it—a business transaction, nothing more to it," he said, voice low, possibly threatening, if it were to be interpreted that way. Otherwise it might have been seen as pleading, humbling—Yaros speaking softly to engender pity from this man of the desert.

Faizal crossed his arms, his eyes turning back to the distant dunes. Reiva followed his gaze, picked out a swirling circle of black specks against the sky.

"Vultures?" she asked.

Faizal grunted in the affirmative. "The camels refuse to go anywhere near it."

Reiva had not been sure until that point whether she actually believed there was something out there—something strange and beyond mortal ken. But if Faizal was honest about the camels...well, animals understood strange things.

"If you do not take us," she said, "we will strike out on our own. You know we will probably die."

Faizal turned back to her, an inscrutable look in his eyes. "There is no probability involved—you will perish." He seemed to deliberate for a moment. "If you truly want to negotiate passage, you would have to convince my father."

"Then take us to him," she said. "Let us make our case."

The tribesman looked between the two of them, back and forth. Then he nodded. "Follow me. Ha'Mithalleik willing, my father will hear you."

If the people had been disinterested in them when they were afar, as soon as Faizal brought them within the confines of the camp, everyone became wary. Children peeked out from behind their mothers' skirts. Men looked up from their dice games. Hands fell to rest on curved knives.

Reiva did not shy before them, meeting every gaze as she passed. She had to admit, she was also curious. She had only seen Mithallkiym camps from afar when she was a girl, only ever spoken to a handful of the nomads in the marketplace. After going to Lazarra, she had certainly never dreamed she would come to walk among them, let alone cut a deal with one of their patriarchs.

Alyat's voice rang in her ears again. *'To train for what you can be prepared for—that is the bare minimum for a soldier. To train for what you will never be prepared for—that is the task of a warrior.'*

Faizal brought them to the center of the encampment, where a broad, open-sided tent had been erected. The *roshbet*—the head of the tribe—was easily identified. All the motion and energy seemed to flow from and to him, as though he was the source of life.

Faizal gestured deferentially. "My father, Jaibul." Then he switched into a dialect of Talynisti and addressed his father.

Jaibul was sitting on a cushion in the shade. Other men with long, full beards like his own sat with him. They would chatter back and forth in their hasty dialect, often making decisive gestures to punctuate their point or dismiss someone else's.

Jaibul himself wore a vivid blue kerchief atop his head, with a yellow band fastened around the temples. It marked him as the patriarch of this tribe, the final say on all matters of significance. When Faizal addressed him, he turned dark-brown eyes upon them, nodding to his son, then scrutinizing Reiva and Yaros.

They stood outside the cover of the tent, sun baking down on them. The men continued to speak, hardly even sparing them a glance.

Yaros looked annoyed, but said nothing. Reiva was glad for it. She didn't know all that much about the nomads, but she knew they were particular about their etiquette. She would follow Faizal's lead—even though her scalp was hot as a pan over fire.

Eventually, Jaibul raised a hand, spoke some words that sounded rather authoritative, though Reiva had no idea what they meant. She thought she might've caught *sun*, but that could've just been her heat-sweltered brain.

The patriarch extended his hand toward his son, who stepped into the shade of the tent, bowed, and kissed his father's hand. They exchanged some brief words. Jaibul looked again to Reiva and her companion.

Faizal motioned them forward. "You are welcomed into the tent of Jaibul, *roshbet* of our tribe."

Reiva stepped forward, Yaros at her heel and slightly back. She bowed and introduced herself in Talynisti.

Jaibul inclined his head, but said nothing.

"Does your father speak Karellan?" she asked Faizal.

"I will translate for—"

But then Jaibul raised his hand. "No, I will speak to this one directly." He leaned forward, dark fire in his eyes. "It is not so common to encounter a creature such as this."

25

THE ADVERSARY'S KISS

ONE BORN to the Worldfather will rule.
    One born to the Windmother will nurture.
    One born to the Warrior will fight.
    But one born to the Wanderer—who can say?
    —*Book of the Nameless Prophet*

                  ~

JAIBUL RAISED A HAND, and servants extended cups of water to Reiva and Yaros.

Reiva accepted, gratefully sipping the water, taking care not to reveal how nervous she felt.

'*A creature such as this,*' he had called her.

"I regret, honored father, that I have no gift for you. But coin I do have, and in exchange for transit across the sands—"

The *roshbet* made a cutting gesture. Reiva fell silent.

His voice was richly textured—a voice accustomed to giving commands, but also to singing songs. "I have not agreed to transport you. Such journeys are sacred things for our people. I do not know if you are worthy." He spoke trade Karellan, but sprinkled with certain Talynisti words—*journey, sacred.*

Reiva kept her tone even, but firm. "Wanderers have taken many other legionnaires across."

"Lack of faith is endemic in these times." He curled his lips as he said it, as though fighting the urge to spit. "What I see before me is a mercenary who reeks of death." He nodded to Yaros. "This is no great thing. But *you*—a woman who carries the arms and armor of a warrior, who wears the red of the Imperial sorcerers. You are something rare."

His eyes narrowed, and Reiva felt as though he were peering into her very soul. "The Lazarrans send their women to war, but you are no ordinary woman. An Adept. A *Talynisti* Adept. Who has heard of such a thing? And you come, no doubt, to replace the man killed in the holy city of Dav-maiir —may it be cleansed. 'The devil of ice,' they called him. And what are you? What manner of weird-working have you brought to our land?"

Reiva swallowed, aware of the weight of dozens of eyes. "I am called Reiva, an Adept of Fire in service to Emperor Dioclete of Lazarra."

Jaibul's eyebrows rose. "Fire. More surprises, more wonders. Fire purifies. Fire is holy. And yet you come here under the banner of the Lazarran Empire, a banner marching amidst the fire-glint of thousands of spears under the sun. You worship false gods, and you make war in their names."

"The Wanderers," retorted Reiva, "are not known for orthodoxy in Talynis."

Jaibul spread his hands. "A difference of opinion, and one in which we will be shown true and faithful in the final days. But you? What do you come here for? Why should I not have you killed here and now, to avenge in blood the shame you bring upon your father's house?"

Sourness curdled at the base of her throat. "Because I would burn your whole encampment to the ground before you could."

In a breath, hands moved to swords. Sand shifted as feet were planted to receive or launch a strike. Out of the corner of her eye, Reiva saw Yaros loosening the great sword on his back.

"I will not attack in anger," she continued, "but if you or your men raised a hand against me, it would be my duty as an Adept to defend myself and the investment placed in me by the Empire."

Of all the Talynisti, only Jaibul had remained absolutely at ease as Reiva delivered her threat. That was good—it meant she had calculated well in pushing back. He could have been offended—maybe he was—but he was also deeply interested, she saw.

"An investment," he mused. "I am a man of trade. I know of investments. What of the investment placed in you by Talynis? Are you not a daughter of the desert?"

Her fists clenched. She consciously eased them, but Jaibul had already seen. "I...do not know." When Jaibul seemed to expect more, she said, "I was sold to a slaver for a bag of silver smaller than a pomegranate. The Empire became my home—I was rescued."

Expressions of disgust rippled through the observers as the story was translated and passed along.

"The one who sold you," Jaibul said slowly. "A Talynisti?"

She gave the slightest of nods. "Yes."

Now, Jaibul spat in the sand. "The curses of the prophets fall upon he who betrays the blood of the people."

He raised his eyes from the earth, and Reiva stood fast under the weight of his gaze.

"I will return you to Talynis safely. As reparation for the evil done to you. But first, you must endure a trial. Judgment."

Something prickled at the back of Reiva's neck. "What sort of trial?"

"A test of your allegiance. If you are an enemy or an ally, this shall be revealed."

"You already know for whom I march."

"A trifle. The unseen weavings of fate lead us along many paths—we Wanderers know this. The Adversary's Kiss will prove whom you serve."

Yaros shot Reiva a questioning look, but she knew nothing of this test. She gave the slightest of shrugs. He shook his head subtly.

"Only a true Talynisti may pass through this judgment alive. Will you submit and be judged?"

For a moment, she surveyed the scene before her. Eagerness glistened in the observers' eyes. Just what sort of spectacle was she getting herself into?

Whatever it is, I'm not turning back now. It will just be some superstitious rite. I can manage it.

"I accept the trial."

Jaibul extended his hand, and an elegant weave of brown and red textile was placed before her in the sand.

"Kneel."

She did so, feeling the heat radiating even through the cloth.

Jaibul barked rapid orders, and his son Faizal left hurriedly, two other men at his heels.

"Now," said Jaibul, "wait. And pray, though I would not trust your gods to save you."

She chose not to, instead centering her awareness on the Flame. As before going into a battle, she let the pulsing of the inner power become her center, the moon drawing the tide.

Sweat trickled down her brow, but she held herself still and upright.

Projecting the proper presence was key in holding the respect of these people.

Yaros stood at a distance, clearly displeased with the whole situation, but he kept silent. That was good—if he had caused trouble, this might have turned into a bloodbath.

It might still become a bloodbath, she thought, *depending on how this goes.*

She searched her memory for what she knew of ritual ordeals. There were tests for finding thieves, for discerning marital unfaithfulness, for discovering idolaters. Some of those involved drinking a potion, supposedly only harmful to the guilty.

Was that why Faizal and those men had gone off?

As if in answer, they returned. The *roshbet's* son held a black box, cradling it in one arm with the other hand placed on top.

Jaibul rose, accepted the box from his son—carefully—and stepped forward.

Reiva noted the tension shift in the area. People stepped backward.

Her whole world became the box.

Her heart was hammering.

Focus. Calm.

"The test is a single minute. If you move, you die. Listen to me," he said severely, "you cannot *do* anything to survive this test. You must *be* one who survives."

Reiva nodded slightly.

"The Wanderer watches."

And with that, he set the box on the sand, and pulled away the cover.

From the confines of the box, a death adder rose, black eyes staring into hers.

Flared nostrils, diamond markings. A flickering tongue.

"*Ssss.*"

Reiva swallowed, eyes fixed on her demise. "You want me," she murmured, "to kiss a *snake*?"

Jaibul stood impassively. "No, Adept. We want to know if the snake will kiss you."

The adder hissed, weaving its flat head to and fro, a hypnotic motion that spoke of winding tracks through endless sands.

Perhaps it was just her imagination—but it seemed agitated.

One minute. Forty-five seconds by now, surely.

Every muscle strained to move, to hold, to give no cause for the creature to lash out with its brutal venom.

She let her breath flow smoothly.

The snake's tongue flickered.

One bite—I could take one. Venom is venom. Aether will purge it quick enough.

"Ssss."

Maybe.

The world emptied of all substance and meaning save her and the serpent, joined together by unflinching gaze.

The Flame roiled inside her. This was a threat. The answer was destruction.

Her heart thundered in her chest like a racing herd of wild stallions. She held still. She fought to quell the Flame's beckoning call for release, but she could not deny the truth that she longed to destroy the beast.

As if it knew her thoughts, it hissed again, louder. Its head quivered.

And then—something shifted.

Looking back on this moment, she would not be able to recall what she saw, or sensed, or intuited—she only saw death lashing out for her.

Her hand darted up, closed into a fist—and lit aflame.

In her grasp, held just below the snapping jaws, fangs dribbling the lethal venom, the serpent writhed and hissed as it burned.

Reiva gasped, the reality of the moment crashing down on her.

She stayed on her knees, staring at the dying beast, feeling it contort and squirm, desperately wrapping its tail around her forearm in a rough-scaled, whiplike grasp.

And in its eyes, she saw pain. And if snakes could feel hatred, she thought she saw that as well.

And then she heard—nothing. A dreadful silence.

The world expanded, and she became aware of the Wanderers, of Jaibul and Faizal, and of the elders. Of Yaros, and his fingers twitching for his weapons.

Slowly, she stood, holding the still, charred body of the serpent.

Jaibul's face was a flickering mask, moving through countless emotions. He was pale.

As if making an offering, she held forth the body.

"Did I pass your test?" she asked, already knowing what she would hear, already counting foes and planning tactics, but hoping against hope the day would not come to bloodshed.

It was the slightest shake of the head. "No."

Her gut wrenched.

New priority: get out alive.

"Then my companion and I will leave you." She dropped the carcass to the ground, where it landed with a crackling hush.

She nodded to Yaros, who began to steadily step toward her, so they might walk out of the encampment the same way they came.

"No."

Reiva stopped in mid-step. She had to turn back to the *roshbet* and stare, just to be sure he had spoken.

"No," said Jaibul again, a measure firmer.

"I failed your test. I will leave you now."

Were swords to be drawn? Had Reiva earned death for herself and Yaros by killing the beast?

And again, the *roshbet* said, "No."

Slowly, Reiva surveyed the faces all round. Bewilderment. Shock.

Awe, even.

"You are no daughter of the desert. You are no child of our enemy." He turned his head aside for a moment, looking eastward. "The House of Jaibul will take you to the holy city. You will eat and sleep apart, you and your companion. Hide yourself during our prayers. Do not work your magic so long as you are in our company."

And just like that, Jaibul gave the order for the tribe to pack up and resume their travels.

As their surroundings burst into motion and activity, Yaros' hand fell on Reiva's shoulder in a vice grip. A fearful grip, she realized.

He hissed in Lazarran, *"What in all the hells was that?"*

She shook her head, dumbfounded. "I saw it strike. And I caught it."

He grabbed her face, forcing her to look at him. "No, no you didn't. I was watching." A manic look was in his eyes. "I know what I saw. No one out-strikes a snake—there are proverbs and fables about that sort of thing. Reaction never trumps action. You moved in unison, *at the exact same time,* and you killed it."

Tents were being folded away, camels and horses laden with livelihoods. All the people gave Reiva and Yaros a bubble, breached only by constant, searching looks. They were muttering something among themselves, something Reiva could not understand.

There were many things, that day, that she could not understand.

It was training. It was reflex. It was instinct.

And did any of those satisfy her? Maybe the last—*maybe*—but like Yaros said, who had ever heard of someone out-striking a snake?

When the tribe moved on, they left the charred carcass of the serpent where Reiva had dropped it.

The two of them were made to follow behind the tribe at a short distance. At regular times, they would be brought food and water—always by a widowed woman who never spoke to them. They slept in shifts at first, then eventually decided the tribe would do them no harm. The Mithallkiym traveled by night, stopping regularly at the minor oases scattered throughout the desert. Once, Reiva and Yaros tried to drink from one, and they were sharply rebuked by Faizal, though he would not explain why.

That strange duality—both welcome guests and mistrusted strangers—persisted. Days rolled by, weeks. Eventually, the sublime moment of catching and burning the snake took on a sort of dreamlike quality. She and Yaros did not speak of it, though she could tell now and then that it was on his mind, that he was observing her with an intense curiosity and bafflement.

And then, one day, the air changed. Like after the first rain of the year, the atmosphere softened. The terrain shifted from loose sands to gravel and rock.

They had reached the sphere of a grand oasis, a *maiir*, and in the distance, sparse greenery peeked at the horizon. For another two days they traveled, then the tribe halted. This would be as far as they went.

For the first time since the day of the ordeal, Jaibul summoned Reiva to his tent. He had regained his typical stateliness, but he regarded her differently now. Almost like he thought she had taken on some quality of the snake in killing it, and now he had to beware a death-strike.

The *roshbet* stood from his cushion, beckoning Reiva forward. Carefully, she approached.

"What is your name? Your birth name."

The world seemed to tilt. How long had it been since she said it?

"Rebbaelah," she murmured.

With both hands, he proffered something small and white. "Then this is a gift," he intoned, "from Jaibul to Rebbaelah. A token that he will recognize her as friend, along with any other Wandering House she should meet. If Jaibul, or any person of his house, ever meets Rebbaelah again, and she is without this token, then he will kill her, for she will not be known to him."

Dumbstruck, she held out her hand.

Jaibul deftly placed a ring carved from bone in her palm. Though the engraving was small and her command of the language weak, she recognized a prayer to ha'Mithalleik etched around it.

Emotion seized at her eyes and throat. "I will always carry this with me, honored father."

"Go in peace," he said, bowing his head.

With that, Reiva and Yaros departed from the tribe, striking out—dusty and slightly thinner, the same as their horses—in the direction of Dav-maiir, the holy city and capital of Talynis.

On her finger, Reiva wore the ring of bone, absently tracing the engravings.

PART II

THE HOLY CITY

26

A GIRL FROM TALYNIS

BEFORE I LED the Ninth to Talynis, I knew of Ego's plans, and I was determined to foil them. Reiva changed things, revealed a new road to a different future—and I decided to go down that road.

History will judge my conduct.

—*The Memoirs of Flavia Iscator.*

～

MEETINGS such as this were meant to take place under the cover of night—but Avi could not help thinking he would rather meet Zageth somewhere open, under the light of the sun.

He did not trust Zageth—how could he? The man was a traitor to Lazarra. Even if he was on Avi's side in this endeavor, he did not have any delusions that Zageth—or the mysterious man he represented—cared a whit for the Talynisti cause.

He was grateful for Stag's presence in that regard. The Karellan may not have been much use with a blade, but his tongue and keen sense of business acumen were worth more in an engagement like this. And, of course, Jackal and Mouse were lying in wait close to here. If Avi or Stag signaled, they would swoop in.

The site was in a rundown section of the city largely destroyed in the looting that took place after the Ninth Legion stormed the gates and drove out King Malik and his sons. Technically, this area was off-limits to anyone

outside the legions, but the Imperials had neither the manpower nor sufficient cause to patrol it.

Avi and Stag arrived first, about fifteen minutes early. Jackal and Mouse
would take up positions in a collapsed house nearby, crouching in the
shadows.

Stag took in the ash-dusted floor, the shattered ceramics, the overturned
furniture.

"It's a garbage heap, but that's why we're here I suppose."

"You're talking about my city," Avi growled. "My people lived here. It
wouldn't be like this if the Empire had stayed away."

Stag shrugged. "Sure, sure."

"Don't you care that the Empire rules your people?" It was something
Avi had never puzzled out about Stag. He'd asked Jackal about it, but she
hadn't cared enough to even ponder the matter—for her, the false names
were of little use if they went about prodding one another's secrets.

Stag picked up an overturned chair, set it aright. "On paper, the Empire
rules Karella, yes, but they do not *truly* rule it. The Krypteia, the five families
—we have our true rulers, and the Empire knows that."

Avi frowned. "The Krypteia. Thought they were a myth."

Stag laughed. "Of course you do—and they like it that way."

Avi's face burned. He hated being outside the know on things, hated that
Stag would not simply tell him. What was the point of asking questions if
you were just going to get laughed off?

He took up a watch in the shadows, listening and watching.

It wasn't long before Zageth arrived with three bodyguards in tow. They
were lean men, with muscled arms that seemed cast from bronze. They said
nothing, simply taking up positions along the wall. Avi could not see any
weapons, but he didn't doubt they had ample iron on their bodies. Hell,
given how connected Zageth's boss Ego was, they might have even had
steel.

Zageth offered a mock bow at the two men waiting in the dark. "At last,
we meet." He spoke proper Karellan, not the trade dialect, so Avi struggled
to keep up.

Stag inclined his head and indicated the other chair. "Please, sit. Zageth,
correct?"

"The same. And you are the one called *Stag*."

"I am. This one is the Wolf."

"An honor to meet you both." His smile took on a slight, self-satisfied
edge. "Will we be introduced to the others lurking in the shadows?"

Stag, to his credit, kept his expression neutral. It was a talent that made him a devil at cards, but clearly served him well in situations besides late-night games and gambles.

Avi, on the other hand, could not help tensing up. Zageth caught that, smiled wider.

"I just wanted to be clear that we are all on the same page. I do not begrudge you for taking such precautions—I would be more concerned if you had taken none—but please do not get any ideas about pulling the wool over my eyes. Ego does not traffic with fools."

"Good," said Stag. "I enjoy working with a man who values competence."

"My employer is without peer in that regard."

"I only wish I could have the honor of meeting him face to face."

Zageth chuckled. "Perhaps you will. Strange things are happening in Talynis these days."

"Strange indeed."

Zageth's eyes flitted to Avi for a moment, and he got the uncomfortable sense Zageth was referring to the *Nihilo* Blade. Did he approve of how Avi had used Ego's gift?

Stag stretched his arms above his head. "While I would love to continue dancing, I'm afraid I am notoriously greedy for sleep, and we are past my bedtime. State your terms so we may discuss."

Zageth wasted no time. "We have already smuggled a great deal of arms into the city. This project has been in the works for quite some time, you see. They are in place, ready for retrieval. In exchange for your sworn cooperation, we will give you their locations, as well as the keys necessary to access them."

"My oaths are an exclusive commodity, friend. I'll need more information before I swear to anything."

Zageth spread his hands. "Ego wants this city to be in total rebellion against the legion and the usurper king before long."

"How long exactly?"

"He plans to arrive inside the gates within the month, and he would like to oversee the proceedings personally."

Avi blinked. He hadn't been expecting that—none of them had, not even Crow.

Stag carried on with total aplomb. "And that is when we may meet him?"

"Indeed. And he has relayed a phrase by which you may know him. 'Behind every door, a secret. Behind every man, a motive.'"

"Properly cryptic."

Zageth smiled. "One must be cautious when dealing in such things as revolutions."

"Naturally." Stag leaned back, rubbing his chin.

Even though Avi knew the display was for show, as they had already decided to accept Ego's offer, he was impressed by how seriously Stag seemed to be considering it.

The Karellan slapped his thigh, as if coming to a resolution. "Very well. The terms are acceptable. You have our sworn agreement."

Zageth nodded and produced a wax-sealed roll of parchment from inside his cloak. "This will lead you to the locations of the armaments, and these"—he held out his hand to accept a small box from one of his bodyguards—"are the keys to the places they are stowed."

"All inside the city, then?"

"Oh, not all of them are locked up—some are buried in the surrounding sands." Zageth smirked. "I hope the Wolf can dig as well as his name implies."

Avi frowned, but said nothing. This was Stag's show. He would follow the Karellan's lead.

"Then I believe we are done here—blessedly fast as well." Stag made to rise, but Zageth held up a palm.

"There is one more thing. Something *you* in particular must be made aware of." He jabbed a finger at Avi.

He perked up. "I'm listening."

Zageth paused, almost as if he was relishing the moment. "The Empire has finally dispatched the replacement for that Adept you killed with Ego's gift."

Avi's heart raced. Another Adept. Another one of those bastards to die under his knives.

"She will arrive in Dav-maiir sometime in the next few days. A fireshaper."

"A woman?" He knew the Lazarrans kept female soldiers—he'd fought some on the day the city fell—but they even brought women into the Adept Corps?

"And a quite deadly one, according to reputation. But I wanted to let you know ahead of time..." Another one of those satisfied grins creased his face. "The Adept is a Talynisti. The only one, supposedly."

Avi was sure he had misheard. "*What?*"

Zageth was standing, raising his hood. "We will be in touch through the usual channels."

Stag rose too, throwing a warning glance at Avi. He made a subtle gesture, palm-down, like one might try to calm a dog that won't stop jumping.

Well, he was no dog. He was the Wolf of Talynis.

"A Talynisti Adept. A Talynisti woman," he said, dumbfounded and far-too loud for a clandestine meeting. "Is this a joke?"

Zageth shrugged, making for the door with his bodyguards in tow. "I assure you it is not, my friend. But since you are so bothered by the idea, I suppose it will not be hard for you to do your job and kill her. You have the relic, don't you? Use it—Ego will be glad to know it has brought an end to another Adept."

And with that, he and his men were gone in the night.

Stag watched their departure, then turned to Avi, clearly concerned. "A Talynisti Adept is unusual, but that is even more cause to think clearly. Be patient. We'll talk this over with the others."

Avi barely heard him. "I *am* going to kill her, Stag. You don't understand —it's an affront, a shame upon our whole kingdom. A *girl* from Talynis, fighting for the Empire and using their twisted magic."

Stag gave another one of his sighs. "Kill her then. Just don't get yourself killed in the process."

"I did it before, didn't I?"

"Then, you were only angry."

"I am angry now."

Stag looked him over, lips curling slightly. "No. Now you are possessed."

27

HORRID SIGNIFICANCE

MARCUS GALLIUS—so named for his decisive role in conquering the land of Gallia—came from a house of meager means and import. Honest, admired by those under his command, he was a man too good to brush shoulders with such blackguards as we.

—*The Memoirs of Flavia Iscator*

PRAETOR MARCUS GALLIUS stepped out from his command tent into the biting winds. Camp Mandelus, the center of the Fourth Legion's effort to subdue Duke Faydn's rebellion, was still blanketed by snow despite the approaching spring. Marcus tried not to take that as an ill omen, though he had learned that this campaign offered little respite.

Today's new arrival would hopefully turn their luck, but...well, there were stories about Adept Sharasthi. Marcus did not doubt she was as formidable a warrior as her reputation indicated. He did doubt, however, whether she was entirely sane.

The sun was still on the rise as Marcus made his way through the camp, acknowledging salutes with a nod and deferring questions about coming operations.

When spring truly arrived, they would make an assault on Faydn's castle. Since the incident with Adept Reiva and the devastating blow to Ironback Company, the rebel duke's den had accrued a certain infamy among the legionnaires. They wanted revenge. They wanted to tear Faydn from his secure position among the stones and make him pay.

Adept Reiva...Marcus had not met the woman personally, but his direct subordinate, the legate of the Fourth, had called in some favors to get her assigned to the Hyrgallian campaign. She had graduated as the premier Initiate in her cohort, and was an Adept of Fire to boot. There had been high hopes for what she could do for the war effort.

Well, look how that turned out.

As he climbed the steps to the parapet atop the camp walls, Marcus felt his troops' rage burning in his own breast. He also felt wary. There had been no more signs of those Beast Relic fighters—the wolf-men—but that didn't mean their enemy had no more in reserve, or that they were not training up more. Seven relics of such power was already an impossibility, and though the Adept Corps officially maintained that it was impossible for Faydn to sponsor the creation of more...Marcus had served in the legions long enough to know that sometimes, you needed to take what the Corps said with a heap of salt.

So it was with a sigh that he caught sight of the familiar red mantle, stark against the white fields. Marcus shaded his eyes. She was traveling alone.

Right on time.

"Get that gate open, men."

The guards set to work as Marcus descended the steps again. Truth be told, he was impressed. Adept Sharasthi was arriving with perfect punctuality—no mean feat given the weather. That sort of thing spoke to soundness of mind, didn't it?

Sharasthi slid down from her horse, patting him on the neck. "Praetor." She dipped her head in greeting.

Marcus nodded back. "Welcome to Hyrgallia, Adept Sharasthi." Senior Adepts like her were not as deferent as some of their younger colleagues. Marcus didn't particularly mind, so long as they delivered sufficient aid for his military efforts.

"Thank you. First, I will need a map directing me to the site of the massacre where Adept Reiva confronted the rebel relic-users."

Marcus blinked. Sharasthi seemed sincere though. "Perhaps first we can get you situated in the camp, and then you may attend the officers' meeting this evening. I'm sure your presence will be much appreciated, given that the Fourth has been without an Adept for many weeks now."

"I'll need my horse cared for, and then I will take a fresh mount. Everything in my saddlebags can be delivered to wherever you'll place me during my time here. A tour really isn't necessary. I know my way around a legion camp."

Now Marcus was frowning. "I am sure, Adept. But I cannot have you going off on your own into territory that we still have not thoroughly mapped out, especially so close to an enemy stronghold. Wait until tomorrow, and I'll send a detachment with you."

"Unnecessary." She was already making her way to the stables, and Marcus suppressed a sigh.

No, of course it couldn't be simple.

Captain Scanlon did his best to look at ease.

He was anything but, staring at the site where nearly two dozen of his legionnaires had been slaughtered.

The stonework stood with an eerie aura, as though by the blood shed here it honored the pagan gods of the ancient people who had crafted it. All the bodies had been burned (save the wolf-men dragged away from the site so the carrion birds could take them), and with time the remnants of blood and gore vanished with the sweeping snow storms and melting frost.

But Scanlon was a professional, so he stood with his hands on his hips, a dour scowl on his face. He had mourned the dead when it was proper, and then came the time to return to his work, his vocation as a soldier of Lazarra.

Even professionalism though, only did so much to keep him from casting a wary eye upon Adept Sharasthi.

He had not carried many expectations when the praetor had assigned him to this duty. He knew Gallius did not hold him in low regard as a result of what befell his company. Perhaps the praetor even thought it would be worthwhile for him to serve with an Adept again. Companies that did so often rose to heights of glory and honor. Ironback needed some of that, gods knew. Scanlon saw it in the hunch of shoulders, the resentment brewing behind dark eyes. Twenty-two legionnaires had died, not even counting the murdered patrol, and they had left almost forty others to carry the weight of their loss. Not all wounds were visible.

So he tried not to mutter prayers as the Adept scoured the site of the massacre, bending low to inspect faded carvings, stopping to stare off into the distant woods, sometimes for minutes at a time.

And all the while, the muttering, the endless whispers. Scanlon was too far off to hear exactly what she was saying, and he had no interest in getting any closer. Thankfully, the Adept seemed about as happy for the presence of

Scanlon and his men as they were, and she had directed them to stand off at a distance while she examined the site.

He found himself wondering, then, about what had happened to Adept Reiva. When he had asked Sharasthi, she merely answered with a perfunctory, "She lives and serves the Empire."

He was grateful for that, he told himself. She was too young to die.

So were Tharrick and Meridi and Erbel and...

Scanlon shook his head. That familiar thorny weight was tangling in his gut again. The one that manifested when he drank too much, or couldn't sleep at night, listening to howling winds that sounded all too similar to the wails of dying soldiers.

It would be so easy to put all the blame on her. He had, more than once. He'd probably cursed her name a dozen times, though he couldn't always recall, depending on how many mugs of that stiff Hyrgallian beer he'd drained.

But he also couldn't help but curse himself for it. He had approved the mission. He had sent an Adept and multiple squadrons into the jaws of death, against his better judgment.

She convinced you.

Then I was a fool to be convinced.

After some time, the Adept approached Scanlon. Her features were a mask.

"Success, Adept?"

Her eyes flitted over the site one last time, lingering longer on the charred, naked branches of the lone tree.

"Indeed."

Thank the gods for that. Days of travel for just a half-hour...

"Shall we begin the return journey?"

She nodded, already making her way to the horses. Scanlon trudged forward to come level with her. Unlike Adept Reiva, Sharasthi superseded Scanlon in rank, but he was not about to look like a whipped dog following at his master's heels.

"Do you bear ill will toward me, Captain Scanlon?"

He blinked. "Excuse me, Adept?"

She hummed. "I did not want you to attend me, but your praetor insisted. Understandably. This area is close to the reported location of Duke Faydn's castle, and you know better than I its horrid significance."

Scanlon shrugged. "We're legionnaires. We do what is required of us."

"Even if that means babysitting a madwoman?"

He coughed. "Adept—"

"I am familiar with the stories, Captain. Some of them are even true."

He stared at her from the corner of his eye. What in all the hells did that mean? "I don't know any stories about you, Adept."

She glanced at him, the slightest arch in one eyebrow. "Truly? I am not sure if I ought to encourage you to seek them out. But enough of that. What matters more to me is what you think of Adept Reiva."

An eerie shudder traced down his spine. A nagging, primal fear that she somehow knew his thoughts lurked at the back of his mind.

"Do you resent her?"

Scanlon walked along in silence for a while.

"Yes," he admitted.

They said nothing more until they reached the horses. Once they had mounted up, Sharasthi said to him, "I do not blame you for it, but I would counsel you against indulging such feelings."

She tipped her head toward the shrine. "What happened there—what brought an end to more than twenty of our comrades-in-arms—has happened before and shall happen again. It is enough to drive a soul to madness."

Scanlon held her eyes, gripped by the need to see what lay within them, petrified by their intensity.

"Would you lead the way, Captain?"

Slowly, he nodded.

They said nothing more to one another throughout the journey to Camp Mandelus. He dreamed strange dreams in the night, but never recalled them upon waking. Only the image of a woman dressed in robes cut from violet and silver hung in his mind. He knew not her face, but thought her familiar. The desire to ask the Adept questions about his dreams weighed heavy upon his shoulders, but he held his silence.

When he returned to the camp and gave his report to Marcus Gallius, he did not speak of the dreams, only telling what his praetor demanded to know of the expedition and Adept Sharasthi's purpose and behavior.

When Scanlon relayed how she had talked to herself as she walked to and fro, inspecting the ancient carvings, the praetor frowned. "They say," he mused, "that she was permanently damaged—psychologically—by her service in the Parthavan campaign."

Scanlon perked up. Was that what she had meant when she mentioned stories told of her?

The praetor must have noticed his interest, because he continued. "Lone guerrilla warfare, far behind enemy lines. Adepts can only use their magic so much before it destroys them, and supposedly she pushed herself to the absolute limit of that capacity. Just think—the paranoia, the sheer drive and will to live that pulls a person through as doomed a situation as that..."

Gallius shook his head.

Scanlon swallowed. "She is an odd sort, my praetor."

"Were your men disturbed by her?"

Scanlon shrugged. He did not intend to insinuate that his legionnaires were a timid bunch, but he could not lie to his praetor. "Soldiers are a superstitious lot. She doesn't do much to convince them otherwise."

"A reputation is a weapon as sharp as the best sword, as strong as the best shield."

It sounded like a quote on the praetor's lips, but Scanlon couldn't place it.

Then Gallius fixed his eyes on Scanlon. "And what about you, Captain? Does she intimidate you?"

The moment seemed to stretch. His instinct—the same battle-honed sense that had carried him through the lethal press of arms and warfare year after year—told him that this was a turning point. What he said next would pitch the outcome of the day.

"Aye, sir. She does."

The praetor nodded. "Good. You're assigned to be her liaison for the remainder of her time with the Fourth. Anyone gives you lip, tell them it comes from me."

Scanlon went rigid. He had feared this would happen ever since word came he was to escort her to the massacre site, but... "Sir, I don't know if—"

"It's an order, Captain Scanlon. And as part of your duties, you will regularly report to me on her. Efforts to repopulate the ranks of Ironback Company are hereby stopped; you will be reformed as a strike force. Keep the name if you like, but you will answer directly to me from now on."

The world spun. "Praetor! I failed my legion!"

"And now you have an opportunity to do it proud. Emperor and Eagle, Captain. Go give your men the news."

Stunned, feeling as though he walked on air, Scanlon stepped out from the command tent and into the cold. The setting sun cast long, thin shadows everywhere he looked, like hundreds of skeletal fingers groping for something.

28

WHAT SECRETS MERITED

THE SECRET SOCIETIES, with their dark cloaks and flickering candles, I have never esteemed. Are they necessary? They certainly think so, and perhaps they are even correct in this. But my father impressed upon me from a young age the value of truth—and truth is a thing of light, a thing of the day.

Woe to the man who finds himself in such times that truth can only survive in whispers.

—The Life and Wisdom of Simeon Binkhok As Told by Himself

~

IF ALYAT HAD BEEN hesitant last time, now he was absolutely certain that meeting with Nuntius was a bad idea.

But he couldn't make himself stay away.

In the same ruined temple as the last time, he waited, mulling over the contents of the scroll he had received.

He had to admit, a startling amount of it made sense. There was a logic to the book's cold—if baffling—claims. Alyat, though, was a man of evidence, reasoning. He would always hear someone out—no matter how impossible they sounded—but he needed more than one dusty and frustratingly short scroll to be convinced.

Particularly when it was trying to convince him that most of the history he knew about the Empire was wrong. That the rise of the First Emperor was an event not of triumph, but of horror. That the Almost King was not a would-be tyrant, but a slandered martyr.

Frustratingly, much of the scroll was written in Old Lazarran. Even when he could puzzle through some of the more archaic linguistic forms, he was still left with a painfully vague narration that forced him to tease out hints.

Alyat perked up at the sound of footsteps on the grass. His hand drifted toward his weapon.

"Adept Alyat," Nuntius said softly. "I am pleased to see you again. Alone. Would I be bold in presuming this to mean you are compelled?"

"I am interested enough that I've not yet put you in chains, but don't assume that will not change."

The man inclined his head. "Of course, of course."

"I have questions."

"Ask away."

"What proof do you have that the text is not some forgery or fake?"

A shrug. "Of the book itself, nothing. If you are so curious, though, you may check the information against other such texts in the Imperial Archive. The restricted sections, naturally."

Alyat arched an eyebrow. "So, why take the risk of smuggling me a copy when you could have just sent me there?"

The man laughed softly. "Adept Alyat, come now. You are a man who spent many years in Legion Intelligence—are you not? The texts kept in the Archive are like the outer strings of a spider's web. Touch one, and it shall tremble."

"So by seeking them out, I'm painting a target on my back. How convenient for you."

"Go look for yourself, Adept. Nothing in this venture is done without risk, and I have no doubt you are clever enough to cover your tracks."

Alyat sized up Nuntius. He still felt uncomfortable with this man—not just him personally, but also this whole matter of the Order he served. The Order of the Sleeping Dragon.

"Who is the Order, and how do *you* know these secrets?"

The man drew himself up a little straighter. "The Order has kept many of these truths down through the years. Since the twilight of the Republic, we have undertaken this duty, remembering the truth of what once was, so that we might one day throw off the veil of lies that has been draped over our eyes."

"How noble," drawled Alyat. "And you've been at this for two centuries? An impressive feat to stay in the shadows for so long." The Adept cast his eyes over a ruined heap of furniture in the corner. Something was bothering him, though he couldn't put his finger on it.

"You would be surprised to learn the names of our forerunners. Great generals, politicians."

Alyat couldn't help but snort. "And that slipped past all the Emperors who possessed that mythic Art you spoke of? The Art of Foreknowledge?"

What was it? Had something shifted in here since last time?

"I assure you, Adept, it is as real as the air you breathe, and it is nothing to be trifled with. At any moment, *he* may be watching, listening. Even our meeting here is—"

He trailed off suddenly.

Alyat realized what had been bothering him.

The animals—the owls, the hounds, the crickets—had all gone silent.

Nuntius drew a knife, steel clearing leather with a distinct *hiss*.

Alyat reached for his sword, but the man raised a hand. He shook his head before running out the gaping entrance, out into the night.

He yelled, "Scatter! They are upon us!"

And Alyat heard the keening shriek of metal on metal, men shouting.

A thousand instincts screamed at Alyat to go out and fight alongside him —but he knew who he would face: Orphans or Legion Intelligence. Both, possibly.

And if he was seen, he would have to kill every last one of them—and judging by how many voices he heard, there were quite a few. A tall order for two men, even if one was an Adept.

Alyat had never been built for open combat. It had made him unusual— even detested—back home. Now it was his strength.

He pulled back to the nearest wall, tucking himself into a nook between a crack-ridden pillar and the dilapidated masonry.

Then, he bent the light, forming a pocket of deep shadow.

Just as he vanished, a squadron of men came storming in. Several blades dripped blood.

"Check for any exits!" ordered their leader. He alone had a pale blue epaulet on his shoulder—the sign of a Legion Intelligence officer. The soldiers who fanned out to search the temple were all Orphan legionnaires.

The Orphans set to their task with dizzying efficiency, checking every corner and crevice with haste as half of their number sped off to scour the back reaches of the place for any other escape routes. There was at least one other way out, Alyat knew.

Sure enough, they came back with their report: "A single exit, but no sign of anyone fleeing."

The officer twitched, a pale scar on his cheek standing out in the gloom. "Check again for any hidden chambers. This was an oracle's temple—there would have been a secret room somewhere."

As he was speaking, two more of the Orphans hauled in Nuntius' body.

Alyat couldn't exactly say he grieved for the fellow. He'd hardly known him, and had felt suspicion for him than anything else...but all that aside, he couldn't help but feel a measure of respect and sorrow for a man who died in service to a cause—whatever that cause was.

The officer searched his body, retrieving some sort of bronze disc. He held it aloft, turning it this way and that. "Should have left him alive," he muttered.

Alyat peered at the object, but from this distance he couldn't make out what it was.

The Orphans, however, seemed uneasy.

Alyat was uneasy too—not just because this meeting had been found out, nor because of whatever that object was. He was disturbed because he still hadn't been able to place the identity of that officer.

He had served with Legion Intelligence for many years, and he still kept tabs on the organization, often working with them as a consultant or coordinating various military efforts with their assistance.

This man, he hadn't the faintest idea as to who he was. The only identifying marker was the blue epaulet on his uniform—no indication of rank.

That was a bad sign.

There was a word for men like him. Ghost. Agents who worked with the barest level of oversight, often handling the most sensitive missions. They oversaw the most restricted levels of intelligence in the Empire—the black archives. Alyat had once worked an operation with a ghost who'd killed three standing senators during his career. They just *did* things like that, and they were accountable only to their handlers—and gods only knew who they were. Praetors. The Emperor himself.

If a ghost was involved, then the Order of the Sleeping Dragon really was something else...and if the Empire was so willing to expend such resources on them, then what did that say about the dead man's claims?

The ghost tucked the bronze into his cloak, taking another moment to survey the ruins of the temple. Alyat felt an uneasy chill as his eyes—for the briefest moment—locked with the ghost's. The moment, thankfully, passed without incident, his camouflage holding.

"One man killed, all others escaped." His voice echoed off the cold stones, dying with an eerie reverberation.

The Orphans were a proud legion. They carried the honor and responsibility of guarding Lazarra, the capital of the Empire, and the men and women who ruled from it. The Palatine Guard—the hand-picked protectors of the Emperor himself—were selected from their ranks.

But even these were cowed by the displeasure in the ghost's tone.

"We will catch them, sooner or later, sir." That Orphan looked like he might have been their sergeant.

The ghost raised his eyebrows. "Indeed? Well, I certainly hope so."

"They've been getting reckless, as of late."

"That they have, that they have. But their brashness only exacerbates my superior's hunger."

Superior. That would be his handler.

As he said it, the Orphans seemed to stiffen. Did they know who he was referring to or was the insinuation enough?

"Shall you deliver the report, Sergeant, or shall I?"

The Orphan who had spoken blanched.

A toothy smile cut across the ghost's face. "Not to worry, Sergeant—even I am capable of telling a joke from time to time. The Carnifex will be displeased, of course, but I will do my best to ensure he does not vent any of his frustration on you. I do *so* value your contributions."

Alyat's blood ran cold.

Forget the ghost—a Carnifex is in the mix? Old gods save me...

After they had departed, leaving the bloody corpse on the tiles, Alyat waited in the darkness. A quarter-hour, a half-hour. Only then did he slowly move from his spot, expertly wielding his *Ars Lumens* to keep himself hidden.

He turned over the corpse to search it for any clues. Nothing. He would have to try to discern what that bronze disc had been.

Gently, Alyat closed the man's eyes and slipped into the open night.

As he made his way through the ruins of the Old City, he heard the howling of dogs making their way to the ruined temple.

By dawn, little more than a bloody scrap of cloth would be left of the man.

Alyat could expect little better if he got caught.

But getting caught was something he'd have to risk.

He wasn't about to let this slide. He was going to find out what secrets loomed here, what secrets had been worth a man's death—what secrets merited the attention of a Carnifex.

He needed to get a letter to Reiva.

29

LEGATE FLAVIA ISCATOR

WHEN THE LION first came to me, what struck me most was her face. Her eyes. She was possessed. Possessed by a hunger, an ambition. When I first saw her, awash with dust and grime, looking at me with those haunted, too-knowing eyes of hers, that was when I knew she was something else.

I could never have known, of course, just how far Reiva's ambition would take her.

—*The Memoirs of Flavia Iscator*

≈

WHILE TALYNIS WAS DOTTED with many oases, only so many were large enough to sustain a true city. The great ones were about as big as major lakes in other parts of the world. It was around these that the *maiir* were built, the watered cities.

And Dav-maiir—so the legends said—was built upon the greatest water of all, the fabled Origin Spring, where it was said the Four Gods had first irrigated the desert and cultivated life, guiding the Talynisti settlers to those rare bastions of survival. According to the stories, the Origin Spring still rested far below Dav-maiir, and from it arose the city's oasis. Some even went so far as to say all water in Talynis flowed from the Origin Spring—a charming myth, to be sure.

It was on that story the religion of Talynis was built, and even after thousands of years, the people were still deeply pious and faithful to their curious ancestral doctrine of a mere four divinities (barring the squabbles between the Mithallkiym and the priestly orthodoxy over the figure of the Wandering God, of course).

Approaching a Talynisti *maiir* was like entering a different world. The rough sand and cracked flat terrain suddenly morphed, as though an invisible boundary had been crossed. There was rich soil, moist and dark. The air cooled. Scraggly bushes were no longer the only flora in sight. Lilies grew from the verdant, fecund land. Acacia trees. Date palms. Even olive trees.

Talynis was a desert unlike any other, but tucked away within the brutal wilderness were a handful of microclimates like this where life flourished.

Reiva had grown up in such a place as this. Shugrith. The Jewel of the Sands, it was called. Second largest among the *maiir*, and the current residence of the royal family.

Former royal family, Reiva reminded herself. The Empire was backing Malik's younger brother, Tamiq. Malik's Loyalist supporters were vicious, however, and they were not keen to allow the Empire to swoop in and elevate Tamiq the usurper.

Thanks to the more temperate climate of this region, Reiva and Yaros had been able to travel during the day. It was on the third day since leaving Jaibul's tribe that they encountered people.

This furthest outward portion of the *maiir* was largely the domain of farmers. It had been the site of battle before the legions reached the gates. Reiva could still make out some burn scars among the greenery. There were sections totally devoid of growth, where all the wheat had been burned or pillaged or simply trampled. The Ninth Legion's path was easy to discern.

People were tending to their crops, driving yoked oxen, pasturing their sheep. Now and then, they would shade their eyes and watch Reiva and Yaros ride by—but no one raised a hand in greeting or shouted curses in antipathy. They just went about their work.

Rivers radiating outward from the center of the *maiir* curled and wove their way through the landscape, and many had been diverted for irrigation. Bridges spanned some of these rivers. There had been more, Reiva could see, but many must have been destroyed as an attempt to slow the Ninth's approach. Perhaps all had been destroyed—now that she looked closer, every one she saw had been constructed according to the Lazarran pattern.

As they crossed over such a bridge, Yaros stretched forward, shading his eyes. "Someone's coming, boss."

Reiva followed his gaze. Her eyebrows rose. "They're wearing Scout colors."

Legion Scouts dressed to camouflage into their environment. They had none of the bright colors or shining armor of typical legionnaires. Often-times they worked alone or in small detachments, trading security of numbers and arms for speed and stealth.

Reiva removed her mantle and waved it above her head. The Scout returned the wave, though they didn't seem hurried in making their way over.

The Adept's heart beat faster. This was her first contact with someone in the Ninth. Odds were, this Scout would tell others what Reiva was like, what her first impression was, whether she seemed tough enough to handle this campaign. Legionnaires were always eager to gossip about the Adepts they were assigned to.

Particularly if that Adept was replacing one who had been killed in action.

When the Scout was nearer, she called a greeting—and Reiva could see now that she was indeed a woman. She carried a strung recurve bow across her lap. Her hair was in a simple braid, her skin sun-darkened. Women weren't as rare among cavalry Scouts as among the heavy infantry, but she still found herself a bit surprised. After the looks she had gotten in the border village, she had wondered whether the Ninth was largely male.

"You must be Adept Reiva," she chimed, not even bothering to hide the way she scanned her head-to-toe, followed by Yaros. "And your bodyguard?"

He shrugged. "More or less."

"Welcome to Dav-maiir. I'm Scout Lieutenant Charas, your liaison. Legate Iscator dispatched me to bring you in."

Reiva perked up. "I am sorry to be late. It was difficult finding a way to cross the sands."

Charas snorted. "Yeah, fewer and fewer people are willing to help legion folks along. Fees keep getting higher and higher too. Wanderers bring you across? What'd they charge you?"

Reiva hesitated. She could have easily thrown out an exorbitant number —but this Scout was her first chance to start building a reputation in Dav-maiir.

"Nothing," she answered honestly. "The *roshbet* of the tribe made an alliance with me, and he brought us here without cost."

She left out the bit about the ritual separation and the serpent ordeal, of course.

Charas tilted her head. "Really? Well, I should expect nothing less of an Adept." And then she grinned, but Reiva got the sense there was something more behind her eyes. It felt like she knew more than she was letting on.

"Well," continued the Scout, "it's hot as hell out here and the legate has been itching to meet you. Ever since Havan went down, Iscator has been hounding Lazarra for a replacement. When word came you were on the way, it did a good deal for morale."

She nudged her horse into motion, bringing him around to lead the way toward Dav-maiir.

Reiva followed along with Yaros, and they shared a glance behind the Scout's back. She raised an eyebrow and nodded toward Charas. He mouthed back '*Unsure.*'

She felt the same. It sounded like Charas worked closely under the legate, given that she had been specifically assigned to keep watch for Reiva's arrival. And Vantelle had warned Reiva that she was suspicious of Legate Iscator's devotion as of late.

Still, Charas seemed likable enough. Scouts could be an odd lot given how much time they spent alone, but there was nothing off-putting about her...besides that odd look in her eyes.

"So your name's Yaros," she said, "and you're not wearing any sort of legion kit. Myrmidon?"

Reiva glanced at Yaros. She had wondered herself whether Yaros had a history with the Karellan's elite army corps, but he didn't seem the military sort.

Sure enough, Yaros shook his head. "Just a mercenary."

She shot a sly look over her shoulder. "*Always* been just a mercenary?"

His smile was easy, though it didn't quite reach the eyes. "Long as I can remember. And what about you? Charas almost sounds Karellan, but based on that bow and the quiver hanging off your saddle, I'd guess Parthavan."

"Dead on." There was a note of respect in her voice as well.

Reiva had to admit, it had been a good deduction on Yaros' part. The bow was the biggest clue—few people in this part of the world had the knowledge or skill set required to make recurves. And the arrows were fletched with black feathers, which wasn't standard legion practice.

"You're auxiliary then?" asked Reiva. Auxiliary troops were not formally legionnaires (and so, not full citizens of the Empire), and were often formed of hired swords or local conscripts from Imperial provinces. Scouts tended to be an eclectic mix, so it wouldn't have been unusual for Charas to be an auxiliary. Perhaps the Ninth had requisitioned forces from Parthava on the march from Lazarra.

But Charas gave a little laugh, saying, "No, there are hardly any Partha-vans in the Ninth. Long story, maybe I'll tell you someday, but the short of it is that I bought my citizenship with sponsorship from Legate Iscator."

"I see. I look forward to hearing how that happened."

Already her mind was racing through possibilities, though. Parthava's relationship with the Empire was complicated. Most of the land had sworn allegiance to the Emperor after Sharasthi's campaign, and officially they were an Imperial territory with a provincial governor...but things were too complicated to say that the Parthavans were a subjugated people.

And how close was Charas to the legate if she could get sponsored for Lazarran citizenship?

"I'm not fully appraised of the most recent developments in Parthava," said Reiva, "but when we skirted by on our way, I heard talk of a mounting armed resistance against Imperial rule and Parthavans who accept it."

Charas shrugged. "Don't pay much attention to home nowadays. I left some years ago. But yeah, I've heard similar things."

A somewhat evasive answer, Reiva judged. Perhaps she had family who were opposed to Lazarra.

"Well, if there's any chance of that, it makes control of Talynis all the more important."

The Scout nodded. "I wouldn't worry though. Iscator is in a class all her own—and besides," she said with a wink, "we have an Adept with us again."

Reiva smiled thinly. "I'll try not to die on you."

Charas' face fell, and she turned back toward the distant city.

They rode on for a bit. "So," Yaros asked eventually, "do you live up to the Parthavan reputation for archery?"

Charas laughed. "Ask around the camp how much money I've taken in marksman challenges."

Something flickered to life in Yaros' eyes, and Reiva wondered if he was considering challenging the Scout.

She had to admit though, she'd be curious to see it. Parthavan mounted archers were legendary across the world. A great deal of Adept Sharasthi's famed escapades during the Parthavan campaign had involved setting fire to their pastures, stealing a dozen horses and leaving them scattered across the countryside, cutting saddle straps so they failed under their riders in the heat of battle.

She wondered if Charas had heard stories of Sharasthi's exploits—from the perspective of those she had terrorized. Well, she could ask about that some other time. For now, she needed to prepare for meeting Legate Flavia Iscator.

They rode along in silence for some time, sipping a weak vinegar to ward against dehydration and the loss of salt. This drink was one of the few adaptations from the previous Talynisti campaign that had remained a standard part of legion practice.

It was not long before they stood before Dav-maiir's walls.

The Imperial banner hung on either side of the city gate—and though Reiva knew well the standard, and she knew well the gates of a Talynisti city, the sight of them together was dizzying.

According to the briefing Reiva had received in Lazarra, the center of the Ninth Legion's operations in Dav-maiir was a garrison constructed near the western gate of the city—that was what lay before them now. From here, they controlled a great deal of trade, given that the Talynisti had very specific protocols about which gate one was to leave from for what purposes. The legion certainly would have checkpoints at the other gates, but aside from perhaps the southern gate, there was hardly any other risk.

To the north lay the fractured and broken land of Zarush, a haunt of exiles, madmen, and countless people cursed by ill fortune to be born in the wake of the collapse of what the world once knew as the Immortal Empire.

Far east, at the distant fringes of Talynis, lay the Endric Pass. The pass was part of the Empire's motivation for taking Talynis—it was the gateway to the rest of the world, the only way through the otherwise impenetrable mountain range known as the Spine.

The other cities of Talynis were scattered about, and they would fall to the Imperial banner in time. As far as Reiva knew, though, there was no expectation that Malik could mount a military offensive to reclaim Dav-maiir anytime soon.

As they rode toward the gates, Reiva counted the legionnaires on patrol. Too few, it seemed. That aligned with the information she had been given at the outset.

The Empire's hold on Dav-maiir was tentative at best. If they did not consolidate power quickly, then the capital stood a good chance of falling back into Malik's hands.

That was part of why Reiva was here, but until all the reinforcements from the Tenth made it across the desert, she would only be bailing water from a hull-torn ship—delaying the inevitable.

Hopefully, meeting with Legate Iscator would provide some better insight as to the situation on the ground, but Reiva couldn't stop thinking about what Vantelle told her after she accepted the mission.

'I shepherded her rise myself. But now I fear the legate has begun to harbor anti-Imperial sympathies. Or perhaps she has simply begun to go soft. I pray it is nothing, but I will rely on you, Reiva.'

Such words spoken of one so highly placed as a legate...it was enough to set the stomach roiling. And, if Vantelle's intelligence was true, a man with a *Nihilo* Blade was lurking within these walls as well. Slipping amongst the shadows. Watching for an opportunity to strike out. There had been several assassinations of Ninth Legion officers, and at least one instance of arson.

This was the man they called the Wolf—the man who had killed Adept Havan, and who would certainly try to kill Reiva with that horrific relic.

This would be a war fought not only with shield walls in pitched battles. It would be fought with intrigue. Clues. Alliances, trust, deception.

Reiva had not been trained for that kind of warfare. The best thing she could do here was burn the whole place down. It would kill the assassin, but somehow she had a feeling that razing the capital of Talynis to the ground was not what the praetor expected of her.

First, she needed to speak with the legate to find out exactly what she could and would be expected to do here. And find out whether this legate was worth Vantelle's concern after all.

Charas led them into the garrison, where they dismounted. The Scout said she would ensure their horses were cared for and their possessions taken to their quarters. Reiva had no doubt—no one would dare steal from an Adept or her entourage.

With some directions to the legate's command tent, they were off.

As she and Yaros walked through the garrison, the mercenary pointed out how several Talynisti were patrolling the parapets atop the city walls. These men bore an unfamiliar design upon their shields and over their hearts.

That, Reiva guessed, was the standard for Tamiq, the new king of Talynis. Never mind that he was a usurper, that he had attempted fratricide—he had quite a few men-at-arms at his disposal.

And what does it say that he has stationed so many here with the Ninth's garrison? Is he merely reinforcing us, or is it a show of strength?

Both were true, she assumed. She doubted Tamiq would betray the Empire—it would be a display of remarkable arrogance and stupidity to attack the force whose strength he had relied on to seize power. But she also doubted that, despite the formal arrangements, there would be no friction between Tamiq and the Empire. Even though Lazarra officially deferred to Tamiq in matters of local rule, there would be certain conditions upon *how* Tamiq ruled. That was always the game the Empire played —and it was a game that brought many benefits for both parties, to be fair.

Reiva just had a hard time imagining the people of Talynis wanting to play along. Of course, some people had not liked the old king and were simply ready for a change. Some people were more given toward revolutionary causes, and so they hopped on board whenever anything exciting happened, hoping that as some sort of new social order emerged, they would be on the right side of things.

These people were on her side. The usurper was on her side; she might very well meet him before too long. Here in the city, he ruled by decree of the Emperor and the spears of the legion.

Even so, she had little respect for opportunists.

On the other hand, she respected Yaros, despite his being a mercenary... though she never quite totally understood exactly *what* he was. Certainly not a normal mercenary, certainly not a typical Karellan.

And of course, she knew she could be said to be the biggest opportunist of all, siding with the Empire after what they did ten years ago...but principles didn't keep a girl alive, not when the threat of lifelong slavery hung over her head.

As she walked amidst the neat, orderly rows of the legion garrison, her trepidation grew.

Legionnaires leered with dark shadows under their eyes, squinting against the sun. Many seemed jittery, exhausted.

Yaros nudged her, nodded subtly to a guard with ill-adjusted armor and a leaning spear. "Either the Ninth isn't up to snuff, or these sand-shufflers have been giving them a run for their money."

Reiva suppressed a grimace. "I'm worried," she murmured, "that it might be both."

The command tent was large, of course, and affixed in the ground before it was the standard of the Ninth Legion. Perched atop the staff was the golden Eagle—the Imperial *Aquila*. Written in silver lettering against a blue background were embroidered the words *Loyal to Our Fathers*, the Ninth Legion motto.

The guards at the tent (who, Reiva noted, looked somewhat more presentable than many of their compatriots) waved her in. They gave Yaros a narrow look, but Reiva explained he was her bodyguard and had proven himself trustworthy.

Although as she stepped through the flaps of the tent, she thought to herself that it would have been quite an impressive feat were Yaros to have been an assassin this whole time.

As soon as she saw the legate, she almost wished he was.

Flavia Iscator was the sort of woman who defied all Reiva's expectations about an officer in the legions. Of course, some ill-suited or untalented dregs happened to rise higher than they ought to have. An influential parent, some money slipped into the right palms—these could get you a commission, even promotions. Sleeping your way to the top was possible, though rumors spread through the legions faster than venereal disease in a dockside brothel.

Whatever Reiva had expected of Flavia Iscator, she had not expected *this*.

The legate was leaning back in her chair (not a typical commander's folding chair, Reiva noted, but a rather elegantly crafted, high-backed thing). Her hair was loose instead of tied back, and it seemed to have recently been washed. She might have even perfumed herself, given the scent of myrrh.

Iscator had a uniform on, technically, but her belt was unbuckled and loosened, and she had a single pearl earring. She held a cup of wine, swirling it gently back and forth.

Reiva saw her lips were tinged purple from the wine, and when she looked closely, she noticed the legate was wearing face paint as well.

So, at a cursory glance, no fewer than four breaches of legion dress regulation.

Reiva cleared her throat. She clutched her fist over her heart in the legion salute. "Adept Reiva, reporting to Legate Iscator."

Iscator glanced up from a book lying on her desk. Blinked. "Ah!" she said at last, flashing a wine-stained smile. "Adept Reiva," she said sonorously, rising from her chair. She did not set down her wine glass as she came to shake Reiva's hand.

Reiva dropped her fist from the salute and returned the gesture. To her surprise, the legate's grip was firm, her hand calloused.

The legate took Yaros in. "And this is...?"

He smiled easily. "Just a mercenary, ma'am. Yaros."

"Mm, a Karellan. I do adore the isles. Where do you hail from?"

Reiva perked up, but Yaros laughed the question off. "Oh, everywhere, more or less. Spent some time in Sophe, then Lakodon."

"Lovely beaches. Excellent wine." She impishly waved her cup as if they might not have noticed it yet.

"While I enjoy discussing the archipelago," Reiva cut in, "as much as the next person, I was meaning to give you my apologies for taking so long in making my way here. There were several delays along the road, but that is no excuse. Forgive me, Legate."

"Oh." Iscator blinked. "Are you really that late?" She swept back toward her desk, cape fluttering (not a single tear or patch).

As the legate leaned over some sheaves of paper, absently pushing them around as she searched for the right one, Reiva got the impression she was watching an actor, like one might see on a stage. Not a real soldier. Not a real warrior in service to Emperor Dioclete.

"Aha!" She plucked a notice off the desk and held it aloft. "Eighth of

Tenthmonth, I received a missive from Cassia. 'Adept Reiva en route, expect her within two months.'"

She looked at Reiva with big, pretty eyes and absolute sincerity. "What is today? The eleventh?"

Reiva ground her teeth. "The twelfth, ma'am."

"Twelfth! Well, that's within a week of it, no? I will report to the praetor that you have made your way here and begun your service in Dav-maiir." Her eyes scanned Reiva head-to-toe. "And did you leave your shield outside, or are you serving *qua paenitentia*?"

"The latter."

Yaros' eyes flitted from Reiva to the legate. He was masking it well, but Reiva could tell he was more than a little perturbed by all this.

How did a woman like this become head of a legion—under *Cassia Vantelle's* leadership at that? Forget bribery, sex, or favors; did this woman have blackmail on the gods themselves?

Iscator dropped back into her chair, crossed her legs. "Now tell me"— she took a pull of wine—"how apprised of our situation here are you?"

Reiva took a breath. "I understand that the Ninth's hold on Dav-maiir is frail. You've sustained severe casualties due to the environment and military engagement with the Talynisti, and—most pressing to why I am here—you have lost Adept Havan, who was attached to this legion when it departed from the capital."

Iscator nodded along. "Quite right."

If she took any offense at being reminded how brutal a time the Ninth had had of things, she did not show it. Some commanders took such things personally—and with good cause. Responsibility for every death, every error, fell upon the leadership. It was the great strength of the legion hierarchy—there was always someone to blame. And every officer answered to someone else for their mistakes. Corporals answered to sergeants. Sergeants to captains. Captains to prefects. And the prefects answered to the legate, who answered only to the praetor.

Praetors, of course, answered to the Emperor, but such things were beyond anyone else's concern—you might as well have wondered about how the gods decided the weather.

Iscator glanced at Yaros, then back to Reiva. Something was hanging in the air. Something that had to do with the death of Havan, she guessed.

Reiva inclined her head toward the entrance. "You'll need to leave for a moment, Yaros."

The Karellan held her gaze, shrugged. "Just yell if an assassin pops out from under the desk."

Reiva caught a grin on the legate's face. Whether she found Yaros funny, frustrating, or just wanted to haul him to bed, Reiva couldn't tell. At the moment, all she cared about was hearing this straight from the horse's mouth.

Legate Iscator had inspected Havan's body herself, according to Praetor Vantelle.

The woman beckoned Reiva closer. She stepped up to the edge of the desk.

"Vantelle," Iscator began in a low voice, "informed you of the circumstances of Havan's death, correct?"

The Adept swallowed. This was the fearful shadow that had lurked at the back of her mind throughout the whole journey. "A *Nihilo* Blade."

Iscator looked away for a moment—and Reiva noticed something flash across her face. Concern?

When the legate turned back to her, a different sort of light was shining in her eyes. Something...predatory. Reiva nearly took a step back, but held her ground.

"You must understand," she murmured, "I have only heard of such things. All legates are initiated into full scope of the relics from the old days but...it is somewhat different to hear those words on an Adept's lips."

"I...understand, Legate." Did she? "Your description of the wound was passed on to several senior Adepts within the Corps, and they unanimously concurred that it matched the profile of a *Nihilo* Relic. And, as I am sure you appreciate, it is not so easy to kill an Adept, under normal circumstances."

Iscator raked her eyes over Reiva, head to toe. "No," she mused. "I suppose it is not."

Reiva thought back to the hard, calloused hand that she had shaken minutes ago—so stark in contrast to the rest of her image.

She thought again of how Iscator reminded her of an actor strutting about a stage, playing a part. Reiva was beginning to get a sense of how this woman had climbed to the office of legate. She would need to ask some questions, very careful and discreet questions, about exactly how her soldiers thought of her.

The commander took another sip of wine, set down her cup. "Tell me, Reiva—what do you need from me?"

The Adept blinked. "Pardon?"

Stupid—never let yourself be caught off guard, and never show it if you were. Alyat would have had his head in his hands if he were watching this.

"You are here, for some reason that even I do not fully understand, by my praetor's orders."

Iscator took a moment to look into Reiva's eyes, her gaze severe. "I don't know how familiar you are with my career, but I trust Cassia Vantelle with my life. Not one of the other praetors is as cunning as her. But since she has not explained to me why she sent a Talynisti Adept to fight a Talynisti war—something I am certain took no small measure of strong-arming your superiors at the Sanctum—I am only left to assume that you are here with some set of orders I have not been made privy to. Is that correct?"

Yes, Reiva could see why this woman had ascended to within two steps of the Emperor himself.

She also could not fathom how to respond properly to such a question without disclosing that Vantelle was not nearly as trusting of Iscator as the other way around...unless that too was an act.

An unnerving sensation pricked at the back of her neck. The legate's eyes rested on her, and she couldn't help feeling as though those eyes could see into her mind, into the places where she held her secrets. What if Iscator already knew or had surmised that Reiva was here to keep an eye on her and report to Vantelle? What if she already sensed Vantelle's suspicion?

Not for the first time that day, Reiva felt overwhelmed by the intricacies of the game she had been thrown into—a game in which she was but a piece, caught between a multitude of agents acting with far more expertise and information than she had. She had trained to fight on battlefields with magic and metal, not behind closed doors with whispers and intrigue.

Thankfully, Iscator seemed to take her silence as enough of an answer. "Well, I am sure Cassia will inform me of what is relevant. If you are ever so inclined as to share such information with me—if you are permitted, of course—then know that my ear is always available to you. Until then, simply ask of me what you require, and if it is within my power, I shall grant it."

Well, she could work with that.

"An interpreter, to start with. Someone who can teach. My command of Talynisti is fragile, and if I am to be the symbol of Imperial-Talynisti unity that Praetor Vantelle thinks I can be, I'll need to fix that."

"Done."

"I will also need to speak with the informants we have in the city—anyone with ties to the local underworld or the Loyalists."

"We have a few of both. There will be a meeting tomorrow night with the senior officers to discuss the matter of the man who killed Havan. There are some new leads regarding the Wolf—we suspect him to be working with several other King's Vipers."

Reiva clenched her fists.

Wolves—always wolves these days.

"There is a barracks under construction as well. Rooms are sparse and few at the moment, but an Adept such as yourself, of course, merits such accommodations. Particularly given the threat to your person."

A room with solid walls, a door to bar. It was better than a tent. "I accept it, thank you."

"Will the Karellan be with you as well?"

Reiva did not see any guile in the legate's eyes—but such questions could have implications.

"He is only my employee, Legate. I've half a mind to dismiss him now that I have made it safely to Dav-maiir."

It was a lie, but one that would hopefully dissuade Iscator of any notion that Reiva was afraid or unconfident in her position.

But then a sly smile crossed Iscator's lips, and Reiva had to suppress a shudder. "Oh, my dear Adept—there is nothing safe about arriving in Dav-maiir."

30

ANGER

I ALSO SAW in her eyes guilt. I saw hatred. I saw fury and pain, and every manner of contempt.

Were it not for the first of these, I would not have recognized that the greatest object of her wrath was none other than herself.

—*The Memoirs of Flavia Iscator*

THOUGH SHE TRAVELED ALL the way from Lazarra without a shield, Reiva had not felt the absence so conspicuously until she walked to the patrol with Yaros.

"Feels like I'm about to be skewered," she muttered.

Yaros shrugged. "That what's I'm here for, isn't it? Besides, I see some pillar pendants. Those are *triarii*, aren't they? Third-liners? Iscator isn't about to let you die for lack of protection."

"An Adept shouldn't *need* this sort of protection."

As they neared the patrol, one of the *triarii* wiped sweat from his brow, squinting at them. "You my new charges?"

"Adept Reiva, and this is my bodyguard Yaros."

"Pillar Belic. Pleasure to have you, Adept. I'll try not to be insulted that you've brought a bodyguard to my patrol."

Yaros grinned easily. "I'm quite useless, really. Just a pretty face."

One of the other legionnaires cackled. "That what passes for a pretty face nowadays? No wonder 'e's got a beard—less skin shown the better."

The man stuck out his hand. "Pillar Mago. I'll be leading the patrol."

Yaros shook it, a twinge of confusion coming into his features. "Didn't realize this was a double patrol."

"It's not," barked Belic. "And he's not in charge today. I am."

Mago knit his eyebrows. "You were in charge yesterday."

"I told you, the legate wanted me in charge for the Adept's first patrol."

"Why in the 'ells would she say that?"

Reiva frowned. "You two...exchange command?"

"Right on the money!" chirped Mago.

She glanced at the assembled soldiers. A few seemed to be hiding smirks.

"If this is a joke, Pillar Belic—"

"Oh it is, but we're dead serious about it."

"Belic an' me been joined at the 'ip together long as we can remember. Thank the 'eavens Flavia got ahold of us—most folks in the top brass don't appreciate how we work. I don't know what we'd 'ave done if we'd been separated."

Yaros was watching the exchange with open amusement. "And here I thought military patrols were dull."

"Oh they are," huffed Belic. "Proper dull, all day every day. And Mago makes the same jokes every time. But the exercise is good."

"Sometimes you e'en get to take a left turn where you normally take a right."

Reiva suppressed a sigh. "Speaking of which, shouldn't we be along?"

Belic made a show of glancing at the sun's position. "Right you are, Adept. Mago, take the lead."

"Thought the legate told *you* to lead."

"I am leading, you're just leading the formation."

"Ah, I see 'ow it is," he grumbled, hitching up his shield as he stepped forward. "Put me at the 'ead so I get caught in the ambush first."

"Ambushes don't come from the front."

"Clever ones do—never expect 'em that way."

Yaros shot Reiva a look of mirth. "You'll have to thank Legate Iscator for this."

"Thank her yourself," she muttered.

The patrol set out from the garrison, passing through the western gate of the city and onto the main west-east thoroughfare.

As soon as they passed beneath the gate's broad shadow, Reiva's stomach knotted. Over seven years had passed since Shugrith. This wasn't the same city, but it felt so alike—the shape of hewn stones, the feel of the dusty road underfoot, the sounds of chattering children and bickering spouses, the rough smell of animals being driven to market intermingled with pleasing aromas from hearth fires.

Yaros nudged her. "Feeling all right, boss?"

She nodded, her tongue in a twist.

The patrol moved in a column two wide, six deep. She and Yaros were in the row second from the back, with Pillar Belic right behind them.

"So," Reiva offered once she found her voice, "where did you get your distinction?"

Belic adjusted the thin pendant of an iron pillar hanging from his neck. "Mizkhar. Same as Mago."

Yaros' eyebrows went up. "Did you see Queen Nethsta?"

The pillar clucked his tongue. "Nah, she was visiting her cousin in Caroshai or something. Good for her. Missed the burning of her own city."

"You saw the razing?" asked Reiva.

"Saw it? We were on duty when it happened. On my left, Mago's got one arm under a private who's missing her left leg, in his other's a broken spear. On my right, the captain's blowing the horn for reinforcements. All the while, the royal palace is in flames behind us."

Belic shrugged, twisting his lips. "We pulled back into a guardhouse. By then, we knew no one was coming. So our captain gives the order to push for the docks—figures if the gods are gracious, we might find a ship and shove off down the river. We were down to thirty by then, only ten of us in decent shape."

Yaros let out a low whistle.

Reiva thought back to her childhood, recalling what it was like to fear fire—to have no control over it, to know it would devour you at the slightest touch. "And you got to the river?"

Belic shrugged. "We did, but I don't remember most of that final push. Mago neither. But we made *triarii*, so someone must've seen something. No boat though, I remember that. We swam for the other bank, trailing red all the way. Ever seen a crocodile? Lost plenty more to those bastards. Three times I felt one brush against me."

Reiva swallowed. "How do you handle it?"

"Hm?"

"How do you handle all that loss?"

Belic twisted his lips from side to side. "Doing the rites helped. And remembering that they all died for us to make it through. It keeps you going."

Yaros nodded solemnly. "Did everyone who made it get *triarii*?"

Belic scoffed. "Yeah. Yeah, we did. All two of us."

Reiva looked ahead. Mago's spear was high in the air as he led the way, the plume of his helmet swaying.

She found herself thinking of Tharrick and Meridi, and all the others who had died at the shrine. What was Gascal doing now? What about Scanlon? Had Ironback Company repopulated, or been absorbed into another unit?

Yaros had thought Iscator put them with this patrol to benefit from the protection of two *triarii* legionnaires. And that was likely accurate. But maybe it wasn't the only reason.

The patrol wound its way through the streets. By now, the legion had been in place for many weeks, so plenty of folks hardly even looked up as they tramped past. Others did look, though, and didn't bother hiding their dour expressions.

And a great deal stared at Reiva. She told herself it was the red mantle—but she couldn't help wondering if they knew who she was. Who she *really* was. Not just an Adept, but one of them.

In the distance, a flash of bright light blazed over the rooftops. For a moment, Reiva thought something had caught on fire.

Then she realized it was gold that had caught the sun's light.

"The Temple," she breathed.

Belic grunted. "Quite a sight, eh?"

As they walked on, a gap between buildings fully revealed the structure situated atop a hill in the city center. Reiva gaped at the majestic architecture.

She had heard about the Temple for as long as she could remember, of course, but to see it in person...

And to see a Lazarran banner hanging from the wall.

A sour taste filled her mouth. She took a slow breath, channeling aether. Energy coursed through her like a shock of cold water. But it didn't settle her. If anything, it only set her further on edge.

"—boss?"

She kept staring at it. The Imperial sigil embroidered in gilt thread on purple, beautiful and hideous against the golden accoutrements of the Temple.

"Boss!"

Reiva snapped to attention, turning to Yaros. Then she realized the patrol had gone further on. She had stopped in the road.

Belic was giving her a strange look. "Something wrong, Adept?"

She swallowed, forcing down an acrid lump in her throat. "Nothing, Pillar Belic. Nothing's wrong."

Belic grunted. "Well, let's get along. I don't like leaving Mago unsupervi—"

Yaros swore, shoving Reiva down.

Something whirred overhead, striking the wall behind her with a *crack!*

Belic echoed Yaros' oath, hefting his shield up just in time to block a stone meant for his face. "Ambush!"

Yaros stepped around Reiva, putting up his own shield. Reiva drew her sword with her left hand, filling her right with fire. Another two stones clanged against Yaros' and Belic's shields.

People were screaming, emptying out of the road.

"That rooftop," huffed Yaros. "I count three."

"Count again," snarled Belic. "We're cut off."

The clash of metal on metal filled the air, and Reiva saw a group of Talynisti fighters swarming from the alleyways. People who had just been standing around moments before drew weapons from the folds of their cloaks.

There were about fifteen men between the three of them and the main patrol. Another five had appeared on the opposite side, hemming them in.

"Get close!" snapped Belic. "It'll spoil the slingers' aim."

Reiva grimaced. "Finally time to earn your pay, Yaros."

In one lightning-quick motion, Yaros grabbed a javelin from over his shoulder and whipped it straight into an attacker's chest. He followed up by drawing his sword and disarming another.

"And here I was hoping I could keep up the charade another week or two."

Belic roared, slamming his shield into a fighter and knocking him off his feet. His spear darted forward and pierced another's throat. His foe collapsed, gurgling blood.

Reiva moved forward, keeping Yaros and his broad shield between her and the stone slingers.

They were outnumbered, but their enemies didn't have proper armor, nor proper weaponry. Just a rag-tag bunch of Loyalist resisters who got lucky enough to catch her off-guard.

She raised her fire-wreathed hand, eyed her target and—

And nothing.

In the distance, the Temple was over his shoulder. She could see the Imperial banner.

And she could see a Talynisti man ready to give his life—ready to charge an Adept head on—to bring that banner down.

She knew that face, those dark, deep-set eyes.

She blinked, and suddenly she was kneeling beside a cot, dabbing his sweltering, sweat-covered forehead.

Father?

Yaros lashed out with a precise kick, snapping the man's knee and then slashing his face. "Reiva! Fire, or they overrun us!"

Another stone cracked against the wall, spitting fragments of brick into her face. It stung, but the sensation was far away.

The Imperial banner was still flying.

Her fingers were tight around her sword's grip. On instinct, she brought it up to parry a thrust, but when she went to return the strike—nothing.

Yaros spat a string of curses. Like a rushing river, he flowed against the enemy, moving from overhead slash to deft parry to shield bash to stab.

He really was worth every last coin she paid him to kill her countrymen.

A hand clamped down on her shoulder. Belic shoved her aside, stepping forward to come between her and his enemies. His enemies—her enemies?

The rest of the patrol was fighting their way through, but Yaros and Belic were about to be overwhelmed. Belic was *triarii*, one of the legion's finest. Yaros was a fighter unlike any she'd ever seen.

A sound pulled her attention from their spectacle. She looked back, noting that Belic had downed all five men who'd come from behind them.

But where there had been five, now another ten appeared around the corner. And they looked enraged at the sight of their fallen brethren.

Rage. She knew rage. She knew anger. Her Flame fed on anger.

Another stone whizzed by her head, missing by an inch.

The ten Loyalists bore down on her.

The bodies in front of her changed. She saw Tharrick, his head staring at her five yards from his body. She saw Meridi, one eye ruined, one shoulder smoking from cauterization.

Yes, she knew anger.

She dropped her sword, channeling aether down both arms, and stretched out her hands.

Tongues of fire burst from her palms, engulfing her enemies in a blistering blaze.

Bile rose in her throat as they screamed, dropping one and all. They sounded like her squadrons in Hyrgallia. They sounded like her father.

She turned toward where the stone-slingers perched. Even at this distance, she could make out the horror on their faces.

Channeling aether to her legs, she burst forward. They panicked, fumbling stones into their slings.

One was faster than the other two, and he whirled the pouch over his head twice before whipping it forward.

Reiva threw herself into a roll, feeling the missile's passage through the air as she tumbled.

She popped to her feet. The other two were swinging, ready to launch.

She conjured a broad plume of fire in front of her, then threw herself to the side. Unable to see her through the screen, the slingers shot wide.

Those were the last shots any of them managed to get off.

Fortifying her legs with a rush of aether, she jumped, caught the lip of the rooftop, and hauled herself over.

The man nearest her drew a knife; she grabbed his arm and snapped it. An aether-empowered punch to the face put his lights out before she threw him into the man furthest from her.

This wasn't the Nine-knuckle House—this was true combat. Aether coursed through her, filling every muscle with superhuman vigor.

The third man tried to tackle her midsection, but it was like grappling a tree. She snapped her knee up into his side, breaking ribs. Grabbing a fistful of hair, she brought his face down on her thigh. His nose crunched, spewing blood, and he collapsed in a groaning heap.

She had barely taken a breath when the one she'd thrown the first into closed in, swinging two knives. She danced backwards, evading as the blades sliced the air.

With one more burst of aether, she threw a blast of fire at his chest. The force of the blow carried him off his feet, smashing him into the barrier at the edge of the roof, where he lay groaning, his torso smoking with the horrid stench of seared flesh.

She heaved a breath, taking in the sight of the battle in the streets—or rather, what was left of it. The main patrol had rejoined with Yaros and Belic, and together they had dispatched the rest of the ambush. The men Reiva had burned were lying in the road, groaning and clutching at their wounds. Or rather, most of them were. Those who had been closest to her now lay still.

A hissing intake of air drew her attention. The man whose ribs she'd broken was getting to his feet, gingerly holding his side with one hand. His face was a bloody mess. With his other, he was drawing a knife.

"Leave it," she said in rough Talynisti.

He got into a fighting stance. A sloppy one.

"Stop. You lost."

He grimaced, holding the knife a little higher. She could already see his plan. He was about to charge her, try to stab her throat.

She lit her hands on fire.

He cringed, fear bleeding into his expression. His eyes reflected the blaze.

"Surrender."

He shook his head. "You'll put us in chains."

Her stomach turned. "Better than dying."

"Hah, you can't understand, Imperial." He winced, favoring his side. "Can't understand us. This whole city would rather die than live in chains to you."

She tasted something sour. The world seemed far away. "Surrender."

He yelled as he attacked.

Reiva quenched her fire and stepped around the stab, disarming him easily before putting him into a hold.

He gasped in pain, curling in on his wounded side. "We're not, *ah*, like all the others you conquer. Talynis will never fall. Talynis will *never* stop hating you!"

Reiva looked up, taking in the Imperial banner hanging from the Temple. "Yeah," she muttered in Lazarran. "I know the feeling."

31

INTERESTING TIMES

SHARASTHI CONSTRUCTED her gambits with absolute precision. Only with great caution and meager scale was she able to avoid the all-searching eyes.
—*The Memoirs of Flavia Iscator*

ADEPT JAN STRETCHED as he stood from his desk. He rubbed his eyes. When he took the job of Imperial Postmaster, he'd thought it would be *less* stressful than wading into battle. Oh, the naïveté of his younger self. If only he had known then the horrors of mankind's most indefatigable foe—bureaucracy.

As he stepped out from his office, the pervasive smells of the Roost—avian reek mixed with the sweet vanillin of parchment—wafted into his nostrils. The cacophony of hundreds of messenger hawks calling to one another hit him in full force.

The Adept stretched out his awareness with his arcane discipline: the Art of Beasts, *Ars Theron*. His mind brushed against every single one of those hawks, and warmth burgeoned in his heart as they acknowledged him.

An animal's mind was a curious thing—simpler than a human's, to be sure, but beautiful in its own way. And Jan adored his birds. During his training as an Initiate, he had often wondered just what enabled him to touch animals' minds, but not humans'. His mentor had waxed on about philosophies and religions, none of the answers being particularly satisfying.

Nowadays, though, he was glad he did not have to bother with the minds of men. Every single hawk had a nobility you could find in perhaps one out of a hundred humans. Ravens had wisdom and subtlety unimaginable. And among the beasts of the earth? Well, he could count on one hand the number of men who could match the lion for its ferocity, or the ox for its stoic determination.

Plenty of people could match the stubbornness of an ass, though.

A postworker wove around him. "Pardon, sir!" She clutched a bundle of scrolls under either arm.

"Have you taken a break yet today, Brisa?"

"I'll get around to it!" she called over her shoulder. "The rookie needs help with the reds."

"Take a break! I'll help him."

Jan shook his head, smiling absently. That was another thing—people who came to work in the Roost were so different from the Adept Corps. Everyone in the Corps was so serious. Not that managing the Imperial Post *wasn't* serious—it was one of the most essential cogs in the machine of Empire. And certainly many people in the Post were stolid, or grumpy, or self-important—but that's why Jan worked in the Roost. You had to be a little cracked in the head, in a good way, to work around hawks all day.

Jan suppressed a smirk as the rookie scuttled by, his eyes wide and lips pressed tightly together. He had started working here barely a week ago. Still hadn't quite gotten the ropes of working in as hectic a place as the Roost, but he had a good ethic.

"Declas! Brisa tells me you're overwhelmed."

The young man nearly tripped over his feet, then spun around and blinked frantically. "Sir Adept Jan! Doing my best!"

Jan waved his hand. "It's Adept, or sir, or just Jan. Definitely not all three at once."

"Right, sir Adept! Er—"

Jan snorted. "Two is an improvement, I guess. What's the trouble?"

Declas' eyes widened again.

"Move it, lad, there's mail to sort and the birds don't wait."

"Yessir!" As he shuffled off to the Red Room—so named because all red-sealed letters were processed there—Jan meandered after him. He reached out again with his magic, noting that there were a few more birds out from the Roost than was normal.

Wonder what that's about...

Declas fumbled around with the few dozen rolled-up letters strewn across a wide table. "It's the sorting, sir. I can't keep it all straight. All reds are high priority, but some reds are higher priority than others, depending on the seal design, and then some of *those* can be handled by us, but others need your direct attention, but then I—"

"I get it."

Declas' mouth snapped shut.

Another postworker delivered a half-dozen more letters, shooting a sympathetic glance at Declas and nodding to Jan.

"Do you remember which seals need my direct attention?"

The rookie screwed his eyes shut. "Red...red with an A, red with an eagle, and red with..."

"With an I."

"An I!"

Another grin tugged at Jan's lips. "Right. And tell me what those all represent."

Declas blinked. "Uhhh... The eagle is for the Emperor."

Jan nodded. "Thought so."

"Sir?" Declas said, wringing his hands.

"Instead of trying to just memorize which seals go to me, make the association in your mind between the seal and what it means. The purpose of a symbol is to convey meaning, yes? So you need to know what they mean. Then it will be natural for you to sort out what needs to go to another department and what needs to go by me first."

Declas nodded slowly.

"Eagle for the Emperor. That's Imperial Post of the highest importance— either sent to or on behalf of Dioclete himself. What about A and I?"

The young man chewed his bottom lip. "Adept Corps? And Legion Intelligence?"

"Good. And you can see why I need to handle those personally, right?"

"Yes! But, sir, why are there so few special reds then?"

Jan cast a sardonic look over the messy table.

"I mean, shouldn't there be even more?"

Jan clapped a hand on the young man's shoulder. "Put your mind to it, son. I'm sure you can figure that out yourself. Now let's get some mail sorted."

And keep me out of that stifling office for a little longer.

Declas grabbed a scroll. "A. Adept Corps." He scrutinized the minuscule writing. "Adept Reiva to Adept Sa...Adept Sha—"

"Sharasthi," Jan read. He had told her a dozen times to use her Lazarran name for the sake of the postworkers, but she found it amusing to think how they struggled with Zarushan phonology.

Ordinarily, Jan would have had to consult a ledger in his office, but he happened to know where Sharasthi was at the moment. He took the scroll. "Bring me a Fourth Legion hawk."

Declas frowned. "That's...Hyrgallia?"

Jan nodded his approval.

While he waited for Declas to return with the bird, he turned the scroll over in his hands. It was large, as far as letters went. Tied with thin, brown string. Adept Reiva had been sent to Talynis, and he imagined it was quite expensive to buy string dyed in more exuberant colors.

The entire Corps had heard of Praetor Vantelle's unprecedented decision to send Reiva to Talynis—and the even more shocking decision by the Circle of Peers to approve it.

Sharasthi, Jan knew, had been instrumental in making that happen.

Jan's training had been unusual, as far as such things went. He had been an Initiate under two mentors. His first—the one who had bored him with philosophy—had been killed in action partway through his training.

Sharasthi had taken over as his mentor then. What's more, she had specifically asked to do so—the Night-cloaked Witch herself. Though she had not yet earned that title, Jan laughed when she did—it certainly suited her. Training under Sharasthi had *never* been dull or boring.

She had also nudged him to take this job—partially because she had known he was better suited to this sort of work than the ugliness of war, and partially because...well, partially because she wanted someone inside the Post.

As his fingers traced along the textured parchment, his heart beat just a bit faster.

The flutter of feathers alerted Jan to Declas' return. He was glad the man knew how to handle a hawk properly—with his Art, he could feel the creature's ease. That was good. Declas may not have gotten the hang of the system itself yet, but if he had the temperament for the hawks, then he had a future in the Roost indeed.

Declas had already unscrewed the capsule, strapped to the hawk's underbelly with a specially designed harness, so Jan inserted the scroll. As Declas closed the capsule, Jan touched the hawk's mind. Instantly, the bird's piercing eyes focused on Jan's.

The Adept pushed aside the manic thoughts of the beast—mouse flesh, the open sky, a warm nest—and sent an image of the Fourth Legion's standard. He felt understanding dawn in the hawk's mind. It was trained to fly to Hyrgallia, and it would know to seek the Fourth Legion's headquarters, where the standard flew high. Then, he buttressed the image with a general area to search out.

This sort of work wasn't necessary when using fixed locations (many other Imperial cities had roosts of their own, modeled after the central Roost), but when sending to an ongoing campaign, it was important the hawk be given some direction.

Then, Jan sent an image of Adept Sharasthi's face. Unlike ravens, hawks did not naturally remember human faces, but Jan's magic could fix a face in a hawk's mind for about a week. If the hawk saw Adept Sharasthi on the way, then he would deliver the letter directly to her.

With that, Jan broke the mental connection. The hawk shook his feathery head, screeched briefly, and began to rustle in Declas' hold.

"He'll want to be off right away," said Jan.

"Aye, sir!" he replied, and hustled off.

Yes, Jan thought the youth had some hope for working here.

He cast another look across the table. Quite a few letters had the Adept Corps' seal. Something told Jan that Adept Reiva would be the subject of more than not.

Declas returned, a few feathers in his hair. He moved to the ledger, set on a smaller table in the corner so as not to risk ink spilling across the letters being sorted. As he dipped a quill, Jan said, "No need to record that one, Declas."

Declas furrowed his brow. "But sir, all red seals need to be logged for—"

"For Legion Intelligence, very good. But not that one." He smiled easily, clapping a hand on his shoulder. "Less work for you, eh?"

"Y-yes, sir. Thank you. And...if any others come through from Adept Reiva?"

"If they're going to or coming from Sharasthi, don't worry about it. Intelligence already knows everything they need to about those letters."

Nothing at all.

Declas nodded. "Will do, sir."

"Before long, you'll be an expert at sorting these, son."

With that, Jan returned to his office, possibilities turning over in his mind, curiosities about exactly what his old mentor was up to that she wouldn't want logged for review.

He had some suspicions, and all of them meant the Empire was in for some *very* interesting times.

32

LUCK OF THE SANDS

HAD TAMIQ BEEN LAZARRAN, I have little doubt he would have ascended to the praetorian office—perhaps even to the vocation of Emperor. He was a handsome man, charming, with the natural force of a leader adored by his men. In many ways, he was more suited to the kingship than his older brother.

But even as I ate at his table and drank his wine, I hated him for the traitor he was, and I hated myself for my participation in that treachery. I do not think the Lion hid it so well as I.

—*The Memoirs of Flavia Iscator*

❧

REIVA LET OUT a heavy sigh as she dropped onto her bed. Her quarters were meager, as was to be expected, but four walls and an actual bed were luxury compared to life on the road. Though she'd only been in Dav-maiir for a week, she already thought of this small room as her home.

A legionnaire's kit contained just the essentials for life on campaign, and so she had unpacked in moments when she first arrived. The room's only furnishings besides the bed were a chair, a small desk, and a trunk for her belongings. It had been intended to house an officer, clearly, and the desk came already supplied with a charcoal pencil and a few sheaves of parchment.

Sitting on her bed, she put her head in her hands. Another long sigh.

Yes, she was moved in. She had been sleeping here for days now. Going on patrols had taught her the roads and surrounding area well.

But she had not been able to settle. She had felt more comfortable sleeping in a tent. Talynis was the land of her birth, the land that had been her *home* for more than half her life—and now that she was finally back, she felt more a stranger than ever.

It was the way people looked at her. The fear. The disgust. And not just Talynisti—she saw it among legionnaires as well. The subtly masked suspicion that she was not wholly loyal.

Well, if butchering Talynisti Loyalists wasn't enough to prove that, nothing would be.

Fighting the deep fatigue in her bones, she shucked off her sandals and began doffing her breastplate. At least she was not in Shugrith. That would have been impossible. She knew the streets, the people. She wondered if her family was still there. Well, what was left of her family—if anyone was still alive at this point.

The grave, though, she could have gone to visit it...

She shook her head, running her fingers roughly through her hair.

Better to leave such things in the past, along with everything else. She was here as an Adept; an Adept was a Lazarran, a child of the Empire. She may have been born here, but her home was in Lazarra. Her people were in Lazarra.

A knock sounded at the door. "Boss," called Yaros, "the legate—"

Reiva suppressed a groan. "I'm not late, so tell the runner to leave."

A moment's pause. "She didn't send a runner."

Reiva's eyes widened. In a moment, she was on her feet and at the door.

Flavia Iscator smiled easily. "My apologies, Reiva, but it's not every day one dines with a king. I wanted to make sure you're prepared."

"I know how to dress myself, Legate."

"In the toga, but I had something special made up for you." She snapped her fingers, and her optio, a man named Felan, stepped into view. He presented Reiva with a neatly folded pile of fabric, expertly dyed and silken to the touch.

After a moment, Reiva realized what she was holding. Something in her skull started spinning.

"Give us a moment, boys," said the legate, stepping in and closing the door.

Reiva swallowed, still staring at the garment. "I'm not wearing this."

"You are here to serve the Empire's interests, Reiva. This is one way you—"

"No. I am dressing as a Lazarran." Her voice sounded hollow in her own ears.

"You *are* dressing as a Lazarran. Here, look at it."

Iscator took it from her hands and unfolded it, letting it hang in front of Reiva's eyes. "You see?"

Her heart began to pound. "I...do see."

Somehow, Iscator had combined the Lazarran toga with a Talynisti dress. Like the toga, it was cut from broad swathes of fabric to drape over and around the body, with a band of Adepts' red and violet that was just a shade off Imperial Purple. Instead of a tunic though, Iscator had prepared a dark undercoat with long sleeves, like a Talynisti woman would wear.

"Fashion," the legate offered, "is but a hobby of mine, but I think the tailor did a fine job realizing my vision. Now stop gaping and try it on."

A part of Reiva still wanted to reject it, but...she couldn't deny she was curious. After stripping off her tunic and cingulum skirt, she slipped into the legate's invention.

Iscator brightened. "Good, I guessed your measurements. Mm, that's not how you cinch that—here."

Reiva bit her tongue. She had grown up tying that sash.

She had also forgotten, evidently, as Iscator managed it right away, and with far defter fingers.

"Now, drape that like this, fold that around your arm and..."

The legate took a step back. "Perfect." A self-satisfied smile crossed her features. "Still think you'd rather wear an ordinary toga?"

Reiva looked down at herself. "It's...striking."

"Oh come now, I can see you love it."

She stifled an involuntary smile. "It's beautiful."

Then the corners of her lips tugged down. Was this what her culture was now? Something to put on for display, an elegantly textiled and tailored metaphor for Imperial dominion?

She grit her teeth. *Not my culture. Not anymore.*

"For the sake of the Empire," she said, "this will do."

"Damned with faint praise, perhaps, but I'll take it. Now, get a washcloth and wipe the dust from your face—we have a king to meet."

~

THE TWO OF them stepped into a chariot, pulled by some of the finest horses Reiva had ever seen. They were Parthavan stock, she guessed. Sleek, limber, and famed throughout the world.

The man at the reins of their chariot was Iscator's optio Felan. He was quiet, but he handled the horses well.

He was also a force of nature on the battlefield, if his reputation was accurate.

A detachment of cavalry rode in formation around the chariot, while a pair of advance riders cleared the way up ahead. This involved quite a bit of shouting and waving, and it was not long before crowds were beginning to form alongside the streets. Heads poked out of windows and doorways. Children hid behind mothers' skirts. Fathers crossed their arms and watched the procession with wary eyes.

Vantelle had warned Reiva the city was still divided over the changing of rule. Tamiq had enjoyed great popularity as prince, yes, but usurping the throne was not something the people took lightly.

"I realize," Iscator said, "that this must be uniquely uncomfortable for you. Seeing your own people stare at you like some foreign invader."

The legate was not looking at her. She had her eyes held forward, surveying the throngs of Talynisti, scanning the rooftops and the road. However she had behaved when they first met, she certainly knew how to project authority when the situation demanded it.

Reiva, likewise, was gazing out over the crowds—but she was careful not to linger too long on any one face. "Am I not a foreign invader? It seems a fair judgment."

Iscator might have shrugged if they were not under such scrutiny at the moment. "You are here as a representative of Lazarra, an Adept of your Corps, but you are also a Talynisti woman. That is not by accident."

"As you said, Praetor Vantelle is a cunning woman."

"She is." Iscator shifted slightly as the chariot bumped over a rock. "But you are not just some tool, Reiva."

"An Adept is a blade in the hand of the Emperor."

A small smile touched the other woman's lips. "A lovely creed, to be sure, but not always practical."

They slowed to turn a corner. Moments like this, Reiva knew, were ideal for someone to spring an ambush. She almost wished it would happen. She knew how to handle knives and clubs far better than whatever she was about to walk into with this strange legate charged with subduing the kingdom.

Regrettably or thankfully, no such attack came. The crowds had only grown larger at this point. Reiva found herself scanning for any signs of a weapon—someone favoring one side of their body, a hand hidden within the folds of a cloak. There were too many people though, and the loose, flowing Talynisti garb was well-suited to concealing a sword.

"It is important that they see you, Reiva, even though that may be uncomfortable for you."

Reiva was beginning to grow irritated.

"As I said when you gave me this garment, Legate, I am quite capable of doing what the Empire requires of me."

Iscator was silent for a little while.

"Yes," she said at last. "Yes, I believe you are."

"Then, with all due respect, stop addressing me as if I am some fragile child. What happened in Hyrgallia was trying, but it has not broken me."

"My apologies then, Adept. I did not intend to cast doubt upon your fortitude."

The optio, who had been silent up until now, glanced over his shoulder. "Haven't heard the legate apologize to anyone in well over a fortnight, Adept." He threw in a wink. "Your presence is a blessing from above."

Reiva blinked, accepting the remark with a nod.

Iscator was rolling her eyes. "Yes, well, hopefully she'll get more done for us than you have, Felan."

"Would you like to drive this chariot yourself?"

"If I did, then we would already have been sitting down for dinner."

"Exactly why I should be the one at the reins, ma'am."

Reiva watched their interaction with acute focus. It took a minute before she realized why she had latched so tightly on to it—this was more what she was used to from the legions. Banter, sarcasm.

She had not had any of this since...since Hyrgallia.

Well, she had Yaros, but he was something else—she had to bear the dread of knowing every joke and wisecrack was subsidized from her own purse.

Speaking of which, she hoped he was not getting himself drunk now that he had a night off for the first time in so long.

AVI SLIPPED through the crowd like a snake through grass. It was a skill he had perfected while he was young—either picking pockets when he first left home, or killing enemies of the throne once Crow found him. There was an art to it. You had to move faster than most in order to get somewhere, but you could not draw attention. You wanted to look uninteresting and unthreatening. A bland, normal man about his business who just happened to be walking along when the woman in command of the legion came riding through with her new attack dog.

And Avi did the act pretty well, he thought. The Adept even looked right at him at one point. She could never have known that she just locked eyes with the man who had a *Nihilo* Blade strapped to his side.

He should not have brought it along, really. It was a stupid decision, a brash spur of instinct. The soldiers searched people sometimes. He doubted that would happen to him while he was in the middle of so many people, but it could have happened earlier, it could still happen later. Things would get messy if it came to that.

But he wanted to kill her. Wanted to avenge those men who had gone after her when she first came to this city. Foolish men—men who'd given their lives senselessly. But men who had stood for the same cause he did.

Maybe men who had been inspired by how he had killed the devil of ice.

Crow had warned him against trying anything. They were going to get more information from Asrah, hopefully, regarding the new arrival. Even if Crow had not ordered him as such, he could not have tried to kill the Adept without condemning himself to a violent death in the process. Both the legate and her optio were carrying swords, even on their way to the palace. You hardly ever saw an Imperial without a weapon of some sort. They probably slept with the damn things strapped to their hips.

That had been the problem this whole time—they were still struggling to amass enough Loyalists to stage a proper offensive operation. There were clumsy attempts now and then, like the one that had gone after the Adept in the streets, but nothing with Crow's keen planning and oversight. And despite Avi's overwhelming urge to try to assassinate the Adept in a precision strike, Crow was adamant that he would be trading his life away. The legion had already lost one Adept—they'd suffer shame if they lost a second. Ever since that atrocious attempt to kill her in the streets, she was always well-guarded, always just beyond his reach.

The chariot rumbled around a corner, out of sight. Avi let the crowd carry him away as they dispersed. His fight would have to wait for now. Once Asrah got them more information regarding the Adept's purpose in Talynis, they would have, hopefully, the intelligence necessary to make actionable plans.

Asrah.

Further cause for his frustration today.

He had gone to her early in the morning to speak regarding the dinner —Crow had some specific information he wanted her to suss out if possible.

"Ready to dine with a traitor?" Avi had whispered when she let him in from the balcony. The sky was gray with pre-dawn light.

Asrah had frowned. "Are you referring to the Adept, or to my father?"

"You dine with *that* traitor every night."

She let out a long breath through her nostrils. "This isn't easy for me, you know."

Avi massaged his hands, working out the tension from the climb. "You're eating in luxury. What could be so hard? The only threat is the Adept, so listen. The Adept is—"

"I can handle the Adept. After all, what I do isn't so hard."

Avi blinked. "Asrah, don't be like that."

She gave him an incredulous look. "Do you hear yourself? In one breath you disparage me, then with the next you try to tell me how to do my job."

"I just want to help. I am *trained* for this sort of thing, you know."

"You're trained to stick knives into people and skulk around the dark. *I* am trained for the court."

"You're trained to be someone's wife."

Asrah darkened. "Someone's wife. Well, I'm not yours, and I never will be. I thought we had made that abundantly clear to one another. So stop treating this like we are anything but what we are, or leave. I can handle an Adept—we don't all need swords to solve our problems. "

Avi tried to swallow around the knot in his throat. "Fine," he muttered. "Sorry to have bothered you, *your highness*." He tossed a finger-sized scroll tied with a string onto her bed. "That's what Crow wants you to find out. But I'm sure he wouldn't mind if instead you just found out how she does her hair or what her favorite perfumes are."

She turned her back and went to pick up the scroll. "Out of my chambers."

He hadn't said another word as he slipped outside.

The touch of small fingers pulled him back to the present.

Avi slapped the hand away from his coin purse. A little boy scurried away, bumping into people and drawing curses as he went.

On another day, Avi might have pulled the urchin aside and given him some tips on how better to manipulate his fingers to avoid detection. He also would have given him a stern talking to on only stealing from Imperials or Revolutionaries. He could steal from his own people when there wasn't an occupation—for now, they had a common enemy.

He found himself walking with a deep scowl. A common enemy—the Adept was a common enemy. Still, that hadn't been enough to keep him from bungling things with Asrah.

Well, fine—if tonight was supposed to be a night away from the fight for him, he could just spend the time at the tavern, like he used to before everything went sideways in this city. The Adept could eat a fine meal with the usurper and Asrah while he played shells and nursed a beer. Let the knives rest for one night.

The Singing Owl was less crowded than usual. Avi guessed it was the procession keeping people busy. That was fine by him; he'd rather not put up with the usual din of the evening rush for a while longer.

He slid into a chair, and almost immediately, someone was at the table.

"Is this seat open?" asked the man, in accented but capable Talynisti. He spoke it like a merchant, but he looked more solidly built than a trader. Hired guard, perhaps, in town while his employer handled exchanges and contracts.

Well, he wasn't dressed like an Imperial, so that was fine by him.

Avi motioned to the seat. "I'm not waiting for anyone else, so it's yours."

The stranger nodded gratefully and eased his way into the seat, groaning softly.

Avi smirked. "You look far too young to be making sounds like that."

The man flashed a charming smile. "Hard traveling, lately."

"Where are you from?" Avi began setting up the table for a game of shells. "You know how to play?"

"Karella originally, and yes."

"Damn—was hoping I could take you in for a few rounds."

The Karellan laughed. "Who knows—luck of the sands, eh?"

Avi snorted. "Whoever told you there's any luck in Talynis was trying to con you."

"You've had a hard time of things lately?"

Avi's smile wavered just a smidge, but he kept his cheer up. "In some ways, yes. Other ways are good. New friends, hardships with...old friends."

A disarming, too-knowing smile. "Friends or a woman?"

Avi looked up from the game pieces.

The man shrugged. "In Karella, we know two things—women and wine."

"I thought the islands are famed for philosophy."

He waved it off. "An invention by men who could find neither."

"Fair enough. First round, I deal?"

"Go ahead."

They went on like that, casting shells, placing bets. Nothing too grand or extravagant. It occurred to Avi that the relic strapped under his clothes would probably be worth more than everyone put together in this tavern would earn in half a decade, maybe more. Could you even put a price on something like that?

"So tell me about this woman. What's the problem?"

Avi shrugged. "She thinks I'm being too protective."

"Hm. I know another woman like that."

"Your wife?"

A bark of laughter. "Gods no, I wouldn't survive her. A business associate. I do have someone but...well, that's a complicated story."

Avi threw another hand of shells, cursed at the result. "They often are, aren't they?"

"Women? Like I said, philosophy was invented by men who—"

"No, stories. Women too, though."

"Well, it's not too complicated in my case; just the fact that she's married already."

"Sorry to hear that."

The Karellan shrugged it off. "I haven't been to the archipelago in a long time. I hope she's happy. Maybe my absence makes her happier."

"You don't think she misses you?"

"I imagine her husband would not be pleased with such a thing."

Avi smirked. "You could kill him."

To his surprise, the man chuckled. "Oh, I could."

The Talynisti blinked. He had heard Karellans were...soft. Stag only seemed to confirm that impression, though Crow had assured him the man wasn't completely worthless with a sword.

"Are you...?" Avi trailed off.

"A soldier?" supplied the man. "In a sense. I work for hire."

"Ah."

The mercenary grinned. "I've gotten used to that sort of reaction. Especially here, people seem to find it particularly distasteful."

Avi leaned back, ignoring the game. He took a closer look at the man now. Yes—he could see scars lining his hands, his arms. His eyes had a perpetual squint from untold days under bright suns. His arms were strong, his shoulders set.

"And are you working now?"

"Not *right* now. I have the night off. But yes, I'm on contract."

"I see." Avi glanced at Zebon the barkeep, who seemed to be going about his business with typical hustle and bustle.

The Karellan laughed, leaned one elbow on the table. "I'm just here for some fun, friend. No names, no allegiances. You've probably guessed I'm attached to the Empire."

"Nothing wrong with that," Avi muttered. It wasn't that he felt intimidated—it was that he had never failed to read someone like this. The way this mercenary had so easily masked cues he was a warrior. It was something—well, it was something *Avi* did.

The man winked. "You're a bad liar, kid. That's a good thing, by the way —reminds me of that business associate of mine. I won't ask who you're backing here or what you think of the occupation. I'm a good enough liar, but I'd prefer I not have to, eh? Just in case someone important asks me what I did tonight. This was just a night of throwing shells with a new friend."

"A new friend," echoed Avi, voice low.

"Exactly." The mercenary stood up, placing a few coins on the edge of the table. "I was going to lose this round—only fair I pay up."

Avi cut his eyes from the man to the money. He picked them up, held his fist out. "We'll finish this some other time, gods willing."

Another half-smile. "Gods willing." He took his coins back and left.

Avi did not wait long before he got up to follow.

Maybe he wasn't the best of liars, but there were other sorts of deception. Soldiers from the western lands rarely appreciated the significance of guerrilla warfare. They saw it as underhanded or cowardly.

The Talynisti were not like that—they understood that just as the lion challenged his foe openly, so the fox needed to be cunning. The gods set all sorts of creatures in the world as models for men to learn from.

And Avi had learned well.

The streets were clearing out, which was both a blessing and a curse. It made it easier to make his way, but it also meant that if his quarry looked back, Avi would be more easily identifiable.

Thankfully, Avi did not need to stay right behind him. The man was tall, easy to follow at a distance. Avi slipped through an alley, getting onto a parallel street. He moved at a fast lope, eating up ground. Occasionally, through the gaps between buildings, he caught a glimpse of the man.

He didn't want to kill him; the man was simply doing a job. There was nothing personal about that. Avi just wanted to find out more about him. Asrah wasn't the only person who would be collecting information tonight.

Sure enough, as Avi expected, the man began arcing toward the legion camp. Either he had a tent there, or he would be reporting in for some sort of check-in. He said that tonight had been a break for him, but that could have been false. The legion and Revolutionary faction certainly knew there were Loyalists still embedded in the city—there were only so many dead officers you could come across without drawing such a conclusion.

The *Nihilo* Blade strapped to his side felt heavier than normal as he stalked through the evening streets. Maybe this man had something to do with the Adept who had recently arrived. The Empire controlled almost every relic in the world—maybe they were putting out feelers to try to track down the man who had killed their last Adept, the ice-maker.

You're getting ahead of yourself, Avi thought, slowing his pace.

What were the chances of that, really? Crow always said that assumptions were the poison of most spies and guerrilla operatives. You got so far down into the weeds of your intuition that it left you blind to what was right in front of you.

The mercenary had spoken Talynisti. That was ample enough reason for the Empire to hire him.

No, Avi would do this carefully. He would ascertain this man's exact role for the legion, and then he would take it back to headquarters so everyone else could weigh in.

At least, that's what he would do if he could actually keep track of the Karellan.

One moment, he had been there. The next, gone. Avi wasn't stupid; he made his next moves carefully—cautious of any possible counter-tailing measures the Karellan had deployed. It was more than he would expect from a mercenary, but better to be cautious.

He ranged closer to the legion camp and barracks, but he caught no sight of the man. And he couldn't stay long, lest his face become familiar to the guards patrolling this part of the city.

So he went back, scouring the side streets for any sort of clue. He knocked at the back door of a few taverns, brothels—no one had seen the man tonight. Their stories stayed the same even after Avi offered a few jingling bits of silver.

All told, the pursuit left Avi fuming in the corner of an alleyway. He had gotten so lost in his own head that he had lost track of one of the tallest men in the city.

Muttering a few choice oaths under his breath, he began making his way to a meeting with Stag. They were going to check on one of Zageth's arms drops.

∾

THE ROYAL PALACE in Dav-maiir was broad and stout. Guards at the gate stood at attention with iron spears and swords at their belts. Their shields were round and wide, similar to the Karellan style.

As the chariot pulled up, a man approached from between the guards.

This would be Tamiq's personal scribe and aide. Reiva knew many scribes—they were the sort of men who never actually picked up anything heavier than a quill.

At least, that was what she had come to expect of scribes. But this man was built as broad as any of the guards on the ground with him, and he stood with calm assurance before her and Iscator.

She could not help but feel a bit proud seeing that.

She wished she could have staunched that emotion.

"*Ave Imperator*," began the scribe. "It is good to see you again, Legate."

"*Ave Imperator*, Katabh. May I introduce Adept Reiva, our newest arrival from the capital."

Katabh smiled, an old scar tugging at the edge of his upper lip. "Welcome to Dav-maiir, Adept Reiva. *Salm.*"

Peace. Welcome. He spoke Lazarran remarkably well—but he still greeted her like that. Like she was one of them.

Was she? Would Iscator approve of that, or find it suspicious?

It is important that they see you, she had said. Because she was an Adept, a Talynisti, or both?

"Thank you," she said flatly. "Your city is beautiful."

"I am glad to hear you are enjoying your welcome."

Reiva faintly returned the smile, her memory conjuring up the scents of blood and gore, the sounds of dying Talynisti men.

"Please come with me. His majesty is eager to host you for dinner."

Katabh led them through the gates, leaving behind their escort. Inside the compound wall was a stretch of lawn, with the edge of the royal gardens visible just around the palace's corner. It was an ostentatious display. Though the *maiir* itself did not want for water, there was always something of the desert in the Talynisti consciousness. Always the fear of thirst.

They left the lawn behind and stepped into the halls. As they passed guards in the hallway, Reiva felt eyes following her. That was normal for guards, she supposed, but they were still allies—assuming none of these men were Loyalists, which was not a guarantee.

More realistically, she guessed, was that they were simply wary of allowing an Imperial Adept near their king. Would any of them have known Havan, she wondered. What did they think of her unusual attire?

After leading them up the stairs, Katabh ushered them, at last, into the dining room. It was luxuriously furnished, with furs of all sorts of animals, domestic and exotic, decorating the walls. Dominating the room was a large, gold-accented couch. The king's, naturally, and the smaller one to the side was likely for the princess.

Katabh directed them to wait on their feet for the king, but he also kept a distance.

Reiva whispered to the legate, "What is he like?"

Iscator considered that for a bit. "Charming," she answered at last.

Tamiq's wife Dialli had died several years ago from an unexpected, and quite brutal, illness. Tamiq was still aggrieved about the matter, as he had yet to take another wife. Iscator had assigned an Intelligence officer to brief Reiva on all of this.

It was also the suspicion of Legion Intelligence that Tamiq had not remarried because he was alert to the possibility of further cementing his political union with Lazarra via marriage. He may have been a lonely widower, but he was still a pragmatist.

The princess was likely to be betrothed before long as well. That was a surprise to have not happened yet, given her age. Reiva wondered if Tamiq had been holding off on negotiating such an arrangement because he awaited the opportunities opened by Imperial provincialization.

Before the king entered, another pair of guards slipped into the room, did a perfunctory check behind the various curtains and beneath the tables (even though these were particularly low and afforded hardly any room for a would-be assassin to hide).

Still, with at least half the country trying to kill their king, it was an understandable precaution.

King Tamiq, when he finally arrived, had such an unavoidably regal bearing that it was impossible to imagine such a time when he had not been king. His beard was full, his hair fell in ringlets to his shoulders, with streaks of gray that suggested he was not too young to rule, but not so old as to seem frail or doddering. He did not wear a crown as it was not the Talynisti custom, but he did wear a golden belt set with four gemstones—a sapphire, an emerald, a ruby, and an onyx. One for every god. He was dressed in layered fabrics of blue and purple, and his skin bore a deep tan.

With athletic grace, he stepped across the room, nodding to his guards and Katabh, before coming to Reiva and the legate.

"Welcome," said the king, voice resonant and rich. "*Salm,* Legate Iscator and Adept Reiva. I had wished to meet you personally much sooner, but I understand you made a long journey in great haste. I hope you have had the time to find some rest since you arrived."

Reiva bobbed her head in a small bow. There would be no clasping of hands here, certainly no embracing. "Thank you, King Tamiq. I'm adjusting well to Dav-maiir. *Ave Imperator.*"

The king was observing Reiva openly, not in an ogling sense, but clearly intrigued by her presence. "*Ave Imperator*," he echoed. "May the gods on high bless his rule."

Iscator smiled warmly, "And yours as well, King Tamiq."

"My deepest thanks. Shall we be seated, then? My daughter should arrive before long."

Iscator subtly motioned for Reiva to wait until Tamiq was reclining on his couch. Then she sat, Reiva following her lead. Their couches were to the left side of the room, with cushions to rest their elbows on. Servants began to slip in, placing dishes on the low tables set before the couches. Again, Reiva and the legate waited for the king.

The king, however, was waiting for his daughter, and Reiva noted the tension in his neck and shoulders.

Reiva was not quite sure whether it was proper for her to address him first, but Iscator had not warned her against it.

"How goes the revolution?" she asked.

Tamiq blinked, pulled out of his thoughts. For a moment, Reiva worried she had offended him, but the man laughed heartily. "Right to the point with this one, hm? Very good." He plucked a flatbread from a dish and dipped it in oil. "The last Adept was far too...well, cold."

The king chuckled at his own joke. Iscator emulated his amusement, though her smile didn't quite reach the eyes. Havan had been attached to the Ninth Legion for quite some time, Reiva recalled.

"Well, since you ask," he went on, "my brother continues to raise a great clamor among the eastern cities, accusing me of illegitimate reign and so forth. Nothing will come of it—the people know he is a pretender to the throne, now that the priests are behind me."

Iscator shot her a warning look.

Politics, Reiva thought, was the worst sort of battlefield. A sword would always be a sword. You knew what to do with it, you knew to avoid one when your enemy came swinging.

In politics, however, the slightest statement could be an ambush, the lightest jest a knife in the back. And she did not know enough to be sure of her footing here.

So, she stuck with what she did know.

"The eastern cities, you say. Your brother has moved to Shugrith, as I understand it. I was born there."

A light entered Tamiq's eyes, part predatory and part curious. "You know, I am quite interested in hearing your story, Adept. Shugrith. A beautiful city. I almost envy my brother for being the one to take up residence there. Alas"—he shrugged with one shoulder—"this is the holy city of the sands."

Iscator motioned for a servant to pour some wine. "A great burden to bear, surely."

The king chuckled. "A burden indeed. Well, before long we will have secured Dav-maiir, and then we may turn our attention to Shugrith. Ah!"

The king lit up as his daughter slipped into the room.

Tamiq extended a hand to the princess. "You have kept us waiting, my dear."

Princess Asrah bowed to her father. "Forgive me, my lord. I was feeling ill for a moment."

Distress wrinkled the king's brow. "And you are well now?"

Asrah kept her eyes downcast. "Well as can be."

Tamiq eased visibly. "Good, good. Well, sit down. I was just hearing from the Adept about how she hails from Shugrith."

As the princess reclined on the couch nearest Reiva, Katabh signaled the servants to bring along the next round of courses.

"I don't know what I would do without this man," Tamiq remarked, extending his wine cup. Katabh bowed gratefully and then accepted the cup from the king's hand. He took a slow sip, then returned it.

For the briefest moment, all the guards seemed to hold their breath. Then, things eased slightly.

Katabh, Reiva realized, had just tested the cup for poison.

The danger cleared, Tamiq took a deep draught. He nodded in satisfaction. "Your legate brought me this cask when we first met. Some of the finest wine I have ever had the pleasure to enjoy."

"A gift," Iscator said, "from my Emperor, of course. I am merely the messenger."

"Well, any messenger who brings wine this excellent and soldiers this fearsome is always a welcome guest in my house."

Iscator accepted the remark with a bob of the head. Reiva marveled at how the legate had so easily put on this quasi-Talynisti manner. She was not submissive, by any means, but she was also not as outspoken as was her wont.

Vantelle had clearly made the right choice in sending the Ninth to Talynis. Reiva hoped that meant she had also made the right choice in sending her.

"Now tell me, how did it happen that you made your way from Shugrith to Lazarra? Were your family merchants?"

Reiva took a sip of the wine, tasting nothing. "No, your majesty. My father was a carpenter. He answered the call to arms when Lazarra last attacked Talynis. He did not survive that war."

Tamiq, to his credit, kept his composure quite well. "My condolences," he said evenly. "There were great losses in those days."

Princess Asrah had perked up. In fact, she seemed to be hanging on Reiva's every word.

"Yes, his death was hard for us. My mother and brother."

Tamiq hummed, taking another bite of bread, diplomatically allowing Reiva to offer as much detail as she chose.

Reiva chose to give as little as possible. "The short of it, your majesty, is that I was taken to Lazarra by slavers. That is where the Adept Corps discovered me and returned my freedom."

Tamiq's eyes narrowed. "*Slavers*, within my borders?"

"This was seven years ago."

"Still, if it happened then, it could happen again. It could still be happening. I assure you, once I have consolidated my reign, I will ensure that our laws are upheld in every corner of the kingdom. My brother failed you, Adept. You have my word that I will not allow that same failure to come upon another."

Reiva dipped her head. "A noble dream, king. But don't the prophets tell us wickedness can never be stamped out until the end of days?"

"Not fully," he conceded, "but I would be remiss in my calling as ruler of Talynis if I did not do my utmost to protect my people."

"At risk," Iscator said, "of the current trend of conversation spoiling our digestion, I must compliment the princess on her necklace. An engagement gift, perhaps?"

Asrah blushed, bowing her head in acceptance. "Thank you, Legate Iscator. Regrettably I am not yet betrothed, though. My father, quite charitably, has not yet been impressed by any suitors."

Iscator took another sip of wine—far more elegantly, Reiva noted, than how she drank when they had first met—and made a sound of approval. "Well, hopefully we will be rid of this conflict soon, and your father can turn his attentions from war to more pleasant topics."

The king scoffed. "You mistake me, Legate. War is eminently more pleasant than the thought of handing away my daughter."

As her legate and the king batted words back and forth, Reiva slipped a handful of pomegranate seeds into her mouth and subtly glanced toward Asrah.

The princess listened to her fate being discussed with absolute poise. They might as well have been speaking of the weather for how little she betrayed any effect it had on her.

Then she glanced back at Reiva. After a moment's eye contact, she offered a half-smile. "So," she said softly, so as not to be heard over the other conversation, "what is it like to be back in Talynis?"

Reiva shrugged as she reached for the dish again. "It's nice enough."

A sympathetic twinge touched her lips. "That bad?"

Reiva's hand stopped halfway to her mouth. She cast a quick look toward the king and Iscator. Then she swallowed another handful of the tangy seeds. "I never thought I'd be back. That sort of change is difficult."

Asrah nodded. "I see. Were you scared, when they took you? I would have been terrified."

Reiva found herself looking down at the extravagant carpet. "I was."

"But now you don't need to be scared anymore."

She frowned. "What do you mean?"

"Well, I've heard about what Adepts can do. If even half the stories are true, then I can hardly imagine you fearing any enemy."

Reiva took a slow sip of wine. "It changes things. I'm sure my experience in combat differs from the typical legionnaire's. But there is good reason why we esteem courage as one of the highest virtues. Fear is universal; the strength to overcome it is precious, worth more than the finest sword or strongest shield. A weapon that can never be taken from you."

"That is a beautiful way to look at it."

Reiva shrugged. "Nothing special about it. That's life as a warrior. I'm sure you have plenty of things to fear as a princess. Plenty of ways to display courage."

Asrah's face fell. "Mm, you are kind to say so. And...well, there is something. Not as a princess, but a woman of Talynis. I must admit, Adept, I am fearful of what you bring to my city."

Reiva carefully set her wine cup on her table. "Do tell, princess."

"There is talk that the legion may set up an image of the *Imperator* in the Temple. Just rumors perhaps, but such a thing haunts my dreams. The thought of how much bloodshed it might bring. My father tells me that our faith will be respected by the Empire, so you must forgive such worries on my part. A woman such as myself—my heart trembles at the slightest of things. But already, your Empire's banner hangs from the Temple wall. Some would call such a thing blasphemy."

"You would do well to avoid such people," Reiva whispered. "Some would call such talk dangerous."

"I am but a princess, Adept. Silly things catch my ear. I miss my cousins, you know, but soon as I say so, a dozen of my father's counselors and viziers are there to tell me of how fortunate I am that the gods saw my father's true quality. And indeed, fortunate am I to have a dozen men, far wiser than I, to remind me of such things. To remind me that my kin is in Shugrith and I am in Dav-maiir by the will of the gods. And nothing is more dear to my people —to *our* people—than our gods."

Reiva flexed her hand. The pomegranate seeds had stained her fingers red. She dipped them into a shallow washing basin.

"Yes, princess. I understand. Undue violence is the last thing I want for Talynis."

Despite her efforts, the color refused to wash off.

YAROS GRINNED IN THE SHADOWS.

It was somewhat unfair really. This young Talynisti man could not have had any idea exactly what sort of person Yaros was. What sorts of skills he had.

He hadn't lied to him—he had been honest. Just a bit selective with what details he shared.

Even Reiva had no idea exactly what he was capable of. She had some suspicions certainly, but if she actually managed to figure it out on her own...well, that would be quite a feat.

He would not have been surprised, to be fair. The Adept was fiercely competent. She was also fiercely loyal to the Empire, which was one of many reasons why it was best to keep her in the dark about certain key details of his past.

If tonight's outing proved fruitful however, he might need to end up sharing some of that.

The man he had played shells with was plainly frustrated at his failure to keep up with Yaros. That led to him making mistakes. Yaros had to be wary that he did not get sloppy himself, relishing the ease with which he was able to tail the man.

He was a Loyalist, that was almost certain, but just a man on the streets? A warrior? He could have been one of the street blades—young men (and women, Yaros suspected, though Reiva doubted that was possible) who slipped knives between the ribs of legion officers and Revolutionary Guardsmen. The king had tried restricting public gatherings, where the killings were common, but the massed throngs who watched Reiva and the legate go through the streets showed about how well that strategy was going.

Yaros had thought he caught some hints that the man from the tavern was carrying a blade beneath his clothing, but that was not definitive evidence of anything. Plenty of men in Talynis carried weapons as a matter of course, in spite of the law. It would have been foolish to do otherwise.

The evening sky had darkened by the time his quarry arrived at his destination. Yaros wedged himself into the gap between two buildings, pulled out a bit of *naza* leaf and began chewing it. Earlier, when he had first shaken off the other man, he had thrown on an overcoat cut in the local style, as well as a headdress.

To the casual observer, Yaros would seem like any other Talynisti man looking for some peace and quiet under a night sky.

From the corner of his eye, he watched the man take up a position, waiting by the look of things. Yaros withdrew further. It occurred to him that he might find himself inadvertently pinned down if the man was here to meet some other folks, but he did not feel particularly worried.

Sure enough, after a few minutes, the man perked up. Yaros smiled as he chewed the leaf. Wait until Reiva heard—

He nearly swallowed the wad. Pulling as far out of sight as he could, he did his best to avoid choking like a short-nosed bull hound with a cold.

It's not him.

Yaros peeked back around the corner.

It's him.

Bafflement turned to amusement, then excitement.

"No luck in the desert, eh kid?"

Reiva approached her chambers, suppressing a heavy sigh. All night, the princess had been like that—saying the most innocuous, innocent things, but somehow always managing to twist a knife in her. And she found it almost impossible that it had not been intentional, at least partially.

Had she been sincere though? Was her goal simply to impress upon Reiva the severity of the Empire's interference in Talynis, or was she after something else? Was she testing Reiva's true loyalties?

She unlocked the door, frowning.

What true loyalties were there to test though? They were all on the same side, they were all—

Reiva jolted to a stop. "How the hell did you get in here?"

Yaros shrugged, sitting in her chair. "You forgot to lock the door."

"No, I didn't."

Another impish shrug. "You didn't."

She closed the door behind her. "I hope you have a good reason for this, Yaros. I'd hate to fire you after our partnership was going so well."

The mercenary smiled, spreading his hands. "Come on, boss, you could never let me go so soon. I'm a valuable tool in your arsenal—as I am about to demonstrate once again."

Crossing her arms, Reiva said, "I'm listening."

"I met a rather interesting young man earlier at a tavern. Loyalist, I'd guess."

"I'm sure there are thousands of young men like that in taverns right this moment."

"He tried to follow me after our game of shells, but I turned things around and ended up following him to a meeting."

Reiva put her fingers to her temple. Was that a headache coming on? "Picking your way into my room, tailing Loyalists...I hired you for your sword arm, Yaros."

"I come with a variety of skills for your use. And the meeting, you'll be interested to know, was with an arms dealer from Karella."

Her eyebrows shot up. *That* was something.

"You know him?"

Yaros grinned, teeth glinting in the darkness. "You could say that. His name is Theimos Atreion, but while I was waiting for you to get back, I went ahead and brought my description of Theimos to Legion Intelligence. Sure enough, they had a profile."

Reiva waited expectantly. When it became clear Yaros was not just going to spit it out, she rolled her eyes. "What did you find, Yaros?"

"He goes by Aleka Vasi here, a merchant specializing in textiles and ceramics, supposedly."

"Handy things to hide weapons inside."

"My thoughts exactly."

"Does our friend Theimos have a local office?"

"As a matter of fact, he does."

33

JUST BUSINESS

THE SENTENCE OF A LEGIONNAIRE, or Adept in this case, serving *qua paenitentia* was a curious one. To go into battle without a shield—the chief instrument and symbol of the legion's military strength.

A general of the Karellan Myrmidons once admonished his men, standing against impossible odds, facing certain death, "The whole of your country exists in the man at your side, behind your shield. Think of nothing but the man you guard with your shield, and you shall guard your wives, your sons, your daughters, your cities."

So why send a legionnaire into battle without a shield, and always at the front lines without regard to rank? Nothing impressed so severely upon the repentant legionnaire the significance of his failure to uphold Lazarran virtue. If he died, his blood atoned for him. If he survived the campaign, he had proven himself worthy of bearing the shield again.

In a strange way, serving *qua paenitentia* may have only bolstered the Lion's reputation though. Talk spread of the Adept who waded into war with both hands ablaze, stepping in front of the shield wall with abandon.

What was meant as a mark of shame begat inspiration for her allies and terror for our enemies.

Rumors spread that she had the right to take up the shield, but chose not to as a matter of faith and valor. I did nothing to dissuade such talk—and indeed, the lie became true.

—*The Memoirs of Flavia Iscator*

~

WITH A SMALL DETACHMENT of legionnaires on standby, Reiva and Yaros knocked on the door.

Yaros waited. A cool morning breeze drifted by.

No answer.

"May I?"

Reiva stepped back, waving him forward.

The mercenary took a short running start, then planted his foot right over the latch. The door flew open with a thundering crack.

Yaros already had his sword drawn. Reiva followed him in, shouting for anyone inside to surrender.

Five men were inside. Four seemed to be clients, while Theimos stood on the opposite side of the foyer, looking irritated and holding a sword up as though for inspection.

Said clients were armed on their own already and did not look inclined toward surrender.

With a roar, two of them rushed Yaros together.

The mercenary parried a stab for his ribs, throwing a kick for the other assailant's knee. The latter danced backward, and Yaros sent out a return thrust to the one he'd parried. His blade took the man in the throat. With a rasping gurgle, he went down.

Reiva leaped forward, intercepting the other with her own sword and hurling a cloud of embers at his face. Yelling in rage, clawing at his eyes, the man went down with a slash across the gut.

Abreast with Yaros, Reiva sidled forward, sword ready, hand crackling with fire.

Having seen their compatriots go down so quickly, the other two didn't look eager to jump into the fray. Their hesitation was answered by a raucous clatter from the back of the building, where the rest of the legionnaires had just stormed in. They fanned out, clearing rooms and closing off exits.

Reiva nodded toward the bodies on the ground. "Surrender." It was a simple word in Talynisti.

The two Loyalists glanced at one another.

They charged.

Even working without a shield, Reiva had years of drilling and combat experience that made her a force of destruction *before* she drew on her magic. And Yaros was, almost literally, worth his weight in gold as a warrior.

It was almost pitiful how easily the two of them brought the attackers down.

Which just left Theimos, still standing by his desk, holding the sword. Reiva could see it was Imperial by make—the same sort of gladius carried by every legionnaire in service.

The arms dealer was eyeing Yaros, though his gaze flitted back toward Reiva's mantle more than once.

"Give it up, Theimos," said Yaros, brandishing his blood-slicked blade. "You're smarter than those others, aren't you?"

The man grimaced, then threw down his sword. "Three hells, Yradas, it's just business."

Reiva shot a look at the mercenary. *Yradas?*

"Why in all the hells and heavens are you in Talynis of all places?" The man looked exasperated more than anything. You would hardly have believed he was surrounded by a dozen Imperial legionnaires and an Adept.

Yaros seemed unfazed. "Just business for me too."

"You're working for the Adept, then?" Theimos cast a bored glance over Reiva, as though the presence of one of the Emperor's arcane warriors had become a trifle to him in the last fifteen seconds. "You know, I could've sworn the Krypteia did you in. Placed bets on it, too."

Now Yaros looked insulted.

Reiva, for her part, felt startled—along with not a few of the legionnaires standing around, judging by their demeanors. She caught more than one uneasy glance between the soldiers.

The Krypteia was the fabled shadow league that practically ran Karella's underground. Even after years of rule, the Empire had not managed to fully bring them to heel. The current state of affairs was more like a business arrangement than genuine dominion. If anything, the Krypteia had only grown more independent with time.

Yaros returned her look with a disarming ease.

Well—it seemed it would be her turn to hand over some information after all this was over.

34

IMPOSSIBLE MARKINGS

IT IS TRITE, though necessary, to speak of the horrors of war. Just as terrible, but hardly acknowledged, are the horrors of indoctrination and propaganda. In the war of arms, I know the lay of the land. In the war of truth, how often have I felt the terror of a midnight fog bank bearing down on me, with nothing in my hands but a frail candlestick dribbling hot wax over my fingers.

—*The Memoirs of Flavia Iscator*

～

ALYAT HAD SENT a letter to Reiva immediately after Nuntius' death. It had been vague by necessity—you could never be sure who was reading the Imperial Post—but she would know there was danger about. And since she was a clever one, she'd doubtless connect it to the Order if anything happened to him.

He had also asked Demman, quartermaster of the Sanctum, whether he had any clue as to what a small bronze disc like the one Nuntius had could have signified. Demman was a reliable man who labored long and quietly in his workshop, and he was discreet in the extreme, which had made him a confidant for Alyat throughout his years as an Adept. He also had an almost obsessive and encyclopedic knowledge of all things metal from all over the world.

When Alyat described the disc, though, Demman had merely shaken his head. "Could be a dozen things—I'd need to see it or hear more about it." He frowned at a steel blade he was clutching in a pair of tongs. "Damn metal—something must have been wrong with the iron. Mines are having trouble again."

Alyat apologized for taking up Demman's time, then set to searching the Imperial Archives.

The Archives were a sprawling place, laden with countless texts—scrolls, clay tablets, bound volumes—constituting a veritable treasure trove of records, reports and all other varieties of information.

While there were constantly ongoing efforts to catalogue the Archives, much of the holdings had either come as part of sudden influxes (such as when the troves of some other library were taken and subsumed) or simply had been present from so long ago they had been forgotten or shuffled around, lost to record and recollection.

Navigating them, as such, was more of an art than a science—and one that Alyat was remarkably skilled at. He had a feel for what trails to chase down, when to branch off a path and follow some other hunch or rabbit trail. He also just had good luck, which was certainly a factor.

His first day had been fruitless—standard Imperial histories and such.

His second, he had found a few breadcrumbs, references to other texts that seemed they might be profitable.

On the third day, he finally hit upon something. It wasn't even a full document—just a scrap of parchment that had been tucked away inside an old set of military supply records.

The text was brief, but evocative:

Adept Bascia killed in engagement with three Gallian Adepts—Ice, Earth, Blood. All Bascia's armor easily recovered. Gallians seemed uninterested in spoils.

Three sentences, three surprises.

First, the report simply mentioned the existence of *three* Gallian Adepts with little fanfare. That was impossible. Now and then, one saw some sort of rogue Adept appear, but they didn't last for long. Without an arcane focus, magic killed the wielder—no exceptions. The strongest could hold out for a little, but hardly long enough to ever be an effective soldier. The timeline was a seconds to, maybe, a few minutes.

But that was where things only got stranger. For one, standard notation would have been to label the Gallians as *rogue Adepts*—either they would have appeared naturally, or they would have been turncoats who left the Sanctum. Why not clarify that? Why break from the standard jargon?

To Alyat, this was a clue that the document was old—*very* old.

He continued puzzling through the strange revelations. The dispatch listed the three Arts of the Gallian Adepts. *Fraja, Terra*—those two were common enough, even among the Sanctum's recruits from Gallia today...but the third. *Blood*, said the report. *Ars Sanguis*.

A sinking feeling hit Alyat's gut.

The Art of Blood was rare; its disciples...unusual. Theirs was the only Art that was not taught within the Sanctum. A child who showed an aptitude for *Sanguis* was taken to a separate location—where he was made into a Carnifex.

The ghost had mentioned a Carnifex. It must have been a coincidence, but...

Alyat moved on from the subject.

All Bascia's armor easily recovered. Gallians seemed uninterested in spoils.

Another divergence from standard language. While the legions always did their best to recover the equipment of fallen soldiers when possible, they took special care when an Adept died.

Not for the armor, though—armor was worth nothing compared to an Adept's focus. The things were priceless. Incredibly arduous and time intensive to craft, arcane focuses were the most valuable, essential artifacts of the Sanctum, more important even than relics. Without a focus, an Adept could not safely channel aether, could not wield their magic—could do nothing beyond the capacities of a particularly well-trained soldier. It was unthinkable—even if a low-ranking officer had written this message—that someone would not explicitly mention the focus.

He read the final line again. *Gallians seemed uninterested in spoils.*

This went back to the identity of these so-called Gallian Adepts. If they were rogue Adepts who had emerged outside the training and cultivation of the Sanctum, then they needed focuses. Only the Lazarran Empire understood the manner by which to create a focus—they had *invented* the damn things.

Alternatively, if the Gallians had been traitorous Adepts within the Sanctum, then they would have known how valuable Adept Bascia's focus was and would have taken the time to harvest it.

Alyat rubbed his forehead.

He took a moment to review the contents of the file he had found this in.

Most of these documents were troop records, but their provenance varied wildly. The most recent he found dated to around seventy years ago, but some seemed to stretch as far back as before the Dark Days, making mention of various offices and political positions that had ceased to exist when the Republic collapsed.

He took the time to examine the dispatch again.

The writing was certainly faded. Ink lettering, neat, without flourish. If an Adept had written it, it almost certainly would have been in the Sanctum's own records, so that suggested to Alyat that the author had been an officer in the main body of the legions, likely whoever Adept Bascia had been attached to.

Alyat tucked the slip of parchment inside his cloak—checking that no one's eyes were upon him—before stepping away to continue his search. Later, he would visit the Sanctum archives and search for mention of this Bascia. Once he had Bascia's records, he would be able to decipher when this had been written.

So Alyat continued to search. An hour slipped by, then another, before he hit upon another nugget of information.

It was a map. An old map, drawn up by a Lazarran cartographer. It was even dated, so Alyat could situate it within his knowledge of history.

The map had been made about a hundred years before the collapse of the Republic. It focused on Lazarra, and as such it outlined the various provinces that had once been discrete territories. While these places still carried their names today, and many still had local governances along the same borders, at the time this map had been drawn, they had been autonomous.

Because of that, Alyat's first guess had been that the cartographer was interested in Lazarran political geography at the time. The closer he looked, however, the stranger he realized this map was.

Indeed, someone taking a cursory look likely would have thought nothing of it. Even someone distinctly interested in reading it would likely have missed the discrepancies—but Alyat had spent years poring over charts of Lazarra from all stages in the land's history.

The borders did not map precisely to what was to be expected. Ordinarily, that could be excused—sometimes borders shifted or records could be slightly off. But as Alyat examined the map, he realized the borders had been drawn *twice*. Once that aligned with the expected lines, and another time that did not.

He had to look closely to see hints of the 'correct' lines—they had been made with a very fine nib. The 'incorrect' lines though—those were thick and dark, clearly labeled.

That was one side. The reverse depicted the whole world west of the Spine—from Lazarra to Zarush and Talynis. The eastern lands were vague, hardly more than splotches, but the cartographer had gotten the locations of the capital cities right.

And there Alyat noticed the other vagary.

This cartographer had used an odd symbol to denote capital cities. At first he had dismissed it as an artifact of the time, or perhaps some unusual style, but as he scrutinized the realm map, Alyat's curiosity—and his discomfort—only grew.

Lazarra was marked with the symbol: two parallel lines struck through by a third line. The same symbol was over the capital of Karella. As with Hyrgallia, Gallia, and so forth. It marked Dav-maiir, where Reiva was right now.

But the symbol *also* appeared in the middle of nowhere—or so it seemed to Alyat. It popped up in a stretch of land currently occupied by Parthavan renegades. It appeared along the northern coast, again far away from any major populations he was aware of.

Most puzzlingly, it appeared in the Gray Wastes in the northeast, and it appeared in the middle of the Great Sea.

Alyat could have perhaps excused the others. Maybe there had been some burgeoning urban centers in those locations a long time ago—though that seemed a strange thing in Parthava. But the middle of the Great Sea? The *Gray Wastes*?

He rubbed his eyes, but the map still bore those impossible markings.

The symbol key was faded, its lines not as bold as those of the map itself, but Alyat peered at it still. By illuminating it from behind with a stream of light from his fingertip, he was able to get a better sense of what the writing may have once been.

The unusual symbol—the two lines with a third intersecting them—it did not mean 'city.' Just as he had suspected, it pointed to something else— something that just so happened to coincide with cities in many cases. Instead, it marked the location of...

Alyat frowned. He did not know that word.

He racked his brain. He had learned Lazarran young, but sometimes he still found gaps, particularly when dealing with old texts.

Together. He could make out that much of the word; it was a prefix still in use today. But the rest of it? It might have been a word for road. That was feasible. Crossroads?

He felt a brief surge of satisfaction, thinking the mystery solved—until he realized the map also identified where major roads joined and separated.

The Northlander huffed, rubbing his forehead.

A place where things come together...what else to call such a thing?

This he couldn't sneak out as easily as that smaller scrap of paper, so he took a moment to commit to memory the symbol and where it had been located. He could work on this with a map of his own later—something more detailed than this old thing.

After returning the map to its place of rest, Alyat stood up to stretch, letting out a long sigh.

It would have been late by now. He wasn't as young as he had once been, and he still had some reports to examine and sign off on. The position of overseeing recruitment efforts for the Sanctum was important, and it came with a great deal of respect, but it was also a brutal one. Much like searching for sources in the Archives, tracking down potential Adepts was more art than science.

Countless predecessors in his position had speculated whether some deeper natural law or order governed the births of prospective Adepts. Certainly, some years more had come to the Sanctum from Gallia and Hyrgallia, others Karella had an impressive showing—but no precise pattern had yet been deciphered. Specific regions of the world bore particular disciplines with greater probability, but reasons as to why were anyone's guess.

There had been a few Adepts in his position who had developed an astonishing instinct for the shifting tides. They would direct attention to Aspagne, and sure enough, the next few years would show a great harvest from there. Then the flow would taper off, and they would cast their eyes eastward, northward.

Others were not so fortunate, and in such years the Sanctum suffered from a dearth of candidates. As it was, so few made it through the process that they needed as many as possible if they were to keep up with need.

There was the one great weakness to the Empire's reliance on their Adepts. If the influx slowed to a trickle, as had happened at certain points in the past, then their enemies stood a far greater chance at resisting, or even at throwing off the shackles of Imperial rule. It had taken centuries for the Empire to expand to the extent it had for that very reason. Now Lazarra was the only great Empire still standing—both Karella and Zarush had fallen to pieces in their own ways—but the failed campaign to Talynis ten years ago had set many people on edge.

Alyat was under-target for Initiates, so far. Not by a catastrophic amount, but still uncomfortably so. As he made his way out from the Archives, he decided to spend the next few hours in the Sanctum's libraries. He could take some time to investigate Adept Bascia, but perhaps he could also make some progress on his recruitment issue as well.

While such thoughts tumbled through his brain, he missed the person approaching him from behind.

"Adept!"

Alyat spun, acutely aware of his sword and the surrounding aether.

Startled, the young archivist hopped a step back. "Oh! My apologies, Adept," she said, bowing her head. "I didn't mean to startle you."

Alyat blinked, feeling a sudden wave of annoyance at himself. How many spies had he sussed out purely by how guilty they had behaved? People were terrible at keeping secrets, if you knew what to look for.

"Not a problem," he said, deliberately relaxing his features and posture. "Is something the matter?"

The attendant brightened. She was pretty, Alyat noted. She easily could have gotten herself a job somewhere more exciting than the Archives.

She offered something, holding it in both hands. "I believe you dropped this."

Alyat accepted it, peering at it with bemusement. If not for years of experience, he doubted he could have kept his face so calm.

The parchment. The dispatch mentioning Adept Bascia.

Alyat smiled at the attendant. "Ah, thank you. Some notes I took down— can't trust the mind as well at my age, I'm afraid."

The young lady said something appropriately deferent, then shuffled off, the tails of her junior archivist's robes sliding along the floor.

All the way back to the Sanctum, Alyat focused on breathing, letting his heart still.

Nothing will come of it, he assured himself again and again.

He made his way back to his office first, taking care to secrete the parchment somewhere out of sight. Then he took down some notes on the map, before it faded too far from memory.

His eyes were straining by now, so he channeled a measure of aether to ease them.

He longed to just end the night there and return to his work in the morning, but there were too many mysteries, too many leads to pursue.

Adept Bascia...

A tapping at the window.

Alyat whirled on the sound, casting a beam of light.

The wooden covering was shut. Slowly, Alyat made his way, drawing his sword in his other hand.

In one rapid motion, he pulled open the covering and brought up his light.

A raven squawked at him, flapping away and screeching as the light blazed in its beady eyes.

Alyat sighed, letting his shoulders droop.

It had been too long since he snuck around like this. Things were getting to his head.

He took a moment to peer out the window—he had a view of the central courtyard—and then he battened it shut again.

He decided to leave searching the Sanctum's libraries for another day. No need to work with frayed nerves and risk a mistake.

Before he slept, he slipped a dagger under his pillow.

35

THE WRATH OF RACHIBRAS

I WALKED atop the vault of heaven, and there I heard one spirit say to another, 'By what device shall we snare men to labor for us?'

And the second answered, 'Do not enslave men to yourself, lest you also find yourself enslaved to them.'

—*Book of the Nameless Prophet*

～

REIVA SCANNED Alyat's letter a second time. It was cryptic, vague—but he was clearly agitated by whatever he was discovering in his research.

He had taught her a simple system of codes for their correspondence— the first letter of the second word after the greeting always indicated something. If it started with a *P*, then everything was all right. A *B* meant he was under duress, possibly being forced to write against his will.

This message, the signal character was a *J*. It meant there was danger afoot, but of an uncertain character.

Well, as long as Alyat was still sending letters, she could count on having someone in her corner back in the Empire. He had also noted that the Sanctum was evidently pleased with her efforts in Talynis, given the reports they had received from the legate.

The pressure was on though, because word had come down from Iscator that Vantelle herself was due to arrive in Dav-maiir before long. The praetor intended to evaluate the progress of the revolution (and the Adept she had chosen) with her own eyes.

All told, it added up to Reiva being rather tense in her interrogation of Theimos, the man known as *Stag* among the Vipers.

"Where are your compatriots?" she asked for the third time, leaning forward in the cramped room where the prisoner was held.

Theimos was inspecting his fingernails, frowning at the manacle clamping him to the table. "You may be the most deadly person in this city, Adept, but I see they did not train you to use your tongue as well as that sword."

"Do I have to draw my sword to make progress?"

Theimos smirked at that. "Physical threats. Always the same with the Empire."

The arms dealer cast a bemused glance toward Yaros, who was guarding the door. "You know," he said, "I'm not at all surprised you conned an Adept into hiring you—but I still want to hear how you made the crossing."

Leaning against the wall, Yaros snorted. "I paid your sister. She always loved to give me rides."

"Juvenile as always, Yradas." He gave Reiva a flat stare. "Do you have any idea who this man is? I know the Empire is rather lax in its standards when it comes to hiring soldiers, but surely you have some inkling of his background."

She did not, really, but that wasn't the point of this conversation. "I want to know who *you* are, Theimos, what *your* background is, and what brought *you* to Dav-maiir."

"You already know I am Theimos Atreion, you can ask him for all the sordid details about Karella, and of course war brought me here—just like all of us."

"When did you arrive?"

"You know," Theimos chirped, shifting in his seat, clanking the chain, "Yradas Letiades is a rather infamous name in certain circles across the islands."

Reiva's next frustrated comment died in her throat.

Letiades?

A satisfied glint shone in Theimos' eyes. "Good, so you are not entirely ignorant."

Damn it, Yaros, why couldn't we have talked this through before *questioning the only man in this city who knows you?*

"Rumors have placed our dear Yradas everywhere from crewing a Northlander raiding ship to marrying an Endric warrior princess."

"Too cold," said Yaros, "and I've no interest in women with more scars than me."

"Yes, you were always fragile in that sense."

"Guilty as charged."

Reiva could *hear* the smirk on Yaros' lips.

"As grateful as I am for your enlightening details about my employee's history," she sighed, "I expect you would rather give me what I'm asking for before my patience wears so thin I hand you over to the common soldiery. Their interrogations are less chatty, and many of them have lost brothers on the points of swords you provided to the Loyalists."

Theimos considered this. "I do business, Adept. At the moment, in arms, but not always. There is nothing personal about this to me."

"Another bona fide Karellan mercenary," mused Yaros.

"Quite so. But I need something out of this besides the hope that I will not be brutalized by your rank and file. I would prefer to avoid it, as you so keenly perceived, but I am not about to take a mediocre deal when something better is on the table."

Reiva leaned back, crossing her arms.

The man looked absolutely at ease. You would think he was having tea in his own home, until he shifted in his fruitless search for a more comfortable position and jangled the chain.

Either he was an excellent actor, or he legitimately had little fear of pain.

More questions to ask Yaros. At this rate, she might just need to threaten him with terminating their contract if he kept holding back.

"Let's deal then," she said. "You give us the names and locations of key Loyalist bases in the city—and any you are aware of outside the city—and I get you a writ of safe passage back to Karella."

Theimos smiled—and it was the first time he hadn't looked contemptuous doing it. "Now we're getting somewhere." The man perked up, seeming to come more alive as he leapt into negotiations. "I want that writ of safe passage to carry the legate's seal, as well as your own signature."

"I can arrange that."

"I'll also need an escort."

Reiva scoffed. "You're a criminal and military enemy of the Empire; you're lucky enough to get the safe passage."

"A writ is just a piece of paper—it won't do anything against bandits or pirates—of which there are many between here and the archipelago. I would be dead before I got halfway. Don't worry, I will gladly pay the legion fair compensation for its services once I am safely returned to the shores of my homeland."

Yaros piped up from his post at the door. "He doesn't need an escort, Reiva. He can handle himself, trust me."

Theimos answered that with a withering glare. "I am a soft man in my age, Yradas."

A snort. "If you're old, I'm ancient."

"If only you could see how old your son is."

The air changed, an unmistakable electric tension suffusing the room.

Reiva was too preoccupied with reading Yaros' posture to worry about the revelation. She would rather not hold him back—but the look in his eyes told her she might need to, lest Theimos die here and now.

But the mercenary eased, a slow breath escaping his nostrils. He still looked like a caged tiger, but there was a margin less murderous intent.

She could work with that.

"In the interest of ending this discussion before you are ripped limb from limb, Theimos, how about you agree to hand over the information, so I can leave with my man and get those papers sorted for you."

"Do I have your guarantee that nothing regarding my activity here in Talynis will find its way into the Imperial records? I wouldn't want one sour business venture to come back and haunt my family, you see."

"Your name will be stricken from any records we have from this campaign."

"And the *other* records."

Reiva held the man's eyes. "Now that's a tall order."

"I would not command such a price if my information were not worth its weight."

Reiva cast her eyes toward Yaros. Begrudgingly, the man nodded. "He's being honest. Probably."

"I always am when it comes to these things."

Reiva stewed over that for a bit. She hated that he was getting away with so much. She also did not have the authority—even as an Adept—to clear something from Legion Intelligence's black archives (and how the hell did a Karellan arms dealer even know about those?) That went all the way to the praetorian level, and she was not inclined to ask such a favor of Vantelle.

At last, she made up her mind. "I will take your request to the appropriate channels. You'll get a writ of safe passage and your name cleared from the formal records of the Ninth Legion. No escort promised, nor anything regarding your other request."

Theimos considered this, then nodded. "Acceptable terms. Shall I expect an army of scribes to descend upon me?"

"We've confiscated your ledgers. Is any of the information encoded in them?"

Theimos laughed. "This isn't my first time in a precarious situation, Adept. It's all between my ears—you'll need me alive if you want to find out even a single thing."

Reiva frowned. "I've already promised you the writ of safe passage. You'll be set free. No knife in the dark."

"Forgive me if I am not so quick to trust the Empire's word."

She stood. "Well, they won't be scribes. They'll be Legion Intelligence officers with a particular hatred of anything that obscures their scent for the truth. I would be forthright."

"A deal is a deal." He offered a seated bow, ignoring the indignity of his restraints.

Just as Reiva reached the door, he spoke up again.

"One more thing, Adept."

She turned, noted the self-satisfied look. It was the look she had come to recognize as his *I'm about to tell you something you'll hate* face.

"The Wolf. The man whose name you have no doubt heard whispered in every alley in Dav-maiir. He bears a unique hatred for you."

"The feeling is mutual," she said flatly. "He killed one of my fellow Adepts."

"No, this is different. He enjoyed killing the other one, of course, but that was all patriotism and militant passion. When he speaks of you, he seems to legitimately think you are a demon enfleshed." He smiled as he said it, as if he had been complimenting her hair.

"I could not say why—it might just be because you are Talynisti, and he finds your treachery abhorrent—but I would stay wary. Don't go off getting killed before you can get me my pardon and ticket out of here, eh? You Adepts do not have a particularly inspiring track record against him and that black blade."

Reiva barely resisted the urge to spit on the floor, but she had a feeling he would only relish the moment.

Instead, she simply turned and walked away. "Acknowledged."

What did make her turn back, however, was a sudden *thud*.

Yaros was gripping Theimos by the hair, the arms dealer's face red and rapidly bruising. There was blood on the table. Yaros followed up with a punch across the face, sending Theimos and his chair crashing to the floor.

Yaros heaved a breath, rubbing his knuckles.

She raised an eyebrow, but said nothing as he followed her out. Theimos watched, head on the ground, one eye swelling closed and blood trickling from his nose and mouth, with disturbing smugness.

Once the door was locked and they were on their way, Reiva said under her breath, "You didn't need to do that."

"That wasn't for you—but I can go back and give him another if you'd like."

"I think he would just enjoy it."

Yaros nodded gravely. "He would."

They walked in tense silence toward the barracks. The sun was setting, a blazing red ball against the open desert sky.

"I can't keep working with you if I don't know who you are, Yaros."

He held her eyes for a few moments. Then, in his typical manner, raised one shoulder in a shrug. "If it's so essential, you'll get what you want to know, boss. It will complicate our relationship."

"Everything about my life seems complicated these days."

"I suppose you hired me to help with those sorts of complications, didn't you?"

"You can't kill every sort of complication."

"Unfortunately. Meet me outside the camp later. We can talk away from all these ears."

She agreed, then set off. There were other things that still had to be handled today—patrols, preliminary investigations into Theimos' information, reports of banditry in the outer regions of the *maiir*.

All the while, Reiva could not help wondering exactly what she was getting herself into.

What had she learned about Yaros, just in the last day?

His real name was Yradas Letiades. That family was well known to the Empire—they were politicians largely, with a storied lineage in the Karellan archipelago. She had first heard of them from Alyat, if she was not mistaken. Warriors, kings, philosophers—the Letiades line had produced all sorts.

So why was Yaros working as a mercenary outside Karella, under an alias at that?

Theimos had expected that the Krypteia would kill him. That likely had something to do with it. Some sort of target painted on his back.

Perhaps he had even done something that merited that sort of end—a frightening thought if she was going to continue retaining him in her employ.

And he had a son, if Theimos was being honest. The way Yaros had reacted seemed to indicate that he had been.

Such thoughts swirled through her mind as she went about her tasks.

Everything after the interrogation was painfully boring in comparison—especially since she knew that at these very moments, Legion Intelligence was ascertaining hosts of critical strategic information from the man known as Stag.

She wondered if the Vipers would try to kill him for cooperating with the legion. Maybe that's why he had asked for an escort.

Then again, Yaros had insisted Stag would be capable of handling himself in the wild. Something about the man's demeanor throughout the interrogation—the calm, self-assured attitude he had throughout, even when threatened with violence—inclined her to believe that Yaros had been right.

Her heart beat a fast rhythm as she went to meet the mercenary. He was waiting outside the garrison with two horses. Without a word, they rode out from the legion camp as the sun sank below the horizon.

There was the risk of bandits, Loyalists, or wild animals—but Reiva was the Adept of Fire, and Yaros was...whatever he was. The only danger would be to anyone brash enough to try to challenge the two of them.

They followed a path that legion patrols often rode during the daytime, looping through the agricultural districts. Neither spoke. Eventually, they got to the drier reaches of the *maiir*. The air here was dustier and abrasive to the lungs.

It was then that Reiva's suspicions about where Yaros was headed were confirmed. Looming overhead was Har-Esh, the Mount of Fire. It was not a volcano; they did not have those in Talynis, so far as she knew. The mountain had been named for a moment of great religious significance for the Talynisti. Supposedly, this was the place where a shepherd had been met by the Four on High—the Worldfather, the Windmother, the Warrior, the Wanderer. The gods had appeared like blazing figures of light, instructing the shepherd in the ways of wisdom and truth that became the heart of the Talynisti religion.

It was deeply sacred—supposedly, anyone who set foot atop the summit would instantly be struck dead if they were not worthy.

Reiva wasn't sure what she thought of the gods of Talynis anymore. By Imperial doctrine, war determined whose god was mightier. If the Empire defeated a nation, that meant Arkhon had defeated the gods of their nation. That was all well and good—Lazarra made it part of their belief system that gods were incorporated as simply as nations were. The gods of Gallia were subject to Arkhon just as the Gallian people were subject to the Emperor. The Emperor, after all, was the divine child of Arkhon, and every subject was part of a grand relationship structure emanating from the throne.

If the gods of Talynis were real, then did that mean she was helping bring them to heel under Arkhon? But if Tamiq was right and *he* had the divine right to rule, then did that mean the gods wanted to be brought under Arkhon's dominion?

For a sacred mountain, Har-Esh was not too tall. The horses picked their way up the slopes with relative ease, the paths well-worn by tens of thousands of pilgrims' feet across the ages.

They stopped on an outcropping, the flickering lights of Dav-maiir in the distance. The legion bivouacs were clearly identifiable by the ring of braziers and cookfires dispersed throughout.

Reiva and Yaros tied their horses to stakes, then went to sit at the edge, feet dangling over the yawning drop.

She had climbed a mountain like this with her brother once—he had been scared to get near the edge. He was scared of many things.

'Promise me...'

Yaros had brought a wineskin, and Reiva held out her hand for it. Wordlessly, he passed it over. The wine was all right. Little more than sour grape juice, hardly fermented. But by a soldier's lot, sometimes that was all you got. Alyat had never permitted Reiva to entertain notions of superiority. Being an Adept came with privileges; letting those privileges go to your head was one of the fastest ways to a career cut short—whether by death or politics.

"So," she said at last, wiping her mouth. "You have a son."

He nodded, watching the torches atop the city wall move to and fro.

"What's his name?"

Yaros swallowed. His voice was hardly above a whisper. "I don't know."

"I'm sorry."

The waxing moon rode high above the desert, bright enough to cast shadows across the sands.

"Well, it was my fault."

Reiva shrugged. "Lots of things are people's fault—that doesn't mean you can't be sorry for them."

"Perhaps. What does it say about me that I'm a better mercenary than a father?"

"Do you intend to go back to him?"

"I've *intended* for a long time—but intentions are fickle things, boss."

"True enough." She took the wineskin for another pull. "I was under no delusion that I was hiring you for your morals. Now though, I'm not sure exactly what I *did* hire you for."

Yaros watched an eagle wheeling below their feet. Now and then, it would let out a piercing shriek, dive for some mouse or baby jackal. "Our terms still hold?"

She nodded.

Yaros leaned back on his hands, face toward the sky. His eyes took on a glassy look as memories welled up from within. "Yradas Letiades is the son of the current High Fist of the Krypteia. He tried to get out and was subsequently exiled from the archipelago. He did *not* stay away from the islands, got someone pregnant whom he should not have, and subsequently had a contract placed on his head."

The mercenary's head lolled toward Reiva, a sardonic grin on his face. "There are more sordid details, but I think I've bought something from you."

Reiva pulled up one leg, rested her cheek on her knee. Yaros' story—brief as it was—was certainly something. The son of the head of the Krypteia, that made him next in line to lead the most powerful assassin league in the known world—effectively the true ruler of Karella.

It was an ignominious tale, to be sure, but it made her story seem...well, less grand.

"I'm not anyone so important," she murmured. "My father's name was Qohl; he was a carpenter. He provided for my mother, my brother, and me. When I was little, the Empire's first Talynisti campaign swept into the country. All the able-bodied men of Shugrith were mustered. He came back to us in a litter, a terrible infection ravaging his veins."

Yaros' face did not betray anything as he listened. As a mercenary, as one of the Krypteia, such stories would have been common as copper to him.

"He didn't last long. In Talynis, the community provides for the widow and orphan. People loved my father. They wanted us to be okay, not to struggle."

She shrugged, turning to watch the moon. "But lots of people died in the war. Lots of mouths to feed. And our mother, she...wasn't the best with money. People started to tire of giving her coin, only to see us go hungry while she wasted it away on drink or honeyed cakes. So they started bringing us food, thinking that would solve the problem.

"She started walking to the other side of the city, just to find someone else she could sell the bread to and came home with enough booze to get her through another night. Every night, she'd get far enough gone that she told me and my brother how she wished we would die already, how she hated the way everyone looked at her. She hated my father for dying and hated him for putting us in her womb."

Yaros listened attentively, saying nothing. He did not look surprised or judgmental—he just listened. So Reiva continued speaking, words tumbling out that she had never shared with anyone, memories that had been locked away for years, only erupting in nightmares.

"One day, a caravan of Zarushan merchants came through Shugrith. It's illegal to enslave a fellow Talynisti, but Zarushans have no such compulsion, so long as things are done discreetly."

Reiva shrugged, a half-mad smile on her face, as if she could hardly believe her own story. "She sold me. The merchant gave her thirty silvers for me."

Yaros frowned. "For a slave?"

"I think she was drunk when she made the deal. Chained up in the caravan, I used to lie awake, imagining that when she came to her senses she would beat my brother out of anger."

She saw Yaros' next question forming, cut it off. "She never struck us while I was there. I don't think she had the will for it. Or the spine."

Yaros took this in. "So, how in all the hells did you get to the Empire?"

Reiva snorted, shaking her head. "Bad weather, of all things. There was a sandstorm that blocked the route back to Zarush, and rather than wait it out, the slaver decided to go west. He wanted some Parthavan horses, I think."

"Good horses," Yaros muttered.

"Indeed," she said, looking back at her mount. The creature was watching her with intelligent eyes. Horses, she had always thought, seemed far more clever than was proper.

"Well, he had good luck in Parthava, but he was hoping to get a better price for me in Lazarra, since we were halfway there by now. I think he also wanted to bring back a souvenir from the capital—something for his daughters."

"Is that so? What a family man."

Another pull from the wineskin. "Without question."

"And you ended up in the Lazarran slave market."

"Almost."

Yaros raised an eyebrow.

"All the stock must be inspected before it goes to the auction. Checked for illnesses, deformities...but what the slaver did not realize was the Empire screens all prospective slaves for magical aptitude."

Yaros scoffed, shaking his head. "Just like that?"

"An Adept passed an arcane focus over my head, and within the minute I was out of my chains and on my way to the Sanctum."

"The slaver must have been happy to have such a payday on his hands."

Reiva laughed—harder than she had been expecting to, harder than she had any reason to. "Oh, not at all. The Adept told him he could either hand me over as a gesture of goodwill, or he could take it up with the Adept Corps. By law in Lazarra I was immediately transferred to the guardianship of the Sanctum."

Yaros grinned incredulously. "So he brought you to Lazarra all the way"—he stretched a hand out to the east—"from Shugrith, only to find out he had given you an all-expense-paid trip to the Imperial capital."

"That he did."

Yaros snorted, taking the wineskin back. "*The gods laugh.*"

Reiva glanced over as he guzzled the sour drink. "I've heard that before."

"Hm?" He wiped his lips, and she saw that his teeth were stained. Hers probably were too. "Oh, it's from a play. Very popular in Karella in the summer. *The Wrath of Rachibras.* Standard fare—demigod hero goes to war, slaughters his enemies, loses the love of his life. In the final act, Rachibras climbs the mountain of the gods out of rage and spite. Along the way, he fends off attacks by eagles, hawks, crows—everything the gods can throw at him.

"Then, right as he crests the lip of the rock, the gods send a dove, and because Rachibras cannot fathom that this little puff of white can be any threat, he ignores it. At least, he ignores it right up until the puny thing pecks out his eyes."

Reiva frowned, keenly aware of how near to the summit they were, but she kept listening.

"So, at the end of the play, Rachibras is stumbling around the stage, blood streaming down his face like tears, and he roars out a hail of invectives and imprecations upon the gods, who stand all around him. He strikes out at them, but they dodge out of his way, turning it into a game. And the Chorus chants, *Before all the plans and purposes of men, the gods laugh, high in their heaven.*"

For a few moments, silence. Then, Reiva blurted out, "And this is a popular production?"

A strange smile crossed Yaros' lips. "Well, there is one more thing you have to understand. The actor who plays Rachibras is blindfolded for that final scene—he really does reel around like a madman, trying to strike one of the actors playing the gods."

Like an orator, the mercenary raised one arm toward the night sky, as though pontificating on some ancient philosophy or hidden lore. "And, from time to time, Rachibras succeeds in grabbing hold of one of the gods, and he wrests the deity from its place atop the mountain, pulling him or her bodily from the heavens and down to the mortal plane. If that happens, then the

Chorus sings, *Against all the power and ploys of the gods, men laugh, low upon the earth.*"

Reiva let that sink in. "So people come because they want to know how the play will end?"

"In part. It is a good story, all told."

"I'll have to see it someday."

Yaros chuckled. "I would say I'll take you, but I cannot set foot within the archipelago without risking my neck."

"I'm sure they put it on in the capital."

"Ah, it wouldn't be the same. You can't hurl Arkhon off the mount of the gods—they'd haul you away in chains."

Reiva frowned, feeling an impulse to defend the Empire, the Emperor.

Yaros caught on. "I understand why the Empire means so much to you. It gave you a new life—not just one far better than what you had here, but better than whatever would have awaited you as a slave. But, if I may ask this question not to the Adept of Fire, but merely to my employer, why all the loyalty? Why not treat it as nothing more than a job?"

She worked that over in her mind. In truth, she had been working it over for a very long time, but she still didn't quite have the full sense of it. "I suppose...that would be nice, if I could. Just get out, like how you got out of the Krypteia."

"Not the ideal parting of ways to say the least, but sure."

"But I still have Alyat, my mentor. I have Domi, a friend from the Sanctum. What do I have here? I lost my family."

"To the Empire."

She shrugged. "War is nothing personal. You're a mercenary, you should know that."

Yaros raised an eyebrow. "Mercenaries are universally despised because we don't treat war personally."

She rubbed her forehead. "I mean, when two countries go to war, there's nothing personal between the soldiers on the ground, you know? If Talynis and Zarush went to war—like they used to practically every year back in the old days—it's not because one man and the other particularly hate one another. Sure, there might be causes that each man holds dear to his heart, but Jashar in Dav-maiir and Kakshi from Zarush might just as easily end up sharing a drink in a tavern if they had met under different circumstances."

Yaros shrugged. "I see your point. But I think it ought to be personal and impersonal at once. Jashar and Kakshi ought not hate one another simply because fate had the ill will to place them on opposite sides of a war. Fair enough. But the two of them also ought to believe in their hearts that they are doing the right thing by fighting for their lands."

"Well of course—why would you fight for someone else's land?"

Yaros chuckled. "I don't know. Why don't you ask a mercenary?"

"You're not in this for coin though. That much is clear."

"Sure, sure. But I'm also not in it for anything noble."

Reiva shrugged. "Noble can be many things."

"Are *you* in this war for something noble?"

She leaned back, looking at the moon again. She searched for something, some grander motive, but the wine was working against her. "I don't want to die, Yaros. That's why I'm here. I screwed up and now my career is on the line, and possibly my life. I don't intend to let one foolish decision be my end."

Yaros waved the wineskin. "One thing we can certainly agree on."

The drink ran out not long after, so they untied their horses and set off down the mountain. Now and then, Reiva would cast a glance over her shoulder, peering at the star-backed silhouette of the summit, imagining the gleaming visages of the Four tracing her path.

The lights of Dav-maiir smoldered in the darkness before them. Their mounts' hoofbeats changed tune as the terrain changed from loose gravel to soil in that curious way known only to the *maiirs* of Talynis.

Reiva twitched the reins, coming abreast with Yaros. "What was her name?"

The mercenary's face was inscrutable. Reiva thought he was going to withhold from her, but then, in a voice hardly audible above the rustling desert wind, he said, "Deila."

"That's a nice name."

She thought that would be it, but Yaros had one more question before they reached the walls.

"While we were traveling here, especially once we entered the desert, sometimes you would say a name in your sleep. I didn't understand it, but now I think it's something like *Qohl*. Your father?"

She could have lied. It would have been easy to just say yes and forget about it.

But when you were on campaign, you needed to know you could trust someone, and trusting someone didn't come from *them*. It came from your own willingness to be honest and forthright, despite your own wishes to keep secret and buried all the dark things you bore.

"No." She felt like she was floating as she said it. Only Alyat had ever heard about this. "Similar, but no. Aviqohl."

It was a common formula in Talynisti. Yaros translated, "My father is Qohl." He blinked. "Your brother's name?"

She nodded. "He's dead now. Dead or a slave."

"How do you know?"

As the camp's gate loomed maw-like before them, the Adept shrugged. "I can't know for certain. But alone with our mother, once I was gone...there's not much else that could have happened to him."

36

A PRAETOR OF THE LAZARRAN EMPIRE

WERE THE CLUES THERE? Could I have cut off the head of the snake?
Yes. Yes. But I had my own plans. I had my own blindness.
I had my own weakness.
—*The Memoirs of Flavia Iscator*

～

HEADQUARTERS WAS A MADHOUSE, even though Avi and Mouse were the only two there.

In the wake of Stag's capture, everyone had gone to ground—pulling in from their assignments and battening down inside the place as though the whole damn Lazarran legion was on its way to lay siege.

Crow and Jackal had left moments ago to meet Zageth—they had a prearranged meeting with Ego's right-hand man, and they intended to raise the matter of Stag's capture.

Which left Avi here, poring over their map of the legion camp, trying to suss out where they might be holding Stag. Crow was certain that they would not kill him—not so soon, at least. He had valuable information, and they would do whatever they could—be it dealing, pleading, or torturing—to get ahold of whatever knowledge Stag might have of the Loyalist operations in the city.

And Stag knew quite a lot.

Avi rubbed his forehead, biting down on his lip. "What did that witness say she saw again?"

Mouse sighed, resting his knuckles on the table. Candles cast his flickering shadow across the map. "Wolf, calm yourself. A frantic mind only benefits our enemy."

"These are Lazarrans. For all we know, they've got his head through a noose—or worse."

He didn't have to say what *worse* was. Everyone in the world had stories of the infamous Lazarran method of capital punishment—the beam and nails. Men slit their own families' throats rather than risk such a fate befalling them.

Mouse tapped Avi's forehead with one big finger. He blinked in confusion, looking from his map to his comrade. "You are still panicked."

Avi scowled.

"One of us should have gone with them," Avi muttered.

Mouse leaned back into a creaking chair. "They can handle themselves." The Endric man's eyes flitted over Avi's contorted features. "You feel guilty."

Avi's hand twitched. *How the hell does he catch these things?*

"Tell me why. Guilt is a burden removed through speech."

He wanted to say nothing, not to this man who had no true allegiance to Talynis, who was here for his own gods' agenda.

But then something pressed in on Avi, an overwhelming urge to drop his guard. It was almost dizzying, and Avi leaned against the table. Without thinking, he began to speak. "I met a man last night in a tavern during the procession. A mercenary in the legion's employment. I tried to follow him after, but he got away. I met Stag right after."

Mouse stroked his beard. "And you think he followed you to your rendezvous with Stag."

"It's too convenient to be anything else."

The Endric warrior hummed, crossing his thickly corded arms. "Quite a coincidence, that would be. We shall have to set to work tracking this fellow down."

Avi found himself nodding. There was a plan. He could work with that. As long as there was a plan, then there was a chance to claw their way back from the brink.

Mouse was right. When Crow and Jackal came back, the four of them would put their heads together and—

The lock rattled. Mouse tensed. Avi was already reaching for his blade on instinct.

When the door opened, Jackal and Crow swept in, the former shutting and locking the door behind them. A sheen of sweat glistened on her forehead in the candlelight. Crow's wrinkled features were etched with deep lines in the tenebrous atmosphere, making him look like some sort of figure off a stage.

"What is it?" asked Avi, already on his feet.

Jackal's lips moved, as though a hundred different words were vying for the right to be most important.

Crow took a deep breath, head bowed. "Our timetable has been moved up." He looked up, and Avi saw an anxiety that had not been there since the morning the legion appeared on the horizon.

"The Lazarran praetor has entered Dav-maiir. Cassia Vantelle."

Mouse blinked. "So soon?"

"That's not all," Jackal managed at last. "Zageth says Ego is here too—ahead of schedule—and he has a mission for us."

"A demand," muttered Crow, almost ruefully.

Avi waited breathlessly—but somehow, he already knew what was going to be asked of them. The *Nihilo* Blade seemed to pull his attention like iron filings to a lodestone.

"Ego wishes to see the Lazarran praetor dead within the week, along with the Adept of Flame. And he wants it done in broad daylight. If we fail to carry this out, then he withdraws support of our endeavors."

The weight of that request filled the room, pressing in on every person. Avi felt more acutely than ever the empty space where Stag would typically stand.

"This is our test," Mouse mused, fiddling with one of the bands around his forearm. "This is how Ego determines whether he thinks we can bring down the usurper and the Imperials."

Avi clenched his fists. "Then we'll do it. We have no other choice."

Theimos lay in his cell, awake late into the night.

He ran through what he knew, categorizing what could be safe to release soon, and what would be better to hold off on for the sake of the others. He could still give them something of a chance even now that he was in the custody of the Empire.

From beyond his door, he heard the shuffle of the guard changing. For a brief moment, he would be vulnerable here in his cell. He was not exceptionally high priority—not high enough to mandate constant vigilance.

The thought occurred to him that the Vipers might take steps to silence him. It would be bold of them—striking right into the heart of the legion camp. If they could pull that off, they might as well sic Wolf onto the Talynisti Adept.

She was an intriguing one, that Adept. Attractive to be sure, but also entirely sublimated by the Imperial body. In Karella, people only acted like they favored the Empire. They still nursed their bruised egos, remembering the olden days when Karella ruled the sea and the lands touched by her waves.

Talynis, still, had never fallen. It would be quite a feat if the Lazarran Empire were to manage what no Karellan ruler ever had. Tame the sands. Bring the desert folk to heel. Theimos doubted that the nomads—the Mithallkiym, that was their name—would ever be subjugated, but they were a case all their own. Even when Talynis had been a vassal to the Immortal Empire of Zarush, long ago in bygone days, the Wanderers remained unbowed.

The sound of the new guard coming into place reached him, and he unwound just an inch. Not time to vie for his life just yet. He could put up quite a fight if things came to blows, but even a man of the Krypteia could only do so much.

He was musing on what he might leverage to attain an armed escort back to Karella, when he heard a key rattle in the lock.

In a flash, he was on his feet. A visitor this late at night...either they had forgotten to ask him something important earlier, or they had decided he was more trouble than he was worth and intended to do away with him here and now.

Either way, he liked to stand to receive guests—however fatal their tidings.

The person who stepped through the door, and summarily shut it, was no one he had ever seen. A uniformed woman, stately in her bearing, blonde hair cropped close, well on its way to turning silver. Her eyes were hard.

And pinned over heart, the golden eagle of a Lazarran praetor.

Theimos' mind raced. This would be, almost certainly, Cassia Vantelle, head of the Ninth and Tenth, superior to Flavia Iscator. Three hells—he hadn't even met the legate yet and here he was, face to face with a praetor.

All this flashed through his mind in a moment as the praetor regarded him with a cold, analytical gaze. This woman was famed across the world for her military exploits—she had climbed the ranks with exceptional ambition, beating out more experienced officers for promotion and crushing far better equipped and better experienced generals in battle. There was even talk among the Krypteia that Emperor Dioclete had already selected her as his successor.

Theimos decided to gamble with that—better to start things on his terms, if possible. "To what do I owe the pleasure of receiving none other than the Lazarran Empire's future lord?"

Vantelle, to her credit, was unfazed by the comment. Either she had dismissed it, or she was not the sort to let flattery get to her head.

She continued watching him, almost unnerving in her manner.

Theimos buried his perturbation. This sort of thing was a common tactic, he knew. An easy way to make your interlocutor uncomfortable, more willing to spill their guts.

He simply looked back, hands behind his back, a light smile resting on his lips.

He noted, in the corner of his eye, the knife strapped to the praetor's belt. He was confident he could disarm her if it came to it.

All that confidence, however, was dashed away with one sentence.

Vantelle brushed hair aside from her forehead. "Behind every door, a secret. Behind every man, a motive."

The world, for a moment, seemed to tilt. Theimos put out a hand to steady himself against the table. Had he really been sitting here just a few hours ago with the Adept?

Was he really speaking now, in this same cell, to the one known throughout the criminal underworld as Ego?

"Excuse me," he stuttered—hated himself for it, he never stuttered. "I am a bit caught off-guard."

A sardonic grin touched her lips. "I would be concerned if you were not."

He swallowed. The game...the game had changed. Irreparably. Unconscionably. All bets were off at this point.

A *praetor* of the Lazarran Empire?

"You were captured, Theimos. That is a wrinkle."

Hells take me.

He swallowed, suddenly acutely aware of how warm the room was. When did he start sweating? "Your...your excellency," he murmured, bowing as steadily as he could manage.

"Does the Adept know about Ego?"

Right to business then. If he had any chance left to save his life—it would be here. He had to prove he was not a complete failure, that Ego could still use him.

"Only in broad strokes, I assure you." He fidgeted with his collar, suddenly feeling that his throat was very, very exposed.

The praetor hummed. "Not entirely incompetent then."

Theimos had only survived in the Krypteia, and in business, by being able to split his mind. You had to predict where your opponent's blade was going at the same time you were planning your next move. You had to compare the trade routes to the climate cycles.

Every ounce of instinct and acumen he had at his disposal, he flung at the enigma before him.

The *Nihilo* Blade—that was a piece of the puzzle. They had known that the Empire controlled all known relics of such pedigree. So simple! It had come directly from the Empire's coffers.

Theimos had played both sides in plenty of deals before. You had to, if you intended to outlast empires—and his family had. What was Cassia Vantelle after?

What could Ego care so much about in Talynis? In Dav-maiir?

The woman continued to regard him with that flat stare—a predator evaluating whether the kill was worth the effort.

"I assure you, Praetor," he ventured, "we can continue to cooperate. I am nothing if not discreet."

"Certainly." She smiled. "I trust your family name, Theimos. I have no doubt that you will keep *this*"—she gestured between the two of them—"private. I have worked a very long time to develop this persona, as you can imagine. I would hate for all of that to go to waste."

"Absolutely, your excellency. Discretion is the lifeblood of House Atreion."

What the hell was that about another persona—who was real: the praetor, or Ego? Or were they both merely faces of some other, more removed person?

"I have instructions for you," she said.

Theimos could hardly keep from blowing out a sigh of relief.

"In your subsequent interrogations, hide any hint of where your compatriots' base is. That must be kept out of play as long as possible. I doubt the Adept—or Iscator—have the stomach to resort to torture, much as they might threaten you with it, so do not fret. Feel free to share anything else, so long as it is not particularly damaging to the cause. I am sure you are judicious enough to make such calls on your own."

"Your faith flatters me, your exce—"

"Do not be flattered by it. Only prove to me that it is not misplaced."

Vantelle stepped closer. She was close enough to gut him now, if she chose. He had given up any delusions of disarming her and making his escape. Even thinking such things seemed dangerous, a risk.

"There are forces moving the likes of which have not been seen in centuries. Forces beyond your comprehension." She leaned in, nearly nose to nose. He was keenly aware of just how tall the praetor was.

"Deviate from my will to the slightest degree, Theimos Atreion. Give me so much as a whiff of treachery from you. Go ahead—try it, and I will show you just how savage the Empire can be when someone stands between her and her aim."

With an iron grip, the praetor seized Theimos' wrist, clamping it with all the force of a vise. Her thumb drove into the soft hollow in his wrist, right where the nerve ran.

The pain was like having a red-hot poker jabbed through his arm.

"I understand, your excellency," he muttered, doing his best not to groan. He had never seen a crucifixion first hand—but he had heard enough stories from those who had to fear it.

And in that moment, he knew he would do anything this woman demanded of him. Betray the Vipers. Betray his family. His nation. His friends. Hell, even betray himself.

Anything was preferable to the agony of a Lazarran beam and half-foot nails.

Sometimes, losing your soul was preferable to losing your life.

Mercifully, the praetor at last released his wrist. Wincing, hissing, he stepped back. He didn't care if it showed weakness; he had already been proven the lesser here. Dogs knew when to show their throats to the pack leader. Humans, if they had any sense, were no different.

Vantelle turned to leave. "You have a great opportunity at your feet, Theimos. Do not forget that. Your name could go down throughout history, if you prove yourself in the time to come. Or it could be forever erased. You have my word on that."

With the clank of the door and a turning lock, Theimos was alone again.

He collapsed into a heap on the floor, sweating and panting. He felt like he had just come face to face with a demon from the underworld.

Maybe he had.

Head in his hands, he began running through his options. Always options—there was always something to be done...

Precious few, this time.

37

HEAVEN-BLESSED AND HELL-FEARED

CASSIA VANTELLE'S brilliance was matched only by her ruthless utilitarian drive. Show her a mountain and she would take it apart, stone by stone, and she would not flinch no matter how terrible the cost.

And somehow you loved her for it. You loved how she could compel you to believe the world really was as terrible as you feared, and the only way to survive was to match it for its horror.

At least, I did. Hearts of greater courage might have rejected her, but I did not. I could not, not in my youth.

Had I been stronger in the early days, perhaps I could have turned her course. By Talynis, though, it was too late, and for all my life I bear the weight of my failure.

—*The Memoirs of Flavia Iscator*

$\sim$

REIVA TYPICALLY WOKE early in the morning—so, when a frantic thumping came at her door, jolting her out of a rare, peaceful dream, she was first, annoyed. Second, worried.

A runner—an anxious, sweaty young man little more than sixteen—brought news that moved her from worried to fearful.

Praetor Vantelle had arrived last night ahead of schedule, and she was calling her first meeting right now.

Reiva thanked the runner and quickly set to dressing. She hesitated for a moment as to whether the occasion called for formal kit. She decided it would be safer to dress for field work. The praetor had sent her here to win a war—better to look like she was actually engaged in that business.

The sky was just about as dark as it had been when she returned to camp with Yaros. A pounding in her temple reminded her with every step how short on sleep she was, so she channeled a drip of aether to take away the edge.

The Flame of the *Ars Vulcana* was difficult to tame at the best of times. It constantly pushed for her to give in to anger, to passion. When she was tired, the voice of the Flame only grew stronger, her will against it weaker.

She prayed she would, at the least, manage to keep it together in front of Vantelle. Her life bore just as much risk from this woman's opinion as from the *Nihilo* Blade.

The guards around Iscator's command tent were unfamiliar. They were dressed in standard legion gear, but they held themselves with a certain assurance that only came from years of military service. Vantelle's personal guard. Elite soldiers, selected for tenacity, courage, and undying loyalty to the Emperor. Quite possibly, many of them had even guarded the Emperor at some point, or would in the future.

That was doubly likely if Cassia Vantelle became the next person to sit the Palatine Throne.

With a brief glance at Reiva's mantle, they admitted her with a nod. She swept in, hoping she looked well put together without looking like she had taken too much time getting ready.

No one was seated. With a quick visual sweep of the tent, Reiva recognized just about every key commanding officer in the Ninth. In the center, behind the legate's desk, stood Vantelle, commanding all attention, even when she was not the one speaking. All the energy in the tent coursed around her, like leaves floating along eddies in a stream.

Iscator was there with her optio, of course, plus the Ninth's head of intelligence and various prefects and senior captains—the men and women whose direction and manpower would push the Ninth to victory, inch by bloody inch.

Vantelle was listening to a report from one of those captains—Reiva could not place his name, to her panic—about the recent attacks from Loyalist agents. The praetor listened with unwavering attention, only looking away to give Reiva a brief nod.

That was good, wasn't it?

When the captain finished his report, Vantelle set him at ease with a wave. He saluted crisply. Reiva glimpsed a trickle of sweat down the back of his neck.

"Thank you, Captain. And thank you for joining us on such short notice, Adept Reiva." A gentle smile touched her features. "You're not late, by the way. I only just sent for you."

A knot in Reiva's gut loosened a bit, and she realized just how furiously her heart had been pounding. All she managed was a salute, unsure if she was expected to speak.

Iscator, Reiva noticed, was watching her very closely. The legate looked rather haggard herself. That was unnerving in its own right. Reiva took issue with some of Iscator's frivolities regarding dress regulations, but she had gotten used to them. Now it seemed Iscator had not slept much either, given the dark circles under her eyes and the slight hunch in her shoulders. Stray strands of hair frizzed from an uneven braid. And—gods above—had she misdone a clasp at her shoulder?

Reiva pursed her lips.

She's not just tired. She's nervous.

Reiva could not help but wonder when it last happened that Iscator was not the most powerful person in the room. What sort of relationship did the legate have with her praetor?

Vantelle seemed to be contemplating something, then clapped her hands once. It ought to have been a clap of thunder for how still and focused it made those present.

"I am satisfied with the progress here. Mostly."

At that last word, Iscator went rigid as an iron rod.

"However, the continued resistance by Loyalist forces within the city remains a nuisance, and one that proves our fight here has not sufficiently demonstrated the might of the Empire."

There was a brief pause. No one dared say anything.

"In order to remedy this, I want a task force organized immediately. A more direct show of strength is needed. Select and round up two hundred individuals of import in the city. Anyone known or reasonably suspected to have ties to the Loyalists. Start with who we know for certain. Any relatives of the royal family, even if distant, will work as well, so long as they have not been unanimously enthusiastic regarding the ascension of King Tamiq."

Everyone, somehow, knew what was coming next. Executions, of course —but this was not anyone giving the orders.

This was Cassia Vantelle. The architect of a half-dozen legendary engagements, any one of which would have assured her recognition as a military genius.

Half-measures were not in her vocabulary.

"The crucifixions will be performed two days hence in front of the southern gate. Public viewing—Captain Ezail, you will be responsible for security and crowd control. Does this present a problem?"

For a moment, everyone was quiet.

Reiva felt something hitch in her throat, waiting for someone to say something.

Surely, there were people present who were uncomfortable with that—even opposed to it. The Ninth had a reputation, Alyat had told her, for being relatively lenient with enemies as far as things went in the legions.

But of course, this was a different sort of war. And this was their praetor—they might as well defy the Emperor himself, so high was her rank and grand her authority.

And Reiva's place in the Empire, her very life, was hanging by a thread. A thread this woman had the power either to cut or pull her to safety by.

She swallowed. She would say nothing. Could say nothing.

And neither could anyone else.

"With all due respect, my praetor, this seems excessive."

Anyone but Flavia Iscator.

Reiva's eyes snapped up.

The legate might as well have just told Vantelle to kiss a horse's ass for how everyone was looking at her. Wide-eyed. Bewildered. Unsure if this was about to have ramifications for *their* careers.

Only Vantelle seemed unaffected. "Excessive." She drew the word out like it was a foreign term, unfamiliar on her lips. "Explain, Flavia."

Flavia. Not *Legate*, or even *Iscator*. Just Flavia. That could have been intimacy, familiarity. It could also be a reminder of just how vast the difference in their power was—a single step that spanned the height of a mountain.

Iscator, resolute, squared her shoulders. "It is not without reason that crucifixions have been uncommon throughout the past century. They are distasteful. Brutal by design, effective to be sure—but not a few minds of import and authority in Lazarra have raised questions."

"Poets and sycophants," Vantelle said, waving it off. "Soft-bodied people who never served a proper term in the legions, never saw real war."

Iscator seemed to bite her tongue.

Ordinarily, Reiva had little interest in the squabbles of Lazarran philosophers, but even she knew that Lucian Sana, one of the greatest minds Lazarra had ever known, had written disparagingly of the practice.

But she didn't say anything about that—she just kept her eyes forward.

Vantelle rested her chin on her fist. "These Talynisti. They are not Karellans. They are not Gallians. We know how they fight—first hand, we know. No pitched battles. No lines drawn, no marches made to the killing field with heads held high and shields locked together. The Talynisti fight like a pack of wolves—a force of nature, acting on sheer killing instinct and the brutal belief that all the world hinges on whether it can defend its territory from the bear that has just crashed through the thicket."

The praetor took the time to look around, locking eyes with every person. These officers had lost subordinates, lost peers. Some of them would lose their own lives by the campaign's end.

"Lazarra cannot win this war the way we win others. Here, our reputation only emboldens the foe to greater feats of bravery. I heard this morning from Captain Ezail that he lost five men to a single Loyalist warrior. Captain Dorien, much the same—except that one could not even be brought down. She fled into the sands, and was lost to our trackers within the hour."

Reiva frowned. A female warrior with the Talynisti? That could only be the one called the Jackal. One of the Wolf's comrades, according to reports.

"We failed to conquer Talynis ten years ago," continued Vantelle. "It was a humiliation for us. For these people, it was confirmation that they are heaven-blessed and hell-feared. It does not matter how well Tamiq rules—however he may delude himself. It does not matter whether their lives are tenfold improved by obeisance to our Emperor. We can build aqueducts and arches and any number of roads, and it wouldn't matter a whit. All that matters to them is freedom, honor, pride. And unless we want to slaughter half this country bringing it to heel, unless we want to soak the sands red, then we must *break* the Loyalists. Before Malik can mount a full effort to take back Dav-maiir. Before Zarush or Endra decide they would rather join forces with Talynis now than face the Empire on their own a few years down the road."

Iscator, admirably, had held the praetor's gaze, which had come to rest singularly on her.

Vantelle adjusted the gold eagle pinned over her heart. Perfectly polished, perfectly straight and shining, the metal seemed almost liquid in the smoldering candlelight.

"They will learn to fear the Empire first, and then they will learn to love her."

Iscator scoffed. "This will cause a riot."

For the first time that morning, the praetor laughed. "I would not be so certain. Not once the people see what comes of such resistance. But if folly endures, then we will stamp it out. Reason will prevail, and with it—loyalty. Something you should have accomplished a long time ago, Flavia."

Iscator took the chastisement with a stoic face and a salute. "Forgive me, my praetor, but it would not be reason prevailing. Only fear."

"Sometimes fear is exactly what a mind needs to return it to its senses. Would you disagree?"

Iscator stiffened, almost imperceptibly. "No, my praetor."

For a moment, Reiva thought she felt something pass between them. Then it was gone.

With that, the meeting was adjourned. Vantelle spoke to Reiva briefly, telling her she would serve on one of the round-up crews later on. It was important, Vantelle said, that the city see her as part of this.

"You represent the power of the Empire and the strength of Talynis united in one person. The people will see how much better it is to throw their lot in with Tamiq rather than hold on to any dreams of Malik's return."

Reiva nodded evenly. "I live to serve the Emperor, praetor. Only direct me and I shall follow."

As she said it, she saw those first men she'd burned. Heard their screams.

Yes, she would follow. She'd long passed any chance of altering course—what was there to do but continue?

Vantelle seemed pleased by her response and dismissed her. As Reiva turned and left, she caught a brief, unreadable glance from Legate Iscator. She left the two women in the tent, wondering what would be said, and also not wanting to know.

REIVA KNUCKLED HER EYES, wishing she could drive a stake through her temple to vent the pressure that had been building up inside her skull. The aether channeling wasn't helping with the headache anymore. It wasn't just from fatigue—it was deeper than that.

She needed more than sleep. She needed peace.

She found herself going to the training grounds.

Hardly thinking, thinking too much, she grabbed a quarterstaff and began wailing on a training dummy. She didn't even bother taking off her armor.

The sun crested the horizon, shining in her face. That irritated her more.

It stoked the Flame.

You should have spoken up.

She rammed the butt of the staff into a dummy's gut, then spun it to crack it against the head.

Faces spun out of the cacophony inside her mind. People she had not thought about in years. Some dead, some possibly living. Talynisti, one and all.

She gripped the staff, whacked two more dummies in quick succession —gut, throat. She went for knees, ribs, nose—vulnerable places. With every hit, she imagined the satisfying crack and crunch of brittle bone.

All the while, she saw those faces in her mind's eye. Pleading, begging, wailing—held down by legionnaires, placed against rough-hewn beams, arms and legs tied down by ropes. Then, out came the nail and hammer.

Reiva swung the quarterstaff right for the dummy's head—*bam*—and it went flying.

She stood, huffing and sweating, in the middle of a field of havoc.

She had slipped outside time, her whole being engrossed in the act of striking, killing.

I should stop.

Out of the corner of her eye, she saw another cluster of training dummies, still upright.

Her fingers tightened on the staff. She took a step toward them, then halted. Fury coursed through her. She reached out to the aether.

Eyes narrowed, she focused on the foremost grouping of mannequins. There were three of them, fifteen feet away.

"Come on," she muttered to herself, thinking back to the guidance in Sharasthi's last letter. "You've been practicing."

Her heart was hammering in her chest. The sun was shining hot and bright. Sweat rolled down her back.

"Come on."

The quarterstaff trembled in her hands.

"*Burn.*"

BOOM!

The mannequins blew to pieces, shredded in a blink by a roaring explosion.

Reiva let out a heavy sigh, melting to her knees and leaning on the staff. She felt like passing out. Her soul strained under the weight of that technique; it was as if she had just torched a field.

And then she laughed, smiling like a madwoman.

She had practiced with her burgeoning skills, but she'd managed nothing like *that* yet. Passion and anger fueled her Flame—and she had finally gotten hold of enough anger to break through.

Her ears pricked. She also was not alone anymore. Some people had trickled in to the edges of the training field and were murmuring amongst themselves. As soon as Reiva's glare fell on them, they skittered away.

They would probably talk.

Let them. Why shouldn't they?

That was the Flame speaking. But why shouldn't she listen to the Flame? Why not let it drive her? Anger had let her pull off that burst of power. Surely, Adept Sharasthi would be impressed to hear how rapidly she was progressing.

"Wow, you really showed those practice dummies what for."

Reiva blinked, looking up, only to be brought up short by an outstretched hand holding a bowl of water.

Reiva blinked, looked at the soldier.

"Even Adepts need to drink, don't they?"

Reiva accepted the bowl, muttering her thanks. In seconds, she had drained it. "Thank you."

Then she put together the Scout's attire with the face.

"Charas."

She nodded, a wry smile on her lips. "Honored you would remember one so lowly as I."

"You were helpful." She waved the bowl. "Still are helpful. I'm sorry to have forgotten you for a moment."

"You seem to have a lot on your mind."

You have no idea.

She shrugged.

"Well, if your arms aren't completely tattered from that exercise, would you mind coming with me to the range?"

Reiva stared for a moment. "I'm no archer."

"That's good—no bad habits to unlearn." Charas set off walking.

"I'm exhausted," called Reiva. "I won't be any good."

Charas shrugged and kept going.

After a moment's hesitation, Reiva followed.

The air was warming now, and Reiva was cursing herself for leaving on her armor. Charas was dressed in a soft leather jerkin with riding trousers. Her hair was tied back in a simple braid. Even though she was not a legionnaire, Reiva recalled, Charas wasn't a foreign auxiliary—she was an Imperial citizen enlisted with the Scouts. That was remarkable—Lazarran citizenship was a coveted thing, exceptionally difficult for a foreigner to attain. It was impressive, too, that she spoke the Imperial tongue as well as she did.

The range had targets set up at twenty, forty, and sixty yards. Along the firing line, quivers filled with arrows were staked to the ground.

The Lazarrans were not known for their archers, their legions being heavy infantry first and foremost. Auxiliary units of archers were typically fielded in cooperation with the legionnaires, and what they lacked in skill, they made up for in sheer number. A company of soldiers all firing at a single target could make up for a lack of individual competence with the bow.

Parthavans were different. Their way of warfare was distinct for the unique brand of mounted archery they employed. The Empire had eventually brought Parthava into the fold through a surrender, in large part thanks to Adept Sharasthi's famed exploits in crippling the Parthavan Coalition's command structure.

Parthavan mounted archers were a coveted resource, but Charas had joined the Scouts as well—apparently building a close working relationship with Legate Iscator, who had had something to do with sponsoring the woman's bid for citizenship.

Charas retrieved a bow from the supply shed, stringing it in one smooth motion. She tested the draw weight. "Shouldn't be too hard for you to pull." With a guileless smile, she offered the weapon to Reiva.

Reiva snorted, accepting the weapon as her Flame flared. "I'll try not to break it."

The range was largely empty at the moment, something Reiva was glad for since she really was not confident in her archery skill. Still, she had learned the rudiments as part of her training. She took up position beside one of the quivers.

Charas indicated a target at the twenty-yard line. "Not too far, hm?"

Reiva nodded, nocking an arrow and drawing. She sighted the target, let fly.

The arrow went wide.

"You're hunching into it. Keep your shoulders level, chin high."

"Is there a reason for this?"

"Like I said—you have a lot on your mind. You're too angry."

Reiva frowned. "I need to be angry. It strengthens my magic."

"Sure, sure, and if you end up toasting a line of legionnaires in a blind rage, that's all part of the plan. This will help, trust me."

Reiva didn't see the point, but she nocked another arrow. She drew, only for Charas to touch her elbow.

"Your breathing is shallow. Deeper, more even."

Irritated, Reiva eased off the draw, took a longer breath.

She saw her grandmother gasping on the beam, suffocating under her own weight.

Reiva coughed, shook her head. Another breath—uneven, still.

"Whatever's distracting you, put it into the arrow."

The Adept turned from the target to Charas. "What?"

Tapping her temple, Charas said, "Whatever is in here, distracting you..." She tapped the arrowhead. "Put it in there."

Alyat used to say things like this—she had never worked well with it.

"Charas, I—"

"That's an order, Adept."

Reiva blinked. There was not a code or bylaw in the Empire that gave a Scout Lieutenant an ounce of authority over an Adept.

There was, however, the matter of who knew the bow better—and that was clear.

Reluctantly, Reiva took up her stance again.

"Now, whatever is haunting you, whatever the thing is that you cannot get out of your mind, no matter how hard you try—let it flow from your mind, down through your arms, and into the arrow."

Reiva took a breath. She had learned to direct her fire through vision exercises like this—pulling the aether into her body, then sending it outward. It was an easy step to apply the same imagery to this.

That horrific image appeared again—her grandmother dying on a Lazarran beam.

Never happened.

She imagined she was standing outside herself, watching herself. A fire raged in her mind, burning away all thought save this moment. The fire coursed down her spine, blazing a trail across bones and veins and nerves. It raced down her arms, swelling into a blazing star at the end of the arrow.

She drew, sighted, loosed.

The arrow struck the target with a heavy *thwack.*

And, to Reiva's surprise, she did not feel elated by that. No sense of pride. She just felt...lighter.

Charas clapped a hand on her shoulder. "Off-center, but not bad."

Reiva absently nodded. She kept staring at the arrow in the target. It seemed like it should be too heavy for the target to hold. She told herself it was just an arrow, but...

The Adept threw a suspicious glance at the archer. "How did you know that would help me?"

Charas shrugged. "I was born with a bow in my hand. Mother got sick—I sent it on an arrow. Brother died in war. Arrow. Boy I liked got engaged to my cousin? Arrow."

She slapped Reiva on the back. "All right, now another."

"I thought we would be done here."

"Oh, your psychological distress was the easy part. Your aim is still atrocious. Ancestors help me if I can't teach one of the Empire's finest warriors to shoot straight."

Reiva shook her head, smirking. "That may be a task beyond even you, O teacher."

She drew, sighted, fired.

The arrow went wide.

Reiva scoffed. "The wind took that one."

Charas cocked an eyebrow, smirking. "Then I guess you'll have to shoot with the wind, Adept."

38

LITTLE FLECKS OF RED

THE KARELLANS MADE a name for themselves as seekers of wisdom and disciples of truth. Indeed they are, but beneath the edifices of marble and the glittering expanse of the sea, they hide terrible things. I confess, more than once I found myself tempted to inquire into these matters, and more than once I nearly convinced myself it was a purely academic interest, purely intellectual.

I came so close to indulging this desire that I even made pilgrimage to the fabled Atelier of Deldus. Ascertaining its location required all manner of secret arts—both inherited and hired—and years of studying the attendant legends. All the while, I assured myself I sought it out of benign curiosity. Seduced by myths of men of iron and tales of fire that burns the sea, I approached the half-ruined threshold—a mere three steps ahead of me did it lie, just three steps after countless miles of travel above and below the earth.

But I have seen the rot that sets into men's souls when they sacrifice conscience for knowledge.

My fear remained greater than my intrigue. My fear saved me.
—*The Life and Wisdom of Simeon Binkhok As Told by Himself*

∾

THE FIRST ROUTE of inquiry Alyat pursued was the identity of Adept Bascia —that would be the quickest and easiest matter to sort out. The Sanctum kept a record of every Adept who had ever served the Empire, and so all he had to do was track down Bascia's name and he would be well on his way to finding when the man had lived and died.

Service records were organized by name primarily, then by time. Alyat started out by searching the *B* records from the earliest point, then began moving closer to the present.

Bescora, was a close name, as was Brasinne.

No Bascia, though.

He made another pass just to be certain, but it confirmed his initial findings. There was no record of an Adept Bascia.

Alyat's first theory was that someone had expunged the record, but then he thought again about the name. *Bascia.*

That was a Lazarran name. A *proper* Lazarran name, not a bastardized form of something foreign, which was how most Adepts christened themselves upon arrival at the Sanctum. *Rebbaelah* became *Reiva. Sharasthi* became *Sarasti* (though she rarely bothered to use the Lazarran form).

That anxious feeling, like falling through the air, was reasserting itself. There were no Adepts born from Lazarran blood, so declared the unanimous testimony of history and Adept Corps doctrine. But Nuntius had said the Emperor was an Adept—something Alyat had no evidence for or against, aside from the supposed impossibility of such a thing.

Suppose Bascia was an Adept, he thought. *Why would he be missing from the records?*

Two possibilities crossed his mind. The first was that it was simply an error and he was reading into this too much; the record had been lost by mistake. The second was that a record had never been made, or it had been made and intentionally removed at some point.

There was a third option, though. Something that could also explain the irregularities he had gleaned from the death report.

What if Bascia had lived before the Dark Days?

While there were documents from those times, many had been destroyed—burned either for warmth or to comply with the Almost King's mandates. The Adept Corps had been formed at the behest of the First Emperor, and it was their presence and power that had enabled Lazarra to establish herself so rapidly as a superpower in the region.

Magic—the Sanctum assumed—had existed and been held before the Dark Days, so it was conceivable that individuals who could channel and shape aether had served in the Republic's armies. The invention of the arcane focus, however, was also part of the Empire's birth. And without a focus, it wouldn't be possible to put that talent to use—not effectively, anyway.

Where did that leave Alyat? A forgotten Adept with a Lazarran name, with no evidence of a focus, killed by a trio of supposedly *Gallian* Adepts, one of whom practiced the rare and disturbing *Ars Sanguis*.

Again, he cursed the vagueness of that scroll Nuntius had given him. Why could secret societies never just hand you a plain, simply phrased charter explaining things? Always riddles, always secrets.

You're letting your speculation run wild, he chided himself.

It was possible that the documentation of Bascia's service had been pulled from the records for some reason—he could investigate that, though he would have to do so more delicately. The sort of information tucked away in secret by the Sanctum, he needed a particularly good explanation to request access to it.

Well, that was something he could come to later. For now, he could still pursue the matter of the map.

He could have gone back to the Imperial Archives and compared hundreds of maps to one another, but Alyat was particularly interested in the holdings of the Sanctum. He was hoping to find a lead as to that strange symbol—the two parallel lines with a transverse third. Mostly cities had been marked with it, but a few locations broke that pattern, and if anyone had a record of unusual symbology, it would be the Sanctum. While the Adept Corps had been the first in the world to tame the arcane power of the aether, many ancient peoples had at least glimpsed some insight into its nature. As such, the Sanctum regularly made it a point to harvest the records of any sects of magicians or wonder-workers found in conquered cities or simply out in the wild.

But after digging through the standard resources and compendia, as well as through more obscure sources, Alyat found himself facing a wall. The symbol was nowhere to be found. Hours had slipped by.

And he was still behind on that report explaining his plans for recruitment.

While he was knuckling his forehead, someone came by and tapped the table where he was immersed in research.

Alyat looked up from his work, not a little irritated. His annoyance only grew when he saw the face of Adept Gylos. Strong-nosed with dark, heavy-set eyes, the man cut quite the figure. He practiced the *Ars Viva*, which made him an incredibly valuable asset to the Corps and the broader Empire.

Gylos cast a disinterested eye over the many books and scrolls strewn across the workspace. "Have an exam coming up, Alyat?"

Though Gylos was about a decade younger than Alyat, he had ascended rapidly in renown and the pecking order of the Corps. He commanded about as much respect as Alyat did—something that grated on the North-lander. Alyat looked at Gylos flatly. "Some of us try to expand our under-standing of things. You ought to try it—when you're not busy expanding your reputation."

As essential as adherents of the Art of Life were, the impact their Art exerted on their emotions often nudged them into compromising positions. *Viva* Adepts were prone to dizzying flights of romance. Some worked that out in marginally more respectable ways; others became well-known patrons of the city's bordellos and the temple of Belletra.

If Gylos took the implication as a slight, though, he said nothing of it.

"Your protégé is in Talynis right now."

Alyat acknowledged that she was.

"Are you at all concerned that she's caught the eye of someone as...*renowned* as Cassia Vantelle?"

Alyat narrowed his eyes. This was a dangerous game. The relative autonomy of the Adept Corps became a tenuous thing when it came to the seven praetors. While the Corps served the Emperor alone, the praetors were extensions of his will.

"Vantelle," Alyat said, "is a famously competent leader and tactician. Reiva will do well under her tutelage."

He didn't think Gylos was the sort to play games, pitting a fellow Adept against a praetor—that sort of thing could have ramifications for the rela-tionship of the Corps as a whole with the seven. But still, better to be wary.

Gylos didn't press on Alyat's diplomatic, if empty, response. He did, however, pull out a chair and sit, scrutinizing the documents strewn across the table. He seized upon a codex of various esoteric ciphers.

"Back to your old interests in cryptography?"

Alyat realized he was clenching his jaw. He forced himself to relax a bit. "No—just hunting leads for something else."

Gylos hummed, taking a moment to inspect the page Alyat had been on. It described a particularly tough nut to crack—a code written in the Karellan alphabet that then had to be shifted over two spaces into the smaller Zarushan alphabet, then put through a particular cipher. Even once you understood the algorithm, picking apart the meaning still required a bit of creativity, and often there were double-meanings embedded in certain sentences.

Alyat had been part of the team that first deciphered it years ago. Now he was going back over that old material, wondering if he might find a single connecting thread—some letter, some signal—that could help him understand what he was looking at.

Gylos looked up from the page, scratching at the stubble on his chin. "So much effort to hide a few secrets."

"A well-kept secret is a currency without peer. Men have killed—and been killed—for less."

"True enough." The younger man leaned back in his chair, lazily casting his eye over the research materials. "So, what secret are you after?"

Alyat was about to blow him off, but he was also at a dead-end.

He was hesitant to share anything—but to be fair, he also had no idea whether this matter of the map would actually be anything significant. It could have just been the idiosyncrasy of some oddball cartographer.

Odds were, nothing about it would have any significant repercussions. Alyat was just chasing down threads, hoping to find something that verified what the book he had received from the Order suggested.

He decided to take the chance.

"I'm trying to figure out what this is." As he spoke, he slid a slip of paper over, on which he had scratched the symbol with a charcoal pencil.

Gylos picked it up, examining it with a neutral expression.

Then, something registered. His eyes widened, his breath caught.

Alyat's heart beat faster. "You recognize it," he said, unable to keep excitement from bleeding into his words.

Gylos nodded softly, sliding the paper back.

There was a moment of silence, as Gylos seemed to be deep in thought, some internal argument working itself out in his mind.

"Wherever you found this...I would suggest you be discreet."

"You have more than that."

Gylos' normally easygoing manner cracked a bit. He seemed ready to up and leave.

"Gylos, I've spent hours trying to tease out even the slightest bit of understanding as to what this is—and I'm not going to give up, especially now that I know there's something to find."

The younger Adept took a deep breath, let it out. His eyes flitted to the distant door, as if it were calling out to him.

"Please, Gylos. Better that I hear it from you than step on the wrong toes elsewhere."

The man rubbed his eyes. "Damn it, Alyat," he muttered under his breath. Then he leaned in, resting his elbows on the table. "I've only seen this in one other place."

Alyat was getting excited now. He called up his mental reference of all the locations on the map that had been marked with the symbol.

"Ouranopolis," he guessed.

Gylos looked startled.

"You're from Karella," he explained, "and I found this symbol on a map, marking out a number of locations across the world, most of them capital cities. There was only one in Karella, and it was over Ouranopolis."

Gylos nodded slowly. "It *is* at Ouranopolis. Well, under it. It's on a wall, deep within the labyrinth beneath the city. As children, we used to play a game—who could go the furthest in and make it back."

Alyat cocked an eyebrow.

"It was a stupid game," he admitted.

"How many died?" drawled Alyat.

Gylos shrugged. "Enough, but no one I knew, so we kept on going. Sometimes you could see gouges in the rock along the ceiling, where the horns of the minotaur had marred the rock. So the myth says, at least. I liked to follow them, imagining I was hunting him, going to save the children who had been sacrificed. Then, one day, I wasn't paying attention, went too far in, and got lost. Hours passed. I had no idea where I was, and my torch was burning down. I was sure I was going to die in there."

The Karellan had a look of nostalgia and discomfort all at once as he told his story.

"I found a wall. It looked different from the others—like it had been cut from a different sort of stone and slotted in. Like some huge block of marble had been dragged through the tunnels and fitted in amongst the limestone. But it was too big to have been moved like that, I remember thinking."

"And this symbol was carved into that wall."

Gylos nodded imperceptibly. "It was huge—top to bottom it must have been close to the height of a man, and it still had some flecks of paint on it. It must have been bright red, once, but by the time I got there, it was a shadow of that."

He shrugged. "I had no idea what it could mean, but by then I was tired and thirsty, and my torch was almost dead. I remember thinking that I must have been in a bad spot, because I couldn't even smell the smoke from it—it was as if I was standing in one of the pastures out around the city, where the shepherds drive their flocks."

"How did you get out, then?"

Gylos shook his head, a haunted look on his face. "That's the strange thing. I didn't. Standing there, my head began to spin. From hunger maybe, but I had eaten a good dinner. So I set my torch down, curled up on the cold floor, and went to sleep. Maybe it was smoke inhalation, but like I said, I couldn't even smell it. You know what it's like to be in a cloud of smoke, like when you're in a siege—you can't ignore that scratching feeling in your throat and lungs."

"So you fell asleep and someone found you?"

"Must have. Because when I woke up, I was outside."

"Outside the labyrinth."

"Not far from one of the entrances—though that particular entrance is hard to find as they go. I was lying in a patch of grass, tall grass, growing by a stream. The first thing I did was drink from the stream—I still remember how refreshing it was, like it was the first real drink of water I'd ever taken. Eventually I was able to get my bearings and find my way back to Ouranopolis—I had ended up about a mile outside the city."

"And what did people think?"

"Well, I'd been gone all night and about a day. My mother was relieved—angry, of course, but relieved. My friends thought I'd been playing a trick on them, making them think I was lost and dead. No one believed my story; they thought I was lying. I never told them about the symbol on the door, though. Something told me I shouldn't have. Like a little voice."

"And have you *ever* told anyone else?"

Gylos shook his head. "Never, not once. Just a few weeks after that, I was found by the Corps and brought across the waves. You know what it's like, having the chance to start with nothing of your past. I wanted to forget about what happened in the labyrinth, so I never told anyone and I never thought about it—except when I dreamed, sometimes. They weren't any special dreams—not like the prophetic oracles you read about in the old epics. No, I just relived what happened. That's why I can still remember that symbol so clearly; I kept seeing it in my dreams, with the little flecks of red paint and the precise lines carved into that marble wall."

Alyat leaned back, the chair creaking under his weight. What was he to make of this?

"So why tell me?" he asked eventually. "You kept this to yourself for so long. Am I just that persuasive?"

A shake of the head. "I would have walked out without a second thought. In fact, I was intending to. But then...that little voice."

"The voice that told you not to share anything about the symbol, and the wall."

"For the first time, I felt it nudge me to tell someone."

Alyat wasn't sure what to make of that. It was common for Adepts to think of their magic as a sort of presence, exerting influence on them. Reiva, when she was first undergoing her training, began describing it as her Flame, and she would speak of it almost like it was conscious, like it had desires.

From time to time, Alyat had thought something similar. He had the Gleam, as he called it. It never spoke to him, but it would sometimes clue him toward paying attention to things he might otherwise overlook, almost like a sort of shimmer in his mind. Following the Gleam had often led him to discover things, or make some sort of revelation.

Alyat asked Gylos if the voice was something like that, but he only shrugged.

"It could be, but I have no idea why my *Viva* magic would ever be interested in that symbol on the labyrinth wall. What I do feel is a sort of unconscious guide, when I'm healing someone, that is. I understand what is damaged, what needs to be repaired and how to do so. I gain access to a knowledge that goes beyond medical treatises and anatomical study."

Alyat understood that; there was something ineffable to the unique awareness one received after spending years coming to understand their Art.

"Well," said Gylos, finally rising. "I came down here to pull out some old training manuals. This new batch of Initiates is a tough nut to crack."

Alyat grunted. "They always are. Maybe we're just getting soft."

"Maybe."

"Thank you," said Alyat.

Gylos shrugged. "No need. It's nice to finally open up about that. Like I said, I don't know why things were different this time. And you said you saw this symbol on a map?"

Alyat nodded.

"Hm. And will you be searching for other walls like the one I saw then?"

"Could be."

Gylos nodded. As he walked off, he raised an arm in farewell. "Let me know if you find anything."

Alyat said he would.

When he was left, at last, alone in the Sanctum library, Alyat sat in stillness.

There *had* been other cities marked with the symbol.

And Lazarra was one of them.

Alyat went in search of another map—this time, for one of the city catacombs.

39

THOSE WHO WILL STAND WITH US, AND THOSE WHO WILL STAND AGAINST

LAZARRANS of greater moral stature than I have questioned the crucifixion, asked whether something so wretched, so cruel—so, dare I say, barbarian—has a place among the repertoire of a people so civilized as we claim to be.

But no one could question its utility, and that, I think, is why we never dispensed with it. For all our talk of honor and superior virtue, we could never let go of something so effective as the beam and nails.

—*The Memoirs of Flavia Iscator*

~

THE DAY of the executions came swiftly. Legion engineers chopped down trees to fashion them into the infamous beams. However, so immediate was the need and so numerous the number of condemned that many trees were simply cut to an appropriate height and trimmed of their branches.

In no way was it thought a defect that the gibbets were rough, splintered, or merely pruned trunks. If anything, it was a feature of the method.

Reiva's stomach had writhed in knots all night. She feared she might need to retch at some point, and so she had hardly eaten a breakfast. Under the baking sun, she worried she might faint. Yaros offered her some mint leaf—it was dry and so lacked almost all the refreshment of the typical article, but she would take anything she could get. With a cool tang in her mouth, she oversaw the setup of the beams.

Reiva saw her first crucifixion when she was sixteen, the fourth year of her training. Alyat had thought it important she be aware of the method. They had been on a mission attached to a legion serving in the southwestern rivieras. Some men—bankrollers of the enemy force—had been captured, and a nontrivial number of local women had accused them of various improprieties.

The local commanding officer had seen this as an excellent opportunity to display what Imperial justice meant.

The young Adept Initiate had heard of the method, of course. It was not unique to Lazarra, though few other cultures had become so notorious for its use. What she had not known, however, was that death by the beam and nails was death by suffocation.

Those men had hung, naked and bruised, backs chafed raw and bloody, for hours upon hours. One lasted nearly two days. All the while, they labored on the beams, hauling their weight against the very iron nails that fastened them. It was the only way to breathe when you were dangling like that—pushing yourself up on the nails for one more haggard gasp.

It was illegal to inflict such a death upon a Lazarran citizen, no matter how terrible the crime. When Reiva had asked Alyat why it was legal to put anyone to death in this manner, he shrugged. "Some questions will only haunt you, kid. If you have the opportunity, try to kill them before it ever gets to this point."

Reiva had not slept for a week afterward.

Now, as she gave the orders, she felt that old revulsion rising in her gut, a lightheaded whirling in her skull. She kept a constant stream of aether flowing through her, taking the edge off her nausea. When she asked Yaros how she looked, she could tell that he was lying when he said, "Same as usual."

Even his indefatigably upbeat mood had been crushed by the occasion. Karella was no stranger to the beams either—from within their own culture or by the Lazarrans when the two nations had been at war in the old days.

"Go to the market square," muttered Reiva. "Make sure it's secure for later."

The mercenary grimaced. "Sure, boss. I'll do that."

Vantelle, on the other hand, was the very image of command and control. The praetor arrived on the site early, clutching a tightly rolled scroll. This, Reiva guessed, was the register of the condemned and their crimes.

Her assumption was proven accurate when the first man was brought forth. Vantelle read the man's name, the deeds that sealed his guilt as an enemy of Tamiq and the Empire.

As man after man was hauled forward, her voice never wavered as she proclaimed what sins they had committed to earn this gruesome end.

As Reiva watched, she had a brief fantasy of sneaking into the place where they had penned in all the condemned to burn them all alive—quick, effective, dispassionate.

They might have praised her name as their skin sizzled.

The Ninth was out in force, both to administer the executions and to maintain control of the crowd that was sure to muster. Capital punishments always drew a spectacle...but Legate Iscator had anticipated this would be different.

"We're using the most feared method of execution in the world against these people for their association with the outgoing monarch. Even if people in the crowd support Tamiq," Iscator had reasoned, "none of them will support the idea of their countrymen dying like this. It's a shameful death."

"Which is why," Vantelle had answered coolly, "we will only put to the beam those who are deserving. We will cow these people while at the same time showing them the good we can do for their nation."

Indeed, a sizable crowd had begun to gather, ranging from the young to the old, all bearing some mixture of curiosity and dread. Some of these would be relatives of the condemned. Sons, daughters, wives, parents.

Reiva imagined what she would have done, were she still a true Talynisti, if she knew her father was going to be nailed to a beam.

She suddenly felt that the security detail, large as it was, was inadequate to the scale of spectacle Vantelle had organized.

The beams lined the road from the city gate all the way to an old watch-tower. The ruined construction had been a small but vital instrument in the defense of Dav-maiir in the days when the desert was split by warring factions and cities. Now, this shambling edifice would be little more than a collective tombstone for two hundred men accused of defying the Empire and King Tamiq.

As the blistering sun rolled on, Reiva catalogued the condemned. The first sort looked lost, as if every rock and stone upon the earth was some facade, a trick conjured up by a nefarious devil. None of this was real, was it?

The second sort of man was openly terrified. These ones had to be forced along, cajoled, struck and shoved. Many were praying for the gods to have mercy, to spare them from this fate or to let it pass quickly. Others were already cursing the gods for allowing such a thing to happen.

The last sort walked with head held high, shoulders squared. The sight filled Reiva with an odd respect. Even pride.

The urge to retch writhed in her throat.

As the line advanced, Vantelle read from her scroll. There were men of renown here. Men who had served in the military. Men who had brought and created much wealth for Dav-maiir. Men who had great reputations for piety.

Their crimes ranged from open support of King Malik to covert support, to conspiracy, and to even greater extremes of intrigue. Some had apparently been caught writing letters denouncing and personally insulting King Tamiq, as well as Emperor Dioclete, with language too foul and heinous to reproduce.

It struck Reiva that these men's language was supposedly too terrible to repeat, yet here they were being stripped naked and nailed to lumber. Heavens, how might they be punished if they had done something even worse than speak? Was there some twisted sense in conjuring up the worst sort of punishment for a crime? Was there a reason that the more heinous the act, the more heinous the retaliation had to be?

Lazarra had built her name through conquest, through force. The might of the legions swept forth with the driving point of the spear.

Reiva found herself wondering what might happen if someday a bigger fish entered the pond.

The condemned were led to their ends under the watchful eye of the legionnaires. While the security detail kept them in order, others would take one prisoner aside and bring him to the beam, which was laid flat on the ground.

The condemned would be stripped, then placed against the beam. The hands were stretched above the head, placed atop one another just so. A single nail, nearly half the length of a man's forearm, did the job. The nailing was done hastily, and always wrenched from the victim a tortured wail, or a succession, depending on their firmness of will and constitution. The nail went directly through the main nerves in the wrists. Then the legs were brought up to an angle and the feet pierced.

Once the nails were fixed, the legionnaires would lift the beam, the base dropping into a pit, such that the gibbet rose high into the air, the condemned dangling helplessly. The legs were at such an angle that almost immediately, the thighs began to tremble under the victim's weight.

This was done again and again. The air was filled with endless screams. Cries for mercy. Cries for justice. Pleas for wrath and vengeance to be visited upon the Empire.

All the while, Cassia Vantelle read the crimes these men were being executed for. Reiva tried not to think about which charges were true, which were invented simply to win the appeal of the crowd. Or, if not to win their appeal, at least to redirect any animosity felt toward the Empire to these men instead. These screaming, wailing men.

Eventually the screams dulled to nothing more than eerie wheezing and choked gasps. Air became a precious resource, every breath a fresh agony, a new hell.

The scene lost novelty, at this point, for much of the crowd. Death would take hours, even days, depending on the person's strength of body and will. People began to trickle away.

The legion had feared an attack by the Loyalists. As the hours dragged by, it seemed no such thing would happen.

The noon sun hung high overhead, its sweltering heat baking the road. Reiva took her helmet off, wiping the sweat from her brow. In search of water, she found some by the city gate. A small cluster of legionnaires huddled in the shade, taking a break from their patrol.

When they saw her, they snapped to attention. At her request for water, they filled a bowl from a copper basin, which she greedily quaffed. The water was warm, but even so, it was unbelievably pleasurable. She had been getting herself through the day so far on aether, denying her body essential needs such as this. Magic was potent, but the body could not live on it. She refilled the bowl from the basin, drinking again.

From the shade of the gate, she cast a glance out across the road.

There was something undeniably impressive about it. Only the Lazarran Empire could manage something such as this—lining a road with executions. No one entering or exiting Dav-maiir would ever forget the sight. There were testimonies written by Lazarrans who had seen mass crucifixions like this. Almost always, the scenes were of horror. There was a deep sense of gratitude that the author need not fear such a fate, being safe as a Lazarran citizen from ever suffering such an indignity. But there was also a profound terror, even to a people as war-soaked as the Lazarrans.

The philosopher Lucian Sana had written: *There is nothing that should shake one's faith in humanity as deeply as the practice of crucifixion. Both that it should have been invented, and that there should have been cause to invent such a thing. We are creatures of violence, and it is to such an image that we are conformed.*

Reiva never cared much for philosophy, but when she had heard Domi read that passage aloud one sleepless night during their training, she had listened. And she had thought back to it often, late at night, on long journeys, and in moments like this.

On the nearest beam, a man was wheezing, blinking his eyes frantically against the sweat trickling down his face. His skin was covered in a sheen, his back red and raw against the wood. As he hung there, he coughed—a dreadful, hacking sound—twisting his body and eliciting a low moan. Still, he coughed, and coughed, and coughed.

Reiva felt an itch in her own throat. Dry winds brought sand and dust from beyond the *maiir*.

She was still holding that bowl of water.

It was illegal for anyone to give succor to one of the condemned.

He coughed again, and again, half-groaning and half-choking.

Reiva took a step, bowl in hand.

One legionnaire cleared his throat. "Adept?"

Reiva turned on him. "Yes, soldier?"

The man looked uneasy, as did his fellows. His eyes were darting to and fro, refusing to stay fixed anywhere, especially not on Reiva.

"Adept," he muttered, "the praetor has made clear that these men are not to be given any mercy, unless they cooperate with the Empire in naming fellow Loyalists."

Reiva remembered what Alyat had once told her of Vantelle. '*A woman of iron, a flawless blade in the hand of the Emperor.*'

"Thank you for informing me, soldier."

She turned, stepping into the sunlight. It seemed even hotter now that she had spent some time in the shade. She went, and with one hand, took up one of the ladders leaned against the gate. It was tall enough, but not too unwieldy for an Adept with enhanced strength.

With one hand, she propped the ladder against the beam. It was unsteady, and she had a bowl mostly full of water, so she took the ascent slowly. The man, she realized, was watching her out of the corner of his eye. His tongue was lolling out of his mouth, swollen and parched. His chest spasmed with weak gasping.

When she came level with him, she did not speak, only held out the bowl, tipping the water slowly into his mouth.

He drank desperately. The last drink he would ever get.

When he had drained the bowl, he looked at her again.

He knew who she was. She had the mantle. She had stood guard as he was marched outside the gates.

She expected him to look hateful.

Instead, he just seemed tired, strung out. A nearly hollow body, the soul almost stripped away.

A rasping sound passed through his lips.

Reiva had to lean closer. "Forgive me," she said in Talynisti. "I do not understand."

Again, the man muttered something, his breath shallow and pained as he lifted himself for air.

"*Salm*," he said. *Peace*.

Reiva cast her eyes down to the sands.

"*Salm*," she whispered, then descended.

She stepped into the shade again, returning the now-empty bowl to beside the water basin. The legionnaires looked abashed. Reiva couldn't blame them. She also couldn't chastise them.

Again, she went into the sun. Slowly, she scanned the land for the praetor. Cassia Vantelle had not ceased to be active, not even when the heat had risen to such a heavy degree. She was on the move, walking to and fro in full armor. Reiva could see her now, about halfway down the line. She seemed to be speaking to one of the condemned.

Reiva could guess at the contents of the conversation.

Vantelle would be offering a swift death in exchange for information regarding the Loyalists. It was not uncommon in these situations. The condemned were at their limits, or past them by now, after several hours in the air. If they would give someone up, a legionnaire would break the large bones in the legs—unable to push up to breathe, the victim would die in moments.

Reiva felt the urge to petition Vantelle for a water detail. She could spin it as a way of getting goodwill from these men in their final moments. It seemed ghoulish, but people at death's door could act in strange ways.

The walk to Vantelle was long, made longer by just how many of the dying she had to pass. Incoherent groans. Pleas for help. Pleas for death.

She made her way. The praetor was coming toward her, so they met about the midpoint.

"My praetor," murmured Reiva.

Vantelle looked hollow, grave as a statue. "Do it," she said, voice sharp. "Have the soldiers give water to those who'll have it."

Reiva stared. "How did you—"

Vantelle's lips were a thin line. "I saw what you did for that one. And I've been in your position, Adept."

"The men," said Reiva, "said that you ordered them against it."

Vantelle's eye twitched, her frown deepening. "I did, and you will not tell them that this comes from me. It was your request, your plea. I granted it, but did not suggest it in any way. You had to fight me for it."

"I don't understand, Praetor."

The haunted gray eyes of Cassia Vantelle bored into her. "You are still young, Reiva. You still have the chance to cultivate a reputation among the rank and file, among our enemies. Let them know you as one of mercy. I must be the hammer, now and always."

The praetor looked upon the nearest victim, writhing on his rugged beam. "*Distasteful*, Flavia once called this. Indeed it is, and if there were any other way for us to make this world a rightful place, I would embrace it."

Vantelle turned to Reiva. "Once you have given the orders for the water, we need to get to the Grand Bazaar. Tamiq's man sent a runner. The crowd grows agitated, and I must address the people before things get out of hand. A necessary horror—that is what they must see this as."

"Will they, praetor?"

"They must. We will divide this city between those who will stand with us and those who will stand against. Indecision is dangerous—better to know exactly who is your ally and who is your enemy." Vantelle turned and left.

Reiva could not stop staring at the praetor's back as she went.

Who was this woman, really? What was she after?

What had made her into who she was?

40

THE WILL OF THE GODS

THERE WAS, and is, much gossip and rumormongering regarding the nature of my relationship to Cassia Vantelle. She was everything to me. A hero, a mentor, a legate, a praetor—but she was not a lover. Perhaps some other skein of fate bears a different pattern, but that is a thing for philosophers and poets to ponder.

Had she asked of me, I would have given her anything. I adored her 'as the moon adores the sun.' But Cassia had one great love that surpassed all others: her love of Empire.

—*The Memoirs of Flavia Iscator*

~

REIVA SET out from the gates with Vantelle, making for the Bazaar. They moved with Vantelle's bodyguards through the streets. Reiva kept her eyes open for threats, but little of her mind could stay focused on the task. Again and again, her mind went to Vantelle's quiet terror.

The praetor, the Emperor's flawless blade...Cassia Vantelle was an enigma to her, one that she desperately wanted to solve, to understand.

"My praetor, I have questions," she managed at last.

Vantelle nodded, unsurprised. "I will do my best to answer them, but not now. In private, we may discuss anything."

"Of course, my praetor."

The atmosphere in the square was taut as a bowstring. The Bazaar loomed large behind a scaffold. Security was unfathomably tight, with as many Talynisti guardsmen as there were legionnaires.

Katabh, Tamiq's right-hand man, was present, and he seemed...not relieved, but at least he obviously preferred Reiva and Vantelle be here than face the crowd alone.

The guard opened to allow them entry to the scaffold, beside which Katabh was standing, sheaves of paper clutched in his hands. His eyes looked hollow, his skin pale.

"Praetor Vantelle," the scribe said flatly. "Adept Reiva. You have done quite a thing on this day."

"A necessity," Vantelle said.

"So you insist. Are you of the same belief, Adept?"

Reiva felt unimaginably small under the weights of the man's gaze and Vantelle's aura.

She hated that they had executed those men. Talynisti men. She also hated that Katabh was trying to drive a wedge between her and her own commanding officer.

"These are challenging times. Extreme measures are necessary on occasion, and today was such a day."

The scribe did not seem pleased by this answer, but he did not press her further on it.

Vantelle threw a glance across the crowd. There were countless of them packed into this square. "Is Tamiq still considering an appearance?"

Katabh smoothed his beard anxiously. "He is. The people are disturbed. They need to hear from their ruler."

"The people will be placated."

Katabh did not seem as confident.

If Tamiq was on his way, there was no word of his coming. The crowd's agitation built.

Vantelle's cool, calculating gaze swept over the plaza. "We cannot wait," she said.

Katabh shot her a nervous look. "Praetor, perhaps it would be better if you simply did not—"

"I have brought peace to cities before. You are not so unique."

With no fanfare or introduction, she strode up the steps to the scaffold.

As soon as she was out in the open, above the people, the discontented grumblings rose to a fever pitch. The crowd was apoplectic. Shouting filled the air, all overlapping and swirling into a deafening wall.

"Murderers!"

"Justice! The gods will judge you!"

"We die standing! We die free!"

That last one spread, at first through a portion of the crowd, then through half, until all the plaza was chanting:

"We die standing! We die free!"

"We die standing! We die free!"

"We die standing! We die free!"

Reiva's stomach twisted into knots. She forced herself to breathe, letting her Flame stoke. Vantelle seemed calm as an autumn afternoon. The praetor could project all the confidence she wished; Reiva was ready for things to go south.

Yaros appeared at Reiva's side, his fingers working open and closed on his sword's grip. Reiva leaned over, practically yelling into his ear to be heard over the crowd.

"It's the death-cry of the Mastayr Two-hundred."

Yaros swore under his breath.

The Mastayr Two-hundred were legends in Talynis, martyrs from the last campaign. Caught inside a fortress, they had all chosen death instead of surrender and slavery.

Her father had lost friends at Mastayr. He'd thought of them as heroes—the ideal to which all men of Talynis should aspire.

And today the Empire had made another two hundred.

Reiva watched Vantelle stand in the center of a maelstrom. The praetor almost certainly knew what the chant meant.

She stood there, observing.

The roar continued. If anything, it grew stronger. People began to push against the Revolutionary Guard. The Guard pushed back. Legionnaires gave each other looks. Shields were hefted, grips adjusted.

Reiva realized she was grinding her teeth. Her fingers twitched like she was about to throw fire.

"We need to pull her back," she blurted out. "There's going to be a riot."

Yaros grimaced. "Great—who wants to yank the praetor off her stage in front of half the city?"

Reiva sighed. She set one foot on the bottom step.

Appearances be damned; she wasn't about to let a praetor die on her watch.

And then Vantelle jumped off the scaffold.

Reiva's heart jumped into her throat.

A shocked ripple went through the crowd.

Reiva hustled around the scaffold, rushing to keep Vantelle in her sight.

She almost wished she hadn't.

Vantelle ordered the Guard to let her through to the crowd.

Alyat had a special curse he reserved for situations like this—'Damn the gods and gild the devils.' Reiva rushed after her.

But as soon as she started running, she came to a stop.

The crowd was parting.

Vantelle pressed further into the mass, and the people were making way for her. And the further in she went, the quieter the crowd became.

For a moment, Reiva thought she was dreaming.

The hush spread as people berated their neighbors.

No one, it seemed, understood what was going on.

The legion was on the same footing as the people in that regard, since Reiva saw a captain arguing with his sergeants about what to do.

Was this what it meant to be a praetor? To have so much power that people fall away from before you, and raving crowds fall silent?

Vantelle kept walking. She seemed to be searching for something, someone.

Reiva saw her kneel, and her first thought was that the praetor had been struck. But after a few moments, she stood up and began making her way back along the trail she'd blazed.

She was holding a little boy's hand, leading him along.

The Revolutionary Guard opened again, letting her and the boy through. They passed Reiva, and the boy looked up at her with a vacant expression.

She knew that look. She had seen it all over the world, starting with her brother's eyes, in their home in Shugrith.

By the time Vantelle had returned to the platform, the little boy in tow, the square was dead silent.

Vantelle held for a moment, as if taking in the whole scene.

"You call me a murderer." Her voice rang out, crisp and clear. A voice that could carry over the pitch of battle, a voice that never lost its steel.

"You say that I will be judged. I *know* I will be judged. I have known it all my life. I am a pious woman, who performs appointed sacrifices and rites just as all of you. I have a family, just as you do. But my family is the Empire. My father is the Emperor."

A pause.

"Many of you lost family today. You lost fathers. Brothers and sons, too. I know that loss. I have lost brothers and sons. I have lived a life of war, and I have paid for that. Yes, the gods will judge me. And it is because I know I will be judged that I can stand here now. Friends, do not call me a murderer because I put to death traitors and rebels."

A noise of protest went up from the crowd, but Vantelle raised a gauntleted arm. "I have put to death men from my own city!"

As the words echoed, the plaza fell silent again.

"I have put to death soldiers young enough to be my sons—soldiers I *called* my sons—because they turned to desert us, their family. Because they slept on watch and put us all at risk. None of it malicious. None of it done out of hate, or moral defect.

"The gods will judge me as one given authority and set over others. I take no pleasure in handing down such a sentence. Not upon the blood of Lazarra, and not upon the blood of Talynis.

"If I could undo any of today's deaths, any at all, I would. I swear it on the seven rivers of death—may they bar my passage if I lie to you today—I would. These are not deaths lain upon villains, but upon men who believed in their cause and found themselves on the wrong side of history. I respect these men. I love these men.

"But you, Talynis, you have a choice set before you now. Your gods have brought me here, by the will of Tamiq, the king they elevated to the throne by divine intent.

"Your families suffer today, but you will prosper tomorrow. Under the reign of Tamiq, you will prosper. With the friendship of Dioclete, Emperor of Lazarra, you will prosper. Our blood will be bound together, and the rising sun will look upon a greater Talynis. If what I do here is the price of that future, then yes, let me be so judged."

Now, she drew forth the young boy, setting her hands on his shoulders.

"What shall you choose, Talynis? What shall you choose for the widows, for the orphans in your streets? This little boy was lost amidst you, with no one to care for him. Anger—anger was in your hearts, and not a one of you saw him. But I knew I would find him, because there is not a city in the world where I have not found such a one as this child.

"Yes, there has been death. The death of the old ways. The death of famines, of pestilence. The death of isolation. Those who fight for such things want no place in our future. Such is their right, but it has always been the will of the gods to put such men to death. What does it matter to you whether they use a child of Talynis or one of Lazarra? Let the gods' will be done!"

The whole assembly seemed stunned—Talynisti, Lazarran, every last one.

So this, this was a praetor.

This was Cassia Vantelle.

For the first time, Reiva thought she understood her.

And she thought to herself, with surprise, *This is someone to die for. This is someone who represents the Empire in all its faces.*

Vantelle leaned down to whisper something in the little boy's ear. He said something in return, then left, sent on his way with a pat on the back.

The praetor watched as the boy returned to the crowd.

Reiva watched too, waiting to see what would happen next.

She was watching when a little troupe of children pushed to the fore, so they could receive him.

She was watching as he melted into them.

And so she was not watching when the arrows struck Vantelle.

41

TO KILL A PRAETOR

Perhaps it was her love of Empire that was her undoing, in the end.
—*The Memoirs of Flavia Iscator*

Reiva channeled aether to her legs, bounding ten feet through the air and landing on the platform. Letting momentum carry her forward, she tackled Vantelle around the midsection, throwing them into a tumble.

Arrows thudded into the wood all around them.

Searing pain like a red-hot poker stabbed through her leg.

Then they were in the air.

Reiva spun so she was beneath the praetor, then channeled all the aether she could manage to her back and skull.

The impact jarred every bone in her body.

But she was alive, and so was Vantelle, though she had been wounded. At least three arrows had slipped between the plating of her armor, half-broken shafts sticking out from her right shoulder and forearm.

Shoving down her own pain, Reiva scrambled to her feet and hauled Vantelle underneath the platform.

The praetor was pale, her lips drawn to a thin line, but she could stand. Good.

Reiva finally looked at her own injury.

The arrow was sticking out of her hamstring.

She grit her teeth and pulled.

Instead of coming out, it just tore into the muscle.

The bastards were using barbed arrowheads.

She sucked in a breath, then broke it off at the skin. A bit of channeled aether, and the wound closed.

A surgeon could cut the head out later. She just needed to survive that long.

Vantelle moved to pull out her own before Reiva stopped her. "Leave it for the doctors." The praetor nodded grimly.

Now that they were out of sight, the attackers shifted their targets. A legionnaire took an arrow through the throat; another barely got his shield up in time.

Where the hell is Yaros?

Then darkness had her. An icy, phantom claw closed around her heart.

If there had been panic before, now was total pandemonium.

Soldiers broke from their posts, covering their heads and bolting like spooked horses. The crowd was a roaring, incoherent stampede, flooding out through every street and byway available.

And Reiva was certain, without a shadow of a doubt, that she was about to die—that her life would be snipped like a frayed thread any second, and she would be no more.

She couldn't breathe. She couldn't tell up from down or right from left.

She needed to be safe.

She needed to get awaysheneedededtorunsheneededto—

An open palm slapped her across her face. A hand gripped her shoulder. Vantelle's hard, gray eyes were an inch away.

"Get ahold of yourself, Adept!" The yell struck her eardrums like a hammer striking a bell.

She seized on the moment of clarity and stoked the Flame to a roaring inferno, and like the rising sun it burned away the fog of fear that had settled into her mind.

Vantelle let her go. Her eyes were wide, face pale. She was barely keeping it together herself.

The realization struck her like a lightning bolt.

Ars Psykana.

It was nigh impossible—it was also the only thing that could account for what was happening.

"They have an Adept. Art of Mind."

Vantelle's lips drew to a thin line. She drew her sword with her off-hand, letting her right arm hang limply to avoid further damage. "Then prove Lazarra's are the only ones worth their salt."

Yaros came barreling into the cover of the platform, his shield stuck with arrows like a pincushion, a spear clutched in a white-knuckled grip.

Like Vantelle, he was barely keeping it together.

Reiva had studied every arcane discipline—she knew how the Art of Mind worked. Right now, the enemy Adept was washing the battlefield with a wave of terror. By sinking into her own discipline, she was able to stave off the effects—but most of their soldiers would be an absolute wreck.

Indeed, it seemed just a handful of officers and veteran troops had kept their heads, barking orders at frayed and fleeing rookies.

Yaros yelled a warning, then sent his spear flying right over Reiva's shoulder in an overhand throw.

She spun as the spear sunk into the attacker's chest with a wet *thud.*

Without hesitation, Reiva smothered him with fire.

As the man's sword clattered to the stones, Reiva's mouth went dry.

Vantelle was first to say it. "He's part of the Guard."

Reiva nodded. "Then we're betrayed, or they're mad."

"Lovely," muttered Yaros, drawing the great sword from off his back.

And more were on their way.

Reiva threw a wall of flame at their pursuers. "Run for the Bazaar, stay low! Yaros, cover the praetor!"

They broke from cover, Reiva throwing fire into the sky to obscure their path while Yaros held his shield over Vantelle.

Legionnaires were locked in combat with traitorous Revolutionary Guardsmen. To make things worse, not all the Guardsmen had turned— adding chaos to the whole mix as men and women couldn't tell friend from foe.

Arrows continued to rain down.

"Where the hell is our overwatch?" snarled Vantelle.

As if in answer, a legionnaire fell from the sky, still clutching his bow as he crashed into the stones with the sickening crunch of shattered bones and crumpled metal.

Reiva cast a glance heavenward, and let out a string of oaths harsh enough to make a sailor blush.

Ropes swung from the roof of the Grand Bazaar, and down slid masked Loyalists, cutting off their escape route.

One drew a black sword.

The Wolf of Talynis.

"Get in close!" she yelled. Their only hope was to make it impossible for the enemy archers to fire upon them without risking harm to their own.

Unfortunately, that meant getting within reach of the *Nihilo* Blade.

Should have sacrificed that extra bull.

There were three Loyalists blocking their way—the Wolf, a woman with a curved shamshir, and a massive man carrying the two biggest swords Reiva had ever seen.

"Yaros!"

"I know," he snapped, splitting off to engage Two-sword.

Wordlessly, Vantelle peeled away to the woman with the saber. The praetor was injured, holding her sword in her weak hand. She wouldn't be able to last for long.

Reiva needed to *end* the Wolf, fast.

She took a breath, narrowing her awareness to his frame. He was small, probably malnourished as a child—

Burn him!

With a surge of will, she detonated a blast of fire right on top of him—or, she tried to. As soon as she willed the aether to burn, the *Nihilo* Blade hummed, devouring every last wisp of fire, sucking it in like steam sucked out a window.

Reiva swore, drawing her sword. She should have tried that on one of the other two—but she'd been desperate to take the *Nihilo* Blade out of play.

Now her soul was strained, and the Wolf was closing in, blade darting forth like a serpent.

Reiva parried, jumped back, and returned the strike.

For a moment, they stood apart, swords tip-to-tip, eyes locked.

"You are the Wolf," she said in Talynisti.

"And you are the bitch who betrayed our people."

The Flame burned brighter, hotter. "Adept Reiva, daughter of Talynis in service to Emperor Dioclete."

Something snapped behind the Wolf's eyes, and he struck forward. It was a clumsy strike, fueled by blind rage.

Reiva handily deflected it, nearly disarming him with a deft twist of her blade.

The Wolf scrambled back. "You *defile* that name."

She swept a low kick, throwing a flaming lash along the ground. The Wolf jumped over it, rolling and jumping up into a rapid sequence of slashes and thrusts.

He's well trained, Reiva observed, meeting every strike with a precise parry. She beat his sword to the side, stabbing at his throat.

He ducked the blow, and she had to jump backward to evade the dangerous edge of the relic. She kept seeking a moment's opening to detonate a blast on either Yaros' or Vantelle's foe, but the second she diverted her attention, the Wolf pressed upon her with another vicious salvo.

~

AVI SAW RED. Every blow, every slash—blind fury drove him forward.

'*Daughter of Talynis,*' she dared call herself.

She was worse than a traitor. She was an affront, an abomination. And she would *pay.*

The sable blade of his relic cut through the air with a foreboding hiss; the Adept scampered backward.

As a Viper, he was good—he could admit that without arrogance. But he was no Imperial Adept. Only the *Nihilo* Blade's grave power was keeping her on the back foot. He could afford to take a cut or two. For her, such a thing might as well be a death sentence.

So he continued to press forward, letting the dangerous power of his weapon compensate where his technical mastery was lacking.

That damn praetor had the devils' own luck—if she had been dropped by the first volley, this would have been a sweep. Three on three was the worst possible scenario here.

Still, he had faith in Jackal to handle a wounded old woman; and Mouse's strength and skill verged on unreality, far beyond the pale of most warriors.

Seeing Mouse fight the man Avi had played shells with just a few nights before, though...

That was a disturbing sight—one that confirmed his hunch of how they had captured Stag.

Avi slashed for the Adept's upper arm, desperate to score a hit, to cripple her magic. She blocked, sliding her sword down along his. He leaped back just before she could liberate his fingers.

The Adept threw another blast of sweltering flames, and like always, his stomach dropped—but he stood his ground and held the relic. Whenever it devoured magic, the blade hummed a deep tune only Avi could hear. It sounded *satisfied,* somehow.

Again, the Adept closed in. So long as she stayed close to him, their archers couldn't risk taking a shot. And, much to his chagrin, it seemed the legionnaires were reasserting battle order—he didn't understand why they had panicked so terribly when the assault began, but he thanked the gods for it.

Now though, it wouldn't be long before the Imperials had beaten down the Loyalist turncoats within the Revolutionary Guard, and then Avi and his comrades would be out of time.

So, time to do something drastic.

Avi turned his back on the Adept and ran.

He felt, rather than heard, the sudden blast of fire coming to engulf him —but again, the *Nihilo* Blade saved him.

The Adept's sandals struck the stones as she chased him.

She would be too slow. She'd grown up marching; he'd grown up tearing through the streets.

Avi knew how lethal Jackal could be with that shamshir. He almost had a begrudging respect that the praetor had survived this long, especially with her injuries.

But the scales were about to tip.

The Adept was yelling something; the praetor's head whipped to him for a moment, then back to Jackal just in time to *barely* parry a blow that should have taken her head off.

Fifteen yards. Ten yards.

Avi was about to kill a praetor.

Jackal's eyes flitted to him as he closed. It was an involuntary reaction— the natural response to something barreling into one's peripheral vision.

It saved Avi's life.

"Down!" she screamed.

Avi let his knees fold, gravity pulling him down, down out of the path of a black-feathered arrow that went right into Jackal's gut.

Avi yelled something. He didn't know what.

Jackal looked down at the bolt in confusion, grasping at it with her left hand, right before she remembered what she'd been doing with her right.

The moment cost her dearly.

The praetor—the wounded, aging praetor—drove her gladius forward in a vicious thrust. Jackal tried to parry, only for the praetor to twist her sword into a precise, almost delicate slash.

Avi threw himself into a run, desperately trying to claw back every ounce of speed he'd lost.

Blood spewed.

Jackal's shamshir clanged to the ground, her severed hand still wrapped around the hilt.

Avi lashed out, driving the point straight for the praetor's midsection.

He struck her armor—then the blade slipped between the plates, burying into her abdomen.

The praetor recoiled, pulling herself off his blade and fumbling at her wound.

Avi practically tackled Jackal, throwing her over his shoulder. Already, he could feel hot blood seeping through his clothes.

"Mouse!" he bellowed. "We're gone!"

Without hesitation, the Endric man disengaged and bolted after Avi, long legs carrying him out of the mercenary's reach in seconds.

Through the wide mouth of the Bazaar, they ran.

REIVA WATCHED in horror as the Wolf stabbed her praetor in the gut, then took off.

Yaros took two steps after them, dropped his shield, then—grasping his sword with both hands—hurled it end over end after them.

Only for the massive man to—barely slowing—spin, bat Yaros' sword out of the air with the crashing ring of iron on iron, and then vanish into the cramped maze of the Bazaar.

Reiva forced herself to set aside the incredulity of what she'd just seen—she needed to get to Vantelle.

The praetor was leaning against the wall, both hands pressed against the break in her armor. Red seeped out from between her fingers. Her face was pale.

Racing with enhanced strength, Reiva nearly slammed right into the wall.

"Hold on," she said absently. "*Hold on.*"

She'd said the same thing in Hyrgallia, she realized. She had been talking to herself then.

This woman had given her another chance after that.

Reiva pressed her hands over Vantelle's, flooding her with channeled aether.

For a second, Vantelle almost looked worse as the immense flow hit her system—then she stabilized.

And if it hadn't been a gut wound, that might have been enough. But there was a chance the Wolf's strike had torn a gash in the praetor's intestines. Toxins could have leaked out in those precious few seconds, and if that was so, it would be a long road to recovery.

She needed a doctor immediately.

Hooves thundered behind Reiva.

The Adept spun, hands raised to throw fire.

She could have raised them to praise the gods instead.

"Scout Lieutenant!"

The Parthavan woman reined in her horse, black-feathered arrows rattling in her quiver. She had already fired most of them, Reiva saw.

"You've got Mercuro's timing, Charas."

"Pray I have his speed too."

Vantelle did not protest as they hauled her into the saddle in front of Charas.

The cavalry Scout wheeled her mare around, kicking her into a blazing gallop.

Already, more reinforcements were sweeping into the square, picking off the remaining pockets of Loyalists. Many scattered, only to be brought down by the arrows of Charas' Scout riders.

Regarding arrows, Reiva realized the Loyalist archers had stopped raining death down on them. Hopefully they'd been killed, but at the point, Reiva would take victory by retreat.

As she let her Flame quell, she noted the heavy drone of fear washing over the place had almost entirely subsided.

Right then, Yaros came striding over to her, having retrieved both his sword and shield. He was bleeding from more than a few gashes, but only one seemed serious enough to merit immediate treatment.

He shrugged it off as Reiva channeled aether to him. "That man fought like a demon," he grumbled.

The Wolf had called him 'Mouse.'

Reiva thought back to how this Mouse had wielded those twin swords in a whirlwind, how he had deflected Yaros' wild sword throw, almost like he had eyes in the back of his head.

If she had seen the enemy Adept today, he seemed the most likely candidate.

The two of them looked into the Bazaar. Countless stalls displayed luxuriant fabrics, spices, perfumes.

"So," he said, obviously frustrated. "What now? We go shopping?"

Reiva shook her head. "Now, we hit back harder."

42

THE ORPHAN BOY FROM SHUGRITH

Soft men and women often ask with horror (or poorly concealed thrill) whether death and violence really do heat the blood of a warrior, and they ask why on earth this is the case. Why should the grit and gore of battle arouse someone to fits of passion?

Perhaps I simply have the benefit of almost dying too many times to count, but the answer is simple—no obstacle seems worth attending to once you've brushed shoulders with doom.

—*The Memoirs of Flavia Iscator*

~

Jackal had her hand clamped over the stump, arterial spray oozing between her fingers. Avi was supporting her, desperately trying to keep them moving as fast as possible.

Mouse swept past them, lifting Jackal off him and slinging her across his broad shoulders in one smooth movement.

"We have to move, Wolf! They are on us!"

Avi chanced a look over his shoulder. Sure enough, a swarm of Tamiq's Revolutionary Guards were barreling down the street after them, shouting curses and orders to stop in the name of the king.

It put an extra kick in his step.

People tumbled out of the way, faces plastered with shock and surprise. Mouse bellowed for people to clear away, brandishing a massive blade.

Avi ran through escape routes in his head. They couldn't just run like this forever—and people would be able to reconstruct their path.

They passed a baker, practically sliding as they rounded a corner.

Avi knew where to go.

"Mouse! Left!"

The Endric man obeyed in a flash, changing course like it was nothing. Avi never ceased to be amazed at the speed with which that man could move, given his size.

They sprinted down an alley. For a moment, they were out of sight—both of pursuers and any bystanders.

Avi skidded to a halt. "Stop! Door on the right."

Mouse didn't even stop to knock—he shouldered open the door. A clamor of youthful shrieks came from inside. Avi swore, slipping inside.

"Quiet for the Madam!" he hissed.

The scene was almost comical. A whole troupe of Talynisti boys and girls—many with flushes on their cheeks and tears welling up in their eyes—all stared at him, choking off their screams.

The room was dead silent.

Even when a massive man carrying a sword in one hand and a bleeding woman over his shoulder stormed into your home, nothing could override the fear of Madam Sahir.

Avi shut the door, dropping the bar. Thank the gods Mouse hadn't broken it off its hinges. He pulled off his mask, sucking down a grateful breath.

"You again!" snapped Madam Sahir, ghosting in from an adjacent room. "What is this?"

"Madam Sahir," he said, bowing deeply. "Forgive me once more. Men are chasing us. Servants of the false king. Just let us into the old sewers, and I *swear* this time will truly be the last."

Sahir's pointed gaze swept over him, then over Mouse and Jackal.

"Always the same with you, eh? Well, tell your friend to put that sword away—there are no blades in my house."

Avi gave Mouse a pointed look. The Endric man complied, looking almost abashed. Madam Sahir could have that effect.

"Follow me," she said, as if she were merely leading them to a dining room.

Jackal, pale, got Mouse to set her down. Somewhat shakily, she followed. Mouse kept up the rear. As they went, children's frightful eyes followed them.

There was a clamor from outside, the thunder of guards on the run, the rattle of swords and spears.

Madam Sahir drew a curtain, then brought them down a series of steps into the basement.

"Move the grain over there," Avi said to Mouse.

Madam Sahir huffed, crossing her arms. "Someday, gods willing, you will come visit me for some reason other than imminent death."

"I pray the gods will be so kind, Madam."

"Ridiculous—first you, now even Samara has caught the fever."

Shoving away his questions as to what that meant, Avi huffed, moving another bag out of the way. Mouse was doing two at a time.

Jackal watched them, leaning against the wall. With her teeth and remaining hand, she was cinching a tourniquet to staunch the blood flow.

Madam Sahir gave her a once over. "You're not his betrothed, are you?"

Jackal made a face like she'd been stuck with another arrow.

"Good—he's not worth the trouble."

"Madam!" hissed Avi, chucking the final bag out of the way.

A booming knock echoed through the house.

Madam Sahir glanced up, disinterested. "Took them long enough. They're getting slower nowadays—almost too easy." She began ascending the steps, only stopping to jab a finger at Avi. "And no, this won't be the last time. Don't swear oaths you can't keep."

Avi sighed, shaking his head. "Come on."

The false wall, compared to the grain, was rather easy to move. It swung on a pivot, opening up a small space in the wall. Avi worried for a moment whether Mouse would be able to fit.

The sound of men yelling reached them from above—followed quickly by Madam Sahir's own. She seemed to be outdoing them in volume and indignation.

Avi might have laughed in different circumstances. At least some things could be counted on in this world.

He ushered Mouse and Jackal into the tunnel, shutting the false wall behind them.

"Down to the end, then left."

So they picked their path in total darkness. Avi had not been in some of these tunnels in some time, but his body remembered all the turns. Madam Sahir made all her children memorize the way.

"It will open up right about now," he whispered.

Mouse sighed gratefully, coming out of his hunch.

As they went, Avi heard Jackal's labored breathing.

"Are you all right?" he murmured.

"Just lost a hand, took an arrow—nothing too serious."

Avi snorted. "What *would* be serious?"

"If the blade were poisoned." Her voice had changed. "Which it may have been."

Avi's stomach lurched.

"Come on, I'll go up front, we make a chain."

The old sewer tunnels were smooth, and though there were access points to them throughout the city, they encountered no one. That surprised Avi a bit, but he was grateful for it. He had avoided using the tunnels in recent weeks out of fear the legion had discovered them, but it seemed his worries had been for naught. That was good to know. Maybe the Four were still with them, even after the cataclysm that was today's attack.

As they picked their way, Jackal began to flag. Her breathing turned shallow; she needed to lean against the wall. Blood loss, and possibly poison, were taking their toll.

Navigating by instinct and memory, Avi brought them to an exit near headquarters. He slipped out first, the exit putting them in a warehouse filled with odds and ends, probably some supply depot for an old war. He had never quite been sure what it was meant for, but it had served him and the Vipers well.

The point of most danger was in crossing to their headquarters. Ten yards across the road—but if anyone recognized Mouse or caught sight of Jackal's arm, it would be tricky.

Thankfully, the havoc they had created had sent the whole city into a panic. People were hiding indoors, barring themselves against the violence that threatened to turn the city into a butcher shop. Always, Dav-maiir was perched on the edge of a knife. Today, things had wobbled.

As Avi opened the outer wall's door and pulled Jackal into safety, he swore that things would fall. The praetor still lived. The Adept still lived. He would change that—whatever it took.

When they got inside and Crow saw the wound, he gave a slight frown and knit his brow. For the old man, Avi knew that meant he was seriously distressed. Jackal's pallor was severe, her face shining with heavy droplets of perspiration. The elder Viper set to work preparing a poultice for the wound.

Crow sniffed at it, and his frown deepened. "Poison. Lutzroot is probable." He shot a dark glance to Mouse as he said it.

Jackal's jaw clenched.

Avi and she had never gotten along the best, but seeing her bear that news, have that suspicion confirmed—something that could have been a guaranteed death sentence—he respected her for it.

He hoped she would live long enough so she could rub that in his face.

"What does she need?" asked Avi.

Crow shook his head. "Nothing we have, or can easily acquire." He was crushing herbs with a mortar and pestle, and a pot of water was on the boil. "This will have to do for now."

Jackal eyed the concoction as the old man mixed the brew. She wrinkled her nose against the heavy odor. "I'll lose my guts if I drink that."

"You'll lose your life if you don't." He poured it into a cup.

She pinched her nose.

She nearly gagged on it twice, but she clamped her hand over her mouth and forced it down.

Looking like she was on the verge of retching, she put her head in her hand. "Next time, just open a vein and let me bleed ou—"

Suddenly, she swayed. Crow had his hands on her shoulders.

Avi blinked, then sprang forward. White as a spirit, her eyes rolled back...

Crow checked her pulse. "She's not dead. The elixir will slow her body's natural processes, her heartbeat, everything."

"You're buying time—for what? I thought we don't have anything for lutzroot?"

"*We* don't." The Crow turned to Mouse, who had already changed his clothes, shucking the bloodied cloak and robes for what looked like traditional Endric attire. Loose trousers tied with a bright-red sash, an open vest that left his powerful chest and abdominals exposed.

Walking outside like that, he would have been the most conspicuous man in Talynis.

And, searching his memory, Avi realized Crow had not explained to Mouse what was to be done...which meant he already knew.

Avi realized, not for the first time, that Crow and Mouse had not divulged everything about their connection. He did not resent it, typically. He understood that not everything was shared in this profession.

But today, today he had failed. He had looked the Adept in the eyes, and he had failed to bring her down. He had the only weapon in the world that could do such a thing, and he was defeated. His comrade wounded, approaching death's doors...

He snarled. "What's going on, Crow? Mouse? What is this?"

Crow gently handed Jackal's unconscious form over to Mouse.

"There are some things, Wolf, that it may be best for you not to know."

Avi slammed his fist against the wall, hard enough to knock things off the shelves.

Crow and Mouse turned to him.

"Am I a part of this outfit, or am I just an arm that swings a sword because no one else is mad enough to go toe-to-toe with those red-cloaked demons?"

Mouse looked pensive. Crow looked annoyed.

"Our comrade," began the elder, "is on the verge of succumbing to a poison from—you said it was a *praetor's* blade? Do you think they play around? It may already be too late." He turned to Mouse. "Go—as fast as you can. I have not spoken to Hatzakh in some time, but he still owes me a debt. Tell him it's paid if he can save Jackal."

Mouse nodded, moving further into the house.

Avi followed, incredulous.

There's a hidden passage, isn't there.

Sure enough, there was—Mouse opened it by twisting a hook on the wall. Another thing he had not been informed of.

As Mouse stepped through, he stopped and turned to Avi, body half swallowed by the shadows within. "I am taking her to the Desert Sages. We have...an arrangement."

And before Avi could say or ask another word—he vanished, the passage slamming shut.

The Wolf stalked for the Crow. The old man watched him approach. "I suppose it was Mouse's right to tell you that, but I consider it unwise."

"Sages?" Avi asked, incredulous. "Those old hermits who live in caves out in the desert and meditate all day?"

"Not all of them are in the desert." Crow stood, brow heavy and pensive. He rolled two stones in his palm, round and round, their soft clicks sounding in the empty halls.

"You could follow them," Crow said at last. "They would not have gotten far yet. If you wish to know...yes, you can go if you wish. Only realize that what you learn down there—it will change your understanding."

Avi threw his hands in the air. "Of the city? Of Talynis? I thought we were Vipers together, Crow. But now I don't even know what I don't know."

Crow shook his head. "Everything."

The entrance to the tunnel Mouse and Jackal had taken seemed to call Avi's attention.

He had always wondered what he was missing out on. He had always been on the outside, even once he found a place to belong—whether it was the street gang in his youth, whether it was the Vipers...now he had the chance to see what was really going on, the reality unknown to most.

There was a scream. It jolted Avi from his thoughts, pulled him from the gravity of the tunnel. Not too close, but a scream nevertheless. A woman, from the sound. Perhaps the riot had spread to this part of the city. Perhaps the legion had locked everything down with the Revolutionary Guard. Perhaps a son had been returned to his mother, weeping holes in his hands and feet, raw scrapes on his back.

Crow was observing him.

Avi sighed and stepped away.

"Not now. Another time maybe."

"Where are you going, then? A dangerous time to be out and about in Dav-maiir."

"If I don't need to know everything, then neither do you. We live our masks, don't we?"

A strange mix of satisfaction and bemusement flickered across Crow's face. "So we do. I can only hope it is not to our peril."

Avi left the hideout, slipping into a world gone mad.

Despite the absolute havoc Dav-maiir had fallen into, Avi was still more than capable of sneaking past the palace guards. As it was, night was fast on the approach and smoke obscured the air throughout the city, rising from fires lit near legion strongholds.

It was almost worrisome, Avi thought, not for the first time, how easily he managed to access the princess' apartment.

Unlike a would-be assassin, of course, he knocked.

He half-expected to be ignored—either because Asrah had no interest in seeing him or because she was occupied by...well, whatever occupied royals when they had an uprising on their hands.

So, when the balcony door cracked open, and Asrah's eye shone through the gap, he was more than a little happy, despite everything else.

She let out a terse sigh. "I was worried. Are you hurt?"

That made his heart swell.

"I'm all right."

The tension in her face eased a bit. "Come in, just be quiet. My guards wouldn't let me out of their sight until I told them I couldn't sleep under their stares."

"You forgot the coded knock."

"Oh, shut up."

The room was dark. Avi padded his way along, tugging off his sandals. It was rather surreal how ordinary things were in here.

Asrah lit a candle and gasped. "Whose blood is that?"

Avi blinked, looked down. In the flickering light, the splatters of dried browns and dark reds looked sinister. "A friend's," he said eventually. "Enemies' too. It all looks the same."

"Is your friend alive?"

He swallowed. "I don't know."

The princess kneeled on a cushion, motioning for him to sit down. He wasn't sure exactly what to do—how close should he be? Would she be offended if he were too far?

He tried to sit somewhere in the middle—whatever that meant—but as soon as he looked up, Asrah's large, soft eyes met him.

"Why did you come here?" she asked, voice scarcely audible. He had to lean closer to hear.

He dropped his eyes, focusing on anything else. The carpet to the side. The earring on the floor, beside the dresser.

"Have you ever seen someone die up close?"

She nodded slowly.

"It makes you think."

"About your own death?"

"And others' deaths. My friend...she has a chance, but she might die from poison, or an infection. Even if she lives, she lost a hand in the attack. That could change a lot."

"She's like you? A fighter, I mean."

"Mhmm."

They sat in silence broken up by occasional shouts from outside—calls for more men, men with spears, men with buckets. Would people die, Avi wondered, because some guards had to be on watch at the palace?

What would the cost be, all told, at the end of this fight? When Malik was on the throne again and the Empire banished—how many lives will they have lost? How many, like Jackal, would still live, but having paid a grave price for victory?

"I should be out there," he muttered at last. "They could use another set of hands." He made to stand. Asrah reached out and grabbed his wrist.

He froze.

"Sit down. Please."

Reluctantly, gratefully, he obeyed.

She held onto his wrist, even after he was seated again. Then, like she realized she had been touching hot metal, her hand snapped back. She looked askance. "I wanted to say...I'm sorry for last time."

"For the day of the dinner? I don't know what there is to apologize for. You were right—it was not my place."

"It is also your duty to be wary of that Adept, and I was about to meet her. What I'm saying is...I don't know, it's understandable."

"A kind way of telling me I was still wrong."

Asrah smiled, rolling her eyes. "I'm not saying you were wrong."

"Then what are you saying?"

"That...that you are sweet, how about that?"

The Wolf of Talynis went rigid. Swords, he could handle. Fire-throwing soldiers, his vocation. But a compliment—that was something else.

Asrah covered her mouth, stifling a laugh. "You look like I just stuck you with a knife."

"I'm more used to knives."

"Clearly, since you came here, concerned for my well-being, even though you have a cut on your shoulder."

"I have a—?"

Asrah prodded at the spot over and left from his heart.

It stung, but when he looked at it, he arched an eyebrow. "This? I've hurt myself worse tripping. It's not even bleeding."

The princess shrugged. "Either way, it should be washed. We can't have the Wolf of Talynis dying from an infection, can we?" She got up, padded across the room and retrieved a shallow basin of water with a clean cloth.

"It barely even broke the skin. I don't see why—"

Asrah shot him a look. He shut up.

"Better." She knelt on her cushion, soaking the cloth in the basin. "Could you, um..." She vaguely waved her hands, pink creeping into her cheeks.

Avi's own face heated. Uneasily, he took off his cloak, then his tunic.

Blushing and worried, Asrah put her hand on his chest. "You said it was shallow."

"It is," he protested weakly.

"Men," she huffed. "You'd die if only to prove you were strong enough to take it."

Awkwardly, but tenderly, she scrubbed at the wound, clearing away the dried blood. Avi winced as she worked the grit out.

"You could be more gentle, you know."

She smirked. "Make up your mind. Either it's nothing or it's something."

But she did ease the pressure. Avi hoped the light was dim enough to obscure the flush on his own face—but then realizing how red Asrah's was... well, at least he wasn't alone in that.

After she had cleaned and dressed the cut—cutting a strip of fabric from one of her dresses to substitute for bandages—she set the basin and wash-cloth aside, both tinged pink.

Avi moved to put his clothes back on, but she stopped him, wrinkling her nose. "Those reek of death."

He froze, awkwardly stuck in the motion of pulling on his tunic. "Well, I can't go running through Dav-maiir in the middle of the night in just my trousers."

Asrah swallowed, looking away. Was it his imagination, or was she even more flushed now?

"Could you...stay? For tonight?"

Avi's throat closed up.

"In case that Adept comes for me, I mean."

"You have guards," he said, realizing how stupid he sounded.

"You have that magic blade."

"But if I'm here then—"

Suddenly, Asrah, usurper princess of Talynis, pressed her lips to his.

Avi flinched back, eyes wide.

She looked sad and amused all at once.

His heart beating out of his chest, he fumbled for what to say. "I-I'm...I'm sorry. I didn't—"

"It's okay," she whispered, dropping her chin. "My apologies. That was improper of me."

Avi was still frozen in his backward-leaning half-scramble, staring at her.

It hadn't been his first kiss—but somehow it still felt like it. It felt like those other girls he had known—from Samara in Madam Sahir's house, to his days in the street gang—were pillars of sand, blown away by a sudden north-born wind.

Asrah was tucking her hair behind her ears, fidgeting with a strand.

"Asrah, I..."

What was he even supposed to say?

"It's all right. I have my guards." Finally she looked back at him, eye to eye. "You can go."

Without thinking, he spoke. "My name is Aviqohl beyt'Avadh."

A flicker of happiness glinted in Asrah's eyes, glowing in the dancing candle flame.

Avi found himself intensely aware of every inch of her. The texture of her chestnut hair. The curve of her jawline. The shallow rhythm of her breathing. She wore a simple robe, not the elaborate raiments of a princess.

The two of them sat there, staring at one another, staring at the floor, at the wall. Until their eyes locked again, and neither would look away, as if this single, fragile moment was too much to step away from, lest it never be recovered.

Asrah swallowed, tucking that stubborn strand of hair behind her ear. Almost immediately, it slipped free again.

Avi reached out his hand, nudged it away from her face, behind her ear. She set her own hand over his.

Her fingers were so soft compared to his. No callouses, no scars. Gently, she tugged his hand to wrap into her hair.

Their eyes still had not broken apart.

Her lips trembled, shaping words that slipped into the air between them soft as a dove taking flight. "Come here."

This time, he didn't pull away.

Their lips meshed, soft and hot, first unsure, then eager. Avi's heart thundered in his chest like a racing stallion. Driven by desire, he wrapped her in his arms, pulling her into his lap.

Asrah tangled her fingers in his hair, then traced them along his face, his chest. Her tongue nudged past his lips, hesitantly, then bolder.

In between their kisses, they caught fleeting breaths of air, scarcely willing to break apart. Asrah's legs wrapped around his waist, her arms encircling his neck. His blood raced; he clutched her as close as he could, as if he could not stand the slightest measure of separation.

A subtle moan came from her throat as he deepened the kiss.

Avi's face, his chest, his whole body felt as though it had been set aflame.

The princess pushed his shoulders, sending him to the floor with a *thud.*

Instantly, the pair froze, eyes snapping wide open, lips pulling apart. In the candlelight, they stared at one another, shock and desire and worry on their faces.

A gentle rap at the door. "My princess," rumbled a guard, concern evident in his voice. "Are you all right?"

Asrah swallowed, licking her lips. Putting on an impressive feigned tiredness, she murmured, "My apologies, I knocked something off my nightstand."

A pause.

Avi was suddenly very conscious of his blade being out of reach, of the princess of Talynis lying atop him—of just how unquestionably dead he would be if that door opened right now.

But then, mercifully, the guard muttered something about her being cautious, and to be sure to yell for them if anything seemed amiss.

She mumbled something grateful about their vigilance in return, then let out a long, tremulous sigh that tickled Avi's ear.

He was very aware, all of a sudden, of the soft press of her breasts, interrupted only by a thin slip of fabric, against his chest.

Asrah looked into his eyes, hers wide as saucers. "That was close," she whispered.

Avi nodded dumbly.

She wiggled, disentangling herself slightly from him, but still straddling his supine form. "Maybe..."

"We should stop?"

She nodded, pain and frustration in her features.

"That's a good idea."

She nodded again, less enthusiastically.

"Asrah?"

"Hm?"

"...you have to move off me."

She hummed, looking away, nodding a few times. "Right."

But they stayed like that a little longer, her palms resting against the muscles of his chest, fingertips tracing the ridges of scars crisscrossing his skin.

Eventually, their breathing evened out. Slowly, she slid to the side, giving Avi the freedom to shift into a seated position.

"I'll stay on the floor," he murmured.

She shot him an annoyed look.

"Or not."

Plainly pleased, Asrah blew out the candle and burrowed into her covers. Avi climbed in beside her. Before he knew it, she had nestled her back against his chest and pulled his arms around her.

"My arm is going to fall asleep like this."

"You took a sword to the shoulder earlier—you can manage."

Avi snorted, but pulled her in tighter. Then, on a whim, pressed a kiss to her ear.

Together they lay like that, until slowly, Asrah's breathing deepened, her muscles relaxed.

Carefully, Avi disentangled himself, rolling onto his back and staring at the ceiling.

And he lay awake like that for a long time, wondering at what could happen next to him, the orphan boy from Shugrith, lying in bed beside the usurper princess of Talynis, in the regal palace of Dav-maiir.

43

EMPTY, EVER-WATCHFUL EYES

Adept Alyat was a man of noble character, a man well-regarded by legionnaires, scholars, and politicians alike. His only flaw—or the one that mattered most—was that he spent so long shining lights into dark corners, he hardly took the time to wonder what, or who, he might disturb.
—*The Memoirs of Flavia Iscator*

In many ways, Alyat was uniquely suited to exploring the catacombs. For one, he had an endless resource of light. There was aether sickness to be wary of, but so long as he only used his magic like a torch, he had nothing to worry about. This was his most basic technique—he could go for hours, and he'd need to sleep long before he felt any weariness in his spirit from the constant pull of aether.

Second, Alyat was excellent with navigation. He didn't have a perfect memory for most things, but when it came to finding his way, Alyat might as well have had a map burned into his brain. The winding tunnels, branching off and looping back on themselves, presented little danger of getting lost, even though he had not come down here in a long time.

And third, he had no problem being around corpses.

Most people in Lazarra never entered the catacombs if they could help it. The ever-expanding network of subterranean tunnels held many of the city's dead. As one walked the cramped paths, on either side were recesses carved into the rock—usually three levels high, like shelves. In the recesses were bones. Sometimes he would smell the reek of a body still decomposing, then wrinkle his nose and turn to go the other way.

Lazarrans burned their dead, sending the deceased up to the heavens in the form of smoke, but some cultures had strange beliefs about the afterlife. The Mizkhari, for instance, often went to great lengths to preserve corpses, elaborately embalming them and tucking precious trinkets into the burial wrappings. Zarushans did not go to the same lengths, but they too preferred to bury their dead as opposed to burning them.

That turned the catacombs into an odd sort of neutral ground among peoples who otherwise were at odds with one another—socially, culturally, religiously. They all buried their dead beneath the earth, and they all received scorn from Lazarrans for their strange superstitions. Parthavans were the strangest, of course—they left their dead out beneath the sky for the vultures and wolves. There weren't many Parthavans in Lazarra, though. There weren't many Talynisti either, though Alyat imagined they used the catacombs as well.

That set him thinking about Reiva. Her reports from Dav-maiir were... well, he would have been lying to himself if he didn't admit they were worrisome. Cassia Vantelle was a foreboding leader, even among the praetors. She had high standards. Reiva said Vantelle seemed to approve of her, thankfully, but Alyat was uneasy about the whole arrangement. There was a sort of person who was masterful at making others into their dogs. They would shower others with praise, then as soon as someone fell a hair out of place, they lashed out.

Alyat had seen merchants like this with their employees, husbands to wives and vice versa, parents with their children, masters with their slaves...

He had to trust that Reiva would have the presence of mind not to be cowed by that sort of behavior. He had instructed her in all the social politicking that went on in the legions, but she was still young as far as these things went. Young and anxious about her station after what happened in Hyrgallia.

Alyat shook his head, alone as he meandered through the tunnels. If he let himself keep ruminating, he would never stop. It was not unheard of for Adepts to get married—either to one another or to someone outside the Corps—but Alyat had never felt the need. Marriage meant children, and he had no need for children—he already fretted over his apprentices like a worried father.

Apprentice, he reminded himself. There was only one now. The others were all gone, either ash carried aloft on heavenward winds, or piles of bones indistinct among countless corpses littering far-flung battlefields.

Alyat had no problem being around death—he had known too much of it in his life.

He turned his mind toward navigating. The catacombs had been mapped out reasonably well—at least, those parts nearest the various entrances littering Lazarra. They were ever-expanding outward as need required and the borders of the city stretched, and so as Alyat walked he could mark out the passage of time. People carved the names of the deceased into the rock, along with prayers for the dead, and sometimes they would even paint little frescoes—portraits of what the dead had looked like, or sometimes religious imagery. Wards against evil spirits and grave robbers. Glimpses of what they expected the afterlife where their loved one had gone to look like.

As Alyat moved deeper into the catacombs, those carvings and frescoes became less distinct. More worn. Even bones, with time, dissolved into dust. Alyat used these markers to guide his passage. Sometimes, even this far in, he would come across a more recent burial. The people who used the catacombs were always wanting for space, as cutting out new tunnels and ossuaries took much time and effort. If an old place was now filled with nothing but dust, why not use it again?

As another hour slipped by though, even that became uncommon. No longer did he hear the distant echoes of mourners moving through the tunnels, or grave robbers after Mizkhari burial treasures.

Now, he *really* felt as though he was alone.

Well, you never felt totally alone among the dead. They left a sort of weight in the air. An Adept could sense the shift in the flow of aether around places where many bodies lay. Alyat had often wondered whether *all* people could recognize that, so strong was the influence of the dead—or whether it was all just in their heads when they spoke of the different feel of a burial ground.

The Sanctum had been filled with debates of that sort over its history—whether all people had some aether sense and the initiation of an Adept merely sharpened it, or whether the sense was only bestowed by the process of becoming an Adept.

Officially, the latter was the position of the Sanctum—though many Adepts quietly (or not so quietly) dissented. Not that it mattered much; everyone knew that even if all people had some awareness of the aether, it was impossible to turn any person into an Adept through training. That was why the recruitment effort was always so essential—the Corps had to search far and wide to find eligible prospects. Much effort throughout the years had been spent on attempts to 'breed' Adepts, but none had come to fruition.

For some reason, no Lazarran could become an Adept. Among those people who could, there was no discernible reason as to why this person showed potential and that person did not. There were trends, but no one knew exactly why.

Alyat wondered if they would have a missing piece to the puzzle once Talynis was brought under Imperial reign. Then they could recruit regularly from the desert and perhaps the cycle would make sense.

Or perhaps it would continue to be an impenetrable mystery to them, and things would go on as they had.

Thinking on these things, Alyat came to a branching tunnel. By now, he was so far in that he had gone beyond the mapped portions—at least, those mapped in the Sanctum's records. Perhaps there was some old, crudely drawn rendition to guide the regular visitors through here, but Alyat didn't have it, so he had to make some educated guesses.

No one knew exactly where the catacombs had first begun—perhaps that used to be understood but was forgotten in the Dark Days. But as far as the Adept was concerned, the right way to go was whichever path brought him closer to the center of Lazarra. If something had been constructed beneath the city, it seemed reasonable that it would lie close to the center. If that hunch was disproven, he could begin ranging out further.

With that in mind, he chose the left tunnel, footsteps echoing faintly as he made his way, the walls lit by the beam of radiance held in his hand.

He might need to make multiple trips down here, if his luck was poor, but he hoped his Gleam would do well to guide him to what he sought. If he found the symbol carved down here, just as Gylos had seen in the labyrinth as a child...well, it would be a grand discovery. It would stand to reason that such sites existed in the other locations marked on the map.

And it would also raise even more intensely the question of just what the things were. Why had they been built? Why had a map been drawn to identify all their locations? Why were some built under cities, but others not?

Alyat realized he was already assuming he would find one here—but by now, he would have been more surprised *not* to find one. That wasn't necessarily a good attitude to have as a researcher, an investigator. But his intuition was strong, and—like it or not—he was beginning to feel convinced of what he had read in that scroll from the Order.

Not that he believed *all* of it. Some of it still seemed wild beyond belief. The idea that the emperors of Lazarra were Adepts following this secret Art of Foreknowledge, for instance.

But the possibility that the Empire was covering up its own history? Alyat had seen with his own eyes how that ghost operative had killed Nuntius. You didn't need to kill madmen—you just let them babble. If you went to such efforts to silence someone, it only proved they had something true to say. Deceit needed protection; the truth was its own armor.

Though Alyat was aging, he hadn't gone soft. A legionnaire was expected to march twenty miles in a day, farther and faster if there was urgency. An Adept's capacities in that regard were bolstered by their intense training and the longstanding exposure and reliance on aether to fortify their constitutions.

Alyat was quite a ways from the training regimens of his youth, but he hadn't let himself get weak, and he always had his aether. As his steps ate up ground, he hardly felt himself tire. That was valuable, since the tunnels weren't a straight shot by any means. From where he had entered them, he would have long ago reached the city center; he probably even could have gotten there and back, but just like intestines, these winding passages could go unimaginably far in what otherwise seemed like a short distance. They hadn't been built for travel, after all. They were built for corpses.

With time, though, Alyat noticed more changes. There were no more intact bodies and bones here—only dust. The carvings on the wall looked ancient, the frescoes were so faded as to be indecipherable.

Alyat stopped. He wasn't even sure why he had stopped, at first, only that he needed to.

He took a moment to pause, breathe.

The air. The air was different here. It seemed...crisper. Almost fresh.

Gylos had said he hadn't smelled his own torch's smoke, that it had been like standing in a field.

Alyat closed his eyes, inhaling deeply. Yes, he could imagine it. He might have been standing atop a rock overlooking some rolling plain in the countryside.

He opened his eyes—and he saw it. The Gleam made it stand out to him like a shard of iron under a rising sun.

There was a narrow tunnel ahead. A hundred people could pass by and have no idea it was there.

As Alyat inspected it, he realized the crisp air was wafting out from this branching passage. Its source, then, must have been further in. And Alyat was confident he knew what he would find as he delved deeper.

It was a tight squeeze, but he got through.

The tunnel had been cut with exceeding care. Unlike the rough-hewn catacombs, the walls here were smooth as a new-forged shield. And as Alyat made his way, he noticed the tunnel was opening up. Soon it was twice as wide as the rest of the catacombs, then wide enough for five to walk abreast.

Alyat strengthened his light, pressing the beam further into darkness.

"Incredible," he breathed. Not only did the tunnel stretch incredibly far, it sloped *downward*.

Alyat reckoned that by now, it must have been afternoon. He had entered the catacombs soon after dawn, which meant if he turned back now, it would take him the rest of the day to get back.

But he sure as hell wasn't about to turn away at this point.

As he made his way down, he marveled still at the masterful workmanship of the walls—how smooth they were, as if they hadn't even been cut by human hands, but the earth had simply opened up in immaculate form.

Frescoes appeared on the walls.

He stopped to examine these—not only out of curiosity, but also out of awe. These renditions were, by any standard, beautiful. Bright greens, cool blues. The rolling countryside of Lazarra. The shimmering waves of the Great Sea. As he walked along, Alyat saw the landscape evolve.

Beasts appeared, grazing along the earth. Then people appeared to tend them. Sails came over the horizon.

It was a visual history of Lazarra.

People took up arms against one another—first with bronze, then with iron. They wrapped themselves in armor, they lifted high their banners. Alyat couldn't make out what families or cities those standards represented.

Of course—this is from the days of the Republic. Before the Republic, even.

A city took shape, and it was the heart of many conflicts. Blood soaked the fields, turning them an ugly red. Then rain washed them green, until another war. The colors the armies flew kept changing, but always the result was the same. Blood and carnage. Then peace, the city building higher and broader. Then blood again.

So engaged was Alyat in these scenes that he hardly payed attention to how far he was walking.

Was someone maintaining these frescoes?

He thought about how Gylos had somehow been deposited outside the labyrinth. Were there keepers of these places?

Alyat felt a chill as he realized he might not be alone after all.

He took a moment to shine his light all around, back and forth. He set the beam blazing as bright as he could—at this strength, he could blind a person permanently if they were at close range.

No one was behind him.

No one—

...wait.

As the tunnel sloped downward, Alyat thought he saw a figure. Two figures, in fact.

He pulled back the intensity of his light, somewhat—they would have seen him by now, of course, but he'd rather not blind them.

They just stood there, though.

So Alyat just stood and watched.

Then he scoffed, shaking his head.

They were statues.

He dimmed his light, jogging to get over to them. They were a ways off, so he passed quite a few more frescoes, but didn't pay them much mind. He could come back and look later to see if they were anything remarkable.

As Alyat approached the statues, he noted they were both very tall, taller than an ordinary human by about a foot, and they were set on high pedestals.

One stood on either side of the passage, and they were cast of bronze. Like the frescoes, they were in perfect condition—not a spot of rust or discoloration.

On the right was a man, on the left a woman. Both wore armor, which Alyat recognized as dating to around the time of the Republic's collapse and the rise of the Empire.

These were *legionnaires*.

Alyat checked the pedestals, but he couldn't see any identifying plaques explaining who these two were supposed to be. Absent that, he checked their kit. Every legionnaire bore their loyalty on their shoulder.

Hand held high, he inspected the pauldron, and he saw...

Alyat frowned.

He didn't recognize this symbol.

And then his eyes widened.

He didn't recognize this symbol.

"The lost legion," he breathed.

He looked into their eyes—their blank, unseeing eyes.

The lost legion, the First Legion. Vanished with their praetor in the calamity of the Dark Days, never to be seen again, their sister legion known to this day as the Orphans.

Alyat stepped back so that he could see the two of them standing across from one another.

Tears were forming in his eyes.

He had come expecting impossibilities, but *this*?

Was he looking at a memorial to the First, or was this from when they had still served? Why was this beneath the city, so deep and tucked away? Who maintained it?

His mind spun with the possibilities.

Then, nudged again by his Gleam, he turned down the tunnel and shone his light.

Further down, another pair. Then another, closer to them.

He began to walk. He passed a pair of bronze legionnaires. Then another. And another.

He felt lightheaded as he descended further and further, but the air remained as cool and crisp as an early spring breeze.

The tunnel wound such that he couldn't see very far ahead of him. He kept going, kept passing under the empty, ever-watchful eyes of bronze sentries.

The tunnel wound down, down into the depths of the earth, though the air remained fresh as the lushest field of greenery. Alyat followed its curve, always wondering when he would at last hit upon the deep-buried destination.

And then there it was. The winding way straightened out. Alyat's light cast the scene in brightness; looming shadows danced against the walls, drawn from the multitude of bronze sculptures. The statues stood, almost in formation, backs to the wall.

That wall was cut in black basalt, a far cry from the granite and limestone that had made much of the way down here. And hewn into it, brightly painted, was the now-familiar three-lined symbol.

He had found it. He had actually made it all the way here—his hunches proven *right*.

He took a step forward. Then the shaking started.

His first thought was *earthquake*, but then he realized it wasn't the land that was moving.

It was the statues, shuddering on their pedestals, sending tremors through the tunnel. One by one, the bronze soldiers *stepped down*, clanking and jittering in a clashing cacophony of marching metal.

First to move was the guard regiment positioned along the symbol-marked wall, but as they quickened, the life spread. More and more came to life, and every one of them honed in on Alyat with those burnished eyes.

Alyat's light glinted off their swords, their flesh, their armor—they shone like an army clad in mirrors.

Damnation.

Seeing the impossible was an arresting experience, but fear of death was as motivating a feeling as any. The Adept turned and ran. His legs pumped, carrying him up the incline, which suddenly seemed far harsher than it had on the descent.

Pulling aether in to bolster his stamina, he raced fast as he could back through the winding tunnel, all the while hearing the increasingly deafening march of bronze legionnaires behind him. As he channeled aether, something brushed at his senses—no, not something, many things.

The statues had an aetheric presence.

"One impossibility at a time, please," huffed the Adept. Statues of the lost legion come to life, chasing him through a hidden underground tunnel connected to the old catacombs...

He almost wished he were back on the battlefield like in his younger days.

The one blessing in all this, he realized soon enough, was that the automatons could only move so fast. Alyat was able to slow his pace to a jog, staying well ahead of them with minimal effort.

His fear was that somehow the soldiers ahead of him would have awoken as well—but thankfully, they continued to stand immobile. Still, Alyat kept his distance from them as he walked.

The raucous marching became quieter, then deadened entirely. He stopped, shining his light down the tunnel behind him, taking deep, controlled breaths.

He waited like that for a minute, then two. Not a single one appeared.

The desire to go and inspect them again seized him. Had they returned to their pedestals, or were they simply frozen in place? What was it that had triggered their awakening? What life gave them movement? What intelligence illuminated them?

Much as it pained him, he tore himself away, turning to finish the ascent. By the time he made it out, he would find himself under the stars —there was no time. Besides, what were the odds the statues would just wake up and chase him again? No, he needed to go back and make a new plan.

He didn't even know where to *begin* researching this, though. He knew of no Lazarran historian who spoke of such entities, but something dwelt in the back of his mind, some suggestion of ancient lore.

Yes...yes, there was something there—some old myth of metal men given life by the whirling of gears and strange magic, rituals forgotten and forbidden as humanity escaped the days of old.

The statues had given off auras of *aether*. The only possible reference he had for such a phenomenon was a relic—was that what they were?

This was too much to handle alone. He needed to bring someone else in on this. Perhaps Gylos, or even quartermaster Demman—he was a reliable man, trustworthy.

Before returning to the catacomb network, he inspected the frescoes on the walls again. He inspected the soldiers, the armies bathed in blood. Then, casting one last look behind him, down into the depths, he began the long trek back through the intestines of the under-city.

44

ADEPTA LEONA

How strange that we know her as 'the Lion,' as though she were the only one. The title was a rare one, to be sure, but not exclusive. She didn't even like the way it stuck to her, but that was outside her control. If only Cassia had known what she was starting.

—*The Memoirs of Flavia Iscator*

By the time the riots—not all of them, just those in the immediate vicinity of the legion camp—had been quelled, Reiva's blade was slicked with blood, her armor painted red.

And, as always, her nostrils stung with the acrid reek of scorched flesh.

It was night now, and there was a doubled watch. Rookie soldiers who were not on duty would lie awake in their quarters, ready to lunge for sword and shield. Veterans would snooze away, accustomed to catching every last wink of sleep they could in a combat setting.

For Reiva, though, there was no time to rest, despite the bone-deep fatigue and symptoms of magical overexertion. Vantelle had called an emergency meeting, apparently while she was still in the surgeon's care.

When Reiva stepped into the command tent, the praetor was seated. Her face was pale, lips drawn thin, but she kept her back straight, her eyes high. Even in obvious pain, she projected absolute control, absolute devotion to her cause. Even though she was the only one seated, she radiated more authority than any other officer in the room—all men and women of great standing in the military.

The sight made Reiva breathe a little easier.

Vantelle's next words, however, tugged back some of the worry. "We are going to strike back. Fast, hard. Today was a humiliation for us, and we must not allow the Loyalists to imagine they have us on the back foot."

"A retaliatory strike," said Reiva. "When?"

They would need to put together a team, draw up a plan of attack, decide upon a target...Reiva estimated they could launch something by tomorrow, if they hurried.

Vantelle, however, had other ideas.

"We will attack now, Adept. Within the hour, you will lead the strike force."

Reiva's eyes widened. "Excuse me, my praetor, but how—"

Vantelle raised a hand.

Sounds of a struggle came from outside. Grunting, shuffling sand and soil.

Through the flap of the tent came a man in a legion uniform, hauling a gagged Theimos Atreion.

The man called Stag had several large, freshly purpled bruises on his face, and when he opened his eyes, it was clear a blood vessel had burst, casting the white of his left eye in crimson.

Reiva's throat closed. She should not have been surprised. Not after Vantelle so easily ordered a mass crucifixion. The only thing remarkable really was how quickly she had acted.

"This," Vantelle said, "is Zageth. My optio."

The uniformed man gave a half-nod to Reiva, gritting his teeth as he heaved Stag into place on the ground. Zageth's knuckles, Reiva noted, were bruised.

Theimos, for his part, looked terrified. The emotion seemed wrong on his face. Reiva had known him only as collected, calm, in command of himself and whatever else he could manage.

Before the praetor, however, he could hardly bear to look her in the eyes. Reiva struggled not to turn away when Theimos gave her a pleading glance.

Cassia Vantelle, once again, had proven to be another sort of power.

The praetor made a small gesture, and Zageth pulled the gag from Theimos' mouth.

The arms dealer spat blood, heaving short, tremulous breaths. Reiva knew that sort of breathing—soldiers got like that in the heat of battle sometimes. Battle panic, Alyat had called it. Sometimes it clung to men long after they retired from war, invading their minds without notice.

The Adept eyed Vantelle's man, Zageth, with renewed suspicion. A few punches could rattle a person, but *this*?

"Did you," Vantelle said, "have any knowledge of the planned assault that occurred today?"

Theimos shook his head violently, eyes screwed shut. "I did not, I did not, I swear it—I was captured before any such plan was made. We didn't even know you were in the city! Crucifixions?" He let out a sharp bark of half-mad laughter. "We never imagined such a thing."

Vantelle pursed her lips.

"Lies."

Zageth struck Theimos across the jaw, knocking him to the ground.

Reiva stole a glance at Flavia Iscator. The legate was not even bothering to mask her displeasure—but neither of them could do anything. They were outranked here.

Zageth hauled Theimos to his knees again, the Karellan moaning, bloody spittle dribbling from his lips.

"What do you know of the Vipers? Give me the name of the man who wields the black blade."

Theimos muttered incoherently, shaking his head. "No names. Nothing. S-secure."

Zageth threw another punch, this time leaving Theimos to languish on the ground longer. "You had better remember something soon, friend." He said it like he was discussing dinner plans.

Theimos cackled, hacking a red spray in the air. "Friend! If only you knew, Adept, what he's saying," he sputtered, fixing Reiva with that disconcerting bloodied eye.

Reiva hardly had time to process that before Zageth put another fist in his gut. The breath rushed out of Theimos in a single *whoosh*, and he was left gasping like a fish out of water.

Iscator rapped her fist on the desk—*her* desk, though she was not the one sitting at it—pulling Vantelle's attention. "This is barbaric. The Adept's interrogation was proceeding perfectly well." She jabbed a finger at Theimos. "That man will hardly be able to remember who was in this tent by the end of the night, let alone anything we need to get out of him."

Vantelle's regard for the legate was one of absolute contempt. "When did you get so soft, Flavia? I trained you to be better than this. Because of men like *him*, legionnaires lie dead in the streets, their blood intermingled with that of Talynisti soldiers and—Arkhon's mercy—civilians."

"Because of your excessive use of force, my praetor."

"I would never have needed to resort to such measures if you had pacified the region sooner. I sent you an Adept, a pristine blade, and you treated her like a switch to discipline children. What next? Will you swat the Loyalists on their asses? Put them in a corner? Nonsense. There has been too much death here."

Clenching her jaw, Vantelle rose to her feet, one hand braced against the desk. "I am going to put an end to this city's incorrigible resistance, and then I am going to bring this whole country under the dominion of Arkhon and our Emperor."

She observed Theimos. "You do not have names? Fine. Give me the location, then. Is there a base? A headquarters? Where do your Vipers nest?" Vantelle lurched forward, peering straight into the Karellan's face. "Consider carefully the truthfulness of your answer."

Theimos shrank under her eyes, wilting like a flower under noonday summer sun. He swallowed.

Reiva pleaded, prayed for him to give it up.

Mercifully, he did.

He told them where to find their base, how many Vipers numbered in their band, how many entrances and exits he knew of.

With every word, Reiva breathed more easily. The legate looked relieved as well. Now the torture could stop.

Vantelle nodded, satisfied. "That is everything you have to say on the matter?"

Theimos Atreion hung his head, abashed, broken. "Yes, praetor."

"And there is nothing more you know that could help us in razing this den of yours to the ground?"

"No, no I have told you everything."

Vantelle nodded, and there was something of finality in the gesture.

Reiva's stomach dropped to the ground.

Even before Cassia Vantelle gave the order, she knew what was coming.

"Well said, Theimos Atreion. Now, for your crimes against the Empire of Lazarra, including conspiracy to murder one of the seven praetors of Emperor Dioclete, you are sentenced to death."

Theimos hardly had time to scream before Zageth raked a knife across his throat.

Reiva's heart lurched in her chest. Theimos hit the ground, gurgling and wailing, unable to scream through the blood filling his mouth and lungs.

And Reiva couldn't look away as he desperately thrashed, looking at her like he might find a savior, a rescuer. With horror, she realized he was trying to say something to her through the foaming red.

She stood there, as his lifeblood seeped across the ground, touching her sandals.

Iscator was apoplectic. "What is this, Cassia? Are we bandits now? Anarchists? We have laws!"

The praetor's glare was ice. "The Emperor *is* the law, and we are but the agents of his will."

The legate threw up her hands. "Where is the Emperor? Show me!"

"His mercy," Vantelle said, "extends across the world. By our hands."

She thrust out a hand to Theimos' still-twitching form. "You call *that* mercy?"

"I call it necessary. And yes, I call it merciful. I could have had him nailed to a beam. I could have had him flogged, sodomized. All that is allowed and even prescribed by our *laws*. I chose to give him an easier end. For his crimes against the Empire, you know a harsher sentence would have been just."

The legate was practically nose-to-nose with Vantelle now. Reiva had never noticed how short Iscator was. Somehow, she made up for it. "Many things are legal, praetor. Rare is the occasion that calls for the limit of the law, particularly when dealing with a cooperative hostage."

Vantelle shook her head, as if the legate's protests were that of a child whining over a broken toy. "Tread carefully, Flavia. Your failures have been too numerous of late to justify such insubordination."

The legate went rigid. Reiva's breath caught.

Insubordination—that was a deadly word in the legions. You were better off if someone accused you of seducing his daughter than of being insubordinate.

"I have been nothing," Iscator said, deathly calm, "but subservient to the will of our Emperor."

"You have been inadequate. I wondered whether I made the correct choice in sending Adept Reiva to Talynis—now I see my true mistake. I should never have imagined you could handle this assignment."

The praetor turned to Reiva. "Unlike the Adept, who has proven her competence time and again. In capturing the Stag, in protecting my own person amidst an ambush by Loyalists. This is what fealty to the Empire looks like, Flavia. You would do well to remember that."

Reiva felt the adrenaline in her system jolting her muscles into readiness. She had to fight. She had to run. She had to do something—she was in the middle of a battlefield, here in a command tent in Dav-maiir.

And like a knife out of the dark, Vantelle delivered a strike she could not have foreseen in a thousand years.

"Adept Reiva," she said, "I hereby bestow upon you the rank of *Adepta Leona*. You are my princeps. I will inform the Sanctum immediately. In Davmaiir, you answer only to me—your hand and tongue carry my authority."

The world spun. *Adepta Leona*—Lion of the Adepts—at just *nineteen*? Horses were more likely to sprout wings, donkeys to start speaking prophecies. It was a rare commission, denoting an Adept who received the honor of bearing the office of princeps. The princeps was a special charge that could only be conferred by three authorities in all the Empire—the Senate, a praetor, and the Emperor himself. A princeps had special authority to act as the manifestation of the bestower's will. To be a princeps was to be the first among many. It was an honor beyond imagining.

And the madness only continued.

"Legate Flavia Iscator, you are relieved of your command here. You will take a brigade and see to the subjugation of the neighboring cities. Be out of my sight by the sunrise after next."

Iscator might as well have been slapped in the face. She opened her mouth again, only for Vantelle to shoot her a look of pure venom. "One more word of dissent, Flavia, and I strip you of your rank. You are dismissed."

The legate stayed her tongue. With naught but a disgusted glance at the corpse on the floor, she stormed out of the tent.

Reiva's knees were on the verge of giving out. A Lion of the Adepts? She could count on one hand how many of those were in service currently. Not a single one was under thirty years of age—let alone twenty.

With a soft grunt, Vantelle lowered herself into her chair. "Your first task with your new authority, Adept: organize and execute the destruction of the Vipers."

45

SANGUIS

ALL THE ARCANE arts leave a mark upon the soul. Like a trellis, they shape one's growth, and the rigorous student of magic learns to turn this to his edification.

But certain paths bear a more horrid weight, and I would caution all but the strongest from seeking out their secrets.

—*The Life and Wisdom of Simeon Binkhok As Told by Himself*

BY THE TIME Alyat was back at the Sanctum, the sickle moon had nearly set. He had taken a brief detour to leave a note in the quartermaster's workshop. It was vague and included instructions to burn it after reading, but it would set Demman thinking, possibly even investigating through channels of his own.

Weariness wore on Alyat, but such was his excitement that he hardly felt tired. What he had seen down there...it was arguably the greatest discovery since steel.

Which only demanded more caution. He couldn't allow himself to forget that this had all come about because he had agreed to meet with the Order of the Sleeping Dragon. If the Order was to be believed, then the Empire was deliberately covering up and obscuring parts of Lazarran history. Did those automatons underground have something to do with that, or had Alyat merely happened upon some fantastical lost trove?

Who had drawn up the map with the symbols? What lay at the other locations?

So many questions, and every discovery only seemed to raise more.

He couldn't go about this alone. Tomorrow, once he was rested, he would begin putting together a plan for how to go about researching all this. He would need to let others in on this—people he could trust completely. The more people you let in on a secret, the more liable everything was to fall apart.

Such thoughts occupied his mind as he trudged through the quiet halls of the Sanctum. He glanced at the tapestries and painted marble busts decorating the walls, and thought back to those frescoes in the last tunnel.

That was history that *had* been lost. The Order was right about that much; but then again, everyone knew things had been forgotten after the Dark Days. That wasn't the same as saying that the Empire had deliberately covered things up, erased them from the collective consciousness.

He rubbed at the bridge of his nose as he climbed the stairs. Now that he was so close to a bed, he realized just how tired he was. A good night's rest would do him well.

He turned the key and, stepping into the darkness, shut the door behind him.

Then he froze.

"You're as perceptive as they say," crooned a soft voice. A voice he didn't recognize.

"You know it's considered rude to let yourself into someone's home."

Alyat kindled light in his palm.

Sitting atop his desk, one leg demurely folded across the other, was a man dressed all in black. His head was shaved, and his eyes seemed unnaturally wide. As he looked at Alyat, he didn't blink.

And he was holding a scroll in his hands.

The stranger clicked his tongue as he unfurled it further. His eerie gaze ran over the text, but Alyat still somehow felt as though he was under the weight of those eyes.

"Someone," he whispered, "has been reading some very inappropriate material."

Alyat's heart was pounding. If this was anyone else, he would have run, shouted, tried to blind him with burning light.

But this...this was a Carnifex. 'Butcher,' literally.

His best chance was to stall until some sort of opportunity presented itself. If it came to a fight...well, his odds were about as good as a deer fighting a lion.

The Carnifex looked up. "No resistance? No fighting back?"

"I've done nothing wrong. I acquired that text as part of a research—"

"You're lying, Adept Alyat." He said it so calmly, as though he were discussing the weather. "Your heart is beating faster. Blood is rushing to your limbs and brain, preparing you to either run away or to kill me. The first option you know will do you no good. The second you know is impossible."

Alyat fought to keep his breathing steady. He took inventory of his immediate surroundings, considered what could be a weapon or a shield—not that it would do him much good against a Carnifex, but it was a habit.

The Carnifex sighed, closed the scroll, and gingerly set it aside. Leaning over, he took a flint and steel to kindle the oil lamp.

"I was hoping for something more...exhilarating than this. Could you give me something more exhilarating?"

Alyat's mouth was dry. "I have information. A tunnel connected to the catacombs."

The Carnifex nodded. "Yes, that is how we knew it was you."

Hells take me.

"The tunnel is the Empire's?"

"The world is the Empire's. And you, Adept, are a traitor to the Empire."

Alyat's heart was pounding.

And then—it wasn't.

Alyat clutched at his chest.

A half-grin quirked across the Carnifex's lips.

Ars Sanguis. The Art of Blood.

Alyat's head spun, black encroaching on his vision.

Then, as quickly as it had stopped, his heart resumed its rhythm.

He gasped, collapsing against the wall.

"Now, would you make this more interesting for me?"

Alyat looked at him with absolute hate—hate, and fear.

He threw a blinding palm of light intense enough to destroy a man's eyes.

Or that's what he tried to do. Instead, his arm wrenched to the side, his light washing the wall in searing white.

Alyat channeled aether into a shell, a second-skin—and he fought with every shred of will he could muster.

Now, the Carnifex was smiling, perched atop the desk as he was.

Aether was aether—Adepts were always capable of matching other Adepts to at least some extent by manipulating the flow of energy. As Alyat's spirit wrestled against the influence of the man's blood magic, he slowly reasserted control over his limbs.

The room was dead silent, save the faintest of groans from Alyat as he poured all his concentration into resisting the building pressure from the Carnifex.

Inch by inch, he pulled his arm back into position.

The Carnifex looked *eager*.

Alyat clenched his jaw so hard his teeth groaned under the weight, threatening to crack. His head felt like a rock had dropped onto it from atop a mountain.

Everything he had was going into a defensive technique. The second he went on the offense, his focus would slip.

He had to take a chance. The one thing going for him was that he could feel the Carnifex targeting his brain—he could localize his defense, betting that the rest of his body would not be assaulted.

Alyat poured every ounce of will he could spare into burning the man's eyes out.

Everything flared white.

As soon as his attack launched, blood magic struck his temple like an awl, and he redirected everything he had to shielding himself again.

And the Carnifex was just sitting there, hands clapped over his eyes.

Alyat wilted.

Always was the weakest in a fight.

His strength had lain in other realms—thinking things through, making plans. In head-to-head combat against another Adept, he hardly had a prayer.

The Carnifex peered at Alyat through splayed fingers. "Good effort, Alyat. Good effort. Your spirit is formidable. Imagine if you had been born to some greater power, like your protégé, hm?"

He tilted his head, like a child inspecting an insect crawling on a leaf. "I wonder what she'll think when she reads the letter you'll write her."

The weight on Alyat's skull intensified. He buckled under the pressure, dropping to his knees. Both hands clutched his head, his whole spirit desperately fighting to maintain the cracking shield of aether.

"Oh do not fret, Alyat. This will be our little secret. No one need know what you were up to. They will think your death was but a twist of fate."

Alyat could barely think—everything reduced to vague impulses, half-seen images. He wanted to survive. Wanted Reiva to know, to be safe. Wanted the Corps to be pure.

The Carnifex slid off the desk, meandering over to kneel beside him.

Alyat was tired of the fight. Tired of resisting.

He knew he was doomed. No one survived a Carnifex.

But he would be damned if he let this bastard kill him with anything short of a herculean effort. He kept his defenses up, a mad snarl on his lips as another gruesome wave of vile power assaulted his defenses.

The Carnifex hummed appreciatively, and Alyat couldn't help feeling a small swell of pride at that.

That's right, bastard. I gave you your fight.

The Blood Adept pressed his lips against Alyat's ear, whispering, "*Ave Imperator*, Adept."

Like a tidal wave smashing walls of sand, the blood magic shattered Alyat's defenses.

Reiva, survive. You have to—

Something in his skull *popped*—and then all was dark.

PART III

FIRE AND DEATH

46

ONE MAN

OF ALL THE many mysteries I encountered, among the most frustrating and enigmatic is the matter of just who the Crow was. I have heard rumors, and I have even thought some of them credible, but I wonder if we shall ever truly know.

We know his name, at least, for Malik told the world. Lereias. A Karellan name, of all things. I almost wish I hadn't heard, because it only deepened the mystery.

—*The Memoirs of Flavia Iscator*

~

IN TIMES OF WAR, an Adept needed to act, regardless of wounds, of fear, of doubt or despair.

Reiva, whatever she felt about Theimos' torture and death, about Iscator's treatment, about her own promotion—she was an Adept, one of the Emperor's servants. She had run the gauntlet of death to make it here. She had crossed the world and back.

She was a soldier. She would do what must be done.

The strike team was assembled and ready in hours, despite Vantelle's wish for an immediate attack. A surgeon finally cut the arrowhead out from Reiva's leg, and she closed the wound with aether. According to Theimos' information, there were four other Loyalist Vipers—and just as many were probable to be there, in the wake of their being beaten back by the legion.

The greatest concern was the matter of the *Nihilo* Blade. If not for that, Reiva would have had no trepidations. As it was, she made sure Yaros had a sizable shield.

"Can't you carry your own again?" he asked. He had taken the news of her promotion with an odd neutrality. She got the sense he was not sure what to make of it. It could have been part of his way of working through Theimos' death, but she never really knew with Yaros. The man had an uncanny ability to feel everything and nothing all at once.

She ran her fingers along the rim of a round infantry buckler. "Despite the praetor's word, I am not a Lion without the will of the Sanctum. It would be improper for me to pick up a shield."

Yaros shrugged. "I'll try to watch for the kid, then."

'The kid,' that was what he had taken to calling the Wolf. It was like calling a spear a splinter, as far as Reiva could tell. He was the only man in this city that presented a mortal threat to her.

That, also, was why she had called upon a selection of veteran *triarii* —'thirds,' so named for their position in a standard battle configuration. You always wanted your best troops behind the novices and the middling warriors. The time for the decisive show of force was after the initial clash, when energy was flagging, when the tide could easily swing one way or another.

There would be no long, pitched battle today. No siege with terms or negotiations. The *triarii* would be at the front, battering down the door and rushing the defenders.

Reiva had also brought Charas. She was looking somewhat out of her element, walking rather than riding, but she had accepted Reiva's call without question. Not that she had much of a choice, given the Adept's new rank.

They marched through the streets of Dav-maiir as dawn approached.

Charas had strung her bow and was jogging alongside Reiva at the head of the column. "Where do you want me?"

Reiva called up the mental map she had sketched based on Theimos' description. "Pull some men into a perimeter patrol, pick off anyone who escapes." She clapped a hand on Charas' shoulder. "No shooting to disable. Bring them down."

Charas nodded, unflinching.

Everyone's mood, Reiva realized, had changed. After so many weeks in Dav-maiir, the legion had grown at ease. Vantelle had been right about that. Their awareness of the knife's edge atmosphere had dulled. They were letting their guard slip.

With Vantelle in command and Iscator ordered away, with news of Reiva's ascension to Lion spreading through the camp—the legion could sense that this occupation was about to take a decisive turn.

And it began with taking the Viper's headquarters, burning it down if they had to. Dav-maiir would bow to King Tamiq and the reign of the Lazarran Emperor, the Loyalists purged with fire from the hand of an Imperial Adept.

When they reached the site, Reiva was struck by just how ordinary it looked. That was the point, of course. According to Legion Intelligence, this place was known as a reclusive aristocrat's villa, property of a merchant who had made his fortune trading along the Endric Pass. Maybe that was true, maybe that was false. What mattered now was who dwelt inside.

"Take up positions," Reiva said, adjusting her helmet. "Prepare to assault."

~

WHEN SHOUTS REACHED HIS EARS, Lereias had been reading.

He rose, groaning in spite of his age. That was part of the act, of course, and no one was around for it, but it had become habit by now. Even within the confines of the base, he had played the role of old master, serving in battle by way of mind instead of muscle.

A part of him was disappointed the others were not here for this. He particularly wanted to see Wolf and Jackal's reactions. Mouse knew, of course, but Mouse knew many things the others did not.

Jackal would be learning some of those things now, if she had not already. Wolf...he had a hunch Wolf would come to understand the deeper secrets too, before long.

But even though it meant he had to face the legionnaires alone, he was glad for the others' absence. Lereias would have felt pressure to keep them safe, to spare them from a painful death at the end of a sword or spear.

There was none of that now. There was only him, his blade, and the enemy. And he had made his peace with death a long time ago. He could fight here, hold out for as long as he could manage, bring down as many Imperials as possible.

Would the Adept be with them? He hoped so—he would like the chance to test her skill personally. Against any other legionnaire, he felt confident of victory, but she posed a legitimate threat, wearing that shackle they called a 'focus' around her neck.

He felt a stab of sympathy for her—she almost certainly had no idea what the truth of the world was. Almost no Adepts did, besides the Carnifexes. In some sense, it was a miracle Lereias had lived so long, knowing what he did about Arkhon and the Empire. The truth was a heavy thing to bear. But he had decided a long time ago not to regret his choices.

Shouts, orders being given. Was that the Adept? She did not sound as young as she was. War did that to people. The Adept Corps, he was sure, did that to people.

He rolled his shoulder around, leisurely making his way to stand in the foyer. He grabbed hold of the key hook, twisted it forty-five degrees, and pulled.

Click, and a panel of the wall popped open. He slid it aside, grasping hold of the sword he had stowed away. He had only told Mouse about this. A part of him had hoped he would never have to draw it again, that he would die some way or other and Mouse would retrieve it, take it to Endra.

He had not picked this weapon up with the intent to kill in...

Well, better not to think about that. He wasn't *that* old.

The grip molded to his hand like it had been made for him, and he drew it from the leather.

And, as he gave it a few experimental swings, he felt the spirit within come to life, a gentle breeze drifting from the iron, rustling his clothes, the papers in the other room.

A distant groan, the splintering of wood—the legionnaires had broken through the perimeter wall, and their footsteps shook the ground as they made for the villa.

Crash!

The door shook and creaked, but held against the first ram.

Crow took a few steps back, set his feet, settled into his breathing.

He raised the blade, ready to fight, to kill, to die.

Crash!

The door was scarcely holding, now. Splinters flew, the hinges moaned. One more hit, and they would be in.

He heard the Adept on the other side. She bellowed the charge. "Give them no mercy!"

A roar went up from the legionnaires.

And Lereias smiled. "I do not intend to."

In an explosion of wood and iron and fury, the door flew off its hinges.

With a subtle twist of his sword, currents of air spun off to the side, no shrapnel or slivers touching him.

This day had been a long time coming.

~

REIVA WATCHED, fingers tight around her sword's pommel, as the first wave charged in.

Shouts, the clash of metal on metal. The Vipers, evidently, had been prepared.

That was fine—Reiva actually preferred it that way. Let them have a fair chance; let the world see that no force on earth could stand against Lazarra.

She only wished she had been at the front herself—but the presence of the *Nihilo* Blade and her own liability to burn the whole place down on her and her own men made that inadvisable.

So caught up in her musings was she, that she nearly missed the impossible.

Yaros straightened up. "Are they...?"

Reiva's lips parted, eyes widening. "Falling back."

The two of them drew their blades, advancing.

One of the men hobbled to them, bleeding from at least three wounds, one of which could be serious if he did not get immediate attention.

"Situation report, soldier," said Reiva.

He gave it, and Yaros nearly choked. "*One* man?!"

But the others confirmed it—one *old* man.

One old man, moving like the wind, fighting like a demon.

Reiva and Yaros shared a look.

Theimos had told them Crow was an unusual sort, secretive even by the standards of the Vipers, but this...they had no indication of this.

Perhaps Theimos had held some things back, despite everything he had been put through. Or perhaps he had not known, and was just in the dark about this as they were.

"The hell is wrong with this city?" muttered Yaros.

"Shut up," said Reiva, "you're getting paid enough."

"For this? We'll see."

From the gaping entrance came a voice, aged but strong. "While you catch your breath, might I offer a solution to the Adept?"

Reiva's head snapped to the doorway. He was out of sight.

She took a quick scan of the area. Charas was not far—and she was in position with her eyes on the door. Good. With a signal though, the Parthavan indicated she had no line of sight on him.

"It's rude to ignore your elders, you know."

Reiva swore under her breath. "Adept Reiva," she called into the building. "Am I correct in presuming I speak to the one known as the Crow?"

"Indeed, indeed," he chuckled. "I must say, the Lazarran *triarii* are as formidable as their reputation. One of your men gave me quite a scratch along the ribs."

A scratch.

"He is dead now, I regret to inform you."

Reiva worked her fingers on the hilt, her free hand twitching and sparking with embers. "The Stag is dead as well." She wasn't sure why she said it. To get back at him, somehow? As some sort of courtesy?

A pause. Then, sounding genuinely mournful, Crow said, "Poor boy. Such is war, eh?"

"You had an offer for me."

"Mm, yes. You know, in the bygone days, they used to settle these sorts of things with champions. One to one, before the armies. I do not have an army with me, but I'm sure yours would suffice."

Yaros shot Reiva a wary look. He clearly was not comfortable with the idea. Neither was she, but...

"I must admit, I was quite ready to stay in here, holding out on my own, but, well, I forgot what it's like to kill young folks. It seems wrong, somehow."

Reiva knit her brow. "I had heard you were strange."

"Not strange, just old."

Yaros snorted, shifting his shield. "It's a trap, boss. We charge him together, or you just burn the whole place down around him if you want to be safe."

"We need their documents," she reminded him.

"Then we charge him—but none of this single combat business."

Reiva sighed, eyes fixed to the doorway.

"Would we fight inside, or out here?" she asked eventually.

"Outside, I imagine. That would suit both of us well."

Reiva's gut was twisting. Something was very wrong here.

He moves like the wind, he fights like a demon.

"Come on then," said Reiva, motioning for her soldiers to clear away. "Step into the light."

Yaros rolled his eyes. "Do you have a death wish, or do you just want to spite me my rightful pay by dying before our contract comes to term?"

"What happened to me being one of the Empire's finest?"

The mercenary shrugged. "Alar the Great died choking on a fig. *The gods laugh.*"

Yes, she thought, *yes they do.*

The *triarii* had formed a semicircle around the area, creating a cordon within the perimeter walls. There would be soldiers around the sides and back as well. The Crow claimed he was alone, but Reiva believed that about as much as she believed a Zarushan money changer.

SLOWLY, with a bit of a hunch, the Crow emerged, blinking against the early dawn brightness. "Lovely day to die," he muttered.

The Crow was indeed old, but he moved with easy grace, like a dancer. His form was concealed beneath loose robes (no armor)—easy to disguise hidden weapons, or hidden strength, apparently. He may have indeed had a wound on his side from one of the fallen *triarii*, but so covered in blood was he that it was impossible to tell.

Reiva's eyes were moving to inspect his weapon, when the *thrum* of a Parthavan recurve bow shook the air.

Reiva had almost forgotten about Charas.

The arrow missed.

Crow glanced at it, quivering in the wall, with amusement.

Reiva shot a look at Charas, who was staring in bewilderment at the old man, like she could not believe what she was seeing.

"I would say that was dishonorable," Crow chuckled, "but I'm not exactly playing fair either, so..." A shrug.

And then Reiva took a closer look at his sword—and swore. She had seen a weapon exactly like that during her training.

"He has a relic. Windsword."

Yaros narrowed his eyes. "Should've burned the place down."

He may have been right.

The Crow gave a sly smile. "I hope this evens things out between us, if you are willing to hold to your word."

"I will," she said automatically. Already she was running through possibilities. He had no armor; he relied on movement to stay alive. Charas—a crack shot if ever there was one—had missed.

As she turned her aetheric sense toward him, she felt the shifting tides of energy curling around and within the weapon, even and rhythmic.

Just as she had suspected—*Ars Ventas*, the Art of Wind.

"How did you come by such a weapon?" she asked, stoking her Flame.

"Oh, these things can be found all over the world, if you know where to look. Not that the Empire would know, of course."

First a *Nihilo* Blade, now a *Ventas*...

Dav-maiir was proving itself a place unlike any other.

"Ego, is that your master's name? Is he the one who supplies you with the relics?"

"I am here to duel you, Adept, not to discuss supply trains, fascinating as they may be."

"Your possession of that relic is a severe violation of Imperial law."

"Many things violate the law, Adept. I am standing before you out of appeal to a higher one. Honor. Forthrightness. Will you fight me here, or will you send more of your men to perish under my blade?"

The Adept frowned. "Take your position, Crow."

The courtyard of the estate had enough room to move, not enough to flee. Along the walls, *triarii* had their spears bristling from among their shields.

It occurred to Reiva that the Crow very well might be able to fly with that weapon—it was a favored skill of Adepts who mastered the ability to seize the winds.

In a normal duel, there would be seconds. The Crow had no one, however, and Reiva did not particularly feel the need to let Yaros know that if she died, he would be on the hook to get satisfaction for the Empire. The man was hung up enough on his contract as it was; he would know how to get his payment if she fell today.

The greater concern, to Reiva, was that civilians could be watching. She had legionnaires locking down the area, ordering people to stay inside, keep their windows shut. But something would slip through—something always did. It would be impossible to keep the existence of the *Ventas* Blade a secret, which would only add weight to rumors that the Vipers had a mythical *Nihilo* Blade. The ramifications would be...hell, she really didn't want to think about it. A duel was the worst time to get a headache.

Maybe campaigns to Talynis really were cursed.

The Crow stood at ease, feet spread, sword lowered. The winds were swirling around him, almost imperceptibly, but the shifting dust about his feet was anything but natural.

Reiva mirrored his posture, building her Flame to as much of a peak as she could without unleashing it.

She planned to strike fast, to overwhelm him. She would have to be careful not to sear any of her own men—but she had confidence in that. The courtyard was wide enough, and if there was one thing that the legions taught well, it was how to control your position on a battlefield.

Looking rather dissatisfied with his role, anxious even, Yaros called the start.

Like an erupting volcano, fire burst from Reiva's fist, swarming for Crow. The old man didn't even move.

She kept the pressure on, pulling aether through her body as fast and as intensely as she could manage. *Triarii* ducked behind their shields, squinting against the blinding, blistering flame.

Then she stopped.

Standing right where he had been, the Crow was holding his blade aloft, a vortex of fire whirling about his body.

It hadn't even singed his hair.

Then he thrust his sword forth—and the winds carried Reiva's fire right back to her.

She tumbled into a sidelong roll, trusting that her soldiers would take care of themselves. There was no opportunity to spare her attention—not against a foe like this.

Crow lashed out with a series of fast cuts, and the wind lashed from his blade in aetheric arcs of power.

Reiva dodged one, the second clipped her shoulder, nearly spinning her around, the third slammed into her side, sending her flying.

She slammed into the ground, rolling along the stones with a clatter. Somewhere along the way, she tossed her sword away, lest she die on her own steel.

Scrambling to her feet, she threw both hands out, fingers splayed. A jet of red fire roared forth.

The Crow barely lifted his feet, but the *Ventas* Blade pulled him along the ground, like a water skimmer along the surface of a lake.

And he glided right along to Reiva's sword, snatching it up in his off-hand.

Damnation.

Reiva threw volley after volley, blast after blast, strafing Crow's position.

In a whirling storm of metal, he leaped right for her, deflecting her fire-balls with the *Ventas* Blade, her own sword poised to skewer her as he dove like a falcon.

Frantically, she threw herself into another roll, throwing off a plume of fire as she went.

As she popped to her feet, a blade whistled by her ear.

Blindly, she threw another blast of fire at point-blank range.

Crow wrapped himself in a cocoon of wind, letting the fire knock him through the air.

And he didn't come back down.

Instead, he spun the sword in a dizzying pattern, and the winds formed up around him, bearing him up high above the earth.

Of course.

Reiva threw jets of fire into the sky like burning lances. The Crow weaved around them with preternatural grace, as if he had all the training and spiritual discipline of an *Ars Ventas* Adept.

Diving like a falcon, Crow dropped for Reiva, swords flashing. She rolled beneath the biting iron, feeling the air tremble with his passage. Another sudden gust of wind ripped through the square, carrying him aloft.

Reiva watched with a scowl. His maneuverability was too much of an advantage.

Fine, I've got my own tricks.

As the Crow swooped around for another dive, Reiva focused in on him —and detonated fire at range.

A ball of flame *boomed* as Crow zipped down on her—unharmed.

Reiva swore, throwing herself into a clumsy roll, barely avoiding his blades. Her soul was weary, weary like she had just pushed a mountain across the desert. Triggering an explosion at a distance used up extreme amounts of aether compared to normal fire techniques.

And even when she did manage it, there was a slight delay between her commanding the requisite aether and the effect's activation.

Which meant she had to compensate.

Drawing in a deep breath, pulling tremendous quantities of aether into her system, she focused on a space just ahead of Crow, letting her mind's eye draw out his path.

Targeting empty air was much harder than a well-defined figure, but something told her he wouldn't sit still for her if she asked nicely.

So, right before he intersected the space she'd honed in on, she triggered the explosion.

A ball of fire burst into being, swallowing up Crow—for a moment. A spinning cyclone of aetheric wind spun off his wheeling blade, dispelling most of the flames.

But he was singed—and he was off balance.

He went in for another dive, even steeper this time.

Reiva held her ground, launching another burning lance—weaker this time. Her head was pounding—the familiar sign of minor aether sickness.

Crow slipped around it like a fish weaving around an oar.

Reiva threw another jet. This one, he deflected with a wind current.

Her soul was heavy—heavy enough that she worried another advanced technique would push her into the next stage of aether sickness.

But she wasn't about to roll over and die.

She built a shell of aether around her hands. She would need to time this exactly right if she wanted to keep all her fingers.

Both swords lashed out like metal tongues.

Reiva activated the reserve of aether she'd been building.

Two gauntlets of bright flame burst alight around her hands—and she batted the swords aside like sticks.

Her head spun from the exertion, but the maneuver had been worth it. Crow tried to pull into another ascent, but she was too close.

She grabbed him by the collar, hand still aflame, and tore him down, slamming him into the stones hard as she could.

In an instant, she was on him, pinning down the hand with the *Ventas* Blade with one fist, bracing her knee on his other arm.

"*Yield,*" she said, nose wrinkled against the smell of burning flesh. Her stomach turned, not just from the stench but from the adverse effects of magic.

A croaking sound came from the older man. Then, a hacking laugh. "A bit late for that."

He let go of the swords; Reiva knocked them away, relieved to see Yaros moving to pick up the windsword.

She extinguished her burning gauntlets and flipped Crow onto his back.

Half his face was a bloody mess, and the wetness of his breathing signaled a punctured lung. Pressing her hand against his chest, she felt ribs move in a way they ought not.

He coughed. "No healing, Adept."

Without it, he would be dead soon.

Reiva's stomach dropped. "You fought well."

"For an old man." He slipped into another fit of hacking laughter. "Out of practice."

Reiva was suddenly very conscious of her *triarii*. Whatever she said here would be known by the whole camp by nightfall.

She tried to think of what Alyat would say in her position.

Reiva got on one knee beside his broken form. "A warrior should be proud when he dies. You earned that."

A faint smile appeared on Crow's features, cutting through his pain like a ray of sunlight through gray clouds. "You sound like my father."

"I will take it as a compliment."

"He was a right bastard."

A chuckle rippled through the soldiers.

"All the same," she said, feeling a mournful smile creep onto her own lips.

Crow nodded, which she took as approval.

She remembered something Alyat had told her years ago:

'The soul across the battlefield, Reiva, is the one you must respect above all. She has been raised since youth to draw the bow and provide for her lands. He has been taught to raise a shield and defend the traditions of his fathers. Of all people, you ought love your enemy, for you are the same.'

"Who are your gods, old man?"

He was silent for a moment. "Give me to the Wanderer."

Reiva couldn't mask her surprise, and the Crow flashed another grin, revealing bloodied teeth.

He seemed about to say something else when a fit of coughing seized him.

Reiva set a hand on his shoulder.

With a final shudder, the Crow stilled.

When she raised her head, she saw all her soldiers standing with rapt attention, deadly serious. More than one among the *triarii* had tears in their eyes.

He had been one man.

47

WAR

When Cassia relieved me of command, she knew who I was. Of this, I am certain. Why not kill me, though? Was it for appearances' sake? Were there yet more machinations she intended to use me for?

Or was it simply a mercy? I like to think she was capable of such a thing —capable as she was of everything else. As I left, I could almost hear the collective intake of breath. The sound of a city bracing for the plunge.

—*The Memoirs of Flavia Iscator*

~

Avi woke, and for a moment forgot where he was. Panic seized him, and with it the need to grab a weapon.

Then Asrah put her hand on his chest, her fingers over his mouth. "It's okay," she whispered, smiling fondly. "You're not under attack."

He blinked, forcing himself to ease up. Was he really safe?

Sure enough, he looked around, and he was still in the princess of Talynis' chambers.

The usurper princess.

Four on High. When would his life have some normalcy again?

Avi let his head fall back onto the pillow. How was it even possible for a pillow to be this soft? Was it stuffed with baby geese or something?

Asrah was watching him, a soft smile playing on her lips.

He had kissed those lips, he realized. Actually, she had kissed *his* first.

On second thought, he could get used to this sort of normal.

"I should go," he murmured.

She nodded. "I am expected soon."

"Can I help you get dressed?"

That got him a slap—but a playful one.

"I would have hit you harder if I didn't have guards at the door."

"Sure, sure."

Asrah bit her lip, shoving him out of bed. "Come on, you need to get out of here before the city is awake."

Avi mumbled a vague agreement, fishing along the floor for his discarded tunic and cloak. Asrah had kicked them all the way to the corner. When he shrugged them back on, he turned to find her observing him.

"Can I help you?"

"Mm..." She tapped her chin. "Take them off and put them back on, but slower."

Avi shook his head. "Four Gods, woman. What if someone came through that door right now?"

"I'm sure they'd be just as gripped by your physique as I am."

"Well, my physique is easily ruined by a well-placed spear, so I will take my leave."

The princess snorted, hopping to her feet to meet him at the balcony door. She gave him a brief kiss, then a less-brief one.

Avi felt lightheaded as he strapped the *Nihilo* Blade against his side. "Concealed?"

"Exceptionally."

"All right." He set his hand on the door, then stopped. "When will I see you again?"

"I have a report due next Avenday." She added a sly grin. "Come at night?"

"For security's sake, of course."

"Of course."

Like a ghost, he slipped outside. Before he could close the door, she grabbed his arm. "Aviqohl," she said, tension in her voice.

Hearing his name on her lips made his stomach flutter. "Yes?"

"Be careful."

He nodded firmly. "I will. I promise. You too."

Asrah held her chin high. "I assure you, I will not go charging into a crowd of legionnaires."

"Thank the gods—I was worried you might."

As he made his exit from the palace grounds, he felt both giddy and somehow empty. He nearly walked right into a guard's line of sight while he was trying to come up with a plausible excuse for going back.

Cursing himself, he pinched the bridge of his nose.

Can't see her again if you're dead, genius.

Forcing himself to focus, he made his escape with no further hiccups. Soon he was well clear of the heightened security around the palace, and he was able to walk along the streets like a normal pedestrian.

The atmosphere, among those few who were already out and about, was tense. Still, there were things to be done, and Talynisti were not the sort of folk to let a little civil unrest dissuade them from their responsibilities. They were made of sterner stuff than that—had to be, living amongst the sands.

Strangely enough, though, Avi did not see many Imperials. Perhaps they had been pulled back to their camp at the western gate.

The calm before the storm?

He found himself worrying about Asrah, chided himself for it.

She's smart—she's been in the palace without even a hint of suspicion for months now. She'll be okay.

Still, maybe he could make sure she knew some basic moves with a knife the next time he went to see her. Just in case.

He was so caught up, he almost didn't notice the commotion in the street.

He slipped into a corner, peering at the Imperials crawling all over the place. Their ridiculous plumed helmets stood out against the brick and mortar, their iron breastplates shining beneath the rising sun's light.

His first thought, naturally, was for Crow—but the man was either dead or far away by now, given how casually the legionnaires were going in and out of the place. He hoped they would not find the tunnels—at least not the one Jackal and Mouse had taken.

Avi swore under his breath. Should he have gone with them after all? How could he get to them now?

He was trying to recall the nearest Loyalist cell where he could contact the network—and then he saw her.

The Adept. Helmet under her arm, hair tousled, sword in its sheath.

Blood spattered against her armor.

And he knew Crow was dead.

He stepped out from the shadows, hand reaching for the *Nihilo* Blade.

He would kill her. Here and now—he would do it.

But as his fingers closed around the relic blade's hilt, Asrah's face flashed through his mind, lips pursed, eyes wide with worry.

And he came up short.

"Hold!" snapped a woman's voice.

Avi whirled on the sound.

She was on a rooftop, and she was nocking an arrow.

Well, he sure as hell wasn't about to wait and see what she'd do next.

Throwing himself into a dead sprint, ducking as low as he could, the Wolf barreled away as the *twang-hiss* of a loosed arrow split the air.

As he ran down the alley, he found his way blocked by two legionnaires.

Fine, have it your way.

They were calling for him to surrender. Why did legionnaires always seem to expect he would just up and obey? Did they not think he had seen what they did to people like him?

Avi dashed straight for them.

Predictably, they braced their shields and set their spears.

Really, these sorts had no sense of imagination.

As he came up on them, he kicked off the ground, running along the wall.

Too slow, one tried to skewer him. Avi grabbed hold of the shaft, dropping behind the legionnaires and wrenching away the spear.

Fast as lightning, he slammed the butt-end into its former owner's face, then spun it around to open up the other's throat with a vicious thrust.

He never stopped moving, dropping the spear and breaking into another sprint. Behind him, cries of alarm were going up—shouts about a Loyalist, an insurgent. He was already gone, weaving between buildings and clambering out of sight.

He didn't have the headquarters anymore, that much was clear, and he certainly couldn't go back to the palace right now.

That was fine—he had another option. And he knew how he would use it.

All throughout the city, the Loyalists had cells. Most only had one or two faithful citizens of Talynis on hand at a time, but their reach was wide.

The nearest was a blacksmith. Avi had never met the man, but he knew him by description.

Looking up from his forge, the heavily built fellow eyed Avi up and down. Before he could say anything, Avi already had the code phrase out.

Instantly, the man's expression shifted. He jerked his head to the door, and Avi wasted no time getting off the street.

Inside was a woman, bouncing a toddler on her knee as she mended a pair of trousers. She looked up as Avi entered. Again, Avi uttered the phrase.

"How can we help you?" she asked, pulling her child to her hip and setting her work aside.

Avi was panting, sweating. Words tumbled through his skull. So many things to say—so much information to get across.

By now, the woman's husband had set aside the piece he had been tapping outside and come within, folding his thick-corded arms across his chest.

There was one thing, Avi decided, that they needed to hear right now, that needed to be spread to every cell across the city as soon as possible.

"Prepare for war," he said. "The praetor and her Adept will try to inflict a massacre in our streets. We will send the message that the people of Davmaiir will not stand idly by. No more waiting for Malik's word, no more holding on for aid. It's time we retake our city, before we lose it forever."

48

INITIATE

THE CONVERGENCES ARE WEAKER than they once were—certainly weaker than in the Golden Age of our world—but even so, not a soul can witness their unbridled abundance and not tremble with awe.

My heart aches to imagine how it all was, in the purest state. Pondering this brings me to tears, like a man far from home, knowing he will never return.

I have seen all the world, but never have I felt so distant from home as when I come closest to what ought to have been, when I come to the places of Convergence.

—*The Life and Wisdom of Simeon Binkhok As Told by Himself*

～

ARTUNIS AWOKE SOMEWHERE COOL, to the sound of running water.

When she first opened her eyes, in fact, she thought she was underwater. Everything was cast in a soft blue light, and the air seemed full of mist.

Then, as her vision resolved, she realized she was looking at cave walls.

The next thing she realized was how much her wrist hurt.

Wincing, she tried to sit up—struggling as hard as she might have trying to lift a mule. She was lying on a cot, a thick blanket spread over her.

When she finally got herself propped against the wall, she let out a puff of exertion.

And she sat like that for a while, staring at the rough walls.

Just look.

It took her another minute of preparation before she finally pulled her arm out from under the blanket.

Sure enough, her arm came to a sudden stop at the wrist, wrapped in thick bandages.

Her head fell back against the stone. She would have grunted at the pain —but she didn't have it in her. Her dominant hand was gone. She was like a lame horse now. What else was she supposed to do—paperwork and planning like Crow? Negotiations like Stag? She had neither Mouse's bulk, nor Wolf's—well, hands.

She would be dropped. It was the only option for her at this point. She couldn't work as a Viper like this.

But even so, melancholic as she was, she couldn't stand staring at the same cave wall forever. For a short while, she distracted herself by inspecting the strange plants giving off that cold, blue light, but even that novelty could only do so much to pull her attention from the gaping pit in her gut, from the ache at the end of her arm.

So, dragging herself against the fatigue, she got to her feet. She had come here—wherever here was—with Mouse. He would have to be close by.

Her other possessions—as in her weapons—were laid out on a sheet of canvas beside the cloth. Out of habit more than anything, she stuck her favorite dagger through her belt. It felt wrong holding it in her left hand— she always used her left for the throwing knives—but she would rather have it with her.

Her shamshir though, that was missing. Her father's last gift to her.

She shoved down another wave of grief. *Work through that later. You still have your life—figure out what you'll do with it.*

Her steps were unsteady—Crow's potion, she guessed, had not entirely worked its way through her system. She was relieved though, that the sweating and the searing pain that had been crawling up her arm were both gone. That was good; whoever Mouse had brought her to had taken care of the poison.

With her one hand braced against the wall, her wrist tucked against her stomach, she padded to the single entrance to her room. Her cave opened up to a larger tunnel, perhaps about one and a half times her own height. As she looked left and right, she saw more of that luminous plant growth, as well as the apertures of more caves.

Tunnels under Dav-maiir were nothing strange, of course, but all those were obviously manmade. These were rough, winding. Where she saw evidence of human occupation (a discarded hammer here, a dropped scrap of cloth there), they stood out as stark contrasts to the otherwise natural environment.

Now and then, she would hear voices, but they either came from further down the tunnel, or they came from curtained-off chambers. Unwilling to poke her head in, she kept on making her way.

The sound of water was growing louder, which she took as a good sign.

As the tunnel curved, something clicked in her mind.

It couldn't be...

Then, just as she rounded the corner, her suspicions were confirmed.

Suddenly, the tunnel opened to a massive subterranean chamber, lush with fruit-laden trees, bright, blossoming flowers...there was even a pair of goats nibbling at the verdant, long-bladed grass. Then, as she looked closer, she saw more animals. Birds nesting in the branches, hares bounding to and fro.

"The oasis," she breathed.

"Jackal!" boomed a familiar voice.

She rounded on Mouse, who was jogging over from another tunnel mouth to the side.

"We're under the oasis of Dav-maiir," she said, awed. "Or close to it, at least."

Mouse seemed both amused and satisfied by her deduction. "*Very* close to it."

"How did you...how is there..."

Mouse put up a hand, forestalling her questions. "I will answer what I can soon. I am sorry that I was not there when you awoke. We were expecting you to remain under the effects of the anesthetic for a while longer."

"I still feel it," she grumbled. "Wait—who is *we?*"

Here, Mouse turned more pensive. "You know them as..." He trailed off, searching for the right words. "The Desert Sages," he said at last.

Artunis scoffed, waving at the underground garden in front of them. "If this is a desert, I'm the Queen of Caroshai."

"The power of the Origin Spring is great."

She nearly lost her footing. "The *Origin Spring?* I thought that was just..."

Mouse smiled softly. "There are many things you know as *just legends* in this part of the world."

As they were speaking, a baby hare hopped over to them, snuffling at their feet, curious. It gave an inquisitive sniff at her toes, only to snort, shake its head, and bound away again.

Mouse watched the scene with open amusement. Artunis' jaw hung as she watched the rabbit go off and rejoin its friend—a fox cub. The impossible pair trotted off into the underbrush, looking to be engaged in a game of tag by now.

"Tell me everything," she murmured. "What's truth, what's fiction—all of it."

The Endric man, for the first time, looked sorrowful. "I wish I could tell you everything, but there are things barred to you, as you are not an initiate."

"An initiate of what? Don't tell me you're a Sage, Mouse—you're not some old crusty man who rolls around in the sand instead of bathing."

"No, he is not," muttered a raspy voice from behind.

Artunis whirled, heart in her throat.

Standing before her was an elderly man, pale, attired in a long headdress and flowing robes belted with cracked leather.

She swallowed. "You, ah...don't look like a crusty old man who rolls around in the sand either."

The newcomer snorted. "I am glad to hear it." He spoke Talynisti with an odd accent, one she had never heard before. He scarcely moved his lips as he spoke, and he ran his fingers along a bushy silver beard, far bigger than was the conventional style in Talynis.

"This," Mouse said slowly, "is Hatzakh. He is the man who saved you from the poison. And yes, he is one of the Sages."

Artunis did her best to maintain her dignity as she offered a brief bow. "Thank you, sir, for your care. Four on High bless you."

Hatzakh watched her impassively. Eventually, she realized he just would not say anything, so she shot a glance at Mouse. The Endric, however, looked similarly uncomfortable.

"So," she murmured, "Hatzakh is a Desert Sage. You are not. But you *are* an initiate, whatever that means?"

"Yes. I am what you would call, on this side of the mountains, an Adept."

49

A WINDING, SCRAWLING LINE

How terrible to lose a father. How much worse to lose one twice.
—Lucian Sana, Lazarran philosopher

∿

The crackdown went well for all of two hours. While Reiva had overseen the investigation of the Vipers' headquarters, Charas had seen and shot at a man she thought she recognized as the Wolf from the previous day's violence. Unfortunately, her description of his face bore nothing unique— he had a short beard, dark eyes, and a small scar over one eyebrow. There were probably thousands of young men in Dav-maiir who matched that description. While fleeing, he had killed one legionnaire and wounded a second before disappearing.

Apparently, he had spread the word that the Loyalists were to get out in force, because Dav-maiir had turned into a war zone overnight.

And it was painfully apparent to the legion how severely they had underestimated Loyalist presence and support in the city.

Quietly, Reiva acknowledged that Vantelle's moves since coming to the city had further inflamed the situation. But now, all of those moves were inextricably linked to her as well—and her ascension.

And as a Lion with the effective rank of a legion princeps, Reiva was in command of the ground strategy, with Vantelle's oversight.

Legate Flavia Iscator had indeed departed by Vantelle's deadline, taking a nontrivial—but still uncomfortably small—force of soldiers with her. Reiva had the sinking sense that she would not see the legate again, not in this life at least. Nevertheless, when Iscator departed, she kept her head high, and her legionnaires did the same. Many of those legionnaires were among the most talented in the Ninth.

Reiva had watched them go, her stomach tying into knots.

While she had watched, Charas rode up to the legate. The Scout Lieutenant had loaded her saddle bags as though she was going to join Iscator's force. They had a brief exchange, Charas seeming increasingly flustered. Eventually, Charas had turned and left, her posture rigid.

Maybe the legate felt certain they would all die out there, and wanted to spare Charas that fate. Maybe she simply wanted a loyal set of eyes and ears in the city.

Reiva hoped it was the latter. Things would be dangerous out there, and the legate had taken just a few hundred troops. Iscator was not on Vantelle's level when it came to military strategy, but she had been trained and hand-picked by the woman. She had a chance of taking some smaller towns, with luck on her side. It would be a costly operation though, and every one of those soldiers' absences would be felt in the city.

All told, the situation for the Empire in Dav-maiir was grim. The palace and the Temple were both effectively secured, as were the western gate and most of the aristocratic homes and businesses in the east. The problem was, that left the legion and the king's forces divided, with the bulk of Loyalist presence and power concentrated in the middle.

Already, blockades had gone up, manned by men and women with not a day of true combat experience, but enough zeal and vigor to make up for it. And given by how many of them carried swords, spears, and shields, it was evident that Theimos Atreion's information had not enabled the legion to completely stop the flow of arms into Loyalist hands.

The first night had been quiet, largely. The second saw several hit-and-run attacks on Imperial patrols and guards. By the fourth night, Reiva had given the order for patrols to cease except in the most well-controlled districts.

In less than a week, the Loyalists had knocked the Empire back on its heels, and the city was locked in a vicious tug-of-war.

Dark circles sat under the eyes of most officers, sleep lost either to sudden crises, or simply to long hours spent writing condolence letters to families.

Even Yaros was beginning to show wear. The mercenary had shown a remarkable aptitude for coordinating the logistics of urban warfare (though at this point, Reiva was hardly surprised by anything he was capable of). With the nature of the struggle changing day by day however, he was constantly tearing out his hair trying to counteract the Loyalists.

"The legion isn't built for this," he grumbled, rubbing his forehead as he pored over yet another map. "You train for pitched battles, for clearly defined engagements."

Reiva slammed her palm on the table. "The legions have gone through guerrilla warfare before and we'll do so again. You have the best army in the world at your fingertips—use it!"

The Karellan gave her a withering look.

Reiva screwed her eyes shut. "Sorry."

"How much sleep have you gotten this past week?"

"My constitution can handle a little fatigue, Yaros."

"For how long?"

"As long as it has to." Her breathing was heavy, she realized. Her heart was pounding. "And I don't need to fight with you while I'm already fighting a war."

Yaros threw up his hands. "I wasn't asking for a fight. I was being realistic about what you're capable of here."

Reiva started pacing the tent. She had hardly sat down all day; any time she tried, she was back on her feet in seconds. Commanding from afar like this, being forced to watch while her men went to battle without her—she was supposed to be *in* the fight, not supervising it.

"Even with our new estimates on the size of the Loyalist insurgency, we outnumber their soldiers."

"We outnumber their *soldiers*, Reiva. We don't outnumber their fighters."

"What, you're saying we should count every last man, woman, and child?"

He stood, bracing his arms on the table. "That's exactly what I'm saying. You grew up in this country, you know how things are."

"I left when I was twelve, Yaros. *Twelve.* Were *you* studying military logistics when you were twelve?" She put up a hand. "Don't answer that."

Yaros sighed, tapping the map with his knuckles. "Did I ever tell you about the time I was hired to bring down a camel thief?"

"Is now a relevant time for that story?"

"Relevant as any."

She waved him on, dropping to a seat.

"When I was in Talynis last, I worked a lot of odd jobs to supplement my main contract. Often, someone would ask me to hunt down some bastard who had done their family wrong somehow. Deflowered their daughter, stolen a sheep, the usual suspects."

"And this was a camel thief?"

"On the surface, yes. But as I tracked this fellow—and I had to track the weasel through three cities, nearly losing the trail twice—I kept on hearing more about him. One man in Shugrith said he had raped his daughter. Another said he broke off an engagement, but made off with the dowry."

"He had a reputation. There are people like that in Talynis—that's why the justice of the desert is firm."

Yaros jabbed a finger in the air. "Exactly. The justice of the desert. Every city I passed through, every person I spoke to, I only built up a bigger and bigger promised reward. By the time I caught up with him, I could have lived for half a year off my earnings."

Reiva leaned in. "So what's the point?"

"When I finally found him, he was in a village. Small oasis town. Everyone knows everyone."

"They wouldn't hand him over to you, would they?"

Yaros nodded gravely. "Not only would they not hand him over, every man and woman in that whole town came out with rocks, knives, brooms—whatever they had. And they told me that whatever claim I had against their man, I would have to go through every one of them."

"And even you are but one warrior."

Yaros was taken aback. "You wound me. I killed the bastard that very night, and I rode his stolen camel ragged halfway across the desert getting away from his tribe. All the way, his head was slapping against my thigh as I rode."

Reiva's eyebrows went up. "So *that's* why you refuse to go to the eastern side of the country."

"And why I no longer take individual bounties unless I know for sure it's a local job."

Reiva chuckled. "Everything in Talynis is local."

"Right, tell that to my ass after a full night of riding. But do you see my point?"

"Tribal loyalty."

"And tribal warfare. That was just one example. I've seen grandmothers hide knives up their skirts so they could stab soldiers. Children use slings to harass war-bands from fifty yards away. Every person in this nation is willing to fight and die."

He slumped into his chair. "When this was just an occupation, that was one thing. Even if people were unhappy with the way Tamiq replaced Malik, or the fact that the legion was here, it still had not elevated to actual warfare."

"Iscator sieged the gates not four months ago."

"But the king fled," Yaros pointed out. "That was enough of a change to give the people pause, to question whether the will of the gods was with Tamiq after all, especially since the Temple threw their support behind him."

Reiva massaged her temples. "But now we've given them every reason to stop treating this as a matter of opinion. We've made it a war, and they've answered in kind."

"So the question remains—how will we end this war?"

She sat with that for a bit, but in truth, there were only two options.

Either the legion left Talynis, admitting for the second time that this expanse of sand was too much for them...

Or they learned to fight with different rules.

"We put together training exercises." She sprang to her feet, breaking into another bout of pacing. "Short, to the point. We have Tamiq's men train our legionnaires in guerrilla warfare. We give the Talynisti no quarter. We wage war like they do. Brutal. Fast. Without warning or hesitation."

Yaros was looking eager, but he held up a hand. "Everything about that goes against the legion hierarchy. It requires that people operate on their own, without direct oversight or approval."

But Reiva was only picking up momentum. "No, we can do this. We increase the autonomy of sergeants and their squadrons. Compartmentalize the command structure."

"I love nothing more than independence, boss, but you'll have to sway a lot of the old guard on this."

He blinked.

"Or...you *would* have had to, Lady Lion."

Reiva's heart was racing.

Vantelle may have been brutal, she may have been vicious, she may have lacked compassion...

But she was brilliant.

"With the praetor behind me, I can do this. She's the only person who can contravene my orders, short of a vote of no confidence from the prefects."

"Is that possible?"

"Doubtful given how stringent our current situation is. In a normal campaign, there would certainly be resistance, but there's not a legionnaire in this camp who's eager about our chances here. The officers will fall in line —especially if Vantelle supports my call here."

Reiva was already on her way to the command tent. She would give Vantelle her suggestion, then call for a meeting of the senior officers. By tomorrow, they would be on their way to winning this war.

But as she swept outside, she nearly collided with a runner.

The youth practically tripped over himself, scrambling into as dignified a salute as he could manage. "*Ave Imperator,* Princeps!"

Reiva returned the salute. She was opening her lips to ask what he had for her, but the man was already blurting it out.

"Praetor Vantelle requests your presence in the command tent immediately."

A thrill gripped Reiva. Perfect—she would already have Vantelle's undivided attention, and she would walk in with a ready-made solution to this catastrophe.

In just a few months, no one would remember the failure of Adept Reiva in Hyrgallia. They would only know of her triumphant success in bringing Talynis under the Emperor's dominion.

This would be the war that made her name.

"Thank you. Dismissed."

"Ma'am!" cried the young man, bringing her to an abrupt stop.

"What?" she said, somewhat annoyed now.

The youth withered under her eyes. "The praetor," he mumbled, "did not seem in great spirits. Just for your awareness."

Reiva's gut twisted. "Thank you. My apologies."

The runner took off on his next errand—or maybe just to be out of her sight.

Reiva made her way to the command tent, doing her best to look at ease, determined, as a commander ought to be before her soldiers.

When she saw Vantelle brooding over her desk, a set of scrolls before her, she realized that, if anything, the runner had underestimated the severity of her displeasure. Perhaps she had disguised it in front of such a low-ranking individual, but now it was clear that the praetor was disturbed, her brow wrinkled, her eyes dark.

"My praetor." Reiva snapped off a salute.

Vantelle looked up, half-surprised. Had she been so engrossed she didn't even notice Reiva's entrance?

"Sit down, Reiva."

The Adept's stomach was sinking as she slid into the chair.

Vantelle bridged her fingers, eyes downcast.

Reiva's heart was pounding, different fears racing through her mind. Had the Sanctum denied her ascension to Lion? Was Tamiq breaking away from them, spurning the Empire in hopes of rallying the populace to himself?

The praetor's stormy gray eyes fixed on Reiva's at last.

"This letter is from the Sanctum."

Gods, here it comes...

"The Circle of Peers has approved your commission to *Adepta Leona*. Unanimously, in fact."

Reiva let go a breath she had not realized she was holding.

Vantelle actually cracked a smile. "They called it unprecedented, but they acknowledged that given just how unprecedented the situation here is, as well as the weight of a praetor's will..." A shrug. "Desperate times."

"Certainly," Reiva muttered. "But if the Sanctum has confirmed my—"

Vantelle raised a hand, rubbing her forehead with the other. "That's not the entire letter. Reiva..."

The praetor stalled for a moment.

"Adept Alyat is dead."

And the world dropped out from under her.

She nearly fell from the chair, gripping onto Vantelle's desk like a drowning man to a rock.

"That is not possible."

With a sympathetic grimace, Vantelle slid the letter across to her. Sure enough, it bore the Sanctum's seal; it followed all the prescribed formulas for official communication.

And at the end, it described how, just a day after the decision was made, Alyat had been found dead in his quarters, evidently from an aneurysm.

He had been writing a letter, the communiqué said, to her.

Reiva's hands were shaking. She tried pressing them into the desk to stop it, but it only made her whole body tremble.

"Alyat..."

Vantelle slid another letter to her, also bearing the Sanctum's seal.

Reiva stared at it, dumbfounded. "Is this...?"

"The letter he had been writing you."

She should have taken it back to her quarters first, but she couldn't. She broke the seal right there, rolling open the scroll so fast she tore the edge.

She forced herself to read it, and sure enough, it was his handwriting. That odd, blocky, precise way he had of forming letters as hard-edged as he was. The overly formal style he always wrestled himself into when writing letters.

Adept Alyat to Adept Reiva,

I congratulate you on your recent appointment to the office of Adepta Leona. *When the decision came down from the Circle of Peers, I could hardly believe it, but you always were prone to exceeding even my expectations. It is my hope that when you return from the campaign in Talynis, we may celebrate your*

The final word trailed off in a winding, scrawling line, and Reiva thought for a moment she could read his death in it.

Vantelle, she realized, was standing, her hand extended.

Reiva rose unsteadily, shook the praetor's hand. "My congratulations and condolences alike, Adept. If only this news had come separately."

"If only," Reiva echoed. She swallowed, rolling the letter back up, fingers trembling. "May I take my leave, praetor?"

"Granted, Adept. I will ensure the troops are made aware of your ascension; you now command the authority of a princeps without question or compromise."

"Thank you, my praetor."

And with that, Reiva turned, tucking the letter carefully into her breastplate.

She had not told Vantelle of her plans to revise the legion's strategy. There would be time for that later.

Adept Alyat to Adept Reiva, I congratulate you

Right now, something more pressing had torn its way into her world.

Every footstep seemed as though she were walking on air at the same time a lead weight hung from her neck.

She was an Adept. She was a soldier. She was always ready to die. Always ready for *others* to die.

I congratulate you

But somehow, Alyat had seemed immortal.

She opened her door, slipped inside, locked it behind her.

congratulate

And somehow Alyat had been murdered.

50

INTO THE DARK WITH ME

I saw a man lying in the street, his body ragged with weeping wounds.

'Who has done this?' asked the child. 'Where is justice in the land?'

And all the world saw the king holding the knife, and all the world turned away.

'I see the man who holds the blade,' said the child. 'I see the man who has worked evil.'

And the people seized the child and threw her from the mountaintop, for they knew the knife-hand well.

—*Book of the Nameless Prophet*

The Imperial galley *Indomitable* sliced through the pristine blue waters of the *Mare Magnum*, the Great Sea. A call went up: "Port in sight!" Straight away, the crew set to work stowing the sails.

"Oars!" bellowed the bosun. A great clatter of wood arose from belowdecks as the oarsmen locked their implements in place and sent them out over the water—but they did not dip them in yet.

They waited, because even though no sails caught the wind, the galley still surged through the waves at great speed—fast enough that if the rowers tried to match it, they would find themselves slammed in the gut as the force of the water ripped the oars from their grasp.

The oars were for precise maneuvering once they got nearer the port, but until then, they could rely on the raw power of the massive wall of water pushing the vessel at the stern.

Yes, there were privileges that came from crewing a ship with an Adept of Sea.

Domi wiped sweat from her forehead, her other hand submerged in the cool waters. She glanced up from her perch near the starboard stern—a special addition affixed to those galleys fortunate enough to sail with a wielder of the *Ars Thalassan*. Her tongue stuck out between her teeth as she peered through the nest of oars hovering above the water, estimating the distance to the docks of Caroshai.

And right...about...now.

Domi withdrew her power, allowing the rushing wall of water behind the ship to fall away.

"Oars!" she called.

"Oars!" answered the bosun. "Ready—stroke!"

In unison, the rowing began. The bosun called out the time; the practiced oarsmen dipped and pulled in perfect rhythm.

Domi clambered onto the deck. She stretched her arms above her head, allowing herself a deep sigh. With no small amount of satisfaction, she noted that the impetus from her magic was petering away at just the proper rate. The galley would only be entirely under the rowers' power just as she came to land, when fine maneuvering would be essential.

Her shoulders squared at that. The Art of Sea was a tricky thing, with not as much potential for precise control as other disciplines. She had been working on getting the timing just right for the last three ports, seeing it as a challenge. The crew insisted she didn't need to provide so much assistance —most Adepts of Sea were content to let them make the last quarter mile on their own. She knew they appreciated it though, and having the goodwill of the crew was worth more than gold when serving at sea.

Domi had little time to relish in her accomplishment, though. She slipped into her private quarters—the only such quarters besides the captain's—and peeled off her soaked clothes. There was a delightfully casual atmosphere to working on board a ship; she got to wear comfortable attire all day, with nothing to indicate she was of a different rank or station than the rest of the crew.

But any time they came into port or pulled along another ship for inspection, it was time to look the part. Domi threw on her uniform and hastily wrapped her mantle around her shoulders. Holding a knife aloft, she grimaced at her reflection. Her hair, her eyebrows, her lashes—all caked with salt.

"Just a couple hours," she muttered, "and you'll get that bath."

During her training days, she used to count how many days it had been since she last washed with freshwater, but that had quickly become too depressing to bear.

By the time she emerged from her quarters, squinting at the sun, the crew had moored the *Indomitable* to the dock, and the captain was negotiating with the harbormaster.

First time for everything, she thought with a wry smile.

Every other port they had come into, Domi had bounded ashore right away—sometimes before the line was even tied. Yesterday, however, the captain had impressed on her that doing such a thing in Caroshai could create problems.

Domi lifted up her gaze, taking in the port.

All ports had some things in common—the frenetic energy, the shouting, the smells. People bustled about, loading and unloading crates. There was a whole dialect composed of profanities only sailors could comprehend. But the port of Caroshai was unique in Domi's eyes, because it was the first she had ever seen without an Imperial banner hanging from the harbormaster's office.

So this is what independence looks like.

The city-state of Caroshai enjoyed an unusual relationship with the Lazarran Empire, possessing the honor of autonomy. Domi had learned the reason for this during her education at the Sanctum—supposedly an ancient queen of Caroshai had given hospitality to the Founders while they were journeying the *Mare Magnum* in search of a proper place to settle. Once the city of Lazarra rose along the coastline of the Ixian Reach, the two states built a mostly positive connection on that history.

Even when the Lazarran Republic fell and the Empire rose out of the Dark Days, still Caroshai remained an ally—not a target for subjugation, but an old friend.

At least, it used to be like that. Nowadays, Imperial navy ships had to pay the same harbor tax as everyone else, and there were even stories of Lazarran marine legionnaires getting thrown in Caroshain jails for rowdiness ashore (which Domi thought was about as sensible as jailing birds for flying).

She tried to look disinterested as the harbormaster repeatedly shot glances at her, but every passing minute rankled her worse and worse. All she wanted was a hot bath, some good food—Caroshai was famous for the spice markets—and a cup or two of wine. By tomorrow, the *Indomitable* would be full of fresh supplies and on her way; the harbormaster needed not worry that a Lazarran Adept would cause any trouble.

He certainly had cause to worry in the long term—it was well known among certain elite circles in the Imperial navy that Emperor Dioclete wanted Caroshai annexed within the next three years—but Domi was not here to bring that about today. Today, she was just a weary soul.

A keening shriek pierced the air.

The ship's messenger hawk flapped its wings, crying out again.

Domi winced. The hawk never acted like this—did it need to be fed?

The answer came a moment later as a shadow swept across the galley. Domi glanced up just in time to catch sight of another messenger hawk's swift form. The creature let out a cry of its own before banking right and flying out over the city.

Headed to the Lazarran embassy then, same as Domi soon as she could step ashore. She idly wondered what sort of message the hawk was carrying, but then dismissed the thought. It was probably just a dispatch—always another dispatch. She used to be excited by messenger hawks before she realized nine times out of ten it was logistics. The Empire *ran* on logistical notices.

Blessedly, the harbormaster finally gave them clearance to disembark—and, as usual, Domi was first off. "I'll see you lot tomorrow," she called with a wave over her shoulder.

All the crew—from the rowers to the marine legionnaires—had acclimated to the way she scampered off on shore leave. All the crew save one, that was. Larco didn't even bother to hide his scowl as she left.

Domi smirked. He should have been with her as an escort—but as far as the rest of the crew knew, he was just another soldier. They had no clue as to his unique assignment, and running after Domi to keep an eye on her would betray that.

She could already hear how he'd reprimand her once he got a moment of privacy—there would be talk of security, of duty and obligation, certainly talk of guilt.

That was something to handle in the future, though. In the present, Domi had a brief moment of freedom and space. Even in streets as crowded as Caroshai's, she had space. People made way for an Adept anywhere in the world. The constant looks were a nuisance, but she'd take it over having to elbow her way around.

In truth, she was not as confident of the route to the embassy as she had indicated to the captain, but she also was not above asking for directions. She picked a storefront and got the attention of the owner.

He made a sound of surprise, followed by some chattering in a language Domi didn't recognize—likely a Southlander tongue. "An Adept at my restaurant!" he said in competent Karellan. "Never have I known such an honor."

Domi smiled easily, and the man beamed even brighter. The world was such a nicer place when people were happy to see you. "Could you point me to the Lazarran embassy, sir?"

"'Sir,' she says—ha! Ghumo is a friend, young lady, call me as such. The embassy is down that way. Take the second turn on your right, then the first left."

Domi bowed her head graciously. "My deepest thanks, Ghumo. Your cooking smells delicious. I've been at sea for weeks now, and my stomach can hardly bear me standing here."

The man clicked his tongue and glowered. "Fed on rations no doubt. *Pah!* Sit, eat, young lady—the finest spiced lamb in the city. Half-price for you, as a welcome to a lovely new friend."

Another smile tugged at Domi's lips. It would no doubt do the man's business well for an Adept to be seen at his table. Even if people were intimidated by her, they would also be curious.

This was something Reiva had never quite gotten the hang of—the social aspect of being an Adept, the back and forth pull of granting another the gift of your presence in exchange for something. That girl saw everything as a battle, but socializing was more of a dance—and it was a dance Domi knew well.

But the memory of Reiva sent a pang through her heart. She hadn't heard anything from her in a long time—far too long a time. Had she made it to Talynis safely?

The itch of salt on Domi's skin called her attention. Her bones felt weary, her muscles strained. Yes, it had been a long few weeks at sea.

"I'm afraid I must go to the embassy right away, but if you are open this evening?"

"Of course! A dish and a place at the table for you—whenever you should arrive. If you make us wait until midnight, we will be here! Well, my son over there will—an old man like myself can only stay so long."

Domi laughed dutifully. "Surely you jest—you could be my older brother."

Ghumo bowed his head gratefully, another wide smile on his features, before he slipped off to attend to a pot hanging over a fire.

Domi spared a glance for the young man Ghumo had indicated when he mentioned his son—broad-shouldered, handsome. He was also looking at her, though he quickly turned aside when she saw him, a flush creeping over his features. He did a remarkable job looking interested in sweeping the floor.

A small smile quirked her lips.

Yes, it could be very nice to be alone with him at midnight. He seemed shy, but that could be endearing.

First though, the embassy. She could report in, take that bath, and get her clothes properly laundered.

Ghumo's directions held true. The Lazarran embassy looked as though it had been ripped right off the streets of the capital and shipped across the sea. In contrast to all the lumber of Caroshai, the embassy was marble pillars and painted sculptures, with the signature purple and gold banner of the Empire fluttering in the wind.

The legionnaires on guard saluted Domi as she approached. "*Ave Imperator.*"

She returned the salute, strutting up the steps with more decorum than she felt energy for. It was always a good idea to look impressive for the rank and file—maintaining the image of the Corps was a task every Adept took seriously.

When she set foot inside the embassy, though, she allowed herself a small sigh. Her shoulders slouched.

So close. Just have to—

Domi stopped short. Two men were locked in an intense conversation at the receiving desk. One was clearly a clerk, but the other had a sash around his waist that marked him as a former senator—meaning that was the ambassador himself. Supposedly, this man had retired from the Lazarran legislative body to lead a more peaceful life in the diplomatic service.

Well, he didn't look to be at peace now. Both men were aggrieved as they studied a parchment unfurled on the desk, muttering to one another as they pointed out different details.

Domi's heart picked up. Was that what the messenger hawk she saw earlier had been carrying?

"Excuse me," she said, "Adept Domi, reporting from the galley *Indomitable.*"

The pair looked up from their study. The ambassador recovered first, straightening and offering her a hand in greeting. "Welcome to Caroshai, Adept. If only you came to happier news."

She stole a glance at the parchment—and her heart almost stopped.

That's the Corps' seal!

"What happened?" she blurted out, fatigue fleeing as adrenaline surged through her veins.

The ambassador grimaced, and Domi saw true pain in his features. "I am sorry to be the one to inform you, but...your colleague, Adept Alyat has passed on. A few nights ago, according to this dispatch. My deepest condolences. I worked with Alyat once when he—"

It had taken Domi's mind several tries to process the words, but they slammed into her like a battering ram. Domi snatched the letter from the clerk's hands, poring over the words herself.

In the neat hand of a professional scribe, it detailed just what the ambassador had said—Alyat was dead.

"Get me parchment," muttered Domi.

The clerk stuttered. "Excuse me, Adept? Do you need—"

"*Parchment!*" she snapped, crumpling the letter in her hands. "Ink and a quill, now!"

The clerk practically fell off his feet rushing to comply.

Domi dipped the quill, splattering droplets of ink across the stationery as she hastily scrawled her message. Her writing was slapdash, her letters strewn across the page like bodies after an ambush.

"Messenger hawk," she demanded.

The clerk dashed off to get hold of the bird.

Domi blinked away tears as she wrote.

Gods above, Reiva, I just heard. I'm so sorry...

∾

AN ANEURYSM, the dispatch said. Adept Alyat had died from an aneurysm.

Praetor Marcus Gallius sneered at the letter, tossing it aside. He had read it several times since its arrival yesterday, his incredulity growing more and more.

Right. An Adept done in by something so pedestrian.

The same Adept who had mentored the notorious Reiva. There were whispers about her as well. Vantelle had named her a Lion and princeps—which could only mean that she was less and less satisfied with Flavia Iscator's performance as legate. His gut told him Iscator would almost certainly be passed over for Reiva when Vantelle ascended to the throne, as she almost certainly would.

Marcus rubbed his eyes. Complicated—everything was so much more complicated these days.

And this damned Adept of Shadows wasn't making this life any easier.

His optio, Viro, poked his head into the command tent. "My praetor, she is not coming."

"*What?*" growled Marcus.

"She says she will only speak to you."

"Then why the hell isn't she standing before me right now?"

But he was already on his feet, striding past the optio.

Fine, Sharasthi, make a praetor come to you. You think I'll just let you trounce over my authority in my own camp?

The Adept's quarters were not far. His knuckles rapped a sharp beat on the door. "Adept, this is your praetor."

There was a pause. Then, the door opened.

A man less trained might have showed surprise on his face, but when he found himself faced with Captain Scanlon, Marcus Gallius merely offered a flat stare.

"Have you been fraternizing with the Adept, Captain? Don't answer that," he quickly added, shoving his way past.

The residence was small, but appropriate to someone of the Adept's rank. It felt constricted though, given everything strewn across the floor—maps, tools, gear, letters.

And amidst it all stood Adept Sharasthi, her hair disheveled and uniform unkempt.

"This is how you appear before your praetor, Adept?"

"You appear before me, technically."

Marcus ground his teeth. "At least Scanlon had the dignity to dress himself properly."

"Dignity or shame. But let's not get into the weeds of that."

Marcus forced a slow breath in, out. He opened his mouth to speak again, but came up short.

Adept Sharasthi's eyes stared into space, hollow, red-rimmed. Dark circles spoke to a sleepless night.

He shot a quizzical look at Scanlon. Where he had seen embarrassment before, now he saw something else in the captain's demeanor. Almost...pity?

Marcus turned back to the Adept, studying the hunch in her shoulders, the way her arms seemed not crossed in defiance, but almost protective of herself.

She muttered something.

"Excuse me?"

"I am not speaking to you."

No wonder she gives my legionnaires the creeps. Maybe try a different tack...

"My condolences given the loss of your colleague, Adept."

Her fingers tightened on her arm, then quickly relaxed. "Accepted."

She thinks he was murdered as well. Has she told Scanlon as much?

As if he'd read Marcus' thoughts, the man cleared his throat. "Praetor, should I leave?"

"You stay," said Sharasthi. "I'm working something out, but once I do, you're both going to know."

Marcus raised an eyebrow, checked the door had been closed. He was a praetor—he wasn't about to hang on every word from an Adept's mouth, no matter how grieved she may have been.

"I know you're used to being the sharpest mind in the room, but even a simpleton such as myself can tell that Alyat's death is suspicious."

"If you were a simpleton, Praetor, I would have lied to you and sent you off."

"You're hiding something."

"I have been, and now I will bring it into the light. Or perhaps I am bringing you into the dark with me."

A cold finger traced down Marcus' spine. She continued that strange muttering, and some primal part of his psyche told him she wasn't just talking to herself. No, she seemed to be pausing, almost as if she was...listening.

Then she straightened, a strange gleam coming into her eyes. A predatory purpose. She crossed the room and opened a trunk—the sort of trunk every officer used to store their belongings—and rifled through it before producing a small, locked box, entirely of iron.

Cradling it almost reverently, she produced an ornate key and turned it in the latch.

Click.

Marcus realized his heart was pounding.

From within the box, she drew out a bronze seal about the size of his palm. Then she handed it to him.

It was stamped with a design he had never seen. A sort of grand beast, curled in on itself, like a hound sleeping. But it was not any sort of creature he knew. And over the beast's head was lettering, faded by the touch of countless years and countless hands.

Even so, he was able to work it out, and his stomach dropped into his boots.

Ordo Draconis Laevisomnis.

"What do you know," whispered Sharasthi, with eyes hard as granite, "of the Order of the Sleeping Dragon?"

51

FOREVER PROUD, FOREVER STRONG

THE TALYNISTI ARE A STRANGE FOLK, in many ways, but nothing is perhaps so strange as their allegiance to a mere four gods—so few that you could count them on one hand. A strange superstition, to our Lazarran eyes. It was thought that once we defeated them, they would do much as every other nation had, allowing their gods to be brought into our pantheon as lessers to the true ruler. Much as mortals were ruled by the Emperor, so divines were ruled by Arkhon.

That this possibility was seriously entertained serves as a testament to how poorly the Empire understood our little foe.

—*The Memoirs of Flavia Iscator*

∽

IN THE CITIES OF TALYNIS, there was no spectacle so regular and central as the rites of sacrifice performed in the temples. And of all the temples, no location was so central as *the* Temple, the House of Four in Dav-maiir. It was said the very foundation stones had been blessed by that ancient shepherd who was to be a great prophet, the man who met the Four Gods atop the looming precipice of Har-Esh, where he received from them the plan according to which the Temple was to be built.

All day, the priests hastened to and fro, hands clutching censers of incense, bowls of water, knives of gold and iron. The endless procession of priests was only surpassed by the procession of animals that came through the grounds. Even in times such as these (or perhaps, especially in times such as these), the people were faithful in their observances of the various rites of absolution.

Even more so than the king, it was the religion of Talynis that bound the people together, reminding them that every man was a brother to his neighbor, every woman a mother to the young girl she passed on the street. The sacrifices were made to atone for the ways in which one failed to love and do right by their brother, sister, father, mother.

The Temple was the ultimate symbol of why Talynis had endured for so long in the desert. The grace of the Four to bless this land with springs of water. The mercy they had to teach men how to regard and respect one another. The sanctity of their instruction regarding how one was to make right failures of conduct.

There was no place so crucial in all the city, in all the nation, to the identity of the people of the desert.

And so, it was the first place the Wolf intended to take back from the tainted grasp of the usurpers and the Empire.

To say that their force was under-equipped would have been generous. Half of them were farmers, the other half were barely old enough to have the build to properly handle a weapon.

That was fine, though.

Avi wasn't trusting in force of arms at this point. He had given up on that when he saw Crow's blood painting the Adept's armor.

Now, he was trusting the Four. If they were on the side of the Loyalists, then surely he would be able to take the Temple.

And if not...well, he hoped Asrah would make it through all of this. He hoped Jackal and Mouse were either far enough away or sensible enough to keep their heads attached.

The throng entered the Temple like anyone else—through the front gates. Imperial legionnaires watched them with suspicious eyes, even pulled aside one or two people to search, but there were too many people to stop every single one.

The legionnaires asked questions—what was their purpose for coming?

'The teaching' was always the answer. Everything came back to the teaching—it was something Imperials did not understand, Avi knew. They could not appreciate the significance of what it meant to have your laws from the lips of the gods themselves.

The soldiers even took the steps of searching men who looked like they might be a threat—humorously, they did not search Avi. He had been prepared for the possibility that they might, so he had given his *Nihilo* Blade to the wife of the blacksmith he met before. Her name was Devra, and she was walking arm in arm with her husband Khador. Their child was at home, being watched over by a grandmother or aunt or some such.

The legionnaires could not enter the gates. They were not recognized by the Four—only a child of Talynis could come this close. It was not unheard of for foreigners to go through the prescribed rituals for integrating their bloodline to that of Talynis (this too was provided for in the teaching), but these legionnaires were years away from ever having that sort of status, if any even desired it.

Avi had no doubt, though, that the Empire would attempt to force such a thing. Already, they tried to control the Temple, to ensure that every Talynisti guard posted within the grounds was loyal to Tamiq the usurper, to the Emperor off in the western lands.

They did not understand, these Imperials, just how valiant the sons and daughters of Talynis were.

They did not understand, as his father used to say, what it meant to fight for something greater than yourself.

Avi muttered under his breath, "The time draws near."

Devra reached within the folds of her robes, handing the relic to Avi. If she had thought anything strange of its unusual form, she had said nothing. Obscured by the crowd, Avi strapped the blade to his thigh, pulling it from its sheath.

He was in the middle of the throng, and the blade was black as night. As he began to press forward, murmuring, "The righteous shall prevail," the others made way for him, letting him slip through. They too would be reaching for weapons, hidden on their person, or on their children, or even tangled within the wool of their sheep.

A man stood at the inner gate. This was the demarcation between the profane outside and the sacred interior, where only those who had purified themselves could enter. This man was known to Avi. He was the captain of the Temple guard.

A sign, if any such thing existed at all, that the Four on High favored the blow Avi was about to strike today.

The captain regarded their mix with suspicion. "Hold back!" he barked. "You know the rules."

"What rules, brother?" called Avi. He was nearly at the front now, holding the blade behind his back.

"The new rules promulgated by Tamiq, anointed ruler in the grace of the Four on High. Orderly lines, space between people. Disperse."

Already, some of the guards were clustering to their leader.

Avi looked them each in the eye. Some watched him with suspicion.

Others had a glint of eagerness, of passion. They were brothers to the cause. They were true sons of the sands.

Avi turned his gaze back to the captain of the Temple guard, and he saw a flicker of fear there.

"Long reign Malik."

Bursting forth like a pouncing panther, he set upon the captain. The man frantically, reflexively tried to guard himself, but Avi's fury, skill, and speed were unstoppable.

With callous precision, he opened the man's throat. Already, he saw the Loyalists among the guards turning on those who had supported Tamiq's Revolution. He felt more than saw the bursting, rising tide of righteous anger from the people.

The captain sank to his knees, hands desperately pawing at the gushing wound in his throat. Eyes wide with shock, with fear, he gaped at Avi, gurgling bubbles foaming from his lips.

Avi held his eyes as he went down.

"We are the true children of Talynis," he said. "We are forever proud, forever strong."

And so began the seizing of the Temple.

It was forbidden for foreigners to enter the courtyard—this was considered a great act of defilement. However, as the clamor of violence—shouts, chants, clanging metal—filled the air, it was inevitable that the legionnaires on guard should burst within, followed both by the dismayed shouts of Talynisti guardsmen, as well as relief from these same guards that they would not be facing the Loyalists alone.

And indeed, were it simply a matter of numbers, the seizure of the Temple doubtlessly would have been little more than a bloody massacre, perhaps even one seeing the death of the Wolf.

But the Four on High, it would be said, favored the cause of Aviqohl beyt'Avadh.

As legionnaires and guardsmen stormed the courtyard, bearing down upon men and women with no great career in war, no lengthy experience with battle—it was then that the priests of Dav-maiir made known their allegiance.

Avi himself watched as the high priest was cut down by one of his own attendants. The man's blood sheeted down over the ritual vestments of the highest religious office within the faith.

Standing over him, a young priest, his beard still thin, his hands trembling. In his hands, a bloodied knife of sacrifice.

Avi clapped the young man on the shoulder. "What is your name, brother?" he shouted over the havoc.

"Lishim," he said.

"Then to arms with us, Lishim. The Four watch and keep you."

Indeed, Lishim did fight with the Loyalists against the usurpers' men and the legionnaires. As did the majority of the priests in the House of Four. They took as their weapons the discarded arms of slain allies and enemies alike. Their armor was their vestments, their valor and courage born of their faith.

Avi moved through the scene like a force of nature, his black blade whirling and dancing through air and flesh, constantly in lethal, elegant motion. At one moment, he was side by side with Lishim and his fellow priests, holding a gate against a further incursion of legionnaires. The next, he was helping Devra stand after a wild charge by a usurper guardsman had knocked her to the ground. One of her eyes had been put out, half her face scarred and slick with blood.

They secured and braced the gates. They purged the grounds of those who still defied the Loyalists' call and cause. Avi carried out many of these executions himself—swiftly, but not without some measure of relish.

He did not kill all of them though—he had more plans.

The last thing to be purged was perhaps the primary instigator of their rage. The standard of the Lazarran Empire, waving proudly, arrogantly, from the parapet of the Temple. Avi tore it away, working with Lishim to cut the ties, and together, they ascended to the highest point in the temple court. A tower, used to spot the birth and death of the day, the exact moments of sunset and sunrise.

From this tower, a tower constructed of brick and mortar, they hung the Imperial standard. Night was just darkening the city, and so when they set the Imperial flag aflame, the spectacle was well marked by the denizens of Dav-maiir.

The streets were filled with proud, resolute voices, singing one of the oldest songs in the land. "Four on High, keep our king. We pray his rule you bless, and for your grace we sing."

A watch was set. Avi fully expected there would be an attempt to take the site back, and he was not about to give up something so costly won.

They had lost brothers and sisters in the fight. Avi went about, looking upon the forever-closed eyes of every single one. He learned their names, burned them into his mind, as it was said the words of the Four were inscribed in immortal fire upon the foundations of heaven.

He did not sleep that night. Every moment he spent either on watch, or deep in reflection upon the battle. He thought back to every moment he might have died—a spear angled just so, a wild strike he might not have ducked...

Aviqohl beyt'Avadh had always believed in the gods. But now, he felt he owed them something. He had returned the Temple to rightful hands, but he had done so by way of the sword. There would need to be extensive rituals and ceremonies done to purify it from the killing, from the improper use by followers of the false king.

Avi intended to repay the Four for what they had granted him today, and he intended to repay it a hundred times over.

This was only the beginning. The Wolf would not rest until every scrap of land in Dav-maiir was under the rightful rule of King Malik, and until the sands of Talynis no longer knew the heavy tread of Lazarran legionnaires.

And that began, he knew, with the end of the Adept. The traitor to this land. The one who had slain Crow.

Eyes heavy, nerves flaring, he made his way across the courtyard.

He was not the only one who had not slept. A huddle of bound and gagged Lazarran legionnaires were here, their backs bent low, their eyes bloodshot.

All night, Avi had been composing his message. In the end, he decided on something simple.

Talynis was the land of his birth. It was the land of his father, who had died defending it. It was the land of his mother, a deeply flawed woman, but still a daughter of the desert.

It was the land of his sister, wherever she was, if she even drew breath still.

He was perhaps the last of their family in Talynis, perhaps the last one alive.

He would ensure that the world, and the heavens, knew his name.

He would ensure too, that the Adept knew it before he killed her.

52

A NEW VISION

Ordo Draconis Laevisomnis. Such a foreboding name. Such a sinister reputation.
—*The Memoirs of Flavia Iscator*

∼

For nearly an hour, Reiva pored over the letter, searching for any possible clue.

Whoever wrote it had forged Alyat's penmanship with startling accuracy —even the jagged line that erupted from the final letter somehow looked like something he would have written.

He could not have written it, though. They had their code—Alyat had abided by it in every single piece of written correspondence he ever sent her. She had forgotten to use it *once,* and he nearly tore halfway across the Empire, thinking she had been captured or killed.

Now those positions were reversed—and she was sure as all the hells that Alyat would never make such a careless mistake. No, he had been killed. Whoever he had been concerned about in his last few letters had caught up with him.

The Order of the Sleeping Dragon, that's who he had been after. Right before she left, he had told her he would be investigating them, that she should steer clear if she caught any hint of them.

A chilling possibility gripped her.

What if Alyat *had* written the letter, and he had done so knowing they were about to kill him? What if she really was staring at his own final scrawl there, the shaking hand of a man pushed beyond the veil?

What if he had broken from the code to warn her?

She had her head in her hands. The image of Alyat, held against his will, being tortured, brutalized, forced to write a letter that would make it seem his death had been nothing but a malicious twist of fate.

No. No, it can't be.

She was up on her feet again, wearing a trail from one wall to the other. They had a code for that sort of thing too—Alyat would have done her more good by communicating that. The letter was a forgery, of that she was certain.

And she was also certain, she realized, that she had been lied to somewhere in that letter from the Sanctum.

She cursed herself, pounding her fist to her head. She should have taken the other letter from Vantelle so she could search it for any clues, any discrepancies.

Well, she could investigate on her own. It would be difficult from so far away, but she had trustworthy allies in the Sanctum. Quartermaster Demman, he was a good man, one of Alyat's longstanding friends. He would almost certainly be as grieved by Alyat's death as she was, and he would do whatever it took to bring justice if the man had been murdered.

Abruptly, she came to a stop, realizing the train of thought she had just been going down.

She was already implicating the Sanctum in her suspicions. The people who had just elevated her to the rank of Lion.

To throw me off their scent.

Reiva snarled, running her hands through her hair, turning around and mindlessly pacing back and forth.

No, I can check that. I can find out when Alyat died, confirm that with other people.

Easily covered up.

She leaned against her desk, hands clamped on the edge.

Intrigue, mysteries, deception...none of this was in her wheelhouse.

She bathed the world in fire. She led the charge with sword held high and fist aflame. Nothing about her training was meant to prepare her for this sort of thing, skulking about in shadows.

Alyat had been good at that, and he had been outmaneuvered unto his own doom.

She couldn't do this herself.

She needed someone. Sharasthi? A letter would take some time, and Alyat had always acted strangely around the topic of Sharasthi. What if she wasn't trustworthy?

Like a clanging bell, clarity struck her.

Of course.

She was already halfway to the door when there was a knock.

Another runner?

Dread piling up in her gut, she opened the door.

Yaros.

Perfect.

"My mentor's been murdered and—"

"The Temple's been taken and—"

The two blinked.

Yaros sighed, shutting the door. "Two crises at once, figures."

Reiva stared at him. "The *Temple*. The Temple we had a double guard on."

"The Temple that had a double guard, half of which were embedded Loyalists, and which happens to be tended and served by a coterie of priests who have evidently decided the will of their gods is most decidedly against Tamiq."

"The *priests* took up arms?"

"Quite effectively. The Wolf was there himself, and he burned the Imperial banner high in the sky."

"The *priests*?" she said again, baffled. "They spilled blood on sacred ground!"

"Reiva, I'm not particularly interested in how this conflates with their theology—because we have bigger issues. The streets around the Temple are all barricaded, and we can hardly even count the number of civilians who have taken up arms to keep it in Loyalist hands."

"Tribal loyalty. Anything else I should know? What's Tamiq up to?"

"Unclear. So far he hasn't publicly responded to the seizing of the Temple, but that can't last long."

"We need to make sure he's on the same page as us."

Yaros snorted. "And what *is* that page?"

"Tamiq needs to categorically condemn bloodshed in the Temple. If he claims the moral high ground, then with luck we can spin this to convince people that he is still the most righteous side in this debacle."

"You think you can convince Dav-maiir that a usurper king has the religious justification over against the priests?"

"There have been plenty of corrupt priests."

"There have been plenty of corrupt kings."

Reiva ground her palms against her eyes. "Well, we need to do something."

Yaros leaned against the wall, picking at his beard in the way he did when he was nervous.

Reiva eyed him and sighed. "We're thinking the same thing."

The mercenary gave her a look. "If you are also thinking our problems could all be solved by killing the Wolf, then I believe that's been on the table for quite a while now. He remains impossibly elusive though, and whenever we *do* know where he is, he is frustratingly out of our reach."

"And even if we could get him, he'd only become a martyr. It would be like the crucifixions all over again."

Yaros grunted. "It could be worth it, though. If we could sort out his schedule, maybe I could take him out. It wouldn't be the hardest job."

"Certainly not for a Krypteian hand," Reiva mused. Then another pang of grief struck her heart. "Speaking of...that world. Yaros, about my mentor..."

"He was murdered, you said? I'm sorry."

She could tell he meant it, but there wasn't much feeling behind the words. He would have lost plenty of people over the years; it was just part of the job.

"I need to ask you," she continued, lowering her voice, "if you've ever heard of a group. The Order of the Sleeping Dragon."

Yaros went pale.

Reiva's stomach dropped.

Maybe it would've been better if he hadn't known.

"Where the hell," he hissed, "did you hear that? Did *they* kill your mentor?"

"I don't know. All I know for certain is that he was investigating them, and he thought that someone was after him recently. Someone forged his final letter to me, and they managed to make his death look like an aneurysm."

Yaros was rubbing his chin, eyes vacant.

"Well? Could they do something like that?"

The Karellan sighed, shrugging helplessly. "Maybe. The Krypteia could probably pull it off, so I see no reason why they couldn't."

"But who are they?"

Here Yaros suddenly looked far more uneasy, fidgeting with a leather bracelet. "I only have rumors. Even my father hardly talked about them. The Sleeping Dragons, they're ghosts. They have some sort of vendetta against the Empire, and they work to bring about their desired changes from within, working in positions of power and intrigue alike."

Reiva frowned. "You're saying..."

"Senators, generals, Intelligence operatives. You've almost certainly met one or two."

"That's impossible though. Alyat of all people would have known about them."

Yaros crossed his arms, taking the time to look Reiva in the eye. "The sort of things people like this get up to—I'm not surprised if your mentor would not have known who they are, and I'm not surprised if they would have killed him for finding out too much."

A chill ran down Reiva's spine. "What do you mean?"

"Reiva, you're talking about people who want to remake the Empire according to a new vision. They're not exactly the sort to be tolerated by the reigning authorities, shall we say." He leaned closer, dropping his voice to a whisper. "To swear yourself to the Sleeping Dragons is to swear that the Emperor is a failed ruler, a tyrant even. The assassination of Gaian Yulo? Led by the Order. The rebellion of the Godsriver Queen? The same."

"Yaros, you really want me to believe that if such an organization existed and had accomplished so many grievous attacks upon the Empire throughout our history that the Adept Corps would be in the dark about them?"

He held her eyes, a grave aura about him. "For all you know, Reiva, the Adept Corps is *owned* by them. Your promotion, your mentor's death—it could all be part of some bigger game."

Reiva realized, too late, that her breath was shaky. She braced an arm against her desk. Desperate for air, she opened the window shutters. The moon was high over the distant gold of the Temple. The smell of food— baking bread and roasting lamb—wafted on the wind.

For a moment, she could almost forget that she was looking upon a city at war, that she was looking at a foe to break, to bind, to bring under the Imperial boot.

Reiva's mind went to Tamiq and his clever daughter Asrah. What would they be thinking right now? Did they regret throwing their lot in with the Empire?

What about Iscator, off somewhere across the sands, on her way to try to subdue another city to secure yet more resources for the legions?

The Adept sighed, rubbing her eyes. She wasn't built for this, wasn't trained for this. She'd start seeing Sleeping Dragons hidden behind every shadow now if she let paranoia get the best of her.

Trust. Alyat had always hammered into her the necessity of trust. You needed someone, anyone, that you could count on.

Yaros—at least for as long as she could pay him, though she got the sense that he was well along for the ride at this point.

Charas. She had not known the Scout Lieutenant long, but the woman had an honest soul and a caring heart, not to mention fierce determination when battle kicked up.

Who else?

Vantelle. She feared and admired the praetor in equal measure, but the woman had done good by her word. That meant a lot to Reiva. That was something Alyat had done for her years ago—kept his word to see her through a trying time. If Alyat had not done that then, Reiva would have washed out of the Corps. If Vantelle had not helped her, where would she be now?

Still, that was a perilously short list.

Legionnaires—she needed men and women on the ground who would rally to her in a crisis, look to her for leadership rather than break away to fend for themselves. That was the sort of dedication that would get them through this.

Her attention was tugged back to the present by pounding hoofbeats, the shout of a soldier crying, "Make way! Make way!"

That would almost certainly be a message for her, perhaps from Vantelle. Two summons on the same day?

She was already dreading what on earth could be the matter as she stepped out from her quarters, when she recognized the rider. It was Charas, her bow clutched in one hand, a riding quiver strapped to her saddle.

She reined in, her mount's hooves skidding.

Reiva was already rushing to her, Yaros close behind. They met Charas halfway, the Parthavan woman shining with sweat. "Adept," she huffed, snapping off a salute. "Urgent news from the Temple."

Reiva clenched her fists. "The situation has changed?"

"That's an understatement," panted Charas. "The Wolf has hostages."

53

WAY OF STONE

WHEN FIRST VISITING the holy city, I marveled at the construction of the Temple and how it seemed beyond the skill of human hands. Upon remarking to my father on this, he made a sign of prayer.

'Your intuition perceives more than you know, my son—blessed is my blood by the one who grants insight! The Temple was constructed by the Peaceborn King, who by hidden arts bound a spirit within his signet ring. By the power of this enslaved spirit, he realized this wonder.'

I asked him, 'Are these the same teachings which you have handed down to me, Father?'

'They are, and they are teachings you too shall pass down.'

—*The Life and Wisdom of Simeon Binkhok As Told by Himself*

~

ARTUNIS FLOPPED onto a patch of dewy grass, head spinning.

Mouse stood over her, hands clasped behind his back. Hatzakh the Desert Stage glowered nearby. He had protested as Mouse explained things to her but had not actually stopped him.

She turned to Mouse again. Somehow, a different energy seemed to exude from him, now that she knew the truth.

"In Endra," she muttered, "anyone can be an Adept." Even as she said it, it sounded impossible. Surely, she had misunderstood him. Surely, it was all a dream of some sort.

But no, Mouse was nodding his head. "We call ourselves *Kshara*, but yes. In a practical sense, this path is not open to everyone. There are strict class boundaries and trials that bar many people from ever having a realistic chance...but yes, in theory, anyone can undergo the Binding."

Artunis threw her arms up. "How could *no one* on this side of the mountains know that? That's ridiculous. It would be like saying that all of Endra knows about a fountain of youth, but no one west of the Spine had heard of it."

Mouse shrugged his burly shoulders. "There are many reasons as to why. Much of the truth was hidden by the Lazarran god, centuries ago. But in part, this was also the choice of Endra and the other realms beyond the mountains.

"Imagine you lived on one side of a river, and there was a village across the water. You encounter them once in a while, to trade, to skirmish. And you notice they have weapons of bronze, with only one or two of iron that happen to come into their possession. All along, you know how to mine and forge steel."

Artunis could see the logic. "You hide how much steel you have, and you hide that you know how to forge it." She waved at Hatzakh. "The Desert Sages, though! You say they're also Adepts, but here in Talynis. How could no one here—"

Hatzakh snapped, "It is our way to be secretive. The powers we hold are blessings from the Four, not to be profaned through popular imagination. Not even the king of Talynis knows the truth of this place."

She gestured broadly at the lush flora. "Why hide the Origin Spring from your ruler?"

A shadow passed over Hatzakh's features.

Her mouth snapped shut with a *click*. "Unless...unless this place holds the secret to making new Sages. A king would turn you into soldiers, just as the Emperor of Lazarra has the Adepts."

"These things," hissed the Sage, "are not for the uninitiated to know."

Mouse shot a sidelong glance at the man, then turned back to her. "Hypothetically, it would be a good guess."

In a flash, she was back on her feet. "We need to get back to Crow. Mouse, if you could use your magic more openly—"

"Crow knew everything, Jackal," said Mouse, softly. "He sent us here, remember?"

Hatzakh folded his arms into his sleeves. "And he is dead, according to our eyes above ground."

Artunis' stomach sunk to her sandals. "He can't be. No one could kill

Crow—the old bastard was too stubborn. He'd never let anyone take him! No one in this whole sand-scrubbed country could ever—"

Mouse rested a warm hand on her shoulder. "It was the Lazarran Adept. Crow had a weapon of lore, a blade ensorcelled with the breath of the winds, but he could not hold for long against a much younger, much more powerful foe."

Artunis' legs trembled. She fell back onto the grass.

Hatzakh sniffed. "Crow deserved it for getting involved with that wretched foreigner Ego."

Artunis clutched grass in her trembling fist. She wanted to strike the man, to make him recant what he had just spoken. Mouse had already moved to interpose himself between her and him, though. That was good— it would not be wise of her to attack a Sage in his own territory. That didn't stop her from wanting to.

"The city," Hatzakh went on, "has fallen into absolute chaos. Blood runs in the streets. The Wolf leads open war against the Empire and the usurpers. The Sages must defend the Origin Spring—all the tunnels will be guarded, some we may collapse."

Mouse heaved a sigh. "Is this your way of telling us to leave?"

The Sage's nod was grave. "I will give the woman some painkilling herbs for her arm, but you must be on your way. For your own sakes." All of a sudden, Hatzakh was looking his age. "Better to bury this place than let it fall into the hands of the False Ruler, the one worshipped by the Empire. It is our oath that only a child of Talynis may glimpse the Spring, or"—he gestured to Mouse—"a true initiate of the Thousand Ways."

Artunis was shaking her head. "No." Now she was on her feet. "No. We need to help Wolf retake this city, save the *kingdom*. We cannot do that without you Sages. The Empire has a soldier who can hurl flames with barely a thought. And the Empire does not like to lose—certainly not twice. The Adept will burn this whole place down. Who cares if you protect this place if it means the death or enslavement of every Talynisti within the walls? What of the other cities? How many will fall because you refrained from getting involved?"

Hatzakh, undeterred, drew himself up to full height. "Any chance that the Imperial praetor finds her way down here is a risk far too great. You are not learned in our ways, you do not understand what is at stake."

She turned on Mouse, spreading her arms plaintively. "We *have* to help Wolf. You're one of them—convince them!"

Mouse snorted. "You overstate the nature of our relationship. I am here because I was sent here. I had a sacred task. The Sages of Talynis have little regard for me beyond recognizing our mutual practice of the arcane paths."

Hatzakh did not seem the least offended by Mouse's unflattering portrayal of them.

"Still," rumbled Mouse, "I would ask you for some form of aid, Hatzakh. Surely you can spare some help for us, enough to give us a fighting chance."

Artunis' heart lifted. She was not a particularly religious woman, but she sent a prayer up to the Four that they would move the old man's heart.

Hatzakh looked between the two of them, visage hard as granite.

Then he sighed. "I will send two brothers with you. Twins. Followers of the Way of Stone."

Mouse brightened. "Infinite gratitude to you, Sage Hatzakh."

The old man waved it off. "Don't get them killed. There are precious few acolytes left to us in these days. The False Ruler chokes the paths of spirit, culling our numbers."

Mouse looked aggrieved. "We have felt this in Endra as well."

Hatzakh vanished, apparently going to retrieve the Sages who would return to the surface with them. Artunis whirled on Mouse. "You keep mentioning the False Ruler as your enemy. You can't just mean Tamiq. Is it the Emperor of Lazarra?"

Mouse looked uneasy. "Not the Emperor, but the one behind him. The god who sits enthroned above all other gods in the western lands, who would set himself up as most high over the Talynisti Four if he had the chance...even over the deities of Endra, should his ambition prove insatiable."

Artunis frowned. Her lips parted, but Mouse raised a hand. "Do not speak the name. It draws his attention. He is the Far-seeing One, many-eyed and eared."

Her voice died. "But then, you're telling me we really are up against the gods of Lazarra?"

"Not all of them. Some are content with the pretender's rule, of course, but others are rebellious, keen to throw off the yoke he has placed them under."

She waved her arms back and forth. "Mouse, you're speaking in riddles. Give me something straightforward."

He took a breath. "You are not initiated, Jackal. It is forbidden that I share these things with you."

"Our enemy knows these things," she said resolutely. "If I go into this fighting blind, then we're at a disadvantage."

Conflict flickered across the big man's features. "I understand, but I am bound by sacred oaths. And besides, you overestimate how much our enemy understands. The False Ruler knows, of course, but hardly any souls in Lazarra, I would wager, know the truth. This is a war of gods, Jackal. Of spirits."

She threw up her arms. "We're up against an Imperial Adept! Of all people—"

"Of all people, she may be kept furthest from the truth. There is no one the Empire fights harder to keep from understanding the nature of the spiritual world than the warriors to whom they grant the power to wield it. Adept Reiva has no idea what the true essence of her power is."

Artunis opened her mouth to ask more when Hatzakh returned, two young men with deep-set eyes in tow. Like the older Sage, they wore sand-patterned robes and simple headdresses.

When they came forward, the younger Sages bowed to Mouse, sparing a curious glance for Artunis.

And then, both bowed slightly off to the side.

Mouse, to her shock, mirrored the bowing, right down to the obeisance toward empty air.

Or air that seemed empty.

'This is a war of gods, Jackal. Of spirits.'

'Adept Reiva has no idea what the true nature of the power she holds is.'

"This," Hatzakh said, indicating the first Sage, "is Wakaram. Follower of the Way of Stone."

"We are glad to have you, Sage Wakaram." Mouse made one of his complex Endric gestures of blessing.

Wakaram made another smooth bow, saying nothing. He did not seem to be carrying any weapons

Before Hatzakh could introduce the second, he spoke up, his voice smooth and slow. "I am Bebar. My brother observes a vow of silence, but you will find no greater warrior among our number." He drew himself up taller as he spoke. "The Four have blessed him with great skill in exchange for his piety; no contest of might can undo him. If you must speak to my brother, do so through me."

Mouse dipped his head. "Thank you for joining us, Sage Bebar."

Hatzakh surveyed the group, sighing. "We will seal the entrances as best we can once you have left. What do you intend to do? Our most recent reports indicate the Wolf has taken back the Temple."

Artunis' mind raced at that. They had countless possible plans for how to proceed in the event Dav-maiir descended into all-out war.

None of those plans, as far as she had been made privy to, however, accounted for the presence of two Talynisti Adepts—Sages, she corrected herself.

"What if we take the garrison?" she asked.

At first Mouse looked startled by the prospect. Then a grin spread across his features.

"What if?" he echoed.

54

ON THE EDGE OF A KNIFE

OSTENSIBLY, chastity is a Lazarran virtue, but our philosophers did more to that word than sailors to a dockside whore. The Talynisti cared more for such things (or at least, they made more of it).
—*The Memoirs of Flavia Iscator*

EVERY NIGHT in the command tent was consumed by meetings. Updates on the legion's supply situation, the unrest of different parts of the city, the rapidly shifting lines of combat as troops pushed and withdrew in a dizzying dance.

Tonight, however, the consuming topic was the matter of the Temple and the Wolf's demands:

The traitor to Talynis shall hand herself in, lest more blood be shed upon this sacred ground. From dawn, every six hours, another shall die.

As Vantelle read the terms aloud, Reiva put her hand to her forehead, screwing closed her eyes. "Shit. How many?"

"Seven legionnaires from Tortoiseshell Company."

"Is Captain Ezail alive?"

"His head is on a stake."

Of course, no one intended to even contemplate giving Reiva to the Wolf. From a purely logistical perspective, an Adept was worth far more to the legion than the handful of hostages he had taken.

Still, they were not about to throw up their hands and simply let the bastard slit their comrades' throats, hurling invectives at the Empire as he did so. It would make them look weak; it would spread dissension in the ranks.

Possible routes of attack to retake the Temple were offered, but few of them would be inexpensive in terms of life lost from the legion. The least bloody route involved a heavy application of Reiva's fire magic—but burning down half the Temple did not seem a prudent way to keep the few members of the city still sided with the legion happy.

Vantelle was obviously bemused by the whole matter, her knuckles pressed against her forehead. Prefects and captains brought forth suggestions, most of which amounted to some sort of variation on the same plan.

Reiva was growing increasingly frustrated as well. The Wolf had taken not only the Temple, he had taken prisoners of war. There were Lazarran men and women atop the hill counting on them.

If they're still alive, even. Reiva frowned, crushing the thought. They were —they had to be. If they turned out to be dead, then the Wolf would have no leverage when it came to handing her over to get the prisoners released.

Not that there would be any handing over, of course.

Guilt settled in her stomach.

She had ended up in this situation, in this country, because she had failed as a leader, gotten two squads killed in a bloody, frozen tableau of guts and horror.

Now she had the opportunity to save lives.

She knew, rationally, that handing herself over was ridiculous, that she would do far more for the Empire as an Adept in service, with many years on the field and in the Sanctum.

But, deep inside her, she could not deny that there was a certain charm to the notion of dying as a sacrifice. There was a sense of ease in it—to hand yourself over knowing your death would accomplish the rescue of your comrades, that you would be eulogized as a hero for it, selfless and coura-geously going to your doom.

There would be no more campaigns, no more politics, no more long days and nights on march, in camps, on bloody, muddy fields of battle. No more lost comrades. No more humiliations. No more failures.

There was an attractiveness in dying sooner, rather than facing down a lifetime of difficulties.

She was so absorbed in the thought train that she almost missed Zageth slipping into the tent.

Two captains were debating the merits of storming the Temple in a night raid, something that would have to be organized and executed immediately given the timetable they had received from the Wolf.

But Reiva had tuned them out, watching Zageth move to whisper in Vantelle's ear.

A cold smile curled across the praetor's lips. She turned her head slightly, eyes dancing with mirth. Though Reiva could not hear her, she could read the words: '*Are you sure?*'

Zageth nodded, a predatory grin on his features.

Vantelle rapped her knuckles on the desk.

All fell silent, turning to their praetor.

"The game," she said with deep satisfaction, "has just changed, friends. It seems the Loyalists have a mole inside the Temple."

Reiva perked up. "That's not particularly surprising. We have suspected for some time that there were spies, possibly left over from the regime change in the confusion." This was something she had been briefed on extensively when she first came to Dav-maiir. Legate Iscator had conveyed such musings to her personally. She felt a stab of anxiety in her gut at the thought of the blonde commander, somewhere across the sands.

Vantelle's smile only widened. "Very true. But *none* of us had suspected that the Loyalists would have in their pocket none other than Tamiq's own daughter."

Reiva's stomach lurched.

Princess Asrah?

She almost said that such a thing seemed impossible—but then she thought back to how intelligent Asrah had seemed at the dinner. How quietly frustrated she had been by her father's incalcitrance. How fondly she had spoken of her relatives, exiled in Shugrith.

At the revelation, everyone seemed to hold their breath.

Then, all of a sudden, it was as though a string had been cut.

"This is an incredibly delicate situation," muttered one of the prefects. "It would be a risky move on our part to make any sort of public accusation of the princess' involvement. It could ruin our relationship with Tamiq."

Vantelle rested her chin on her fist. "Indeed. We are on the edge of a knife—but if we are wise in how we go about this, it could win us much more than merely the captives. This could turn the tide of the war." She gestured to her optio. "What other sorts of information do you have on the matter, Zageth?"

The man crossed his arms. "It's not clear if there's a regular pattern to this, but we know a Loyalist agent meets her on her balcony, often in the middle of the night. One of our informants, a maid to the princess, has sometimes overheard them."

"So the princess," said Reiva, "would pass information from within the palace—from within the king's own inner circle—to the Loyalists."

Zageth smirked. "Not only that—our woman thinks there may have been a romantic dimension to the relationship."

That was leverage, then. Not only was she the princess, whoever she was connected to among the Loyalists had been taking her to bed. That was a death-knell for her honor in Talynisti society. She might be disowned for such a thing, if not corporally punished. It would be a shame upon Tamiq.

"We have to handle this carefully," said Reiva. "Talynisti culture could have severe ramifications on the entirety of Tamiq's family if this comes to light. It could make him seem like a weak father, a weak king."

Vantelle nodded. "Ample opportunity and risk abound—but we must move quickly. We call a recess, and then within the hour I want a plan for how we can get those legionnaires to safety. It doesn't need to be perfect, but we need something to work with. The Wolf's deadline looms before us. I'll not be out-maneuvered by that thug again."

Something popped into Reiva's mind.

"I may have something for you already, my praetor. A way we can leverage what we know about the princess without tipping our hand too much."

The praetor leaned forward, expectant. "Do tell, Adept."

55

LIKE LIGHTNING ACROSS THE SKY

MUCH AS OUR CULTURES DIFFER, Lazarra and Talynis are alike in how we esteem the household. In Lazarra, we call the Emperor our father and the Empress our mother, and we understand ourselves to be part of the Imperial domicile.

The Talynisti way of things is more complicated—there are many patriarchs and clans and households—but I felt a sympathy of sorts for it. Certainly, I understood the importance of the king, and how much it mattered that the royal household be strong.

We exploited that belief, of course.

—*The Memoirs of Flavia Iscator*

～

ASRAH YAWNED, shaking out her hair. She was tired, not only due to the hour, but also tired in her spirit.

Aviqohl had taken the Temple. He had hostages.

She was both incredibly proud and extremely fearful. The city seemed a bundle of kindling inching closer and closer to the flame. Who was in control? Her father? The legion? The Loyalists?

And while all that went on, here she was, on a soft bed, in a comfortable room. Gods—she wanted to be out there, to be in the middle of it all.

She wanted to be at Aviqohl's side rather than working in the shadows like this, spying on her own father.

The room was dark as she sat on the edge of her bed. Her hands were folded between her knees, her head bowed.

By all measures of family duty, she was a failure. A traitor. She heard how Aviqohl spoke about the Adept, Reiva. That's how her father would view her once they found out that she had been against them all this time. They would learn how she had been against them from the start, since the legion first came knocking, since her uncle Malik was first driven out the gates.

And if Malik came back—what then? He had two sons; there was no need for him to bring her into the family. He might, out of gratitude, to give her honor she would lose as the daughter of a usurper king. But, for all the wrongs Tamiq had done, it was undeniable that many found him more likable than Malik. Sure, now Dav-maiir was in absolute chaos, fires burning at all hours, smoke and cries for blood in the air. But would the people be so welcoming of Malik? Or would they decide they'd rather keep what Tamiq had promised—openness, connection to the world, the advantages of Imperial allegiance.

It was a frightening reality that her place in that world was dreadfully uncertain.

Her eyes were heavy, one shoulder stiff from sleeping poorly the night before. But she couldn't bring herself to lie down. She had tried earlier. Tossing and turning. Sighing. Huffing.

Sleep was elusive. Her thoughts raced like lightning across the sky.

And there was no one in the palace she could open up to. There would have been a Loyalist or two, of course, but she had no clue who they were, and she couldn't simply call people into her quarters at all hours of the night and unload her worries. That wasn't what they were here for. And besides, she was no wilting lily.

She would endure this. She would survive it—whatever the chaos and havoc. If she had to endure it all from the sidelines, then so be it; she had been born in Talynis. She was used to being the woman on the sidelines. Fine. While all the world thought she was sitting in the shade sipping honeyed tea, she would do her duty for her people, for her gods.

Aviqohl was off doing that right now. He was taking action. His name—the name she knew at last—would be remembered, she was sure of that. What about the daughter of Tamiq? Would Asrah of Talynis be remembered for siding with her uncle? Or would she merely become a footnote in some chronicler's tale? Would she even gain so much of a mention? Scribes were strange with the stories they told—somehow, every single one was the same.

Somehow, women like her were either villains, problems, or just plain absent from the page.

What could she say to that? Could she write her own story?

That was a risk, of course. That was dangerous, the possibility of that being discovered.

But maybe she wanted danger. Maybe she actually wanted to be found out, to have her life on the line. Maybe she was sick and tired of being the only Loyalist in all of Dav-maiir who did not have to worry whether she would get a knife in the gut by day's end.

Intellectually, she understood that her work was important for the fighters like Aviqohl doing work on the ground. But in her heart, she wanted to be among them.

She let herself be carried off by a fantasy of running through the streets of Dav-maiir, her little dagger in hand as Aviqohl ran ahead, fallen legionnaires littering the ground. They were freeing Dav-maiir. Freeing Talynis.

The reality of the lonely room constricted her heart. She should have been asleep, but sitting on the edge of her bed, all she could do was imagine a different now. A different past. A different future.

A knock sounded at the balcony. Soft, short.

At first, Asrah only stared, certain she had misheard. He couldn't be here right now, could he? Surely he was hemmed in at the Temple, busy coordinating the retaliation against her father and the legion. What could he...?

The knock sounded again—still soft, but more insistent.

What if he wanted her to come with him?

She was on her feet, padding across the room. She wasn't dressed for running through the city—but surely he could hold on for a moment.

Before he could knock a third time, Asrah sidled up to the door. She rested her fingers on the latch, ready to unlock it.

She tapped two short knocks, paused, and then a third.

Now Aviqohl would answer with his own code—he had always chided her for forgetting to use hers.

But there was only silence.

Asrah's heart leaped in her chest.

In an instant, every shred of her awareness honed in on the knife tucked inside her nightstand. The knife she should have had in hand already.

She threw herself across the room right as the door crashed inward, splintering.

Asrah screamed for her guards as she finally got hold of the weapon.

In an instant, shouts rang out in the halls. But that door, she remembered even as she yelled for them, she had locked as well.

So here she was, clutching a knife, face to face with a man much larger than her, holding a strange sword.

A cool breeze curled through the air.

The assailant flashed a broad smile. "Sorry for the door, princess."

"I'll kill you," she snarled, dagger clutched in front of her.

"It wasn't *that* nice of a door."

Asrah lunged forward, thrusting the knife at his gut and twisting to avoid the sword.

The sword didn't touch her, but her knife didn't touch him, either. The man nimbly stepped around her stab, catching her wrist and with one quick twist disarming her—fingers splaying open in a painful reflexive motion.

But it didn't stop there. The man grappled her, pinning her arms to her side. Her legs flailed, madly trying to kick his knees, his ankles. Nothing connected.

Grunting, the man hissed for her to hold still. "Wouldn't want to drop you three stories, hm?"

Asrah hardly even had time to process what he'd said before her room tore away from around them. Suddenly, they were in open air, the palace grounds below them.

And they weren't falling.

Asrah screamed again, thrashing like a landed fish.

The man swore, clamping down on her with one arm, his other holding that strange sword aloft, pale green light bleeding from its edge.

Asrah nearly stopped fighting in bewilderment.

They were *flying*.

Then, she saw the side of a building rushing to meet them, and screamed again.

The man swept the sword, and a sudden gust of wind sent them careening to the side, tumbling through the air.

Asrah felt her stomach lurch as they spun and whirled on the gales, and she sighed with relief when they finally stabilized.

"My apologies, princess," he said.

Well, what was she supposed to say to *that*?

"Let me down, and we can call things settled."

He chuckled. "If only."

Asrah wondered if she could pull a knife off his belt—he seemed the sort to have one or two—but her arms were still pinned to her side.

And, of course, they were still zipping over the city.

Watching buildings slip by below, she got another strange feeling in her stomach. She tried staring at the horizon instead, but all was dark.

The stars were shining, and she wondered what the odds were of an angel descending to rescue her.

No star left its winding course, regrettably.

"So, how does one come to own a flying sword?" she called over the rushing winds.

"Take it off a dead man."

"That hardly seems legitimate."

"People do it with kingdoms all the time."

Fair point.

They were about to fly over the western wall.

"That's the legion camp."

He chuckled. "Trying to earn the goodwill of your kidnapper is normally a sound strategy, but I'm not trying to avoid them."

Suddenly, they dropped through the air, Asrah's stomach going into her throat. Another gust of wind caught them and bore them aloft, wheeling them down to the sands.

He hit the ground at a run, kicking up a cloud of sand. As soon as they were on solid ground, Asrah kicked at his ankle.

With a grunt, he dropped the sword and grappled her, pulling her arms behind her back. "Some thanks I get for a smooth landing."

The princess stomped and kicked, praying she could crack a bone in his foot, but she just kept shuffling her feet around in the cold sand.

"Easy on her, Yaros," called a familiar voice. "She's a princess, not a mule."

"Oh, my mistake—I normally tell the difference by how they kick."

"Adept!" shrieked Asrah, spitting hair out of her face.

Reiva was approaching from the direction of the legion garrison, fire burning in her palm.

"I'm sorry to meet you under these circumstances, princess."

"These circumstances," she echoed flatly. "You sent this man to kidnap me by *flying through the sky*. You could have simply come for dinner again."

"And you could have simply stayed out of the war—but things aren't that straightforward these days, are they?"

Asrah's face hardened. The Adept was eyeing her like one might size up a wild animal, or an opponent on the battlefield.

To her surprise, she liked that feeling.

She also felt afraid, though she fought to hide it.

"I would rather we speak about this civilly, without a burly man holding my arms behind my back."

The Adept nodded. "That sounds preferable."

56

THE DAUGHTER OF A USURPER

THOUGH I SPENT many years searching, I did eventually discover the means by which the Peaceborn King bound a spirit to his signet ring and engineered the Temple.

Precious few magicians still remember the spells and rituals involved, and many only know pieces of a greater whole that—in spite of all my strivings—may be lost to time forever.

But this I have discerned for certain: the magic originated in the Immortal Empire of Zarush, likely during the reign of Ahura Darius the Second.

—*The Life and Wisdom of Simeon Binkhok As Told by Himself*

AVI SLEPT IN FITS, often waking to do rounds of the Temple.

Now the sun was soon to rise, and he was well and truly awake. He got up, rubbed his face, and after checking that he still had the *Nihilo* Blade secured, he began another pass of the grounds.

Some small part of him, that little boy who had made his life on the streets of Shugrith, marveled to think that he was walking round this place with impunity. He could remember the awe with which his father explained the four sculptures at the cardinal points, promising that someday he would see them in person.

Now he was the protector of those sculptures.

To the east stood the Worldfather. Bearded, paternal, at his forehead he held the sun, his hands in a vertical triangle.

To the west, the Windmother. Source of life, mother of all, at her pelvis she held a lush garden, her hands in an inverse triangle.

To the south, the Warrior. Youthful, raising a mighty arm against the enemies of his people. Son of the father.

To the north, the Wanderer. Hooded against the sands, watching with keen eyes and holding something amorphous in his hands—the chaotic unknown. Son of the mother.

The Four on High, the Four Gods of Talynis.

Avi did not care what this pretender king said, did not care what any high priest had to pontificate about it. The gods of Talynis were not to be mocked, not to be cowed, not to be made subservient to some foreign lord. The people, whatever they thought of Malik, would never abide that. Talynis and her gods would stand proud against this threat, as they had for centuries before, all the way into the time unknown when the Four first watered this blessed land.

As the golden red rays of the approaching sun colored the horizon, the Wolf climbed the inner stairs to stand atop the parapet. From here, in the beating heart of the Dav-maiir, he could see everything. The reaches of the desert all around. The burned sections of the western farms. The arrogant blue banners of the Ninth Legion.

And the palace to the northeast, where Asrah was sleeping. Or maybe just waking up.

His chest ached for her. The thought of her soft lips quirked in that half-smile, her hair loose and tousled. The desire to pull her close and hold her forever burned in his heart.

Soon, he told himself. Soon the city would be back under their control, and then...

And then what? What was the daughter of a usurper to do?

There were difficulties there. Challenges. He was sure Crow had plans for that—he would not have contracted with Asrah if he thought that aiding the Loyalist cause would be a death sentence for her.

But, realistically, they would have to convince King Malik of her trustworthiness. Which meant *Avi* would have to convince King Malik, considering Crow's death and...whatever the current status of Mouse and Jackal was.

He needed them to get back soon. He needed their help, assuming both were still alive...

The thought of the Vipers in Dav-maiir being reduced to just Mouse and him was jarring, unnerving. It seemed an impossibility the gods should will such a thing. Him, the mongrel. Mouse, the Endric warrior.

The gods, however, were famous for strange things. Who would have poured water into a barren desert and said, 'Here make your dwelling, for one day it shall grow lush and verdant'?

The same gods whose house he was currently using as a military base. No one had been struck dead yet, though, so that was a good sign.

The real test, of course, would be this very hour. The legion would have to hand over the Adept. The traitor to Talynis.

He would have spit if he were not on sacred ground. The Loyalists had already labored for much of the night to clean away all the spilled blood they could find, discarding the bodies outside of the gates—friend and foe alike. They were much reliant on the assurances of Loyalist priests—the faithful priests—that the temple's sanctity and purity was unimpeachable, so long as the rites and observances were upheld.

Already, he could smell incense rising from the pre-dawn prayers. There would be songs sung. Requests for mercy and strength, for absolution for the sinner—the small-hearted, the vicious...the murderer.

'I never want you to have to kill like I did, Aviqohl.'

He felt that sour taste in his mouth again.

"Well then, why did you die and leave us?" he whispered to the winds.

A shout from the Temple floor caught his attention. Avi turned and saw one of the men who had performed most valiantly in the assault. A middle-aged fellow named Nubul.

Nubul had the responsibility of receiving messages from the legion and bringing them to Avi. Avi waved and set off down the steps, heart racing.

Would this be it? Would they capitulate to his demands and hand over the Adept?

Nubul made his way up, slower. His joints were bad, he said. It certainly hadn't stopped him from helping to cut down their foes, though.

As they drew closer together, Avi realized he looked distressed. With every step down, his stomach seemed to drop lower in tandem.

"What is it? What did they say?" he asked, unable to hold it back any longer.

Nubul huffed, scratching at his black-and-gray hair. He cast a glance toward the hostages under guard in the corner of the courtyard. "New terms from the Empire. New demands."

"They can't demand anything," snarled Avi. "We have seven of theirs—they have nothing."

Nubul looked pained. "The runner outside says...he says the Adept has taken Tamiq's daughter as a prisoner."

The world spun for a moment.

"He says they discovered she was a spy for the Loyalist cause, and have taken her into custody."

Avi braced a hand against the wall. His knees suddenly seemed weak.

Nubul watched him with obvious concern. "It's true then? She was with us?"

He nodded shakily. "She was. Is."

Nubul rubbed his forehead, muttering an oath, then looking toward the central structure of the Temple in fear.

Avi huffed, feeling as though he were short of breath. Nubul watched him inquisitively. "She was important, then?"

Important to me.

"Yes," he said. "She brought us essential information from within the palace. How many people know?"

Nubul shrugged. "Only us and two of the boys at the gate right now. But, son, if we do an exchange—"

"We'll do it."

"The whole city will know."

"The whole legion already does, odds are."

Nubul shook his head. "Four Gods. What'll this do to the divide?"

Avi was rubbing his eyes. "If we're lucky, people will see her as an inspiration."

Nubul seemed like he'd swallowed something sour. "Or they'll see her as a renegade daughter."

"Yes, they might."

Suddenly careless of his presence on sacred ground, Avi swore very loudly. "Why can't anything in this city ever be simple?"

57

THE DAUGHTER OF A KING

WE WERE proud of the Imperial succession. The notion that only the most fit to rule received the throne—it was a delusion, but it was a delusion we adored, for it spared us from the democratic excesses that had presaged the Dark Days, as well as the hereditary buffoonery that characterized neighboring lands.

But Princess Asrah...such a woman as her may have been enough to convince even the most stalwart of senators that a line of kings had merit—so long as they were born of *her* line.

—*The Memoirs of Flavia Iscator*

∿

EVEN WITH AN ARMED GUARD PRESENT, Reiva still had to fight the urge to grip the hilt of her sword. Now she had to project strength. She had to show the Wolf that she would not be cowed by him, that the Empire would not be cowed by him.

She stood, helmet on and armor fastened, at the edge of a contested street. Not fifty feet away, Loyalist barricades stood as ramshackle barriers. Now and then, she caught a furtive glance from one of the Talynisti.

Her own soldiers were keenly observing the barricades, as well as manning their own defensive battlements. The legion engineers were constantly on call, constructing and repairing where they were needed. It was said by many a tactician that the legions won their wars not by the sword or shield, but by their technical prowess. Reiva hoped that was the case—the men and women of the engineering divisions had been laboring ceaselessly. Fatigue showed beneath their eyes, a slight tremor in their hands.

Always, however, their work was superb. No soldier was worth their salt who could only perform in ideal conditions. The entire point of training and drilling was to prepare for *real* war.

Reiva, for her part, was feeling the drag as well. Her mind bore the toll of constant alertness and paranoia. Her body was in fine shape and health thanks to her aether channeling, but her spirit was fraying. She'd kept so frantically busy that she hadn't even had time to read a letter from Domi that had arrived by hawk in the middle of the night—no doubt on the matter of Alyat's death and how Reiva was coping.

So, facing down a prisoner exchange, she was more than a little concerned that something would drive her to snap.

The runner who had relayed the Wolf's response vowed he would execute none of the soldiers. If he did, then the deal would be off. There was always the chance that he could have pulled some sort of bait and switch though. They would need to verify that all the people he handed over to them were truly legionnaires and not imposters.

Yaros came over to her, sweeping his eyes over the barricades as he walked. He still had the *Ventas* Blade on his hip. He drew odd looks from the other soldiers. Rumors had spread about what it was, of course, but they had also spread regarding who *he* was. Soldiers from their raid on Theimos' establishment must have let word slip that he was somehow connected to the Krypteia. But people were far and away more baffled by how he managed to spirit a princess out of her own room in the middle of a war-torn city from a locked-down palace.

For his part, Yaros looked frazzled. When he drew up to her, he didn't even flash a smile, only nodded. Reiva returned the gesture.

"Princess is comfortable," he said.

"Who's watching her? I'd rather have you there."

Yaros cracked a smile. "Belic and Mago. They're good men."

"I know, but still, we can't afford to screw this up."

"I'll get back soon—but she doesn't seem very sweet on me."

"Gods only know why."

Yaros nodded absently, peering at the Loyalist barricade. "How close will you get to him?"

Reiva gave him a look. His eyes were haggard, wary, almost like a beast at the end of a long hunt. It was disconcerting to see him so frantic, and given how well he normally masked such things...

He's worried.

"Ideally, we stay on opposite ends on the square."

"Ideally, I'd be lying in bed with some spiced wine right now."

Reiva shook her head. "It will be fine, Yaros. Get back to the princess."

Wordlessly, he departed, giving her one last tense look.

Reiva realized she was gripping her sword again. Deliberately, she eased her fingers.

When the Wolf arrived, Reiva didn't know it by seeing him. The first indication was a roar of acclaim from the Loyalists at the barricade.

In response, the legionnaires tensed, adjusted their shields. Archers tested their draws.

Reiva felt the Flame burgeon inside her. She willed it to quiet, to calm. She was furious. Everyone was furious. Their brothers and sisters in arms were being led here in bondage by the man receiving those cheers.

But anger would only stymie her chances. The Flame needed to quell, for now.

But she did not let it quell *too* much—just in case.

Reiva stepped out partially from behind the battlement. With her crimson Adept's mantle, she would be impossible to mistake.

Behind the battlement, a *triarii* with a tower shield stood ready to leap out. Reiva was also keeping a constant drip of aether flowing into her system.

Still, when the Wolf revealed himself, that terrifying black blade on his hip, her heart shuddered, her jaw clenched. She was sweating, she realized. Gods send that her voice didn't fail her.

This man, the Wolf—last time, she had regarded him as little more than an agitator, a young man with more passion than skill who had killed Adept Havan thanks to the unanticipated factor of the *Nihilo* Blade.

In hardly a week, he had turned this conflict on its head. Maybe that was a fluke.

Maybe Reiva surviving their last encounter was a fluke.

She was the first to raise her hand, palm outward. The universal symbol for parley. If anyone struck out in violence from this point on, there would be no quarter given.

The Wolf, thankfully, answered with the same gesture.

"You have seven of my people," called Reiva. Her voice echoed off the stones, filling the square.

The Wolf laughed, sharp and mocking. "It continues to amaze me, Adept, how you have forgotten who *your people* truly are."

Reiva's shoulders stiffened. Hopefully, he could not see the effect his words had on her. She hoped her own legionnaires did not notice either.

"Bring them out," she said.

"Bring out the princess."

"Your *spy*, you mean. I seem to recall you are not in favor of the king and his family."

"Tamiq," snapped the Wolf, "is no king of ours. The princess Asrah is a true daughter of the desert, faithful to our gods and our traditions."

Reiva grit her teeth.

'*True daughter of the desert.*' It was impossible not to hear that as another accusation.

She waved to a legionnaire, who went to fetch the princess.

Reiva let her eyes slip off the Wolf for a moment. Even at this distance, she could see the animosity the Talynisti had for her. One of their own by blood, standing underneath an Imperial banner.

Don't let him get to you, Yaros had said. She had thought he only meant with the *Nihilo* Blade. Now she realized physical distance might be the least of her worries.

When Yaros returned with Asrah, she was shackled with either arm to the two *triarii*. She held her head high, despite her state. When Yaros took her, she had been in her nightclothes. They had found some more suitable garments for her to wear, but nothing worthy of a princess.

Her hair, Reiva realized with horror, was left unbound. She looked more like a woman who might stand at the corner and offer services than the daughter of a king.

Reiva cursed herself for not thinking about the problems that might cause. She met the princess' eyes—hard, proud—then she turned to Yaros. Hissing out the corner of her mouth, she ordered him to make her look more presentable.

Yaros cocked an eyebrow.

"Dress her hair or something."

Understanding dawned in the mercenary's eyes. Belic and Mago looked baffled as the Karellan suddenly stepped in and began putting the princess' hair into a braid.

"And someone cover her head!" Reiva turned back toward the Wolf, scrambling for a way to buy time. "You see your princess once I see my legionnaires."

The Wolf crossed his arms. "The princess first."

Reiva clenched a fist. "I'm willing to wait, dog. Shall I have some wine brought, maybe a tent? It's a lovely day to watch barbarians strut about."

The Wolf looked like he'd been slapped in the face. He seemed to be turning over the logic of her statement (there wasn't much, admittedly—which was part of the point).

Thank the gods though, he went back behind the barricade.

Breathing a sigh of relief, Reiva turned back to the incredulous scene at her side.

Princess Asrah snorted. "I've never had a man dress my hair before."

Yaros shrugged. "I assure you, my lady, I am quite capable."

The princess frowned. "Heathens. Your women fight in wars; your men dress their hair…"

"Wait until you hear about our gymnasiums."

Asrah shot him a scathing glare. "I am familiar with the concept. The depravity of the western lands is famous."

"Well, I assure you, the real thing is incomparable to the rumors."

Mago and Belic shared a baffled glance around the princess. Reiva almost cracked a smile at their befuddlement. Even as a veteran in the legions—there were some things you could just never expect. This would certainly provide them ample stories to tell over wine and campfires.

The princess was watching Reiva again. She seemed like she wanted to say something.

Reiva preempted her. "I enjoyed our dinner, for what it's worth. I am sorry for this."

She held up her chin, looked askance. "You were a pleasant conversation partner. I am sorry the legate has been sent away. She was a kind woman."

And Vantelle, of course, was not.

Yaros stepped back from his work. "Not bad for a rushed job, eh?"

Reiva frowned. "As good as we'll get I suppose. And where's that head-dress?" She turned back to the barricades. There was a flurry of activity, but still no sign of the captives. Reiva was beginning to worry the whole thing was a front, when the Wolf appeared again.

"I have all seven here."

"Show me."

He made a gesture, and a gap opened in the Loyalist ranks.

Reiva's stomach seized up.

She had been worried that they would have to inspect the hostages closely to ensure they were truly Lazarrans, not just Talynisti trussed up in stolen gear. That wasn't a concern anymore.

All seven were naked, hands bound to one long length of rope. All were bruised, bleeding. It was obvious from their builds, as well as their hair-cuts, that these were legionnaires, but the tattoos confirmed it beyond doubt: the standard military sigil, with an IX. They were *Legio Nona*. Ninth Legion.

Reiva fought to keep steadiness in her voice. "You know, if we had treated your princess with as much disgrace as you treated our legionnaires, I imagine you would seek to gut me here and now."

The Wolf shrugged. "I already wish to gut you. And I won't have any of this posturing, Imperial. We all know what the Empire does to its enemies."

Reiva scowled. "Bring her out," she growled.

Belic and Mago stepped forward. Asrah kept pace with them, not needing to be coerced or shoved along. Thankfully, Yaros had managed to find what appeared to be a hastily-cut swathe of sackcloth and draped it over her head. Even so, she had all the bearing as she might at an official function.

As soon as she was in the open, a change came over the Wolf. His hand crept for the *Nihilo* Blade. She imagined that if they had been closer, she might have noticed his breathing change.

He was angry. He was relieved. He was willing to kill for this woman.

"Send them over," she called, letting her own hand rest on her sword.

The Wolf shook his head. "These seven sods are my only insurance against your betrayal. And we know how much you love to stab your own in the back."

Reiva ground her teeth. She hated how easily he got under her skin. She wanted to grab him by the shoulders and shake him, shout in his face that this was never her choice, that this was her only way to survive, that she was just a girl from Shugrith who lost her family and was doing what she had to.

Instead, she crossed her arms. She stared him down. She let the weight of the moment hang there. "A walk-by then."

Again, the Wolf laughed. "You expect I would allow seven Imperials to pass by Princess Asrah? For all I know, they would pounce on her like a pack of hounds, eager to extract some final revenge."

"The Empire," bellowed Reiva, "is honorable. And these men and women are under my command. They will do no such thing." She looked at the legionnaires as she said it. She had no delusions that they would even consider such a thing—it would mean certain death—but she wanted to put the Loyalists at ease.

Still, the Wolf was intransigent, calling for the princess to be sent across first, so they could ensure the Empire upholds their end of the bargain. "A harmed princess is more of an injury than wounded soldiers."

"She's a spy," Reiva said again. "Not a civilian."

The Wolf was opening his mouth again when Asrah piped up.

"Let the legionnaires go first."

Everyone whirled on her. The Wolf gaped. Reiva blinked.

Until then, the princess had been an asset. When she spoke, it was as if a stack of bronze had given its opinion on tariffs.

Reiva remembered this woman's keenness at the dinner. Even when she was being exchanged in a deal, she refused to let herself be reduced to a bargaining chip.

You would do well, she thought, *in our depraved western lands, princess.*

"The legionnaires will cross over," said Asrah, "and then I shall cross."

The Wolf seemed perturbed by this. Reiva almost laughed—he denied she had the right to be princess, yet here he was being ordered how to conduct a prisoner exchange by and for her.

"The Adept," she said, "is a trustworthy woman."

Now it was Reiva's turn to look startled. That could have been a dangerous thing for Asrah to voice. The Wolf looked even more incredulous.

And he kept on staring.

And then he gave the order for the legionnaires to be released.

Reiva's heart was beating out of her chest as they crossed. She kept expecting an arrow to strike one in the back, or a hurled stone to crack open a skull.

But sure enough, they made it to the other side. Reiva laid a hand on each one as they passed her. "Emperor and Eagle." Every one met her eyes, viciously proud.

"Emperor and Eagle," they echoed.

She saw something else in those eyes, and in their postures as their bonds were cut and cloaks thrown over their naked, bruised bodies. Guilt. The guilt of survivors.

"Are you the only ones?" She had to confirm it before she sent Asrah back.

One of them, a woman with a nasty gash over her left eye, said that they were. "All the others were butchered, left in the street for rats."

Reiva accepted the news with a nod.

Belic and Mago had overheard that. She could see that they were barely keeping their rage controlled.

The Flame, to her surprise, was hardly in a blaze right now. A part of her was angry, of course. Another part looked at everything that had transpired here, and simply ached.

Her peoples. Her nations.

"Release the captive," she said. "At once."

The two *triarii* produced keys, each undoing the other man's shackle. Then they opened the manacles on Asrah's wrists.

The princess took a moment to rub at the bruises. The raw skin looked starkly out of place on a princess' body.

"Thank you," muttered Reiva. "You made that easier than it would have been."

Asrah accepted it with a nod. "If only this could all end so easily."

"If only."

With that, Asrah made her way across the square, a hundred pairs of eyes fixed on her every step. She was dressed like a pauper, her hair in an unkempt braid. But no one could deny that she was the daughter of a king.

58

NO STRAGGLERS

THOUGH SHE MUST HAVE ENTERTAINED the possibility, Cassia certainly doubted the Talynisti had managed to maintain a cabal of Adepts—Sages, as they call them. I am glad I was not there for the storming of the garrison, though. I have seen Cassia Vantelle thwarted, long ago, and it is a terrifying thing.
  —*The Memoirs of Flavia Iscator*

〜

THE LAYOUT of a Lazarran legion camp was universal. Anywhere in the world, someone could enter one and know precisely where to find the command tent, the blacksmiths, the farriers, and so forth.

This presented a unique advantage to the strike team led by Artunis and Mouse. Composed largely of Loyalist warriors, they were making their way toward the garrison in near pitch blackness, the only light coming from a single torch. Any more would risk smoke buildup in the tunnel—the tunnel Wakaram and Bebar were digging beneath the city with naught but forceful waves of their hands.

The Loyalists they had pulled to their mission were baffled as they watched, but there was also an undeniable exhilaration washing over them. Until now, the power of the Adepts had been held only by the Lazarrans. Now they were privy to a great secret. They knew that Talynis too had been blessed with such arcane strength, and the Four had sent these two men to turn the tide of the struggle for Dav-maiir.

Artunis was uneasy, though. Wakaram was silent, always, but Bebar was willing to speak. And he had been very clear to them—do not engage with any Imperials until the two of them were well ahead. The two Sages would do their best to take the garrison, and it was imperative they not accidentally do any harm to the Loyalists. Collateral damage, Bebar warned, was a real risk.

The positive side of that advice was that, if all went well, Artunis would not even have to cross blades with a legionnaire. Still, it just didn't seem right that they should have *magic* in their arsenal now. She had always understood the Talynisti attitude toward magic as a fearful one. It was a dangerous practice—one relegated to the more eccentric of the Mithallkiym tribes, or the far-flung peoples of distant lands who did not know the Four.

Back in Zarush, there had been ample number of sorcerers. The night before her father died, he had told her that was their downfall. Now here she was in Talynis, fighting alongside Talynisti Adepts. Mouse had said there was a difference between the sort of magic Adepts did and the darker arts that had proliferated in the twilight of Zarush, but he had not elaborated. Yet another truth that was, frustratingly, only for the initiated.

Bebar raised a fist. Wakaram was running his hands along the roof of the tunnel, eyes shut. What was he feeling for?

After a moment, the silent Sage turned to his brother and nodded severely.

Bebar addressed the party. "We are immediately beneath the legion garrison. Remember our instructions. Four save us."

And that was all he said before he and the other Sage thrust their arms diagonally upward.

Up to this point, they had been making the tunnel with a soft rumbling. The sound of earth shifting was not by any means quiet, but Bebar had assured them that at this depth no one would hear them. At the most, someone would think a minor earthquake had occurred.

This was quite different.

Rock and gravel split with a roar like thunder, and in seconds the tunnel expanded, racing upward and exploding into bright daylight.

Wakaram and Bebar were already outside, the earth pulling them upward in a single step. Shouts of surprise, fear, alarm echoed down.

Artunis was stunned by the abruptness of it all—then she ran for the slope.

The others took up King Malik's name in a chant. Mouse drew his two fearsome blades and waved them high above his head as they burst into the garrison.

Artunis nearly tripped over herself when she saw the havoc. They had only been seconds behind the Sages—but already this part of the garrison was littered with bruised and broken bodies, strewn amongst spires of jagged rock and heaps of earth.

Mouse called out, one sword pointed toward the western gate of the city. "They're pushing the Lazarrans out!"

She nodded, breathless. That was according to plan. "Then we do our job," she shouted. "Clear out this side—ensure no stragglers remain!"

Though they were few in number, the remaining legionnaires in this part of the garrison were confused, unprepared. Many who saw Mouse simply turned and ran—an effect, Artunis guessed, of his magic.

If the legionnaires were struck with fear by Mouse's powers, then the opposite happened to the Loyalists. Bold and courageous, they hunted down warriors far better equipped than them. As they went, they scavenged legion shields and helmets, snatching javelins from racks.

The legion garrison theoretically should have been ready for an attack on this side of the city—but there was hardly anything to defend against. The biggest threat was from inside Dav-maiir; lookouts would have been able to alert them to anyone trying to circle around the city. And, of course, no one was ready for an attack from *underneath*.

They had been caught completely unawares.

And the Loyalists were riding high on that psychological victory, fueled further by what Mouse called his Way of Soul.

Artunis shouted at her soldiers, pulling them away from their looting. "We follow the Sages! Sweep this place clean, stay together."

A roar of acclaim met her. Her heart was pounding with exhilaration as she led the advance.

Here and there, she came across a moaning, injured legionnaire. She dispatched them without a fuss. Every throat slit set her soul burning brighter.

She had feared that she would never again fight, wounded as she was. Now, she was seizing a Lazarran garrison, warriors from the gods paving the way.

Artunis couldn't help a mad smile. Dav-maiir was going to be theirs again.

"Are you watching, Crow?" she whispered.

Her feet struck the ground in a frantic rhythm—she hadn't even realized when she started running. She ran faster. Shouts from behind told her people were struggling to keep up. That was their problem—they should have been moving faster. Didn't they know there was a war to win?

Just as she came around a barracks, a massive hunk of rock ripped itself from the ground and went flying. Artunis gaped as it bowled over a cluster of legionnaires in their tortoise formation, shields locked together.

Shields that had served them no purpose, as they now lay broken and bloodied in a mangled heap of flesh and metal.

Wakaram was standing there, observing the scene with a dispassionate gaze. He noticed Artunis, frowned, but merely turned back to his work.

Another squadron was making a mad dash for their position. Wakaram held out his hands, palms up, and then snapped his fingers to the vertical.

In an instant, jagged spires of rock burst from the ground, skewering the legionnaires through gut and limb and throat.

The Sage glided across the ground, every step lengthened as the earth clutched at his feet and carried him forward.

In awe, Artunis watched him go.

Then she shook her head. No time to gawk—there were legionnaires to send on.

She began systematically going through the different tents. Most were empty, some held a wounded soldier who had crawled in, desperately hoping to escape notice. Unfortunately for them, Artunis had made a career of bringing down foes who would otherwise prefer to remain in the shadows.

As she went, her eyes swept to and fro over discarded blades. She dismissed dozens of gladius swords, scanning for a different shape. Then, just as she was losing hope, she found it. Her father's shamshir.

Her heart soared as she stuck her short sword through her belt and snatched up the weapon she had known all her life. Its grip in her hand felt *right*, and she felt like a missing piece had just slotted into her soul.

Before long, the other Loyalists caught up to her. Together, they rid the garrison of any stragglers. Mouse had a deep-set frown on his face.

"The Adept of Fire is not here."

Artunis turned her head toward the gate. Mouse was right—if she had been here, they would have known by now. They were confident their two Sages would be able to match her, but if she struck them from behind, or flanked them such that Wakaram and Bebar were not there to intervene...

"Keep close behind the Sages," she ordered. "If you see the Adept, or any senior officers from the legion, scream bloody murder. We need to hamstring their forces as much as possible."

It was an inspiring call, but as they moved forward, they still played little role besides mopping up the work of the Sages. And as Artunis' adrenaline-shot heart slowed, and her mind cleared...

She found herself angry.

Callously, she slit the throat of a legionnaire with both arms broken. It was a mercy, really—but it didn't stop him from looking at her with fear.

The twitch of a Sage's fingers had broken this man. Half the surrounding buildings were messes of rubble. All this done in mere minutes by two men.

Where were they when the Ninth Legion stormed the western gate? Where were they when Malik fled his own city? Where were they when Imperial banners, banners bearing the sigil of a foreign god, adorned the House of Four?

Hatzakh had said the Sages preserve the greatest of Talynis' glories and traditions. So why had it taken so much to pull them out from underground? What about the *people*?

A hand dropped onto her shoulder.

Mouse was looking down at her, concern etched in his features. "You are troubled," he said. Something brushed her soul. "Angry. Resentful."

Why hadn't Mouse told her what he was? Why hadn't *Crow* told her any of this?

Were they even really trying to win? Or did they have some other sort of goal?

She sighed, wiping the blood from her blade with a ragged Imperial banner. "It can wait. For now—let's finish this. Half of you, go back through the tunnel and find more fighters to man this place. There are ample arms and rations here to support our cause. Gods willing, this will all be over by week's end."

59

BETWEEN PRAETOR AND KING

TAMIQ HAD A MORE natural inclination to rule than his older brother, but he lacked one crucial attribute Malik had in abundance—the virtue called *apatheia*. Without this, his dignity and honor soon departed.
　　—*The Memoirs of Flavia Iscator*

～

THEY COULD NOT RETURN to the garrison with the rescued legionnaires. On the way, riders intercepted them, Praetor Vantelle at their head.

Reiva was instantly on guard, calling on the Flame. In their faces, she saw anger, fear. Vantelle did an admirable job looking unperturbed, but the rigidity in her posture was evident. Her hands flexed on the reins, knuckles white.

"The garrison is lost," barked a senior captain.

Reiva nearly tripped. "How?" she blurted out. "An attack from the desert? Mithallkiym raiders?" Such possibilities had been discussed and prepared for. How could the Ninth have lost—

Vantelle was seething. "Rogue Adepts. Two of them. *Ars Terra*."

Reiva's words died in her throat.

The *Nihilo* Blade, the *Ventas* Blade—those were difficult to explain, but possible. Relics that could have been created by an Adept and somehow lost by the Corps, or devised by some madly lucky pagan sorcerer in bygone days. But two living and breathing Talynisti Adepts...

The strange realization that she was not alone struck her—there were other Adepts born of the desert in this world.

And they would try to kill her. And she would have to kill them.

More steps down the path she had chosen.

On came greater numbers of legionnaires from the garrison—many half-dressed, others missing a sword or shield. All battle-shocked. All bowed with shame and anger.

Yaros appeared at Reiva's side, scanning the newcomers. "Pursuers?"

Vantelle shook her head contemptuously. "They drove us out of the garrison, erupting from the earth beneath the westernmost wing, then pushed us through the gate and into the streets. Loyalists have harried us the whole way. Nothing more than tossing rocks, but it's the affront of it that smarts the worst. We nearly lost the Eagle. They killed Vexillarius Batro and took the standard of the Tenth Legion reinforcements."

Reiva grimaced. The vexillarius was one of the most honored positions in the legion—they would perform a ritual in his memory. The Tenth's standard was less important than the *Aquila*, but still a heavy loss.

The praetor touched heels to her horse. Reiva jogged alongside her commander. She wondered whether her horse was still in the stables, whether it had been taken or slaughtered in the attack.

Yaros kept close, agitation obvious in his movements. His first job was keeping Reiva safe—and now there were two rogue Adepts who could travel underground.

She was glad she had gotten the *Ventas* Blade into his hands. Inexperienced as he was with it, at least it would provide some additional might against the earth-shakers. Besides, Yaros being inexperienced with a weapon was about equivalent to an average man being proficient with it.

As they moved through the streets, an escort of the Revolutionary Guard joined them. Riders had gone on ahead to the palace. Perhaps Tamiq already knew what had transpired.

Reiva did not ask the praetor what the plan was—this was not the place for such a thing. The enemy had knocked them back on their heels. Now of all times it was crucial they project strength and certainty—to their own ranks and to the observers peeking out of homes and shop windows.

This was a moment of humiliation. They would need to strike back decisively. If it could be retaken, the garrison would be a priority. Otherwise, they would need to take some other high-value target. The Temple perhaps, though that might necessitate killing priests, which would not bode well for their reputation with the dwindling number of Talynisti who still thought Imperial provincialization was a wise move.

Then a chill ran down her spine. What if there were more than only two Adepts? What if this whole city was about to swarm with a heretofore unknown enemy asset?

What in the world was happening here in Dav-maiir?

The path they traveled was secure, but even here, their grip was slipping. People looked on them with open hostility and contempt. Others subtly stole glances, trying not to be seen. Reiva made a mental note to order patrols here reinforced—then realized that they may not have the numbers to do so.

She would need a casualty report, interviews with soldiers who had seen the mages at work. There would be head counts and executive meetings. Depending on who was killed or missing, possibly promotions.

Either careers would be made in Talynis, or they would be forever destroyed. Reiva had never heard of a praetor being stripped of rank, but she wondered whether such a thing could happen. Whether such a thing *would* happen, if the Emperor were sufficiently displeased by Vantelle's leadership here.

When the legion train reached the royal palace, the gates were already swinging open for them. As they trudged inside, Reiva remembered how she had last entered this palace—dressed in formal attire, riding in a chariot. That had been a triumphant moment. This—this was shame. This was a retreat, a failure.

Vantelle slid from her horse. As she walked, she slightly favored one side, keeping her arm tucked close to her torso. Perhaps her wound from the Bazaar was troubling her.

If it had, the praetor was not about to be delayed by something so transient as pain. She ordered Reiva to follow with a motion, and made straight for the throne room. Reiva recognized some of the guards here from her last visit. A handful she did not know tried to stop them—one sharp remark from Vantelle and a hasty intervention from their better-informed fellows dissuaded them.

Vantelle strode forward, almost bursting with fervor. With every step, the praetor seemed to accrete more and more rage.

And she was about to go before the throne.

The guards at the doors here were not easily cowed—though they did regard both Reiva's mantle and the golden eagle on Vantelle's chest with concern. The praetor demanded to be admitted.

One guard swallowed, knuckles tightening around his spear. "Your presence is known and welcomed by the king, but his majesty is occupied at the moment."

Vantelle clenched her fist against her side. "I am praetor under Dioclete, Emperor of Lazarra. Your king answers to *my lord*, and so he answers to me. Open this door before I order my Adept to incinerate you for obstructing the will of the Empire."

Reiva grit her teeth, hoping that was an empty threat. Knowing Vantelle, she doubted it was.

The guards shared a look. For a moment, Reiva feared they were really about to defy her.

Then a knock sounded from within the throne room. One of the guards opened the door, only for Katabh to poke his head out. The scribe seemed in ill health, pale with lips drawn. A sheen of sweat covered his forehead.

"King Tamiq," he said, "bids you enter." He gave the guards a severe look before vanishing within.

Suppressing a sigh of relief, Reiva followed Vantelle inside.

Whatever she had suspected, it was not this. Katabh had already left, exiting through some side passage, presumably. Alone in the room, Tamiq was seated on the throne, one arm propped up, knuckles to his forehead. His hair was in disarray, as were his robes. When he turned to inspect Vantelle and Reiva, his eyes shone with dark fury.

"This is how you enter my home?" He scoffed, rubbing his eyes. "The audacity."

Vantelle, never one to be thrown off balance, raised her chin. "Audacity, King Tamiq? The only person here I see with anything of the sort sits upon the throne of Talynis."

In a flash, Tamiq was on his feet, hair whipping about his head as he shouted. "You take my daughter for a bargaining chip! You lose hold of your garrison! You come to me with your tail between your legs! Don't think I will just roll over and take this, Vantelle. I know what you want—you would turn my palace, my home, into your new playground. A garrison with a wine cellar and golden cutlery."

The king was coming down from his dais, step by heavy step, naked contempt painted on his features.

"Well," he continued, "I won't have it. You can go pitch tents in the street, or stuff yourselves into warehouses. This is the palace of the Talynisti king! Not the doghouse of some Lazarran bitch."

His face was flushed as he spat his words. Reiva thought she caught him slurring.

Vantelle, it seemed, had noticed too. "The Talynisti king," she snarled, "is drunk in the morning. He has failed to control his own daughter, creating the shameful situation which the Ninth handled. His grip on the city is like a grip on sand.

"I know why you won't let me dig in here, Tamiq. You realize, deep in your heart, that all of this"—she spread her arms wide, toward the golden fixtures and elaborate tapestries—"is only yours by the arm of my Emperor. You were born a second son, you would have died a second son. *We* gave you the throne. *We* gave you the palace."

If Tamiq had been flushed before, now he was a tomato. "This city is mine!" he sputtered.

"Yours by the will of Lazarra. And you will lose it if you bite my hand once more." She stepped in, nearly nose to nose with Tamiq.

The moment seemed to hang there, the entire world condensed around this one encounter between praetor and king.

"Call me a bitch all you like, Tamiq, but only one of us is on a leash. Now give the word for your men to set themselves immediately to aiding and installing my legionnaires on the palace grounds and in the barracks. Before any more violence transpires today."

Tamiq held her eyes. Then he shrunk away.

"Good," said the praetor. "And while you do—think of how you will explain to me the presence of two rogue Adepts in Dav-maiir."

The king wheeled, eyes wide and brow furrowed.

"I hope for your sake that your surprise is genuine, king. Because I lost a lot of men and women in the garrison to an enemy we had no idea existed."

60

THE PERFECT SYMBOL

High Priest Barmoshe Zadiq said, 'A wayward daughter brings great pain to a household. A wayward priest, a wayward king—these bring great pain to a nation.'
—*A Chronicle of Talynisti Reign, Vol. I: Temple and Throne*

As Asrah walked across the street, Avi's heart lurched, every muscle fiber tensed and ready to spring into action.

Surely, the Lazarrans would enact some treachery. They'd fire an arrow. The Adept would burn her alive. When she was so close to safety, they would take her again, just to spite him. They would take her forever.

But then, she slipped behind the barricade, and Loyalists folded around her, protecting her from the opposing side with their shields and bodies.

Avi fought the urge to heave a sigh of relief. He had to keep his calm now. He couldn't show weakness to the Imperials.

He couldn't show what he truly felt—not to anyone.

So he dropped to his knees, face bowed low.

"You are a champion of the people, lady. A true daughter of Talynis. The Four have delivered you to us."

Asrah's feet shuffled before him. "A true Talynisti is one such as you, Wolf. May the gods bless your fight for the freedom of our people."

The soldiers couldn't help raising up a cheer.

Avi felt some of the tension bleed out from him. He had been afraid they would not trust Asrah, would not believe that a daughter of Tamiq could have been on their side.

But this would give them heart. The news would spread—he would make sure of it—and the whole city would know that Princess Asrah was loyal to the true king, Malik her uncle.

Avi rose to his feet. "Quickly, princess, we must take you to the Temple." Then louder, "I do not trust those Imperial dogs to honor our arrangement."

Something shifted behind her eyes. She said nothing, but Avi could tell she would have disputed his words if they were alone.

Why would she call the Adept honorable? They're practically exact opposites! Asrah stayed loyal to Talynis, despite a thousand riches that would have been hers. The Adept has thrown her lot in with the Empire, despite the hundreds of thousands of lives that will suffer for her choice.

The barricade stayed manned while Avi led Asrah and a detachment of his most skilled Loyalist soldiers back toward the Temple. One street down, they had prepared a chariot liberated in a raid from one of the Revolutionary Guard's armories.

Asrah refused to get in, though. "I want to walk the streets, sir. I want to see what has become of my city."

Avi was displeased at first—the sooner she was behind the Temple walls the better. But he saw how the remark affected his men.

"Your servants will escort you, princess."

She nodded, maintaining the appropriate regal bearing. Looking at her, it was impossible to even notice the mismatch of her clothing to her station. The way she carried herself though, she might as well have worn the finest of robes.

Still, he would have to ensure she received more appropriate attire. It wouldn't do for the princess of Talynis to be seen in servant's clothes, even if her station was not in accord with the Loyalists' beliefs.

What a strange web we live in...

As they walked, people peered out from windows. Avi's neck tingled, like when he sensed he was being snuck up on. It would be all too easy for someone to strike with a missile—a javelin or dart, or even a sling—but he had to keep trust in the people. He had to maintain control.

The people would know that Asrah was on their side.

Word went ahead of them, and before long, there were throngs along the streets. Children pointing and whispering, adults doing their best to hold them in check.

And then, someone gave a sign of deference, bowing his head. Then others followed.

"I have to admit," he whispered from the corner of his mouth. "I didn't expect this."

Asrah gave the slightest of nods. "They know I can never return to the palace now. I both am and am not a princess to them. The perfect symbol."

The atmosphere was not missed by the Loyalists guarding her, who seemed to stand up straighter, honored by the significance of their task.

A part of Avi's mind whirled with possibility. The Imperials had handed them something they could never have dared to use on their own—the open defiance of Tamiq's own daughter.

Of course, it was with good reason they had not considered such a thing. There were other spies within the palace, but none of them so closely placed to the usurper. Not to mention, even though some people accepted Asrah, doubtless others would cast shame on her for betrayal of her father's house. Those who supported Tamiq, certainly, but even Loyalists might. Talynisti could be strange in that way.

Well, the Lazarrans had forced this upon them. He would have to use it for all it was worth.

That was one part of his mind.

The other half, though, the other half felt jealous—jealous and ill, even. Jealous because she had been his—his secret, his confidant. Only he and precious few others had known Asrah's true beliefs and allegiance, and now that was out in the open. Ill because the first thought that had come to mind was how he might use her for the sake of the cause.

But wasn't that all any of them were? Tools, weapons, symbols—he inhabited that role readily. Why did he feel so unsure now about using others the way he used himself?

Because she's not others—*she's Asrah. She's not just a colleague or an ally. If only Crow could see things now...*

The Temple gates swung open to admit them, where they were received by an assembly of Loyalists and faithful priests. As they shut behind them, Avi breathed a sigh of relief.

But the day was not over yet, he saw.

"So," said one priest, suspicion plain in his eyes, "this is the usurper Tamiq's daughter, his only child."

It begins already.

"The people have received her as one of us," Avi said. "She is loyal."

"She is a traitor, just as her sire. Either she is a traitor to Talynis, or she is a traitor to her father. Both of these things are sinful and will corrupt the people."

Avi bristled, already opening his mouth to retort, but Asrah raised her hand.

"You say," she began, "that I am trapped in wickedness either way. I tell you I am loyal, and there are those like the Wolf who can testify to how I have risked myself for the Four Gods' chosen ruler, my uncle Malik. You would cast blame on me for doing what is right?"

"Our ways are our ways," snapped the priest. "Handed down from the Four to the prophets and priests of old. To transgress is to bring the gods' judgment upon the people. We can have none impure among us."

Avi's lip curled. He had never been one to get too involved or interested in the intra-religious disputes of the Talynisti priesthood, but he had heard of factions like this. They upheld the most rigid interpretation of the laws, disputing the notion of any gray areas.

He could see that some priests were in accord with the man—maybe even most of them. Others looked less certain, but they were in the minority.

It made sense, he supposed, that a majority of those priests who remained loyal to Malik's kingship would be those who maintained the strictest interpretation of the faith. They would not waver to Tamiq's clever argumentation for being rightful claimant to the throne.

But he was not about to let Asrah suffer for that.

"I don't care what you say about the law—with all due respect," he said quickly. "Of course I care about what is right, but I'm here to fight for the true king. The princess is an ally in that fight. You would not have your Temple back if it were not for me and my Loyalists. Are you going to cross me so soon?"

The objecting priest scoffed, turning red. "You speak to us like this within the walls of the Temple itself? You, a man of the sword and blood. The Four would have delivered the righteous by a method they chose—you are inconsequential to this."

Avi flexed his fingers. An internal dispute of this magnitude was really not what he needed right now.

"Then how about this," said Asrah, drawing all eyes to her. "I swear to you I am loyal first to my gods, the same gods whom you worship, and to the rightfully anointed king of Talynis. If you think I have done wrong, then let that be adjudicated once the proper rule of law has been restored—once my uncle sits the throne again."

Avi felt a smile tugging at his mouth.

Clever—she's casting her fate upon Malik.

And the priest certainly caught what she was up to, based on his scowl.

Either they refuse to accept Asrah, and risk incurring Malik's wrath when he returns and learns how they treated the niece who stood by him, or they compromise on their position.

"Let justice be upheld," said the princess, "by the man chosen as ruler of these lands."

One of the minority priests spoke up. "This is right," and soon others joined him in the chorus.

The objecting priest was clearly unhappy, but he also took note, Avi saw, of the Loyalist men standing about with their weapons. Men who had clearly thrown their support behind the princess.

The air was thick with the tension—and then, the priest who had objected to Asrah's presence in the temple took a half-step back. "Long live the king," he demurred.

Though it was hardly perceptible, Avi noticed Asrah's shoulders sag with relief. He felt that as well—this was a problem that could be put off until they had quelled the bigger problems of Tamiq's treachery and the occupying legion.

Although...who was to say Malik might not punish Asrah simply for her relationship with his brother? It wasn't without cause that these priests had cast aspersion on her. A woman in Talynis was part of her father's house.

With a sinking feeling, Avi realized just how precarious Asrah's position would be in the future. He would need to have her placed under strict watch, now that the Adept's pet had that windsword—which had apparently been Crow's, another revelation he just didn't have time to properly consider.

Logistics tumbled through his mind. There were few quarters in the Temple, and even fewer that were properly situated for a woman's residence according to the holiness precepts of the space.

He would need to make allies among the priests who had been amenable to Asrah's entry, and maybe even—

A shout from beyond the gates pulled Avi out of his planning and sent one hand to his weapon. Were they under attack? Was the legion already trying to—

A messenger boy scampered through the barely opened gates, making a beeline for Avi despite the crowd and commotion.

"The Imperials are going to the palace!" he huffed, hands on knees as he gasped for air.

Avi frowned. The Lazarrans and Tamiq were in league; why would that merit such an urgent message? "How many?"

The boy stretched his hands wide. "*All!* The garrison—taken."

In an instant, murmurs broke out throughout the courtyard. People called out for more information, for explanations.

Avi silenced them all with raised hands. He felt a moment of satisfaction at that—good, they all recognized his leadership.

"Boy, you're telling me the legion's garrison has *fallen*? To *who*?"

"Desert Sages," he wheezed, then, before Avi could blurt anything else out, "Talynisti Adepts, sir! Leading a band of Loyalists!"

Avi was certain he had misheard, but he couldn't ask anything else amid the raucous shouting and consternation of the crowd.

He and Asrah met eyes, and he only saw the same bewilderment and confusion he felt.

Talynisti Adepts!

61

SINGING OWL

KINGS AND GENERALS may rule the world, but barkeeps make it livable.
—Attributed to the Dog, mendicant philosopher of Karella

AMID THE HAVOC of setting up camp in and around the palace grounds, Reiva wanted nothing more than to retreat to her newly assigned quarters and sleep. There wasn't nearly enough space, so nearby buildings had to be requisitioned as well, which meant dealing with grumbling aristocrats.

When she finally made it to her quarters—one of the more desirable rooms in the palace complex—she was ready to collapse in a heap. Instead, she had barely gotten off her armor when someone knocked at her door.

Charas' voice piped up. "I know you're in there."

Reiva sighed. "Is this urgent, Scout Lieutenant?"

"Yes."

She opened the door.

Charas was dressed in her uniform but didn't have her weapons on her. "Wow—so you *do* take your armor off to sleep."

"Which is what I was planning on doing," she grumbled. "What's so urgent?"

"You need to drink."

Reiva stared for a moment. "I need to sleep."

"Nope—and Yaros agrees with me. Come on, get some proper clothes on. We're meeting him at a tavern."

Reiva considered ordering her to leave, but she doubted Charas would even obey.

"Fine," she sighed. "Give me a minute."

The tavern was called the Singing Owl. By the time they arrived, Yaros had already claimed a spot for them—a table in the corner, well-positioned from a defensive perspective: good sight lines, and with a fair bit of space separating them from anyone else who might sit down.

From her satchel, Charas laid out a selection of cakes—which looked as mouthwatering as she had promised during the walk.

The barkeep came around with their drinks, assuring them he'd keep things open on their side of the room. Yaros nodded his thanks, slipping the man a few silvers, which were accepted gratefully.

Charas took a hearty bite from one of the cakes, sighing in pleasure. "I'm not one for Talynisti food, but this almost makes it all worth it." She chased it with a swallow of her wine. "And that's not too bad either."

Yaros gave a half-smile. "Some places serve better stuff when they know you're with the legion, others serve you worse."

"Always doing reconnaissance, we are."

"Indeed."

Reiva snorted, shaking her head slightly. "You two..."

Charas flashed a wide smile. "Are your only hope in this world."

"Not what I was thinking."

"Then what were you thinking?"

Reiva's smile wilted a bit. "Nothing."

Yaros cocked an eyebrow, but Charas wasn't about to let it slide. "No, you weren't thinking about nothing. In fact, you're always thinking about a hundred things, and it's so obvious that sometimes I swear I can see them buzzing around your head like a flock of ravens."

Reiva winced. "That bad?"

"More or less. And that's why we brought you here and we're paying triple what we should."

Reiva sighed. "I...appreciate that. I do. But really, if I'm not sleeping right now, then I should be overseeing the relocation—"

"No, you shouldn't," Yaros cut in. "There are other officers there right now. Too many officers, if you ask me. They'll be fine."

Reiva knew he was right. But she clenched her jaw. "It's not...it's not about whether they need me, it's about—"

"Looking like you're needed," he said. "Because you're worried people will think you're not doing your part."

Charas rolled her eyes. "All day, dawn to dusk and beyond, you're running around this city. Overseeing patrols, taking reports, making reports. I can hardly believe you ever sleep. You do sleep, right?"

"I do, and why does it matter? Once this is all over, I can sleep however much I want. I can take time to rest in the capital. I can take my next assignment somewhere less fraught. Right now, though, I need to do this job right."

Charas leaned back, crossing her arms. Her eyes were low, sweeping side to side like she was working on something.

Then her eyes came up. "What happened in Hyrgallia, exactly?"

Reiva went rigid. Yaros looked surprised, but said nothing.

That's not your concern. That's irrelevant. You're out of line, Scout Lieutenant. I'm leaving.

All things she could have said, and yet...

Her heart twisted like a wrung-out rag. She couldn't write a letter to Alyat anymore. She would never sit down in his office for another debriefing. Domi was somewhere on the seas—who knew when they would have another chance to speak face to face?

So, who did she have left? Who did she have left who she could honestly talk to—without fear they would undermine her career with talk of her insufficiency or weakness?

"I lost two squadrons," she said softly. "On a mission I pushed for, against the captain's judgment. It was a bloodbath. I nearly died."

Charas listened to all this with an even expression. Reiva didn't know if there were rumors floating around the legion about what had happened, but given how closely Charas had worked with Iscator, it seemed fair to assume she was apprised of the broad details.

So, she talked about how she saw soldier after soldier drop, painting the snow red with their blood. She talked about Sergeant Tharrick and Sergeant Meridi. How she had known them for just a few weeks, but how they had easily integrated her into the life of the company. How they had died for her sake.

"A few minutes ago," she murmured, "when you asked me what I was thinking about—I was thinking about them. You—both of you—remind me of them, in some ways."

Charas nodded slowly. Then she reached a hand across the table and rested it on Reiva's shoulder. "Well, when I was a little girl, my favorite horse broke his leg, and I had to put him down at the tender age of six—so, I know the depths of your pain."

A wry smile split her features.

Reiva snorted, then chuckled. How did some people do that?

"Thank you for telling me," Charas added. "And really, that's a brutal story. People have gone mad for less."

The gaunt expression of Adept Sharasthi flickered through Reiva's mind. "Maybe I already have gone mad."

"Well, you're not parading naked through the streets wailing about the end of the world. On the other hand, you've been working yourself to the bone for weeks. So we'll hold off on passing a verdict just yet."

"But now you know *why*. I need to prove that I'm capable."

"They gave you your own bloody title, O venerable *Adepta Leona*. You received emergency promotion to the rank of princeps. You've proved yourself plenty well. Did you even celebrate that, by the way?"

"That all just means I need to work harder. What if I fail here? What if the legion is driven out of Talynis? I could lose it all. Vantelle gave me another chance to salvage my life and here I am, barely more secure than when I started."

"You're plenty more secure," Yaros drawled. "You're so secure that *I'm* secure, and I'm not even legion. Charas is right, we should celebrate your promotion—late as we are."

Charas tipped her cup toward him. "I'm surprised you didn't think to do that."

"I was busy working out how to kidnap a princess by flying through the air."

"As if that's a worthy excuse to keep you from wine."

Yaros snorted. "Fair enough."

Charas waved to the barkeep. "Another round! All right, so here's what we do. First off, we finish these drinks before the next round gets here—no more dainty sipping from either of you. Next, we don't talk about anything that has to do with this war, or ambitions, or anything like that. Ranks were checked at the door—we're just drinking."

Reiva frowned. That did sound nice, but...

Charas rapped her knuckles on the table. "Oy, sullen face. You said we remind you of your dead friends. Well guess what, neither me nor this one are planning on dying anytime soon. So you owe it to us, and to yourself, to enjoy one night. Who knows when we'll next have a good time for this?"

"This *isn't* a good time."

"Exactly—because there's never a good time. Aha! Thank you, sir." Charas readily took her next cup.

Reiva accepted hers mechanically. Yaros was already a fair way through his.

She looked down at the violet drink swaying in her cup.

Well, I can always burn it off if I need.

She swallowed it quick as she could, welcoming the burgeoning lightness inside her head.

And she didn't burn it off, nor did she burn it off after the next round. Or the one after that.

~

CHARAS WIPED tears in her eyes, her face red with laughter and the flush of alcohol. "Swear it on all the graves of my ancestors! He looks at me, dead innocent, and says, 'Well, I guess we'll have to cuddle for the night.'"

Yaros cackled. "And did you?"

"Well, it was that or freeze to death, but I made sure he knew I had my knife on me."

Reiva realized she was laughing too—she didn't remember how long she had been laughing, or even how Charas' story had started. But it felt good. Everything felt lighter.

"Didn't matter anyway," she chuckled, wiping at her eyes, "since I was taller and had a warmer coat, so I was on the outside facing the wind. He had his back to my front, couldn't have pawed at me if he tried."

Yaros snorted, polishing off another cup. "All those carefully laid schemes."

"I don't think he was *scheming*, just trying to make the most of a bad situation."

"Never said I fault him for the attempt," he said seriously. "Scheming your way into someone's arms is a time-honored vocation in Karella."

"Right, right. Your turn then—tell us a story."

Yaros leaned back, crossing his arms. Reiva was eager to hear this, though she didn't see how it could top Charas' for sheer incredulity.

"Do you know Kleisaph?"

Reiva moved her lips silently, trying to place the name. "The poet?"

Charas snapped her fingers. "She's the one lovers are always quoting. *'I've glimpsed the moon within your soul'* la-la-la and so forth, you know the one?"

Yaros nodded. "That's her. Well, I grew up in the same town as her—

she's a year or two younger than me, prodigy and all that—and there was a shipwreck not far off the coast. And regarding that shipwreck there was a legend that among its various treasures was the necklace of a mythical Mizkhari she-king."

Charas furrowed her brow. "You mean queen?"

"No, she-king—there's a difference in Mizkhar. Anyway, my sister hears this legend and—"

Now it was Reiva's turn to cut in. "You have a *sister*?"

Something flickered across Yaros' face. "Look, do you want the story or not? My sister cons me into diving for the necklace, saying I should give it to Kleisaph for her birthday and maybe she'll write a poem about me. Anyway, next thing I know I'm in the hold of a sunken ship, I've cut my hands on coral, my lungs are in agony, and all I have to show for it is one measly necklace, ruined by the salt water."

Charas gave him a flat stare. "That's not funny at all."

"Well, what's funny is that as soon as I got out of the ship, I found myself face-to-face with a scarred-up, thousand-toothed shark twice my size."

Charas swore, giggling. "And then what?"

"I did the only thing I could think—tossed the necklace at him and took off fast as I could. I think the glitter of the jewelry distracted him a bit. I got back to shore, kissed the sand, and went home. And as it turned out, Kleisaph did write a poem about the incident, beginning like so: '*The deep knows all things, knows no fool so great as Yradas / Of all Karella's men, there is no greater bumbling ass.*' People recited that to me for months afterword."

"Never heard that one," drawled Charas.

"Well, that was before she got famous with all those love poems. Not her best work if you ask me, but still, thank the gods I survived that ordeal with all my limbs intact."

"I don't know if I'd thank them," scoffed Reiva. "I have to put up with you thanks to that."

Yaros cackled. "Make an offering to the sea god, maybe he'll send another one after me."

Charas waved her cup. "I'll pour a libation."

Reiva laughed, a small voice in the back of her mind chiding her that such talk would be upsetting to any Talynisti listening—what if the barkeep was a Loyalist, what if such talk pushed him over the edge and drove him to poison their wine?

She drank again.

"So," Charas purred, "what about you, fearsome Lion? What do you got for us?"

Reiva shook her head. "I've had a dull life."

Charas and Yaros scoffed in near perfect unison.

"Sold into slavery," he said.

"Made an Adept," added Charas.

"Nearly killed in action."

"Youngest Adept to ever receive a special commission."

Yaros saluted with his cup, sloshing a bit of wine onto the table. "You're a champion, kid."

Reiva ducked her head, feeling another flush creep across her face. "Wait —*kid*? What happened to 'boss'?"

"I'm twenty-three. Or four. Something like that. Point is, at this table you're a kid. You're 'boss' again if you prove you can out-drink me."

A look of consternation crossed his face. "*Without* magic," he added.

"Or I could just stop paying you."

He clutched at his chest in mock agony. "You wound me, sir-madam-of-Imperial-magicness."

"I'd take 'kid' over that."

"I'd shut up if you'd just give us a story."

"Fine, fine. Let me think." She knuckled her brow. The wine fuzzed her head, but she didn't want to burn it off, so she just kept plumbing her memory.

Then something came to her.

No.

And she would have kept searching, but something in her face must have changed, because Charas was knocking at the table. "You've got something. Spill."

Reiva frantically tried to think of something else, but now her mind was locked on that one memory.

Oh, to hell with it.

"Well, I grew up in Shugrith. It was a lot like here, if you strip away the military presence. Children played outside when we had no chores. And I— had a little brother."

Charas' eyebrows went up, but she stayed quiet.

"By then, our father was gone. And one day my brother was playing with some other kids, and came back with some scrapes. It wasn't even that bad —like he'd taken a fall or something. But he was upset. Anyway, turned out some other boys had been bullying him. I don't remember why. Maybe there was no reason other than kids being cruel.

"He wouldn't go to our mother. I wouldn't have either. But I wrung out of him the name of the boy leading the bullies. There's always one of them."

Reiva shrugged. "I couldn't fight a gang of boys. So I waited until the other boy was alone and got the jump on him. I think I broke his nose. And...might've kicked him a little. And maybe bit his ear."

Yaros snorted. "No wonder you fit into Lazarra so well."

She smiled thinly. "Well, it worked. My brother was upset with me, though. He said it was a man's job to fight, and he *was* the man of the household, what with our father being gone. But he was a small kid, and I was older and bigger. He could learn to look after himself when—"

She trailed off, her stomach dropping. "When I left," she muttered, then finished her drink.

By now, the tavern was mostly empty. Maybe people had been put off by the loud trio of Imperials in the corner. Maybe it was just that late.

The barkeep brought another round to their table. Yaros tried to wave him off, but the barkeep shook his head and pointedly pushed a cup toward Reiva. "On the house," he said simply, and then ghosted off.

Reiva stared at her cup, some paranoid corner of her mind musing about the possibility of poison.

She drank it down. Charas and Yaros drank as well, commiserating in the silence.

"Well," said the Parthavan, "that was a good night."

Yaros nodded. "Tomorrow, back to some fresh hell, eh?"

Reiva set her empty cup down. She watched the barkeep as he bustled about, wiping down cups and mugs, studiously ignoring their table.

"Thank you for this. I needed it."

"Well, next time you can pay for it," Yaros said with a smirk. "Put that salary to good use for once."

"Right, I've only ever wasted it on useless things like Karellan mercenaries."

"Exactly—who spends money on something like that?"

62

HUNTRESS OF THE HEAVENS

CHARAS, an archer without peer, and with laughter pure enough to make you think you overheard the revels of the gods. I had always thought something was unique about her. I could never have imagined the full extent of who she was, or what she would become.

—*The Memoirs of Flavia Iscator*

BEFORE BEDDING down in her tent, Charas checked her new arrows. The night was dark and the warm fuzz of alcohol still lingered in her limbs, but this was a task she'd been doing her whole life. Working by touch alone, she inspected the alignment of the fletching. Every feather seemed in line—not a one would have to be adjusted. She felt a glow of satisfaction in her heart as she stowed them in her quiver. Drawing her coat over her like a blanket, she lay down to sleep.

She had been away from the Parthavan plains for quite a few years now, but she had never lost the skills ingrained into her by her people. Even serving with the greatest army in the world, she would forever shoot Parthavan arrows—whether bought or made herself. Her mastery with the bow ensured her career with the legions would never end, so long as she was of age to serve and combat capable. Lazarrans were notorious amateurs with the bow—their only saving grace at range was sheer numbers.

And yet, none of that had been of aid when those earth-shakers came ripping through the garrison like a pair of raging boars. Charas had been startlingly near to their first point of attack, working on these arrows. In an instant, she had grabbed her essentials and taken off, weaving through the camp like she was racing a horse through the Bildani Woods.

That was another thing—Lazarrans thought it was disgraceful to run. They considered it a shame if they had to retreat.

Charas preferred to stay alive, and that she had. She had also fired at the rogue Adepts, of course, loosing quite a few arrows, which was why she had spent much of the evening fletching new ones.

She wished she could say it had been worth it, but every single shot had either missed or been deflected by the ever-swirling shield of rock and grit surrounding them.

Her father had told her once, the farther you go from home, the more surprises you'll find. Only an idiot misses out on novelty.

An idiot, or someone blessed by the gods, because going up *against* an Adept was never something she'd thought possible. Half the reason the Parthavans had made peace with Lazarra was due to their Adept Corps, those hellish arcane warriors.

Then there was the Bazaar attack, when she had felt a wave of terror wash over her. In her panic, she almost sent her horse into a panic. Only falling back into one of the old Hunters' Songs had stilled her heart. That had been the work of an Adept—she was sure of that.

But Adept Reiva was not hellish. She seemed quite all right, in fact. For all Charas knew though, that was part of the problem.

The Lazarran legions didn't conquer half the world without some questionable decisions—many of them involving Adepts. A woman who could throw fire? If you believed half the stories, then you would expect Reiva to be the sort who'd burn down a barn packed with folks, just because the order came down.

Maybe Reiva had done that. Maybe she would.

But Charas couldn't ignore the nagging feeling that if she did, she would not do so with a clear conscience. She seemed like she'd rather fight them head-on, give each one a chance to prove their right to live.

She scoffed, shaking her head as she lay down, tugging her overcoat up like a blanket. She'd been working too long. The day had been too gruesome. She hardly even knew the woman, really—what gave her the right or the reason to speculate about her heart like this?

Well, Reiva was important enough for Legate Iscator to order her to stay in Dav-maiir instead of joining the outgoing brigade, all for the sake of keeping an eye on the Adept and watching her back. That was something, to be sure. Iscator hadn't explained *why* Reiva mattered so much. Maybe just being an Adept was enough, but Charas knew there had to be more to it.

She had that ring, for example—the ring of bone, etched with Talynisti lettering. There was something strange about that ring; it was one of only a handful of things Charas had encountered that warped her sight. Reiva said it had been a gift from a Wanderer *roshbet*—but how could a Talynisti nomad have known how to make something that foiled a Hunter's eyes?

Yes, there was something special about Reiva. And she was nice enough—even if Flavia hadn't told her to keep an eye on the Adept, Charas might have befriended her.

She lay there in the dark for a while, but sleep evaded her. Thoughts swirled, nagging.

Eventually, she got up. She needed to walk this off—the drinks from earlier as well as the turnings of her mind.

After fastening her belt and shrugging on her coat, she slipped away.

The green around the royal palace was a mess by anyone's standards, which meant it was a pigsty by the standards of the legion. As she went, she observed the hustle and bustle of an emergency camp construction. It was almost comical, seeing how the palace of Dav-maiir had been turned into an army camp inside of a few hours. Even this late, the work still went on.

Some soldiers had been put up in the barracks nearby, but many had been forced to spread bedrolls (commandeered from the Talynisti) on the palace grounds. Lush gardens were filled with sweaty, swearing soldiers. Pathways were lined with torches and spears stuck into the earth. There was talk of requisitioning some of the aristocracy's estates for use by the legion, but Tamiq was intransigent on the possibility—at least, so the grapevine said. Word also went that he was at an impasse with Vantelle. Charas half-expected that by morning people would say the two had come to blows. Hell, she might even believe they had. Vantelle may have been the praetor, but she had the Ninth's loyalty through fear. There was awe as well, but it was impossible not to see Cassia Vantelle without your knees knocking. She represented the absolute peak of accomplishment in Lazarra; people said she could be Empress someday. And she was living proof of how brutal ambition looked in this world.

Charas found herself thinking of Legate Iscator as she picked her way through the makeshift camp. The legate was the Ninth's true leader, far as Charas was concerned. Sure, she was scatterbrained from time to time and she lacked some of the steel demanded of a battle commander, but what she lacked tactically, she made up for with inspiration and morale. The Ninth had never fought harder or more valiantly than when Flavia Iscator gave their orders—at least, so the veterans said.

Now, Charas worried how many legionnaires believed in this war. A war fought through unconventional means. A war that had already claimed one Adept's life. Rumors abounded that the city bore some sort of curse, unearthed by the legions' bloody entrance into the city. Talk of strange sights and sounds—ghosts, some said, even demons.

And now, these Loyalist rogue Adepts? If Charas had thought she had half a chance, she was of a mind to ride out this very night. It wouldn't be honorable, of course (it was the exact opposite of honorable), but Iscator was gone, possibly dead among the dunes. The struggle for the city had gone sour in six different ways. It was tempting to just slip away and vanish into the Parthavan plains. Folks there would hide her, if anyone put in the effort to come looking. Parthava may have made peace with the Empire, even bent the knee, but they had never bowed in spirit—certainly none of *her* kin.

Suddenly, Charas didn't want to go back to her tent. Instead, she went for the gate. It took some convincing, but she was able to talk her way through. There was no curfew for the Scouts—they had so many missions and assignments at all hours that it would be impossible to enforce. Making the guards believe she had some nighttime reconnaissance was child's play.

The air outside seemed a little clearer, somehow. Maybe it was just her imagination, but she had also grown up on the Parthavan grasslands. Space was a way of life, there. When she first stepped inside a city, she had thought she might lose her lunch.

Out of habit, she tapped the hunting knife strapped to her thigh. It would take a bold soul indeed to attack an Imperial soldier this close to the royal palace, but better to carry a blade and never draw it than find yourself wanting.

The roads around the palace were the broadest in Dav-maiir, so Charas found herself with ample room to stroll. This was more like it—she could almost forget that she was in the heart of a desert city. Now if only she had been atop a good horse, tearing her way down the central boulevard, wind whipping and hooves thundering...

She sighed, kicking a pebble and sending it skittering across the stones. She thought of running rivers, lush hills. Drums at dawn, hunting dogs howling through night hunts.

Yes, she wanted to go back. Not in a fleeting way, not in a temporary longing for home. Her heart ached for the plains and pastures. She had tired of Dav-maiir, of its high walls and ceaseless strife; tired of the desert, of its scorching winds and dry sands.

Most of all, she had tired of the legion. The ranks, the formalities, the cold efficiency. They were the strongest in the world, sure, but they were not for her. Not even a veteran's pension could justify twenty years of service.

That was it—it wasn't worth it. She had finally admitted it to herself.

But she was a woman of honor, still, even if she could not say the same for the commanders who had ordered this war. Lazarra was bent on expansion, everyone knew. Expansion for the sake of it, it seemed. Expansion in the name of their High God, many-eyed Arkhon. Expansion to prove their way of life truly was the culmination of human civilization, and that all the world would gain to be sons and daughters of the Lazarran Emperor, Dioclete. It was a sour name, Charas thought.

Parthava was not truly free, but at least if she returned to Parthava she could get away from all *this*. She would use her arrows only on game and bandits. She could even spend a year or so on her own, drifting along with no one but her horse, maybe a hound if she could find a good, sturdy pup. She knew how to build a shelter, to skin and sew new garments. Finally, she'd be dressed properly instead of in these ridiculous uniforms.

And then, ancestors willing, she would find her way back to her clan. Parthava was a broad land, but eventually she would manage. "Where does the Son of Thunder hunt nowadays?" she would ask, and people would think a moment, scratch their chins.

"He's ranging among the northern reaches," they would answer, or maybe "Back to the coastal raids, holding the old border treaties."

Then, they'd scrunch up their eyes, peer a little closer. They might notice the cut of her jawline, the flecks of gold in her eyes. But before they could ask, she'd be gone.

Maybe word would fly ahead of her, and by the time she found home— wherever it was—her father would be there, his hair wild and his bow strung with the hair of a goddess (so the story went, and she believed it). He'd be sitting on a rock, carving one of his little talismans, votary icons to Kashakran, huntress of the heavens. He'd look her over with his blazing eyes, eyes flecked with gold like hers. And after a moment, he would say...

What would he say? Would he welcome her back? Would he be mad at her for leaving? Would he send her away forever, or would he finally understand why she had gone in the first place?

Charas realized with a start that she'd gotten far from the palace. Her feet had carried her until the spire atop the royal dwelling was a distant shadow against the sky.

But she couldn't walk far enough to reach the plains, not from Dav-maiir. She would see this campaign through to its end, and then she would apply for a discharge once this leg of her service was over. That would be, what, three months from now? She could manage three months.

She turned, heart lighter and faster now, beginning the return journey.

And made it all of five minutes before she came to another stop.

Charas pressed herself up against a wall, eyes narrowed. Her attention fixed on the mouth of a side street, where a man had just slinked off.

She would stake her life that the man was Vantelle's optio. Zageth. He was wearing a cloak, but she recognized him by his gait, the way he hunched to the side so his sword arm was always a bit forward.

Let it go. Three months.

But she started trailing him.

You'll be home by summer. Forget about it.

And against her better judgment, she kept following. She had heard about this man from Reiva on their patrols. The Adept was remarkably tight-lipped about most things, but after Zageth had killed the Loyalist arms dealer, after Vantelle had taken the reins from Iscator...Reiva had been a bit more open, in the days that followed, tongue loosed by anger. Anger and something else, some sort of worry Charas could not quite pin down, but that wasn't her concern. The Adept had her right to secrets, just as Charas did.

Vantelle's hound skulking through the streets, though, that *was* her concern. Reiva had painted this man as sadistic, eager to kill the Stag and eager to organize Vantelle's most gruesome plans.

Typically, she would be happy to play soldier and just carry out orders— but that had been under Iscator. Now Vantelle was in charge. Now Talynisti Adepts had taken the garrison. There were more than a few rumors of traitors in the ranks (though there were always such rumors).

She was tired of being in the dark.

For all she knew, Zageth was just off to a tavern or brothel. Maybe this was all for nothing, and she would just miss out on some sleep for no good reason.

But by night's end, she would know for certain—and that was worth the excursion.

63

RIGHT-HAND MAN

THERE IS something strange about the Hunters of Parthava. I suspect their traditions come from a wholly different source than the mores and norms of the broader culture, but so secretive are they that I have never proven worthy enough to hear their stories.

Some things one must be satisfied with never understanding. In this matter, however, I am forever flustered.

—*The Life and Wisdom of Simeon Binkhok As Told by Himself*

AVI PULLED JACKAL INTO AN EMBRACE.

She stiffened at first, then threw her arms around him in return. It was a very forward gesture in Talynis, never something that would happen between a man and a woman. But they weren't a man and woman; they were Vipers. Warriors in service to the true king.

After they broke apart, Avi looked at her stump with a grimace.

"It doesn't hurt anymore," she said with a shrug. "Save some aches now and then. I still have it in my dreams."

"Where did Mouse take you?" he asked under his breath.

Jackal glanced at the small contingent of fighters they had with them on this mission. "Tell you some other time."

Avi took that with a nod. The world was an unfathomably different place than it had been even days ago. Wherever they had gone, they had returned with two Talynisti Sages, men who wielded arcane power over the earth in the same manner the Imperial Adept shaped fire.

Those Sages were currently watching over the seized garrison and ferrying more Loyalists into its walls. Mouse had stayed behind to oversee that project.

Jackal *had* mentioned that Mouse was a Sage of some sort in his own right as well. Avi wasn't sure what to make of that. They had three magic-users on their side—vastly outnumbering the Adept of Fire—but Mouse's talents were apparently not as destructive as the two Desert Sages. He could influence the mind, so she said, for good or ill.

He wished that Mouse had been with them now, about to meet with Ego's man Zageth.

At this point, the city could fall either way—and since they had the momentum, they needed to press onward.

They needed to kill the Imperial Adept.

The site of the rendez-vous was inside Revolutionary lines, but this part of the city had lost much of its Guard presence in the wake of the garrison attack. The legion was consolidating its strength around the palace, and many Talynisti had turned to the Loyalist cause by now. The people were all but ready to cast off the usurper Tamiq; they only needed the strength to do so.

Ego claimed he could deliver that final piece to them.

The building had been ransacked in the fighting. The door hung limply from its hinges, and the furniture was overturned.

Inside, Zageth stood alone.

Avi was surprised by that. "Are you confident, or just careless, friend?"

Zageth fixed him with a withering look. There was a tension in his features that had not been there at their last meeting. Avi somewhat enjoyed the sight, but he did not like it. He needed *strength* now. He needed to over-come the Empire.

After directing their escort to take up guard around the area, Jackal joined Avi inside. She eyed the man almost contemptuously. "I hear you have something for us."

Zageth nodded, chewing on his thumb. "I do, and despite appearances, Wolf, I am not alone. My people are simply subtler than you appreciate."

Jackal shot Avi a look. He let the jab slide off—now was not the time to antagonize this man by descending into a verbal spat. "Can we count on your people to bring an end to Tamiq's reign over this city?"

Zageth regained some of his composure. "Naturally, my master can give all this and more. He is quite pleased with your capturing of the garrison.

Although I must admit, the appearance of the Earth Adepts was...unexpected."

"Despite what you may think," Avi scoffed, "Talynis is not so unequal to the Empire's might."

"I meant no disrespect, Wolf."

Jackal crossed her arms. "Why are you so uneasy, Zageth? Last we met, you seemed far more sure of your position."

Now it was Avi's turn to shoot *her* a look. So much for stepping lightly.

Zageth, however, shrugged the comment off. "Things have developed at an unusual pace. Ego weathers such things with equanimity, of course; I am but a mortal."

Avi's gut tightened. It must have shown on his face, because Zageth smirked.

"A figure of speech, I assure you. Ego is just as flesh and blood as the rest of us. It is his mind and spirit that are so...transcendent."

That did little to allay Avi's disquiet. "What will he do, then, with his oh-so great mind?"

"And oh-so great resources," Jackal added.

Zageth smoothed his cloak, looking contemplative. "You want the Adept of Fire, correct? Reiva the Talynisti."

"She's no Talynisti," said Avi, "but yes, her capture—and death—would be a great asset to us. It would break the legion's might enough to inspire open rebellion across the city. No more pockets here and there, no more need to coordinate strikes. We could take back the palace and pave the way for Malik's return."

Wearing a look of naked satisfaction, Zageth clapped his hands. "She will be yours. It is within Ego's power to arrange an ambush. The bait will need to be significant—yourself, for example—but if the Adept were lured to you, could you bring an end to her under your own power?"

"Yes," said Avi and Jackal in unison.

Zageth nodded. "Excellent. I have some suggestions prepared, but this operation will be in your hands. Perhaps it will go something like this..."

Avi listened to the proposal with rapt attention. Now and then he would shake his head, demand a change. Jackal asked probing questions about how the plan would be executed.

But in the end, they had a strategy.

They had a way to kill this woman who called herself a Lion.

Avi's heart was racing at the prospect. In mere *days*, the city would be theirs again. They would force the legion to flee the city and never return. They would *win*.

"One more question," said Jackal, crossing her arms. "What does Ego get from this?"

"No need for such obvious suspicion. I am being honest, Jackal. What you want, and what my master wants—they are one and the same. After power is returned to Malik, it is Ego's hope that he will be in a unique position to profit from the restoration of order. Surely, Dav-maiir will be in need of trade, of reconstruction, of *friends*? Ego can provide all this."

"And," Jackal cut in, "he will get access to King Malik through us."

The man shrugged. "It would be a fine way of repaying your debt to act as a bridge. But all of that can come later. For now—"

There was a call of alarm from outside.

Knives came out, eyes darting everywhere. The *Nihilo* Blade gleamed like obsidian in the dark.

"Found something," grunted a man outside.

Zageth eased. "One of my guards."

Avi lowered his weapon, but did not sheathe it. "Let them in," he called. Jackal gave the door a wide berth.

Avi recognized the man who entered—he had been one of Zageth's bodyguards at their first meeting. Tall, tan, heavily muscled—yet he moved like a cat.

And he was carrying a person, arms dangling limply from his grasp.

The bodyguard dumped a woman on the floor unceremoniously.

With a start, Avi realized he recognized her too. She was the archer who had shot at him. Her chest rose and fell in a shaky rhythm.

"She's Imperial."

Zageth cast a weary look at him. "You don't say?"

"Found her lurking nearby," said the guard.

Jackal frowned. "She couldn't have been close enough to hear anything."

At this point, Avi noticed the man shoot a significant glance at Zageth. Zageth, for his part, masked any reaction. "Still," he said, "if she saw me, then that would jeopardize my place in the legion."

The guard spoke up, "The others have already swept the rest of the area —nothing."

Zageth nodded, though Avi could tell he seemed perturbed still. "We will interrogate her elsewhere. If anyone knew where she was going, then this whole area is suspect." He swore under his breath. "Inconvenience after inconvenience."

Jackal frowned. "Just kill her now. It would be a mercy."

Zageth glared. "I do not leave loose ends. I also do not allow myself blind spots. Stick to your own work, and I shall handle this. We are through here," he said with a cutting motion. "If anything changes, I will be in contact. Otherwise, expect everything to go as planned two days from now. Remember the proper field, be there at the proper time, and the Lion shall fall into your hands."

Jackal was plainly irritated by this, but already the guard was gathering up the Scout, and Zageth was drawing up his hood.

Avi nudged her toward the door. Without a word of parting, they left Zageth and his men behind.

They collected their own people as they departed, making their way back to the security of Loyalist territory.

Under her breath Jackal said, "When did you become so conflict averse? I half-expected you to demand he hand that woman over to us—or just slit her throat there yourself."

Avi scowled. "I pick my battles more carefully now. When I saw Crow's body lying in the street...I'm done taking chances, Jackal. If winning this war means quelling my passion and using my head, then so be it. Without Crow's mind guiding me, I can't afford to be little more than a blade."

She looked impressed. They moved in silence for a while. "He would be proud of you for leading like this."

Avi scoffed, despite all the weight on his shoulders. "He can be proud of me once I end this."

After a moment, she asked, "And how does this all end, Wolf?"

He didn't even need to think—he had dreamed of the moment for weeks.

"When I drive my blade through the Adept's heart."

~

THE FIRST THING Charas felt was the searing ache against her skull. It burned hottest right at the back, and with every moment it sent waves of pain radiating through her head.

The second thing she felt was the rough rope binding her hands behind her back. Her ankles were similarly restrained. The cold stone floor bit into the side of her face and dully ached against her hip and shoulder.

In spite of herself, she groaned.

"Awake at last," crooned an unknown voice.

Charas eased open her eyes. There was light, and the light hurt. She shut her eyes tight again.

"My apologies for the severity of that blow," continued the man. "My people are professionals, but sometimes they don't quite know their own strength."

Charas swallowed, suppressing a sudden urge to empty her stomach. She had a concussion for certain. "Who...are you?" she muttered, clenching her abdominals and keeping her throat tight.

A brief pause. "Zageth. You may know my name."

She forced herself to look, bracing against the piercing agony shooting through her eyes and brain.

Sure enough, it was him. Vantelle's optio.

The praetor's right-hand man who had been meeting with the Wolf.

Reiva...Reiva needs to know...

Zageth leaned in close to her, nearly nose to nose.

She spat.

The traitor grimaced, wiping his face. "You have remarkable eyes, you know. Very...*rare* eyes."

Charas' heart nearly stopped.

"Pardon me for gawking, but it's not every day one sees a bloodline such as yours."

64

THE WOLF OF TALYNIS

IT SOUNDS LIKE A FAIRY TALE, does it not? Like a legend, an old myth?

And yet, it happened in our world, in our time. And never shall we forget that day in Talynis.

—*The Memoirs of Flavia Iscator*

~

REIVA DISMOUNTED FROM HER HORSE, taking a moment to survey the farmlands. This was a routine sweep of the agricultural districts beyond the wall...or rather, that was what it was meant to look like.

Heads of barley stretched out across the land, all the way to the distant edge of greenery that marked out the well-watered heart of the *maiir*. Loaves of barley bread were a staple food all throughout Talynis, and the safety of these fields was essential to avoiding a famine. The people weren't satiated by any means—especially given the added burden of the legion forces—but at least they weren't starving.

All of that added up to the very obvious anxiety of the man approaching Reiva. He was dressed like any farmer, and he was a rather sizable man, though hunched in the shoulders and deeply tanned by long hours under the sun. His head was covered, and he kept his eyes low as he approached.

"How may I be of service, Adept?" He spoke the trade language, but with a Talynisti affect.

Reiva let her eyes flit over him for a moment. Dirt speckling and streaking his face from toiling away in the soil. A perpetual squint from the harsh rays. In his hand, he clutched a sickle, wickedly sharp by the look of it.

She had to admit—it was a good disguise.

She nodded toward the granary he had just walked out of. "Do you have any objection to my soldiers searching this storehouse?"

He bent even lower, stammering. "We-well, yes. Er, no! A thousand apologies. Go wherever you please, and you will see that I have withheld nothing."

"Good." She ordered the detachment of soldiers that had come with her to go inspect the granary. "Rumor has it you've been skimming for yourself, but I'm sure that will all be proven wrong, hm?"

He sputtered indignantly, but he also shied away. "Who accuses me of such a thing? I would have him say as much to my face! Was it Jaboam across the road? He's a conniver, Adept, not worth trusting."

Reiva half-listened as he went on a tirade about how his neighbor was a no-good scoundrel. She gave a signal to her soldiers. They moved toward the granary doors to inspect the holdings.

Reiva's heart beat faster as the final legionnaire passed the threshold. She did her best to look disinterested.

One second passed.

The man was rambling on about how his neighbor's sons were rascals.

Two seconds.

Reiva let her hand rest on the pommel of her sword.

Three seconds.

A wall of sandstone burst from the ground, sealing up the granary—with nearly all Reiva's soldiers inside.

Reiva drew her blade.

A patch of earth twenty yards away exploded, and up and out poured a sudden mass of Loyalists, first among them a man wrapped in elaborate brown robes, his hands cutting through the air in sharp, powerful motions.

Her horse was screaming, taking off for safety in a mad dash.

The farmer wailed, dropping his sickle, and making to run away in much the same manner. Reiva grabbed him in a hold and put the edge of her sword to his chin. As Loyalists fell into a circle around her, she hauled her captive so that her back was to the newly risen sandstone, his body between her and the assailants.

Shouts came from within the granary. Her soldiers would be fine—for now, at least. Whether they stayed safe would depend on whether the rest of this went according to plan.

The Talynisti Adept stepped forward. His attire reminded Reiva of how the nomad tribes dressed. He looked her up and down like she was a troublesome pet.

She readied defensive techniques in case he tried to attack, but all she sensed was his own readiness. At the slightest twitch, either one of them could turn this place into total carnage, but for now, they held their positions.

Reiva pressed the sword closer to her captive's neck. He made an appropriately displeased whimper—though she also may have just been a bit too close for comfort.

"So," she said, "are we standing like this all day? I do have an army that will come looking for me before long."

"We are well acquainted with your legion, Adept."

Reiva swallowed, recognizing the voice. So he had come indeed.

From behind the line of bristling Loyalists, a Talynisti man with a black-bladed sword in hand approached. His men parted for him, and he stepped forward so that when they closed ranks again, they hemmed him in with her.

"The Wolf of Talynis. Once again, you prove you are only capable of ambushes and underhanded stratagems."

He gave a mocking half-bow. He wore a mask over his mouth and nose, but she could see contempt burning in his eyes. "And you are the coward who hides behind civilians."

"There are no civilians in Talynis; that's become quite clear."

The Wolf laughed. "I wish you were right! But you have scared far too many of my countrymen from taking up arms. I hope that your death will change things."

"Funny, I don't feel very dead."

Her captive let out a small squeak.

The Wolf waved his *Nihilo* Blade toward her. "You so much as bruise that man, you die, as will all your men inside. I need only give the word and Wakaram will collapse the building."

Reiva felt a subtle shift in the aether around the Talynisti Adept. She had no doubt he was capable of such a thing.

He was the biggest problem, in fact. Everything else could be handled fairly easily if that earth magic was cleared from the table.

"You let him go," continued the Wolf, "you drop your sword, and you hand over that magic talisman."

"And then you kill me without a fight, is that it?"

The Wolf shook his head. "We kill you either way, Adept. We have you twenty-to-one. I killed your predecessor in Dav-maiir single-handedly."

"You act like that makes lying down to die a better option."

"Surrender now," he said, "and your men may go free. So long as they also surrender their arms."

Reiva held his eyes for a moment.

"Ten seconds, or we collapse the building. Ten."

Her fingers flexed along the hilt.

Her aetheric sense screamed a warning as the Talynisti began to gather the aether for a massive shifting of earth.

"Nine."

The Loyalists inched forward, like horses champing at the bit, ready to be unleashed.

"Eight."

Reiva dropped her sword.

Everyone froze, waiting to see if this was really it, or if she was about to throw a wave of fire at them.

She shoved her captive forward.

All the Loyalists, the rogue Adept, the Wolf—they all kept their eyes on her, paying no mind as the man scrambled along the ground, scampering away from Reiva. So no one saw, or no one cared, that he picked up his sickle as he went. They were all watching Reiva as she reached up to take off the focus around her neck.

So not one of them was able to react in time when Yaros slipped near the mage and took his head off with one deft slice from the sickle.

Yaros dove *back* toward Reiva, hitting the ground and rolling just as she poured power into a singular detonation of force. Flames exploded right in the midst of the Loyalists, billowing with such blistering speed and intensity that Reiva feared she'd burn the city's food supply.

Yaros sprang to his feet, sickle at the ready. Reiva snatched up her sword and stepped forward to stand beside him, shoulder to shoulder.

Most of the Loyalists had gone down, either instantly killed or far too wounded to fight.

Only a small number still stood; all of them beside the Wolf, steam curling off his *Nihilo* Blade.

Reiva and Yaros were still outnumbered, but it only took one look at the Loyalists' faces to see who had better odds. Fear, hatred—absolute malice and rage, in the case of the Wolf.

It was almost unfair.

Reiva threw a quick burst of flame, stepping forward in time with Yaros. The Wolf licked it up with his relic, the black blade sucking in the fire like smoke snatched away by a strong wind.

Four Loyalists and the Wolf, two on either side of him.

Reiva closed the distance, sword coming down in a vicious overhead cut.

The Wolf parried and returned, moving with the savage reflexes of a knife-fighter.

Reiva stepped back, throwing a blast of fire to ward off One and Two.

Yaros swung the sickle low, gashing open Four's thigh, then smoothly bringing it up to deflect Three's slash.

The Wolf leaped forward, closing the distance to Reiva. His sword darted out like a striking snake, sparking off Reiva's armor. She danced back, not daring to risk a cut from the wretched relic. She swept for his neck; he ducked and moved back in, clamping a hand over her wrist.

Reiva sparked a shell of aether, lighting her arm on fire and forcing the Wolf to disengage with a pained grunt.

There was no space to breathe though, because One and Two were advancing again.

But now, the *Nihilo* Blade was too far to protect them.

Mustering the aether for a searing jet of flame, she thrust out her hand and washed them with fire. Not enough to kill them right away, but enough to drop them to the earth in a groaning heap.

In the same moment, Yaros lopped off Three's hand, his sword hitting the earth with a dusty *thud*. Four scrambled for him, but the mercenary easily parried the clumsy blow and disarmed him.

Reiva leveled her hand toward them.

"Surrender, Wolf. You still have men you can save."

To say that the man's eyes were full of hate would have been an understatement. Reiva thought he was about to run in for a suicide attack.

"Drop the sword and they go free, right now."

He faltered for a moment, hesitation flickering through his eyes.

That gave Yaros the opening he needed to step in and disarm him. In an instant, he had the Wolf on his knees, sickle at his neck.

"You're a slippery bastard, you know that?" Yaros was bleeding from a few shallow cuts, and he was drenched in sweat.

Reiva felt a wave of relief once Yaros had him restrained, but there was still the matter of his comrades. Three and Four were the least injured—she singled them out and ordered them to get out of her sight, taking along anyone else they could.

Their faces were a contorted mix of pain, shame, and fury—but they went, tails between their legs, rousing what allies of theirs could still stand and flee.

The Wolf's eyes were fixed on Reiva, practically daring her to renege on her word and blast those men to ash.

She sheathed her sword, stepping forward to gingerly pick up the *Nihilo* Relic. One nick from this metal and her life as an Adept would be over. This sword had killed one of her peers and wounded her praetor.

And she had finally brought down the man who held the blade. This thorn in the Empire's side.

She couldn't help feeling exultant as she stepped forward and tore his mask away.

Up close, he looked younger than she'd expected, but there was something vaguely familiar about him. Had she seen him unmasked some time other than the prisoner exchange?

"So, this is your face. Now, your name."

He spat on her boots. "I am the Wolf. I became the Wolf for the sake of Talynis. That is all that matters."

Reiva frowned. "I thought we Talynisti prided ourselves on honoring our names and the names of our fathers."

His face twisted in rage. "You are no Talynisti," he hissed. "You *dishonor* your father!"

"At least I wear my name openly instead of hiding behind an epithet like a coward."

Fire burned in his eyes. "Whatever I am, I am no coward. When you nail me to the tree, Imperial, announce my name. I am Aviqohl beyt'Avadh."

Reiva's heart stopped.

The world spun.

She had heard him wrong. That was it—she had misheard.

But Yaros was looking at her, eyes wide.

"Another deception," she muttered. "Another lie. Your name is not Aviqohl. Your house is not Avadh. You are lying. You are *lying!*"

She lunged forward, grabbing his shoulders and pulling his face to within an inch of hers. "Who told you that name? Who—?!"

Her yell died in her throat as pieces clicked together.

Her father's nose. Her mother's eyes.

Her brother's face—marked and twisted by anger and time and dust.

Her brother's face.

She dropped him, hands trembling.

Yaros was looking between her and his prisoner. "Reiva," he called.

The Wolf looked just as confused.

Feeling like she was walking on clouds, she stumbled off. She needed to...needed to break out the soldiers still trapped in the granary. She had an obligation to her legionnaires. To the Empire.

"I want him locked up by himself," she called back. "Gagged. No one speaks to him without me there."

She had an obligation.

She had many obligations.

'Promise me...'

PART IV

THE LION AND THE WOLF

65

HER FATHER'S HOPE

QUEEN ASRAH SAID:

'I remember there were many—and I think there still are many—who would make the Adept of Fire, born of the name Rebbaelah to a Talynisti man and woman, to be an enemy to our laws and people, a traitor. It is not often considered that, had the people of Talynis abided by our laws, she would never have been made into what she became.

'I do not speak here of what her mother did—I speak of the clan Avadh, of the city Shugrith, and ultimately, of the governance and the kingship itself. It was the sins of Talynis that enabled what transpired, for if we had protected the Talynisti girl Rebbaelah, the Lazarrans would not have adopted and forged the warrior Reiva.

'This too, perhaps, is divine will, and a lesson for our proud people. Have the prophets of old not warned as much? Did they not say that judgment would come with fire and the sword?'

—*A Chronicle of Talynisti Reign, Vol. II: Usurpations*

~

IN HER ROOM, Adept Reiva held her head in her hands. This room was originally the chamber of a distinguished Talynisti commander who had perished defending the walls when the legion broke through the gates.

But she was not thinking of him, of how at night she rested her head where his would have lain—this man born of the desert as she was. No, she was thinking of another man killed by a Lazarran legion. Killed in a war, though death was far too slow to catch up to him.

'Always remember...'

Light crept through the window. She had not slept. Night had passed in an impossibly long, impossibly short haze. All the while, the same memory, the same tableau, wheeled through her mind in endless motion.

REBBAELAH PEELED the cloth from her father's forehead. It had been cold just a few minutes ago. Now it was hot.

The infection worsened by the day. The doctor was not even coming anymore; he had given them some herbs to ease the pain (they weren't working) and told them to beg the mercy of the Four.

Her mother was catatonic. Her little brother Aviqohl didn't understand. "Dad came back from the fighting," he kept saying. "That means he's okay!"

She didn't know how to explain, so she just forced a smile. And every moment she was not caring for her father, she made prayers to the gods. She prayed to the Worldfather that he would tend to this body he had made. To the Windmother, that she would not call back the breath she had spirated into his lungs. To the Warrior, that he would look with favor upon this man who had drawn iron in defense of Talynis.

And she prayed even to the Wanderer, harbinger of death, traverser of all realms. To him, she prayed he would not collect her father's soul. She asked him to walk by a different road, so he would not come to their doorpost and smell the doom that had settled upon it.

Qohl beyt'Avadh moaned softly, tearing Reiva from another battery of prayer. In a flash, the girl raised water to his lips. He drank but a sip.

"You need more," she murmured, as if even speaking too loud would do him harm.

His smile was weak. "Too late, little princess. I can hear him coming."

Rebbaelah twisted her skirts in her hands. Her head shook from side to side. "No you don't. No—he's not here, I asked him to stay away."

It sounded foolish to her, even as the tears welled up. That a little girl's will would stay the god of death from visiting. Maybe she had only drawn his attention closer upon their house.

This was why no one prayed to the Wanderer.

Qohl's hand trembled on the sweat-soaked bedsheets. She took it silently.

Her cheeks were wet. She tasted blood—she was biting down on her lip to stifle the sobs.

Qohl squeezed her hand, his grip frail. "Brave girl."

She was shaking her head again. "You c-can't. We need you here. I need to g-get the neighbors. The doc-t-tor." Every word tore itself from her lips, tremulous and fragile, and vacant of hope.

"It's okay to cry." He squeezed her hand again, even weaker. "You can cry. The prophets cried."

She shook her head even harder. By now, she couldn't form any words.

"Promise me..."

"Promise me you won't go first."

A quirk of the lips. "Can't do that. Promise me you'll watch over your brother. You only have each other. When I'm gone. When Mother is gone. The two of you together."

She was biting down on her knuckles, her other hand shaking in her father's. His frail grip was warm. Too warm.

His fingers were slipping. "Promise, my girl."

And like a geyser, her grief burst out. "Promise! I promise I promise I promise but please don't go away!"

Qohl beyt'Avadh's eyes were closing. "Take care of him. Always...always remember..."

Rebbaelah screamed.

They found her with her head buried in her father's still chest. She was sobbing, the words of her father's hope ringing in her ears.

Three years later, she would be in a slaver's caravan.

'PROMISE *me you'll watch over your brother.'*

'Take care of him.'

"I didn't have a choice," she hissed through gritted teeth. "You left us with *her*. She sold me off. None of this should have happened."

Something hit the floor.

A teardrop.

Reiva scoured her face. She had soldiers to command. She had a praetor to report to.

But she had a brother.

How could she have a brother, still?

Staring at her from the opposite side of the room, atop a small chest, was a bronze plate, propped up and etched. The design was of a mountain, and atop the mountain were four pillars of fire.

She sprang across the room, grabbing the votive etching and hurling it against the wall. The metal rang with a foreboding hum after it struck the floor. Her eyes burned as she looked down upon the bronze, sacrilegiously dropped to the ground.

None of this would have happened if the gods had acted.

Three knocks at the door.

Reiva scowled, huffing. She took a moment to smooth her uniform and dry her eyes.

It was Yaros.

He had a look in his eyes that said he had heard the crash.

Before he could get a word out, she was talking. "I need to speak with him."

The Karellan crossed his arms. "Charas is still missing."

A dull ache struck her stomach. "Even more cause to speak with him. He could know something."

"Is that *really* why you need to talk to him?"

Reiva clenched her fists. "I am acting princeps to the Ninth Legion's praetor. I have apprehended one of the figureheads of the Loyalist forces. This is my duty."

"It would have also been Legion Intelligence's duty if you had not ordered the Wolf not be approached without your consent."

Reiva opened her mouth, but Yaros wasn't stopping.

"I understand, Reiva, but your personal connections with him cannot jeopardize—"

"*Personal connections?* He's my *brother*. He's my brother and I would have sworn on every god I know that he was either dead or long gone from Talynis by now."

"So you convinced yourself of a fiction to comfort yourself. That's fine—everyone does that—but now this is reality, and there is a Legion Scout missing at a time when our forces are perilously thin. A time when we have reason to expect an imminent attack, given how unstable our position in Dav-maiir is. So are you going to fulfill your duty now, or shall I inform Legion Intelligence that they have the go-ahead to interrogate the Wolf?"

Reiva recoiled. Then she grit her teeth. Shoving her way past Yaros, she muttered, "Since when does a mercenary care so much about Lazarran honor?"

If he had a response, she didn't hear it.

THE WOLF OF TALYNIS, Aviqohl beyt'Avadh, was under strict restraint in the palace's dungeon. He was the sole prisoner, and at all times two *triarii* guarded the only stairwell into the depths.

Reiva did not recognize these two, but they waved her through immediately, bobbing their heads and saying, "*Ave Imperator*, Lion."

Reiva nodded in return, but said nothing. In the back of her mind, something marveled at how she had just swept past a pair of soldiers with years of service on her. Things had come a long way from fearing that her career was on the verge of collapse.

The stairs were rough hewn, cut directly into the stone. A host of barred spaces, lined with shackles and chains, littered the place. All the prisoners who had been held here were freed or executed when Tamiq took power. Since then, no one had been locked up down here.

Not until now.

The Wolf was slumped over. Not entirely though, as thick ropes bound him to a straight-backed chair, iron manacles locking his ankles to the legs. His eyes were shut. He might have been dozing, deep in thought, praying.

He still did not look like Aviqohl, thought Reiva. His chin was too sharp. He had a beard, like a full-grown man...which he was, she realized. He would have reached the age of majority about a year ago. She could not remember his birthday exactly, but she thought he had been born in the fall.

The only light came through small apertures spaced alone the western wall. As the day was early, someone else would have had to bring a torch down here to see anything more than vague impressions. Reiva held out her hand and conjured flame.

As the flickering light cast the room in dancing shadows and sudden warmth bloomed outward from her palm, the Wolf opened his eyes.

For a while, the only sound was the hunger of the fire.

His eyes did not look like Aviqohl's either. Too hard. Too hateful.

It made her heart turn in on itself.

'Take care of him.'

"My name was once Rebbaelah beyt'Avadh."

His expression did not change. He just kept staring at her.

"We grew up in Shugrith together. Our father died when I was nine. Our mother sold me to Zarushan slavers three years after. They took me to Lazarra, where my talent for magic appeared and the Adept Corps took me in."

That same stare.

"You are my brother."

The Wolf spat on the ground. "Even if you were telling the truth, you're not my sister."

"I—"

"Even if we came from the same womb, you are not my sister." His eyes blazed with reflected fire and naked fury. Fury and pain. "You are a traitor to Talynis. You defile my family's name. You dishonor my father's memory and everything he stood for."

He was shaking against his bonds.

"The Empire killed my father—and now I see it killed my sister. You are *no* family of mine! You are *no* daughter of the desert!" Tears shone in his eyes as he spoke through gritted teeth. "I thought—I thought my sister ran away. I thought she left me there, alone with my mother. For *years* I hated her for that, until finally I thought I could forgive her for it, if only I could see her again. I thought that would make everything right, because at least I would know you still lived. Now I see the folly of my wishes. You are a liar, a coward, and if the gods have any justice in them, your body will rot unburied outside these walls."

To her own astonishment, Reiva kept her Flame steady as he yelled.

His chest heaved. Sweat glistened on his face. Heavy breaths echoed off the cold stone.

"I did not choose this. I did what I had to do to survive, and I *am* your sister, whatever you think."

"Go to the hells." He wasn't looking at her anymore.

If Reiva's heart had hurt before, now it lay in shreds. Not even because of what he had said. She understood him there. She had thought much the same of herself, many days and nights, in the turmoil of her soul.

It was his face that had destroyed her. The way he curled his lips when he was angry, just like their mother. How he stuck out his chin when he wanted to emphasize a point, like their father.

This was her brother, and she had done nothing for him, nothing until she came to the walls of his city with a Lazarran army.

Push it down. Serve. You are not Rebbaelah beyt'Avadh. You are Reiva the Adept. Reiva the Lion.

"I still have questions for you, and if you do not answer to me, then Legion Intelligence will replace me. And they won't ask the questions until after you're bleeding. Where did the two Talynisti Adepts come from?"

He shrugged against the restraints.

"One of your Vipers?"

"We did have to get creative after you killed half of us." He fixed her with a glare. "Is your dog enjoying his new toy?"

"You mean the *Ventas* Blade."

"*Crow's Ventas* Blade."

"If that's Crow's *Ventas* Blade, then whose *Nihilo* Blade did you use to kill Adept Havan?"

The Wolf shrugged again in his constrained manner. "Do you bed him?"

"Excuse me?"

"The Karellan mercenary."

Reiva's fire blazed hotter. "I have not, and if I had it would not be your concern."

He sneered. "I thought brothers are supposed to care about such things. Can't collect a bride price if you've already gone and screwed half your regiment though, eh?"

"Watch your—"

"Tell me, how long did you last in Lazarra before someone pulled you into their bedroom? Lots of eager men and women curious to get a taste of a Talynisti girl. Or did you even make it that far? Zarushans are famously—"

"One more word and I burn out your tongue."

Aviqohl snickered. She hated that it was still his laugh, after all these years. He used to tease her with that laugh when she tripped. Now this.

She took a breath.

I'm not about to let a captive—brother or not—get to me like this.

"There is a missing Legion Scout," she continued after a moment. "A Parthavan woman. Did you take her?"

To her surprise, pain flickered across his face. "I did not. But I know who did."

Reiva frowned. "Explain."

The Wolf scoffed. "The same person who gave me the *Nihilo* Blade."

"*Who* is that person?"

"You know, if you were really my sister, then you would spit in Ego's face for me."

Ego? He was a figure of the Lazarran underworld, supposedly helping the Loyalists.

"I've never met the man, I'm afraid. But if you help us catch him, it might lessen your sentence."

The Wolf snorted, shaking his head. "Ask whoever sold me out to you."

Reiva's hand twitched, the fire swaying for a moment. "What?"

He stared into her eyes again. "Ego betrayed me to you. He was going to get you into that field for me so we could lay an ambush, but you were made wise to things. And now..." he shrugged against his bonds. "Here I am."

Reiva let her fire die. She turned on her heel, sandals slapping against the stone as she left.

"Like I said," called Aviqohl, "spit in his face for me."

66

OF AN ASURA

In Talynisti, *ruakh*. In Lazarran, *genius*. In Zarushan, *ahura*. In Karellan, *daimon*. The most elaborate taxonomy I have found is in Endra, with many nuances and subtleties the beginner need not concern himself with.
  —*The Life and Wisdom of Simeon Binkhok As Told by Himself*

Charas' head was getting better. Not much, but still better. The ropes had long rubbed her wrists raw, and no matter how many times she changed positions (much as she could, given her restraints), she could not get away from the persistent aches.

Zageth came in regularly to check on her. He brought her meager food and drink. Every time, he would ask about her lineage. She never answered him, save with oaths that would have made even her uncle blush.

He tried to entice her with the promise of more sustenance if she would answer his questions. Still, she gave him nothing.

That went both ways. He refused to tell her where she was, nor for how long she had been in his captivity. She couldn't see the outside, so she had no clue to the passage of time. It could have been two days, it could have been a week, depending on how long she had spent out of consciousness.

Eventually, Zageth came to her again, this time with a blindfold. He took her gag out first.

"I don't suppose you've had a sudden change of heart and would like to share something pertinent with me?"

She spat. "Bite me."

When she was gagged and blinded, he tossed her over his shoulders. She could have tried to struggle, but it wouldn't have done much good. Her heart was beating fast. Being moved was a chance to escape.

She needed to conserve her energy much as she could. For all she knew, they planned to kill her today. Maybe that was where she was being taken—to be dumped into some cistern or tossed over a dune.

When he set her down again, it was into a tight wooden container. Her legs had to be unbound so she could curl up to fit. The lid was shut and locked over her.

Then the movement began, rattling and tossing her around inside, and she surmised from the motion that she was probably in a trough being pulled through the cobblestone streets. Now and then, she heard voices through the wood.

A part of her wanted to scream, to kick against the box, to do *something* —but she suspected she would only be ignored (what would people find more likely, a person or a dog?), or she would earn herself an even quicker death.

So she bided her time. She tried to still her breathing. To ignore the ache in her head and her bones. She didn't bother trying to track the turns and lengths of travel—if she were in a better state, she might have been able to reverse engineer their route once she got free, but she doubted she could pull that off as she was.

The air inside heated, so the sun must have been up. That was interesting. If *she* were secretly transporting a captive, she'd have done it at night.

Were they under some sort of time constraint?

Eventually, they came to a stop.

Charas heard two voices—Zageth and a woman. Zageth spoke softly, while the woman was loud, furious. Charas' head ached at the racket, and she closed herself off even as she felt curious.

With a rattle, the box was unlocked, then unceremoniously tipped over. Charas hit the ground with a groan, her bruises flaring with pain.

"As I said," Zageth quipped, "consider this a gift from Ego. He considers you of worth—perhaps you can use this in your negotiations."

Charas rolled over, but still she was blindfolded and gagged. As she heard the crack of a switch and the patter of hooves, she knew Zageth would be beyond her reach.

So who had he handed her over to?

She lay still. She could sense a presence near her.

Everything was still for a moment, save Charas' own breathing.

"Hold still," said the woman. With calloused fingers, she freed Charas of the blindfold.

It was the woman called Jackal, staring down at her with obvious confusion and frustration.

"Scream and I gut you, understand?"

Charas nodded dully.

The gag came off.

Recognition dawned in the woman's eyes. "You shot me in the stomach."

"Nothing personal, I assure you."

Jackal scoffed. "So, who are you, and why didn't Zageth kill you after what happened?"

Charas was still restrained, but she managed to roll up into a sitting position. She recounted how Zageth's men had knocked her out, and how he had chosen to keep her alive.

She left out anything about *why* Zageth had decided to spare her. She still felt unease in her stomach at that. Why had his guards trained to recognize Hunter blood? There were even more mysteries about Zageth and Vantelle than she had thought.

Zageth, she knew for certain now, was a traitor. He was in league with Ego. She had never heard of such a person, but the strange name alone was enough to evoke suspicion. The only question remained then, was Vantelle in on this, or was she blind to Zageth's treachery?

Her gut told her not to trust Vantelle. Her gut had saved her life many a time.

Besides, what Vantelle had done to Legate Iscator...

But Charas wasn't about to play buddy-buddy with a pack of Loyalists just because they hadn't killed her yet. She needed to find out what was going on here, what these 'negotiations' Zageth had mentioned were.

As it turned out, Jackal readily gave her the answer to that.

The Wolf had been captured. Reiva and Yaros had sprung a trap when *he* had been trying to trap *them*.

Charas' gut pushed another hunch toward her.

When the Jackal learned Charas was but a Scout, she was plainly disappointed. They weren't about to trade back the Wolf in exchange for one Scout. They had already swapped one princess for seven legionnaires. Princesses, though, were born to be bargaining chips. The Wolf was a military enemy, a criminal in defiance of their new regime.

Charas wasn't worth enough for that—not to the Lazarrans, at least. She would get an honorable commendation beside her name in a report some-where; funerary rites would be held (with or without her body).

At some point, a large Endric man came in. The Mouse. The price on his head alone was astronomical—a warrior of supposedly unparalleled strength and bravery. He surveyed Charas with neutral eyes. Then, straight away, got her some water and bread. As he held the bowl to her lips, he eyed Jackal reproachfully.

Jackal was bemused. "Really?"

"Mercy is demanded of us always; cruelty leaves a stain upon the souls."

Charas liked the sound of that—not the least because it reminded her of something her grandfather might have said. And, you know, food and water were a welcome blessing as well.

She also liked the image of Cassia Vantelle's soul being grim and splotchy black for all eternity. In Parthava, they said such a person would never hunt with the gods—they could only scavenge with the carrion birds.

Jackal, for her part, brushed off Mouse's comment. "She's no good to us. A strain and a risk if we put her up here."

"We won't kill her."

If she hadn't been so hungry, Charas might have been more invested in the discussion over whether she got to live. With her teeth, she tore a chunk of bread from the loaf Mouse held out to her.

"What makes this any different?"

"Trust me," rumbled Mouse. "There is something here, though I cannot name it."

"The only reason I can see," huffed Jackal, "is that Zageth wanted to foist more troubles upon us."

Mouse chuckled. "I'm surprised you didn't cut him down where he stood."

"We still don't know what Ego's capable of. Besides betraying Wolf to the Lazarrans, of course."

Mouse folded his arms, his brow creasing. "Which leaves the question of why Zageth would give this one over to us."

"Still have ears," mumbled Charas around a bite of bread. She was intensely curious about where this was going though...she might have reason to show her cards soon.

Jackal rubbed at her forehead. "He's playing both sides. Ego wants the Empire and the Talynisti Loyalists at each other's throats—somehow that helps him accomplish his own goals."

The Mouse gave Charas a sympathetic look. "I do not suppose you could help us with figuring that out?"

Jackal scoffed. "If she could, Zageth would have separated her head from her shoulders."

Charas swallowed. Now seemed as good a time as any. "No idea what this Ego person wants. But I *can* tell you that Zageth is the optio to Praetor Cassia Vantelle."

And now was the time for the hunch.

"You've been dealing with a Lazarran praetor this entire time, the commander of our forces. She's Ego."

She knew how crazy it sounded, but as soon as she said it, she *knew* it was so. Whether that was from the head injury, or it was from something deeper...well, she hoped it was the latter.

The Vipers stared at her.

Jackal was the first to break. She rolled her eyes, scoffed, and practically walked off all at once. "She's crazy then. Either that or she's telling us a mad lie, and this is another crackpot, back-alley plan."

Mouse, however, did not look as suspicious. He *was* skeptical, but Charas recognized in him a glimmer of belief, of expectation.

"Just a moment," he said. "We can find out rather easily whether she's lying."

Jackal whirled back. "What?"

Mouse tapped his forehead, and Jackal's eyes widened.

Charas suddenly felt uncomfortable, even as her curiosity burgeoned. "You could really find that out?"

"I could even find out whether she's just gone mad."

She nodded firmly. "Do it."

"Hold on a shake," said Charas, "what exactly are you—"

Mouse touched his fingertips to Charas' forehead, and everything went white. The last thing she heard was a murmured, "My apologies."

Rolling green plains.

Sweet winds and sour berries.

Rushing rivers and roiling thunderclouds.

A bay mare with a white cross on her muzzle galloped by.

Braana?

It couldn't have been Braana. Her first horse had died when she was but six years old.

And yet, she knew it was her.

She flew beside Braana, found herself suddenly in a copse of trees beside a river. Braana was gone, but at the bank, a young man was washing his face with the brisk water, smiling through the cold and humming an old tune.

Gerol.

Charas' heart twisted. She hadn't thought of *him* in years.

But then he was gone too, and she was flying across the plains again. Flowers bloomed and withered. Storms raced by and stars whirled.

She saw her father next. Tobron the Son of Thunder. His hair was grayer than last she saw him, and he looked straight at her. She wondered if he was actually looking at her right now, looking with those divine eyes of his, as she spiraled through this vision.

She was in the clouds then, looking down over the whole realm. In the far west, she saw the glittering surface of the sea cut across by white-capped waves. Then she was soaring away, into the east.

Beneath her was Parthava, and then it wasn't. The grass dissolved into sand. Trees transformed into city walls and towers.

The garrison of the Ninth Legion sprouted from the dust, and through the churning sands strode Cassia Vantelle, proud and icy-eyed, with Zageth dogging her heels.

The sun fell and the world was dark, and Charas was in the dark. But still she saw, saw in a way that should not have been possible for an ordinary person to see. She saw Zageth, and she saw Jackal, and she saw the Wolf. No one else could have seen so far through such gloom. Only a Hunter had such eyes.

And if it had not been for her own surprise at what she had seen there in the dark, she'd have been wise to her preternatural senses and the approach of a vicious man about to strike her across the skull.

Then, as quick as it had all began, it ended.

Charas' head jerked back. She was gasping, soaked in sweat.

Mouse's fingers hung in the air. His face was a mask, but she knew he had witnessed everything.

She felt naked under his sight.

"She is telling the truth," he said.

Jackal looked bewildered. "You tap her forehead and that's that?"

"He did more than that," snarled Charas. "You had *no* right to see me like that!"

Mouse looked deep in thought, unperturbed by her anger.

Then, all of a sudden, he dropped to his knees and prostrated himself, forehead to ground.

Charas almost preferred when he had been scouring her mind.

"I apologized before," he said. "I apologize again. I did not expect this."

Now Charas felt just as confused as Jackal looked.

Mouse raised his eyes. "Fool that I am, I did not recognize the signs—

though now they are clear as day to me. You are descended of an *asura*. You are a child of the gods."

67

A CROWN AWAITS

BETTER TO STARVE, better to suffer any pain than be a slave to guilt.
—Lucian Sana, Lazarran philosopher

VANTELLE HAD TAKEN up office in a converted room. When Reiva entered, she found Vantelle reclining, examining the *Nihilo* Blade taken from Aviqohl. It seemed so strange, seeing the weapon that had killed her peer, Adept Havan, now in the hands of her commanding officer.

When Vantelle saw Reiva enter, she gingerly set aside the relic, though her gaze lingered on it.

"A great treasure for the Empire," said Reiva. Might as well start off with something benign.

The praetor nodded. "It will be good to have it in the Imperial Reliquary. Your superiors at the Sanctum will be overjoyed to hear you brought back not only this but the *Ventas* Relic as well." She smiled easily. "I'm sure not a single skeptic of your ascension to Lion will remain."

"I hope you are right, my praetor."

Vantelle frowned. "What is it? The Wolf didn't manage to kill himself in that cell, did he?"

"No. No, I just spoke with him."

"And he so thoroughly disturbed you? Tell me what's going on, Reiva. I need all my soldiers at their best right now."

Cassia Vantelle, for all her military bearing and severity, had a remarkable capacity to look matronly when she wished. Far more than Reiva's own mother ever had.

It almost made Reiva want to lie. To let her past finally die, once and for all. She could see her future in this woman's eyes—a Lion, an Adept without peer, renowned leader of the Imperial Legions, reared by the Sanctum of the Adept Corps. Vantelle would raise her to all of those heights. Had already begun raising her to those heights.

'Take care of him.'

'You only have each other.'

She swallowed.

"My praetor, there are two things to speak of here."

"Well, you'll have to begin with one of them."

Reiva nodded, breaking eye contact. What was worse—to accuse her of a connection to Ego, or to reveal that the man they had been hunting this whole time was Reiva's own brother?

She decided the latter might be safer, if only marginally.

"The Wolf of Talynis, whom we now know as Aviqohl beyt'Avadh by name..." She reasserted eye contact. "He is my younger brother by blood."

What flashed across Vantelle's face then—Reiva had never seen such naked shock and surprise from the praetor. Not even when the Wolf had descended from atop the Bazaar to assassinate her. Until this moment, Reiva had never seen Vantelle truly caught off-guard.

"You are certain of this?"

"My name was once Rebbaelah beyt'Avadh. I was born and raised in Shugrith, with my younger brother Aviqohl named for our father."

Vantelle pressed a fist to her lips. She eyed Reiva for a moment. "Can you fulfill your duty to the Empire in this situation, Adept?"

Reiva had thought long and hard all night about this. The words came out just as she'd rehearsed them—though with every moment she feared more and more that they sounded frail. "For Emperor and Eagle, I shall. But if I could be so bold, my praetor...might he receive clemency, if he cooperates with us?"

A sympathetic smile lit Vantelle's features. "He cannot be pardoned, Reiva. It is an impossibility. The lives he has taken, the war he has waged against us. His life is forfeit."

"Of course." Reiva's throat was dry. "But if he were to cooperate, then perhaps the method—"

"You want him spared the beam."

She swallowed. "Yes."

The praetor sighed, bridging her fingers. "In the report I received regarding the dead rogue Adept, it specified that no focus was found on his person. You did not take it, did you?"

Reiva shook her head emphatically. "I would have informed you of it. There was no focus, but that is impossible."

"It *should* be impossible, but here we are."

"I imagine an autopsy will discover it below the skin somewhere."

Vantelle raised an eyebrow. "Such procedures are fatal for Adepts."

"Eventually, but there are some stories of Adepts putting themselves at such peril in order to temporarily unlock greater power."

Vantelle hummed, but shook her head. "You won't find one."

Reiva blinked. "Excuse me? My praetor, not to discount your opinion but—"

She waved it off. "Call it a hunch, an informed guess, whatever you please. But there are reasons to suspect that the Talynisti Adepts are not using arcane focuses."

Reiva was baffled. "That just can't be true." Everything she knew about the arcane Arts, everything she had learned in the Sanctum railed against what Vantelle was suggesting.

The praetor seemed remarkably confident in her assertions, though. And then she got a glint of fire in her eye. "Perhaps there is a deal to be made with the Wolf. A way he can be useful to the Empire and earn his way to a lighter sentence."

Hope kindled in Reiva's heart, though this matter of the focus still bemused her. "What terms should I ask of him?"

Vantelle waved it off. "This is a matter of personal interest to me, Reiva. Of personal interest to the Emperor, in fact. I will handle the negotiation myself."

Reiva blinked. Had Vantelle just implied this was above her rank?

The praetor chuckled. As if she'd read Reiva's mind, she said, "Believe it or not, some things are above even a Lion's clearance. But rest assured, the way you are ascending now, you will attain to greater heights before long, even younger than I did, perhaps."

The possibility was dizzying, but Reiva still didn't see what her brother could know about magic that was beyond *her* reach. Even if there really was no focus, why would Vantelle know of such a thing? Even the highest ranking of the Imperial Adepts wore a focus. An Adept's focus was integral to her identity. Surely Alyat would not have kept such possibilities from her.

If there was a way to manipulate aether without a focus on one's person...Reiva knew firsthand the effects of aether sickness. First came minor aether sickness: headaches and dizziness. The second stage, severe sickness, brought nausea and minor hallucinations. After that came extreme sickness—full-on delusions, loss of bodily control, and even mutations and deformities in rare cases. By then, your fate was dire. Psychosis was the fourth stage, and by that point, death was almost assured.

She had only ever heard of one Adept surviving the fourth stage—she had used her Art almost ceaselessly for days at a time, trapped far behind enemy lines. Adept Sharasthi, follower of the *Ars Tenebrae*, the Art of Shadows. She had seen for herself the haunted look Sharasthi still bore years later. And Sharasthi—by all accounts the most aether-soaked Adept known to the Corps—still wore a focus.

She needed it, just like the rest of them, to regulate the flow of aether, to stem the ocean of power to a mere trickle.

An Adept who performed magic without a focus died in seconds, minutes if they were strong. The human body—even with years of aetheric exposure and conditioning—was not capable of such a strong influx of energy. There was the odd pagan sorcerer who managed to harness a drop of aether, but they came nowhere close to the power of a genuine Adept. Channeling aether like an Adept did, you could get off one, maybe two techniques if you worked quickly. Then you would collapse, seize up. You would fall apart in mind, body, and soul, ravaged by the uncontrolled tide of mystical power rushing through you. Death came with inane babbling, a chewed-up tongue, and brutal spasms.

Vantelle tapped her desk, pulling Reiva from her grim musings. "You had something else."

Reiva swallowed. Now that the moment had come, she was even more hesitant about voicing this...but she could not turn back now. She had to speak, whatever the risk.

"The Wolf had an accusation toward you."

An arched eyebrow. "It must be an interesting accusation to merit you bringing it to my attention."

Already, Reiva felt heat creeping along the back of her neck.

"Yes, he...he said that you have a connection to the criminal Ego."

Earlier, when she had revealed the truth about her brother, Vantelle had looked shocked. Reiva expected something similar.

Instead, she got amusement.

"Oh, please go on." She propped her chin atop her palm, eyes sparkling. "I hope there was more to it than a wildly hurled suggestion like that."

Reiva flushed, but she pressed on, feeling more and more embarrassed with every word.

"The Wolf says that he had arranged the ambush intended to kill me with one of Ego's lackeys. Instead, he claims, Ego sold him out to the legion and gave us the information on the ambush so that we could capture him."

The praetor's expression had not changed.

"My praetor, it was you who first raised the matter of an informant who knew of the ambush. This informant delivered the Wolf into our hands."

Vantelle nodded. "Indeed, it was profoundly useful intelligence."

"Was that informant the man known as Ego? Or one of his men?"

Vantelle smiled softly, almost pityingly. "Reiva, I can tell you with absolute sincerity that I have never met Ego, nor have I collaborated with him in any way."

Reiva's gut relaxed a bit, and she nearly blew out a heavy sigh of relief.

"However, what this makes clear to me is that you are not in a right state of mind right now."

It was like a slap in the face.

"Since you learned your brother is the Wolf, you are under incredible duress. You have warring loyalties in your heart. You are uncertain."

"My praetor, I *swear* to you, I—"

Vantelle stayed her with a raised hand. "I am not accusing you of anything, Reiva. Nothing but being human. This sort of thing, after all, is why the Adept Corps forbids its acolytes from serving in the land of their birth. It is confusing. It tears you in two directions.

"You are a loyal servant of our Emperor. You are one of his children, as much as I am, and I trust you will be fully loyal to him all your life. But as an older sister to you, and as a fellow servant of the Palatine Throne, it is my duty to take you off any paths that may lead you to fall away."

Reiva couldn't believe what she was hearing. "Praetor Vantelle, I am nothing if I fail to uphold my oaths. If I have sworn something, I will adhere to that vow whatever it costs!"

'Promise me you'll watch over your brother.'

Her heart lurched, her throat closed.

'My life and blood for you, my Emperor.'

"I swore to..." She swallowed, pressing her lips together to stop their trembling.

Vantelle rose. "This is for the best, Reiva. I am taking you off any operations concerning the Wolf and his allies. You will continue to serve in logistical and military matters pertaining to the Loyalist cause, so long as you adhere to your oaths of service."

Operations concerning the Wolf.

"From now on," she continued, "I will personally oversee the matter of the Wolf's interrogation. I promise you, I will still endeavor to reach that cooperation you suggested so that I may justify a more lenient sentence for him."

"But I—"

"This is my word as praetor, Reiva. There is no discussion."

Her face felt hot. She feared her hands were shaking, so she closed them into fists. Fingernails dug into her palms.

"Yes, my praetor."

She felt hollow as she gave the salute.

"*Ave Imperator.*"

Vantelle set her hand on Reiva's shoulder. "*Ave Imperator*, Adept. Now go, take some time for yourself and be ready to deliver your findings at the meeting tonight. I would recommend you not mention the matter of your brother. It will be enough that they know I am handling the matter."

And then she gave a squeeze that should have been comforting. "This is a severe trial, Reiva, but it is not the first you have overcome. I selected you for this campaign because I saw your potential. And you have done nothing but exceeded it. Look at you—princeps, *Adepta Leona*, the living image of Imperial might."

Reiva nodded along. Once, these words would have meant everything to her.

"You know, there was a time when I intended to adopt Flavia... such a shame, such wasted opportunity. But you, Reiva? I know you will never fail me as she did. So I want you to know that when we return to Lazarra, after the triumphal procession, I intend to name you as my adopted daughter and heir."

Reiva's head spun. She was going to be sick. She was going to collapse. The world went gray and black and sideways.

Words tumbled out of her. "You do me too great an honor, my praetor. A terrible honor."

Vantelle smiled, and it was so warm a smile it burned. "A crown awaits in your future, Reiva."

Breathless, lightheaded. Her lips failed her, and so she could only bow.

As she made her way back to her quarters, her head rang with every step, and the words, those words etched into her brain for years, buried deep under edifices of ambitions and hopes and fears, those words continued to sound:

'*Promise me you'll watch over your brother.*'

68

AN UNRELIABLE ASSET

IT IS SAID that history turns on small things. A king sees a woman from across the banquet hall, and he breaks off his engagement to the princess of a neighboring land. A sudden gust of wind turns aside an assassin's dart, and a merchant lives long enough to forge a trade deal.

The historians, no doubt, will forget his name, so I set it down here: Zageth. It was Zageth who time and again proved himself the key to all of it. How strange, how terrifying, to consider that, if Vantelle had not turned away, she might have caught him in his lie. Where would we be then? History is built on fragile moments such as that.

—*The Memoirs of Flavia Iscator*

~

As SOON AS Reiva was gone, the door shut, Vantelle's smile dropped away.

Scowling, she looked down at the hand she had rested on the Adept's shoulder. Slowly, her fingers closed into a white-knuckled fist.

Cassia Vantelle was an individual without peer. The Emperor ruled all of Lazarra and the Dominion, and beneath him were the praetors and the Senate.

Everyone with eyes and a brain, however, knew that among all praetors, Vantelle stood head and shoulders above. Though her authority was equal to the others on paper, no one doubted that her will and influence were greatest.

No one doubted that the Emperor favored her to be his heir, and that when he passed on to the higher realm, she would be Empress of the world —a world she had played a significant role in conquering.

Talynis would be part of that world. This scrap of desert would bow and scrape if she had to break the knees of every sand-scrubbed buffoon she saw.

Lazarra would rule the world, that was certain. Already, nearly all the world this side of the Spine was either subservient or irrelevant—two centuries of blood had bought them that. Only Talynis remained truly defiant, and only Talynis contained a traversable route through the notorious peaks of the Spine. The Legion Scouts had tried crossing the mountains by climbing, tried sounding out some heretofore unknown passage. All had either died or come back in shambles. Vantelle had once visited the forward base for those operations—an expensive trip, a dangerous journey through the Gray Wastes. It was an impressive site—the epitome of legion efficiency and drive.

The Spine had defeated it.

With Talynis in hand, Lazarra would control the Endric Pass. Oh, the princes of Endra would surely resist their coming. Vantelle had plans to lead that war herself, carving her way into the land of strange songs and stranger gods.

Yes, there was ample cause to take Talynis. No one was surprised that Cassia Vantelle was spearheading the campaign here. It would be an essential move in the longstanding dream of dominion and civilization.

But it could all go to hell for what she really wanted.

What the Emperor really wanted was right here beneath the sands.

The only way the world would bow to Lazarra was if their gods bowed to Arkhon.

Aside from the Parthavans—an unusual exception finally subdued seven years ago—Talynis alone had survived the crippling strike, the blow that had stripped the nations of their mystical defenses. What the world knew as the Dark Days, those who had been initiated into the truth knew as the first steps toward domination. When Arkhon, endless-eyed spirit, had claimed the high throne over all gods and chosen the First Emperor, anointing him with the *Ars Prognoscens*, the Art of Foreknowledge.

With the power to glimpse the future, the Emperors and Empresses of Lazarra subdued the Ixian Reach, and they had launched an unprecedented conquest, bursting forth from the ashes of the lost Republic and toppling every other regime. Gallia fell. Hyrgallia. Even Karella, despite the formidable resistance of the Myrmidons and the Krypteia, eventually bowed.

With knowledge of political movements and intrigue, troop deployments, even a twist of fate as simple as a monarch's infidelity, the Imperial lords were a force unmatched.

But it came with a price.

The truth behind why Adepts could only come from beyond the borders and bloodlines of Lazarra. The Emperor alone could be made a Lazarran Adept. None but the highest in the Empire knew this. Only two or three praetors at a time, their closest advisors, and a handful of high-ranking senators had this knowledge, along with one or two of the most learned and trustworthy in the Sanctum.

Vantelle picked up the *Nihilo* Blade from her desk, running her finger along its length. This weapon had wounded her—ironic, since she had been the one to remove it from the Reliquary and had it smuggled into Talynis in the first place.

A part of her wondered if she should just have Zageth kill Reiva in the middle of the night. Or she could do it herself. The young woman had done so much for her, it might be the least sort of courtesy she could offer.

But no, that would be too extreme. Reiva's talent was exceptional. This business about her brother was a snag, of course, and no doubt it would be several years before Vantelle could ever reveal any of the truth to her...but Reiva would serve as a suitable heir. With time, she may even surpass her as a leader. She told the truth on that day Reiva had rejected her proposal—she always chose the right people. And she would manage this snag and right the course of history.

Yes, Reiva would be her daughter and successor. It would take quite a bit of finagling to pull off—both with the Senate and the Sanctum. The former would be resilient to the notion of an Adept on the Palatine Throne, but most could be bribed or strong-armed. The few who defied, she could handle in other ways. And as for the Sanctum, there *were* some records of how the old mages used to follow multiple arcane disciplines at once. That was impossible for modern Adepts, of course, given the way their powers functioned, but Arkhon could bypass that, Vantelle suspected. Even during Reiva's training, there had been talk of her exceptional attunement to the aether. If anyone could revive the ancient forms of magic, it would be her. Such an offer could sway even the most stolid on the Circle of Peers.

Yes, she could use Reiva, shape her into a worthy successor, a worthy Empress. She would need to handle this matter with her brother with great care, so as not to evoke any ill will. But Vantelle was nothing if not precise.

She had to be, in order to lead a seventh of the largest army in the world while also maintaining her network of contacts as Ego. Thankfully, she had Zageth to handle much of that.

And just as she was thinking that, he entered. When he saw her, he balked a bit. Even after years of working for her, even after the myriad of things he'd done in her service, he was still wary of her when she was angry.

That was good—it was how she could trust him to stay subservient.

"Developments?" she asked, still fingering the *Nihilo* Blade. Zageth never wasted her time; he had learned that lesson long ago. If he was here, he had something important.

"The Loyalists are reaching a fever pitch. Not everyone believes we captured the Wolf, but most are reacting with fury. I suspect there will be movement tonight, possibly a press against the district lines."

That was good. The more unrest there was, the more cover for their plans. They still needed to win in the end, but the state Dav-maiir was in when that happened didn't particularly matter.

Vantelle turned aside, inspecting the fine ebony edge of the relic, letting her mind turn over the dozen forces at play in all this. "What of that hostage you mentioned? The Scout?"

Zageth grunted. "A waste of time. Hardly could string a sentence together. She's floating in a cistern."

Vantelle hummed. "No loose ends."

"Never."

"Good. I want you to accelerate things. The Adept is an unreliable asset at the moment. She will stabilize with time, but I do not want to take any chances in the short term."

Now she finally looked at him. "The Wolf is her brother, and he has a connection to the Origin Spring."

Zageth's eyebrows shot up, and Vantelle took some satisfaction in seeing his reaction.

"The Sage killed in the ambush did not have a focus, as we anticipated. They've maintained the Binding."

Zageth's lips were moving, brow furrowed. He was working out logistics, estimating timespans. "How soon do we need the attack?"

"As soon as possible. You said you expected movement tonight? Tomorrow I want outright war. Blood painting the walls, flowing through the streets. I will wring the way to the Origin Spring from the Wolf if it kills him, and when the city screams with the agony of countless dead and dying..."

Zageth nodded. "We make their gods bow."

A smile cut across Vantelle's lips. "For Emperor and Eagle."

69

ONE BROWN, ONE BLUE

Much is made of the man who can walk in a straight line. But what happens when the road twists?
—Proverb among the Mithallkiym of Talynis

For hours, Avi sat, alone with the roiling storm in his heart.

He hated it all. Hated the Adept. Hated who she was. He hated his father for dying and leaving them. Hated his mother who had lied about his sister. He hated the world for conspiring against their family.

He hated himself for what he had said, but as he thought about it, he didn't think he would take it back.

Where had she been for him? All his life, scrounging for food, sleeping on the streets. Scraping by however he could to stay alive. All along, she had been living a life without want or need. She had been an elite in the Lazarran Empire. He had wrestled with his gods for the pain they sent him; she had left them behind and lived according to Lazarran decadence. He was sure she had—he could see it in her eyes.

If only he had stuck her with the relic—if only he had sucked away every last shred of magic and power from her body. That would have been a just end to her betrayal. That would have—

The door above opened.

The door shut.

Footsteps, the flickering light of a torch playing off the walls.

The visitor rounded the corner, and at first, the bright fire of the torch blinded him, but as she drew closer, he recognized who had come. The praetor. The one he had wounded, but failed to kill.

She had his sword on her hip.

The praetor fixed the torch in a brazier on the wall, then stepped closer. Avi held her gaze every bit of the way. He wasn't about to be cowed.

"If you think I'll talk, you're—"

She struck him across the face.

Reeling with the blow, Avi tasted blood.

"You'll talk when I say you can."

He spit a glob of red, mouth burning. For a moment, he feared he'd bitten his tongue off. It was all numb and painful at once.

"You know, now that Reiva told me, I can see the resemblance." She grabbed his face, leaning down so they were nearly eye-to-eye. "You have the same eyes. You scowl the way she does too."

Avi tried to spit, but she saw it coming. Her hand shot forward and clamped around his throat, choking him. He thrashed against her grip, but she only locked down tighter.

When he was seeing stars, as his head lolled, she let go.

Desperate, agonized, he sucked down a breath. Then he coughed, hacked, fought for another breath.

With a sinking feeling, he realized just how well she understood how to do this.

"She wanted to come talk to you again, you know. She wants to stop me from nailing you to a beam."

Avi did not consider himself a fearful man. He knew going up against the Empire meant that crucifixion was a very real possibility. But hearing that from a praetor, tied to a chair in a dark dungeon...

His spirit waned a bit, much as he tried to keep his defiant gaze.

"You look like a toddler," drawled Vantelle, "trying to keep your lip from quivering. Blinking back the tears. Thinking I'll believe you're as brave as you wish you were."

"I'll die for Talynis."

"Yes, I've already decided that." She rammed a fist into his gut, knocking the wind from him. "But I haven't decided you can speak yet. We're still warming up."

Sputtering like a fish, Avi slumped against his restraints. Vantelle grabbed his hair and yanked up his head, forcing him to look at her.

"You answer my questions, and I stop. I'll even let you die by hanging, or beheading if you're a particularly good boy. The more you resist me, the worse it gets. Understand?"

Avi grimaced. He was trembling, he realized. He couldn't will himself to stop. He looked at the praetor with unbridled anger and pain mixing in his eyes.

Silently, he nodded.

A wolfish grin appeared on her features. "The dog can learn. Good. Now, where is the tunnel that leads to the Convergence? How can I find the Origin Spring? You may speak."

Avi croaked, murmuring the words. "Don't know what—"

"Louder, dog."

"I don't know what you mean."

She flexed her grip, tearing hair from his scalp.

"I know the tunnels, some of them." he groaned. "I don't know what a Convergence is."

She eased her hold. "Below this city is the lifeblood of all Talynis. The source of all water in this desert, every oasis, every river."

"Just a myth," he huffed.

She lashed his head to the side—except this time she kept pulling, yanking, until Avi and the chair he was tied to tipped and crashed to the stones.

On impact, he yelped, shoulder lit on fire, one side of his face aching.

"Indulge me and pretend it's real. I know you have access to it—there is no other way you could have brought those Earth Adepts to fight for you."

At a different time, in different circumstances, Avi might have been able to keep a mask. As it was, however, as soon as things clicked in his mind, his face betrayed the revelation.

Vantelle smiled. "You know. Tell me."

"I don't—"

Her boot collided with his side. Something inside him *cracked,* and every breath set his lungs on fire.

"Let's try something else, hm?"

She kneeled, pulling the *Nihilo* Blade.

"It's a bit too big to be precise, but I'll try my best, hm? Now, I asked you for the tunnels. Which tunnels do you know?"

Avi took in the sinister gleam of the black blade. When he had held it, he had found it mesmerizing. Now it was a terror.

"I know how to get almost anywhere in the city. There are entrances all over the place if you know where to look."

"Good. And where should I go to find the Spring?"

Avi shook his head.

Vantelle shrugged, setting the tip of the blade to his groin.

He swallowed, his heart pounding.

He managed to hold his tongue until the edge parted the fabric and pierced skin.

"Beneath the headquarters!"

"Where?"

"A hidden door in the innermost chamber. I think you turn the second hook from the corner."

"You think."

"I never opened it myself."

"Mm, good to know; I don't need to keep you alive to serve as a guide then."

Avi screwed his eyes shut.

But then the blade pulled away.

He opened his eyes. The praetor hauled him upright again, dusting off his scraped cheek. "Now was that so hard?"

Avi said nothing, every breath quivering as he tried not to aggravate the fractured rib. At least, he hoped it was only fractured.

Vantelle let the *Nihilo* Blade drift toward his face. He flinched away from it. "Funny. I put this in your hand."

Despite himself, Avi recoiled and stared at her.

She was smiling in that predatory way again. "Yes, I retrieved this from the Imperial Reliquary and had it sent here. Just as I laid the trap for you, making you think you would finally kill your sister. Just as I fed you all the information that you used to win every meager victory you ever achieved in this gritty, sweltering excuse for a city."

Avi was gritting his teeth. His lungs still burned, but now he hardly noticed.

Vantelle touched the edge to his left cheek, the one spared in the fall. "How does it feel to know you managed nothing on your own?"

She drew the blade across his skin, slicing a stinging line. Leaning, she took his chin and forced him to look at her. "I've had this city on strings since the start. Everything you think you achieved, every victory you think you won—impossible, if not for me. And now it's all led to this. You, here, tied to a chair, bruised and sniveling. Me, standing over you, as is right."

Her tongue flicked out, lapping away the blood trickling down his cheek. His stomach twisted into a knot.

"I was born to step on small people like you. You were born to be crushed. Do you understand? So stop sitting there, looking so sad and depressed, would you? There's nothing sad about this—it's simply the way of things. A hundred years from now, everyone will understand that what I did for Lazarra was in the world's best interest. I bring enlightenment and civilization to all corners of the world. You were one of some hundreds of thousands of barbarians, ill fated by the gods to be born in the dirt. There's nothing personal about that. It's just the way the world is. When all is made right, when all is Empire, then people will know this and be glad. They will embrace it, and they will strive to have the power that is rightfully the strong's. The weak will know their place, and no longer will those like me have to dirty ourselves rolling in the muck with you.

"You are part of the making of peace, little dog. Can't you see that?"

Avi felt tears at the corners of his eyes.

In her face, he saw every enemy he'd ever faced. He saw the big cousin who used to fight him in front of all the other kids. He saw the girls who would tease him for not being manly when he tried to run.

He saw his mother, screaming and coming at him with a bronze pot still steaming from the water she'd just tossed at him. He saw the gangs that chased him off their turf. He saw the one that welcomed him, then tried to pin a theft on him.

He saw the rolling banner of the Ninth Imperial legion, unfurled and free in the wind, casting a shadow over the city gate, over the Temple of Four.

Every bully, every killer, every last threat and obstacle life had put in his way, he saw incarnated in the form of Cassia Vantelle.

But he didn't see a road or rooftop he could flee down. He didn't see an adult to run to for help.

He had always had a way out. Always had a plan. Always had *something* that could turn the tide and buy him another day of life.

He saw none of that here.

So he closed his eyes, so he didn't have to look anymore. So he could just hide in the darkness for a little while.

Vantelle sighed. "There there, little dog. It's almost over."

Kill me then.

But she let go, his chin dropping to hit his chest. He heard her take the torch and leave.

At some point, Avi started crying. He didn't know when. But he was in the dark, and much as he hated that, he was glad for it. He hated that he was alone here. At the same time, he was grateful no one could see him.

His thoughts turned to Asrah. The princess who was not his princess. His heart turned inside out. He would have given an arm to see her now, to feel her gentle touch on his bruises. To hear her murmur softly as she washed the blood away and dressed his wounds.

Every sob that racked him, his lungs burned. He wanted to stop crying. He wanted to cry forever.

He wanted to be nothing. To be a puff of dust on the desert winds, indistinguishable from every other handful of sand. He wanted to become a vague memory, a name spoken with approval, known for greater things than he ever truly accomplished. He could be nothing, and they could remember him for more than he was.

Because he *was* nothing. He had stripped away half his name. Born Aviqohl. 'My father is Qohl.' Then, only Avi. Avi and empty space where there should have been a sound. My father is nothing. Nothing begets nothing. *I am nothing.*

He felt as though he was sinking. He hoped it was so—that some maw had opened in the earth to devour this place, bury him forever. He did not open his eyes, so the fantasy could stay with him a little longer.

And in the silence of a dark and lonely dungeon, he hissed with agonized breath, "Why bring me here just to die?"

And heard no answer.

He stayed like that, alone in the dark, drifting on the tides of the mind. He opened his eyes and saw inky blackness. Strange shapes swirled at the fringes of his sight, but when he turned his head, the same empty void met him.

He sat there, hanging his head.

And then something changed. Looking back, he could not say when the change had occurred, only that it had. Something was different about the reality folded around him, like the ozone charge in the air as a storm gathered.

Footsteps—he heard footsteps. Not the heavy tread of an armored warrior, though. These footsteps were light, almost too soft to hear.

He turned to the door, and in came a man, and though darkness lay thick throughout the dungeon, the man appeared as though lit by a full moon.

"Who are you?" croaked Avi.

The stranger said nothing as he approached. He was dressed, Avi realized with a shock, in the garb of Mithallkiym, the desert Wanderers—wrapped in linens with a kerchief drawn across his face.

Avi looked up at him, and something fuzzed in his mind. The man had a face, Avi was sure of that. But he could not see it, not properly. He was peering through thick fog, barely catching the arch of an eyebrow here, the line of the cheekbone there.

The stranger bent down, coming almost nose-to-nose with Avi.

Again, Avi spoke, though scarcely in a whisper, his heart quivering in his chest. Whoever—*whatever*—this person was, something very deep within him, maybe the deepest part of him even, was utterly terrified.

"Who are you?"

And the stranger raised a single finger and tapped Avi's forehead.

In less than a heartbeat, the world changed.

The blinding light of day exploded into being. Avi found himself standing in the desert. No, not in the desert—right at the edge of the desert, at the place where the waters of the *maiir* reach furthest before dissipating.

A weak river, hardly more than a stream, trickled beside him. The sun beat down overhead, but Avi could not feel its heat.

And standing at his side—the stranger.

"Where are we?" asked Avi, voice trembling. But as soon as he'd asked, he realized he knew it—he was at the fringe of Shugrith, the *maiir* where he had been born and raised.

The stranger raised a hand and pointed to the south. Avi followed the gesture, squinting on instinct before he realized his eyes did not hurt despite the blazing brightness.

Far to the south, barely visible, was Shugrith itself, the city, built atop the oasis from which this little river was a meager outflow.

And something was coming. As it drew nearer, the blotchy shapes resolved into more familiar forms—camels bearing goods, camels bearing people, and lastly he saw people trailing behind the camels, their hands bound to leads.

Avi turned to the stranger, but he could not find the words he was looking for, the question he wanted to ask. The stranger showed him a hand sign, one Avi knew well, for the Vipers used it.

Watch, signed the stranger.

So he did. He watched as the caravan approached, coming close enough that Avi could hear the voice of the man riding the foremost camel. He was dressed in fine garments, and heavy rings were on his fingers. He was laughing about something.

Avi wanted to hide, but somehow he knew—just as he had known where he was—that they would not see him.

As they drew nearer, Avi saw that the lead binding the hands of the people trailing the caravan was not a rope, but a chain. In horror, he saw how cloth had been haphazardly wrapped around the manacles to prevent the metal from burning the prisoners' skin under the sun.

No, not prisoners. Who would bother to transport prisoners under the noonday sun?

The slaver called a halt, and Avi realized with a start that he had spoken in Zarushan, and he had understood it.

"Drink up!" he barked. "Won't get water like this for quite some time."

Again, Avi turned to the stranger, and this time he did not lack for words. "What are you showing me? It was night—when is it now?"

And again, the same sign. *Watch.*

So Avi did, and his stomach knotted. He watched as the caravan guards moved to take the chained slaves to the stream, and then the man called out, "Let 'em off this time. After all, where would they run?" He laughed again. Then, somewhat belatedly, he remarked to one of his men, one carrying a bow, "If any do, shoot them."

So the guards went from one to the next, unlocking the manacles and shoving the people toward the pathetic little stream. Many put their faces right into the water, only coming up to gasp for air. One drank too quickly and disgorged what he had drank back into the river—he went right back to drinking.

"There are Talynisti here," Avi murmured. "They are free on this soil—it is our law, handed down from the ancient fathers." He turned to the stranger. "You have power, don't you? Free them! Kill that man so they can go home."

And for the third time: *Watch.*

And this time, Avi was about to lash out, to grab hold of his garments, but he stopped cold.

A little girl stumbled from the chain, dressed in tatters, her hair tangled in clumps.

"This isn't real," whispered Avi. "This is a dream." He turned pleadingly to the stranger, and even though Avi still could not perceive his face, he sensed the recrimination directed at him.

His sister, his older sister become a little girl again, dropped to her knees beside the dusty waters. She bent low, cupping her hands to draw out water.

"Rebbaelah," he croaked.

She didn't hear him, staring at the particulate water in her hands, trickling through her fingers. She took a drink.

"Rebbaelah, it's me. It's your brother!"

Tears streaked through the dust on her face as she plunged her hands in for another drink.

"*Rebbaelah!*"

She gasped, her head snapping up.

Avi stared, awestruck—but then he realized she had no idea he was there at all.

A man had splashed through the stream, and every frantic step kicked up dust and dirt.

The slaver snorted. "There's always one." And then the man with the bow nocked an arrow, drew, and fired.

It took the man in the lower back. Likely a kidney wound, Avi thought. Excruciatingly painful. Slow to kill.

The man dropped to the ground, wailing. He tried to crawl.

The archer nocked and drew another arrow, but the slaver put up a hand. "No need to waste a second."

Slowly, the archer eased off the draw, his face impassive.

The man's cries echoed across the desert. He was cursing—by the Four Gods, he cursed the slaver and the hand that had drawn the bow. Avi recognized with a deep shudder that he was quoting lines from the Holy Poets.

"*May hands of fire break you over boulders,*

"*And feet of flame trod you in the press!*"

As he writhed in the dust, every eye was fixed on him, and no one moved. The slaver made a face like he'd eaten something sour, but he did not allow the archer to fire again, nor did he give the word for them to move on.

Avi turned to his sister. She had seen this?

Rebbaelah looked around, and something dropped inside of Avi. She wasn't going to run, was she?

She's alive today, fool. She can't die here...

But then what was going through her mind?

Her hand plunged into the stream, and closed her fingers around a rock, withdrawing it with a white-knuckle grip.

She looked around again.

All eyes were on the dying man.

Her mouth curled into a horrible rictus snarl. For a harrowing moment, Avi thought she was about to attack the nearest guard with her rugged little rock.

He didn't even have time for his heart to lurch when she held it high and brought it down on her own temple.

Or, she would have, if the stranger's hand had not closed around her wrist.

"Rebbaelah," said the stranger. "You are not to die today."

And she saw him—plain as the sand or the stream, she could see him, kneeling beside her at the waterside.

The rock fell from her grasp, and soon as it struck the earth, the sun vanished.

Restraints closed around Avi's body. Slick, sweat-drenched clothes hung on his frame. His wounds stung.

He was in darkness again.

And the stranger was standing before him.

"What happened? Tell me what happened! What happened to my sister?!"

Soon as the words left his lips, something cleared. No longer was he peering through a haze.

The stranger looked back at him with mismatched eyes. One brown, one blue. And he said, "You know."

And as Avi opened his mouth to speak again, he saw he was alone.

70

NO VIRTUE MORE ESTEEMED

WARS ARE WAGED by soldiers and spies and supply trains, yes. But often victory comes to the one who forgets not the 'small people.' History bears witness to us of the battle turned by a shepherd who knew the back road, or the prostitute who lay with the general.

Who was thinking in Talynis of the small people? Who had the humility to think how they might turn the tide?

—*The Memoirs of Flavia Iscator*

~

ALL NIGHT, Reiva tossed and turned. She got up, paced the room. She sat down and meditated. She went through her aether drills and exercises. Everything designed to carefully regulate an Adept's spiritual state so she could find enough peace to rest.

Rest never came. In fits, she slipped into unconsciousness, only to wake again right away. Had an hour passed just then? Ten minutes?

When the dawn arrived, she was scoured mentally, everything reaching her through a layer of fog. A jitter had set into her nerves, and at the slightest sound she whipped her head around.

Getting dressed, she hardly paid attention to whether she was tying off that cord right, affixing the insignia properly. When she slung her sword belt on, it hung loose at her hips, pulled half-taut as she walked out the door.

She was supposed to go first to an officer's meeting. She would be late, if she made it at all. Her first priority was seeing her brother.

But when she got to the dungeon, the two *triarii* on guard stopped her. Nothing—not her rank, not her title, not even the threat of disciplinary action was enough to get them to uncross their spears.

"On orders of the praetor, Adept," said the one on the left, apologetically. And perhaps a bit fearfully.

Reiva pinched the bridge of her nose. "Of course," she managed. "My apologies for troubling you."

As she left, she felt their nervous eyes on her. These were hardened men of the Ninth, and she had just badgered them to defy their orders and let her see a high-value prisoner.

What was happening to her? She had been the picture of legion discipline...

After Alyat had molded her, that was. Had convinced her that following the rules and sticking to the codes was the best way to go about things.

Was this the real her then, finally exposed after years under the surface? Snapping at soldiers under her command? Trying to go behind her superior's back and contravene a direct order?

As she made her way to the officer's meeting, she realized she was getting odd looks. Scowling, she adjusted her attire as best she could—properly fastening the sword belt, smoothing out the wrinkles, retying her hair.

She couldn't be sure how she looked, but either way, she was sure Vantelle would notice the state she was in. That had been a foregone conclusion. That woman could have probably just looked into her eyes and read the sleepless night of a troubled mind.

All the while, in the back of her skull, echoed the constant refrain from her dying father.

'Promise me.'

"Well, we can't keep all our promises," she said under her breath, turning a corner.

She was late for the meeting. No one seemed to mind; she was a Lion, a princeps, an ascendant star who had just brought in the enemy's peak agent. Surely she would have been up to something important.

All except Vantelle, who ran her eyes over Reiva with her typical analytical gaze. Her face was a mask; she was good at wearing masks. She had total control over everything at all times.

She also had bruises on her knuckles.

Reiva stared at the praetor's fists while a prefect gave a report on some attacks that had occurred during the night. She realized at one point that

Vantelle was looking right at her. At that point, she finally tore her eyes away. But she didn't hear another word of the meeting. All she could think of was Stag getting executed right in front of her, with so casual an order from Vantelle.

Her brother, she was sure, was alive. He had to be. The guards were in place. She had struck him, but he was alive.

When bigger kids hit him, she used to tell him to hit back. If they were much bigger, then she would go to fight for him sometimes. They never wanted to fight a girl, and afterwards, they wished they hadn't.

Now this was happening for her nation. Her Empire. There was no bigger kid—there was one of the most powerful people in the world, someone with the Emperor of Lazarra's ear.

Why couldn't he have just handed over the information she wanted?

If he even had it. If she didn't strike him anyway.

As soon as the meeting was over, Reiva was on her feet and on the move. Vantelle didn't hold her back. Reiva wasn't sure whether she was glad for that.

Today she was supposed to be overseeing defensive efforts along the district lines. Last night, the Loyalists had made some headway in pushing back the Ninth and the Revolutionary Guard. Some men had been pulled from the line to run another inspection and investigation of the Viper's headquarters. Apparently, the Wolf had clued that there may be something hidden there.

She was half-considering going there herself (who would stop her?) when a hand touched her elbow.

Jerking to a halt, she turned on the person.

To call her a woman might have been overstating things, though in Talynis most had to grow up quick. A servant girl two hands shorter than Reiva, she was clutching laundry in her arms, and she looked like she'd seen a devil.

"Forgive me for touching you, Adept. I tried to say something, but you didn't..."

Reiva frowned, waving it off. "That's fine, what is it?"

"Would you...?" Awkwardly, she indicated they move out of this central hallway.

Bemused and half-expecting the girl to try to stab her, Reiva followed, not even sure why she was indulging this. *This had better be something meaningful, not just some nonsense about—*

"I have a message for you."

Reiva blinked. "Who sent you?"

The girl shook her head. "All I know is that someone is waiting for you at the stables with the farrier. That's all I was told, I swear it."

She was pale, eyes wide and darting.

She was truthful, truthful and terrified.

Reiva got the same feeling as when she'd been pressing the *triarii* not an hour ago. But those had been war-hardened soldiers with armor and weaponry.

This was a girl, practically, with nothing but some linens and commitment to a cause.

Reiva could have killed her right then. She was a Loyalist collaborator, that was obvious. Reiva had the authority. Or she could have had her hauled before Intelligence to undergo questioning. She thought of Vantelle's bruised knuckles.

How much courage did it take, Reiva wondered, to face down an Imperial Adept, a woman who could throw fire from her fingers, in the beating heart of legion power? In hallways traversed by the highest-ranking officials in the Ninth, save the conspicuously absent Flavia Iscator?

"Go on," muttered Reiva. "And be careful."

As the young woman slipped off, tension in every muscle, Reiva felt that tension in her gut turn for the worse. It wasn't just discomfort anymore—it was revulsion.

There was no virtue more esteemed in the Lazarran legions than courage. Bravery. The willingness to face down an enemy who had every chance of slaughtering you. The heart to look fear and death in the eyes.

She used to aspire to that.

When had she become the person others had to stand up to?

71

IN ONE VOICE, THE PEOPLE ROARED

Go to war, my son, and do not e'er return,
Lest victory you've won, or to ashes you were burned.
—A Lakodonian mother's words of parting, later taken up throughout Karella

Artunis had never seen such a flurry of activity. Even the day they had seized the garrison, the energy in the city had been frantic and fearful, but this—this was confident. It was brazen. It was determined to win or meet its end trying.

She had hoped that today would put an end to the occupation. She believed they could do this.

Zageth—the bastard—had sent word that the Wolf was to be executed soon. Vantelle had nearly expended her need of him. And though he would not explain exactly what that meant, he had been insistent that if things did not end today, the Loyalist cause was good as finished.

Whose side he was on, Artunis had not the faintest clue—but it didn't matter, because the end had already been prepared for today, and no word from him could have hastened or delayed it.

Artunis buckled a leather breastplate on, double checking the straps and testing the laces on her boots. It was almost startling how quickly she was adapting to having but one hand, and she found herself grateful for Crow's training long ago. She had never worn this much armor before, but today was a day for breaking new ground. She even had a full-sized shield, strange as that was for her. Doubly strange given that it was strapped to her right arm, and she would fight with her left.

Mouse wore his usual loose, open attire. He seemed to carry no anxiety on the matter of setting Charas free. He'd even insisted they put one of their moles inside the palace at her disposal. Jackal still didn't have half a clue as to exactly what he thought she was, but he'd been certain she would serve them better on the loose than dead in a gutter. And his magic could supposedly discern her honesty when she swore not to fight against them today.

Too late to second guess any of that now. Focus on the battle.

When she asked if he feared getting hurt in the melee, he only smiled.

"Too restrictive. Besides, in my culture, a warrior has two duties: fight with honor, die with honor. So long as I achieve this, I will be pleased with myself, and my true self shall receive its due reward."

Artunis wasn't particularly familiar with the philosophies and religions of Endra, but she felt peace radiating from the big man. "Just don't go getting yourself killed if you can help it, all right? Some of us would prefer you put off that destiny as long as you can."

He laughed a rich laugh. "My wife would say the same, I am sure."

She blinked.

"You didn't think I had no one back home, did you?"

"I don't even know your name, so I can't say."

Mouse chuckled, adjusting his headdress. "Arjun," he said.

She turned, eyes wide. "What?"

"Arjun." He patted his chest. "That is who I am."

She nodded, awestruck. "Artunis." It sounded foreign on her tongue, like she was talking about someone else. "Ha, what are the odds? They're so similar."

Mouse—Arjun—smiled toothily. "May the Great One watch over you, Artunis."

She dipped her head. "You as well, Arjun. I don't care if all that matters is fighting and dying with honor—you get yourself back to your family or I'll find you in the afterlife and throttle you."

He laughed. "Just because I am at peace with death does not mean I intend to meet it today."

Most of the Loyalists wore gear scavenged from the garrison or from watch points they had stormed and seized in the night. To distinguish themselves from the legionnaires, they splashed their heads and helmets with black tar.

An elder woman had made up a new banner, bearing the sigil of the Talynisti king—an olive tree inscribed by four stars. This was raised on as tall a spear as could be found, and would be carried to the palace gates.

There would be no negotiations under that banner. No parley, no discussion.

This was a fight for the city, and the outcome of the day would decide everything.

The entire western half of the city, by now, was on their side. Even Revolution-allied aristocrats, when surrounded by Loyalists, had turned. Whether or not they liked Malik, they weren't very confident in Tamiq's chance of holding onto the throne. That gave Artunis some hope, but she couldn't let herself get overconfident about this.

Even with their sheer force of number, the legion was still fighting defensively. That gave them an advantage, and the palace was nigh impregnable.

Thankfully, they had a man who could move stone.

Bebar had taken the death of his twin severely. To say he wore his grief did it a disservice—every ounce of his frame seemed to buzz with barely constrained power, as if a thread might snap and set the whole world rumbling. Artunis asked him if he would be ready. He looked into her eyes, and she saw refined anger blazing. With a single nod, he gave his answer.

While the siege occupied the palace guard and the legion, the Sage would tear open a path, moving through earth and rock and masonry. Mouse and a group of other more experienced fighters would make a mad rush directly for the throne room.

It was a suicide mission, but with Bebar, and with the element of surprise...

The one wrinkle was that the Sage would not kill any Talynisti. It was part of his creed, apparently. He would kill any legionnaire they saw, but he would not kill the king or any of his soldiers.

That was fine—maybe she would get to end this with her own hand.

But, she wondered, *what if he comes across the Adept? Will he count her life as forfeit?*

As final preparations were made, as last prayers were being said, as farewell embraces and kisses were given—Artunis let her mind move over everyone who they had lost.

A restless energy rolled through the people. The moment would come soon—the moment they would step into the streets and fight life and limb.

Mouse nudged her. "You should say something."

She gaped at him, feeling the color drain from her face. "That—that's not what I do."

"Trust me, they'll like it." He added a wink. "I can guarantee that."

Artunis swallowed, a sour knot of dread forming in her gut. Magic or no, she felt more comfortable fighting one-handed than addressing a crowd.

As a girl, she'd trained as a dancer. She had even performed with her older cousins once or twice. She had enjoyed that. She had enjoyed speaking without words, reciting a poetry whose rhymes were motion and balance.

That had been taken from her. *Everything* had been taken from her. And one thing had led to another, and now she was here.

And Mouse had a point—she had to say something. Besides, by now they all knew who she was. They didn't even care, as far as she was aware, that she was Zarushan born.

The Endric man nodded toward a stack of crates. "Well?"

Pressing her lips together, she nodded, scampering up to stand over the throng.

Then, for a moment, she froze. How was she supposed to get their attention? Whistle? Yell? Wave her sword around?

Mouse took care of that for her, bellowing a call to attention. Hundreds of faces turned, conversations died away.

Standing above all those faces, knowing that many more were in wait throughout the city...it was impossible not to feel nervous.

But that was all right. Nerves meant you were alive. They meant your body and soul were girding themselves to perform beyond their natural limits. This was the place where the torch burned brighter, pushing back the dark curtain to reveal unknown land.

Today would be a day songs were written of. Historians would remember what was about to take place, for good or ill.

She opened her mouth.

And nothing came out.

She swallowed again, her throat feeling impossibly dry.

An uneasy ripple moved through the crowd. Artunis felt the urge to hide. Her knees felt weak—were they shaking? Did she look terrified?

But then a calming pulse coursed through her. Her breathing evened. She caught a wave rolling through the crowd—the irresistible sense of importance, solemnity.

Thank you, Mouse.

She took another breath.

Just like dancing. One step, then the next.

"Many have died for this."

The crowd's silence deepened.

"Many who fought for us. Who lent us their arms in battle, risking their bodies and blood to slay the foe."

Wolf.

"Many who lent their brilliance to our cause, staying awake on long vigils through the night to outwit the predators stalking our streets."

Crow.

"Many who lent their wealth when we had need for food, shelter, equipment."

Stag.

"And many have died whose names we may never know. Many lie in gutters and shallow graves, some even burned to ash, others suspended in the air by the cursed hooks of the Imperials."

Now the crowd stirred. Murmurs rippled through them. Heads were shaking. Angry oaths were going up to the sky.

Artunis raised her voice.

"Today is where we prove that every last sacrifice made—every family that has lost a father, every home that has been smashed to rubble—that every last measure of pain and drop of suffering *means* something. That the people of Dav-maiir are not about to be cowed. That you will not bow knee and head to clanking foreigners who know nothing of honor."

A shout went up.

"That you will not abandon your faith in the Four on High to follow some unknown god from a far-flung coastline."

Another shout, louder.

"That you will fight and die for your true king, for your true gods, for your true country!"

They were roaring now, fists and swords in the air.

"This is the end, Talynis! Many have died for this. Will you run and cower, or will you bleed and die with them?"

In one voice, the people roared, "*Death!*"

"Then to death we go!"

So thick was the air with cheers and the clamor of swords on shields, fists on chests, that Artunis would not have been surprised if they heard it all the way in the palace.

She hoped they had.

72

SINKING FURTHER AND FURTHER

IF THERE IS one story I have found the world over, it is that of the descent into death. There is even a name for it in Karella, the *katabasis*. What is burned into our collective imagination that time and again in such diverse places, we ponder this harrowing, hellish journey?
—*The Life and Wisdom of Simeon Binkhok As Told by Himself*

THE ROYAL STABLES were not far from the palace. Reiva and Yaros made their way there with but a few minutes' walk. The horses there were the property of the king—save a few that came from the fallen garrison—but now the Ninth Legion's horsemaster had taken control of the stables.

The grooms were ready and willing to point them to the farrier, assuming Reiva was here to claim a mount. As soon as the man himself saw her, however, his eyes widened a bit. "You simply must see this, Adept," he said in a carefree tone. "Some of the most magnificent horseflesh I have ever seen. I suspect Zarushan ancestry, but the build suggests not a small degree of..."

He went on babbling like that, and for all Reiva knew he really was talking about a horse that resided here in the stables. His name, he mentioned, was Sacaro. He had worked with Legate Iscator for many years, across many campaigns. She wondered if that signaled something about how he evaluated Vantelle as a leader.

The stable he took them to was rather sizable, even grand; there were guards around—Talynisti men. They did not seem particularly happy to see Sacaro, but he was in charge, so they let the three of them through. Reiva wondered in passing what had happened to the king's horsemaster, to which Sacaro could only shrug. "Skipped town a while ago, so I hear. They've been without proper leadership for some time. These poor horses—some of them looked like they hadn't been brushed in..."

Again, she tuned him out, swimming in curiosity as to what this message was. Yaros had, of course, brought up the possibility that this was a trap, but if it was, it was a strange one. In enclosed spaces, Reiva practically had a radius of instant death should she unleash her magic.

Sacaro produced yet another key. "Here we are—my apologies for the long walk, but some things must be specially guarded."

Reiva entered and saw Charas. The Parthavan woman was sitting with her back to the wall, fishing straw out of a trough and tossing it to a majestic mare, who cantered around a small, private field.

What kind of horse got its own enclosed field?

Well, a king's horse.

When she saw them, the Scout smiled faintly. "I'll be damned," she said. "Thought I'd waste away here."

Reiva gaped. Sacaro was beaming. Yaros just shook his head with a wry grin. "Should've put money on you surviving."

Charas snorted. "I should go gambling when all this is done, luck I've had."

"Why are you here?" Reiva gestured to the stable. Charas looked like she'd been through hell. She didn't have any obvious wounds aside from a bruise on her cheek, but from the fatigue in her features, Reiva guessed her last few days had been anything but pleasant. "Were you captured by Loyalists?"

Charas scowled. "If that was it, I would've come right back. Thank my ancestors I could trust at least one person here." Sacaro half-bowed at the comment.

Yaros frowned. He put things together a moment before it clicked for Reiva. "Someone inside the legion took you. Or handed you over."

Charas nodded wearily. Reiva felt her headache coming back on.

The Parthavan recounted the night of her disappearance. How she had seen Zageth meeting with the Wolf and the Jackal, how Zageth caught and interrogated her, then eventually released her back to the Loyalists after the Wolf's capture.

"And you escaped then?" asked Reiva.

Charas threw her hands up. "They let me go."

Everyone stared, except Sacaro, who had apparently heard this whole story already.

"Why on earth would they—?"

"It's a long story," she sighed. "The tall Endric man with two swords? He's an Adept."

Reiva went stiff. She had suspected as much on the day of the Bazaar attack, but now it was confirmed. Pressing her palms into her eyes, she huffed. "Just how many Adepts can one city fit? He was *Ars Psykana*, yes?"

"If that means he can read minds."

Yaros made a choking sound as Reiva blurted out, "*What*?"

That was not something she had ever heard an Adept of Mind could do.

Then again, the reports of the rogue Adepts' handiwork in the garrison also defied what Reiva knew about the *Ars Terra*...

Charas slapped the ground. "I'm dead serious. He went into my head and saw that I was telling the truth about Zageth. They thought Zageth was just a mole inside the legion for someone named Ego, but once their plan got turned on its head and you captured the Wolf..."

Reiva had that too-familiar sinking feeling. "And you were able to tell them Zageth is Vantelle's optio..."

"They realized Ego is working with Vantelle," finished Yaros.

"Or *is* Vantelle," said Charas.

"That seems a bit much," protested Reiva. It was a weak protest, though.

"No, wait," muttered Yaros, "think about it. Somehow, the Loyalists get ahold of a *Nihilo* Blade—something that even among relics is almost impossible to find. They're almost always one step ahead, and even when we catch them off-guard, we're knocked back on our heels before long. We suspected there was a spy but—"

Reiva put up her hands. "We can talk details later. Right now, we need a plan. We can't just hide in this stable forever."

Charas shrugged, tossing some hay toward the horse. "Well, *I* can, but I'd rather not stay too long."

Yaros crossed his arms. "Are you well enough to ride?"

Charas looked insulted.

He turned to Reiva. "The city is about to fall one way or the other. Odds are, your brother won't be in a good spot once that happens."

The knot in her throat closed even tighter. She knew that.

Charas blinked. "Excuse me, brother? The brother from your story in the tavern?"

Reiva clenched her fists. "He's the Wolf."

Charas swore in a manner Reiva had only heard from sailors.

She nodded, her mind going back to the bruises on Vantelle's fists.

She closed her eyes. The words she needed to say were right on her tongue, but she knew once she said them, there would be no going back.

But she didn't have time. Death could come at any moment; the world could change like the weather. Alyat had been on the verge of something massive before he was killed. Something that terrified him.

Vantelle was also onto something massive, something involving her brother. Something that had to do with Adepts who could bend aether to their will without wearing a focus.

"We're leaving." She almost whispered it. "We're leaving. We take some horses and go."

Charas looked skeptical. Yaros looked like an excited child. "Been a while since I last made a hasty getaway under pain of death." He rubbed his hands together. "Who gets the royal steed over there?"

Sacaro frowned. "I am hearing none of this, of course, but I would sooner die than let a Karellan ride this beauty when a Parthavan is but ten feet away."

Charas looked triumphant; Yaros seemed about to pout.

Reiva knuckled her forehead. "Can we do this later? My brother is still under guard, and I'm not going to leave him behind."

As soon as the words were out, a weight dropped off her shoulders, and the echo in her head went quiet. Her head spun, like it had been off-kilter and set aright.

I'm going to look after him, she thought, as though it was a surprise someone else had sprung on her.

She suddenly felt a stinging heat behind her eyes. Surreptitiously, she wiped at her eyes, trying to make it look like she was just tired. If anyone noticed, they said nothing of it.

Yaros scratched his chin. "I found some places outside the city. Not anything that could last for long, but at the very least it could hide us for a while."

Charas held her hands up. "Fine and dandy, but where are we *going*? Most the world this side of the Spine would either kill us or truss us up and toss us at the praetor's feet, reward or no."

"We're not fleeing the Empire," Reiva said, resolute. "We're not traitors. *Vantelle* is the traitor. Whether she's working with Ego, whether she *is* Ego... whatever's going on, she has to answer for this. I can take this to the Circle of Peers in the Sanctum. Even a praetor can't touch us if we have the protection of the Adept Corps. It would take a direct order from the Emperor to get to us."

An unspoken terror scratched at the back of her consciousness.

And what if she isn't acting as a rogue agent? What if this is sanctioned?

What if Alyat's murder was sanctioned?

The possibilities and implications behind that...she shoved them out of her mind. That was too much. Cassia Vantelle was the enemy here. They would see justice done, and the world would be right again.

She might have to leave her brother somewhere else, of course, since he was still an enemy agent, but she could deal with the logistics of that later.

Sacaro was stroking the neck of the mare. "Again, I'm not hearing any of this, but if I was, I would suggest you take this lovely girl with you. My life would greatly lack if I were to never see her again."

Charas raised her eyebrows. "That wouldn't reflect particularly well on you, if we were to get away with her."

"So tie me up, hit me on the head. Surely you've done things like that before." He shrugged as if he were merely discussing dinner plans. "I've fought in wars too, you know. I didn't spend my whole life with a brush and food pail in my hands."

Charas seemed amused. "I guess not."

Yaros clapped his hands. "Settled then? We're doing this?"

Reiva nodded. As did Charas.

"So how do we break your brother out?"

Reiva had been racking her brain on the matter. "Tonight, perhaps, I can go in and get him. Either way, I'll need to get through his guards; seems best to do so when the guard inside the palace is lightest."

Yaros nodded. "Then I meet you tonight to spring him, and we come here to escape together—horses and all."

Her head was whirling. She felt like she did right before the front lines of two armies crashed together. A pit of fear, but also a rush of adrenaline. This was the moment warriors lived for, Alyat had taught her, the moment when skill and challenge met together in a maelstrom.

She would do this. For her brother, for her father. For Lazarra—the true Lazarra, that had taken her in and raised her, giving powers incomprehensible to a little girl from Talynis.

She would do this.

"Then, Charas, you stay here and get ready however you need."

"I'm fine with that," she said, stretching out her legs. "But I do have some personal effects I'd rather not lose, assuming my belongings haven't been ransacked yet."

"The quartermaster would have taken them in."

"I'll handle that," said Yaros. "What do you need in particular?"

Charas got a strange look, almost bashful. "It's...a small carving of a horse. It's religious, you could say."

"If that's all, should be easy."

"My bow and arrows, of course."

"Goes without saying, doesn't it?"

Reiva let out a breath. "All right, then all that's left to do is make it through the day."

Sacaro pointed across the field toward the distant wall. "Right around there is a secret passage, big enough to ride horses through. I'd imagine kings have used it to escape the city in the past."

"It will take us outside the gates?" asked Yaros.

"Not quite, but it will place you near the eastern gate."

"That's probably the least secured gate in the city right now," mused the mercenary. "Should work. I'll go take a look now."

Reiva felt like she was looking over a great drop. As soon as she stepped outside, she would be acting against the interests of a standing praetor of the Empire. Every legionnaire she saw would be an enemy to her, even though they wouldn't know it.

"Well," she said slowly, "I guess there's nothing else to do but put the plan into action. Gods send that it survives first contact."

Yaros snorted. "What plan does?"

～

REIVA LEFT the stables by herself. Charas was conferring with Sacaro about which horses they should take while Yaros inspected the secret exit so he would be ready to lead them out when the time came.

When did he manage to find hideaways, anyway?

Then again, he had come from the Krypteia. Maybe she should have been more surprised if he had not.

Her plan was to collect a few minor things from her quarters—Alyat's letters, especially—and then go about the rest of her business as normal. That could entail fighting if the Loyalists made a move today. She very well might need to talk her way past some officers inquiring about why she was still moving around the palace despite her standing order from Vantelle.

She could deal with that. If she were to meet Vantelle herself, though...

She continued to be haunted by the chance that this wasn't all Vantelle acting on her own. That this really was something bigger, something the Empire willed.

The praetor had told Reiva that she was in Talynis for something of great interest to the Emperor...

She could only hope the Emperor was not as enlightened as to Vantelle's motives and methods as the woman had implied. She had been deceptive for who knows how long about her connection to Ego. She had been engaging in traitorous activity, sedition practically.

No, Reiva had to trust that the Empire was still intact. That she could set things right by going to the Sanctum. Alyat's murder, Vantelle's scheming— all of it would come to light, and then the world would straighten back out.

Shouts pulled Reiva from her thoughts. Shouts were not uncommon in the city, especially recently, but Reiva had been a soldier for years. She knew the difference between yelling about business or some personal dispute and crying out for murder.

This was the latter.

Her sword was already coming out of its sheath, feet pounding the stones. The clash of metal reached her. Keening voices, Lazarran and Talynisti alike wailing for aid, for blood, for mercy and for mothers.

The streets were a battleground, centered around the palace.

The Loyalists were a swarming mass, and what they lacked in formal tactics and discipline, they more than made up for with fury and numbers.

They were coming along the roads from the west and south—both the garrison and the Temple must have poured forth their fighters, and doubtless more were rising up from houses and businesses across the city, joining the fray.

Legionnaires organized quickly, and already they had formed a line— but there were only so many of them. While they held the line, Loyalists scrambled over rooftops, raining down rocks, spears. Some launched themselves down directly into the legion forces, who were sweeping their blades with lethal effect in the melee.

In a blink, Reiva took it all in—and she threw herself into the fray.

The road from the stables came toward the palace from the east, so Reiva was behind the legionnaires. Rushing forward, she channeled aether to her legs and with a single forceful bound, leaped high into the air and set her feet on a rooftop.

Before her were three Loyalists, all gaping at her sudden appearance and gnashing with fury to bring her down.

She threw a blistering wave of fire, dropping them all in a sizzling, screaming mess.

As they screamed, she thought she saw bruises on her hands.

The sight was gone in an instant, but it jarred her, threw her off balance.

I am loyal to the Empire. These are still enemies.

A stone whizzed by her head, and she threw herself to the ground. A few inches to the right, and her skull would have been caved in.

But she wasn't one to stay down—that wasn't how Adepts were made.

Rolling and springing to her feet, Reiva left her sword behind and threw both hands out in a fanning motion. A wide sweeping plume of fire broiled over the Loyalist horde. A move like that could have scorched thirty men, bunched up as they were.

But her father's face had flickered through her mind, and at the last second, she had pulled up, letting the flames lick overhead.

The Loyalists were still shaken by the display, though. Seizing the moment, the legionnaires pushed forward, carving a wedge into the enemy ranks. Reiva retrieved her sword, shouting orders for the legionnaires to hold the line and withdraw to the nearest choke point if needed.

She didn't wait to check that some officer in the mix would carry out her orders—they would. They were Lazarran legionnaires.

As she dashed for the palace at breakneck pace, she infused her legs again with aether. The palace guard was forming defensive lines, though most of them would be within the gates.

Not all the streets had held as well as the one she'd just come from. The Loyalists had just about reached the palace.

Reiva's mind raced. The tactical choice would likely be to pull everyone inside the gates, then hold out. But that didn't account for—

An earth-shaking *crack* split the air.

Reiva whirled on the source of the noise.

She couldn't see it, but she knew what had happened.

The rogue Adept had just broken through the palace wall.

Reiva made another running start. She sent so much aether into her legs that her skin rippled with goosebumps, every muscle tingling.

It had been a long time since she made a jump like this.

Throwing in all her concentration and might, she rocketed through the air, clearing the walls of the palace grounds. Talynisti guards along the parapet stared in utter shock as she soared over their heads.

Dropping into a roll as she hit the ground, enforcing her body with aether to dampen the impact, she broke out into another run. As she went, she shouted as loud as she could, "They're inside the walls!"

She tore across the grounds, crossing the southern length of the green in moments. Soon as she reached the western wall, she found that the palace guards and legionnaires here had already learned firsthand about the intruders.

Half a dozen legionnaires were dead, another dozen grievously wounded. The Adept of Earth was a force of utter destruction, hammering legionnaires with spires of earth, with boulders ripped from the ground, with whirling storms of dirt and gravel.

She recognized the Jackal among the Loyalists here. She cut down a palace guard, then blocked another's sword on her shield.

It was surreal, as it had been the last time, seeing a woman outside the legions on the battlefield. She wondered for a second if she might have found herself fighting alongside the Loyalists on this day, had she never been taken to Lazarra.

The thought flashed through her mind and was dismissed.

Life could turn out any number of ways—there was no sense in dwelling on what might have been. All she could do was strive to make her way in the particular strain of destiny afforded to her.

And Reiva knew well how to make her way.

First, she threw a wall of fire along the grass. It would leave an ugly scar when all was said and done, but she put her will behind it to keep it from burning toward the palace itself. It would act as a barrier for the attackers, funneling them right toward Reiva.

She locked eyes with the rogue Adept.

Reiva had seen hate before—but this was enmity stoked by crucible to its whitest heat. And she had also seen this man's face before, she realized. It was the same as the face of the man Yaros had decapitated when they sprang their trap.

Brothers, then.

Aviqohl's face flickered in her mind's eye, interposing itself over his.

A pang of guilt racked her heart. She threw that guilt into her Flame.

Reiva wreathed both hands in bright-red fire.

All around, Loyalists were locked in combat with Reiva's soldiers. It might as well have been a war between insects around them, for the two arcane warriors had eyes only for one another.

He spoke first, his voice harsh. "Today a Desert Sage shall make justice against your sins, wicked one. Today you die, and the world is set right."

Reiva narrowed her eyes. "If only it was that easy."

The Sage made the first move, driving a spear of rock from the ground straight for her chest.

Reiva ducked around it, answering with two quick blasts of fire, then a broad wave.

In an instant, the Sage built up a cocoon of earth, her flames washing over it harmlessly. The cocoon burst apart into a hundred projectiles, each whistling through the air.

Reiva threw herself down, casting a dense plume of fire forward.

As their two magics met, the aether in the environment charged with sudden intensity, almost as if the fabric of the world trembled at their conflict.

The Sage's missiles struck many of her fighters, but some got through the volley, ducking behind shields or diving for the dirt.

Already, Reiva was back on her feet, kicking out to sweep a burning lash along the ground. Again, the Sage pulled up a protective wall, this time only knee height, to block. Seamlessly, he transitioned from that movement into an outward push, sending the wall of stone out like a ripple along the surface of a lake.

Reiva jumped over it, throwing more blasts as she cleared the barrier. From the crashing and the screams behind her, she guessed that not everyone had been so fast.

Only a few times in her life had Reiva ever felt such concentration, such *thrill*.

Adepts were a force of nature—and it was a rare privilege for two to ever meet on the field of battle. But *this*, this was beyond even that. She had trained alongside *Ars Terra* Initiates in the Sanctum; they could never touch this level of control, of power.

Even as she tried to kill this Sage, she couldn't help but feel respect for him.

As soon as she hit the ground, the earth swept away beneath her, nearly knocking her off her feet. As she flailed, a spire of rock tore from the earth, speeding right for her face.

At the last moment, Reiva threw a tremendous blast of fire in a kick, and the force moved her enough to clear her of the attack—mostly.

The attack clipped her shoulder, sending her spinning through the air. When she hit the ground, she hissed in pain, clutching at her shoulder. If not for the aether infusing her, that would have broken her shoulder.

She pumped more aether to the wound, dulling the pain.

As she scrambled to her feet, rekindling the fire on her hands, she saw the Sage speeding toward her, carried by a rushing wave of earth.

She threw herself into a dodge—not fast enough. The Sage slammed into her like a charging bull, shoulder into her side, knocking the wind from her lungs.

As she rolled across the turf, her hair came free in a wild tangle. The Sage was standing over her, readying another technique.

Reiva yelled, throwing out power in a radial burst.

A sphere of fire burst into being around her, spiraling like a whirlwind.

The Sage pulled himself back along the ground, throwing up more earthen defenses to guard himself.

When Reiva dropped the blistering sphere, she saw burns along the Sage's arms. She smiled madly, brushing the hair away from her face.

The Sage's expression flickered like a sheet snapped in the wind. He looked disturbed, dumfounded. "You are a falsehood," he uttered hoarsely. "That form is beyond you."

Reiva swallowed, marveling at the rushing power coursing through her. She had never pulled off a technique like that, not without nearly knocking herself unconscious from the effort. The amount of aether she'd just unleashed should have cast her into the throes of aether sickness.

Instead, she felt like she'd just woken up after a full night's rest—every wound and ache melting away as if it were nothing.

She was *back*, back in a way she hadn't been ever since that fateful night in Hyrgallia. In her mind's eye, she saw the blazing tree, the fire that had saved her life, the beacon she should not have been able to light. Its glow burned away something deep inside her—some scar that had festered in her soul.

And she found herself laughing.

She *was* an Imperial Adept, she *was* a Lion, and she *was* going to rain hell on those who stood in her way.

Reiva pulled more aether into her, readying for another massive burst of force—something strong enough to turn the Sage to ash where he stood.

The Sage threw out his hands and twisted them around himself.

Reiva braced for his attack, half a mind to take the blow with another cloak of flame at the same time she readied her final technique. It felt like her power was *limitless*—like she could call upon every ounce of power she had used in the last month all at once and not feel worn.

The Sage waved his hands, and the earth around Reiva exploded upward.

Reiva's eyes bulged. She jumped, only for an arm of rock to wrap around her chest and pull her back. Stones piled up, packing together into a one-woman prison.

She roared, throwing all her might against the rocks, blasting them with fire. But no matter how much she poured out, the prison held.

The Sage approached, making a sharp gesture. A great spear of rock tore from the ground, its point aimed right for Reiva's head.

She sucked in a deep breath to blow fire.

The Sage clutched one hand closed in a fist, and the stones crushed in on her, squeezing her lungs of air.

Reiva gasped, channeling as much aether as she dared to save her body from breaking under the pressure.

The Sage stood, his massive weapon at the ready, point hovering inches from her forehead.

Reiva swallowed, looking from it to the Sage, back and forth.

He had tears in his eyes. His teeth were clenched, bared in a horrible snarl.

If his beard were grown out a bit more, if she took away the scar over his eye, he looked exactly like the Sage Yaros had beheaded with the sickle.

She thought again of Aviqohl. How she had just been ready to do anything to protect *her* brother.

Something in her withered. Too late. She hadn't been strong enough for him. "Do it."

The earthen spear trembled in the air. The Sage cocked his head to the side, his eyes losing focus.

She screwed her eyes shut. "Do it!"

A terrible sound—rock cracking, stones splitting.

And her earthen prison dissolved.

She opened her eyes. The Sage was gone.

Her lungs heaved for air, her head swiveled.

Nowhere. The Sage was nowhere to be seen.

She readied another protective technique, bracing for the inevitable attack. She stretched her aetheric sense as far as it could go, cutting through the morass of aggravated energy in the surrounding air.

Nothing. She could sense no other spirit like hers.

"Adept!" cried a legionnaire. Reiva snapped to him, realizing that the hole in the wall was crawling with Loyalists. She scanned the ground— mangled and scorched as it was—and didn't see the body of the Jackal.

Idiot.

Reiva threw a scorching wave of fire at the Loyalists, funneling the power she had been planning to use on the Sage.

But as soon as the magic flowed through her, nausea struck and set her head spinning. Black encroached at the edges of her sight.

The vertigo nearly brought her to her knees.

How—?

In another sudden wave of nausea, she vomited onto the grass.

Second stage of aether sickness. Severe.

Just as quickly as her newfound well of power had opened, it had shut on her.

Blinking against the shaking world around her, she saw with relief that she had done enough damage to push back the Loyalist incursion—but that wouldn't last for long.

Clenching her jaw so hard she feared she'd crack a tooth, Reiva wobbled to her feet. "Hold them if you can," she huffed. "If not, fall back to the palace."

The state of the defense was bad. The gates were still holding, but Loyalists were scrambling over the walls with ladders. It was only a matter of time before someone managed to force another opening, and then they would really be in trouble.

As she ran, legionnaires and guards swept past her, going to join the defense of the breach Reiva had just left.

She stumbled her way inside the palace. Another wave of vertigo hit, and she had to brace herself against the wall.

Taking long, slow breaths, she screwed her eyes shut.

You're no good to anyone if you hit the ground in a babbling mess.

"Pull it together," she hissed. "Come on!"

She cracked her eyes open. The world was still uneasy, but she was able to keep moving.

She mapped out the path she'd take to the throne room. She'd get to the next hallway, then turn left and—

To the right, at the far end of the passage, Cassia Vantelle vanished around the corner.

Reiva's heart was beating out of her chest. She felt like she'd vomit again.

With the palace on the verge of collapse, the king at mortal peril—why would Vantelle go *that* way?

Because that way was the dungeon.

That way was Reiva's brother.

'Perhaps there is a deal to be made with the Wolf.'

Reiva stumbled after her. She had to slow her aether enforcement to a trickle. Already she could feel her thoughts losing coherence. Her father's voice was ringing in her ears again, telling her to protect her brother. So was Alyat's, telling her that he was onto something impossible, something monumental.

So was Aviqohl's voice, telling her she was a traitor to him, to their family, to Talynis.

Every step, she nearly passed out, walking that hair-thin line of pulling on enough power to stay conscious without driving herself further into the pits of aether sickness.

Hand to the wall, she made it to the mouth of the dungeon.

Amazingly, *triarii* guards were still present, likely held there by Vantelle's orders not to leave their post no matter what.

What had Alyat seen? What was Vantelle chasing?

It wasn't just any two guards on duty. It was Belic and Mago.

Looking at her, they shifted stances. Their expressions were plainly conflicted, pained even.

"What did she tell you?" snarled Reiva.

"Just leave, Adept," said Belic. "The praetor said you specifically were not to be permitted entry."

Reiva couldn't help but laugh. She waved the arm that wasn't supporting her in the air. "Do you hear this? See this? The palace is about to fall, and you think this is where you're needed?"

Mago looked at her, plainly uncomfortable. His eyes darted down the corridor she'd come. The sounds of combat echoed down through the halls.

"They could be within the walls by now," she pressed, clutching at her stomach as another wave of nausea struck.

Mago said, "Apologies, Adept, but we were instructed to let no one enter, lest our lives be forfeit. The praetor was clear that we 'ave no 'igher task."

"I see," she said. She had left her sword behind—not that it would have done much good against two *triarii*. Her connection to the aether was too tenuous, unstable. Her body and spirit were reacting negatively to the overflow of power that had gone through her.

Still, she wasn't about to turn around. What could she do, even if she survived the day? Could she live with herself after that?

Shakily, she pushed herself off the wall, fighting against the dancing black spots before her eyes. Steeling herself, she tapped into her magic.

Her hands lit aflame, but the fire was frail and meager. Even this little draw sent ripples of exhaustion through her. It felt like iron bands had wrapped around her lungs, lead weights locked around her wrists.

The two *triarii* looked at her with...not fear. Not even hostility. They just looked sorry.

Reiva huffed, shoulders heaving as she fought for breath. Through gritted teeth, she said, "Well? Strike. Don't make me kill two men who haven't leveled arms."

Belic fidgeted. "So to speak, if we were to be disabled..."

A spark of hope kindled in her heart.

Mago nodded, grimacing. "Rendered incapable of stopping you."

"Never much liked how things were run after the praetor sent our legate away."

"Not at all."

Reiva felt tears building in her eyes.

"No face though, I'd like to keep my looks."

"'ands and feet, very important."

"Not the jewels neither. Still hope to get some use out of them."

"We're not *that* old."

Reiva let out a sound that was half-sob, half-laugh.

"I'm sorry for this."

They took it rather well, all things considered.

"Ooooh," groaned Belic, balled up on the floor. "Never thought I'd smell myself cooking."

Mago was clutching at his burn as well. "'Ang on a moment, Adept. Maybe a bit more—make it look convincing. Might get an honorable discharge outta this."

Reiva was on her knees, gripping her skull.

"Ah," hissed Belic. "Apologies."

She shook her head, not trusting herself to speak. It was like a spike had driven through her eye and out the back of her head.

"I'd offer to help," muttered Mago, "but I'm in a bit of a state as well, 'ere."

"Stay," grunted Reiva, reasserting her will. "I'll manage."

Shaking like a leaf in a gale wind, the Adept rose. She remembered the time she lay against the lone evergreen in the middle of a snowy field. She'd thought she wouldn't be able to get up again—and she wouldn't have, if it hadn't been for that fire in the tree. That impossible fire.

Could use that fire again.

Step by step, every move battering against her consciousness, Reiva pushed open the door, unlocked. Vantelle must have had the key with her.

Vantelle. Reiva didn't know how she'd stop her. She didn't know how she'd save her brother.

But she knew that *trying* was the only thing she could do—anything else, she might as well drop dead here and now.

So, inch by inch, yard by yard, she descended the winding subterranean stairway, sinking further and further into the darkness.

73

ONE MOVE

PERHAPS BECAUSE DEATH is the one ague no magic has ever triumphed over. The one foe we can never slay.
    —*The Life and Wisdom of Simeon Binkhok As Told by Himself*

∽

NOT TRUSTING her constitution to hold through another burst of fire, Reiva felt her way down through the dark, fingers groping along the rough-hewn stone.

Twice, she collapsed. The second time, she struck her knee against rock and hissed, stifling her cry of pain. She dragged herself back up, feeling warm blood trickle down her shin. The rest of the way, she limped.

The pain was a gift, though. It focused her, cut through the fog of the sickness.

All she had against Vantelle was her magic. That would have to be enough—she would have to kill the praetor. Gods willing, she would live long enough to explain herself to a tribunal. To reveal what had transpired here in Dav-maiir.

But if she didn't climb out of this dark hole in the earth, if she died here...she hoped she could at least get Aviqohl out. Free him from the Empire's grasp.

She could face her father after that. She could face Alyat.

Would she even see them?

Never did offer up that extra bull, she thought, a wry smile on her lips in spite of it all.

The winding passage, pregnant with gloom and shadow, began to light up. Flickering shadows danced on the wall.

And voices, she could hear voices.

Cassia Vantelle, her praetor.

Aviqohl beyt'Avadh, her brother.

Reiva didn't even take the time to catch her breath. If she stopped here, she would never take the next step.

This always looked more impressive in the plays.

Dragging one leg, clutching her stomach with one hand and bracing the other against the wall, Reiva turned the corner.

Illuminated by a single torch, which seemed almost suffocated amidst the subterranean gloom, stood Cassia Vantelle, Praetor of Lazarra, over Reiva's little brother.

He had been taken out of his chair, his wrists locked together in manacles.

Vantelle delivered a savage kick to his ribs.

Aviqohl sputtered, eyes wide as breath left him.

Vantelle knelt down, grasping his tunic. "Stand and walk, or we go back to the knife." She said it almost casually. There was no malice in her voice, only a vague annoyance at being delayed.

Reiva saw her brother's suffering. She thought he might have seen her, from how his face changed, but then it was gone.

She was in the darkness, still.

It was time to enter the light.

"Vantelle!" shouted Reiva, with as much confidence as she could muster.

The praetor spun, surprise writ plainly on her face.

Reiva's heart sank.

Brandishing the gleaming, night-black blade of the *Nihilo* Relic, Vantelle sighed. "Reiva. When I tell you I wish you were not here...I swear, I say it with absolute sincerity."

The praetor stepped over Aviqohl's form, placing him between the two of them, then hauled him to his feet. She put the sable edge to his throat.

"Stand straight, boy. If you so much as dip your chin, your jugular opens."

Aviqohl strained against her grasp, but he stilled. Blood trickled from his mouth and nose.

Vantelle turned her attention to Reiva. She looked...disappointed. Melancholic, almost.

"Adept Reiva. I gave you a second chance. I gave you the name of *Lion*. You owe me your life, your station, your *future*—and now you come to throw it all away over some forgotten desert mongrel."

"That mongrel," she growled, "is my brother."

"I lost a brother when I was half your age," she said flatly. "And I overcame that loss. That's what we do when we have *ambition*, Reiva. When we understand what it takes to ascend. I thought I saw that same ambition in you. That same desire. I thought you had what it takes to burn the world if it meant getting what you need."

Reiva took a shuddering breath. "I have what it takes, Vantelle. And what I need is to save my brother from you."

Vantelle gave her a baffled look. She let out a sharp bark of laughter. "Are you certain you didn't hit your head up there? You don't look well."

"I'm well enough," snarled Reiva.

Vantelle shook her head. "You were never a good liar, Reiva. Stick to killing—that's something you can do honestly."

"You're one to speak of honesty." As her anger built, Reiva let herself take another step forward. Without the support of the wall, she moved further into the chamber. She felt as though she were floating, the only thing anchoring her to this world the constant roiling and raging of the Flame in her soul.

"You're the most celebrated general in the Empire, but all along you were working with a criminal. Subverting the Emperor's will. Who knows how many deaths you've caused to our own ranks. All for what—money? Did you lack for luxury as a praetor?"

Vantelle scoffed, then actually laughed. Aviqohl winced as the blade trembled against his skin, opening up tiny, weeping cuts.

"*Money*? Nothing so pedestrian, Reiva. Everything I do here, everything I *have always* done, has always been for the Empire. You have no idea what this is about. You have no idea how many years I've labored to get this far. I didn't work *with* Ego—I *am* Ego. I created him, another weapon in my arsenal, for those things a praetor must not be known to engage in. Everything that's happened in this city, I orchestrated it all to this end. The one thing I lacked was a guide, and now your brother is going to serve as such."

"A guide to *where*?" she shrieked. "Why Talynis? Why here?!"

"Magic, Reiva. *Power*. The secret to arcane power beyond your wildest dreams. It is by magic that Lazarra has conquered, and Lazarra alone must have it. My one miscalculation, I admit, may have been bringing you here. There were documents that suggested the presence of a Talynisti Adept may aid in the discovery of the Convergence—and perhaps it did. Certainly, without your work, things could not have come to this. But now, I have no more need for you. You have spoiled yourself from usefulness. First Flavia, now you."

She swept her gaze around the chamber, eyeing the walls. "I'm amazed I didn't realize it sooner—it was staring me in the face. A chamber of rock so far below the surface. Built beneath the royal palace—or more properly, the site upon which they built the palace. And do you see the walls here? So smooth, not roughly hewn like the passage down. So few vents, yet do you not feel how crisp the air is?"

Reiva's anger was only building. "You love hearing yourself talk, don't you?"

Vantelle snorted. "It's all I have to do. Eventually, someone will either come down here and arrest you, or you'll try to kill me. The *Nihilo* Blade will stop the latter."

"And if it's Loyalists who come down here?"

"They won't. They all think the palace is the real treasure, not what lies below. Besides, I have their dog by the scruff of his neck."

"So *this* is the—what, the Convergence?"

"Arkhon's eyes, no. But it connects, somehow. A secret passage—quite a lot of those in this city, if you haven't noticed. Some of them carved out by the Desert Sages countless years ago. Others...even older. You can find these tunnels all over Talynis, even out in the desert. The remnants of a bygone era." She clicked her tongue. "Such a shame."

Reiva's head felt like it was going to burst.

"You used us all like tools, just so you could find this Convergence."

"Just? Just so I could ensure Lazarra remains the sole arcane superpower this side of the Spine. The eastern lands will be more difficult, of course, but we will bring them to heel. None are so united and expansive as us."

"It won't happen."

Vantelle scoffed. "You should see yourself, Reiva. You look like a cat someone threw off a cliff. So angry at the world. So powerless to do anything about it. I would have made you *my* heir. I had plans for you, child. Plans you've doomed as sure as you've doomed yourself."

Reiva took another shambling step forward. "I'm here to end *all* your plans, Vantelle. Not just the ones you had to control me."

"You speak so confidently. Do you think I'm blind to what's right in front of my face? I hold all the cards here. I hold the *Nihilo* Blade. You are the traitor. You are the beaten one."

"I am no traitor. I am loyal to what matters, to the heart of Lazarra that gave me life and strength. And you, you're scared of me. If you weren't, you would have ended this already."

"Really, Reiva, you are speaking nonsense at this point."

"Spare my brother. The two of us can handle this between ourselves. Before you have to deal with any interference from above."

"I'm afraid I need him. Have you not been paying attention? Is your bright mind so polluted with vainglory?"

"No, you don't need him," she huffed.

Something had clicked for her when Vantelle was speaking of the passages.

She had a guess. A hunch.

A last possibility.

Bracing herself, she cast out her aetheric sense.

The *Nihilo* Blade left a gaping hole in the space before her, devouring any aether that touched it. It looked wrong—like a flat tear in an otherwise rounded space. A splotch of ink against a painting.

But all around, the aether flowed—and it flowed strong.

She sensed it curling along the stones, the walls, in pluriform tides and currents.

And as she stretched her perception—nearly buckling to her knees with the effort—she sensed how it went deeper. She could see in her mind's eye how this chamber connected to another tunnel, how the back wall, right over Vantelle's shoulder, was false.

"I can take you down there," she breathed. "I can see it."

Hunger kindled in the praetor's eyes. "Prove it to me."

"You said it yourself—I'm a bad liar."

"I didn't get this far by taking chances. Show me the entrance."

"It's over your shoulder."

Everything was still and silent for a moment. It seemed impossible to Reiva that a war was raging above their heads.

Then the praetor nodded. "Try anything and you die," she ordered Aviqohl, then began hauling him to the side. "You," she said to Reiva, "go open the door."

Reiva grunted, setting herself into motion again. She kept her aetheric sense open just enough to sense where the door lay.

Keeping her eyes on Vantelle's, she shuffled across the stone.

When she could at last set her hands against the wall, it was a great relief. She tried not to show how weak she was, but even that seemed a losing battle.

"Open it," commanded Vantelle, a harsh edge in her voice.

Reiva didn't know how. But she could feel how the aether flow—ordinarily so uniform throughout the rest of the chamber—was stilted here. Almost like it was being blocked.

Slowly, she channeled aether, just like she might if she was healing someone, sending it to enter and mend a wounded body, except this time she was sending it into the stone.

Her channeling met resistance.

She feared the strain on her spirit if she tried to push further.

Then, suddenly, the weight on her eased. She gasped, feeling energy return to her.

It felt like a far smaller occurrence of when she had suddenly tapped into that limitless well of power, fighting against the Earth Sage.

With a great rumble, the wall before her dropped away, swallowed by the earth.

Reiva almost fell forward, staring down another downward tunnel. Like the dungeon, its walls were remarkably smooth, almost organic in appearance, like no tool had touched it.

Vantelle gave a gasp of astonishment. "Right there. Not so much as a seam or draft to give it away."

Reiva was still in awe, feeling how the aether from this room had connected to that of the tunnel. "That...it was like a gate, a key. How?"

"Aetheric constructs," breathed Vantelle. "Mentioned in the records, but to see one myself..." Her voice hardened. "How far down?"

Reiva turned to her, desperately hoping the sudden boost of power she felt in her would not depart again. It wasn't as much as before, but she would take what she could get.

She cast out her spiritual sense. "I don't feel any more gates like that," she said honestly. "The aether is strong, continuous. It—"

Reiva yelped, clutching her head.

"What? What is it?!" Vantelle sounded almost manic, which worried Reiva even more.

"It was like—like looking into the sun. A well of power greater than anything I've ever felt."

"That's it," said the praetor. "The Convergence."

Reiva cracked open her eyes again. "Let my brother go, Vantelle. We can go down together. You have the relic. I'm no threat to you."

The praetor looked back at her, almost in a daze. Then, clarity returned to her eyes. "Like I said, I don't take chances."

"Well, you don't have much time. Let him go, or else we stand here until someone else finds us."

Vantelle worked her jaw back and forth. "Your focus."

Dread cut Reiva to her core. "What?" It was hardly a whisper.

"Throw your focus over here. Even with a *Nihilo* Relic, I don't intend to step into that narrow tunnel while you have your magic."

Reiva faltered. Her mind was racing, a thousand different avenues branching out before her. None of them seemed desirable.

She was clutching the focus around her neck, she realized, fingers aching from how tight she gripped it.

"Do it now or I kill him!"

Without thinking, Reiva tore the chain from her neck and threw it.

As soon as the focus was gone from her person, Reiva felt her skin tingle. Her stomach lurched like she was falling. Even after deadening her aetheric sense, she still felt the uncomfortable buzz of unimpeded aether all around her, like being blind but staring into the noonday sun and still feeling its fearsome burn.

The focus clinked along the stones with unceremonious rhythm, coming to rest near Aviqohl's feet.

Vantelle looked down at it with satisfaction. Her eyes came up to meet Reiva's.

"Now, was that so difficult?"

And then she stepped forward and smashed the focus underfoot.

Reiva's hope, whatever of it remained, snuffed out like a naked candle flame in a midnight gale. She had been surrounded by enemy soldiers, outnumbered ten-to-one, and she had felt like she had better odds than she did right now.

She was utterly stripped of her magic. She couldn't touch aether, not without instantly dooming herself.

And then, with a professional, callous twist of her blade, Vantelle opened Aviqohl's throat.

Reiva screamed.

The praetor dropped her brother. He fell to his knees, clutching at his throat with mad fear and terror, a sickening gurgle bubbling from his lips as red blood sheeted down.

Vantelle didn't even spare him another glance, stepping over his body like it was a piece of furniture, inconveniently placed.

Reiva was trembling with grief—but that was only a drop in the ocean compared to the fury she felt.

She may not have had her focus, but the Flame still burned within her.

Vantelle flicked the *Nihilo* Blade, spattering blood along the stones. "How shall we do this, Reiva? Shall I kill you, or would you prefer to do it yourself? I hear aether sickness is a dreadful way to go."

It was. Reiva knew it was.

She also knew the *Nihilo* Blade would nullify any fire she threw—even detonating fire at range would fail, given the relic's devouring field. Vantelle was untouchable, and the second Reiva tapped magic, it would tear her apart from the inside out.

On the cold ground, Aviqohl was staring up from a pool of dark crimson, pale as death. The too-elegant slit in his throat pulsed a weak flow of lifeblood.

She knew that her body and soul were battered and wrung out like an old rag. She knew that, in every possible engagement set before her, the only way this ended was with Cassia Vantelle killing her, then going down to claim her long-awaited prize.

All this rushed through her mind in an instant, and then, over and above it all sounded an overture, the voice of Alyat echoing down the corridors of memory—

'Whenever you're up against the wall, remember: you've always got one move left, kid. You just have to figure out what it is.'

She couldn't throw fire. She couldn't blast at range.

But in a flash of intuition, she realized there *was* something else—something she had never considered before, never practiced, never proved possible.

But it was all she had.

Reiva threw up her hands.

Vantelle raised the *Nihilo* Blade, eyes narrowing.

The Adept channeled aether and felt it rip through her like a maelstrom.

Every ounce of strength she had, every shred of will, Reiva threw it into one last technique—one daring gambit she had never before attempted. Every last sliver of power she pulled repaid her in mind-shattering torrents of spiritual pain, wrenching her apart at the roots of her being. It was a thousand knives plunged into her flesh, ten thousand spears hammered through her bones.

Everything she had, she channeled into one move.

And the last thing she saw before the darkness claimed her was a look of utter confusion on Vantelle's face.

Because there had been no fire.

74

THE ADEPT WHO WAS HIS SISTER

YOU ASK if you are your brother's keeper? Then you have already erred.
—*Book of the Nameless Prophet*

~

AVI WAS GOING TO DIE.

He had known he would. There was no other way out of situations like this. He had even gotten the visit from the Wanderer—no sense in thinking it could have been anyone else.

People who were going to live didn't get to see the Wanderer. It was practically a letter informing you that your presence was expected in the afterlife.

But when the blade sliced through his throat, when his hot lifeblood spurted and poured out from him, every heartbeat disgorging his veins of yet more precious life—only then had he accepted it. Only then, choking on the fluid of his own life, did he finally accept that this was how it would end for him.

At least, he had for all of two seconds—two seconds until *it* showed up.

The Adept was screaming. He might have screamed too, if his throat weren't a mangled mess.

What else were you supposed to do when a man made of fire appeared, floating in the air behind your long-lost sister?

It was almost enough to make him forget, for a moment, that he was seconds from bleeding out.

Avi had heard of men hallucinating in their final moments, saying crazy things, seeing glimpses of heaven, of hell. He hoped that whatever this was, it was on fire because it came from the storehouses of lightning in heaven. The other option was markedly less appealing.

Particularly because it was looking right at him.

Then it raised its hand, set it on *Rebbaelah's shoulder*, and...something passed between them. Light, blinding light, coursing through his arm and into hers, out through her fingertips.

And it coursed through the air, zipping around the praetor and her devouring relic, and it pressed into Avi.

It was like getting thrown into cold water. Every inch of skin rippled with goosebumps, painfully sensitive to the slightest touch.

And then the gash in his throat closed.

The shadows at the fringes of his vision pulled back.

The man of fire vanished from his sight.

He was not going to die.

His sister's eyes rolled back in her head, and she dropped.

Between the two of them, the praetor was standing stock-still, staring at his sister's trembling body.

Well, Avi hadn't survived this long by taking his time.

The Wolf of Talynis sprang to his feet, startled by how *vibrant* he felt, like he'd just woken from a yearlong rest, the sort he hadn't enjoyed in ages.

And he swung his manacled hands just as Vantelle spun on him, total shock and—he was more than a little pleased to see—fear, written on her features.

The iron struck her across the temple, carried forward by as much momentum as he could put behind it.

The praetor dropped like a sack of rocks, groaning.

The *Nihilo* Blade clattered to the floor.

Avi lunged for it, awkwardly gripping the handle and trying not to dwell on the sight of his own blood streaking the blade.

He turned to Vantelle—

But saw his sister first.

Rebbaelah was convulsing, foam at the corners of her mouth. Her eyes showed only the whites. Inhuman groans emitted from her lips as her limbs seized and spasmed wildly.

Later, when he thought back to this moment, he realized he didn't have any guarantee what he was about to do wouldn't kill her.

But Avi hadn't survived this long by taking his time.

Lunging forward, pinning his sister down as best he could by straddling her midsection, Avi held the *Nihilo* Blade over her and drove its point into her shoulder.

Soon as the midnight blade pierced her flesh, Rebbaelah gasped—the deep gasp of someone trapped underwater who finally broke the surface. Her back arched, her eyes fluttered, and suddenly she went limp.

Avi pulled the weapon back, staring at his sister with more than a little trepidation. When he saw her chest rising and falling—albeit barely so—he eased a fraction.

Then he remembered they were not alone.

Scrambling to his feet, he spun toward Vantelle—only to see the praetor barreling toward him.

Avi awkwardly stuck the blade out, but Vantelle merely deflected it off her bracer, sparks flying, and delivered a savage punch right to his ribs.

Avi yelped as the blow struck the same bruised spot where she had struck him before. His knees buckled; his lungs burned. All he could think was *pain*.

Pain was something he was accustomed to though.

Gritting his teeth, he rolled, torso screaming in white-hot agony, and popped up to his feet, blade forward.

Vantelle was grimacing, her eyes flickering through a half-dozen emotions. One hand went up to her head, then came away with blood. She stared at it. Strangely, she looked calm.

With one final look at Avi, then Rebbaelah, she turned away and slipped into the tunnel. She did not have even so much as a torch.

Avi stared at her retreating form. "Hey!" he shouted, voice echoing off the stones. "We're not finished!"

Cassia Vantelle did not answer him.

He had an impulse to chase her. To drive this sword through her heart and leave her dead in the darkness.

But then he heard a calamitous scream, a sound he last heard many years ago, when an earthquake had rocked Shugrith. The scream of stone torn asunder. The ground shook beneath his feet, dust and pebbles raining down from the ceiling.

As soon as it had begun, it ceased.

But Avi wasn't one to chance things.

Contorting himself, he stuck the *Nihilo* Blade through his belt.

His sister was still lying there on the floor. Was it a trick of the light, or did she look far more pale? For a moment, he feared he had sliced an artery, but even with his hands shackled, he was better than that.

Would it be so bad if I did, though?

He scowled.

She had saved his life. Did that make up for a lifetime of treachery? For leaving him?

He thought about it, and he didn't know. He did know that she didn't have to save him like that. That she could have enjoyed absolute prestige and decadence for the rest of her life in the Empire, had she simply left him down here to die.

Instead, she'd come down to stop that praetor. She'd been willing to trade her life for his.

He thought of the Wanderer's face again. How he should have been seeing that face right now, being taken to whatever came next. He thought of the dirty stream at the edge of the desert.

It took some fumbling, but he got her onto his right shoulder. He had to walk at a slant, his left arm burning as he stretched to hold her in place, his lungs protesting every step. That healing, though it hadn't totally fixed him up, had done good work. He certainly wouldn't have been able to do this otherwise.

The ascent through the tunnel was pitch black, and more than once his sister's sandals tapped the wall, letting him know it had come time to turn.

Before long, he heard noise. Shouting, next. Combat.

He swallowed.

He was one of the most prominent figures in the Loyalist movement, and he had over his shoulder perhaps the most notorious soldier in the occupying legion.

Whoever he ran into, he doubted he would get a chance to explain anything before one or both of them found themselves on the end of a spear.

What a boring end that would be, he thought drily.

He rounded the final turn, and in the air above hung a window of light. Freedom—something he had almost been certain he would never see again when he came down this way. The only way out would have been directly to an execution, he'd been certain.

Now he was carrying the Adept out. The Adept who was his sister.

When he asked the Four to save him, he had not expected them to do so like this. Certainly hadn't expected that it would involve him saving her.

Worried that if he set her down, it would take too long to pick her up again, Avi inched up to the door, which was ajar.

There was a raucous din echoing through the halls of the palace. Most of the activity seemed to be centered on the direction where the throne room lay.

The hall running *away*, however, seemed blessedly vacant—an opportunity too precious to wait on.

Avi ducked out of the passage, and he was on the move again.

He wondered, of course, whether Tamiq was still alive. How ironic if he wasn't—that Avi had come so close to his person, only to run away.

There were a thousand questions about what came next—what would become of the monarchy, would Malik return triumphant? Would the legion depart?

Avi had no time to dwell on such considerations. He pumped his legs fast as he could without dropping Rebbaelah.

He didn't really have a concept of where to go besides *away*. Gods willing, he would find a hideaway somewhere nearby, or even just slip away into some nearby ruination—hopefully people would be too busy with the palace to worry about such things.

Would his sister make it through that, though? She had looked pale earlier, barely breathing. Was this something she'd recover from like any other wound, or was it more grave?

Avi's luck ran out once he hit the inner courtyard.

The place—once a tranquil, lush garden—had become a bloodbath between legion forces and Loyalists.

And the legion had just won the struggle.

Before his eyes, a legionnaire drove her sword clean through a Talynisti fighter's throat. As the man crumpled, she locked eyes with Avi—then realized who was over his shoulder.

Avi turned, making a break back down the hallway as shouts of alarm and threats chased him. Heavily shod feet slammed against the tile floor, and Avi cut to the left, down a different hallway.

A javelin zipped past. He nearly fell on his face pulling away, teetering as he tried to keep on his feet.

Drop her.

As he tore through the passage, he had little reason not to. He just knew that he wouldn't. He could face the consequences of that later.

Ahead, another open portico led to the eastern grounds of the royal estate.

Avi had no idea where the attack had come from; for all he knew, this could be legion turf, or it could be Loyalist. Gods willing, he could get his pursuers tangled up in a confrontation with more Loyalists, buying him time and cover to get away.

Soon as he was into the sun, his stomach sank.

Legionnaires, one and all.

His feet faltered for a moment.

He might as well have given up then. He'd made his attempt; he'd gotten further than he thought.

He promptly cursed himself and kept running. Like hell he'd go down like that.

By divine intervention or blind chance, most of the legionnaires were focused on the walls, defending against Loyalists trying to siege the grounds, he guessed.

The eastward gate was sealed, barred.

He'd have no chance of making it out.

The shouts of his pursuers reached him again. They had spotted him after the initial disorienting shift from the cramped halls of the palace to the body-strewn lawn of the exterior.

As the shouts went up, legionnaires along the walls turned. A squadron that had been making double-time for the north side stopped, began making their way toward him.

His shoulder was aching, his lungs strained, his side smarting. In that moment, he would have forgiven himself for giving in. He still had the blade; he could have dropped his sister and killed himself, like the Mastayr Two-hundred had when faced with the previous legion incursion, years ago.

A legionnaire barreled down on him, eating up ground like a battle charger. His sword had blood on it. Soon his blood would be there too.

If he set his sister down, that would be the end of it. No chance in hell he could pick her back up in the midst of all this; all he could hope for would be to kill one or two before they brought him down.

The legionnaire was fifteen yards away.

Avi dipped his shoulder.

And in that same moment, a high-pitched whistle screamed past his ear, and an arrow sprouted from the legionnaire's eye socket. He dropped instantly.

Avi gaped, turning right as a pair of thundering horses raced past.

On one horse, a woman with a bow sat, steering with her knees and loosing shot after shot in smooth, sustained rhythm. On the other, a man with a sword in each hand—one Karellan in make, the other lashed by glowing green ribbons—swung his blades down with ruthless lethality.

And it finally clicked that he was looking at the mercenary who always dogged the Adept's heels, the same mercenary who had played shells in the Singing Owl with him.

And that mercenary was slaughtering legionnaires.

The soldiers on the walls looked on in shock and confusion, shouting for someone to give them orders. None of the officers seemed to have a better handle on the situation though.

The mercenary wheeled his mount back around, slamming his Karellan sword home to its sheath. The windsword he kept free, ribbons of wind swirling and dancing around in frantic rhythm. His horse skidded to a stop on the grass, snout huffing, eyes wide.

The mercenary stuck out his hand. "Long time no see!"

For a heartbeat, the world froze.

Not the first time that day, Avi felt like he didn't really have much of a choice.

He pressed his sister toward the mercenary, who gripped her by the armor straps and draped her across his horse. He wheeled around, sword held high, winds ripping around them in a tumult.

Arrows and javelins fell on them, but the sword's power knocked them all aside.

"Charas!" he shouted. "Let's move!"

The archer's horse thundered after them, as she still launched shot after shot.

Yaros kicked his mount into motion, yelling "You're with her!" over his shoulder.

Avi hardly had time to think as the archer swept by, one arm stuck out.

He jumped, catching her arm and throwing himself onto the horse. The wind was knocked out of him as his stomach collided with the beast's rigid back.

Just as he righted himself, she yelled, "Hold on to something!"

Avi clutched the saddle as the horse careened right, dodging another squadron of legionnaires.

They came even with Yaros as they turned the corner.

A gaping hole lay in the perimeter wall, and it was still a site of combat. Legionnaires swarmed over the rubble, trying to plug the breach with their shields and bodies.

They were riding straight for the gap.

Again, Yaros swept his sword through the air, conjuring a raging wall of wind that deflected every missile launched at them.

The field was absolute chaos. Screams of dying warriors, of officers trying to reassert order amid the confusion.

As they charged across the grass, the soldiers in the opening spotted them and began to brace, yelling for aid. Their comrades began tossing them spears, which they set against the earth and rubble in a bristling hedge.

Avi's stomach dropped at the sight.

Charas fired arrow after arrow, dropping soldiers, clearing the space bit by bit.

Not enough, though.

"Hang on!" she shouted again.

"Already am!" he yelled.

Their horses leaped as Yaros twisted the windsword, sending a wild cyclone into the legionnaires, stumbling some, knocking some clean off their feet.

As they passed through the wind, Avi felt like he'd been slapped across the face—then it dropped away instantly.

Hooves came back to solid ground, clattering against the cobblestone roads of Dav-maiir.

The fight out here was far messier than inside the grounds. Streets were littered with bodies, shields and spears, professional soldiers and everyday people. The roads were painted red.

They headed northward, against the tide of Loyalists. Yaros led them through the streets, avoiding masses of people as best he could, but even the least-crammed ways were still rife with threats. The windsword fell again and again, its elegant form streaming blood.

On the rooftops, people with javelins and slings tried to bring them down. Charas returned their attacks with precise shots, dropping each with a single arrow.

Avi stared at the havoc in the streets, feeling helpless. He should have been fighting with them right now. This was the final push, it had to be. Everything would be decided today.

But something kept him rooted to the back of that horse. Something kept him from scrambling off and going to join the fight.

Curiosity, yes. Curiosity as to what had happened down there in that cave, and why these two had suddenly betrayed their own legion to rescue him and his sister. But there was also something deeper, something he couldn't explain. Something that drove him to stay wherever he was being taken.

As they neared the northern gate, instinct nudged Avi to throw a glance over his shoulder.

A pack of legionnaire cavalry was after them.

"They're after us!" he yelled.

Charas stole a glance, scowling. She pulled another arrow from her quiver—one of her last.

"*Lean right.*"

Avi got as low as he could, twisting himself sidelong. As he went right, Charas turned leftward, bow first, drawing.

One legionnaire fell from his saddle, the other horses trampling him.

Charas nocked another arrow.

Avi's jaw hung as she downed another rider, then another, all the while, turned in her saddle, giving the horse free rein.

Their pursuers dropped back a bit, pulling out of bowshot.

Charas turned ahead. "Keep an eye on them."

Avi nodded wordlessly. He had heard of Parthavan riders who could do that—turn and shoot backward as well as most could standing—but seeing it was something else entirely.

Yaros waved at them, pointing ahead. The city gate lay open before them.

"Bless the ancestors," she sighed, pressing her horse to speed onward. Avi peered over his shoulder. The cavalry was still after them, but out of range.

Charas' bow thrummed.

Avi turned back just in time to see a legionnaire drop from above the gate and strike against the stone with a sickening sound.

They blew through the gates without resistance, hooves striking dusty roads as they reached the farmlands. People stared at them as they sped past, some shouting questions about the city, others scrambling to get as far away as they could.

Avi looked and saw dark plumes of smoke rising from Dav-maiir, much of it concentrated around the area of the palace.

And he saw more cavalry coming after them.

"They're still on us!" he roared.

Yaros swore. "There's a wadi half a mile ahead. If we can break line of sight—"

"Terrain's too flat," snapped Charas. "They'll stay out of bowshot and follow until we can't go on."

Avi's mind raced. He thought of ways they might escape, routes they might slip away by. If it was just him, he might even be able to do it.

But he'd already made his choice in that regard—he wasn't leaving his sister behind, not until he could get some answers.

"If we go into the desert," he shouted, "we might lose them. They can't survive out there."

"They just picked up reinforcements, and they're closing!" warned Charas, nocking another arrow.

Then, just as she turned and drew, a horrible tremor shook the world. The horses screamed. Beneath them, dirt and grass and sand gave way as a massive sinkhole tore open the earth.

They all screamed, falling into the pit.

Darkness swallowed them.

75

THE MOUSE AND THE KING

THE ENDRIC DOGMAS ARE CURIOUS. Beautiful in their way, but also terrifying. Nowhere is this so clearly mirrored as in their warrior class, the *Kshara*.
—*The Life and Wisdom of Simeon Binkhok As Told by Himself*

ARJUN VARIDABRH, *Kshara* in service to an Endric prince, knew no fear.

His great twin blades tore through flesh and bone in an ever-whirling cyclone. Many Talynisti—young and old, male and female—were at his back, coming to fight the false king set up over them.

Arjun had immense respect for them all, and he wanted them to know they were not alone in their fight. Never throughout the battle did he waver in his onward press, always ensuring that the Loyalists saw his broad-backed form.

With every foe that fell under his swords or turned and ran, their roar grew ever greater.

"*Ma-lik! Ma-lik! Ma-lik!*"

They chanted the name of their rightful king, and their chant set the beat for their advance.

Arjun lopped the head off a legionnaire, then watched as the two soldiers who had been at her side melted before him. Eyes widened, knees trembled.

Yes, he had been born for the battlefield.

His *asura*, Vathi, appeared at his shoulder. The four-armed spirit held her hands high in *mudra*, the signs of power. Those hands pointed to the enemy line were *doubt* and *terror*. To the people at Arjun's back, she showed *courage* and *faith*.

Only Arjun could see Vathi, but her influence was affecting hundreds of souls in that moment.

He led a charge for the walls, bringing the people through the great gaping break in the outer wall of the palace grounds. The legionnaires of the Ninth were fighting desperately to secure the breach in their defenses.

When Arjun leaped atop the crumbling masonry, swords held high above his head, their line disintegrated.

A brave remnant held their ground, and these Arjun met in battle with a broad grin—love, even. These were the true warriors, their souls burning bright like torches in the gloom. Many, Arjun was sure, would transmigrate through the cycle of being and be reborn as *Kshara,* like him. That was the way of things—life-by-life they would ascend across the stations of service.

Arjun, in this life, had been born to serve as a warrior—and he would do his duty with great dedication.

A pair of legionnaires bearing spears rushed for him, threatening to skewer him where he stood.

Arjun leaped, reinforcing his legs with aether, and twisted in midair. His swords flashed, and he hit the ground a moment before their heads rolled across the grass.

He had been born to be a warrior, but that did not mean he took pleasure in killing. Battle, the contest of will and spirit—there was the joy. Pain was the curse of a world not yet brought to its fullness. Someday, all would be right; until then, the cycle of existence would continue, souls moving through various lives, ascending and descending as they learned the proper ways of being.

Arjun ran atop a legionnaire tortoise formation, launching himself over and behind before laying into them.

At first, he was outnumbered—and even with his prodigious skill, for a moment, he thought death was possible. His heart pounded in his chest.

But then the Loyalists he was leading caught up, and they swarmed the legionnaires.

A Lazarran gladius darted out and took him in the shoulder. Arjun cut the man's arm off at the elbow before bringing his other sword down in a vicious slash that bit from shoulder to heart.

As blood sprayed him, as blood flowed from his wounds, Arjun felt no fear.

If he died today, he would die as a warrior. That was all he could ask for. With a rallying cry, he led the Loyalists into the palace.

~

VANTELLE HAD BEEN wrong when she called Tamiq a second son—in truth, he had been born third son. The throne should never have been within reach. Malik, always, was expected to reign—the Four had chosen him, gifted him to their father the king as heir to his legacy.

The brother between them had been frail, though, and died of a fever in Tamiq's seventh year.

Suddenly, Tamiq had known opportunity. He had felt what it was like to be elevated in the eyes of men.

He had come one beating heart closer to the throne.

And he had known then, that when the opportunity arose, he would make himself king. No matter how many years it took, no matter how long he had to play the part of dutiful, supportive brother. He was a man possessed by the need—by the *destiny*—to rule the sacred sands.

So, when the opportunity made itself known in the form of the Lazarran Empire, he knew the heavens—whether it be the gods of Talynis or the gods of Lazarra—had extended their favor.

His only regret now, was that he hadn't killed Malik and his sons with his own hands. That would have settled it all.

That was the wrinkle, wasn't it? Much as the priests expounded on the law, and the necessity of caring for those who suffered—if you truly wanted anything in this life, you had to take it for yourself. Real life wasn't like the stories, where the runt of the litter received his just reward after a long life of obedient toil. No—the small needed to claw their way to the top, no quarter given. Those born at the top of the pile didn't understand that. That was why Tamiq had always had the people's favor. He had fought for them. He had given them blessings that Malik would never even have considered.

And he would have had this city, this nation, in his hands for the rest of his life, if only it hadn't been for that bitch of a praetor. She had turned the people against him, crushing them underfoot with iron-shod boots. They saw him as her ally, and so now, now they had come to see him as their enemy.

If he ever saw her, he'd wring out her neck himself. Just like he should have done to his brother. He'd make her spread her legs for him too. Just like he should have done to Malik's queen. That was all women were good for— if the Emperor had sent a *male* praetor, then maybe none of this would have gone to hell like it did. Men knew how to rule; women couldn't be trusted with a thimble of authority. If the Lazarran Empire fell, it would fall because of a woman.

Such thoughts occupied Tamiq, king of Talynis, as his armor-bearer placed the sword in his hand.

"You have a son, do you not, Eved?"

His armor-bearer nodded, double-checking the inside buckle on Tamiq's breastplate. "He polished your helmet this morning, my lord."

"Take him. Take him far away from here."

Eved's eyes widened. "My lord, it is my honor to die for—"

"Your king orders you, Eved. Take your son. *Go.* Quickly, before it is too late. I have already sent Katabh away. Let your tongues tell a different tale of my reign than my enemies will spew."

The man's lips trembled, then drew into a line. "Four on High keep you, my king."

"And you."

The door shut, and Tamiq, king of Talynis, waited alone for death to find him.

THE PALACE WAS in absolute chaos. Half the Revolutionary Guard had turned on the king, aiding the Loyalists in their onward storm. Fighters broke off hallways, moving left and right, in search of Tamiq's followers, his court—and, of course, his treasure.

For Arjun, the only goal worth considering was the throne room.

He ducked a spear, shredding the guard's thighs and moving forward. Momentum, he needed to keep up momentum.

He swept through the hallways, blades singing and slicing. Always at his side, Vathi directed him with her piercing sight, unbroken by walls or matter.

"Left," she said, "then a quick right."

Arjun obeyed unquestioningly.

They were moving away from the main doors to the throne room—those would be too well protected. The Loyalists at his heels had stopped to try to batter down the high doors, so Arjun was running alone.

Following Vathi's directions, he kicked in a small door leading into a narrow servant's hallway. He had to twist his body to fit, leading with one sword.

A manservant saw him coming, yelped, and turned tail.

Arjun didn't begrudge him for that; any battle in which the casualties extended beyond the warriors was a wretched one.

Moving fast as he could, he wound through the passage, coming to another locked door, the wood reinforced with iron bands.

Arjun took a deep breath, letting aether strengthen the big muscles in his leg, and *kicked.*

The door cracked. Shouts came from within.

Again, he kicked.

On the third strike, the door shattered inward, and Arjun barreled through the narrow doorway.

Immediately, he was faced by two men with swords, one young and one old.

Arjun brought his weapons up in an X, catching the young's overhead. He lashed out with a kick to the old man's chest, knocking him back.

Quickly, he disengaged, batting the young man's sword aside and swinging for his throat.

"Wait!" screamed the old man, throwing down his sword.

On instinct, Arjun stopped.

There had been great pain in that scream. Arjun had felt it deep in his soul.

He took another look at the young man, weaponless, then at the elder.

Father and son.

Arjun had children. He had certainly killed fathers today. Fathers and sons. That was the way of things in war.

But one should never have to see the other die.

"Go," he said. "Do not turn back."

The father looked pained. "I am no traitor to my king."

Arjun admired that, but he wasn't here to argue—save with iron.

"Tamiq will no longer be king within the hour. You can die trying to stop that, or you can go and survive. Leave by the eastern gate if you can."

The man hesitated for a moment, then dipped his head in thanks, pulling his son with him.

Arjun noted they left their swords. Not particularly wise—but that too was something he could respect. If you set your sword down, leave it. Fate was not kind to those who tried to live the path of the warrior without commitment.

He hoped they could get out alive.

And he hoped he could find the king alive.

The last time he'd stormed a palace, the man had thrown himself off the roof rather than face the invaders.

Was Tamiq a coward? He would find out.

Again, Vathi guided him through this wing.

As he tore past a hallway, he saw a detachment of guards stacked against two massive doors, bracing it with their bodies. Any moment now, the Loyalists would break through.

"Bolster them," he said. "I want some time alone with the king."

Vathi extended *mudra* of valor and endurance toward the Revolutionary Guardsmen, and Arjun heard the swelling pride in their shouts as they held the doors.

Arjun ran down a hallway, meeting another pair of guards, each with a round shield and a scimitar. These two seemed better trained than most, hefting their shields and holding their blades high.

In an ordinary situation, two men with shields had an inordinate advantage over a single man with two swords.

Good thing Arjun was more than a man.

He bellowed, feeling another pulse of bravado from Vathi, just as she assaulted their minds with fear.

These were hard men, men who had known the ugly glory of battle.

Still, for a heartbeat, they flinched.

Arjun ran up one wall, reinforcing his legs with superhuman strength and stamina, then threw himself over the guards, hitting the ground in a roll.

Rather than lash out at him, they pulled behind their shields.

It was a costly reflex.

They couldn't pivot fast enough, and Arjun had already hamstrung one by the time the other had his sword on the down arc. Arjun parried with one sword, slipped the other around the man's shield.

Just as the man he'd hamstrung collapsed, Arjun slammed a knee into his nose, then flayed open the other's sword-arm.

The shouts from the doors redoubled, and the sharp groan of straining wood filled the halls.

Arjun turned and left the guards. They did not give chase.

Few who survived him ever did.

The throne room had another set of impressive doors. His heart sank, until Vathi, in her ever-equanimous tone, said "They are unlocked."

A single nudge, and the doors swung open.

Arjun reset his grip.

He moved in, expecting a trap.

There wasn't one; Vathi would have warned him if there had been, but old instincts never went away, even with a spirit forever at your side.

Standing alone, with a breastplate and coat of mail over his chest and a sizable sword in his hand, Tamiq the usurper loomed large.

Arjun had to admit, he had the bearing of a king. He had never met Malik, but he wondered if this man's older brother would have stood and fought in the same manner. Malik was shrewd, they said, but not one to get his hands dirty.

He offered a salute to the king, crossing his swords over his chest.

Tamiq dipped his chin. "I presume you are the Mouse. A warrior of your capabilities is wasted on this rabble. Come to my side, and you will have more riches than you know what to do with. You would have any virgin daughter of Talynis as your bride whom you chose. Your children will lack for nothing."

Arjun appreciated the offer, even though there wasn't a snowflake's chance in the Naraka of him accepting. It meant he had proven himself well to his enemy, and there was always pleasure in that.

"Funny, pretender king, because though they are rabble, they are taking back the kingdom you stole. Besides, I am not sure how much you could offer me, given that your riches are being looted as we speak."

Tamiq merely grunted and set his feet.

Vathi raised a hand to send an emotive pulse against him, but Arjun gave a subtle signal that she ought not. Man to man—he wanted to keep this more even. He was curious what this throne-seizer could do.

For a moment, they stood like that, the Mouse and the king.

The king struck first, feinting left, then changing into a sequence of quick slashes and thrusts.

Arjun stepped backward, rolling with the tide of his enemy's momentum. The usurper fought with the confidence and skill of a seasoned warrior. Arjun didn't doubt that against many veteran warriors, Tamiq would have held his own.

But he was against a *Kshara* today.

Arjun easily parried with his left hand and wove around the attacks, stepped around and into Tamiq's guard. With a vicious kick, he snapped the usurper's ankle. A quick flick with his right sword and Tamiq's sword went flying, taking a few severed fingers with it.

The usurper was down on one knee, clutching at his injured hand and glaring up at Arjun with unmasked hatred.

"Kill me then," he snarled. "Parade my head before the masses and receive the glory you are here for."

But Arjun could only shake his head. "I am not here for glory. And it is not my place to kill you."

Vathi's calm voice rang out, "The Loyalists have broken through the defenses—they will be here soon."

Arjun nodded subtly. "This was not personal to me, Tamiq. I do not know what they will do to you, but if we should never speak again, know that you had the dignity of a king, if not the rights of one."

The usurper's head bowed. Stampeding feet sounded from down the hallway.

He murmured something, but Arjun did not catch it.

After the Loyalists stormed the room and—after a moment of shock—seized Tamiq and hauled him away, Arjun inspected the throne of Talynis. It was not the first throne he had seen. He did not think it as fine as the seat of his prince back in Endra, but even so, he made the proper bowing obeisance.

Vathi flashed several complicated *mudra*. After a moment, she said, "The throne guardians of this place bear us no ill will for shedding the usurper's blood."

Arjun hummed. They could have been more grateful than that, but perhaps they were anxious to have a true king returned to their watch. He also doubted they had ever beheld a *Kshara* in this place—though the Imperial Adept of Fire had likely been here, which was more or less the same thing.

He offered one final bow, then turned and left.

76

VANTELLE ALONE

I DO NOT KNOW, nor do I wish to know, the fullness of what confronted Cassia Vantelle in those dark depths. I have heard inklings and pieced-together suppositions, and they are too terrible to consider. No doubt, historians and poets will consider them long and shamelessly, but for me, for me it is too terrible. For one who loved her as I did, it is all too terrible.
—*The Memoirs of Flavia Vantelle*

THE DARK of the tunnel was heavy. Vantelle could make her way only by groping along the smooth walls and trying to follow the gradual downward slope.

She had left Reiva and the Wolf behind. She could have killed them, but what did it matter? Reiva was dead—her spirit would destroy itself as aether ripped through her.

Foolish girl. Giving up the life set before her for the sake of a brother she hardly knew. A man who had been trying to kill her ever since she set foot in this city.

Every day of her life, Vantelle only saw more and more evidence that people had no idea what was truly valuable. What was *real*, could be depended upon. The only thing she had ever found to be reliable, to be consistent, to be trustworthy—it was power.

Power ensured you were not betrayed. Power kept your enemies at bay. It kept those who would spite you under a shroud of terror.

Lazarra would rule the world because Arkhon the All-seeing was powerful beyond all gods. Arkhon would reign, and the Emperor would reign by his divine appointment.

That would be her, someday.

Today, she would destroy the Convergence point of Talynis. The place where this world and the spiritual world mingled, like fresh and salt water coming together.

There was an old story in these realms, that the world had been born from the mingling of two such waters. Barbarian superstition—but Vantelle found it an apt consideration.

Once the Convergence collapsed, the Talynisti would lose their meager store of Adepts. The spirits of this land would be crippled, accessible only through an arcane focus. An arcane focus that only Lazarra understood the secrets of.

This was the great innovation of the First Emperor, enlightened by Lord Arkhon. This was what would bring the entire world to heel.

This was what would ensure Vantelle's ascendancy. It was all but guaranteed, of course. Who else could the Emperor name as his heir? No one—not a soul even came close to Vantelle in their service to the Empire.

Her whole life had been building to this moment. Even before she had known the secrets of this world, the erased histories, the cryptic lore, she had known she was destined for greatness.

How could she not have been? She was descended of the Vantelle lineage, one of the most storied families in the Empire, their pedigree reaching back even to the days of the lost Republic. Always their family had served Lazarra, always they had been faithful to the heavens. And they had been blessed for it, granted prestige, esteem, and glory.

Take Dario—from birth, her older brother had fit the mold perfectly. Strategically brilliant, culturally gifted. He was going to be the ideal Vantelle. Their parents had expected so much of him. He was perfect; he was everything their parents had wanted.

He was the only one they had ever wanted.

But he had grown ill and wasted away, and the perfect heir to the Vantelle legacy was gone.

But they still had Cassia—even if she was a poor replacement. Even if she had never been as clever or charming, she had earned the accolades. She had climbed the ranks faster than anyone before.

Even though always, until the day they died, Mother and Father had looked on her with that quiet, melancholic grief, that grim certainty that Dario would have done better.

Frowning in the dark, she slowed. She never thought of her brother anymore. She never thought of her parents. That was all buried, that was all forgotten. Once a year, when she had to perform the rites for deceased family, they crossed her mind.

It was Reiva. That was it. The girl had found her brother, and it had sparked the memory in Vantelle. It was just a reminder. It was—

It was him, standing before her, barely ten years old, wrapped in grave clothes that scarcely covered a gaunt, sickly frame covered by blood-weeping sores.

Vantelle scrambled backward, nearly tripping over herself.

Everything was dark. Pitch black, grim as a moonless, starless night.

But he had been there. She had seen him.

Her heart was pounding out of her chest.

"An illusion," she whispered to the empty (it *was* empty, wasn't it?) air.

Inch by inch, she made her way forward.

At once, she lunged forth, waving her arms.

Nothing.

She felt along the floor, getting on hands and knees.

No blood. Nothing but dust and stonework.

Nothing but Vantelle alone.

Slowly, she got to her feet again.

The dark was playing tricks on her, that was it. Or perhaps there was some force in here, and it feared her. Yes, that was it—the power in this place feared Cassia Vantelle. It knew that she had come to destroy it.

The praetor continued her descent.

Fear—she understood fear. It was a tool. It was a weapon. Cassia Vantelle struck fear in the hearts of her enemies *and* her allies. Why wouldn't the power of the Origin Spring fear her too? She who had come here as the envoy of Arkhon the All-seeing to destroy this Convergence.

Someone whispered in her ear.

Vantelle flinched, slapping at the air.

No one.

The whisper came again, soft, but undeniably close.

"*Unworthy.*"

"What did you say?" she hissed.

"*Desecrator.*"

"Yes, yes I will desecrate this place. And you will know what it is to bow, at last. You and all of Talynis."

"Failure."

Vantelle did not answer again. It was a deception, clearly. A diversion. Some vain attempt to slow her, to turn her back. Only a sign that she was going the right way.

Not that there was any other way—she could only descend or go back. The wall was an endless, unbroken face of smooth granite. From time to time, she thought she heard the earth shifting, far ahead, but with every step she still felt the ongoing slope.

How deep could she have been by now? They said the foundations of the world were born up by the pillars of the underworld. Was that how deep this tunnel went? Was the Spring there at the boundary of worlds, bridging not just this place and the unseen presences here, but also the world of death?

The faces of the dead came to her. Dario, her brother. Her father and mother. A friend from officer training, killed in their first real engagement; he'd died in her arms after taking an arrow to the throat. They'd slept together the night before.

She pounded her forehead with her fist.

Why was she thinking of this? She hadn't thought of any of this—any of these people—in... in how long?

How long had she been here?

The Spring.

She was here for the Spring. She was a praetor of Lazarra.

She had to keep going.

They stayed, though. The faces. At first she thought it had just been in her head, but now she was certain they were there—right at the edges of her vision. Splashes of ghoulish gray against an otherwise totally black canvas.

She had company—good. One should not be forced to change the world without witnesses. Let the dead see her achievement, her accomplishment. Let them be the attendant audience to the final subduing of Talynis. The breaking of its spirit, in the most literal sense.

Ghosts...what fragile spectators.

Where was Flavia? Where was the bright-eyed young captain she picked out after a decisive battle and clapped on the shoulder? They had planned to go so far together.

It had hurt so much to discover Flavia's treachery. And after everything Vantelle had done for her, after all those late nights sipping wine, talking grand dreams of a better world forged in the fires of their ambition...

Something dripped on her. Something was dripping on her face, running down her cheeks. She put out her hands. Nothing.

The cave narrowed.

At first, she took this as a good sign, an indication that she was getting closer to her destination.

But then it narrowed further and further. She was forced to stoop, then to bend. She was practically on her hands and knees. Then she *was* on hands and knees, crawling through the cramped tunnel.

And then there was Reiva. She was more stoic than Flavia. More possessed by ambition, more concerned with duty. Surely that had been the problem with Flavia—she was too eager to break the mold. Reiva, Reiva had been another chance, someone she could offer a steady hand and raise up to heights undreamt of.

How stupid—how stupid a girl to throw away what Vantelle had offered her.

How stupid Vantelle had been to place her hopes in someone, yet again.

Again, something dripped—this time on her hands. She wiped her face.

Strength. Hers was a strength that never failed. A strength devoted to the Empire. She would always have the Empire—she *loved* the Empire. It had always recognized her, always rewarded her for her sweat and blood and tears.

And when she had learned the truth of the world, she had known there was nothing she would not do for the Empire's sake.

The air remained plentiful—it was coming from the Convergence. All the life in Talynis did. The people spoke of how the gods had first placed water in this desert; what they really meant was that a Convergence had formed here, and that Convergence had been the catalyst for the creation of some great new resource.

The Lazarran Convergence had created great veins of ore, a wealth of minerals upon which the Lazarran Republic had been built. It was those mines that shod and equipped the legions. Iron beyond measure, and more recently the discovery of steel, monarch of metals that would shatter any blade raised against it.

In Talynis, the resource was life itself, practically. An endless font of water. Air in these underground tunnels that crisscrossed the whole desert. Once, those tunnels had carried water from the Origin Spring. The whole desert had been a lush landscape in those days. A garden.

But things always happened. The Convergence was polluted, or diminished somehow. In Lazarra, the greed with which the predecessors had dug for the minerals had evidently been... displeasing. Now, they had to delve deeper, fight harder to disgorge the treasure of the earth. There were cave-ins, pockets of noxious fumes.

She did not know what transgression had occurred in Talynis, but it had turned the place into a desert. Precious few cities still had lifelines to the Origin Spring here; all others had vanished into history. The veins of the desert, the subterranean canals feeding every oasis across the land, all came back to this one place, deep beneath Dav-maiir.

She didn't know exactly what would happen when she destroyed it. When the Praetor of the Seventh and Eighth Legions had destroyed the Parthavan Convergence, it had been startlingly anticlimactic. Would that hold true, or had that been merely another instance of what Emperor Dioclete had called 'the idiosyncrasies of the Parthavan spirits'?

How...how *would* she destroy it, for that matter?

She was on her stomach now, crawling inch by inch, her breastplate scraping the rock.

She had a plan for that...a way to shatter the connection between realms...what was it...

No, no there was no plan, because she didn't need one—it was simple, simple as stepping on an insect. How could she have forgotten something so essential?

Vantelle rubbed her eyes. This place was working against her again. Let it try—no one had ever broken her will.

She continued to crawl, to crawl for what felt like hours. All she knew was the constant forward slither, belly to the ground.

The voices were still whispering—she ignored them. The faces still floating there at the fringes of sight—she paid them no mind. Her single purpose lay ahead, and she would not be dissuaded.

They began to yell at her. To shout. To scream. They got in her way. They made her go right up to them, pass through them.

All she did was set her jaw and keep moving.

On she went, and on, and on—until ahead, she spotted an aperture. A circle of light. The light burned away the ghoulish faces.

And her ears, her ears caught the sound of water, flowing and lapping. The voices were gone.

She crawled through the light, her eyes burning, and all at once, the narrow tunnel opened wide. She was no longer on rock, but grass, soft and green, dewy grass.

Before her stretched a vast lake, crystal blue, surface smooth as glass.

So wide was this place that she couldn't even see the opposite side of the lake—it just stretched onward.

This was it. She had made it. She had arrived at the Origin Spring, the Convergence of Talynis.

Still moving on hands and knees, she crawled to the edge of the water.

Her face looked...strange, reflected in the Spring. It seemed warped somehow. At first, she thought it was someone else looking back at her—this person was distraught. This person was lost. This person was afraid.

That wasn't her. That had never been Cassia Vantelle. She had been born for power and strength. She had never known weakness save when it was beneath her boot.

Across the water, rising gently from the azure lake, was an island of greenery.

"I would not go any farther, if I were you."

A man was standing over her shoulder. He was dressed like one of those desert nomads. In the reflection, she could not quite make out his face.

"I will not harm you, Cassia," he said. He spoke Lazarran, but what was the accent?

"How do you know my name?"

"Is it such a wonder that I should know Cassia Vantelle? You have come to destroy this place."

Slowly, Vantelle got to her feet, turning her back on the waters. Behind the stranger, she saw the small hole from which she had crawled. Looking to her left, following the edge of the water, she saw another part of the shore— there were people gathered there, all dressed in robes. They were looking at her, discussing among themselves frantically.

"Are those the Sages?" she asked.

The stranger nodded. "They fear you will destroy the Convergence, but they hesitate to approach while I am present. They cannot see me, as you can, but I have made my presence known to them."

"And who are you then?" She found herself reaching for a knife, but some part of her said that it was a futile gesture, that she was not speaking to someone she had a prayer of harming.

"Are you a spirit?" she ventured. "A god?"

He shrugged. "Questions of definition—and by some definitions, yes. Certainly I have been taken as both of those things, particularly by the Talynisti, despite my efforts. I am simply someone who has walked many paths, and one of them brought me to here and now, to counsel you this: do not attempt to cross the waters."

"So you are a Loyalist of Talynis, and therefore an enemy of Lazarra. My enemy."

Though most of his face was covered, she read displeasure in his expression. "I have an affinity for the Talynisti, but it would be incorrect to say I am allied with them. In different circumstances, I could be allied to you. Nations, worlds—these are small things to one such as me. I serve something higher. I am brought to those who brush against that higher ideal."

Vantelle swallowed. "What...what is it?"

He seemed to smile. "It is not something you are ready to be told of. But leave this place now, and you may begin the journey toward that truth."

Something tugged her toward him. She wanted to believe him.

And then she caught herself.

"More deception," she spat. "The Convergence is on that island over there, is it not?"

The stranger grew solemn. "It is. If you were to make it across the water, you would find a thread of crystal spun between two flowers. Simply shatter it between your fingers and the bridge between worlds in this place will collapse."

"So what is the trap? Are there beasts in the water? Riptides?"

"Nothing of the sort—in most places, it is shallow enough to walk. But you would die, Cassia. Arkhon has no power to protect you here—this place is beyond even his sight. The water is judgment. Once you enter it, you may not turn back. You will be judged—and not only by the waters, but by yourself."

Her fists clenched. "What do you mean?"

He spread his arms. "This place is not only a bridging between spirits and mortals. The unseen realm is pregnant with all potentialities of being— every set of identities that may become realized. In the waters, you confront the fullness of everything you could have been. Your highest self, your highest ideal. A vision of Cassia Vantelle so unfathomable that if you saw her you might drop to your knees and worship her as a god."

His voice did not carry a shred of falsehood—but it did carry warning. Pleading, even.

"I said I came here to counsel you, Cassia. I come to you at the crossroads of life and death. If you turn back now, you will live."

"And what life," she breathed, "will await me there? Will I find what I want?"

"I cannot tell you what will happen—save that it would be the first step to finding what you *need*."

He stretched out his hand. "Come, let us return to the surface."

And she realized something had changed—she could see his face now. He was looking at her with a strange, mismatched gaze.

With trembling fingers, she reached for his hand.

And smacked it away.

"No," she snarled. "I know what you offer. Failure, mediocrity, the slow slide into insignificance."

She turned her back on him.

"Why would I need you?" she snapped, staring at her own face in the water. "Why would I need *anyone*?"

The stranger was silent. She glimpsed his reflection and saw he was aggrieved. *Pathetic.*

"I am here, I alone. I am by myself, and I am all that I need. *I am all that I need!*"

This water—this place, this nation, this world—it was hers, hers by right of conquest. She was the judge; she was the one who rendered rule.

On her knees, bent over the lake, she plunged her hands into the Origin Spring, the cool waters of life and creation, and drank.

It was cold. It was refreshing.

It was scalding. It was caustic.

Vantelle screamed as the liquid flowed through her, cutting a burning trail through her mouth, throat, stomach.

And it spread, tendrils of white-hot agony curling and lancing through her.

Losing herself in the pain, she pitched forward and fell into the Spring.

For a moment, all was bright and blinding and boiling—and then, nothing.

The waters stilled.

77

INTO THE DEPTHS OF THE EARTH

I SAW a messenger with lips of gold and legs of bronze descending from the clouds in a burning chariot, and he told me to write down this revelation.

'In this way shall Talynis be humbled:

'By fire and the sword shall a wayward people be made to remember the source of their strength,

'And by the lowest shall kings be returned to humility.

'The law to which the mighty make false obeisance shall be restored,

'And the wisdom which the proud hide shall be proclaimed in the streets.'

—*Book of the Nameless Prophet*

~

THE HORSES WERE SCREAMING. Avi felt the vibrations of their shuddering all around him. He had been buried to his chest.

He spat sand from his mouth. At least he could breathe.

"Are you two alive?" he huffed. The darkness seemed to press in on his eyes.

"Yeah," groaned Yaros. "Reiva's still out."

Charas coughed. "Hang on, I can just about free my legs."

Then a deeper rumbling began.

The horses' wails grew more shrill. Avi's stomach turned in on itself.

He braced himself to be crushed.

He didn't even have time to say a prayer before blazing bright light burst into the gloom.

Avi squinted at the little sun. The light was casting two shadows against the earthen wall.

A oil lamp, he realized.

Two men had come into the cavern through a tunnel.

And with a start, Avi realized he recognized one of them—Wakaram's younger brother, who had seen them off the morning of their ill-fated trap. "Bebar!" he cried.

The Sage glanced at him, but quickly turned his attention away.

Avi turned, taking in the sight.

The cavern might have been about the size of Madam Sahir's basement, were it not packed with so much sand. What's more, pillars of rock rose from the ground, holding up a ceiling of too-smooth stone.

Yaros grunted, wresting an arm out of the sand, clutching a knife. "Right, now it makes sense. Come for revenge?"

Bebar's jaw clenched. "Someday I will have it, brother-slayer. But what is happening now is greater than the evil you have done to my blood."

Yaros groaned as he struggled for freedom. "Sure, you opened a sinkhole and trapped us here to chat."

"We brought you down," intoned the elder Sage, "for *her.*"

Yaros scoffed, snaking his free arm around Rebbaelah's unconscious form, trapped at his side. "Not telling me anything I didn't already know. What—couldn't kill her in a fair fight, so you figured you'd seize your opportunity after she saved your boss over there?"

The elder scowled. "The Wolf is an ally, but not our leader. And if you keep talking, she will die on her own."

Charas cut in. "Yaros, there's something beneath us. Like Reiva's power, only a thousand times stronger."

Yaros shot her a look. "And how the hell do you know that?"

Bebar raised his chin. "She is a god-hunter. Half-trained, but she has the sight."

The mercenary sighed. "You know, I'm getting real sick of people talking about all this magical babble like I'm supposed to know what it means."

"What it means," said Bebar, "is that the world is bigger than nations at war. The Adept's *ruakh* has pled her case, and it is required she undergo the test."

Avi suddenly remembered the man of fire he had seen as death closed in on him, the one who had seemed to send power through his sister when she healed him.

"You said she would die if we don't do anything," he said. "Does that mean you can save her?"

Bebar sniffed. "She may die either way, but this is the only way she has a chance."

Yaros laughed. "Charas, tell me you're not buying this. They're going to put her through this 'test' by feeding her poison or throwing her down a pit."

But the Parthavan's lips were pressed together. She seemed to be concentrating on Rebbaelah, looking with an intensity that seemed at odds with her impish features. "Reiva's soul is...mangled. She's fading quickly. We might not have a choice."

"You do not," said the elder Sage. "Agree to cooperate, or we leave you buried here."

Avi looked at his sister's unconscious form, her head tipped to the side, blood smeared across her features.

He swallowed. "She's my blood. I should get to—"

"Oh piss off!" snapped Yaros. "This morning you would have slit her throat and danced on her corpse."

"Why would they have kept us alive if all they wanted to do was kill us?"

Yaros faltered. He glanced at Rebbaelah.

"We go with them," said Charas.

"But she stays with me. Any of you try anything—"

Bebar spread his hands, and the sand holding them slid away.

The horses reared up, but Charas quickly got hold of their reins and shushed them.

Yaros cradled Rebbaelah in his arms, one hand still holding his knife. He cast about, only for Bebar to wave his hand. More sand melted away, revealing the windsword. The earth rustled and shifted, carrying it to Bebar's feet before it sunk out of sight again. "Place your weapons here. The place we go is sacred. Blood must not be spilled."

Yaros frowned. "I'll put it away, but I'm not handing it over." He sheathed the knife. "I'll be sure to wait until we're topside to gut you."

"Sensible," drawled the elder. "But you must hand the Adept over to the Wolf. Only one of Talynisti blood may present her to the test."

Yaros opened his mouth to protest, only for Rebbaelah to let out a faint groan. Charas knit her brow. "Do it, Yaros. She doesn't have long."

Reluctantly, Yaros handed her over to Avi, who took her in his still-shackled arms. Immediately, he was startled by how light she seemed to be. That didn't make sense—it wasn't like she'd been wasting away for weeks. Yet somehow, she seemed not just frail, but almost...hollow.

What was happening to her?

As they went, Bebar widened the tunnel enough so the horses could fit. They seemed nervous, but somehow Charas was able to keep them calm. Avi had heard about the Parthavan skill with horses, but this seemed almost supernatural. Then again, based on what the older Sage had said, maybe it was.

As they descended, the air did not thin. In fact, the lower they went into the depths of the earth, the cleaner the air felt.

"We're going to the Origin Spring," said Avi.

The older Sage turned to look at him, then nodded. "The lifeblood of Talynis itself, the locus of our arcane might. It is the only way she can be healed from the injuries sustained to her spirit."

As they went deeper, his sister stirred. At first, he thought she might wake, but the longer it went on, the more it seemed like someone having a bad dream, unable to escape.

When they came to the end of the tunnel, Bebar pushed his hands forward, and the wall opened up. Pale blue light flooded in.

The place was expansive, lit by strange glowing plants Avi had never seen before.

And it was filled with Sages.

Yaros grew tense, but Avi wasn't worried about him.

He *was* perturbed by how keenly they all seemed to watch Rebbaelah, how they pointed and whispered to one another. She was trembling in his arms now, like she had a fever, but her skin remained cold.

Just what was going on with his sister?

These were Desert Sages—they had been just as intent on killing her as he had been. Now they wanted to save her? Because of, what had the Sage said, her *ruakh*?

The elder Sage motioned for Avi to follow, but said that Yaros and Charas would have to stay here. Yaros protested, but the Sage was resolute.

"Only children of Talynis may go further. The power of this place is too great, and it will drive you mad if your ancestry is not of the desert."

Yaros clenched his fists. "I'm bound by contract to protect her."

"You can hardly fulfill that obligation if you are dead." With that, he turned.

Yaros stepped forward, but a younger Sage interposed himself.

It was the wrong move. In an instant, the mercenary had the younger man in a hold, knife to his throat.

The air charged with power as a half-dozen Sages prepared to attack.

"Don't want me spilling blood in your sacred space?" said Yaros. "Let us in."

The elder Sage darkened. "You are not worthy of—"

"I am a hand of the Krypteia, and a scion to House Letiades, keepers of the seven deadly arts of Orcaes, god of the underworld, in whose mysteries I am a full initiate. I am more than capable of setting foot in here."

More than one Sage went pale.

Charas spoke up. "And I am the daughter of Tobron, the Son of Thunder, favored servant of Kashakran the Heavenly Huntress. With the divine sight I have glimpsed the star-ways and shot the black-feathered arrows. You *will* allow us entry."

"Oh, let them in," snapped Bebar. "Time is too short for squabbling. And the mercenary's life is mine to claim, I remind you all."

Yaros smiled thinly and released his hostage.

The elder Sage looked ready to burst out in a fit of rage, but he turned to lead them on. He muttered something to Bebar, who simply shrugged.

Avi followed through another tunnel. This one was smooth, like the one he had seen going down from the dungeon, the one Vantelle had taken.

Where was she? Was it possible she had made it down here?

Avi marveled as they walked. The further they went, the more lush the place became. They passed through gardens so vibrant and diverse with life they made the palatial grounds look plain by comparison. He nearly tripped over his feet as he saw a lamb dozing in the grass, side-by-side with a jackal. The horses whinnied gleefully and broke into a run.

"What is all of this?" he asked breathlessly.

"Talynis as it ought to be. As it was." There was a wistfulness in the old man's voice.

Rebbaelah was struggling in Avi's arms now, and he had to be careful not to drop her. "What's happening?"

"She is like a man with withered legs being made to stand. This place can heal her, but it will be painful. She is being made to stretch beyond her current strength, frail as she was made. You said she saved you. Here she might be saved."

They came to a grand set of doors, seemingly carved right out of the rock. Engraved in them were countless scenes, vistas, emblems. Avi felt like he could have studied them for weeks and still found new details—but most gripping of all was a massive symbol at the center composed of three lines: two parallel and one that intersected them.

Avi couldn't even see hinges on the doors, yet they slid effortlessly along the ground. Yaros let out a low whistle. Charas muttered something in Parthavan.

"Gird yourselves," said the elder. "Do not go near the water. Do not touch it."

Before Avi could ask anything, they stepped through the gate, and the world opened up.

The chamber was so grand, Avi wasn't even sure whether *chamber* was the right word. It stretched so far that he couldn't even see the other side—it simply faded into a hazy horizon.

And filling the place was a broad, endless lake, crystal blue. Wisps of mist curled off its surface, and the sound of flowing water suffused the air with a soft rushing sound.

The ground here was flat and grassy, and countless different sorts of flowers bloomed everywhere he looked.

"Remove your sandals before you go any further," said the elder, who Avi noticed was already barefoot.

Avi knew the stories of course—you took off your shoes when you came to somewhere holy. If this place wasn't sacred, he wasn't certain what could qualify.

Avi was reluctant to set down his sister, but he didn't have to. They were not alone in this place—other Sages, old like the one who had brought him here, but seeming subordinate still, stepped forward to take her.

Yaros tried to step forward, but Charas stopped him.

One of the Sages inspected Rebbaelah's face, his features hardening.

"She is not strong enough for this, Hatzakh."

The elder Sage turned to him, severe. "Her injuries are too severe to be healed any other way. This is what must be done."

The other Sages did not object further.

Avi's stomach was sinking now, now that the time had come. "You said she might die, still."

Hatzakh shook his head.

"She *will* die. The question is whether the Spring will judge her to be worthy of rebirth. If she is found so, then the Spring will heal her, both her physical and her spiritual wounds. She will emerge from the waters with the insight."

Avi didn't know what that meant, but all he could think of was that today he would either see the last surviving family he had die, or he would witness something so mythical he had never even heard of it.

The Sages who had taken his sister were all dressed in white, spotless and pure. They bore her between them, four of them carrying her, and stepped into the waters.

As they touched the water, little sparks of light flickered.

Avi stared, mesmerized.

"The waters of the Spring destroy all that is impure. Death, filth—it cannot survive the touch of creation."

The Sages lowered Rebbaelah into the waters, then stepped away.

Avi's heart stopped as a blazing bright light burst from beneath the surface.

78

UNDYING FLAME

AND AGAIN THE MESSENGER SPOKE, planting one foot in the desert and the other in the sea.

'Let the righteous understand, for this is a great mystery, and one that shall cause many to stumble:

'By a perverse nation will the children of heaven be disciplined,

'By the godless will they return to faith.

'Pride shall shut many eyes and ears to this instruction,

'And wicked iron shall split open many bodies before they understand.

'Heaven shall use the outcast to punish the ruler,

'And the wicked to correct the righteous.'

I recorded this instruction, and for many nights wept and tore my hair over its meaning. My sons, do not be deceived.

—*Book of the Nameless Prophet*

~

DARKNESS.

Everything was darkness, and darkness was everything.

Reiva had expected death to be cold, but instead it just...

It was not. It was not cold, but neither was it warm.

It simply was not. There was no sensation to it. No value. Like staring with wide eyes into total blackness, every one of her senses strained and found nothing.

Time seemed empty too. She could hardly remember when she had come here. Had there not been blood? Was it her own?

Faces. She remembered faces.

Slowly, the darkness resolved. Her eyes ached like she was staring into the sun, but she could not shut them.

The faces were drifting out from the nothingness.

Her father. He was the first. Him laughing. Him as the infection worsened, still forcing a smile for her sake.

Alyat. Brusque, irritable. Proud, now and then.

They were dead. Did this mean she had finally reached them? Was this what the afterlife was—fleeting touches, brushing up against the souls of those whom you never had enough time with during life?

That seemed a torment.

If she was being punished, then her torturer was only just beginning.

She saw her father die again, lying on the cot before her, making her promise.

The promise. Had she kept her promise? She wanted to sob, but she didn't think she could.

Alyat. Alyat was on the floor of his office, clutching at his skull.

Was this how he had died, all alone?

No—not alone. Someone else was there. She wanted to see their face, to know who she needed to kill to avenge her teacher.

The tableau dissolved into void.

More deaths came to her. Legionnaires on the battlefield—some from engagements that had happened years ago, others from today.

Had it been today, or had it been lifetimes ago? How long had she been here? Had she already wondered that?

Then she saw snow, blood on the ice. She saw faces frozen in terror and unbridled agony as their bodies broke. She saw men wailing for their mothers, clutching at spilled intestines as blood gushed from them.

She should have died with them that day.

She should have died underneath that tree.

Who lit you?

She could see herself, a bloody, mangled mess, sitting in the snow, pale as death. She had been so tired...she had let go. You weren't supposed to come back once you got to that point—Alyat had always told her as much. You gave up, and that was it. People could stave off death for a time, if they set their will to it—but death was a courteous one. If you were ready for him, he appeared straight away to spirit you off.

Why hadn't he come for her?

She saw a river, a river she had seen many years ago, flowing through the snow. She saw herself kneeling beside it, saw her younger self beside her older self, both inches from death. She felt her hand close around a stone, and she felt the determination to crack open her own skull with it. And beside her, clutching her little wrist in a gentle grasp, a man with mismatched eyes. "Rebbaelah, you are not to die today."

And she saw that same stranger standing over her. He knelt down, and she realized that someone else was there—someone with a form akin to a man's, hardly the size of her fist. This one lay in the snow, shuddering, his body woven from trembling tongues of flame.

The stranger breathed on the man of fire, and he burst into impossible brightness, the brightness of a sun. And the man of fire grew, and he bowed deeply to the man with one brown eye and one blue. And the man of fire turned, and he sent forth a jet of white-hot flame that took to the frozen leaves as to dry kindling.

The burning one dimmed then, but he did not return to his meager stature.

The tree was blazing against the night sky, blazing with an impossible fire.

She looked into it, feeling in her spirit the familiarity that came from only her fire.

It was *her* fire. It could only have been hers. She knew it like she knew her own hands and feet.

Impossible, impossible for a hundred reasons.

And yet there it burned.

As she looked into it, it expanded, growing to fill her whole vision. All she saw was the fire—and then she saw *within* the fire.

She saw herself, strangely enough. Herself as a little girl. Herself in chains. Herself dressed for the first time as an Adept.

Someone was talking to her. Murmuring.

It was familiar. Familiar like her fire, though she couldn't place who was speaking. She couldn't understand the words, either.

She saw her brother. How he was when had she been taken from him. She saw him growing up.

She *felt* him, felt how he had when she vanished. Angry. Scared. Resentful.

Angry at her. Angry that she wasn't there for him, even though he also worried for her. It was all hurt, hurt and suffering, whenever he thought of her.

Then, when he learned what she had become, that anger returned, hotter and more furious. He had wanted to kill her.

Hadn't he? Was that not why she was here?

She kept moving deeper into the fire, and she saw herself again. She saw her brother too. She saw Vantelle, holding a blade that tore holes in the fabric of reality.

Reiva watched herself channel aether without a focus, closing her brother's mortal wound, healing him. She watched herself collapse as uninhibited power tore through her soul.

She saw her brother take the *Nihilo* Blade and rip apart her magic, ruining her soul forever.

That was when she fell into the darkness.

But why wasn't the darkness still here? How had the fire kindled again?

A voice, an alien voice that was impossibly familiar, spoke.

"Reiva..."

The flame flared hotter, brighter.

Who are you?

"Arise, Reiva."

The fire blazed hotter and hotter with every word. Her skin, once numb and dull, came alive with sensation. A thousand needles pricked her, and as she looked, the fire washed over her, but did not consume her.

She saw herself curled up inside that fire, saw plumes of vile smoke blacker than night billowing from her skin, from her mouth, her eyes.

"Arise, Reiva."

Why did the voice sound so familiar?

How do I know you?

Tongues of flame resolved again into the scene in the dungeon. She watched Vantelle slit her brother's throat. Watched herself intervene.

But there was someone else now. How had she not seen before—there was someone over her shoulder, but when she tried to look at him, it was like her mind rebelled. She could not understand what she was looking at.

A man, but not a man. He was formed of fire, and he bore the likeness of a warrior. His arms were thickly muscled, wrapped with bands of red-hot iron, and his torso was marked with a hundred words she could not read. At the waist, his body turned to a plume of fire, and he hovered over the ground like a falcon hovered over the desert.

His eyes—his eyes were blazing coals, white and radiant, red and raging.

He turned those eyes upon her and spoke.

"Reiva!"

She opened her eyes.

She saw above her a blazing light, as though looking at the sun from underwater.

Her lungs were burning, burning for air. She *was* underwater. Every inch of skin was screaming, like she had been scoured by a boar bristle brush.

Reiva burst through the surface, gasping for air.

Why was everything so bright? Why was everything so loud?

The water was cold as ice and hot as steam all at once.

Everything was disorienting—but she could see the fire. *Her* fire.

She kicked toward it, feeling solid earth beneath her feet. She stumbled, falling headlong into the shallows, then pushed herself up again.

Her armor was gone, vanished. Naked as a newborn, she felt everything —every mote of silt and every whisper of air. Head to toe, it all stung.

Everywhere except one spot—one circle around her finger. Jaibul's ring of bone, etched with a prayer to the Wandering God. That alone had survived the waters.

Arms bore her up, pulling her from the water. She winced at their touch, then groaned as they wrapped her in a robe. Every thread scraped her skin.

"She is worthy," said an elderly voice.

"Worthy is she," chorused others.

Reiva blinked water from her eyes, squinting against the incredible *loudness* of everything. The grass was too green, its blades too sharp.

Still gasping for breath, she put down a hand to support herself, then pulled it back, hissing. She looked at her palm, half-expecting to see blood.

There was none—but there were also no callouses. She stared at the too-soft, too-pink hand, not recognizing it as her own. She tugged the robe down from her right shoulder, the shoulder that bore her military tattoo. Again, only tender skin.

People were speaking, too many people. Their voices battered her eardrums in an incomprehensible thunder.

She tried to look around again, steeling herself against the needling in her eyes.

They were wearing robes, the people around her. Robes like hers. The Talynisti Adept of Earth was there, an odd bemusement on his features.

Her brother was standing there, looking at her like she'd just sprouted wings.

But none of them held her attention for long, because *he* was there as well. Burning and bright, built of undying flame.

He was watching her with those blazing eyes, and she recognized him. Not only from her vision beneath the water—from before.

She recognized him in the first moment she kindled fire.

She recognized him in every moment of meditation, every exercise and discipline.

She recognized him in the burning tree in Hyrgallia, lit without cause— so she had thought.

"You are my Flame," she whispered.

And though she had barely breathed the words, the spirit nodded to her, approvingly.

"I am Rukhesh."

79

HERALD THE DAWN

WHEN ONE'S LIFE IS WAR AND mayhem, there are ugly necessities. The only way to bear them, I have found, is to seek out beauty and peace whenever possible. Always, there is another curse. Always, another blessing.
—*The Memoirs of Flavia Iscator*

MALIK RETURNED to Dav-maiir soon after his brother's defeat. The Lazarran legion had called a retreat—a disorderly one, given the sudden disappearance of their high commander, Praetor Cassia Vantelle. Rumors floated around that Legate Iscator, who had held command before Vantelle's arrival, had taken back control of the legion, reuniting with them somewhere in the desert. People also said that Iscator had brokered some sort of allegiance with the lord of the city Nadari while she and her detachment were away from Dav-maiir, but people were skeptical of such stories. After all, these were Lazarrans they were talking about.

The returned king had been in the city for ten days by the time the festivities began. Some particularly eager folk had started festivities of their own as soon as his banner appeared on the horizon—but those efforts paled in comparison to the jubilation the king himself sponsored.

First, though, there had been the matter of Tamiq.

The trial was held the day after Malik's return. The execution followed the day after that.

Tamiq was led out of the city, far beyond the walls, where his blood would not stain the life-giving soil. He was taken to one of the scarred patches of land to the west, where the Imperials had first laid siege to the city.

Malik was there, of course. He wore his armor, a sword strapped to his side. This would be the last act of the war his brother had sparked.

A great crowd of people was present—mostly men. What women and children had come stood further back.

Avi flowed easily among the crowd. He was dressed like anyone else today. He felt he owed it to Crow and Stag, to every Viper and fighting man of Talynis who had died as a result of Tamiq's betrayal. He owed it to them to see that the man responsible for their deaths finally received justice.

Tamiq stood alone, barefoot and naked to the waist. One hand was wrapped in bandages—fresh ones, which was quite a courtesy. He favored one leg, the other held in a splint. His hair was matted, his beard unkempt.

But he still stood tall. He still stood like a king.

As Avi looked between the two brothers, he saw the same resolute fire burning in both's eyes.

"My brother," said Malik, his voice carrying easily over the assembled throng. "You who nursed at the same breasts as I, you who lifted up my arms when I was weak—you who betrayed me. The priests and elders of Davmaiir have sat in judgment and found you guilty of transgression against our law. Do you deny your crimes?"

Tamiq's eyes narrowed, but his posture never wavered. "What crimes do you accuse me of? Let me hear."

"Treachery against the Four Gods. Murder of men who swore to defend Talynis. Declaring yourself king, a power that is only the gods' to give. Attempted murder of your own brother, the rightful king of Talynis, anointed of the Four, shepherd of our people."

With every charge levied, the crowd stirred more and more.

Avi was silent, watching Tamiq. He didn't care for the theatrics, though he knew they mattered. The story of what transpired here would fly through the whole city by sundown—the whole country within weeks.

But all Avi cared was to look the man in the eye, if only for one moment.

Tamiq spoke. "My brother, you say I am a criminal in all that I did. But all I did, I did for Talynis, I did for—"

He went on, but now the crowd was in a frenzy. People were spitting, shouting accusations, curses, shouting their support of Malik alone—anything to drown out Tamiq's words.

Still, Avi had not held Tamiq's gaze.

Malik raised his hand. He was standing on a hill so all could see him as he oversaw the proceedings.

Yet this did not quiet the crowd, and so Malik's honor guard had to raise their own voices over the clamor. Even this did not bring silence—only a constrained grumbling.

"High priest," intoned the king. "What is our law?"

The (recently installed) high priest stepped up beside Malik, holding in his hand a scroll of the law. He unfurled it—this too was for show, for he would have known every word by heart—and opened his mouth to speak. "This we demand of you: you shall not suffer the murderer. You shall not suffer the blasphemer, the one who falsely acts in our names. You shall not suffer the one who acts against his father's house, or who is treacherous to the one we raise up to lead you."

"So be it!" yelled one, and others took up the cry.

"So be it!"

"So be it!"

And the high priest bellowed the final words, "So you shall purge the evil from your midst, lest all be led astray!"

"So be it!"

"What," said Malik, "are your last words, brother of my blood?"

It was almost impossible to hear, but Avi was listening, straining all his awareness to catch the final words of the man who had upended his world.

"I only laugh," answered he, "to see how many of my once-loyal men now raise their hands against me."

And he swept his gaze over the crowd, and for the briefest of moments, his eyes met Avi's.

And Avi saw he had no shame or guilt within him.

Someone pressed a stone into his hand. He looked down at it, and for a moment he thought he saw his sister holding that rock from the river.

He cast his vision about, searching for the stranger with mismatched eyes, but did not find him.

He did not see who had pressed the stone into his hand, nor who cast the first stone, but more quickly followed it.

Tamiq had stood proud under the sweltering noonday sun—but he was only a man. As the stones struck him, he doubled over, his hands feebly moving to cover himself as massive bruises weltered his skin and bones broke with sickening *cracks*.

Avi took a breath, smothering the raucous din of the crowd. Narrowing his whole perception to only Tamiq.

He had come here for Crow and Stag. He had come here for the dead.

But he had come here for Asrah, too.

He drew back his arm, sighting his target. "So be it," whispered Avi. And he hurled the stone with an assassin's precision—and a mercy that might have been a son-in-law's. It struck true, opening an ugly gash in Tamiq's forehead.

The usurper's head whipped back, blood and brains spattering. His eyes rolled back, consciousness fleeing him.

Avi let out the breath he had been holding. Stones continued to fly, piling into a heap.

He turned, half-expecting someone to stop him, but all eyes were on the usurper. So, as was his way, Avi slipped out of sight.

After a seven-day period of cleansing, so that those who had participated in the stoning could purify themselves of the blood they had shed, the proper celebration began. It was a spectacle like nothing in living memory—not even at the birth of Malik's first son had Dav-maiir been so exultant.

Roasted calves, the finest spices, rich wines—it was a banquet to rival the feasts of heaven—and all at the expense of the royal treasury, which certainly lifted the mood. If there was one thing folks didn't mind the king spending their taxes on, it was food and drink for the people.

On every street corner, some new song was being raised to the glory of the true king and his triumph over his wicked brother, Tamiq the Accursed, the Usurper, the Imperial Lapdog.

There were even some lines, surprisingly, about the valiant service of a handful of King's Vipers who had survived Tamiq's purge. It may have been the first time in history that the Vipers received such plain acclaim, the necessity of their existence having always been one of shadows and ignominious acts.

Even more surprising, though, was that the king affirmed the truth of the songs when, in the sight of all Dav-maiir, he set a ring on the finger of Aviqohl beyt'Avadh, draped a fine cloak over his shoulders, and hung a golden chain around his neck.

Avi knelt on a scaffold erected before the palace, receiving these honors with a burning face. He had no mask, no hood. His hair had been oiled, his beard trimmed.

His eyes flitted to the side, where Malik's children stood—his two sons, and his recently adopted daughter, who had displayed unfaltering loyalty to her uncle by risking her life for the Loyalist cause, even unto kidnapping by an Imperial Adept.

Asrah gave him a small smile, but Malik's words drew his attention back.

In contrast to how he had extolled Avi's service moments before, now the king spoke softly so that only Avi could hear.

"You should know, son, that Lereias spoke quite highly to me of you. He thought you might one day succeed him."

Tears stung Avi's eyes, and he dropped his gaze.

Crow...I never knew your name, and now you're gone.

"Your servant," he croaked, "only wishes that such a day may have come many years from now, my king."

Malik made a sound that was half agreement, half approval. But Avi did not think the king would be dissuaded from carrying out Crow's wishes.

After Avi stepped down, another went up, and so the ceremonies continued. There was much honor to dispense and valor to recognize. All the while, Avi wished he could disappear, but he stayed. Now and then, he'd cast a glance at Asrah, but she always kept her eyes studiously on her uncle and the proceedings.

After the pomp was finished, there was much feasting to enjoy. Wine flowed freely, and more than one person sought to congratulate Avi (and curry favor, of course). Avi suffered this for as long as he could manage, but after an hour or so, he worked to disentangle himself and get away. This was wonderful—but there was another gathering he needed to attend.

"I'm telling you, my betrothed spoke to the Adept!"

He stopped, turning to look at the man who had spoken.

Stories about Rebbaelah had spread like, well, like fire. No one seemed able to agree on *exactly* what had transpired during the chaos of that day, but the prevailing narrative seemed to have it that the Adept—a Talynisti woman by birth—had suddenly switched allegiances in the climactic moment, killing the Lazarran praetor and throwing the legion into disarray before disappearing into the desert without a trace.

Avi had not seen fit to speak of his role in those events, nor to confirm or deny what was true, though he was sure someone would eventually put together his hand in all of it. He would likely need to recount it all to the king before long.

"Bah! You're telling tales again."

"Swear on my sword! In the palace we stand before, my betrothed was a spy, and she brought a message to the Empire's Lion."

Avi's better judgment told him he should move on, but...

"Your betrothed sounds like a woman of courage," he said, stepping into the gathering of soldiers. These were men at arms who had come from Shugrith with Malik. They gaped at him, fixing upon the golden chain Malik had set on his neck.

Avi smiled easily. "What is your name, friend?"

"Bareli, son of Eliasab, my lord." He seemed awestruck. Avi felt a twinge of humor as he realized Bareli had never seen him before, given that Avi had always been on a rooftop or leering from an alleyway.

"And what is your betrothed's name?"

"Samara, my lord!" he said, more vigorously this time. "Your servant would tell you her father's name, but..."

Avi clapped a hand on Bareli's shoulder. The man froze.

Avi let his smile grow, and he realized—with a measure of surprise—that it was wholly genuine. "May the Four on High bless your marriage, friend. Your bride-to-be has served our king well, as I am sure you have as well."

"Th-thank you, my lord."

Avi nodded to the rest of the soldiers, taking some pleasure in their expressions. "Long live Malik."

"Long live Malik!"

And with that, he left, tucking the chain beneath his clothes as he stepped into the night. From a barrel, he retrieved his familiar hooded cloak, tattered and worn. And he felt like himself again, as he made his way through the street of his city, a city finally at peace again.

If the celebration at the palace was grand, the mood in the Singing Owl was nothing short of ecstatic. Old Zebon must have been feeling the jubilant mood as well, because he produced a cask of fine Karellan wine, and was filling cups at no cost.

He also knew how to take care of reliable patrons, and he had a sharp eye. Soon as he spied Avi, he glided over and took him to a back room. He also assured Avi, no matter his protests, that there would be no charge for the room or whatever they ate or drank.

"You've saved the Owl, son—hardly be fair of me to charge you after that."

Avi nodded his thanks. Malik had handsomely rewarded him, so he wasn't hurting for coin, but he still appreciated the gesture.

"For this week, at least," chuckled Zebon.

Avi grinned. "Fair enough."

If the barkeep thought Avi was more subdued, he said nothing about it. Avi was glad for it. He wasn't sure why he had been feeling like this either, and he didn't feel particularly inclined to speak on it.

He wouldn't be able to avoid that with Asrah, though. He wasn't sure whether he was grateful or nervous about that. Maybe both.

In silence, Avi nibbled on some cakes (honeyed, with dates and figs) Zebon had set on the table. Before long, he brought in two people—one of them looking like a bear draped in a cloak, the other with an elegant, blue silk headdress, one of her sleeves falling longer than the other.

Mouse and Jackal took their seats without a word. Zebon served wine and then left them be, telling them to knock on the door if they had need.

For a while, they nursed their drinks in silence. For the past week they had been swarmed by various obligations—Mouse had helped keep guard over Tamiq and acted as a liaison with the Sages, Jackal had seen to their old headquarters and the search of the legion garrison, and Avi had been overseeing efforts to lay the foundation for the reconstitution of the Vipers.

Now that they had freedom, they didn't feel in a rush to use it.

Mouse was the first to speak up. "Feels strange, does it not? Relieving and sad, all at once."

The other two muttered their agreement.

"You come to expect it, over time. In Endra, we perform rituals at the end of every battle, recognizing that we have survived and others have not. Giving thanks and grieving. At the end of a war, we take a month for such things."

"And that helps?" asked Jackal softly.

Mouse shrugged. "It does, but no ritual can ever fully heal you. That takes time."

They fell into another lapse of silence.

Eventually, Avi brought himself to ask the question that had been on his mind this whole time. "So what now?" He nodded to Mouse. "Going back to Endra?"

The big man scratched at his beard. "Eventually, yes. I miss my wife and children, of course. I made a promise to Crow, however."

"Crow is dead," murmured Avi. "And you captured Tamiq almost single-handedly. You don't owe anyone here anything anymore."

Mouse nodded solemnly. "Perhaps. Debts can transfer, though."

"To who?"

Mouse smiled lopsidedly. "To *you*, little Wolf."

Avi snorted, shaking his head. "I shouldn't take over. I think Malik wants me to, but..."

Jackal rolled her eyes. "If not you, then who?"

He shrugged. "There were two Vipers with Malik in Shugrith—Hawk and Hound. They would—"

"Not be anywhere near as good as you. They practically got a vacation while you were here, and you stepped up when we lost Crow."

"What about you? Front-line fighter, wounded in the line of duty, partially responsible for establishing contact with the Sages—"

"And a woman. A *Zarushan* woman. Besides, I'm tired of skulking around in shadows. I only joined up in the first place because I owed Crow—and that's settled now. I'm not going to play attack dog for Malik."

"Are you leaving Talynis, then?"

She gave a noncommittal shrug. "Not necessarily. Dav-maiir, perhaps, but there aren't many places in the world that are still free of Lazarra's grasp. Might head up to Zarush, see whether things have gotten any better. Or who knows, maybe I go retire in Karella, finally see those beaches Stag was always on about. We'll have to see. For now, I'm enjoying living off our just rewards for getting Malik back in his chair."

Avi caught the displeasure with which she spoke of the king. They had all had their own reasons for why they fought against Lazarra. For him, it had been for the cause, more than anything. For Mouse and Jackal, it was more out of loyalty to Crow—and now that tether was gone.

Stag had been around for business reasons. He wondered what he would have been up to now. Probably complaining that he hadn't been fairly compensated.

"So what *do* you want to do?" asked Jackal. "You're going to stay here?"

Avi nodded.

"Still sneaking into a certain upper-story room?"

Avi flushed, setting Jackal snickering.

"I haven't talked to her yet," he said honestly.

She stopped laughing, giving him a look of disapproval. "It's been weeks since we pushed out Tamiq and the Empire. Don't you think she wants to see you?"

Avi squirmed uncomfortably under her gaze. "Things are different now."

"Yes—her father is no longer the king you spent every waking moment trying to dislodge. Malik would have been well within his rights to imprison Asrah, even to kill her. The fact that he was swayed to adopt her as one of his own is nothing short of remarkable."

Avi nodded along—he knew all that. He may have even had a hand in making sure Malik knew the role Asrah had played in the Loyalist movement.

But now she was back in the palace, and that left them in an odd spot. Admittedly, he hadn't thought too extensively about what would happen afterward. He had just planned to sort things out once it came to that. Now, that time had come, and she was still somehow the daughter of the king—only this time, the rightful king. The king Avi had put back on the throne.

That didn't bode well for their chances.

Mouse was watching his expression, and reached over to clap a hand on his shoulder. "Listen, little Wolf. I may not look it, but I am a wise old man."

Jackal snorted, but Mouse kept going.

"There is never such a thing as a perfect time; there are only those that are better and worse. The right time, often, is simply whatever is before you. You know how I met my wife? I conquered a city for my prince. I was a vanguard fighter at the fore. And after the dust had settled, as we were driving out the last of the fleeing enemy warriors, some woman walked up to me, lifting the hem of her skirt so it wouldn't drag through the blood, and said, 'Three of my brothers died or fled today, and my parents are long dead. I refuse to let my family line break off in such a disgraced manner. Either marry me today, or kill me here and now.'"

Avi stared. "And you said *yes*?"

"I was too scared to say no," he chuckled.

Jackal sipped her drink. "Maybe I should visit Endra before going to Karella," she mused. "Get to know her."

Mouse cackled. "She would think you're a bad influence on the children."

"Every child should have an aunt to be a bad influence."

Mouse threw up his hands. "I just survived another war and you're trying to get me killed at home!" But he was laughing, and Avi was glad to see his friends' mirth.

"So you're saying I should stop shuffling my feet in the sand."

Mouse raised his cup. "You never know what happens tomorrow."

Avi couldn't argue with that, so he just took another swallow of wine. By now, he was feeling a buzz building in his skull. It took him back to lost days, youthful days spent sneaking drinks, passing out behind buildings with friends, waking up with a pounding headache. The people in the tavern, despite the wall separating them, were carousing and reveling so boisterously that Avi felt as though he were right in the middle of them—but he didn't share their cheer.

He caught a glimpse of himself reflected in his drink—and he was startled by how old he seemed. He looked like his father, he thought.

As soon as that thought happened, his mind turned back to his sister.

He hadn't seen her since that day at the Spring. She was with the Desert Sages still, apparently undergoing some sort of training.

Now and then, he would think about that man of fire that had been standing over his sister, who he had seen for those brief moments he was at death's door.

He wanted to ask her about that. He wanted to ask her about many things.

He wanted to clear the pain and scars that lay between them, most of all. He wanted to find out why she had saved him in the end.

Maybe, somewhere inside, he even wanted them to be siblings again. He had no idea what that would mean, what was going to happen to her now. Would she be a Sage the rest of her life? That just didn't seem possible. He was fairly certain he hadn't seen any women among their number during his brief time down there.

He also wondered what had become of Yaros and Charas. He was not surprised that he hadn't seen them—too much of a risk if anyone recognized them as being with the legion—but he also found it hard to imagine they were living down there in the caves.

The conversation turned to other things. Small remembrances of how life had been before Tamiq's usurpation. Recollections of Crow and Stag— good-natured ribbing of the departed, as well as one another.

Eventually, they slipped out. There were embraces, words of well-wishing. All three went in different directions.

Avi wondered if they would meet again.

On an impulse, he looked up to the sky. The moon was full again, casting the city in pale brightness.

Avi turned around, looking here and there.

He was all alone, as far as he could tell.

So he muttered under his breath an old prayer to the Wandering God:

"Bless and keep those who walk along unknown roads, along the edges of the world. Go before us and bring us to our graves, and to what lies beyond, that we may take comfort in knowing we do not go alone."

And though he walked alone, he went on his way knowing he had been heard.

～

THE PALACE WAS A STRANGE SIGHT, in the wake of the last battle for the city— the Retaking of Dav-maiir, as it was coming to be known. Guards manned the gaping holes in the outer wall, as reconstruction efforts were still ongoing.

The allegiances of many of the guards were a confusing web, so many times had sides changed and changed back. Malik, wisely in Avi's estimation, had chosen to be generous with his pardons. There had been executions too, of course, mostly of those who either had been instrumental in helping Tamiq take power, or of those who witnesses testified had abused their power. The sword was used for those—the spectacle of stoning one man had been enough for a city so weary of death.

All that to say, the guards who were on duty tonight were particularly vigilant—both out of caution in the wake of such tumultuous times, and out of a desire to prove that they were willing and able to serve Malik.

Vigilant as they were, though, Avi was still a Viper. He took care, but he was able to make his way across the grounds with all his usual stealth.

The walls had suffered some damages, though this side was more or less untouched. As he climbed, he benefited from a couple of new handholds.

It was only once he reached the balcony that he realized he had no way of being certain this was still Asrah's room. For all he knew, she had moved elsewhere once Malik's own children returned.

Then again, she *was* one of Malik's children now—adopted and severed from the family line of Tamiq the usurper.

She had been popular while Tamiq was in power; when the people heard she had been loyal to her uncle all along, they fell even further in love with the princess.

Avi knew what that was like, but he also wasn't as thrilled about the adoption. Princesses got married off to princes, as things went.

He realized he had been lurking outside the door for nearly five minutes, thoughts tumbling.

Well, either knock or go back.

Eventually, he chose to knock.

But he also scrambled back over the lip of the balcony, dangling from his fingertips, just in case.

After a brief lull, the door eased open.

Avi peeked over the edge.

It was Asrah.

And she was holding a knife.

Avi pulled himself over. "Long time no see."

The princess stifled a shriek, nearly lashing out with a knife. She gave him a flat glare. "Last time I opened this door, a man kidnapped me and took me flying over the city."

Avi hummed. "Well, I can't fly, but I brought some wine."

Asrah snorted, a smile crossing her lips. "I suppose that will have to do."

It was almost startling to Avi how easily they fell back into normalcy.

The wineskin was, admittedly, small—short notice and he needed something he could easily strap to himself for the climb—but it was a good drink. They handed the skin back and forth, sitting on her floor, talking of what had happened since they last met.

Asrah told him how she had stayed in the Temple until her uncle returned, and how only once Malik gave assurance of her safety did the people allow her to leave.

"You would think they all saw me as *their* daughter."

"The people love you," he said easily. "That's not insignificant. It's a good thing."

She nodded absently.

"How are you getting along with your cousins?"

A shrug. "Politely. The eldest seems to have a dislike of me."

Avi snorted softly. "Is being heir to the throne not enough for him?"

Asrah tensed. "Maybe not. It's understandable, I suppose. He saw his father nearly lose the kingship. He's going to be skeptical of anyone who had a part in that."

"Even though you helped his father reclaim the throne."

She shrugged. "Men in power have strange fears."

They passed more of the time in silence. Avi told her about his sister— how she was the Adept, how she had been taken from Talynis, sold into slavery by their mother. He tried to explain what had happened beneath the city, but kept stumbling over his words as he tried to describe. Through it all, Asrah listened attentively, asking a question here and there.

"What do you want of her?" she asked as the story wound down to a close.

"I don't know."

"Yes you do, you just need to be honest with yourself about what it is."

He admitted she was probably right about that, and that was the end of that discussion. He was grateful that she didn't press him on it. He would tell her when he was ready for that. If ever he was ready for that.

Eventually, the skin was empty, and they set it aside.

At some point, they ended up lying down on the bed, her head resting against his chest as he ran his fingers through her hair.

It was comfortable to be like that, but neither of them were relaxed.

Asrah pushed herself up, propped up on one arm. Their eyes met in the dark.

"I'm still a princess," she said. She sounded regretful of it.

"You are."

Her eyes dropped away. Avi reached out to caress her cheek, and she took his hand, wrapping it in both of hers. She pressed a kiss to each of his knuckles, then turned back to him.

A sad smile lit her face. "You're crying, Aviqohl."

"Hm?" He touched his cheeks, surprised to feel they were wet. "Sorry, I just...I was thinking of the others."

She nodded, but didn't press him further. They held one another in the dark, arms wrapped around and legs tangled together. Avi had no idea how much time had passed. He hoped it had stopped, just for them. He hoped this night would stretch and stretch and stretch, and the moon would hang eternal in the sky, and they would never have to leave or speak to another soul.

He hoped—but he knew things like that didn't really happen. People died in wars. People were separated. People had their hearts broken. And all the while, the sun and moon kept up their dance, marching onward day by night by day, and bringing forth new pains, new pleasures.

"What are we going to do?" he whispered, soft as he could, as if even voicing the question might shatter the moment.

Asrah didn't have an answer for him at first. She just held him, looking into his eyes. Not to intimidate, not to interrogate—just to understand. To open to one another and be wordlessly understood.

Finally, she spoke. "We'll figure something out. We'll make plans. We'll sort through our options."

"We will."

"But..."

Avi's heart lurched. "But what?"

She paused, and Avi could see some internal back-and-forth tugging behind her eyes.

"But will you promise me, right now, that whatever happens, whatever obstacles lie in our path, whatever or whoever tries to stop us—promise me you won't give in."

Avi sat with that. He let it turn over in his mind.

There really wasn't anything else he *could* do, when he thought about it.

"I would never let it be any other way, Asrah. I'm not going to give up. And if you think I'm going to let anything less than an army stop me, then you can go talk to the legion."

She was smiling. "I'd rather not go back—they don't wash well, many of them."

"Ever the princess."

Her laugh was soft, and when she pressed her lips to his, they were even softer.

When she pulled away, she ran her fingers along his cheek. "I love you."

Heart in his throat, he answered. "And I love you."

In one another's arms, they heard the first crow of the rooster herald the dawn.

80

SCENT OF THE POWER

'TEND to all the creatures of the earth, of the sea, and of the sky—for the breath of humans rules the breath of animals, and so you must steward them well. By this you shall honor the Windmother.'

So say the Talynisti scriptures. I have often puzzled over that line about the breaths, but I have an inkling as to its significance. You can see it among the Parthavan Hunters—who, even as they slay beasts, do so with a sort of love. They see, with those strange eyes of theirs, the unity of it all, the way it all holds together.

But what, I wonder, is the center around which it all holds?

—*The Life and Wisdom of Simeon Binkhok As Told by Himself*

~

THE RAT SCAMPERED ALONG A HALLWAY. He paused, sniffing the air. The human—one of those rare humans who could sense and touch the power—had fixed the image into his mind. It was a hazy image, but the human trusted him to figure it out.

That gave the rat some cheer.

As he sniffed, he sensed a whiff of power coming from the right. The rat headed for it, whiskers twitching. His paws made a soft pattering sound in the dark, loud to his ears but unnoticeable to most humans. The rat was sneaking, after all—he was quite good at it, which was why the human had chosen him.

What a strange moment, that. There was his whole life in memories—emotions, desires, sensations. The delight of finding a discarded rind of cheese. The surging terror when that scarred-up cat came after him while he nibbled.

Then, the human had touched him, had put some of the power *into* him, and somehow everything had *clicked* together in a new way—suddenly there was something more than just a collection of impulses and wants.

And amid that new something, he had received direction from the human. He had seen the building and what he was supposed to find within it. He knew he had to be quiet and careful, especially of the humans who could touch the power.

The rat saw one of those now. A human with red fur around the shoulders—that red often grew on humans who could touch the power. Other humans feared the humans who grew the red; the rat had smelled that fear many a time. There had been many humans in this place, and on all of them, he caught the scent of fear.

He could understand why—as his nose twitched, he caught the scent of an unseen one, a creature of the power. Such creatures lingered around the humans who could touch the power. They built connections with them.

A twinge of fear seized the rat. The old instinct—perhaps the oldest—told him to freeze, to turn tail and flee. There was death on this human. The smell of blood and power used to kill.

For a moment, the rat's mind shook, like the rafters of a building when the humans started demolishing it.

The rat stiffened. Instinct hammered at his nerves, demanding he obey—demanding he set aside this new thing he had received from the human and return to the rule of the instincts.

But no, the rat did not want to hand control back to them. Not yet. He still had to repay the human who had given him this gift.

The blood-power humans could lurk around these hallways as much as they liked, they could guard as many doors as they pleased—the rat was not one to be deterred.

Rather than go near this human, the rat squeezed through a crack in the wall, finding himself in a pitch-black tunnel. Water, rainwater by the scent, flowed across his paws. The smell masked the waft of the power, but the rat recalled the direction. He scampered through the dark, his little paws going *splish splash splish.*

Yes, the scent of the power, stronger here. The rat squeezed through another crack and found himself in a massive room. Humans did not often build rooms so large, but even rarer was a room that reeked so strongly of the power. Why, it practically buzzed his ears, so great was the concentration.

Again, the rat's mind trembled. The morsel of power the human had placed inside him wavered.

The rat squeaked to himself, the way mother-rat used to squeak to him when the sky flashed bright. He was close—so close.

Guided by scent, he sought out the power that smelled of beasts. The rat knew it well—it was the same sort of power the human had placed in him.

There were many things that smelled of the power here though, and it took time to sniff out the many odors. The things that smelled were not visible—they rested inside stone boxes with chains around them. There was etching on the boxes, but the rat knew not the scratch-marks of the humans, so he had to rely on the whiffs of power that wafted free.

Some smelled of fresh breezes, others of the great saltwater. On the rat went. There was fire-scent. There was the smell of shadows and the smell of light.

There were even some things that smelled like nothing, and the rat took great care to stay away from those because they made the little spark of power inside him tremble.

And then, at last, he found the right ones. He smelled wet fur—fur like that of a dog's, only older. This was the beast smell.

The rat's little heart beat quickly in his chest. He had done it, he had found—!

Dark place. Cold floor. No food, need food. Leaving dark place cold floor. Looking food.

Going way came. Avoiding blood-death-power-smell human.

Finding way out. Looking food. Looking warm and safe. Quickly going find.

Open air. Rain falling on fur. Food smell? Food smell! Going food smell.

Human beast-power-smell. Familiar.

Food in human hand.

Caught! Fear-run need!

The power touched the rat, and he stilled. The human's hold on him was gentle—yes, it was the same human!

The human looked intently into his eyes, and the rat felt power going between the two of them, carrying his memories of the big, dark place that held the things of power.

The human muttered something to the rat—it sounded like mother-rat's soothing squeaks—and set him down.

The rat looked up at the human. He understood then that the power would not stay with him for long. It would leave him again, and he would return to the instincts and impulses.

The human offered him the food—a handful of nuts. One by one, the rat ate.

When the nuts were gone and his stomach was full, he looked up at the human again.

The humans had so many complicated sounds—most did not bother to understand rat sounds. But this one, the rat hoped, would understand his gratitude squeak.

The human patted his head. Yes, he had understood—the rat knew it without a doubt.

Off scampered the rat, taking in the world around him with the mind granted by the power. He sought out the hole where the other rats slept.

As he squeezed inside, he shook off the rainwater. He sniffed out brother-rat and sister-rat, going to bed down beside them.

As he lay down and closed his eyes, he felt the power tremble, and—

Tired. Stomach full. Need sleep. Sleep safe?

Brother-rat warm. Sister-rat warm. Many rats around.

Sleep safe.

ADEPT JAN ENTERED HIS ROOM, locked the door, and took a deep breath.

Hawks, hawks were easy—they could hold on to the consciousness conferred by the Art of Beasts for a week. Rats were eager little things, but they didn't have quite the same mental presence as a predator of the skies.

But his plan had worked. He knew the layout of the Imperial Reliquary, and he more or less had a sense of where the guards—including the Carnifexes on duty—patrolled.

And he knew exactly where to find the Beast Relics Adept Reiva had recovered.

Now he just had to steal them.

The Imperial Postmaster laughed to himself, alone in the dark room.

"Sharasthi," he muttered, "what the hell are you planning up there in Hyrgallia?"

81

THE VOICES OF THE DEAD

AT YOUR PERIL, hearken to the dead. At your peril, ignore them.
  —Proverb among the Mithallkiym of Talynis

~

ZAGETH HAD GROWN up in a slum of Lazarra. His name had been...well, he preferred not to think about it. Names were an easy way to slip into another identity, leaving the old one behind like a cloak with too many tears.

His mother had died giving birth; his father nowhere to be found. It was a miracle the Downriver Gang took him in. Most children in his position would have simply ended up in slavery.

Downriver was a home, the boys were his brothers, and the leadership expected great things of him. His sharp mind and agile body had made him one of their best—not to mention his astonishing talent for acting, which came in useful for all sorts of jobs—and everyone who knew him believed that someday he had a shot at running the whole operation...but he hadn't been satisfied with that.

Neither had an interested observer, who had offered Zageth a way out of that life. There had been strings attached. There always were.

But as he learned what they were, he had been eager to accept the terms.

The fact that he would have been killed if he refused didn't count for nothing, though.

Trundling his way by camel across the cold sands of Talynis, bundled against the chill winds of the night, Zageth did not think himself a traitor. Not to the true Lazarra. He may have been a traitor to Cassia Vantelle, to Dioclete, to the legions, to the Senate—but he was not a traitor to Lazarra.

And neither was the woman he was on his way to meet.

Legate Flavia Iscator had marched out of Dav-maiir with a lone brigade under orders to subdue the neighboring cities. A punishment for her failure to bring Dav-maiir down with the haste and efficacy the praetor had expected of her. But then, Iscator made way for Nadari—an unusual choice, given that it was not the nearest city and its walls were famously strong. It was practically a suicide mission.

Zageth had known she would survive. He had missed her in Nadari, regrettably. Word of the Ninth's retreat (along with the praetor's disappearance and the Adept's defection) had reached the city, and Iscator had led her men out on a rapid march to rejoin with the fleeing troops.

Zageth had only spent a few hours in the city, buying supplies for his journey, as well as the camel. But those few hours had been long enough for him to hear some stories—and it was hard not to grin.

A fragment of the Ninth Imperial Legion had staked out a position before the city gates. These gates were not as impressive as Dav-maiir's, to be sure, but the people of Nadari saw how few the legionnaires' numbers were, and they had faith in their walls. They did not intend to surrender, and they certainly did not expect to lose.

The Imperials sent forth a messenger to the gates. He was a young man, nervous but holding himself aright—that was proper of a lad at war, respectable.

The man at the gate who received the message gaped and asked the legionnaire to repeat it. He sent a runner to the sheikh's estate.

It did not take long for the sheikh of Nadari to appear in person, dressed in finery and openly curious.

When he reached the gate, the legate of the Imperial force—a blonde woman of all things, may the gods witness it to be true—came forward, and she engaged the sheikh in a private conversation, out on the sands, beyond the protection of the walls.

Now everyone was gaping, Talynisti and Imperial alike, because the two seemed to be speaking with familiarity, even friendliness.

Eventually, the sheikh laughed loudly and—again, may the gods witness it—took the legate's hand in both of his and pumped it furiously.

The legion had walked through the gates without a weapon drawn, and they had been hosted within the walls at the sheikh's expense. Not a single infraction occurred, for the legate had placed her soldiers under strict orders not to cause so much as an ounce of trouble, not to so much as leer at a pretty girl two streets away.

When word of Dav-maiir came, Flavia Iscator had vanished within two hours with her regiment, on the way back to their Empire. The people were still marveling over it, and likely would for the rest of their lives.

They had asked Zageth if he was part of the legion. He had answered honestly that he was not. Merely an associate. Talynisti knew a private man when they saw one; so long as his silver was good, he could keep all the secrets he wanted.

The torches of the legion camp lay ahead of him. Tents outlined by the flickering glow stood out easily along the otherwise flat landscape, as though human presence here were not only unnatural, but unwanted by the desert itself.

Zageth let out a breath of relief. If he had fallen too far behind, the wiles of the desert would have buried him, he was certain. Now though, he saw at the far end of the camp the distinct profile of Wanderer tents. They would be able to make passage safely.

Zageth made his way nearer the camp, eventually dismounting from the camel and tying it to a shrub. The merchant had assured him the beast was well-tempered, but just in case, he took his most valuable possessions with him.

There was a watch, but to a man with Zageth's skills, that did not count for much. The legionnaires were exhausted one and all, drained during the day by the blistering heat and cut in the night by the biting winds.

The legion had set up around the ruins of an old town. The central oasis had shrunken considerably, no longer able to support a full settlement, but even a trickle of water was enough when you were just passing by.

It wasn't hard to guess that Iscator would be in the largest structure— sand-swept and doorless as it was. A makeshift curtain hung across the entryway, and a pair of legionnaires were on a lazy watch. Certainly they didn't expect anyone to make a move for their commander out here.

Zageth would have to let her know about that, he thought as he slipped past. It was unfair putting him up against the rank and file, but he should have at least had to *try*.

Inside the house, Iscator was still awake, reading something by candle-light. When Zageth ghosted inside, she glanced up from her book, then went back to it without much of a reaction.

"Zag. You're alive," she murmured.

He stepped away from the entrance, keeping his voice low. "More or less. Took a while to catch up."

The legate nodded, slipping a ribbon between the pages and setting the book aside.

"Good read?"

"Mirkor's *Histories*."

"Illegal read."

"That's what makes it good."

Zageth snorted, dropping to sit on the sand-strewn floor. "How have you survived this long?"

Iscator leaned back in her chair, eliciting a haunting creak from the old wood. "Sometimes if you're obvious enough, people just think you're stupid, not dangerous. An armchair revolutionary who'll hide under the bed at the first sign of risk."

"Vantelle is not the sort to take chances."

"She has her blind spots."

"So I hear."

Iscator raised an eyebrow.

"Senseless rumors, Legate. I assure you."

"Right."

Zageth absently ran his fingers through the sand, tracing patterns. Iscator watched with mild amusement. "The real question is how *you* survived being so close to her all the time?"

"What, you think I just doodle sigils on my reports to her?"

"It would be rather entertaining if you did."

"Right until she broke my legs and made me swallow my own knife."

"No, that would still be entertaining."

Zageth rolled his eyes.

Iscator stretched her arms above her head, smirking. "I assume you didn't visit for banter, Zag. What happened in Dav-maiir?"

"How much have you gathered?"

The legate looked off, brow furrowing. "Vantelle clearly failed to reach the Spring. Malik is almost sure to regain total control of the city before long. There may be some changes in how things are run, but overall, Talynis is on its way back to normal."

"My analysis is the same so far."

"As for the Adept...did she really attack Vantelle?"

Zageth grimaced. "I'm less clear on that. I had to make my escape while the place was still in chaos, but there were reports that the Adept rode out of the northern gate with a small party."

"Yradas Letiades being one, I imagine."

"Almost certainly. As for the remaining two—one was likely the Wolf, the other a Hunter."

At this, Iscator gaped. After staring for a moment, she scowled. "Enough with the dramatic pause—explain."

Zageth smirked. "The Wolf is Adept Reiva's younger brother."

"You're joking."

"Not at all. If it weren't for that, she likely would have stayed with the legion when the final insurrection rose up."

"Instead, she tried to rescue her brother from Vantelle—"

"—who was trying to wring out whatever information she could get regarding the Origin Spring. And somehow in that whole mess, Reiva sprang her brother and fled the city."

Iscator rubbed her eyes. "Gods above. Cassia would have found her way to the Convergence."

"Fortune favors us."

"For now. Let's hope it stays that way. What about this Hunter?"

"Your favorite Scout."

"*Charas?*"

"I stole a glimpse at her records one night—I'm amazed you didn't think to investigate her sooner. Unparalleled successes as a tracker, forward reconnaissance, you name it."

"No physiological signs, though."

"She has the eyes, but they're dim. You could miss them if you weren't looking closely."

Iscator grimaced. "I was careless, then. How the hell could that get by me?" Now she was leaning forward, elbows resting on her knees. Deep in thought, she bit her thumb, eyes flitting to and fro as thoughts collided.

Zageth hadn't worked too often with Flavia Iscator, but when he had, he rarely saw her this worked up. He sat there in silence for a while, sweeping away the designs he had traced into the sand.

At last, she said what was on her mind. "It's too much. Too much to be a coincidence."

Zageth nodded slowly. He had been thinking the same, but had not wanted to voice it, for fear he was letting his hopes get the best of him.

Gingerly, the legate padded over to her trunk. Drawing out a key, she unlocked the latch and began rifling through the contents. Removing uniforms, records, and other supplies, she eventually pulled out a small object wrapped in plain linen.

Zageth's heart picked up. He had one too, but his was secreted far away from here, buried in the corner of the Old City in Lazarra. The nature of his operations meant it was too dangerous to carry anywhere near him.

Reverently, Iscator unwrapped the object, taking care as she did so, setting the wrappings aside.

She held a bronze seal, disc-shaped and masterfully cast. It bore the resemblance of a fearsome beast, reptilian and great-toothed. The creature lay curled up, outlined by a neat circle. And along the outside of the circle were engraved three words: *Ordo Draconis Laevisomnis.*

Iscator held the seal between them for a moment. Then she turned it over. Along the backside, smaller and less neat, were more words. Instructions. Guidance. Dreams. The charter of the Order of the Sleeping Dragon.

Zageth had those words memorized—every member of the Order did—but it was still moving to see them set in metal, these words that could only ever be whispered between the most trusted of allies. These words that could bring an Empire's wrath down upon your head.

The minuscule etching on the seal was intensely abbreviated, but all members of the Order knew the full text by heart:

The Republic of Lazarra is going to fall. Dark days are coming. My children, do not trust yourself to the smooth words of the thousand-eyed spirit who makes himself out to be lord of all. Verily I tell you, his words are but vain seduction, and he will free you only to make you his slave.

You must make for yourselves friends, allies. I have long seen this coming, and made preparations. You will find brothers to the cause wherever you go, if you know the proper signs.

Secrecy shall be your blood, the darkness your cloak. We who would safeguard the light must do so now with covered lanterns—such is the nature of our all-seeing foe.

If you have not the stomach for the task set before you, either build yourself into one who does, or forget you ever knew my name. We have need of stern stock, of souls willing to take up arms against brothers, to lie to loved ones, to hate one's very flesh and blood, one's own country, all for the sake of the truth.

Only by this can we endure. Only by this can we free ourselves.

Find my archives—those that have not yet been destroyed. There are copies hidden in all the great libraries of the world; I am sure at least one will survive.

For now, our enemies drive us into the shadows, beneath the ground. For now, we lie dormant.

But a day will come when the Dragon is roused from slumber, and the tyrant's reign is broken. I pray it comes soon, but if it does not, then do not give up hope. So long as these words are etched in metal, so long as they reside in the hearts of those who cherish truth—we have not lost.

Ciell Aenan, Last of the Lazarran Consuls

Iscator ran her thumb along the etching, feeling the immortal imprint of Aenan's final wishes. The last ruler of Lazarra before the Dark Days.

"She is going to do it," whispered the legate. "She will wake the Dragon. She will break the Empire."

Zageth sighed. "She's powerful. But she is young."

"She'll have others. Already she has the heir to the Krypteia at her side, as well as a Hunter."

"One is in exile, the other is far from what the legends describe."

Flavia Iscator pressed the seal to her chest, turning to look at the pale moon through the gap in the roof. "We don't need legends, Zag. We need heroes."

"That sounds like the same thing."

She snorted, shaking her head. "Legends are born; heroes are made. We can make them into what we need."

"And if they refuse?"

She rose, moving to put away the seal. "Then we die, and someday, someone else becomes the one we need. But I do not intend to sit by while a chance like this is set before us."

Zageth straightened his back. He could get behind that. Hell, he could get behind most things when it came to the Order. That was the majesty of it—if you failed, if you died, the Order would persist. Someone else would take up the cause, and if you had done your job well, then you may even have paved the way for them. Given them ever so slightly a better chance.

For hundreds of years, their predecessors had been doing that. Laying groundwork. Making plays—some successful, others not. There had been betrayals, massacres. They had nearly been wiped out before. But they always persisted. They always stood up again, bleeding and broken, but not yet ended.

"What's our next move, then?"

Iscator squared her shoulders. "First, we reconnect with Sharasthi. Based on her most recent reports, Marcus Gallius may yet be swayed. At the very least, he has not turned her in. That's a good sign."

"As good as any," muttered Zageth. He had always been wary of Sharasthi's plan to bring the praetor into the fold, but he had to admit it would be a great boon if successful.

"Then we contact the Krypteia. We'll need to alert them as to what's coming."

"You think they'll cooperate?"

"Not all the families, but I'd bet my life on a few. Do we have anyone inside the Sanctum still?"

"Sharasthi had a man inside the Roost. If there's anyone else, they're embedded deep. Alyat's death would have been a severe warning."

She nodded gravely. "But Alyat was a clever man. He would have left something behind for Reiva. Something no one else could find."

"We'll have to trust her to get ahold of it then."

"Sure, but who's to say we can't help her along?"

FLAVIA SPOKE with Zageth late into the night, but eventually she dismissed him, saying she needed to sleep.

And that was true, she did. But she was not going to. Not just yet.

Instead, clutching the dragon seal in her fist, she returned to her trunk. With one hand, she rifled through it, searching for another memento—not so old as the seal, but almost as meaningful.

Then she had it.

Her fingers closed around the knife's leather sheath, and she drew it from the depths.

The sight of it twisted something inside her, kneeling all alone with only these ramshackle walls to hold back the cold desert winds.

There was a Talynisti myth that the winds carried the voices of the dead, that they spoke to those still living whom they had left behind.

Flavia hoped it was just that—a myth—but myths had a strange way of being truer than one would like.

Still keeping the seal pressed into her palm, she slowly drew the knife. It was an ornamental blade—meant to be worn on the hip opposite a sword at formal ceremonies.

As the blade slipped from the leather, she caught sight of the lettering.

That twisting inside got worse. She almost rammed the blade back, stowed it away. Or maybe she could throw it out to the sands so she could never see it again.

Instead, she took a long, tremulous breath, and drew the knife all the way out.

Honor to you, Captain Iscator. May High Arkhon and all the gods witness your service above and beyond.

So formal, so grandiose.

Then, on the reverse side:

Good work, Flavia. I'm glad to have you with me. The Empire will sing your praises some day.

Cassia.

She screwed her eyes shut, feeling the hot prick of tears.

How had it come to this?

She pressed the fist holding the seal to her heart.

Memories came unbidden. Cassia with a legate's insignia, slapping her on the back after a battle, wiping blood off her face. *'Keep your shield high, Iscator. Be a shame for a face like that to scar like mine.'* A lopsided grin that tugged at that same scar.

Another campaign, another victory. Celebratory wine. Too much wine. A flush on Cassia's face as Flavia and the others lifted her up on their shoulders.

Flavia had ascended to prefect by then, and she had started the cheer: *'Praetorship! Glory to Vantelle!'* And soon enough, the whole company, then the whole legion, was shouting it to the heavens, demanding laud for their legate, demanding her ascension.

Whether it was the gods who listened or the Emperor, their cry was answered—within the month, Cassia Vantelle was named Praetor of the Ninth and Tenth Legions.

And later that night, another night of too much drink, she had taken Flavia aside and said she would take her place as Legate of the Ninth.

'And always keep that lucky dagger close, hm? You can't go dying on me.' A wine-stained smile. *'Some day, you and I, praetor and Empress.'*

"Cassia...how did it all come to this?" she whispered, fighting a sob as tears trickled down her cheeks.

Outside and all-encompassing, the desert winds howled.

82

WHAT ONCE WAS

EVERYTHING REIVA HAD LIVED THROUGH, from Talynis to Lazarra and back, was only the beginning. She was only finding her feet, strange as it is to think. Stranger still was the path she was yet to walk.
—*The Memoirs of Flavia Iscator*

～

REIVA HAD GOTTEN USED to the robes of the Sages, but she still felt strange walking about without armor.

When she had come up from the Origin Spring, naked and reborn, they had pronounced her worthy of initiation into the Sagehood. She was the only woman they had ever done that for—at least, for many *many* years—but the will of the Spring was immutable.

She had been chosen.

And she still was not sure whether to be glad for it.

Today was one of those precious days when she could leave the endless tunnels beneath Dav-maiir. Hatzakh, the leader of the Sages, kept a close eye on her, but he said that with time, she would train at other cells throughout Talynis.

She hoped the day came soon—she needed the sun.

Standing on Har-Esh, she took in the land she had been hauled from in chains and returned to with the sword. The moon-bathed sands stretched far as the eye could see. Dav-maiir sat nestled, a sudden eruption of swaying flora and proud masonry amid the wilderness. East lay the Spine. Before that would be Shugrith, where she was born, and after it was Endra.

The Empire had failed to take this land.

Her land, now. Hers when she was born, hers again now that she had passed through the waters.

Lazarra...what was she to make of Lazarra?

What had Lazarra made of her? Had she been branded a traitor, or simply declared *Missing in Action*? Had Domi heard by now? Her stomach turned. She needed to find a way to communicate to her, but what could she say? She had never even read that letter Domi sent her in the wake of Alyat's death. And what of Sharasthi? What of Quartermaster Demman, who would be grieving Alyat only to hear of what Reiva had done?

Maybe it would just be better to stay missing forever, let them all think I'm gone.

But even as she thought it, she knew it was a vain hope. Her *ruakh* had told her as much.

Rukhesh hovered behind her. She was always aware of his presence now. They spent many hours a day deepening their Binding. The Sages instructed her in countless disciplines—many of which mirrored practices she had learned in the Sanctum—but most important was that she learned to work with the spirit from whom her magic came.

He had been with her, he said, ever since she was a little girl. He had attached himself to her around the time her father died, and he had gone with her to Lazarra. She remembered how angry she had felt in those days. That, he admitted, had indeed come from him in part—but it was first from her. It was her anger that had drawn him to her, for anger was the emotion that drew spirits of flame.

It was odd, never being alone now. He said that with time, she would learn to disregard his presence. She wasn't sure that really counted as being alone, but many things were changing now.

"How many of you are there?" she asked.

Rukhesh made a sound like a crackling campfire, something she had come to identify as an expression of displeasure from him. "Countless."

"You seem upset."

That sound again. "Few of us are strong enough to forge the soulbond."

He had explained that to her as well. He had explained many things to her. Things that seemed impossible. Things that would force her to totally rewrite her understanding of the Empire, of history, of reality itself.

"What would it take to change that?"

"I have already told you this."

Reiva sighed, looking again at Dav-maiir, far below. She glanced back at the cave, but decided she'd rather stay a moment longer. Har-Esh, the sacred mountain, connected to the Sage's network of tunnels—though they hesitated to claim all the tunnels as their own. They spoke of the underways as a gift given long before the Sages were first organized.

This tunnel connected to a few caves like this one, almost invisible from below, affording a view of the land around Dav-maiir.

Reiva had asked about going to the peak, but Rukhesh had been adamant that she not.

"The Great Four consider it their own," he had said.

When she had asked Hatzakh about this, he was evasive. Apparently, even the gods had politics. And Rukhesh hoped she would get involved in a war.

She turned the ring of bone around her finger, brushing the etched prayer to ha'Mithalleik.

"I cannot overthrow an entire Empire."

Crackling. "One man is not an Empire."

"You said yourself how powerful, Ar—" She stopped herself. "How powerful the Farseer is."

"Things are changing. There is opportunity where there has not been for many years."

This was where she got uncomfortable, always.

The opportunity was her.

"A *ruakh* of flame has not forged a proper soulbond in decades," he persisted. "We will grow strong together, and then you will overthrow the tyrant. You will free us all."

"You are already free."

The spirit growled, which sounded like a roaring wildfire. "Hardly free. The Convergence of Talynis is weakened. Most others in this part of the world are long since destroyed. All because of *his* rule. His betrayal."

"If the Emperor truly can see the future like you say, then what hope do we have?"

"He can *glimpse* the future, but the future is always shifting. He will know what transpired here, if hazily, and he will seek to strike out at you. He knows of the woman named Vantelle's death, of that I assure you."

That was another thing she had learned. Just hours before she had gone below the water, Vantelle had died in them. The Sages had been watching her as she went. She had been talking to herself at the end. Hatzakh had said the Spring makes a person confront their true self. Reiva wasn't sure what that meant for her. She had only seen death down there.

"Why me?" she muttered. "Why bind yourself to me? Why did I survive the waters? Hatzakh said the Spring shows you what you might be—but I only saw who I was."

Rukhesh drew himself up, squaring his shoulders. "You survived the judgment because you confronted your sins. You admitted fault and chose to do right; instead of pursuing death, you chose to heal, even though you knew it would doom you. I chose you because I saw, even when you were a little girl, the potential that you would be one who made such decisions. A Sage of Fire."

"Adept," she protested. "Don't make me into one of them."

"You already are." The crackling sound again. "Your power only exists through our allegiance. Our Binding. I have risked myself more than once for you, going beyond the ordinary reach of my influence."

The burning tree. The sudden tidal wave of power she had tapped into against Bebar.

"I know, Rukhesh."

"For years, I bore that...*shackle*. So many did, in the hopes that one day, your eyes would be opened to us."

'Shackle,' that was what he called the focus. The Lazarran Empire's unique arcane technology, an artifact that could simulate a full soulbond, forcing the spirit to channel its power through the Adept. She had never heard Rukhesh sound so close to being in pain as when he described how those like him willingly submitted themselves to that imprisonment. They had a deep desire, he had said, to be mediated to the world through a human. That was what Adepts did—make the unseen world manifest in the material. Ordinarily, that was done through a soulbond, a mutual relationship, but long ago Arkhon had inflicted some sort of wound upon reality, a wound that had affected not just the spiritual world, but mortals as well. Rukhesh had said that by harming one, he had causally damaged the other.

The intricacies and the metaphysics escaped her, when Rukhesh began speaking of such things—particularly because he seemed to think it was all so obvious. But she knew one thing for certain: she didn't need a focus anymore, now that she had been fully initiated as a Sage. The water of the Origin Spring had done something to her soul, enabling her to bond fully to Rukhesh, completing the process he had started many years ago.

"I understand I owe you much, but I also had no idea how any of this works. *None* of us do, as far as I know."

"Very few in your Empire understand, but there are those who do. And as I said, they will not suffer your defiance for long."

"I *have* no defiance."

"Not so. Your Emperor and the Farseer—their hegemony relies upon the stranglehold of the spirit realm. You threaten that."

"I only did what was right. I did what my father asked me to do. I saved my brother. I can't change the world—all I've ever done is change it for the worse."

Rukhesh glowed like a stoked bed of coals. "You did right once, you say. You must do right again. What else would you do—would you while away the rest of your years as a hermit in the desert? I bound myself to you, Reiva, because I saw you have the potential to change things for my kind—for my kind *and* your kind. I pled your case to Bebar's *ruakh* so he did not kill you. I risked my existence by pushing through the veil and setting fire to the frozen tree."

"You ask too much of me. I am a killer, not a protector. Does saving *one* person change that?"

"It is the beginning of change. You are not carved of stone, Reiva. You are like me—shifting, always taking new shape in accordance with your will. I am not one to beg for sympathy. I speak the truth, and it is the truth you know, even if you have not come to understand it. Your life is no longer your own. Your enemies will come for you. You can kill them, but not forever. You can run, but you will only find the same despair waiting everywhere you go."

Rukhesh stretched out his burning hand, as though reaching toward some future, dancing just outside his grasp among the stars. "The people in this city fought for freedom from the Farseeing One. You did not understand then, but now your eyes have been opened to the truth of the world. You wish to find redemption? You wish to be free of the guilt you confronted beneath the waters? Then set the world free. Set it free, Reiva, and find freedom for yourself. Restore the rightful rule. Return the world to what once was."

83

WHAT WILL BE

MANIFOLD, perhaps innumerable, are the arcane arts. In theory, almost anything is possible, but my father impressed upon me from a young age the significance of caution and skepticism, for there are many who make outlandish claims for purposes of charlatanry or esteem.

And yet...I saw something when I visited the most elite of the Karellan magicians, something that defied belief and reason. I saw a man foretell what was yet to come, and he did so without error day after day for three hundred and sixty days. He did not speak like an oracle, in riddles and sophistry, but plainly, with the same certainty I speak of the sun rising and setting.

And on my last day with him, he told me the manner in which I was to die. I have no doubt he told me the truth, and not a day goes by that I am not tormented by this knowledge.

—*The Life and Wisdom of Simeon Binkhok As Told by Himself*

～

THE PALATINE THRONE, contrary to most expectations, was kept in darkness. Of course, the room was lit when there was some sort of function or ceremony, when there were senators to press upon or guests to entertain.

But when Emperor Dioclete was blissfully alone, undisturbed, he kept the seat of power plunged in gloom. The light of the immediate world was a distraction; he needed to see what lay far beyond the confines of this chamber, this palace, this city.

It was by such farsight that the Imperial lords of Lazarra—the sole Lazarran-born Adepts, followers of the *Ars Prognoscens*, the Art of Fore-knowledge—had brought so much of the world to heel.

There were gaps, however. The future was not set in stone. Seeing what was yet to pass was more of an art than a science, not unlike the oracles and divinations of the ancient cults and mystery religions.

Dioclete knew one thing for certain, though. He knew that Cassia Vantelle was dead. She had failed him. Talynis remained unbowed.

How one scrap of desert had managed for so long to defy the will of the Empire was...*vexing*. They had the advantage of an intact Convergence, of course, which made creating new Adepts far more feasible than for most. They did not need to give a focus to their Adepts either.

Fighting Adepts with Adepts had given Talynis a chance, but Dioclete had thought himself assured of victory. He had *seen* Vantelle returning triumphant through the gates of Lazarra with the spoils of war in tow.

He knuckled his brow, eyes staring blankly at nothing, at everything.

"We underestimated the girl." His voice echoed off the marble.

Arkhon's presence weighed upon him like a cloak of iron. *"Traitors in our ranks. Servants of the Order."*

Dioclete hummed in agreement.

When Arkhon spoke, he often did so in brief snippets, or half-thoughts.

At any moment, the vast stores of the god's energy were devoted to the domination of the realms under his control. Lazarra primarily, but also the provinces. Lazarra still had an intact Convergence, so it demanded more energy to keep the spirits in line. There was a cost to that; not only were most of the Lazarran spirits too weak to form a soulbond, those who could refused. They saw Arkhon's ascension as a tyranny—not the glorious turn of history that it was.

Either way, the Empire did well enough harvesting Adepts from other lands. It took more effort—tracking them down, indoctrinating them into the Lazarran way of life, creating the arcane focuses—but the alternative? To allow the spirits of Lazarra free rein? Never. They were a squabbling mass, just like the people. They needed a firm hand, an iron law.

Just as it was in the nature of some mortals to serve, and others to rule, so it was with spirits. Arkhon, above all others, was destined to rule—and rule he did. Rule he would. Rule over all. There was nothing malicious in it; he simply performed what was his vocation. Just as a shark hunted the seas for prey, so did Arkhon the All-seeing hunt for power. He had been born to do just that, born from the rising tide of human ambition, from the insatiable hunger to reign over everything enumerable in this world. Most spirits were born of passions, or fears, or ideals—Arkhon had been born of a dream. The dream of a united world, single-faced and singly ruled.

Dioclete understood that dream—he lived it, he cherished it, he bent his every waking thought toward its achievement. That was the dream of the First Emperor, greatest of his forerunners.

He had hoped for Cassia Vantelle to be the next to carry the mantle of that legacy, that vision. Still, there were others, and in the wake of her death they would be eager to vie for his favor.

But one did not maintain an Empire that would span the world by leaving loose ends.

"Enter," he said, voice resonating in the empty chamber.

The person who had been about to knock let himself in by a side door— a secret way that no attendants or members of the Palatine Guard would observe.

"*Ave Imperator*," crooned the soft voice.

Dioclete did not look at the Carnifex—not with his eyes, at least. He was perfectly capable of seeing him without resorting to anything so pedestrian.

"Bryg. What did you make of Adept Alyat?"

The Carnifex paused for a moment. "Perceptive," he said at last. "Most are not so quick as he."

Dioclete concurred. The clues Alyat had found were intentionally left behind as a trap—a way of sussing out those who suspected that the history of the Empire was not all that it was made out to be.

Suspected it, or were *encouraged* to suspect it.

"The Order of the Sleeping Dragon," said the Emperor. "I see them making their move."

The Carnifex perked up at this. "Are there any *faces*?" He said the word almost reverently.

Dioclete shook his head. He knew that would disappoint Bryg, but he was not entirely empty-handed. "I see how their web moves. They are making preparations. They expect their time draws near. And it all centers around the traitor Adept. Reiva from Talynis. The one Cassia named a Lion."

Bryg's enthusiasm returned. "Alyat's protégé." His smile was eerily bright in the gloom.

"If you can bring her in alive, do so. But I want no chances taken. Requisition a Krypteia team."

The Emperor paused. Delving into his foresight, he used Bryg's soul like a torch, casting light out into the hazy fog of possible futures, inspecting the branching paths hinting at what will be.

In many, he saw Bryg kill the Adept.

In too many others, he saw the Adept kill Bryg.

And all throughout, there was the disturbing touch of...*that one*. The one who spurned the clarity of his foresight. The one whom Arkhon could not see. The one the Talynisti worshiped as a god.

His influence hid Reiva from Dioclete's vision—direct vision, at least. He could still glean some sense of her future by observing others whose fates intersected with hers—such as Bryg's would—but he had no sense of probability. And that was the most maddening part; always, he won by knowing how to play the odds, by anticipating how his will would cascade onward and bring about the world he desired.

The Emperor rubbed his temple. "She is dangerous prey, Bryg."

"So I hear," he crooned, seeming almost giddy at the prospect. "But I shall be more so."

Dioclete grunted. He had no doubt the Carnifex would pose a grave threat, but the blindness set his teeth on edge.

He took a breath, about to order Bryg to take a second Krypteia team.

The Carnifex cocked his head. "My lord?"

If there was one great failing of the Lazarran emperors, it was overconfidence in their Art. Sometimes, fate *resisted* attempts to meddle with it. Many of his predecessors had gone nearly mad wrestling against the future, baffled by the manner with which it seemed bent on defying their wills.

"I only meant to say that I have full confidence in your skills, Bryg."

The blood-worker's grin was beatific. "I live to serve you, my Emperor."

"Then go and do so. Quickly."

Bryg swept an elegant bow, practically gliding as he made his exit, his black-fringed mantle shimmering in the gloom.

No, Dioclete was not like his forebears. He understood these things required precision, subtlety. The way to shape the future was not by brute force, but by seduction. A light touch, a gentle suggestion.

Then, you could take what you wanted.

And Dioclete intended to take the world.

∾

THE END

LEARN HOW THE JOURNEY BEGAN

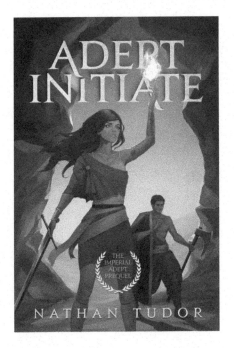

From the blistering desert to the storm-whipped sea, experience the beginning of Reiva's story.

Get a free copy of *Adept Initiate* at nathantudor.com, or by scanning the code below:

ACKNOWLEDGMENTS

Writing and publishing a book is a herculean task, and I could not have accomplished it without the support (and perceptive eyes) of my family. Mom, Dad, Noah—you've waited so long for me to get these words written, and were it not for your love and support, they would still be rattling around inside my head.

Emiko, you always told me I was a great writer even when I was certain I would never create anything worth reading. Thank you for encouraging me from across one ocean, and then another.

Everyone in the Writer's Guild who has offered feedback on my writing throughout the years, thank you. And for laboring by my side in the day-to-day trenches of writing, special mention is well-deserved by my comrades-in-arms: Austin, Daniel, Cade, and Graham. I've shipped, lads, now it's your turn.

When *The Empire's Lion* was little more than a barebones concept and a few thousand very rough words, Michael McClellan met me for coffee and gave me the kick of encouragement and inspiration I needed to buckle down, face Resistance, and do the work. Michael, it's been an untold blessing having you as a friend and mentor. Our conversations have given me special insight into what it means to be an author, and this book would have taken far longer if not for your generous commitment to paying it forward.

Beta readers are essential to something I call 'making sure the book is actually decent.' My thanks to everyone who took the time to read and offer feedback. The story I wanted to tell grew stronger thanks to your comments. In particular, thank you Mom & Dad, Austin, Terrel, Isaac, Cade, and Graham.

Worthy of special acclaim—whether for keen perception or just sheer comedic force—are:

Daniel, who hears the snow cronch [*sic*];

Cade, who not only *got* the heart of the story, but also caught the Steven

Pressfield reference in chapter 37, along with a continuity error so minute he proved himself worthy of being a Legion Intelligence code-breaker;

Austin, who will forever remind me of what the audience *really* wants to see;

And Graham, who described Wakaram and Bebar as doing 'Toph-level earthbending in an R-rated story,' which might just be one of my favorite comments ever.

I could never have created this story and the world it is set in without the myriad influences of my professors. They have guided me in studying the ancient cultures I've drawn inspiration from; they have apprenticed me in writing, critical thinking, and aesthetic judgment; and most importantly, they have been excellent models of character. I wish I could thank you all individually for everything you've done, but that would take another book's worth of pages :)

Daniel and Austin (once again), thank you for the incredible surprise that was the *Imperial Adept* role-playing game, and thank you Wes and Cade for joining the experience. Someday we'll need to get around to publishing that, eh?

And finally, thank you, reader. I hope you enjoyed the journey, and I hope you come along for the next.

ABOUT THE AUTHOR

Nathan Tudor has researched ancient religion at Oxford, traveled the seven continents, and mastered the art of speaking in the third person. His debut novel *The Empire's Lion* tells an epic story filled with action, identity, and the struggle to do what is right in an upside-down world.

When he's not writing or reading, Nathan can be found debating matters of no particular consequence with his friends, falling down research rabbit holes, and fiddling with a hand-crank coffee grinder that's been stuck for the last few months.

Allegations that he hired an alchemist to give him the tread of a cat and the ears of a fox are categorically false.

Allegations that nathantudor.com is the best place to find him online? The reader may judge.

ALSO BY NATHAN TUDOR

The Imperial Adept
Adept Initiate

The most-up-to-date version of this bibliography can be found at nathantudor.com

Made in USA - Kendallville, IN
91461_9781957611006
02.09.2022 1516